FIRST EDITION

THE READER'S DIGEST ASSOCIATION LIMITED
25 Berkeley Square, London W1X 6AB

THE READER'S DIGEST ASSOCIATION
SOUTH AFRICA (PTY) LTD
Nedbank Centre, Strand Street, Cape Town

Printed in Great Britain by Petty & Sons Ltd, Leeds
and Ben Johnson and Co Ltd, York.

Original cover design by Jeffery Matthews M.S.I.A.

For information as to ownership
of copyright in the material in this book see last page

ISBN 0 340 25268 5

READ

CONDE

Reader's Digest
CONDENSED BOOKS

YANKS
Christine Sparks

THE CAPRICORN STONE
Madeleine Brent

THE MASSACRE
AT FALL CREEK
Jessamyn West

WHIP HAND
Dick Francis

COLLECTOR'S LIBRARY
EDITION

In this Volume:

YANKS

by Christine Sparks *(p.9)*

It was a wartime invasion, but not by the enemy. When the Yanks came to a beleaguered Britain in 1943, there were many mis-understandings before the reserved natives and open-hearted Americans came to terms with each other.

This story follows the fortunes of three GIs and the girls they met and wooed in an English country town. Based on the script of John Schlesinger's highly acclaimed feature film, it is a poignant tale of romance, humour and heart-break played out beneath the ever-menacing shadow of war.

The Capricorn Stone

by Madeleine Brent *(p.119)*

Bridie Chance and her younger sister Kate had been brought up to expect a privileged position in life. Their ador-ing father, although seldom at home, provided them with all they could pos-sibly desire. Then, suddenly, news came of his death—a death under the most scandalous circumstances—and everything changed.

Madeleine Brent's latest bestseller tells how Bridie was forced to go out and fend for her family in the glittering world of the Victorian music hall, and how it was her father's last cryptic mes-sage, with its strange reference to the Capricorn Stone, that led her to the brink of disaster.

The Massacre at Fall Creek

by Jessamyn West   (p.281)

In 1824 in the state of Indiana, five white men murdered, in cold blood, a small band of peaceful Indians. Enraged, the Indians' proud kinsmen threatened massive and bloody reprisals unless the killers were brought to justice. But to the pioneers at Fall Creek, hanging a white man merely for killing an Indian was unthinkable. Based on a true and long-forgotten incident, Jessamyn West's latest novel unerringly captures the strain—and joy—of life on the American frontier, where even brutal murder can't dim the beauty of the land, or of a love newly born. It is a book to be savoured, and remembered.

WHIP HAND

by Dick Francis   (p.407)

Sid Halley, ex-jockey turned super sleuth, is back. Dick Francis's most popular hero, the star of Yorkshire Television's *The Racing Game*, returns in style to hound some of the underworld's most devious villains—and to exorcize the one terrible fear deep in his own soul.

This is the eighteenth novel by this hugely successful author, himself an ex-jockey, who has made the turf his very own corner of the thriller-writing field. *Whip Hand* is certain to add still further to his crowd of enthusiastic fans.

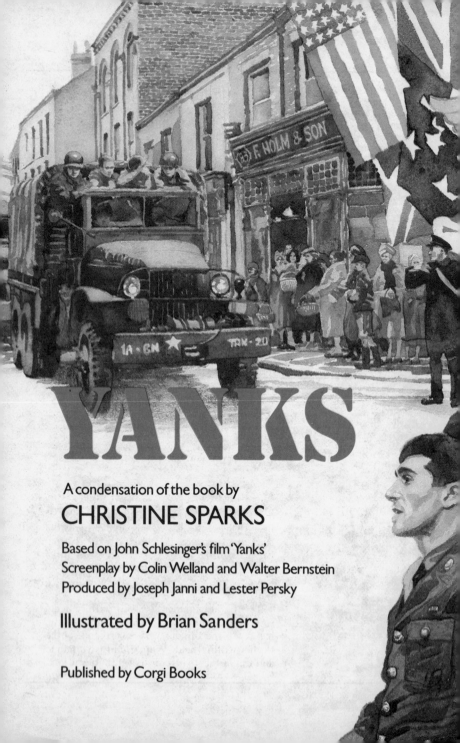

YANKS

A condensation of the book by
CHRISTINE SPARKS

Based on John Schlesinger's film 'Yanks'
Screenplay by Colin Welland and Walter Bernstein
Produced by Joseph Janni and Lester Persky

Illustrated by Brian Sanders

Published by Corgi Books

"To Washington they were officially 'The United States Army–Europe'. To themselves they were GIs. To the war-weary British, who watched the invasion by their supposed saviours with relief and curiosity, turning often to resentment and suspicion, they were simply 'Yanks' . . ."

This is the story of seven months in the lives of three of those Yanks, and of the three girls who tried to make them feel at home in England—an England under siege, racked by wartime austerity and so very different from their own land of plenty. For Molly, the cheerful clippie on the bus, the path of love was simple and straightforward. For her friend Jean, working in her parents' shop, it was fraught with problems; and for Helen, living alone in the big Hall, it was almost impossible. To each of them, however, the Yanks brought something far more precious than chewing-gum, Hershey bars and nylon stockings. . . .

Christine Sparks's novelization of United Artists' film presents an unforgettable picture of the Home Front and of those very special allies who travelled so many miles from home, many never to return.

1

The rain was everywhere. It trickled down their necks and up their shirt-sleeves. It crept into their socks so that their boots became cold and evil-smelling. It saturated the chilly air, casting a sodden blanket over the grey morning world that greeted the three hundred American soldiers as their convoy rumbled through the Lancashire countryside.

Frozen, dirty and unshaven, weary to the soul from the three-week crossing on the troopship, queasy with hunger and the joltings of the truck that had collected him from Liverpool docks and was now transporting him inland, Sergeant Matt Williams threw a glance of hatred up at the misty October sky, and uttered a fervent silent curse. Damn Hitler for starting the war! Damn Roosevelt for wanting to interfere in a scrap that was none of America's concern, and damn the Japanese for attacking Pearl Harbour and making it impossible for the Americans to keep out of it! And damn this rain!

It rained without ceasing as the line of trucks emerged from bomb-scarred Liverpool and into the open countryside to bump over muddy roads to the small town of Conleigh, beyond which lay the US army base established a year earlier, in 1942. Within sight of Conleigh itself the rain stopped suddenly and the sky began to clear, but the cramped and uncomfortable young man stared without enthusiasm at the uninviting aspect of the country to whose help he had been sent.

9

Matt accepted a cigarette from Danny Waterman, a fellow sergeant he had met on the boat. Danny was by nature a cheerful, straightforward young man. Matt, quieter, more questioning, had found Danny's easy buoyancy a prop to his sagging spirits. Their new friendship had made the dreadful crossing bearable.

Conleigh turned out to be a shabby little place, full of bomb-rubble and depression. Middle-aged policemen directed the convoy down the main street, over a bridge and through a vast, neglected bomb site. In the shopping area queues were forming already in front of the baker. The Americans' eyes flickered idly over some of the other shop fronts—Daniels, with a window full of plain Utility clothes, Moretons—general groceries and post office, Collins Ironmongers—

"Hey Matt," said Danny.

"Yeah?"

"What's an ironmonger?" Danny twisted his head to see the sign better as the shop slid past.

"Beats me," said Matt.

Another soldier said, "Hardware store."

"Why can't they call it a hardware store?" said Danny, bewildered. "You sell candy, it's a candy store. You sell hardware, it's a hardware store."

Matt shrugged, too depressed to speak. The women in head-scarves standing on the pavement looked, to his critical eye, dreary and apathetic. The night-workers, coming off shift, struck him as dispirited and dispiriting. They bore no resemblance to the image of the brave little islanders heroically defying German might, which was how a thousand news broadcasts had taught him to think of the British.

At that moment his eyes locked with those of one of the workers, a man of about fifty. And he knew at once that they shared the same opinion of each other. Matt remembered his own unshaven face, his stained uniform, and the thought did something to restore his sense of humour. He ran a hand over his chin and began dreaming of the steaming hot water waiting for him at the camp.

As the road narrowed and curved on the other side of the town, the truck had to slow down to pass a bus which had pulled in to the far side of the road. Molly Dawlish, the clippie, hung from the platform to get a better look at the new arrivals. The smile on her fresh young face and the gleam of her blonde hair brought a cheer from the truck.

"Hey, sugar," called Danny, "You want a hitch?"

"How about riding in here with us?" another young voice ventured hopefully.

Molly grinned back at them, and pointed to their packed truck. "There's more room in a tin of sardines!" she yelled.

"Yeah, but not as much action," Danny assured her fervently.

She joined in their laughter before vanishing into the bus. Danny kept his eyes on the flash of blonde hair that he could just see through the bus windows. He made a mental note of her— just in case.

Molly was clipping a ticket for a middle-aged woman who regarded her with frosty disapproval.

"Like Yanks, do you, miss?" the woman sniffed.

"Beggars can't be choosers, can they?" said Molly cheerfully.

"I've two sons in Burma," said the woman.

"Aye, and I've got two lads in the Desert Rats, but they're not much good to me there, are they, love?"

The woman snorted as the other passengers laughed, and Molly nipped upstairs where she could get a better view of the vanishing convoy. The day had started well. She'd have something to tell her friend, Jean Moreton, when they met later. Though come to think of it Jean probably already knew. If the trucks had come down the main street then they'd passed Moreton's, the little shop where Jean worked for her parents. And if Jean hadn't spotted them for herself, that young brother would have told her. Geoff was eleven, and like most youngsters of his age, Yankee mad.

THE CAMP SEEMED like an endless area of Nissen huts interspersed with piles of supplies under canvas, vast packing cases, and guns and machinery waiting to be assembled. There was water all right, but it wasn't steaming hot as Matt had dreamed of it. When he and three hundred others had climbed stiffly down from the trucks and been herded into the shower room to strip off so that their uniforms could be deloused, he had braced himself in happy expectancy. The showers consisted of wide, flat concrete dishes, from the centre of which water spurted ten feet high, leaving them to huddle beneath the downward spray. As the first relentless jet

11

of icy water hit, a single bellow of pain and disillusion went up.

"Help!"

"Turn on the heat."

"I'll complain to the landlord."

"I thought this was England, not Alaska."

Through the window they saw a Red Cross van drive past. It contained two women, one young and very pretty, the other in her mid-thirties, classically beautiful.

"Hey, get a look at that," said Danny.

Matt edged closer to the window. "I feel warmer already."

"Save it," Danny advised him. "They're Red Cross. They only do it for officers."

"Just don't put on your uniform," said Matt, grinning. "They'll never know the difference."

When the shower was over they felt better—still cold, but better. Their uniforms were clean, or at least fumigated. There was room to move. And there was the promise of hot tea and doughnuts dished out by the two Red Cross women.

Danny and Matt found that they were to sleep in the same Nissen hut. It was a long low building with beds down each side, but with a few rooms partitioned off at the end. Matt made sure he bagged one. That morning the hut was alive with young men busily making the place look as much like home as possible. Photographs of family and sweethearts went up on the walls, sometimes side-by-side with pin-up pictures of Ann Sothern, Lana Turner or Rita Hayworth. Each bed and the small table beside it took on an air of individuality.

Danny, whose career as a promising boxer had been interrupted by the war, shadow-boxed his way down the hut and into Matt's room, making jabbing motions in the air. He was a light-weight who, beside the tall rangy Matt, looked less than his five feet eight inches.

Matt was pinning up photographs of his family—a father and brother who were as dark-haired and fine-featured as himself. When he began to hang a map of England Danny stopped and peered.

"What do you need that for?" he demanded.

"I like to know where I am."

"You're in England," Danny explained kindly. He took out a

pencil and deliberately circled Merseyside. "See?" he said. "That's us—right there."

Later Matt, who was a sergeant cook, went to the mess hut where he would be working. Danny accompanied him to the door, then wandered on. The sun was well up now, casting a pale October gleam over the soggy camp. Hitler was a long way away, and suddenly it felt great to be young. England was no doubt full of pretty girls like the blonde one on that bus, and all just dying to offer home comforts to lonely GIs. He began to whistle.

2

To Washington they were officially "The United States Army —Europe". To themselves they were GIs. To the war-weary British, who watched the invasion by their supposed saviours with relief and curiosity, changing often to resentment and suspicion, they were simply "Yanks".

In a land turned grey by years of austerity the hundreds of thousands of young men who began to arrive in January 1942 to man the US bases in England seemed almost indecently wealthy and well-catered for. Their camps were supplied with their own food, their own films and their own newspapers. They even had their own radio programmes beamed from America.

A country in the grip of ever-increasing rationing felt less than charitable towards young men who were well supplied with things like razor blades, cigarettes, sweets and soap. The rationing of soap was a particularly sore point with the women and with the arrival of a swarm of young, admiring and open-handed soldiers the matter of cleanliness had assumed a sudden importance. Englishmen, who saw their previously sane womenfolk behaving— as one jilted swain had put it—"like a flock of chickens in a thunderstorm", became increasingly resentful. The snappy jibe "over-paid, over-sexed and over here" had gained swift currency.

It was indeed the younger women and also the children who had most cause to bless the American invasion. Let the old folk complain that the Yanks treated Britain more as though it were an occupied country than an ally (an accusation that occasionally had some truth), to the youngsters, nurtured on film-fantasies of an

13

opulent paradise across the seas, the presence of men who actually lived there was like a dream come true. The children found that sweet rationing, once seen as the end of the world, could be man-oeuvred around. The cry of "Got any gum, chum?" was usually productive of a strip of chewing-gum, or even a Hershey chocolate bar. And for the girls there were nylons.

Before the war there had been silk stockings, but these had been banned in 1940, to be replaced by Utility stockings which were ugly and shapeless. The girls hated the dreary leg-wear, so the sudden import from America of delicate sheer nylons seemed to them like a gift from heaven. And the boys who distributed this largesse did so with such charm and attentiveness, and gave such flattering boosts to a girl's ego that—well, it seemed only fair to offer a little something in return.

All this was duly noted by an older generation watching its daughters come home late and its sons pick up horrible slang. It was noted by English servicemen returning on leave to find their girls no longer waiting for them. And the population gradually hardened into the pros and the antis, while between them the Yanks managed more or less well.

On the morning of Matt and Danny's arrival, eleven-year-old Geoff Moreton had been roused from sleep by the trucks rumbling past his window, which was directly above his family's grocery shop. He leaped to the window, excitedly pulling back the curtains.

"Jean," he called, "come here quick! There's Yanks. Hundreds of them!"

His sister entered in her dressing gown. She was in her early twenties, dark-haired, with brilliant eyes set in a face of youthfully solemn beauty. She joined him at the window, looking down sympathetically as the convoy containing hundreds of haggard young men rolled by.

"They look tired out, poor beggars," she said in her soft deep voice. "As if we haven't enough of 'em already."

"Aye. Me mother won't be pleased," Geoff reflected. Clarrie Moreton's strictures on Yanks were well known.

"But *you* will?" Jean smiled. "Eh?"

Her question took in the whole of his bedroom with its walls covered with examples of Americana—US insignias, car advert-isements, empty packets of Lucky Strike cigarettes.

14

Geoff followed her gaze round the room. "Aye," he agreed. "I like Yanks, don't you?"

"They're all right," she laughed. "In small doses."

But their mother disliked and distrusted Yanks to a degree that seemed to Jean to be beyond reason. She didn't argue with her mother. At heart she loved and admired her too much for that. But she tried to let the prejudice wash over her.

The sound of voices downstairs told her that her father had returned from his stint as a special constable. Probably he'd been one of those directing the convoy through the town. He'd be having an early cup of tea now before going upstairs to change into his overalls before setting off for his job at the mill. Clarrie nagged with loving insistence, trying to make him see that two jobs were too much for a man of his age, but he, so often dominated by her in other things, was stubborn in this.

When Jean went down he and Geoff were already sitting at the table. He was admiring a GI cap that the boy was wearing proudly. Both of them were studiously trying not to meet the eyes of Clarrie Moreton who was regarding both her husband and her son with equal disapproval.

She was a tall, thin woman with an expression that could change from gentleness to rigidity with astonishing speed. Had she allowed her face to relax more often it would have had a sweetness close to beauty. But somewhere too far back for her to remember she had decided that strength lay in firmness, and strength was necessary to survive. Over the years her face and her personality had set in hard lines. Only the heart beneath remained tender, and that she strove to hide. Indeed, it was easier to hide it these days when the pain of her illness gnawed at her guts. Fear and the strain of keeping the truth to herself put a snap in her voice.

"Very smart," James Moreton was saying to his son, indicating the cap.

"Billy Rathbone give it me," Geoff told his father eagerly. "Swopped it for two Chesterfields and a Lucky Strike."

"The packets or the cigarettes?" Jean said, sitting down with a smile at her mother.

"They *smoke* the cigs," said Geoff with kindly patience. "We collect the packets."

"What shift are you on?" Clarrie demanded of her husband.

"Nine till seven," he told her.

"Not again. You've been up all night."

"It's the same for everybody, Mother. Least I can do."

"You'll kill yourself, that's what you'll do." She hid her concern beneath a waspish tone.

"And where did Billy get the cap from?" James asked his son.

"What he calls the chip run," Geoff said. "He goes and gets their chips—on his bike—in a box, fish and chips. Takes them back to camp. They *pay* him. And they gave him this cap. He's letting me help him on Saturday."

"You'll do no such thing," said Clarrie at once.

"Aw, Mother—" he began to protest.

"They're very good to the kids, Mother," said Jean.

"And to you too, given half a chance," Clarrie snapped back, clutching her stomach beneath the table. "Is that what you want? To be a source of amusement to some foreigners with more money than sense? Your Ken'd have something to say about that."

Jean flushed, both at her mother's scathing tone, and at the reminder of the young man with whom she'd been going steady before the war swept him away to an army camp in the south. She was fond of Ken, loved him even, she supposed—but she wished her mother would stop pushing him at her and give her a chance to make up her own mind.

"They're just lads," her father was saying. "Soldiers—thousands of miles from home. We should be grateful."

"I am grateful," said Clarrie unexpectedly. "God knows we need all the help we can get. But we're not obliged to make them more welcome than common courtesy demands. They're aliens, and there's no real place for them in any life that calls itself English."

ON THE FIFTH day after their arrival, Sergeant Danny Waterman, his face wreathed in smiles, hurtled into Matt's room.

"We got it!" he yelled joyously. "We got it!"

"Well, don't lose it—whatever it is." Matt didn't look up from the letter he was writing to his father.

"A pass, dummy," said Danny. "We got a pass!" He was jigging in delighted frenzy. "I hear some of these girls have been without a man for years. Can you imagine—years," he breathed. He became aware that Matt was still lying there in his undershirt. "Will you get some clothes on," he nagged.

"They waited years, Danny," Matt assured him. "They can wait a couple more hours."

Danny threw his shirt at him. "Yeah, but I can't."

There was no transport available for pleasure jaunts into town, so a group of men lined up in the late afternoon at the bus stop. Danny crossed his fingers and sent up a prayer to Eros.

He knew Eros had been listening even before the bus stopped. He could see the gleam of blonde hair framing the bright, vivacious face that he remembered. No need to look any farther. She would most certainly do.

Once on the bus Matt studied his fellow passengers with the interest of an anthropologist considering another species. An old man with watery eyes and highly polished shoes rested his hands on a military cane and stared ahead of him. Two middle-aged women in headscarves gossiped. Immediately opposite Matt and Danny a soldier sat with his baby son on his knees, his wife asleep against his shoulder.

Danny studied only Molly, whom he guessed must have seen him although she gave no sign. The bus drew to a halt and she tapped the old man with the stick on his shoulder.

"Coach 'n Horses, Dad," she told him.

Danny wondered how she knew. There was nothing to be seen in the darkness outside. But the old man struggled to his feet. Matt leaped up to help him off the bus, not letting go till he was safely on the pavement.

"OK now, sir?" he asked.

"Thank you, Sergeant."

He raised his hat and hobbled off into the darkness as Matt jumped nimbly back on board.

"Will he be OK?" said Matt to Molly as the bus moved off.

"Who, the Sergeant Major?" she said. "He could find the Coach 'n Horses with his head in a bucket—been suppin' there sixty years. How far you going, lads?" Quick as a flash she intercepted Danny who had opened his mouth. "And no cracks from you, cheeky face. I've heard it all before. Town, is it?"

Danny nodded, smitten.

"First time?" she asked.

He nodded again.

"Cat caught his tongue?" she asked of Matt.

"He's shy," said Matt solicitously. "Women scare him."

"Aye, and I'm the Queen of the May. Two fours."

She punched their tickets and took the money Danny held out. He didn't take his eyes off her.

"One sixpence—two pennies," she said, picking coins daintily from his palm. "Ta, love, now put it away before you lose it. Any more fares, please?" She moved off.

"You hear that?" demanded Danny, jabbing Matt painfully with his elbow. "She called me 'love'."

"I don't think it's personal." Matt tried to make out where they were, staring through the window, but there was only darkness. Finally, the vehicle pulled up.

"Town," Molly sang out. "Terminus. All out, lads. Far as we go." Her eyes challenged Danny for a fraction of a second. "Couple of minutes' walk to the centre of town," she assured him.

The soldiers trooped off the bus. They had gone a few yards into the darkness when Molly's voice reached them. "Hey, cherub."

"Me?" Danny said, turning immediately.

"Here. Just in case you get lost." She caught up with them and thrust a small folded note into his hand. A moment later she had disappeared.

Danny struck a match and studied the note.

"What's it say?" demanded Matt.

Danny glanced up. In the light of the flickering match his smile seemed to stretch from ear to ear.

"It says we're going to the movies," he said triumphantly.

"IF THEY COME," said Jean furiously, "I'm not talking to them."

"Don't." Molly sounded casual. "I'm not bothered."

They were sitting in the cheaper seats of the Ritz Cinema while all around them the audience bellowed "I've got sixpence" to the accompaniment of an organist on a high perch who kept turning round and displaying his teeth. Now and again Molly joined in the chorus. Jean refused to. She was too angry. What on earth did Molly think she was about, turning up at the teashop where they'd arranged to meet and announcing that she'd invited two Yanks to join them: two Yanks she didn't even *know!* She'd met them on the bus only that evening if you please! But that was Molly for you, never a thought before she acted, and then got surprised and hurt when you complained. Now she wouldn't be able to relax and enjoy the film.

"What's up with you anyway?" Molly demanded. "They're only lads."

"They're only *Yanks*," said Jean, exasperated at her friend's lack of understanding. "Me mother'll kill me."

The organist had finished his stint, and began to sink beneath the stage, flashing his teeth over his shoulder as he went. The lights dimmed and Gaumont British News came up on the screen. Just as Jean was beginning to think she'd been let off there was a small commotion in the row behind them, a head leaned forwards on Molly's side, and her friend gave a little squeak.

"Oh my God," she whispered. "They're here."

Jean shrank down in her seat, hoping that the two men wouldn't realize she was with Molly.

"Sorry we're late," Danny whispered loudly into Molly's ear. "It's so goddam dark outside—we couldn't find the place."

"It's a blackout, Chuck," Molly threw over her shoulder. "Show them a light and they drop a bomb on you. Like that, Jerries— nasty."

"The name's Danny," he told her.

"Molly."

"This is Matt."

"This is Jean."

Matt leaned forward. "Glad to know you, Jean."

She didn't answer but sat looking straight ahead. In the semi-darkness Matt and Danny looked at each other. After a moment Danny shrugged. What did he care? He had the live one.

Matt, watching Jean, could just make out that she was stubbing out the butt of a cigarette. He took his chance.

"Cigarette?" he said quietly into her ear.

"No thanks."

It occurred to her that his voice had sounded pleasant, but it was the voice of the serpent and she would ignore it. Like her Mum said, give a Yank an inch and he'd take a yard. She settled back and concentrated on the screen.

The film was an American comedy and since a good half of the audience was American the show went down well. Jean sat isolated in her annoyance while waves of laughter washed around her. She could just make out the chuckles of the two young men behind them, and mingled with her irritation was a guilty feeling that her behaviour had been needlessly ungracious.

When the film was over and they traipsed out into the darkness she preserved her distance, aware that Matt was giving her puzzled looks. But he courteously did not try to force himself on her.

Danny, his arm round Molly, demanded, "Where's to eat?" and they groped their way to a fish and chip shop. Jean at once announced that she would wait outside while the others got what they wanted. When Matt declared politely that he would keep her company she felt guiltier than ever.

Danny blinked as they entered the chip shop, which from the outside had been totally blacked out. He left the ordering to Molly while he looked round, taking in his new surroundings.

The large friendly chip lady bustled out and placed their order on the counter. "Fish and chips four times," she recited. "Eating them now?"

"I am," Molly enthused. "I'm starving."

"What about you, soldier?" the woman looked at Danny.

"I'm just playing follow my leader," he said meekly, grinning at Molly.

She laughed back at him. "Are you now?"

Danny, he told himself, you struck it lucky right off. He spared a moment's pity for Matt, trying to make out with a glacier.

"Two and six, please," said the woman. She gave a glance at her husband bent over the hot fat, then winked at Molly in a conspiratorial manner that took in Danny as well. "That's the way to treat 'em, love."

Danny mentally noted that "love". Evidently Matt had been right and it wasn't personal. At least—he regarded the chip woman's fourteen stone—in this case he hoped not.

It was cold as the four of them made their way along the darkened street. Jean pulled her headscarf closer round her face, and warmed her hands on her packet of fish and chips. She found herself walking with Matt, but kept a respectable foot apart. She was embarrassed both by her own rudeness and by his presence.

She glanced scornfully at Molly, walking happily with Danny up ahead of them. Danny's arm was round her, and they were giggling together. Had she no pride, thought Jean, to act like that the first evening out?

"You know, I got a theory about blackouts," said Matt to break the silence between them. He waited, but she might not have heard. "My theory is, they're the wrong idea. I mean, you can't tell me that if you black out London the other side doesn't know where it is. So I think that you do the opposite. Light everything up. Really *see* the enemy planes. You'd knock them right out of the sky. What do you think?"

"I'm sure the army's thought of it," said Jean primly. "Anyway, the blitz was two years ago—you're a bit late."

"Oh boy!" he said glumly.

Why, he wondered, didn't he just beat it? He sure as hell wasn't going to get anywhere with this icy lady. Yet he couldn't rid himself of a sneaking desire to find out what she was really like once those defences were down. He'd had one really good look at her face when the cinema lights came up, and he'd been startled. She was really lovely, in a serious, almost nun-like way. She was a lady, he told himself, and a lady didn't like having strange guys forced on her.

"Is it that you don't like Americans," he tried again, "or you just don't like me?"

"I don't even know you."

"That leaves Americans."

"A girl gets a name going out with Americans."

"You worried about *that?*"

"I'm worried about my mother. She has a shop here—"

"I don't want to go out with your *mother*—"

A cry from in front interrupted them. Molly flashed her torch. "See you tomorrow, Jean! Behave yourself!"

"Molly!" Jean called, alarmed. "Wait—"

But the torch had vanished. Molly and Danny had gone off together. Jean stared into the blackness in dismay.

When the silence grew strained Matt asked gently, "What are you so scared about?"

"I'm not scared," she said at once.

He gave her his best winning smile which she could only just make out. "I'm more scared than you," he told her. "Here I am—God knows where—for God knows how long, out with the first English girl I've ever met, and she turns out to be Miss Icicle. I mean, that's scary. I've got to figure out, are they all like that?"

"Some *are*—some aren't." She began to walk on and he followed.

"Then it's got to be me."

"I told you," she said, a touch unwillingly, "it isn't you."

He looked at her, and after a moment light dawned. "It's somebody else."

"Yes," she said quietly.

"English? Well, sure, that's a stupid question—in the army?"

"Yes, he's down south."

"And it's serious."

"We're getting engaged as soon as he gets leave." He couldn't see her face, but he was listening intently to her voice, and he thought he detected a troubled note, but it was gone before he could be sure.

"But you're not engaged yet," he persisted.

"It's all fixed."

"So you can see me again."

"I really don't understand you," she said, exasperated. "There's no point."

"I'd just like to see you," he said simply. "Take in a movie some time, have a bite to eat—take a walk. No fancy moves. Nothing to be scared about."

"Look, you just want a girl."

"The woods are full of girls," he said, thinking of Molly.

"Well, pick yourself one. This is where I turn off. Thanks for your company. Good night."

Without warning she was gone, and he was alone in the night as if she had never been there.

"Hey!" he called. There was no answer. "How do I get back to camp?"

Her voice floated back to him. "Turn left at the war memorial."

He nodded before he realized that in the darkness this was no help.

"How do I find the war memorial?" he muttered.

He stood for a moment retracing their steps in his mind. With luck he should make it back to the bus terminus. He thought about

Jean as he picked his way carefully back the way he'd come. He wasn't despondent. Yanks didn't admit defeat easily. Hell, why else were they here?

3 Helen St. John plunged her fork into the ground and paused to survey her morning's work. She found the results moderately satisfactory. She was standing in a potato patch that had once been her favourite flower bed. To her left was a wheelbarrow almost filled with potatoes. Two hours of work had left her with bright eyes, flushed cheeks and an aching back.

She perched on the side of the wheelbarrow, permitting herself a few minutes rest while she surveyed the scene about her. She had been one of the first to "dig for victory"—the acres that surrounded her home, Lime Hall, had become vegetable patches within a month of the war's start. With the help of a couple of land girls the lawns and flowerbeds that had been her pride had vanished under a sea of brown upturned earth.

Potatoes were especially valued. To eat potatoes instead of bread saved scarce wheat. This was Helen's fourth crop and they were getting better all the time. At least, that was what her American friend, Captain John Docherty, said when he came to buy these and other vegetables from her for the nearby army base where he was in charge of supplies.

John had been her friend since the day they met at the camp just a year ago. He had just arrived and was homesick for the wife and children he had left behind. She was lonely for her husband at sea and her children at boarding school. Over Red Cross tea and buns they had talked. The following week he had come to a concert where she had played the cello in an amateur string quartet. Afterwards he had driven her home and they had talked some more. He had promised her the loan of an army truck to help transport some of her harvested vegetables. Thereafter, he had borrowed the truck for her whenever she wanted it.

She felt happy to think she would see him that day. There was no one to whom she could talk as she could to John. The two land girls who had been allocated to her to help cultivate her acres

23

were goodhearted and friendly, but more than ten years her junior. They had no interests in common and although she enjoyed having their company in the large house, she was inwardly as lonely as if they had not been there. Her only other companion was Ivy, her living-in "treasure". Ivy had the strength of a horse and a will of iron. She mother-henned Helen with ruthless devotion. Helen loved her, but she could not talk to her.

She waved at the land girls as they trekked wearily into the kitchen for tea and a natter, and decided she would just finish digging the row before joining them. She still had hours of work ahead of her. In the evening she would change out of the old tweed suit, wellingtons and headscarf that were suitable for digging potatoes, and into her Red Cross uniform, then head for the army base hospital.

She had joined the Red Cross early, studying hard to pass the tests, and giving long hours of her time to the base hospital, or wherever she was needed. There was no compulsion for her to do this. Although the government had finally resorted to conscripting women into war work, Helen, as a mother of two children, was exempt. But it was not her way to dodge what she considered to be her duty.

She was a tall, handsome woman in her late thirties, with the slender elegance of a racehorse. She had married into an old wealthy family with a tradition of service that made it inevitable that Peter, her husband, should volunteer for the navy, even though he was forty and as a doctor might legitimately have stayed at home. The St. Johns had lived at Lime Hall for four centuries and had always sent their men to war. So Peter St. John became a navy doctor, leaving Helen alone with their son Tim and their daughter Anna. A week after Peter's departure the children returned to boarding school, and the large house seemed to echo hollowly without them. Helen's comfort lay in the drawing room with its view of the moors and its perfect acoustics for the soaring tones of her cello.

The cello, once the centre of her life, was now its solace. As a young girl her future had seemed clear. She was going to complete her musical studies and become a concert performer. She had never thought of marriage or love, except that sometimes the piercing sweetness of her heart's response to a phrase, or even a solitary note, had made her wonder if love was like that. But she had dismissed the thought. She was a musician.

And then her teacher had suggested—very kindly, knowing the full strength of the blow he was dealing her—that perhaps she would care to consider training to be a music teacher. She was an excellent player of the cello, but she lacked the special quality that made a performer.

In her youthful fierceness she had rejected out of hand the idea of becoming a teacher. She had never been able to tolerate second best. It must be all or nothing. And since the "all" was to be denied her (since she was "unworthy" was how she had put it at nineteen) she precipitately embraced the nothing. The lovely instrument was locked away, and the following year she married Peter St. John.

She loved him well enough. They were warm and close, and there was something in his devotion that would have been hard for any woman to resist. Love, she discovered, was not soaring music, but gentle happiness and contentment. And once she had come to that conclusion it had been possible to take out the cello again and remember wryly her youthful dreams. Her mind ran ahead now, to the time when she would return from the hospital late that night. She would play then to drive the hospital sights from her mind.

She heard the first sounds of the truck coming up the drive, and went on digging while it stopped and the driver got out and came over to her. She knew, without looking, that it would be John. And she knew that he was watching her for several moments before she acknowledged him.

"You're not much help standing and staring, you know," she smiled.

"I'm not staring. I'm admiring," he said frankly.

She pushed back a stray wisp of hair. "How I dig potatoes?"

"How you look."

The compliment both pleased and embarrassed her. She made a little sound that was half a gasp, half a laugh. He had heard her do it before and he found it oddly touching.

"You're early, aren't you?" she said, looking at her watch.

"I'm always early. Haven't you noticed?" He took the fork from her. "Here, give that to me."

"You'll get dirt on your uniform," she protested.

"I'm used to dirt. Worked my way through law school collecting garbage." He tossed some potatoes expertly into the wheelbarrow.

The front door opened as he bent again to the fork. Ivy, huge and capable in an all-enveloping cross-over apron, stood there.

"Phone, Mrs. St. John," she called. "Master Tim." Her tone gave nothing away.

"Not again," said Helen with a sigh.

John indicated the potatoes in the wheelbarrow. "Want me to take these in?"

"Would you, please?" She gave him a quick half-smile. "I won't be a moment."

She went indoors and he trundled the barrow round the back to the kitchen door. He wondered what she would say to her young son who had presumably phoned her for the same reason he always did—to beg her to allow him home. John felt a wrench of compassion. The English habit of sending children away to school struck him as something barbarous. Helen's willingness to go along with it in the face of her child's unhappiness troubled him because it jarred his vision of her as a gentle, loving and deeply feminine woman.

He thrust such thoughts out of his consciousness as he carried potatoes into the kitchen. There he found the two pretty land girls finishing tea. They flung him smiles of pleased recognition.

"Hiya girls," he chaffed. "Listen, we just got a new crop of GIs in from the States. Just kids most of them—" He raised his eyes to include Ivy's solid frame entering from the hall. "This includes you too, Ivy. I don't want you breaking their hearts. We have to turn them into ruthless fighting machines."

The girls giggled and Ivy gave him a broad grin. John was a favourite with all of them.

"Would you like a cup of tea, Captain?" she offered.

"Thanks, but I'm floating in the stuff. I'll just wait in the living room—" he caught himself, "excuse me—drawing room."

He turned and crossed the hall to the drawing room, wandering over to the window where a grand piano stood. The lid, which was closed, was adorned with pictures of the family, mostly of Peter St. John with his children or dressed for rugger. John ran his fingers over the keys. He was a lover of music, but an indifferent player, whose ambitions outstripped his talent. It had been a bond between himself and Helen, who had confided that the same was true of her. But having heard her play he could not concede that her deficiency was in the same league as his own.

After a moment he became aware of Helen's voice through the open window. She was on the phone in the study next door. "Now Tim . . ." she was saying, "this phoning is getting absurd. Why aren't you at school now? . . . Well, shouldn't you be playing rugger too?" There was a long pause. "I see. Well, you'll be landing yourself in hot water if you're not careful."

Her tone, the words, the inflexibility of her attitude all made him wince. To cover her voice he sat down at the piano and began to play.

In the study Helen was trying to finish the conversation quickly —while she could still bear it. Tim was being ridiculous, it was just weakness to think of giving in to him. But the pathos in her son's voice made her clench her hands. "It's terrible for all of us," she said. "Do you think Daddy likes being away?"

He agreed that Daddy didn't. A resigned note crept into his voice.

Helen heard it with relief. He was going to be good after all. "That's better," she said. "I'll write tonight. Chin up. 'Bye."

The sound of the piano reached her as soon as she replaced the receiver. John was playing "The Harmonious Blacksmith" laboriously and with great concentration. She left the study and went to stand in the open door of the drawing room, watching him. As soon as he saw her he stopped.

"Don't stop," she said.

"I can't play while you stare at me."

"I like watching you play the piano. So angry with yourself when you make a mistake . . . as though you weren't allowed to. It tells me something about you. I like that." She gave him an affectionate smile.

He shut the lid to the keys firmly, refusing to be drawn. Ivy appeared behind Helen in the doorway, carrying a tray with a pot of tea, milk and sugar, and two cups and saucers. With heavy significance she placed it on a low table, announced, "You don't have to drink it," and departed.

"What was *that* about?" said Helen, bewildered.

"I said 'no' to a cup of tea," he confessed.

She gave a husky chuckle. "Tch! Tch! Sacrilege." She sat on the couch and began to pour. He sat beside her.

"I got a letter from Ann today," he said, speaking of his wife. "She's sold up," he added flatly.

"Whatever do you mean?"

"Sold the house, everything. Moved upstate to her family, took the kids."

"Your lovely house?"

"Well, I guess she's right," he said bleakly. "We discussed it, you know, when I was drafted. My chances of coming through— we sort of talked about it then. But now she's done it—" his voice trailed off. For a moment there was such misery on his face that Helen was shocked. The other woman's premature assumption of widowhood (for that was what it amounted to) was, to her, incomprehensible. It was something that could not have been done by a woman who loved, of that she was sure.

Being Helen she tried to understate: "It's a bit pessimistic, isn't it?"

"Ann'd call it realistic."

She faced him. "Peter and I, when *he* went away, we resolved to play the whole thing *down*—try to take it all in our stride. Everybody did. We had to . . . I mean, where would the nation be now if we had all been 'realistic'?"

He gave her a look of admiration that was not for herself alone. "You know, Helen, when I got off that boat—and looked at the bombing—then at the people, I don't know . . . maybe I shouldn't say this, but . . . maybe you people are different. Back home we could never have taken it."

She took his hand in a gesture of pure spontaneous affection. "Of course you could. The trouble with you Americans, you take your wars far too seriously."

GOING BACK to camp John wondered if it was not rather his way to take everything too seriously. He did not lack humour. It was there for all to see, built into the mobile lines of his face. But it had had to fight for its life.

He had been born in a part of New York City known graphically as Hell's Kitchen. The youngest of six rowdy children he had benefited from his place in the line. By the time it became obvious that he had the family brains his older brothers were working and there was enough money to keep him at college—just.

He had chosen to go into law because it seemed to offer him the most straightforward way out of the poverty of his background. He had joked to Helen about working his way through law school, but the reality had been a tough dreary grind. He had got through and graduated, but it had almost broken him.

He had emerged as a fully qualified lawyer at the end of the twenties to find that the crash of 1929 had made a mockery of his childish dreams of prosperity.

Finally he had gained a partnership in a firm, once prosperous and honoured, but almost ruined in the Depression and now fighting to survive. The partnership was offered to him at a bargain price. In the circumstances each was the best the other could afford. The transaction proved a turning point for both of them. Bit by bit he and the firm helped each other out of the doldrums.

He married in his thirties, a plain girl as lonely as himself. He had known that he was Ann's last chance. She was not his. By waiting longer he could probably have married a girl who more closely approximated to what he had once thought a successful lawyer's wife should be. But he had been fighting alone for long enough. He wanted a home and children, and a wife who put him before all else.

And that, on the whole, was what he believed he had, until America entered the war. It had been, on the whole, a good marriage; not a passionate but an affectionate one. He loved his children and felt content with his home. When war came and he knew he would be sent away he clung to the thought of them as an anchor. Then Ann had dealt her blow.

It would be foolish, she said, for her to simply sit around waiting to see what the outcome of the war was going to be. Far better for her to sell the house and return to her old home town, near her parents, where she would at least have people whom she knew. He had agreed to everything, too stunned by this easy way of writing him off to argue. Ann was not perceptive enough to realize that she was once again casting him adrift in an ocean of loneliness.

When he first met Helen at the camp hospital, he instantly recognized a kindred spirit. It was as though she dared offer only

29

a half smile till she saw his answering expression. Only then did she risk offering back warmth for warmth. It was as though she too needed a hand held out to her.

He pursued her after that as a man freezing to death will seek a fire. As supply officer he could find excuses to visit her frequently. When he discovered that she played in a local amateur orchestra he began to slip away to their concerts, sometimes letting Helen know that he was there, but often not. He would stand at the back of draughty halls and churches listening to some piece of baroque music, completely alien to any culture he had known before. But he had eyes only for Helen, for her beauty and mystery, and her air of having come from another world.

4

At times it seemed that the British were involved in two kinds of war. There was the war they were fighting in Italy, Burma and North Africa, and which seemed very distant. Sons and husbands returned for short tense leaves, and spoke of their war with floundering words that conveyed little. They did this because they had no wish to think of the life they had left and to which they must soon return.

Alongside this there was the war fought by the civilians at home. At first the two wars had not been so far apart. During the blitz the civilian war had included fear and death, but after the heavy concentrated bombing had effectively ended in 1941, personal fear was no longer an inevitable part of every day. It slipped gradually away like a tide down a beach, revealing beneath it a grim bedrock of deprivations and restrictions.

Most unavoidable was the blackout which had begun the very first day of the war. Every light that might be seen by an enemy in the air must be covered, no matter how. Cardboard, brown paper, black paint, blinds, thick curtains.

Everything was in short supply, either because the seas were no longer safe for bringing imported goods, or because the factories that made goods at home could no longer do so. Jean, working in her parents' general store-*cum*-post office, was acutely aware of the war waged at home. Let just a hint of a sugar delivery get round the town and a queue would form within minutes. Even before the shop opened a line of weary grey-faced women would be standing waiting to have the coupons clipped out of their ration books, and to return to their homes trying to work out how to make their little windfall last till next time.

Like most shops of its kind the Moreton's was an information exchange. Women with menfolk back from the front came to pass on what little they'd been told. Old Annie, for example, usually had a new story to tell. She had lost two sons in the 1914–18 war, and had four grandsons serving in this one. One of the lads had got back three nights ago, bearing a German helmet which Annie had promptly taken over.

She was wearing it now as she marched stiff-legged round the shop to the admiring chuckles of the other customers. Her goose step was a perfect imitation of what she'd seen on cinema newsreels. With her finger held straight under her nose to represent a moustache and one arm raised in a Nazi salute, the imitation of Hitler was complete.

"Where did you get that helmet, Annie?" Jean leaned over the post office section of counter, where she was sorting stamps.

"Our Jane's lad brought it home," said Annie without removing her finger or ceasing her jerky walk.

"The one that was wounded?" queried Mrs. Shenton, who was being served at the post office counter.

"Aye, from Africa." Breathlessness brought Annie to a halt. "Said he'd've brought the bloody head'n all if they'd let him."

Jean finished her sorting. "Here's your stamps, Mrs. Shenton."

As she pushed them across, her eye was caught by something in the window over Mrs. Shenton's shoulder. Her lips tightened. How dare Matt lurk outside the shop window waving to her! She turned her head away from his smile. He needn't think she was going to be flattered. If she hadn't made herself plain enough the other night, now was the time to do it. She noted with relief that no one else seemed to have noticed him. Her Mam was packing up Annie's little order, thank goodness.

As Annie handed over her ration book, Jean took a furtive glance at the window. Matt was still standing there. She made frantic little movements with her hands indicating for him to go away. To her vast relief he vanished.

"I wish I were a lass again," Annie was gloating. "They're having the time of their lives with the Yanks."

As Annie stopped speaking, Jean was horrified to see Matt ambling in through the doorway.

"Hi," said Matt politely.

"Can I help you?" said Clarrie. No one could have faulted her manner.

"That's very kind of you, ma'am. Is it OK if I just look around?"

"Yes, of course." She nodded and turned away.

Matt began to browse, meeting the eyes of the other three and bestowing his warm smile on them.

"Will that be all, Mrs. Shenton?" Jean demanded with more abruptness than courtesy. Mrs. Shenton reluctantly withdrew her attention from Matt.

"I think so."

"Goodbye, then."

Clarrie glanced up in surprise at her daughter's tone but said nothing. As Mrs. Shenton made for the door Matt got there ahead of her, opening it with studied gallantry. She rewarded him with her best smile before sailing out. Having closed the door Matt resumed his browsing. He appeared to be riveted by the merits of an all-purpose cleanser. Jean  was torn between annoyance and reluctant amusement at the performance. Who did he think he was fooling?

Clarrie, having mentally sized him up as an unlikely candidate for a packet of cleanser, nudged him along a little.

"You're sure there's nothing . . . ?" she pressed.

"As a matter of fact—" he sounded as though light had just dawned, "—do you carry bicycle clips?"

Clarrie's face was expressionless. "We do."

"Do you think I could try them on?"

She regarded him closely, unable to decide if he was being funny.

"Certainly," she said at last. "Jean, would you take care of Annie, please?" Jean crossed to the other side of the shop, and began snipping away at Annie's coupons. She snipped with fierce abstraction until Annie interrupted her.

"Them's clothing coupons, love," she said kindly.

"Oh, yes—sorry."

She began to fumble over the pages to find the right ones. Annie looked at her, then at Matt, her wise old eyes bright with intuition. She gave Matt a broad wink and received his smile in return. Clarrie, who had her back turned, saw nothing.

"Thanks, Annie." Jean returned the book. "Shall I book this for next week?"

"Please, love. It's pension day Thursday." She straightened the helmet on her head, gave Matt a wink, then goose-stepped out. She left Matt chuckling and Jean stony-faced.

"They're on the top shelf, Mother," Jean called to Clarrie who had not found the clips. "I'll get them. You see to Dad's tea."

"Which shelf?"

"Go on—you're not climbing ladders."

"Thank you, Jean." Clarrie gave her daughter a pallid, grateful smile. "I'll be in the kitchen if you need me."

She departed after giving Matt an icily polite glance. Jean descended from the ladder and thrust the bicycle clips into Matt's hands before he had a chance to reach up and help her down.

"Why did you come here?" she demanded, keeping her voice low, mindful of the open hatch between the shop and their kitchen. "I told you—"

"You want to go to the movies Saturday night?"

"Please go away."

"I *am* away," he said with comic pathos. "Five thousand miles—"

"From *here*," she broke in, exasperated. "From me. You'll get me into trouble."

He stepped back and made an elaborate performance of trying on the clips. Jean glanced at the hatch in agony.

"You think these fit?" he asked brightly. "How do I look in them?"

"Why are you doing this? If I was rude to you the other evening, I apologize. Now please, I really mean it."

This time Matt followed her gaze to the hatch where Clarrie's puzzled face could be seen looking at them.

"OK," he capitulated suddenly. "How much for the clips?"

"A shilling." He gave her the money. "Thank you."

At the door he looked back at her. "Now all I need is a bike," he said and vanished before she could gasp out her indignation.

The shop suddenly seemed very quiet and empty after his bright presence. It was the jokes, she decided. How long was it since she'd heard anyone make really silly jokes, not just the black defiant humour hurled in Hitler's face? Oh well. . . .

To escape her mother's still curious gaze from the hatch, she began to pile milk bottles briskly into a crate. As soon as she could she staggered out with it to the place behind the shop where the empties were stacked. Keeping her eyes down while she negotiated a short flight of stone steps she saw nothing else until a pair of warm brown hands descended on hers, the crate was pulled from her grasp, and a voice that was becoming all too familiar said, "You know, one year I was in the state championship game . . ." Jean had no idea what he was talking about. She was just watching him with a kind of resigned fascination. ". . . Biggest football game of the year."

"Why me?" she demanded despairingly of an unhelpful sky.

"Who knows?" said Matt. "But I don't want to cause you trouble. You want me to go away—I'll go away."

"Thank God for that!"

"I'll just come back tomorrow."

A reluctant smile played round her mouth. He gave her a beaming grin in return, confident that he'd won.

Oh, her mother was right. They were so sure of themselves, they thought they had you for the asking. It would serve him right if she turned back and slammed the door in his face. But she couldn't do that because against her will her smile was stretching further in answer to his, and deep inside her was an admiring chuckle for his persistence. And anything would be better than having him park on her mother's doorstep and create a scandal.

Their eyes met. She sighed.

"All right," she said. "Saturday night."

Her muddled thoughts were still with her when she slipped out on Saturday evening, after telling Clarrie that she was going to the pictures, but not with whom.

It was still early evening and some daylight lingered, but there was a fog that shrouded other pedestrians. Figures loomed at her suddenly, revealing themselves as GIs in little groups, eyeing her speculatively. Here and there one of them had a girl on his arm. How she had despised girls who went with Yanks!

But he was different, she told herself. It was just for the evening, to stop him pestering her. She was going to be faithful to Ken. She certainly wasn't going to be like Molly Dawlish (whom she hadn't seen since their last night at the pictures). But Matt was probably a very nice boy and pleasant company, so what was wrong with a cheerful evening for once?

Her steps had brought her to the Ritz Cinema. Matt wasn't there, and she told herself that her stab of disappointment was dismay at having to stand alone in the crowd that was gathering on the pavement outside.

A glimpse of American uniform caught her eye and she turned in relief, but neither of the two GIs who stood there was Matt. They were studying the posters and the girls and they looked half drunk. They noticed Jean standing alone and made their way carefully up to her.

"You alone, sister?"

She turned her head away sharply, her eyes searching for Matt.

"That's a shame," said the second one giving her a blast of whisky-scented breath. "A looker like you. You shouldn't be alone. It ain't safe."

Some instinct warned her that if she showed her fear it would only egg them on. But her heart was thundering as she realized that she was trapped and none of the rest of the crowd seemed to have noticed anything. She stood like a stone, trying to give no sign of having heard them, hoping they would get bored and give up. Only her eyes, frantically flicking from side to side, betrayed her. If Matt didn't arrive soon she felt she would scream.

"Stick with us," the first one was saying, "we'll protect you. Here—have a little drink." He produced a half-empty bottle of whisky. She shook her head. "Come on, honey, protect you from the cold."

"We're just looking to warm you up, baby." The second soldier had put an arm round her shoulders, blocking off her retreat. Now he tightened it suddenly so that she couldn't move. His free hand grabbed the bottle from the other man and forced it to Jean's lips. She twisted her head, gagging at the smell, feeling the stuff run down her chin. She put her hands up in front of her face and felt the neck of the bottle jabbing against them as he tried to push it between her fingers.

Then suddenly the bottle was gone, and to her vast relief there was Matt's voice, gently chiding, almost not angry at all.

"What's the matter, you got no respect?" Jean pulled down her hands to find him regarding the other two soldiers, shaking his head as though explaining something to a dim-witted child. "That's good American whisky—" he admonished them. "You don't want to waste that on some limey broad."

Then he moved. He moved so swiftly that Jean was still feeling a resentful surprise at his words when she realized that he had one of the men jammed up against the wall. He was holding him there with his left fore-arm, while his right hand held the whisky bottle. With a sharp, brutal movement Matt rammed the neck of the bottle into the GI's mouth.

"You drink it, soldier," he said quietly.

His forearm had moved up till it was against the man's windpipe, pressing, while he fought for breath and the whisky bottle filled his mouth, spilling its contents down his coat. Jean watched, frozen.

The second soldier had moved in to help his friend.

"Hey," he bleated.

Matt whirled on him, his eyes full of a cold, blinding rage.

"You want some?" he asked, still without raising his voice.

The man backed away. Choking sounds came from the one up against the wall. As if just remembering him Matt removed the bottle. Then he put his face very close to the man's and said clearly, "You can't hold your liquor, you shouldn't drink."

He released him, stepped back and tipped the bottle so that what was left of its contents flowed into the gutter. He tossed the empty bottle back to the soldier who was clutching his throat.

"That wasn't nice," said the other one plaintively. "That was real bourbon. You shouldn't have done that."

He might not have existed. Matt was giving Jean a polite smile. The dreadful look of casual savagery was gone from his face.

"OK," he said. "Where would you like to sit?"

"I've seen this picture." She could hear her voice shaking. "Why didn't you tell me?"

"You didn't give me much of a chance, did you?"

"OK. Let's go. I've seen it too."

He took her arm and led her away without a backward glance.

He didn't make her walk far, but soon steered her into a pub. She didn't often find herself in pubs, and the unusual surroundings made her self-conscious, but she had been very upset by the incident with the drunks and wanted to sit down. It was Matt who had shaken her to the soul. His complete calm as he had dealt with the two GIs had frightened her more than hot temper would have done; it served to underline his matter-of-fact acceptance of his own violence.

She felt that if one of her own countrymen had dealt with a similar situation in an equally savage and efficient way it would have left him either exhilarated at his own prowess or shocked at his own brutality. Matt was neither. He appeared not to give it a second thought. As Jean sat in an alcove watching Matt ordering at the bar she had the feeling that he had already forgotten the matter.

He returned to where she was sitting, handed her a glass of sherry and put a pint of half and half on the table for himself. Then he sat down, took some bars of chocolate out of his pocket and laid them out in front of her.

"I brought them for the movies," he said.

"Thank you. That wasn't necessary."

She hadn't meant to be ungracious. She knew nervousness was making her sound sullen, but she couldn't equate the cruelty of this man with the bright presence that had almost won her over the other day. She made an effort to be more pleasant and give him a smile by way of contrition.

"Do you mind if I save them? I've a little brother."

"I can get more for him," said Matt without thinking.

He suddenly knew he was saying the wrong thing. Big mouth Yank! Throwing his goodies around. Thinking he'd impress the local girls! Jean wasn't the kind of girl to fall over herself for a flashy guy, and now she probably despised him! The evening suddenly bore all the signs of a monumental foul-up. He sipped his beer. It was warm and awful.

"Sometimes I got a big mouth," he said at last.

"What?"

"I say things I shouldn't. Boasting about being able to get chocolate bars."

She was staring down at the table with a glazed, almost dead

38

look in her eyes. "Why were you so vicious outside the pictures?" she asked quietly.

Understanding dawned at once. After a moment he said, "Do you know something, Jeannie? I never thought twice about it. Back home in Arizona, a guy like that—it's just something you do. Maybe we got violent natures. It worried you, did it?"

"Yes," she said simply. "It did."

"I can understand that." His voice was gentle.

She smiled at him, and the shuttered look was quite gone from her eyes. They were warm and friendly now. She was no longer afraid of him.

Suddenly he wanted to tell her more about Arizona and the family he'd left behind. He fumbled in his pockets for his snaps and as soon as he produced them Jean instinctively moved her chair closer to his, liking him better for the vulnerability he had suddenly revealed.

She could just make out the small neat building where Matt's father had his business. In front of it stood a large genial-looking man. On either side of him stood two tall young men, one of them Matt. She studied it. This Matt was a chirpy young man with a beaming smile and not a care in the world. He had matured since into the thin-faced, weary looking soldier beside her. A moment's pity stung her.

"That's our diner," he was saying. "Right outside Tucson. We own it free and clear. Well, my dad does—that's him there, and my brother Ed, and that's me. I'm the short-order cook mostly. . . ."

"Short order?"

"Yeah—quick eats ya know. . . ."

"Snacks."

"I guess so," he said quickly, anxious to say it her way. "Snacks."

"It looks nice," she said, meaning it. "What about your mother?"

"She died when I was a kid. I don't remember her too much."

After a while he said, "Does your guy have a violent nature?"

"Ken? No. At least I haven't seen it."

"You known him a long time?"

"We grew up together."

"Well, that can be nice," he said carefully. "No surprises anyway. You in love with him?"

"He's everything I've always wanted," she said at once.

"I didn't ask you that," he said, looking at her steadily.

She looked steadily back, refusing to let him unnerve her.

"I heard what you asked. Everybody loves Ken. My mother does."

"Your mother's opinion mean that much to you?"

"I respect my mother, respect her judgment . . . Ken is the sort of man my mother wanted for herself . . . someone to take her over, lead her to better things. She thought she had one—but he just turned out me dad." She gave a wry smile, full of love and compassion for both her parents.

"You're still the one that's got to live with the guy," he pointed out.

"Yes, I am. And what's wrong with that?"

She began to look through the snaps again. Matt realized that she had turned away from the subject not as though she were afraid of it, but as though she considered it fully dealt with.

"After the war, are you going back to the diner?" she asked.

He shook his head. "Know what a motel is?"

She smiled. "Tell me."

"It's a kinda hotel on the highway—only you have your own little cabin with a bathroom. They're springing up all over the States. I'm gonna build me one . . . got a place picked out—lots of traffic—nice view over the desert—I'll make it."

His eyes warmed with anticipation and sudden nostalgia for the desert which had never seemed so desirable as now.

She realized she had been allowed a glimpse of a private dream, one that made his face change when he spoke of it. He looked younger, full of enthusiasm.

He took a quick gulp of beer, then pulled a face. "How d'ya drink warm beer?" he demanded fretfully.

"Should be easy with a big mouth."

He gave her a startled look to see if she had spoken with malice. But her chin was resting contentedly on her hand and the brown eyes that regarded him were full of amusement. She began to laugh at his expression, her face alight with warmth and friendliness.

He put down his beer and joined in her laughter. Without thinking he put his hand out and squeezed hers and she did not take it away.

40

5 The queue had begun before dawn. As the grey light of a November morning grew brighter it revealed a line of about thirty women waiting patiently outside Moreton's. On the shop door hung the notice that had brought them there: TINNED SALMON—WEDNESDAY—8 a.m.

Old Annie, standing with Mrs. Shenton at the head of the queue (a place she somehow always contrived to be in), shifted her feet and peered at a large clock on a building opposite. Her face wore a nagging expression. The clock said one minute past eight.

"We must be bloody mad," she announced. "I've been 'ere since six this morning. All for a tin of flippin' salmon."

"Be worth it when you get it, Annie," said Mrs. Shenton.

A cheer went up as the blind obscuring the shop window was raised. Annie peered in and gave Jean a cheeky wave. It wouldn't be long now if the lass moved herself. There was Clarrie pushing up the blinds of the other windows. Any minute—oh, flaming heck! What did the two of them have to start a barney now for? Didn't they know it was bloody freezing out here?

Jean released the blind with more force than she had intended. Her respect for her mother forced her to try to keep the irritation out of her voice, but it was getting more and more of a strain. "For God's sake Mother, he's a *friend*. I'd like you to meet him. I've always brought my friends home. He wants to meet *you*."

"Well, I've no wish to meet *him*."

Jean's fragile control snapped. "And who the hell are *you?*" she demanded in exasperation.

"Don't talk to your mother like that, Jean." James Moreton had just come in from the backyard carrying two large boxes of tins. A mild man, he seldom admonished his young son, and almost never his grown daughter. But when he spoke in that tone they had to listen. "Where d'you want these?" he said of the boxes.

"Drop them behind the counter," Clarrie told him. "And do me a notice will you?"

She began busying herself about the shop, trying to make it plain she considered the subject closed. But Jean wouldn't let it go. "He's different, Mother—he's decent," she pleaded.

41

"Decent." Clarrie faced her crossly. "How d'you know he's decent?"

"Plenty of them *are.*"

"Oh! You know plenty do you?"

"Pity I don't! Give you something to moan about."

"Jean!" Her father's head went up. "I'll not tell you again!"

He returned to chalking ONE TIN PER PERSON—NO EXCEPTIONS on a small board while the two women began to stack tins of salmon on the counter.

"And what about Ken?" muttered Clarrie.

"He *knows* about Ken. He understands."

"Understands!" There was a world of shrivelling contempt in Clarrie's voice.

"He does. I *know.*"

"How do you know?"

"Because in three weeks—" she hesitated, embarrassed, "—in three weeks—he's never touched me."

She turned away so that Clarrie should not see the flush that rose to her cheeks. She had hinted at something never mentioned in the Moreton household, and she had taken herself to the brink of a subject that she had steered away from even in her own mind.

It was true that Matt had never touched her, apart from holding her hand. But how could you ignore even that when it had sent such a sweet shock running through you? After the brash confidence with which he had started that first night he had changed. There was a gentleness and hesitancy about him now that puzzled her.

After a moment she looked back to see her mother's eyes fixed on her, shrewd and sharp, yet containing another quality that might have been compassion if she hadn't masked it so quickly in response to a rap on the door from Annie.

"Patience, ladies," Clarrie called. She went on stacking tins, still talking quietly. "How can you jeopardize you and Ken for this—this American. Knowing how people feel."

"Oh for God's sake, Mother! We enjoy each other's company that's all. He asked me to tell you—before someone else did. It doesn't affect Ken and me."

"Right then—let's feed the five thousand." Clarrie crossed towards the door, but before she opened it she looked back at Jean and calmly delivered her thunderbolt. "If I *am* prejudiced, I've no wish to be. Ask your friend round for tea on Sunday." She pulled back the first bolt. "And pray to God nobody tells Ken."

The door opened and suddenly the shop was filled with cheering women. Jean tried to catch her mother's eyes again to let her know with a smile how happy and relieved she was. But Clarrie had vanished in the pandemonium.

"You set a lovely table, Mother." Jean warmed the words with a smile to show her appreciation.

To her disappointment Clarrie's face was little more relaxed than usual and her prim "Thank you. Let's hope it's appreciated", was not encouraging.

"Geoffrey," she nodded, "pop in the shop—some chutney, my homemade. Quickly now."

Geoff, neat and unnatural in his Sunday best, slipped into the darkened shop. Only his GI cap looked familiar.

"You wouldn't know we were rationed," said Jean, pointing at the table.

"Bit of foresight, prudence—goes a long way," Clarrie said.

James spoke from behind his paper. "Aye—and living in a shop helps."

Clarrie chose to ignore this, and Jean suppressed a smile. She felt her mother was entitled to her pride. It wasn't just a question of food. The table groaned under the good china that Jean didn't remember seeing since before the war. The glasses were perfectly polished, and there were even flowers on the table.

If Jean could just have rid herself of the unworthy thought that her mother was really trying to intimidate Matt she would have felt happy. But increasingly she had the feeling that the invitation, which at first she had taken as a sign of her mother's relenting, was nothing but a more subtle stage in the hostilities.

She still doubted this, however, until her father folded his paper and said, "Family here lost three lads. On the same ship—torpedoed," and Clarrie replied, "Don't mention that in front of the American, James. It wouldn't be tactful—him not being on active service."

Jean opened her mouth to protest that once a man was in the army he had no choice where he was sent, but before she could get the words out her mother departed for the kitchen. Jean fought down her indignation.

She checked her appearance in the mirror. The dress was an old one from before the war. The material was soft and pretty, and its honey colour made her skin glow. She had put on only the briefest touch of make-up. Something inside her made her flinch from letting Matt believe she had gone to great pains to do herself up for him.

Geoff had no inhibitions about showing his eagerness. He was standing in the shop, chutney in hand, peering through the curtains into the dusk. He turned urgently as the bell rang and Jean came in. "It's the Yank," he hissed in a stage-whisper.

"Well, open the door then," she told him, cross with herself for a quick shiver of nerves that ran through her.

Geoff grinned with the knowingness of an eleven-year-old. "He's not coming to see *me*."

After a quick pull at her dress to make sure it was straight she opened the door. Matt stood there looking neater than she had seen him before. For a moment the impression of Sunday best tidiness made him so much like Geoff that she wanted to laugh.

"Hi!" he said, making no move to come in. He was laden with parcels.

"Hello," she said, formally. "Would you like to come in?" She stood back for him to enter. Geoff's eyes were fixed expectantly on the packages. "This is my brother, Geoff."

"Hi. I'm Matt."

"Hiya." Geoff readjusted the angle of his GI cap.

Matt held out one of the smaller parcels. "Took a chance maybe you liked candy—there's also a couple of comic books. Jeannie said you liked them."

For a moment he wondered if he'd overdone it, but Jean's eyes were friendly. Geoff was in ecstasies.

"Oh ta. I do, aye." He made fumbling efforts to look at everything at once, to the imminent danger of the chutney.

"Can I take your coat?" said Jean.

Matt removed his army greatcoat, carefully shifting the remaining parcels, one of which was large, from one hand to the other as he did so. She reckoned whatever was in there must be important, but he didn't offer to tell her what it was. She hoped

44

he hadn't bought her a big present. That would be embarrassing and would draw frowns from her mother. And she did so want tonight to go well.

"Wait a second," he said, as she went to hang the coat up.

He reached deep into a pocket and removed yet another package.

"OK," he said. "All set. Lead me to the slaughter."

Her father rose to his feet as they entered the living room, her mother appeared from the kitchen and Jean made the introductions.

Matt murmured, "Pleased to meet you—appreciate you asking me," with an easy courtesy that gave her a small feeling of pride in him. Surely her mother must see that this was no roughneck?

Clarrie gave him a smile that was brief but kindly enough, and said, "You're very welcome," as if she meant it.

Matt held out the large parcel to her. "This is for you, ma'am."

"Oh? Thank you. Matthew is it?"

Jean wanted to cry out—no it isn't. It's *Matt!* Don't put him at a distance! But Matt just said, "That's right, ma'am."

"After the apostle." She made no move to open her parcel.

"Hope you won't be offended by this, sir." Matt had handed the smaller parcel to James, who opened it at once to reveal a bottle of Scotch. There was no two ways about her father's reaction.

"Nay," he breathed. "There's easier ways of offending me, son. Thank you very much."

"Aren't you going to open yours, Mother?" prodded Jean.

Methodically Clarrie began to open the parcel, untying the string, wrapping it round her fingers and putting it thriftily into her apron pocket. The brown paper crackled as she pulled it open, then the lid came off. At once the four Moretons crowded round the box and stood regarding the contents, stunned.

It contained a cake. But what a cake! It was a cake such as they could hardly ever remember seeing. Certainly there had been nothing like it since the start of the war. It was exquisitely iced in pink, with workmanship that had plainly been done by the loving hands of a craftsman. Iced roses and leaves intertwined round the side, and the centre was almost wholly taken up with the one piped word—Thanks.

"I made it with real eggs," Matt couldn't resist saying.

Jean's eyes shone. It was a beautifully thought-out gesture—

generous but not vulgar. Surely her mother must see *now*. *Surely*.

Clarrie was looking at Matt as though he'd only just appeared. "You made it?" she said.

"Yes, ma'am. Just me."

Her family were watching Clarrie as she regarded the lovely thing, waiting for her response, her delight. When she finally spoke again her words clattered into the silence like small stones. "Well—thank you Matthew. It's lovely. But we won't have it tonight, if you don't mind. We've more than enough already."

She picked up the cake, wrappings and all, and took it into the kitchen, leaving them feeling as if she had hosed them down with cold water.

James didn't allow the silence to last more than a second.

"Well, we're having *this* tonight, no danger." He held up the bottle. "I'll get a couple of glasses." He trotted off happily.

"You must have worked on that all day," said Jean.

"Special event, Jeannie. I wasn't going to make just cookies." He opened the last package. It contained two tins of fruit salad. "Give these to your ma later," he said in an undertone.

She nodded, silently blessing him for his understanding.

In the kitchen Clarrie set the cake carefully on the table and regarded it. Then she thought of Matt. He was a nice boy, that was obvious—as nice as Jean said. He had pleasant manners, and had obviously been properly brought up. Bitter despair filled her. Oh, it was worse, much worse than she'd feared.

The evening proceeded upon correct, nervous lines. James offered Matt a glass of his own whisky, and Matt accepted only the very smallest amount. They said "Cheers", and sipped slowly, till Clarrie announced that it was time to sit down for the meal.

Clarrie said a silent prayer as she sat. It was nothing to do with Matt. It was just to ask that this time the pain that savaged her insides after every meal might hold off a little—just long enough for her to form an accurate judgment of this man who was a threat to her daughter's happiness.

Matt behaved impeccably over the tea of tinned ham and salad. He bestowed special praise on Clarrie's homemade chutney and Jean was amused to notice a perceptible thaw in her mother after that. Even Clarrie had her vanities.

It was unpatriotic to waste food, so when Matt laid his knife and fork down to indicate that he had finished Geoff gave an expectant look at the piece of ham that still lay on the plate. At any other time it would have been his for the asking. Tonight, to his appalled disbelief, Clarrie scraped it into the waste bin for all the world as if they had food to spare. Clarrie wasn't going to have Matt thinking that the Moretons *needed* his largesse.

As Clarrie stacked the plates together Jean permitted herself a hope that her mother might relent about the cake. Clarrie said, "Are you coming in the kitchen with me, Jean?"

Jean followed her out and watched as Clarrie stacked dishes into the sink. No word of approval came from her, and the cake stood on the table in isolated splendour. It might not have been there for all the notice Clarrie took.

"At least let's have his fruit salad," Jean pleaded. "Geoff would love it."

"Geoff can have some then."

Geoff picked his way through his helping of fruit salad with the air of an explorer. Some of the fruits he was encountering for the first time in his life.

"What's this, Matt?" He held up a small yellow chunk on the end of his fork.

"Pineapple."

"Never seen it before. Saw a banana once. They raffled it at school—help the town buy a Spitfire."

"D'ya get it?"

"What?"

"The banana."

"No. But we got the Spitfire."

After the meal Matt and James sat by the fire, sipping whisky and swapping yarns. James brought out his World War I album, and from it an embroidered postcard.

"Sent *that* to Clarrie from the front," he said proudly. "Hand done, you know. They brought them round—silks, needles and that. . . . We *all* did them—to send home."

"That's real pretty."

"Aye! It is, isn't it?" James's face saddened as he remembered Clarrie then, pretty and ardent, and totally in love with him. She had known nothing of caution then, nor of fear. Why had she changed, learned to hold back?

47

When Clarrie and Jean had done the washing up, Geoff was pressed to perform his party piece, and went reluctantly to the piano. Jean gave him a smile that took the worst out of the moment, and Matt winked understandingly, so he sat and played a children's piece.

Clarrie sat slightly apart from the others, the better to see them without being seen. She knew she could not wipe from her face all the trace of the pain that had seized her now. It dulled her perception of the scene, confused her mind, so that Jean was no longer her daughter, but had somehow become herself long ago. When was it—1918, the last year of the war; herself twenty-one, married to James Moreton, ten years her senior. How she'd loved him, or she'd thought she had anyway, and wasn't that the same thing as long as you didn't know the difference? Ah, if only she could have gone on not knowing the difference!

But *he'd* come—Ian—invalided home on three weeks leave. And they'd met, by chance, and her life had changed in one afternoon. She'd promised herself that night that she'd never see him again—make the resolve *now* before it's too late, her heart said—and the words had mocked her because it was already too late and her heart knew it. Oh God, save Jean from a love like that! Three weeks. So little time, and then he'd gone back to the trenches. He needn't have gone. It was a bad wound, he could have had a safe job. But he'd insisted on going back.

He'd gone. And the war had ended, and James had returned to her, his eyes alight with joy after four years of loving and missing her. . . . Then the long months, waiting and hoping for some news of Ian that never came. He had vanished in the slaughter. No gravestone bore his name. He was listed with a hundred others on the war memorial, and that was the only trace that he had ever lived. Three years later Jean had been born.

Save Jean, let her not feel like that, still less about a man so different from herself, one who could be posted away tomorrow and never heard of again. Save her from the long agony of wondering about a man and having no way of discovering his fate.

Through blurred eyes Clarrie could see her daughter sitting on a stool by Matt's chair, her hands clasped round her knees, one of his hands on her shoulder. Her eyes took in James, puffing happily on his pipe, his gaze resting fondly on his daughter. He was a good man, a kind man. He'd treated her well throughout their married life, and in her way she had always loved him. If only she'd never known the difference. . . .

Matt, too, was barely listening to Geoff's valiant efforts on the piano. His eyes were moving slowly round the room. At last he found what he was seeking.

It was a small picture, showing Jean as he guessed she must have looked two years ago. She was standing with a young man who had his arm round her shoulders. He was wearing a uniform which looked crisp and new. But it was the faces that held Matt's attention. The couple were gazing at each other, laughing into each other's eyes with uncomplicated affection. Even in the poor photograph Matt could make out the man's features. This was a good face, broad and rugged but intelligent and amiable. He would make a good husband for Jean, Matt knew that. The thought made his heart contract with a moment's loneliness. He pushed it aside. It was no good thinking thoughts like that. Jeannie and he were good friends. That was all it could be, that was all he wanted it to be. He was glad that she had a good guy to marry.

The piano piece came to an end and the adults applauded. Geoff grinned self-consciously, and got off the piano stool quickly before anyone could ask him for an encore.

But nobody did. The evening was breaking up. Matt had to get back to camp. Clarrie bid him a goodbye with a cordiality that gave nothing away. Jean went to the door with him and stood with a cardigan huddled round her shoulders against the November air.

"How'd I do?" Matt demanded.

"Well, the Scotch made Dad's war. And Geoff'll never leave you alone now."

He shrugged. "Guys are easy. It's the women give me the trouble." He looked at her steadily, suddenly serious. The presence of her mother seemed to stand between them.

"Don't rush it, Matt," she said. She looked down, aware that merely by saying the words she had pushed their relationship a step forwards.

"I gotta rush it, Jeannie. Who knows how long we got?" He added in a bitter tone. "Who knows who's going to make it?"

He turned away but she took his arm and pulled him back to

face her. "Come on. You've not done so bad so far. And I like my Yank optimistic."

It was the first time she had called him that. She made it sound like a term of affection. He gave her a sudden grin.

"Your Mom. I think she likes me. How's that for optimistic?"

She smiled back. Then impulsively she leaned forward and touched her lips fleetingly against his. His arms began to slide easily round her. She drew away, chilled by the immediate glibness of his reaction. He relaxed his arms and stood searching her face, waiting for her to make the next move. When it came it was equally unexpected to them both. Her hands reached up to his face, drawing his head down to hers while she kissed him again, strongly this time. Before he could recover from his amazement she had retreated inside and shut the door.

Matt walked to the bottom of the street and unchained his bicycle from a lamp-post. He was grinning.

Jean found her mother tidying up when she returned to the living room. "Well?" she demanded.

"He's a fine lad," James said at once. "Good head on his shoulders."

"He said he'd take me on the base," said Geoff. "Let me get in a tank."

But they all knew whose reaction it was that Jean was waiting for, and her eyes never left her mother. Clarrie went on pulling things straight.

"He's very pleasing," she said. "I'll say that for him. Well mannered . . . thoughtful. I can see what you see in him. If it wasn't for Ken. . . ."

She left the implication hanging in the air, and got into the kitchen as fast as she could.

6

Some of Helen's most useful work at the base hospital was talking to lonely men, or writing their letters home. This might involve simply taking down dictation or advising with the actual composition. The latter course was fraught with complications—the most common being that the British and Americans supposedly spoke the same language. After a few sessions Helen could have said otherwise.

". . . and I wish you were here. . . . Goddammit, how do I say that?" The young man with bandaged hands waved one of them in frustration. "Lady, I'm aching for the dame!"

"Say *that*," Helen advised, her pen poised over the pad on her knee. "Tell her you're aching for her."

"How?"

She thought for a moment. "I ache for your closeness . . . I pain for your presence." *No!* cried a voice in her mind the moment the words were out. You make him sound like a stuffed shirt.

The young man obviously thought so too, for he regarded her uneasily.

"Hell, ma'am—she'd think I'd got educated out here." He sounded outraged. He thought for a moment. "How about 'I ache to have you around'?"

"Nice," said Helen hastily.

When she had finished her batch for the day she departed, promising to return with the typed letters next morning. Typing them was her own idea. It seemed to her that if Peter had been so injured that he was unable to write to her himself, then she would rather receive a letter typed on an impersonal machine than written in another woman's hand.

She typed at a desk in her study. It had been Peter's before he went away, and was still a favourite room because it was here that she felt closest to him. The desk was crowded with photographs of Peter and their two children, a constant reminder. Helen resisted the thought that she needed reminding. She only wished that Peter, with whom she had always been able to discuss her worries, could be here so that she could talk to him now. She wished this even though she wryly acknowledged that the doubts that had troubled her heart these last few weeks were not such as could ever be discussed with him.

"Morning." The postman's voice reached her through the window.

"Morning, Albert."

He handed her a bunch of letters. "Nothing I'm afraid," he said, meaning nothing from Dr. St. John, whose writing he knew well. Helen forced herself to smile. She could have done without

Albert's knowledgeable perusal of her post, but she would never have hurt the elderly man's feelings by saying so.

One of the letters was from Tim and she opened it first. In a large childish scrawl he had written,

"Dear Mum,
    Please let me come home. I hate it here. I'm no good at games. I try but I'm no good. I want to come home so much. Please let me as I am still very unhappy. *Please!!!*"

She read the letter several times, her face troubled. Her eye fell on the photographs near her hand. One was of Peter, at about Tim's age. He stood, dressed for rugger, in the centre of a smiling group. His face was alight with enjoyment and achievement. Next to it stood another picture, taken just before Peter left for the Atlantic. He was smiling broadly, wearing his brand new naval uniform, and Tim stood beside him. As Helen stared closely at the picture of her husband with his son, for the first time it struck her that Tim wasn't smiling at all.

She put the letter away. She would answer it when she'd had a chance to talk to John who was coming to dinner that evening.

IT WAS no conscious striving for effect that made Helen turn the lights down as she and John sat by the drawing-room fire after the meal. There was no artifice in her nature. She only thought that the drawing-room fire, piled with logs from the Lime Hall acres, was cosy and inviting and the dimming of the lights seemed to draw the room about them like a warm cloak.

"You think I should bring Tim home, don't you?" she asked him.

"I don't believe a kid should stay in a school where he's miserable, just for the sake of tradition. Come off it, Helen, you don't either."

"It's not that easy, John. He's at a very good school. He may get over his problems. Peter went to that school. I wish I could discuss it with him."

The forlorn note in her voice on the last words caught at his throat, hurting him, making him speak roughly.

"Tim's not Peter."

"He is Peter's son."

"He is also *your* son."

"I couldn't take the risk of upsetting his whole future. We are in England, John, not America. The trouble is," she said smiling, "we English take our schools far too seriously."

A log fell in the fire, so that a star of jagged flames danced and spurted, throwing shadows across her face. John knelt to prod the log back into position. He stayed there, looking into the fire, wondering what to say to her. He was confused. This beautiful, sensitive woman with her deceptive air of simplicity, this woman that he wanted, perhaps loved—talked to him of good schools, meaningless abstracts, that she rated above her son's happiness. She had gone away from him in spirit, damaged the fragile link that he had thought could exist between her way of life and his. Or had she just shown that the link had never really existed?

Then her hand against his cheek made him look up. She was reaching down to him, touching his face as if she were blind, as though her fingertips could tell her what her eyes could not. Something in the set of her jaw told him she was close to tears. "I wish I knew how I felt," she whispered.

He took her hand and held it. "I think you know," he said quietly.

"I *don't* know." As if to herself she added, "Without Peter I almost can't decide."

John spoke very gently. "You English kill me. You know damn well how you feel. But you'll turn yourself inside out not to show it."

"You make it too simple," she hedged.

"I come from a simple, primitive people," he said with heavy irony. "Savages, no tradition." He met her eyes again and his tone changed. The mockery left it, and instead there was an urgent tone that made her pulse throb dangerously. "Trust it, Helen. Trust what you feel."

When she did not answer he rose slowly to his feet. She took a sharp breath. "John. . . ."

"Helen—I've got to go."

"Well—have a brandy." Her voice was shaky.

He took her face in his hands and looked down at her. "Helen—I've *got* to go. I don't *want* to but I've got to." He searched her eyes, understanding what he read there. "Haven't I?"

"Yes, John."

He bent his head and kissed her on the lips. She laid her hands gently on his shoulders. She was fighting an impulse to throw her arms round him, beg him to stay. She could have wept when he let her go.

She followed him into the hall and opened the front door for him. "Goodnight. Take care."

" 'Night. I'll call you."

She watched him grope carefully to his car parked outside. The dimmed headlights went on, the engine started, and he pulled away down the drive. She waved once into the darkness before, with an aching heart, she shut and bolted the door.

7

Molly Dawlish reckoned the war wasn't so bad if you didn't let it get you down. There were shortages, of course, and if you were a girl who liked to dress nicely (and she did) clothes rationing was a nuisance. How was a girl supposed to make anything of herself on a ration of forty-eight coupons per year, when a pair of knickers cost two coupons?

But war had given girls like Molly a freedom that they couldn't have gained in any other way, and it more than compensated for the shortages. Before the war, with unemployment being what it was, Molly's chances of a job would have been slim. She'd have been expected to stay at home and help Mum look after Sal and the twins. And when you were stuck in the house under your mother's eye, without a penny to call your own, fun was hard to come by. So when the young men started to be called up, and the appeal went out for women to take over their jobs and keep the country running, Molly was one of the first to volunteer for the buses.

With a bus that passed the US army base several times a day Molly found herself in heaven on earth. The Yanks, as she had confided to Jean, saw her before they saw any of the other girls, and by the time the bus reached the depot she'd made her selection and turfed off the rejects. From the evening she'd met Danny, however, Molly had eyes for none of the other Yanks. He was the one she wanted, she knew that straight away. She knew he felt the same about her. They laughed a lot and they were good in bed together. What more did anyone want?

Once he said to her, "Molly, I ain't never known a girl like you before. You're sure gonna be some sensation back home."

She'd been putting her stockings back on, sliding them gently up her legs so as not to ladder the delicate nylon. She was sitting in her slip on the edge of the bed in the tiny hotel room they'd taken for the evening on the far side of town. She looked back to the other side of the bed, where he too was getting dressed. "Am I going to see 'back home' then?" she asked.

He hesitated a moment, and she wondered if she'd been wrong to push it.

Then he smiled and said, "I guess you are," as if he'd come to a final decision.

He'd never actually mentioned the word marriage but after that he talked as if it was a settled thing that their future would be together. And Molly, who never worried about tomorrow till it came, was content to leave it there.

Increasingly these days Jean and Matt came out with the two of them. That was a laugh. And Ken due home any time, and everyone expecting him and Jean to get engaged.

"What's Ken going to say?" Molly demanded of Jean one day.

"Nothing, because he won't know," Jean answered shortly.

"You're not going to tell him?"

"There's nothing to tell, Molly. Matt's just a friend, he knows about Ken. Anyway, I'm not engaged to Ken yet."

"I thought you loved him."

"Oh, for heaven's sake, Molly, you sound like my mother. I do love Ken. I'm going to marry Ken. Now leave it, will you?"

IN THE SECOND WEEK in December Ken came home on leave. The sight of his familiar burly figure and heavy face warmed by love for her sent a rush of guilt and affection through Jean. He was her Ken, the man she had always loved. Her life would be with him when Matt had gone away for good.

She kissed him when he slipped the engagement ring on her finger, his eyes shining with pride, and nodded when Clarrie proposed a party to celebrate.

"She wants to make sure no one can miss it," Jean thought

wryly. "This is her triumph, and she's not going to have it slip by unnoticed."

But then, why not? Jean told herself that she had always intended to marry Ken. She hadn't changed her mind. Matt hadn't asked her to marry him. They had been honest with each other right from the beginning. They had both just been passing time.

And so on and on, arguing with herself, and explaining and going over the same ground again and again, trying to deaden the little ache in her heart.

She discovered that it was possible to feel strongly about two men at once. Nothing had altered her love for Ken. What had changed was her standpoint. She had thought that what she felt for him was all there was to love. But she knew the difference now.

When she was alone with him all was well, and it was this that gave her the decisiveness to go on with her engagement. The day before their engagement party he borrowed two bicycles from his father's garage, and they went off for the day together. Jean remembered Clarrie's face as she waved them off. She looked happy and well for the first time in weeks.

"I can't hurt her," Jean thought. "I can't hurt Ken. I love them both too much. It'll be all right."

They rode up onto the moor, where the air was cold and dry, whipping colour into their cheeks. They stopped by a hedge and he took a blanket from his saddlebag. They sat on it to drink tea from a flask, and hugged each other against the chill.

Ken took his right arm out of his jacket. Keeping his left arm still in the jacket he pulled her tight against him and wrapped the free side of the jacket round her.

"There's not room for two of us in here," she protested, not very convincingly.

"There is when one of 'em's a tich like you," he grinned.

"Who's a tich? I'm tall—"

"Yes, but there's nothing of you. All skin and bone. Before we get married I'll have to fatten you up, otherwise you'll vanish under me."

She laughed and blushed slightly, and his arm tightened round her. "Do you ever think of it, Jean? Us—together, after we're married? I think of it all the time when I'm away—oh Jean—"

He had pressed her down on the blanket and was kissing her

with passion. She put her arms round him and kissed him back, hard, praying for some sweep of desire that would wipe everything but Ken from her mind, would push away the obtruding image of Matt.

She felt Ken's arms relax, releasing her. When she opened her eyes he was getting to his feet, breathing hard.

"What's the matter?" she said stupidly.

"You know what's the matter, Jean. I'm stopping while I still can. It's got to be the proper way for us, or not at all. I'm not going to risk giving you a kid before we can get wed."

"Ken—"

"Yes, love?"

She spread her hands helplessly. "Yes, you're right. Let's get off home."

THE FOLLOWING EVENING Danny found himself sitting in the cinema in Conleigh. It wasn't the way he'd have chosen to spend the evening. He'd rather have been with Molly. But she'd gone to Jean Moreton's engagement party, leaving him with no company but an increasingly vile-tempered Matt.

While the newsreel was on Danny tried to keep one eye on the screen and the other on his friend. Matt simply stared in front of him, until abruptly he stood up.

"Where are you going?" Danny demanded.

"Let's go get a beer."

Matt began to push his way out. Danny shook his head sorrowfully and rose to follow him. He knew his friend well enough by now to recognize that Matt was in a thoroughly dangerous mood, and the knowledge left him floundering helplessly. His own love for Molly was a simple, uncomplicated thing based on their happy personalities that were so alike, and their instant physical harmony. The brooding secretive nature of whatever it was Matt felt for Jean would have been quite foreign to him.

He followed Matt doggedly from pub to pub, matching him drink for drink, trying to divert him, take the edge off his mood. He knew he was failing. Matt grew quieter and more sullen and his eyes glittered ominously. Eventually the beers began to get to Danny. His head was thickening and he wouldn't have been sorry to go back to camp. But when he mentioned it, Matt ignored him and strode into a nearby club. Danny paused to take a deep breath and plunged down in after him. He was no quitter.

There was an orchestra, of sorts, playing scratchily. Couples danced in sleepy fashion. They found a table and ordered beers.

"Look," Danny said, attempting a light touch, "so she's getting hitched to a limey. Big deal!" Matt turned two thunderous black eyes on him and Danny backtracked hastily. "OK. To you it is a big deal. That don't make it the end of the world. You ever hear of other fish in the sea?"

"Like that one over there?"

Matt's eye had picked out a table where two women were sitting with two British marine officers. One of the women, a hard thirtyish blonde, had been looking at him.

"She's been giving me the eye since we came in," Matt said complacently.

Danny scented danger. "You don't need a broad. She's already with a guy. The joint is full of unattached females. All you got to do. . . ."

He was talking to empty air. Matt had risen unsteadily and managed to make his way over to the table. With a sigh Danny followed him. He would no more have left Matt to cope alone at this moment than he would have sent a baby to cross the road.

Matt swayed gently before the woman, drunk but killingly polite. "Excuse me, ma'am. Would you care to take a little twirl round the floor?"

Before the woman could answer both marine officers broke in.

"The lady's busy, Yank."

"She doesn't want to dance."

Matt regarded them with dangerous courtesy. "*You* say she doesn't want to dance. I didn't hear *her* say it." He turned back to the blonde. "You want to dance or you don't want to dance?"

"I don't want to, thanks," she said shortly. She was embarrassed.

"You don't dance with Americans?"

"Toddle off, Yank," said one of the officers.

Danny held his breath while Matt looked solemnly at the marine. He would have tried to steer him away, but he knew instinctively that if he touched him he would precipitate an explosion. To his relief Matt appeared to decide to let the remark pass. He groped around in his pocket and pulled out a packet of cigarettes. He grabbed a handful and threw them on the table in front of the blonde.

"You don't want to dance—you want cigarettes? You'll take cigarettes from a Yank, won't you? Or I'll tell you what—whisky. Here, the drinks are on me."

He had taken a bottle from his back pocket and unscrewed the top. He poured the liquid into the glasses on the table, not caring if they overflowed. Some of the whisky began to splash into his audience's lap. The two girls rose and drew back from the table.

"Watch it, Yank," snapped one of the officers. "You're pissed."

"Piss on you, buster," Matt told him sweetly.

Danny, the experienced lightweight boxer, got his first blow in before the man was properly on his feet. The other marine managed to land a punch on Matt before Danny laid him out with a hook to the stomach and a right hand to the jaw. Then he grabbed his friend.

"Let's go," he said lightly.

They could hear the cries of "Get those Yankee bastards!" floating after them as they raced out of the club and up a pitch-dark staircase. Their feet seemed to find their own way in the darkness. Miraculously they managed to go some distance without falling over, or into anything, but the sound of enraged pursuit was getting uncomfortably close. They found a small passageway and swerved sharply into it. A little way along was a recessed door and it was open. They raced through it and slammed it behind them.

As they listened to their pursuers racing past outside Danny rubbed his knuckles tenderly.

"Look what you made me do," he mourned. "I could have broke a hand on those limeys. I got to look after these hands. They got to make me a living."

There was no answer. Matt had slumped to the floor, practically comatose.

"You OK?" said Danny anxiously.

Matt muttered something. Danny strained closer to hear it, and this time made out a word. "Jeannie."

Danny sighed. "Come on . . . we ain't home and dry yet."

He could just see that they were in some sort of storeroom. They couldn't stay there all night. Danny pulled open the door a crack, listened a moment, then hauled Matt to his feet and out into the passage.

They were no sooner back in the main street than a jeep rounded a corner at speed and drew up beside them. Lights flashed, the voice of an American military policeman said, "These two?"

"Yes, that's them," said an English voice.

"OK, come on, you two."

Matt and Danny were unceremoniously bundled into the back of the jeep. As they were driven away, Danny looked across at Matt. He was mumbling incoherently, oblivious to his situation.

JAMES MORETON was coming to the end of his party speech. Normally he hated speaking in public, but it was coming easily to him now because the words were from his heart.

"Jean, you're a grand girl. I've watched you grow up with pride— and I don't give you away easy. It'd take a pretty special kind of lad to persuade me." His eyes rested on Ken, standing beside Jean, his face aglow with love. "But Ken here *is*, and has, and I must say I'm delighted that he did."

There was laughter and applause from the little group gathered in the Moretons' living room. Ken's mother and father stood looking fondly at Jean. This was a match that they

too had hoped for. From time to time Clarrie caught their eyes. Molly, observing closely, swore afterwards that Jean's Mam came as close as she ever would to winking. This was her moment of triumph all right. She had even asked Mrs. St. John, for whom she occasionally did some dress-making up at Lime Hall, to the party. And that Yankee captain was there, too. She wondered what Clarrie thought.

James held up his hand to silence the murmurs. He had more to say, and his voice had taken on a deeper note. "Us old'uns do our best here at home, but it's the youngsters like these two who bear the brunt—the danger and the separation and the worry. So—" his tone lightened again, became determinedly cheerful, "good luck to you both, and let's hope this bloody war's over by the time we all get together again to put the rubber stamp on things." He raised his glass. "Jean and Ken."

"Jean and Ken." More applause, laughter, glasses being raised.

Helen St. John eased her way through to Jean. She noticed how tired and strained the girl looked. It must be hard for her, getting engaged like this and knowing that Ken was going off again in a couple of days. And who knew when he'd be back—if ever.

She handed Jean a beautifully wrapped parcel.

"Congratulations," she said, kissing Jean. "He's a lucky man."

"I'll say," said Ken at once.

Jean unwrapped the parcel to reveal a cruet made of silver and cut glass. It was exquisite.

"Mrs. St. John, you shouldn't—it's beautiful," she gasped.

"It's been gathering dust for years. I knew you admired it."

"Admire it! I love it!" She had loved it since she first went with her mother to Lime Hall fourteen years ago.

John handed Ken a bottle of champagne he'd brought. "Here— to help out," he said.

Ken had barely touched it when he found it whipped away from him by Clarrie, all smiles and mock indignation.

"Thank you, Captain," she said. "We'll save that for the wedding." She scuttled away with it to the kitchen.

Jean felt as though she were living through a dream. Nothing seemed to be happening of her own volition any more. Once she'd given Clarrie the nod for this party she couldn't have stopped her any more than she could have stopped a runaway horse.

"Come on, sunshine," Molly said to her. "You've jumped in the bloody deep end. At least enjoy your flaming swim."

Jean managed a smile. She could see Ken watching her from the other side of the room, and she brightened her face even more for his benefit. Her father was sitting down at the piano, strumming the first few bars of "We'll meet again".

And suddenly they were all singing, standing round the piano. Ken moved over and put his arm round her shoulders.

"We'll meet again—don't know where, don't know when—"

She leaned against him and joined in. All round the room she could see people singing the trite words as though they had just gained a new meaning. Jean watched her mother, until at last Clarrie turned and looked at her. At the sight of her daughter's face Clarrie's singing faltered, stopped. For a moment there was a look of dreadful uncertainty in her eyes. Then it was gone, and Clarrie joined in the song once more.

". . . But I know we'll meet again—some sunny day."

THE FOLLOWING MORNING, cleaned-up but bleary-eyed and violently hungover, Matt and Danny were escorted to Captain John Docherty's office, for the charge. A master sergeant stood beside John's desk consulting the military police report.

"Sounds like you were looking for a fight," John said.

Matt stared ahead. "I was, sir."

John looked at him. "You're the one who's been going out with the Moreton girl, aren't you."

"I took her out a few times. Nothing serious."

The master sergeant read from the report. "Prisoner while in detention was heard continuously repeating the name 'Jean'."

"Look, I got drunk. I made a damn fool of myself. No excuses," said Matt furiously.

John remembered Jean's face the previous night. She had not seemed as radiantly happy as he would have expected in a newly-engaged girl.

"It's very easy to get involved while you're here," he said, conscious of a certain irony. "But you'd better remember it's their country, and you play by their rules." (Rules, traditions, outdated beliefs, seemed to mean more to them than people.) "Even if you can't figure them out sometimes," he added. "Now I'm confining

63

both of you to quarters for a week. If I catch you fighting again you'll lose your stripes."

"Yes, sir," said Matt woodenly.

"Yes, sir," said Danny.

"Dismissed."

8

Ken's train was due out at six in the morning. Jean went to the station to see him off. Even at that hour it was busy. Here and there was the blue uniform of a sailor or an airman, but mostly they were brown-uniformed soldiers, and almost all were with girls, or saying goodbye to their families as they waited for the train to come in. Jean clung tightly to Ken's arm as they walked down the platform. At this moment he was all she could think of. His face was dear and familiar, and soon he would be gone.

He dropped his kitbag and stood looking down at her. "Well, love?" he said, "It's shaken us up a bit, this war, hasn't it?"

"It has everybody."

"I suppose so."

A loud burst of laughter behind them made them both turn. A small group of GIs was walking along the platform, their arms round laughing girls. They all looked cheerful.

"Nice to have something to laugh about," said Ken.

"It must be."

He looked at her. "I'm asking for a simple life, Jean—after all this. A chance to make a real go of it. The garage—me Dad says it's mine when it's all over. I'd like it. I can build something for us out of it—honest."

She knew he wanted her to say something, but all she could think of was, "I know you can, Ken. I *know* that—"

It wasn't enough. She could hear that. His voice took on a wistful note. "It would have been plain sailing, Jean—you and me. Maybe *too* plain. Me—having to hop out of it for a while—it *has* shook us up. If we come through it—the same—" his eyes held hers, "—at least we'll be certain, won't we?"

She wondered how she could ever have thought Ken easy to

fool. There was understanding and compassion in his eyes, and love—a deep love for her, that would never judge her whatever she did.

"Just come back, eh?" she said. "Come back safe."

It was as much as she could do to get the words out. Guilt was churning through her, fear of what he would say next. And regret —regret that she did not love him more, that she had met Matt, that Matt too must go away, that life had to be so complicated. She reached up and kissed him, trying to put into it all the warmth of which she was capable. But she could feel that he did not respond to her fully. While she held him the train pulled in beside them and pandemonium broke out.

Suddenly he pulled her to him with a desperate urgency. He did not kiss her, but wrapped his arms right round her and held her tightly against him. His face muzzled into the side of her neck, and she could hear him whisper, "Jean . . . my Jean . . . my darling. . . ."

He released her, picked up his kitbag and got into the train. He stood leaning out of the window. Whatever expression had been on his face when it was hidden from her had left it now. He was calm again, even humorous.

Her eyes burning, Jean reached up and clasped his hands.

"Ken, there's something."

"Jean—" he interrupted her.

"Yes?"

"When I get out there—where I'm going—they've got a special force—the Chindits. A sort of Commando."

A terrible dread seized her heart. "And you're joining them," she said. It was a statement, not a question.

"How did you know?"

"Well, trust you—if there's a hard way of doing it, you'll find it." She could hear her voice trembling.

He looked at her, as if waiting for her to say something else.

"Ken, there's something I want to tell—"

The whistle cut her short. His hands seized her shoulders. His mouth was pressing hers, and that frantic urgency was there again. The movement of the train jerked them apart.

"I love you, kid," he said hurriedly. "Be happy on *your* say so. I'm asking *nothing*. OK?"

She clung to his hand, running to keep up with the train.

"Ken—Ken—there's something—"

But he would not let her speak. He pressed his fingers against her lips, leaned out at a dangerous angle to kiss her to silence. The train gathered speed, taking him farther away from her. He shouted out to her, his words reaching her faintly, "Look after yourself, kid. I'll be thinking of you—every bloody minute. . . ." His voice became distant, ". . . Love you, remember. . . ."

The words died. She watched him growing smaller and smaller. A dreadful anguish assailed her. He was gone, her Ken, that she loved and had grown up with. He was kind and good and he loved her with complete generosity, and she had sent him off with that sad knowledge. For she knew now that he had understood.

And he had freed her. His last words had been unmistakable. "Be happy on *your* say so. I'm asking *nothing*." Despite the ring on her finger she was free, because he had made her so.

And through her tears the wonderful knowledge asserted itself, until it overcame the consciousness of all else. She turned and began to walk back down the platform, her eyes bright, her head up, relief sweeping her.

She was free.

9

No daughter of Clarrie's could fail to be clever with her fingers, but Jean knew she wasn't in her mother's class. The dress slithered about under the needle of the sewing machine, and obstinately refused to go the way she wanted.

She heard the phone ring in the shop and sat up, very still, listening, as her mother answered it. But Clarrie did not come to fetch her, and after a moment Jean heard the ping as the receiver was put down. She relaxed, trying not to feel so absurdly disappointed.

She had neither seen nor spoken to Matt since Ken had come home on leave. Now it was the day after Ken's departure. Matt would know now that Ken had gone, because Molly would have told Danny, and Danny would have passed it on. So why didn't he seek her out?

Clarrie came through the curtain that divided the living room from the shop. Her face was set hard.

"It was your American. He hasn't wasted much time, has he?"

Jean turned to look at her mother. She knew the shining of her eyes was giving her away, but she couldn't help it.

"I told him you were busy," Clarrie said shortly.

"*Mother*—"

"He said he'd be around, tonight, just after six. You've to wear something special."

Clarrie came over to the table and half sat, half collapsed into a chair. Her face was white. Jean pushed the sewing machine aside and took her mother's hands in hers.

"Mother. What's the matter?"

There was a long pause. Clarrie's hands lay limp, unresponsive in her daughter's. Then she began to speak in a quiet, acid voice.

"I can *see* your stupid excitement. I tried to shield you from it —preserve you and Ken." She gasped with pain, then said bitterly, "He isn't even English."

"What does *that* mean?" Jean's indignation momentarily wiped out her realization that her mother was ill.

"*Think* about it, Jean. When you start up again—you and your Yank. You go where *he* goes—you *are* what he is."

"Wouldn't it be the same with Ken? Around the corner—but just the same?"

"We *know* Ken. What he's shaping up to, your Yank, d'you know what his *best* is—or, God help you, his worst?"

Jean didn't answer. She couldn't. Oh yes, she told herself, she knew his worst. And it frightened her, she didn't deny that. With all her heart she wanted to learn about Matt at his best, how he would be with her, what their good times would be like. It was that thought, and the discoveries they would make together of each other's best that made her draw in her breath.

Clarrie, her face white and defeated watched her daughter.

"Anyway—you're old enough. It's your choice."

"Oh Mother—" Jean got up and hugged her. "We'll see, eh— let's just wait and see."

"Yes," said Clarrie. "We'll see."

Jean looked more closely at her mother, taking in the frail, sick face. "Why don't you see Doctor Harris? Just a check up."

"No. I've had a hard day in the shop. Ration Day. Now—"

She hauled herself up from the chair, moved over to where Jean had been sitting a moment before, and pulled the machine towards her. She took out the dress, inspected her daughter's workmanship critically, and put the dress back with expert fingers.

"Didn't he say you had to wear something special?"

Jean looked at her mother, overflowing with affection. You never knew when Clarrie was going to capitulate suddenly, giving just a glimpse of the loving heart that lay so well-concealed. The doorbell jangled in the shop. Jean went out to serve the customer. Her heart was singing.

SHE WAS READY by a quarter to six. She was not wearing the dress she'd been making earlier that day (even Clarrie's nimble fingers had been unable to make it acceptable in time) but the one made of honey-coloured material that she'd worn on the Sunday he came to tea. She knew he liked it.

She made herself up with care, brushed her hair till it shone, and came downstairs to wait for him. She had half feared her mother's reaction, but Clarrie had only nodded, brushed a hair from Jean's shoulder, and commented gruffly, "If he doesn't like the way you look tonight there's no pleasing him."

Which Jean rightly interpreted as a compliment.

When Matt collected her his behaviour towards her in Clarrie's presence was almost distant. Jean understood and was grateful for his good taste. He would not commit the vulgarity of seeming too obviously pleased Ken had gone.

But when they were out in the street his hand grasped hers, and she knew by his face that he was holding himself back with difficulty. "Where are we going?" she said.

"Wait and see."

"Are we going far?"

"Let's just say I have a late pass."

"How late?"

"Enough to get to Manchester and back."

"*Manchester?* Matt, are you mad? Why are we going to Manchester?"

"Wait and see."

"Matt, is this a sort of joke?"

"Why must you always mistrust me? I've simply arranged a pleasant night out with some friends—there they are."

A bit farther up the road Molly and Danny were waiting for them on the corner. Molly was done up to the nines. She waved when she saw them coming.

"We're going to Manchester with Molly and Danny?"

"You're a bright girl, Jean. You only have to be told something twice and you take it right in."

She began to laugh. His mood was infectious. "Why are we meeting them here and not at my home? My mother knows Molly."

"Yes, but she doesn't know Danny. I don't want to give her any nasty shocks."

They reached the corner as he spoke and Danny heard the last words. "Hiya, Jean. What's he saying about me?"

"I was saying I can't take you anywhere. If Jeannie's mother knew I had a friend like you I'd never be allowed back." He ducked the friendly punch Danny aimed at him.

"You practically weren't," Jean told him as they began to walk to the railway station. "Mother wasn't keen on you ringing me so soon after Ken left."

"Hell, Jeannie, she knows how I feel about you. I'm not ashamed of it. Are you?"

"No—but—don't rush me, Matt. Ken only went yesterday."

"Does he know about us? What did you tell him?"

"Nothing—but he knows. I'm sure of it. He said—"

But she stopped herself. Even with Matt she could not share that moment of Ken's farewell, the generosity of his love. It was too intimate, too personal between Ken and herself.

Matt watched her face as she fell silent, and did not press her to go on. He slipped his arm round her shoulders and they finished the journey to the station like that.

The two girls waited together while Matt and Danny went for the tickets. Despite the gloom of the station they felt an air of excitement.

"Molly, have you any idea what all this is about?"

"Not the slightest. I just got a message to be ready early, and to look good because we were going somewhere special."

"Me an' all."

They looked at each other, savouring the pleasure of such a secret adventure, until Matt and Danny came back with the tickets. Danny looked bemused.

"It's the porters," Matt explained. "He just can't get over them."

"*Girls*," said Danny, outraged. "They're girls."

"Well, of course they are, love," said Molly. "All the fellers got called up."

"But they're dragging these heavy suitcases around, just like they were guys."

"Yes, well we're a lot stronger than we look, so you watch out," she told him.

Danny nuzzled her fondly. "Lady, you can twist my arm any time."

Jean watched, happy for them, marvelling at the change in herself. It seemed such a short time since that night she had met Matt, when she had been so furiously embarrassed at the way Molly and Danny carried on together. Now, in the light of what was in her own heart it seemed that they had always known something she had only just learned. She found Matt's eyes on her and smiled.

"There's a train in fifteen minutes," he said.

"I'm glad. I was afraid there might not be one. They keep cancelling them these days."

He looked offended. "Honey, don't you know I'm a *Yank*. And there's nothing Yanks can't do." He was laughing both at her and himself.

"Big mouth," she said. And kissed him.

The train was cold and dirty, the carriage smelled of smoke and was poorly lit. But the ten-mile trip to Manchester was merry. Matt and Danny kept their secret and resisted all the girls' attempts to tease it out of them. They were still arguing as they left the train at Manchester.

"OK, girls," said Danny. "This is where we have to give in because we don't know the way."

"Way to what?" said Molly.

"The Hippodrome."

Molly squealed with delight. Jean gave a smile of pleasure. The Hippodrome meant a variety show, with the bill topped by the comedian Tommy Trinder. Matt was looking at her questioningly, anxious for her approval. She squeezed his arm.

The theatre was a warm, brightly-lit oasis after the murky streets. The colour and glamour of the show was breathtaking. Some of the acts might not be up to peacetime standard, but folk who had been starved for glitter were in no mood to be critical. And there was nothing second rate about the famous comedian himself. There was a fair number of Yanks in the audience, and Jean had to admit that his jokes were cleverly calculated. They played on the slight tension that existed between the Americans and the British—even the friendliest of them—without being actually unkind to either side.

Amid the applause Jean leaned across and kissed Matt's cheek reassuringly. She knew Danny would enjoy the jokes, but you could never be quite sure what Matt would take the wrong way. But when he looked at her his eyes were glinting with amusement.

10

The troop of GIs from the camp filed into Lime Hall to prepare for the village children's Christmas party.

"My God! It's the bloody invasion," Ivy boomed. Matt led a crocodile of five men, including Danny, into her kitchen. Each of the others was carrying a large ice-cream tub. His own hands were taken up by something he was keeping hidden behind his back.

"Just think of us as Santa Claus," he grinned at her. "Where d'ya want the ice cream?"

"Put it in the larder for now."

She threw open the larder door, but couldn't resist halting Danny in his tracks, lifting the lid of his tub and sampling the wares with the tip of a finger.

"My God—it's real," she breathed.

Matt whipped a bottle of sherry out from behind his back.

"Merry Christmas, ma'am."

Ivy gave him a spontaneous hug that almost knocked him over. Danny, emerging from the larder, glared at both of them.

"He's jealous," Matt explained.

71

He left Danny clutching Ivy in an amorous embrace that had her roaring with laughter and holding her corsets, and went to see if he could be of help in the big dining room. Mrs. St. John was carefully unpacking decorations from a tea-chest. Between her and a big Christmas tree Matt could see two children who looked too much like her to be anything but her own.

There seemed to be at least a dozen GIs in the room shifting furniture around under the direction of Captain Docherty. At the moment he was giving all his attention to the moving of the dining table which was being put up against the far wall.

"How's that?" he appealed to Helen for approval.

"No, I want it in the middle," she said.

"It's *in* the middle."

"Not quite—a bit over to the left."

She squinted as the soldiers moved it. "Too far—back right." Obediently they moved it back. "Now left."

"Come on, Helen," John protested. "Let's have a look."

He went and placed his face next to hers to match her eyeline. The two children by the tree watched, unmoving.

"She's right, fellas," John sang out amiably. "To the left— two inches." They moved it back, and John breathed a sigh of exaggerated relief. "Boy, does that make a difference!"

Helen joined in his laughter and returned to her unpacking. She had not noticed that her children were still watching her intently.

"These are nice." John picked up a pair of Christmas angels that she had taken out. "Where did they go—here?"

He turned and went to put them on the mantelpiece.

"No. Don't put them there! *Daddy never put those there!*"

The shrill childish scream had come from the little girl, standing tensely by the Christmas tree. It was so piercing that for a moment everything stopped. Jokes broke off in mid-air, surprised faces turned towards the child. Nobody moved, till the small boy stepped forward and put his arm protectively round his sister.

Helen gave a half-laugh. She sounded self-conscious. "All right, Anna. John's only trying to help."

She took the angels from John with a look of apology. Talk broke out again. The incident was over.

The party itself was a great success. Jean turned up to help. She and Matt exchanged a brief kiss but, after that, they were mostly occupied with their duties.

Apart from the party, Matt and Jean saw little of each other over Christmas. They spent one night out cheering Danny to victory at the US army v. RAF boxing contest, and helping him and Molly celebrate afterwards.

The big fight was not that night, however, but at the New Year's Eve ball held in the Town Hall. As many GIs as possible had passes and the base up on the moors resembled a ghost camp for that one night.

The Town Hall ballroom was brilliant with lights and colour. In the centre a silver bell spun under spotlights. On one wall hung a banner proclaiming "Happy New Year—1944" On another wall hung the British and American flags and the slogan "These colours never run".

The dance was already in full swing when Matt and Jean arrived, most of the girls dancing with men in uniform, with a preponderance of Americans. A group of black GIs sat at a corner table—alone.

Matt and Jean danced with no one but each other. Neither had any desire to be close to anyone else. Jean danced with her eyes half closed, taking in Matt's warmth, the feel of his hands, the joyous sense of how dear to her he was. She rested her head on his shoulder, trusting him to guide her wherever he would on the dance floor. Her mind was turning over the moments that had brought her here, the memories that had all contributed to this sweet aching sensation in her breast, this feeling that never again would she feel so utterly happy as she did now.

Suddenly the music finished. There was a roll of drums from the bandstand. The bandleader was looking at his watch.

"Ladies and gentlemen! It is now—officially—nineteen forty-four. *Happy New Year!*"

Everyone began singing "Auld Lang Syne".

"Happy New Year, Jeannie."

"Happy New Year, Matt."

They kissed in the middle of the dance floor while all around them couples did the same. Danny and Molly waved from the other side of the room.

The band began to play "Chattanooga Choo Choo", one of the

tunes from America that seemed to dominate English music now. Matt led Jean over to a table, where they watched benignly from the sidelines, content just to sit together. The music swelled. Cheerful yells punctuated the notes. Jean gazed at Matt, wondering, as was every other girl in the room, whether she and her lover would still be together next New Year's Day. And if not— why not?

Suddenly she saw him stiffen. Following his gaze her eyes fell on something that had caused a ripple of reaction amongst the dancers. A black Yank and a white girl were dancing together, dancing superbly, their bodies at one with the rhythm and each other. At first Jean watched for the pleasure of seeing a skilled display. Then she became aware that some of the nearby couples had stood back, making a space round the pair.

An air of tension had gripped those who were sitting at the tables. Near Jean and Matt a group of white GIs watched with undisguised hostility. She looked round. Everywhere she seemed to see white American faces tight with anger. The black soldiers sitting apart at their table were smiling happily, except for one or two who were beginning to look nervous.

Suddenly a white Yank got to his feet, and crossed to the pair who were dancing. A path was cleared for him as he approached. The white man tapped the coloured one on the shoulder and started to elbow him aside, putting out his arms to take the girl. The girl backed away, shaking her head, and at once her coloured partner squared up to the white man, prepared to defend his rights.

The smiles had gone from the faces of the black soldiers. They watched, tense now, as the black man and white girl got back together and tried to resume dancing. Nearby a group of white Americans got up from their table. Their faces were ugly. At last the English seemed to find their feet, moving in between the two groups to keep them from each other.

Then it erupted. The two dancers were pulled apart. There was a scream, and to her horror Jean saw the coloured dancer lifted high over the head of the crowd. Another group of whites had seized him from behind. His friends started to go to his rescue, but were hopelessly outnumbered. The English, trying to cool it down, also found themselves outnumbered and ineffectual.

74

The dance floor was bedlam. Indiscriminate fighting had broken out. The Negro was being passed over the heads of the others in the direction of the door. He was screaming and struggling frantically. The bandleader began yelling through his microphone, but not a word could be heard.

The lynch party had left the room now, carrying their terrified victim. Guided by the screams, Jean began to fight her way out into the hall, followed by Matt, trying to call her back.

Once in the hall, she looked up and saw the group of Yanks standing by a large window. They were holding the Negro's feet, which were the only parts of him visible. The rest of him was out of the window. The man's demented screams continued to reach Jean, standing frozen with horror at the foot of the stairs.

Suddenly there was the welcome sound of a police whistle. The front doors were flung open and a stream of British bobbies followed by military policemen came flooding in. For a moment it seemed as if the startled Yanks might drop their victim by accident, but the police reached them, hauled the half-crazed Negro inside. Jean leaned against the wall, shaking.

The military police were inside the dance hall, breaking up the fights that were still going on. That done, they stationed themselves round the edge of the room to see that order was preserved. The band began to play again.

Jean let Matt lead her back to their table. She badly needed to sit down. Molly and Danny were there waiting for them.

"Never thought I'd be glad to see an MP," Matt remarked.

"That guy was asking for it," said Danny.

There was a moment, while Molly and Jean looked at each other in sheer disbelief. It was Jean who spoke.

"They did that for dancing with a girl?"

"A white girl," Matt explained.

Molly fixed her eyes coldly on Matt, then on Danny. Very deliberately she rose to her feet and headed for the table where the black soldiers were sitting. Jean watched Matt for a minute, then got up and followed her friend. She had never admired Molly so much.

Molly planted herself four-square in front of the table where the little group sat, looking nervous. In a voice that was meant to be heard as far as possible she said, "Excuse me, would any of you gentlemen like to dance?"

After a stunned hesitation one of the Negroes rose to his feet. He paused a moment, looking round him. He saw tense men in Yankee uniform, but beside them he saw British faces, glaring at the Americans, threatening. One of the British soldiers nodded at him. At once he put his arms round Molly and the two of them moved onto the dance floor.

Jean, arriving a moment later, only had to put out her hands invitingly, and another Negro rose to his feet.

As the two couples moved out onto the dance floor other English girls detached themselves from their partners, walked over to the table in the corner, smiled an invitation. Within minutes every coloured man was dancing with a white girl, and every British soldier was giving his Yankee counterpart a look that meant—Watch it!

As the music ended and the couples broke up, Jean accompanied Molly back to their table, knowing what she would have to face. She could see already that both the men waiting for them were upset, but even at this distance the difference in their anger was clear. Danny was plain old-fashioned angry in his typical hot-tempered way. He and Molly would have a barney about it, and then it would be all over. But Matt—she could see that cold rage in his eyes which had frightened her before.

Matt stood up as she advanced towards the table. He confronted her silently for a moment, his face icy and furious. Then he seized her hand and half led, half dragged her from the room.

Ten minutes later, they were in the lounge bar of the Hurst Hotel where they sat a good two feet apart, only barely at the same table.

The barmaid-cum-manageress, whose name was Mrs. Moody, stood before their table wearing the fixed smile of someone who delights in their power to say no. "I'm sorry, sir. No more orders after midnight. Residents only."

"It's New Year's Eve," said Matt coldly.

"Not any more it isn't, sir. It's New Year's Day. We only had an extension till one. It's now five past—mustn't be greedy, must we?"

"I've been waving to you for five minutes."

"Have you?" She smirked. "Aren't I a monkey. I didn't see you. Sorry, sir—it's the law, you know."

"What law?" demanded Matt.

"You have to be staying at the hotel to drink after hours," said Jean, staring into space.

"That's right. As I say—if it was up to me I'd be delighted . . ." She turned to speak to some returning guests. "Sleep tight, Colonel . . . and to you . . . yes . . . let's hope it will be. . . ."

While she rambled on, Matt's mind was moving quickly. "Got any rooms?" he cut her short.

Mrs. Moody's smile froze slightly at his question. She was out of her depth. "Yes, sir," she ventured, "I think we can find you one— or two—?" Her eyes frantically studied Jean whose stony face gave nothing away.

"Matt, it's not necessary."

"OK," he said to Mrs. Moody. "I'll have one."

"Yes, sir." Another glance at Jean. "Single or double?"

"Single," said Matt firmly. "Now, am I a resident?"

"Yes, sir. What would you like to drink?"

"I'd like a double whisky to go with the single room," he said smoothly. "And a sherry for the lady."

Mrs. Moody smirked again. "My pleasure."

She bobbed across to the bar, leaving a bottomless silence between the other two.

"You like getting your own way, don't you?" Jean said at last in a tight voice.

"I needed a drink. Jeannie, listen."

"You listen, Matt. I left with you because I didn't want to make a scene. But if you ever do that again . . . as if you owned me . . ." Fury prevented her finishing the sentence.

"What about what you did?" he demanded angrily.

She blazed at him. "I danced with another man. Do I need your permission for that?"

"You weren't just dancing. You were making a point. He wasn't any other man."

"Oh no, of course not," she cried sarcastically. "A coloured man. The kind you're allowed to beat half to death. . . . And *you stood there*, Matt. You didn't lift a finger!"

"There was nothing I could do," he said sulkily.

"You didn't even try," she spat.

Mrs. Moody waddled across with their drinks. "Here we are then," she said obsequiously. "Your key, one double Scotch and a sherry." She shimmied away.

Matt took a large gulp of his whisky.

"Listen," he said, "they dig me out of goddamned Arizona, which wasn't even a state fifty years ago, dump me in a town the Romans built, and you expect me to act the way *you* want me to act."

"I'd want you to act the same in Arizona."

He sat in silence for a long moment, digesting this.

"Look, Jeannie—we're not the same. We may look the same, talk the same, but we're *not* the same. And I like it. Can't we leave it at that?"

"I don't want to leave it, Matt."

"You want to keep on·arguing?"

"I don't want to leave what we have," she said softly. Her anger was slipping away. She was tired and she recognized that they could argue about this forever—if they were given the chance.

"I can try, Jeannie. That's all I can promise."

She smiled at him. It was enough. It would have to be.

"Finish your drink and take me home," she said gently.

He nodded and tossed back the drink. He picked up the key and looked at it. Then he held it out to her.

"Seems a shame to waste a good room."

She realized it was what she'd wanted, but not now—not this way, with the evening in ruins about them. "Home," she said.

"Home," he sighed, resigned.

As they passed the bar Matt dropped the key in front of Mrs. Moody. "Changed my mind about the room, ma'am. But thanks for the hospitality."

He was gone before she could think of anything to say.

11

After lunch on the day she had taken Tim back to school, Helen sat in the study with her cello, drawing the bow gently across the strings, trying to make the beauty of the music blot out the memory of her son's face as she had said goodbye to him.

"It's for the best, Tim," she had said. "Believe me, if Daddy were here he'd tell you."

The child had not answered, just gazed up at her with bleak eyes that silently accused her of hiding from the truth behind a shield of platitudes. "It's for the best." How did anyone know what was for the best? Unnerved by that tearful stare she had taken refuge in another cliché. "One day we'll laugh about this—promise."

She had smiled at him, but he had not given her one in return. His throat was working hard, and she knew he was trying to prevent the tears from falling. He clung to her desperately when she kissed him, then pulled away from her suddenly, turned and walked into the school. She stood watching him as he went farther from her, towards the old ivy-covered building with its generations of tradition and famous old boys. It was huge and impressive, and her young son looked very tiny in comparison.

All the way home on the cold train loneliness and confusion seemed to batter her. She was thankful that Anna made no trouble about returning to school. Now, so intent was she with her cello, that she did not hear the doorbell ring, nor Ivy answer it, nor the firm footsteps across the hall. She looked up, startled, when the door behind her was flung open to reveal John, his face all smiles.

"Get your coat on," he ordered without preamble. "We're going on a trip."

"A trip? I can't go on a trip. I've got to work—"

"You work too hard. Don't you know there's a war on? Take a day off. *I* did."

Gently but firmly he took her hands from the cello and made her lay it aside. There was no possibility of resisting him, nor did she try very hard. Her heart was racing.

"Where are we going?" she demanded as he urged her out.

"Ireland," he said.

He refused to say any more. Pulling her coat around her shoulders, Helen found herself bustled out and into the jeep. John was whistling to himself as they drove off towards the nearby air force base.

She watched his hands on the wheel. They were strong decisive hands. It was so long since anyone had told Helen what to do and not listened to her argument. She wanted to laugh aloud.

Within minutes of arriving at the base they were in the air in a light plane that looked as though it had been designed to carry supplies. They were over the water almost immediately after take-off. Helen pressed her face against the window to see the gleaming waves rushing beneath her. They looked close enough to touch, yet at the same time she had the sensation of soaring high, high in the universe. If only John and she could fly away like this for ever and never come back.

Once she would have checked that thought before it was properly formed. Now she let it float freely in her mind. She was no longer herself, but a woman who could reach any height with the man beside her. But at the same time she was afraid of the strange feeling that had taken possession of her. All the fixed points of her life no longer meant anything now that the flying had set her free. She laughed aloud, drunk with exhilaration.

She felt John press closer to her and turned to speak to him. Even so she had to shout to make herself heard above the noise of the engine. "What's he going to Ireland for?" she shouted, meaning the pilot.

"Top secret," John yelled back. "Ever been before?"

"No—always wanted to. I never dreamed of going like this."

The plane lurched, and there was his arm round her shoulders to steady her, his eyes smiling reassuringly into hers, telling her not to be afraid because he was with her.

Now they were over land again. Ireland. The plane swooped low over a small airfield. Its perimeter was surrounded by boxes and crates. Obviously a place for the transit of supplies.

The wind, whipping across the flat surface, stung her face as they left the plane. She felt a few drops of rain. The sky was grey and already dark clouds were building up over the sea.

John turned to the pilot who had clambered down beside them. "We'll be back at six." To Helen he said, "I'll try and grab a car."

"I'll give you ten minutes," the pilot bawled back into the wind.

"*What!*" John yelled in dismay. "Are you crazy?"

"Look at those clouds!" shouted the pilot. "I'm not supposed to be here. Just you hang about and don't go too far."

John and Helen looked at each other and began to laugh. Around them GIs had begun loading crates onto the plane. One of them began to check off the items with the pilot.

"You've got the usual—bourbon, cigarettes—a little low on

cigars. I think some bastard's stopping us back at embarkation.''

More crates changed hands. "You also got three dozen best kosher salamis,'' said the GI laconically.

"How do I get rid of three dozen salamis?'' demanded the pilot.

"How should I know. Drop them on Berlin.''

While the loading continued John led Helen away through the rain to one of the larger huts at the edge of the airstrip.

Entering the hut was like stepping into another world. It was done up as a bar and recreation room. The bar was well-stocked with liquor, with special beer taps that served only American draught beer. There were a couple of pinball machines, a juke box playing a current hit song. Scattered about were tables at which sat an assortment of officers looking as though they had all the time in the world to spend in these pleasant surroundings.

One of them looked and smiled cordially at John.

"Nice to know you,'' he said. "Why don't you folks have a drink —on the house.''

"Thanks,'' said John. He led Helen to the bar.

"Top secret indeed,'' she said.

"You don't understand, Helen. Wars are not fought with bombs alone. You'd know that if you took them seriously.''

A GI appeared behind the bar. "What can I do for you folks?''

"Beer for me.''

"Could I have a cup of tea?'' asked Helen.

The bartender gave her a smitten glance. "You can have anything we got.''

As they perched on bar stools John said, "Look at it this way. All that stuff is just going to generals and war correspondents. We're diverting a tiny bit for the common people.''

"Nothing like good honest corruption to raise morale,'' she mocked him.

The bartender returned with their drinks. He began to hand the tea to Helen but John intercepted him with, "Allow me.'' Taking the cup he walked to the end of the bar where there were jars of pretzels, peanuts, hard-boiled eggs, sweets and doughnuts. He selected a doughnut and returned to Helen.

"Welcome to Ireland,'' he pronounced.

At that moment the sound of the plane's engine revving up was heard outside. The door was flung open and a GI made frantic movements for them to board the plane. They fled, Helen still clutching her doughnut. They made it to the aircraft in lashing rain, just as the last crate was loaded on. The pilot made the thumbs-up signal, the door slammed shut behind them, the propellers turned, and they were climbing again.

This time they could see nothing out of the windows but the endless grey and the rain lashing against the glass. Helen chewed on her doughnut like a greedy child, loving every moment of the unexpected adventure. John, looking at her, suddenly saw her as she must have been at seventeen, full of life and passion. He wanted to keep her up there, where he could make her happy, for ever.

"Thank you," she shouted over the engine's bellow.

"For what?"

"Showing me Ireland."

They both laughed, and she leaned back against the side of the plane. They were both sitting on the floor which was lurching beneath them. The plane shuddered suddenly, and seemed to drop fifty feet before continuing. John laid a hand on her arm.

"It's all right," he said. "It's only turbulence. It doesn't mean anything. We'll get back safely."

To her surprise she found she was completely unafraid. She seized John to steady herself against another shudder, and when he drew her close to him she slid at once into his arms. His lips touched hers, gently at first, then with a passion too long repressed. She kissed him back demandingly, no longer able to think of anything but that she loved him.

With a sigh of disappointment she realized that they were descending. They sat up decorously, but she kept hold of his hand. It was an effort, when she left the plane, to smile and thank the pilot, and try to sound her normal self . . . she would never be her normal self again.

They were both silent as he drove her home. John had long known that if Helen came to him it would be seriously, with a total giving of herself. The awesome completeness of such a gift had frightened him. It was more responsibility than he had wanted to bear. But now he knew that loving her as he did he could not be less generous in taking than she in offering. He must be what she believed and trusted he was—or give her up.

He stopped the jeep at her door, but made no move to get out.

"Helen—is this what you really want?"

She nodded, but all she said was, "You'd better not park here. Put the jeep under the trees."

He thought—under the trees, where a passer-by could not see from the road a jeep that had stayed all night. When she had got out he drove slowly round the side of the house and parked. Then he followed her in.

He had known—because he knew her—that she would not make love to him in the room where she slept with her husband. Instead she took him to a small spare room where there were twin beds.

The room was in a far corner of a wing that he guessed was not much used. He felt the silence of the house around them, as though no one but they existed on earth. And that was how he felt their loving to be, something that had no links with anything that had happened to either of them before. He only knew as he held her tenderly that everything that had happened to him before this moment felt wrong and stupid.

"What are you thinking?" she said to him in the dark, kissing him.

"I was thinking that now I'm glad that Ann has wiped me out of her life. I don't have to feel guilty. I don't exist for her any more. I only exist for you. That's how I want to be."

"But you can't exist for me," she whispered.

"I shall love you all my life. What we have now—we shall always have. Even when we can no longer see each other or be together."

She put a hand over his mouth. Her eyes were shining unbearably.

"Don't speak of that. I don't ever want to think of that. We have tonight. Let's cling to what we have."

HE LEFT HER just before dawn. She lay in bed and watched him dress, smiling. When he bent to kiss her she reached up her arms and wound them round his neck to give him a long, tender kiss.

When he had slipped quietly out of the front door she went back to her usual room, where her bed lay unslept-in. She crept in between the cold sheets and lay, feeling the chill creep over her, as the sound of the jeep grew fainter.

12 Jean was down early, opening the blackout curtains onto the poor light of a March morning. But what caught her eye was the convoy of trucks rumbling down the street. She remembered the last time she had seen this sight—the day Matt arrived. Who would have known then how he would change her life?

As the last truck went past it revealed a wall on the opposite street. Someone had painted SECOND FRONT in huge letters. The smile left Jean's face and a chill hand clutched her. For weeks everyone had been talking about the Second Front. Hitler was busy fighting the Russians. The best way to defeat him now—everyone said—was for the Allies to attack across Europe. It was an open secret that some time soon a huge Allied army would land in France and begin the long, liberating march that would hopefully end the war. Nobody knew exactly when or where, but everyone knew it was going to happen.

Suddenly the new influx of Yanks gained an ominous significance. Many troops had already gone to the South of England to begin massing on the coast. It could not be long before the Conleigh army base was broken up, the soldiers sent south—taking with them Matt, who might either be killed in the fighting or just go back home to America and never think of her again. She stood for a long time at the window, feeling a blackness spread through her. They had had so little time.

She heard her father in the living room, and composed her face before going in to him. He was just putting on his bicycle clips.

"They're pouring in," she told him. "Truckloads of them—" She became aware of something strange. "Where's mother?"

"She'll be down shortly."

"Is she all right?"

"Just tired," said her father. "Doing too much—you know your mother—she'll not be told."

Jean had gone past him and up the stairs before he'd finished speaking. She knew her mother had often looked white and strange recently but she had put that down to disappointment over her own behaviour with Matt. But if it were more—if in her own happiness she'd neglected her, how could she forgive herself?

She found Clarrie sitting on the edge of her bed. She was fully dressed but her face was ghastly.

"Mother."

"Stop fussing up here, Jean. There's a shop to open." She made a forced effort to stand and just managed it by holding onto the bedside table.

"I'm calling the doctor—" said Jean.

"*You'll do no such thing!*" Clarrie's voice was sharp. As long as there was no doctor to tell her officially what she had, she could pretend it wasn't true. "I'm perfectly all right. My tummy pain again, that's all. All this wartime rubbish that we have to eat. Now open that shop. There'll be people waiting. Go on!" She summoned up a smile.

Jean did as she was told, but the nagging worry inside her would not be completely silenced. All morning while she served, her mind was on Clarrie, and twice she gave the wrong change.

Geoff, on his way to school, was hailed by Billy Rathbone. He sounded full of news.

"Geoff! Geoff! The golf course!"

Geoff dodged between the cars and reached the other side of the road. "What's wrong with it?"

"It's not there any more. Come and have a look."

The boys raced up the hill at the edge of town, and when they reached the crest, stood looking down.

"See," said Billy triumphantly.

Rows and rows of GI tents covered what had once been the golf course. Where the ground had been cleverly designed to undulate for the better entertainment of golfers a bulldozer was busily flattening it out.

"So that was where all them trucks was going," Geoff mused. From where he was standing he could make out a Red Cross van standing in the centre of the new camp. There was a lady leaning out with cups and buns. Geoff recognized her as Mrs. St. John.

"But what's it *for?*" demanded Billy. "What they bringing all the Yanks up here for? We're not fighting the war up here."

"Don't suppose they'll be here long," said Geoff wisely. "Anyway, it'll be good for the chip run. Guess they'll want some an' all."

They continued their walk. As the two boys passed the entrance to Lime Hall an American jeep drew up at the gate. Inside it was a soldier and a boy of about their own age. Geoff stared when he saw who it was.

"What's *he* doing here?" he said.

"Who?"

"That lad. Tim St. John. He's supposed to be at boarding school."

Billy sniffed. "Looks stuck up to me."

"Well, he ain't stuck up, and he hates that school. He was telling me at the party. He keeps asking his Mum to let him leave, and she won't. Hey!" he breathed out ecstatically as the thrilling possibility dawned on him. "Happen he's run away."

They watched as the boy climbed down from the jeep, thanked the soldier politely and began to walk up the drive to his home.

"Aye," mused Geoff sympathetically. "And happen he's going to get it in the neck when Mrs. St. John comes home and finds him there."

TIM MANAGED to get into the house by the back door and slip up to his room without being seen. He wasn't afraid of Ivy. If she'd caught him she'd have taken him into the kitchen and made him tea. He could have told her about school and how he hated it and she wouldn't have said anything about sticking it out for the sake of his father. Nonetheless he was glad to avoid her because in his present state of wretchedness all he wanted was to be left alone.

The room was freezing cold. He couldn't even get into his bed and huddle under the covers, because it wasn't made up. After a while he thought of his old overcoat in the wardrobe. It was a bit tight on him now, but better than nothing. He wrapped it round him and sat on the edge of the bed and waited.

There was a hard pain in his chest. It was made up of fear and loneliness, and something else that he didn't understand. He only knew that it had been there ever since he came home for Christmas.

He had dreamed of home all through the term. To him it was a haven of peace and safety. He had thought of how when he got back at Christmas he could tell his mother all the things he hadn't been able to put into the letters. He could tell her of the night six other boys had seized him, pulled him out of bed and dumped him in a huge wastebin.

But somehow, over Christmas, there'd never been a chance to talk to his mother. She'd seemed preoccupied, as though she had something on her mind that she couldn't tell anyone. For a dreadful moment Tim had wondered if his father was dead and his mother knew and wouldn't tell. But that was impossible. She would never have been so happy if Daddy was dead. And she was happy. Several times Tim had seen her laughing with the Yank officer who came over about the supplies. Tim couldn't remember ever seeing his mother laugh like that. And, he couldn't understand why, there was a quality of happiness about her that seemed to menace him.

At last, he heard the gravel scrunch as the Red Cross vehicle came up the drive. His heart began to thump. As the front door opened, he went to the top of the landing and called down to his mother. She ran swiftly upstairs to where he stood, facing her with an attempt of defiance. He was shivering.

"I'm not going back, Mummy," he said as bravely as he could. "I'm not—I won't." He could hear his voice beginning to shake. "I won't go back," he whispered as the tears coursed down his cheeks.

But there was no anger in his mother's eyes, only a kind of shocked pity. After a moment she came to him and took the trembling body in her arms. She held him tightly and laid her cheek against his hair. "It's all right, darling." she murmured soothingly. "It's all right."

THE FOLLOWING EVENING Danny had made plans to meet Molly at the Ritz Cinema. He and a few hundred other Yanks had spent the day on the moors, in full battle kit, practising landing on a strange beach while trying to dodge an attacking enemy overhead. Again and again they had dashed from mock landing-craft and crawled across the heather to imaginary targets, while all around them explosions thundered. "You'll do it till you do it right!" the master sergeant had bawled. "Hitler ain't gonna give you no second chance!"

They had marched back to camp at the end of the day, weary to the soul, cold, and apprehensive about facing their girls that evening with their new understanding of the immediate future showing in their faces. Danny, not a sentimental man, spent the journey into town thinking about Molly and the news she had given him over the telephone that morning.

He met her by the cinema, kissed her briefly, and took her inside without a word. Very soon, his fingers entwined with hers, he could feel himself nodding off, until an explosion from the screen made him jump and open his eyes. For a moment he thought he was back on the moors, dodging blank shells. But Molly's hand tightened over his reassuringly and when he looked she was smiling at him in the darkness. The explosions had come from the screen where a newsreel was showing.

"Allied heavy artillery pounds enemy positions south of Rome," declared the announcer heartily. "Already in full retreat before the victorious Red Army in the East, Hitler must now regret his folly as he glances towards the coast of Europe and the fresh onslaught which soon must surely come."

They looked at each other. Her eyes were full of apprehension.

He kissed her hair, wondering whether to say what was in his mind now or wait till later in the evening.

But in the end it was Molly who said it. Taking his hand and placing it on her middle where the swelling was barely visible, she said, "When are we going to make him legal?"

ON SUNDAYS, whenever Matt could get an all-day pass, they would take their bicycles and go for long rides in the country. They could not help noticing that little by little the roads were getting more crowded with army vehicles moving south. They knew that the much talked-about Second Front was getting very close.

One day, as a convoy passed their bicycles, Matt stole a look at Jean. Her loveliness struck him with a force that almost stopped his heart in his breast. His eyes fell on the engagement ring that still glittered on her finger. Out of deference to Clarrie she would not take it off, even with him. But now he knew that he could not go away and leave her while she still officially belonged to another man.

He had tried to get her out of his heart, and failed. His savage pain on the night she became engaged to another man had shocked him. The week he had been forced to spend apart from her, confined to quarters, had been unbearable. When he was free to leave the camp and see her again he had sent her the message to be ready for him and "wear something special" with a confidence he was far from feeling. Joining up with Danny and Molly for that night had been an act of pure cowardice. He had been afraid that their relationship might have changed.

For at this point Matt had discovered fear in himself, fear of the strength of his feelings for Jean. He envied Danny, now happily preparing for his wedding to a girl he loved in a simple uncomplicated way. Of course Molly was carrying a kid, but Danny could have got out of it if he'd wanted to. He'd never have given it a thought. He wanted to marry Molly and he wanted to have that child. While Matt knew that, whatever he might feel for Jean, he was not ready for her to have his child. And yet—how could he just go away and leave her?

13

Once Helen had acknowledged to herself that she loved John Docherty she was honest about her love. She was incapable of those little mental evasions by which women and men pretend to themselves that a situation is other than it is. She loved him. She had no right to her love. She was married, so was he. Soon the war would take him away from her, and she knew it would be for ever. There was no hope that they could marry. What they had now was all they could ever have. They could take it to the full or spend their lives wondering how it might have been.

Take what you want, and pay for it. Helen knew what she wanted and she was taking it. And if the payment should come afterwards in tears and loneliness, she would take that too, and never complain.

She had hoped at first that they would be left to enjoy their time together in peace, but when Tim came home she knew that hope was vain. She could not sleep with her lover while her son was under the same roof. Yet it never occurred to her to send Tim back to school. The unhappiness in his eyes had answered all doubts about the wisdom of her decision.

As for her husband Peter—he was another world, one she could forget when she lay warm and content in John's arms. And during her solitary nights following Tim's return she yearned for those arms with a passion and a longing that once she had thought could belong only to her music. She would lie alone in bed and watch the dawn gradually lighten the curtains, feel a sense of terror lest she should never feel John's arms about her again, and wonder how she would bear it.

Her heart leaped towards him when one day he asked her diffidently if she would come away with him for a night. She knew how close their parting might be, but shut her mind to it, shut out everything but the thought of the day and the night they would have together.

It was early April when they set off in the army car he had borrowed, the brightest April she could remember. The pale spring sun cast a pallid sheen over everything, the fresh wind whipped against their faces, and her spirits soared.

The wind grew stronger as they neared the sea. The Grand Hotel stood at the farthest point looking out directly onto the waves. Ahead of them at the entrance stood a civilian car out of which a British colonel and an American WAC were climbing. A porter was taking their bags out of the back. He saw John get out of the car and nodded.

"Checking in, sir?"

"That's right."

"Back for your bags in a moment. Just go right in."

While they waited John went round to Helen's side and opened the door. She smiled and climbed out, stretching luxuriously.

"Tired?" he asked.

"Just a little cramped."

"Longer drive than I thought."

Now they were here she felt an unexpected sense of constraint. On the journey something had changed. She tried to put her finger on it. She remembered the couple who had gone into the hotel ahead of them, the way the porter had turned to John and herself, his easy acceptance of them.

I wonder how many couples come here, she thought. And the answer was there, disturbingly ready in her mind. Quite a lot. It's handy for the army base.

But we're not like that, she wanted to cry. We're different. I love him, he loves me. And she remembered the porter's face again, the total absence of interest in his expression. To him one couple was just like another.

John was watching her face. "Would you like to stretch your legs?" he asked.

"Yes, I think so."

They walked a little farther down the path till they came to a wall which made a boundary with the beach. They looked out over the sea, which was a heavy grey with many white flecks.

"You know, it's a very pretty country, England," John said.

"Actually this is Wales," she laughed, and pointed. "England's that way."

"So that's the Welsh sea, right?"

"No, actually that's the Irish sea."

"Remember Ireland?" he said.

"How could I forget?"

They laughed together. She relaxed slightly. Perhaps it was going to be all right after all. . . . She turned and began to study the balconies of the hotel rooms above them. A girl had appeared on one of them. She was wearing a dressing gown and carrying a pair of stockings that she appeared just to have washed. She spread them carefully on the balcony rail to dry. A man, also in a dressing gown, appeared behind the girl. He said something to her that could not be heard from down below.

"Think he's British or American?" said John.

"Does it matter?"

"I like to think we get the pretty ones."

Helen continued to stare upwards. Her heart lay like lead within her.

The girl turned back into the bedroom. The man smiled and followed her into the room and closed the window behind them.

"She might be a terribly nice girl," said Helen.

"Why not?"

"They might be very much in love."

"Could be."

She met his eyes, hesitantly. "Perhaps I'm not a woman of the world. I've felt no guilt at all until now. And yet—why should the place make any difference? And here I am *feeling* guilty."

"About Peter?"

Her eyes swept the hotel with its blank professional front that had seen so many lovers come and go, and judged them all the same.

"About coming here," she said in a low voice. "In this way. Do you understand?"

"Yes."

In the silence that fell between them she gave one of her laughs that was almost a gasp. It wrenched his heart.

"I'm sorry," she said despairingly.

In reply he leaned forward and kissed her forehead. No other words were necessary between them. He took her hand and they started to walk back to the car. The porter was there taking out the luggage.

"Don't bother," John told him. "We're not staying."

"Ah?" The porter looked from one to the other, then shrugged. Helen had the feeling that even this situation was one he had encountered a dozen times before. It was the last touch necessary to complete her feeling of cheapness.

John handed the porter a pound. "Thanks, anyway."

When they were sitting together in the car he started the engine, then let it idle for a moment. He shook his head, with a rueful chuckle.

"What's funny?" she said.

"I just wish Tim had been happy at school."

She reached over, took his face in her hands and kissed him fiercely.

About a quarter of a mile from Lime Hall she asked him to set her down.

"I think I'd better finish the journey by myself," she said.

"In case of Tim?"

"Yes." She reached up and touched his face. "Goodbye, John— my dear."

"It isn't goodbye. I'll still be around for the supplies."

"Yes, but—I may not be there. Ivy will know what to give you."

"Helen—"

She turned and walked away from him quickly. She knew he would watch her till she came to a bend in the road for that would be her last chance to turn and wave to him. As she approached the bend she took a deep breath, clasped her case more tightly and walked on without turning. It took all her courage.

14 It was the sight of an American warship gliding down the nearby canal that gave Matt the determination to try and reach a decision. Earlier on during their walk, he had talked, in the most general terms, about the possibility of their marrying after the war, of his taking Jean back with him to America. Jean had been non-committal. Now, as they both stood on the bridge watching the warship slip away beneath them, he found himself pushing her for at least a partial answer. Meanwhile, on the towpath, children danced excitedly and cried out, to the ship, "Where are you going? Where are you going?"

"Newport News," a sailor called back.

"Is that America?"

"Sure is."

A chorus of shouts: "Take us! Can we go? Take us with you."

As the cacophony moved off into the distance, Jean said, "I've told you, Matt. It'd kill my mother. She's ill. What do I do? Take her a cup of tea up and tell her Ken and me's over, and all she's fighting to live for is finished? I love you Matt, but I can't do it."

"All over the world guys meet girls—fall in love—get married. Simple. What's so different about us?"

"Five thousand miles, that's the difference."

"That scares you does it? It's not just your mother?"

"Yes, it does scare me—but I want you so much I don't care." She was looking down into the water. "If it was just *me*, there's no scare big enough to keep me away. But not *now* Matt, not just yet."

His eyes followed the ship's wake, right down to the boat itself, distant now. "I want to take you home one day." He turned and touched her cheek. "So let's just say we both got things to do before we go, OK?"

She smiled at him gratefully. "OK, Matt."

He kissed her then and there, in broad daylight, something he had never done before. He normally shied from demonstrations of affection in public. But now he was too happy to care. They both felt now that as long as Matt were not killed, nothing could happen that their love could not cope with. Just as long as he were not killed. . . .

Jean felt, with sudden fear, that she would never be as happy again as she was at this moment. But the fear passed. She would not allow herself to believe that she had found Matt only to lose him again so soon. He was so dear to her now, his smile, his eyes, the way he touched her, something in his voice as he spoke her name.

It was dusk when they reached the shop, and everything was closed.

"Come in for a moment," she whispered.

She knew something was terribly wrong in the house from the moment they were inside. She could see a light coming from beneath the curtain that divided the shop from their living room, but there was no sound coming from behind it. Normally the radio would have been on, or someone would have been talking. Now there was nothing, just the complete silence and that crack of light that seemed to menace her. She hurried across and threw back the curtain.

Her father sat hunched by the dying fire, wracked with misery. Clarrie sat in her dressing gown at the table, a cold cup of tea in front of her. She sat upright, ramrod stiff, her face dead white and terrible. Jean's heart began to thump with fear.

"Mother—are you all right?" There was no answer, but Clarrie's eyes, full of a shocking accusation, turned on her daughter. "Mother, what's happened?"

But she knew. She knew before a word was spoken that only one thing could bring that look of fierce hatred—for both Matt and herself—to her mother's face. And her heart gave a silent wail of anguish, begging, no, no—please no.

It was her father who spoke, jerking the words out between sobs.

"It's young Ken—he's been killed. His sister came round—they got a telegram—teatime. Killed in action."

The tight pain in her throat was unbearable. She stared speechless at her father. Then she staggered and felt Matt's firm hands support her.

Clarrie turned cold eyes on Matt. "I hope you're proud of what you've done to us," she said bleakly.

"I'm sorry, ma'am—"

"That lad *knew*—knew about you and your dirty little goings on behind his back."

94

"He must have." Even Jean's father, a gentle man who made few judgments, agreed. "He must have. Them Commandos. That's why he joined."

"Dad—" Jean tried to protest but words would not come.

Clarrie's unforgiving eyes were boring into her. "He lived for you, miss—you know that, don't you? He didn't *want* to come back." Her voice rose hysterically. "You've killed him, the pair of you. That's something you'll always live with."

"You're wrong," said Matt's voice quietly behind her. "I'm sorry, I really am, but you're wrong."

Jean had begun to shiver as horror invaded her. Her mother wasn't wrong. She knew that.

James addressed Matt. His voice was not unkind, but it was flat and final. "Just go, will you, son? That's the best you can do for now—just go."

Matt's hands were still on Jean's shoulders. He turned her slightly to face him. "Jeannie—"

"I'll be all right," she controlled herself and took hold of his hands. "I'll see you tomorrow."

"Yes," came Clarrie's bitter voice. "You'll see him tomorrow, and the next day, and the next. It's what you've hoped for."

"Mother, you've no right," Jean begged. "Please—"

"I'm sorry," Matt said over her head to Clarrie. "I'll see you tomorrow, Jeannie."

He turned and left them. Nobody moved or spoke until they heard his footsteps echoing through the shop, and the shop door closing behind him. Then Clarrie broke into sobs that seemed as though they would break her frail body in two. Jean ran and flung her arms round her mother, pressing Clarrie's head against her own breast. She too was sobbing.

"Oh, Mother—Mother—" The tears flowed down her face seemingly without end. Her arms tightened on the grief-wracked body. She could feel Clarrie's fingers biting deep into her back.

James Moreton sat oblivious, sunk in his own pain as the two women held each other.

After a while Clarrie lifted her head and spoke to her daughter, but she did not see her. Her eyes were blinded with tears. "My grandchildren—I'll never see them now. I know that. I'll never set my eyes on them."

LATER THAT NIGHT Jean sat in her own room, trying to blot out the memory that tortured her. But it would not be blotted out. For the rest of her life she would have to live with the knowledge that Ken had known the truth about her and Matt, had released her to love Matt, and had then joined the Commandos.

Wherever she turned in her memory, there was Ken, looking at her sadly, telling her that he loved her enough to set her free. "Be happy on *your* say so—I'm asking *nothing*—"

He had freed her—no strings—no claims—she had been free to do what she did. Why should she feel guilty? But she knew in her soul that she had seized hungrily on that freedom, grateful for the gift and never reckoning the cost to the giver.

She sat there, turning her engagement ring over and over. She took it off at last, and put it gently away in a drawer in her dressing table. Then she sat with her head resting on her hands while the tears fell through her fingers.

TO MATT his presence in the parish church seemed almost sacrilegious. The very knowledge of why he had come made him feel a trespasser.

Over his head threadbare flags hung from the vaulted arches. Centuries old, they were the battle honours of the South Lancashire Regiment. They had hung there as, over the years, the list of the regimental dead had grown and grown. Today yet another name was being added to the big memorial book in the regimental chapel.

By moving forward a little Matt could just see Jean standing beside the lectern on which the memorial stood. She took up the pen. He knew what she would be writing:

Kenneth George Thomas. Sergeant. The Second Battalion. Burma. Died of his wounds 16th March 1944.

She replaced the pen and stood looking at the stark inscription that was now all that could remind her of the man who had loved her with self-forgetting generosity. Her throat constricted. She dropped to her knees in front of the chapel altar.

Matt, seeing her kneel, bowed his head and waited for her. He lifted his eyes as he heard her footsteps returning over the stone floor. She was wiping her eyes, but she smiled when she saw him and took his arm to go out into the fresh air.

Once there Matt breathed deeply, and put his cap back on his head with a feeling of relief.

"Thank you for coming," she said.

"I was honoured," he said, meaning it.

Jean was holding very tightly onto his arm as they walked out into the spring sunlight. There they were halted by the rumble of jeeps and tanks rolling down the High Street. There had never been such a convoy before. To Jean, its message was unmistakable. Soon she would be parted from the only other man in the world who had understood her.

"Matt—" she said abruptly. "Please—take me away for the weekend."

THE HOTEL corridor seemed to go on for ever. The elderly porter who conducted them down it churned out a monologue as he went. "Yes, we've had them all here one time or another. Old Prince of Wales, Lord Derby, the lot. We've had 'em all."

Jean cast a critical eye over the furnishings of the obscure Midlands hotel to which they had come, tried to reconcile them with this tale of its past history, and failed.

She and Matt were walking a couple of feet apart, not wanting to seem too intimate. But the porter had no eyes for them. He was deep in his reminiscences.

"Tore the bloody place apart and all, God bless 'em—Ha! I could tell you a tale or two."

The room when they reached it was pleasanter than the shabby corridor had led them to expect. It was clean and the furniture was in good repair. The double bed looked soft and comfortable.

The porter drew the blackout curtains and switched on the light. Matt gave him a generous tip, took the key and stood waiting for him to be gone. When the door had closed behind him they stood looking at each other.

"What did you tell your mother?" he said.

"I'm staying at Molly's, helping with tomorrow's wedding arrangements."

For a moment, Matt found himself pondering rather wistfully how differently things had turned out for himself and Danny. His friend was so totally committed to the forthcoming marriage, so sure of the future.

"Time for a bath," he said, hastily dismissing all further comparisons, and giving Jean a brief kiss.

"Mind if I have first go?" she said.

"No, go ahead."

She came back from the bathroom along the corridor twenty minutes later, wearing her dressing gown.

"Best I can do in five inches," she laughed.

"Five inches?" he looked puzzled and she remembered that he always washed at the base where, presumably, things were different.

"Go and have a look," she chuckled.

He gave her a puzzled frown and departed.

He saw what she meant as soon as he reached the bathroom. Five inches above the bottom of the bath a black line had been painted.

Above the bath a notice proclaimed: "Five inches of water only. Every inch above—Hitler loves."

When he'd finished he crept back along the corridor, his clothes tucked under his arm, a small towel covering him inadequately.

Jean was already in bed, the clothes drawn up to her chin.

"Open the curtains," she said, smiling. "No—" as he turned towards the window. "Turn the light out first. The blackout."

"Ooops." He switched off the light, then drew back the curtains.

Soft moonlight filled the room. She could see him standing clearly by the window. She lay back watching him, totally relaxed and happy. Her last doubt had fled. Nothing could have been more right than to be here now, this moment, with this man that she loved so much.

"Now, come here," she said softly.

"Yes, ma'am."

He dropped the towel, and came over. Then he sat on the side of the bed and brushed his hand gently down her cheek. She let go of the covers and he pulled them back so that the moonlight flooded her face and breasts. He began to caress them softly.

"How long will it be?" she whispered.

"Will what be?"

"Before you have to go?"

"I've got a weekend pass—"

98

She stopped his hand, her face serious. "You know what I mean. Before the invasion."

He smiled reassuringly. "They don't tell sergeant cooks."

"How long, Matt?"

"It's building up fast. Soon, I guess."

Her eyes held his. It was what she had always known in her heart. More than ever she wanted to belong to him before he went away from her. She took his hand and held it against her breast, feeling the excitement stir deep within her as his fingers began to move.

After a moment he pulled back the bedclothes so that he could see all of her. Like him she was naked. She knew her strong young body was beautiful and she rejoiced. She wanted to make him a perfect gift. As he kissed and caressed her, she pulled him to her violently.

"Matt—"

She felt swamped in her love for him. From the moment he touched her she had known that she was doing the right thing. For perhaps the first time in her life she was ready to let everything go, to forget that there was a world outside these walls. The months of anguish and anxiety were gone as though they had never been.

For a moment the force of her joy overwhelmed her. Then suddenly she realized that he was not going to commit himself to her with that totality with which she had committed herself to him. At that moment she understood, sensed the escape he was seeking, seized him in an agony of protest.

"*No, Matt!* Oh no, Matt," she begged. "Please don't stop—"

He pulled away from her violently.

"Matt—oh *no*, Matt. No!"

She rolled over to the other side of the bed and her body heaved with sobs.

Matt knew that he could not make her understand. "Jeannie— oh God, Jeannie. I'm sorry—" he whispered. "I'm sorry—" He reached towards her.

"Don't touch me," she said hoarsely.

He buried his head in the bedclothes, ashamed, bitter and confused, knowing he had done something for which she would never forgive him.

THE JOURNEY HOME was like dying. She sat in the corner of the dim train, staring out into the corridor, her face resolutely turned away from Matt. In the mirror's faint reflection she could see him, watching her anxiously, waiting for her to turn and speak to him. She closed her eyes, trying to wipe his face from her consciousness.

Every pulse in her body seemed to be throbbing at once with the force of her hate and rage. She felt she would drown in her humiliation if she had to look again at the man who had taken the heart and soul that she had offered and given only a cold body in return. The searing realization that at her moment of profoundest joy he had not been with her, but somewhere far off seeking to escape from her left her shuddering with pain and sickness.

She wanted to tear him with words, make him suffer as she had suffered. But they were not alone. Another GI lounged in the opposite corner with an English girl nestled against his shoulder. The sight brought bile to her throat as she realized that just a few short hours ago she and Matt had travelled this route in that same spirit of happy contentment.

She had insisted on leaving the hotel at once, and he had immediately agreed. To have spent the rest of the night sleeping in the same bed would have been intolerable for both of them. She had not spoken to him as they dressed, nor as they walked to the station. She had not spoken to him since.

The milk-train got into Conleigh at five o'clock. Matt and Jean were almost the last off, walking carefully apart. They made their way between the bundles of newly-delivered newspapers with their startling black headlines giving the latest war news. For once neither of them paid any attention to what would ordinarily have drawn their eyes at once.

As they emerged from the underpass he said, "I'll see you later today then?"

She bit back the retort that he would never see her again, because she had suddenly remembered that it was Molly's wedding day and she wouldn't spoil it.

"Yes," she said shortly. "Later today." Then she turned away.

She walked slowly because she did not want to arrive home too soon and face Clarrie's suspicious eyes. Through her head, like a bitter refrain, a voice repeated endlessly that Clarrie had been right all the time.

15

If the journey home had been bad, the wedding was a hundred times worse. She sat at her table at the reception and thought that you'd never know the bride was pregnant and the groom going off to war. You'd never know that they were all in the grip of wartime austerity. Andy Dawlish had lashed out for his daughter. The marriage took place at the Town Hall registry office and the bride and groom made their appearance in the street to a bagpipe accompaniment.

Afterwards they all repaired to the pub where Matt had taken Jean on their first date. Ted, the owner, had laid on his best "do". It was noisy, musical and heartily obscene. Looking round at the smiling faces Jean thought she had never seen people enjoy themselves so thoroughly. If things had only been different she would have been one of them instead of sitting here looking at them as though through a screen, her heart dead within her.

And look at lucky Molly, she thought. Molly knew her Danny loved her and wanted her and her baby. A band of pain seemed to tighten round Jean's heart. She rose unsteadily, backing away to the door. Matt was standing at the bar, his back to her. Ignoring the puzzled stares from the others Jean fled from the pub.

She ran without looking where she was going. Two laughing, tipsy British soldiers made tentative attempts to waylay her, but gave her a wide berth when they saw her burning eyes.

She came to a bus stop where she knew she could get a bus home if she waited long enough. She hesitated. Two girls eyed her from a nearby doorway. Buses were uncertain. It could be a long wait. Better walk.

She was about to stumble on when she saw Matt loom out of the dark towards her.

"Jeannie—please—"

"Leave me alone, Matt."

Fury and misery choked her.

"Look, forget about me. Think about Danny and Molly."

"You hope I'll forget, don't you?" she said in a bitter voice, not looking at him.

"You tell him, tarty!" The call came from one of the girls in the doorway who was enjoying the scene.

Matt flung the girl an embarrassed glare. He took Jean's arm, his voice was low and urgent. "Let's not talk about it here, OK?"

"You don't want to talk about it anywhere," she accused him, not caring if she were overheard or not.

"Not here," he said through his teeth.

The other girl in the doorway joined in. "Serves her bloody right, Yankee tart."

Matt turned on the girl. "Hey, cut it out, huh?"

"My mother was right," Jean muttered, half to herself.

"What's up with our lads?" the first girl called to Jean. "You too good for one of your own?"

"*Shut up!*" Jean spat the words out, her eyes full of a cold savagery which the girl barely saw in the dark.

"Look who's saying shut up," called the other girl. "Yankee tart!"

The first girl began to chuckle, but the noise was choked off suddenly by the hard slap that Jean delivered across her mouth. Driven beyond endurance by the words that echoed an accusing voice inside her, Jean launched herself onto the girl.

Hissing, spitting, filled with blinding hate, she began to lash out, seeking any way she could to hurt. The first girl that got the impact of Jean's blazing fury rolled away, whimpering, her nose streaming with blood. The other one fought like a cat and got a black eye for her pains.

Horrified, Matt grabbed Jean and dragged her away from her victim. Her coat torn, her stockings full of holes, her knees bleeding, she fought free of him.

"Get off me," she screamed. "Don't you *touch* me!" she faced him in the road, her face swollen, tears coursing down it. "You did this to me!"

She struck out blindly through the laughing jeering mob that had gathered round them. She ran fast as though by running she could get away from what she had become, from what Matt had turned her into.

Matt found himself grabbed by the injured girls, by the spectators. By the time he had thrown them off he had lost Jean in the dark. He began to run after her, calling her name.

She heard him a great distance off, and fled faster. At last, exhausted, she collapsed against a lamp-post, heaving with sobs.

Her face burned where it had been scratched, and she felt as though she would never feel clean again.

She managed to stumble all the way home. She found the shop by instinct, fumbled with her key and burst in. Her father, sitting alone by the living-room fire, looked up in amazement as she rushed by. But she didn't stop.

She slammed the bathroom door behind her and locked it. She began to tear her clothes off in a frantic sobbing frenzy.

Matt found the door to the shop standing open and walked in. He faced James Moreton in the living room. "Where is she?" he said quietly.

"Upstairs, lad."

He nodded and went on up. On the landing he could hear the sound of the bath taps and guessed where Jean was. While he hesitated he saw a crack of light under the door of the bedroom Jean's parents shared. After a moment he went and knocked. Clarrie's feeble voice replied.

He was shocked at the sight of her. She had grown visibly older and more ill since he had last seen her barely two weeks earlier when she had told him of Ken's death and hurled her accusations at him. He stood by the door. "I hope I'm not bothering you—"

"No—you can come in."

He took a step further into the room. He did not want to get closer. After the riotous life-affirming celebrations at the wedding, the air of death about this woman struck him as more horrifying than ever. And in the face of her implacable hatred he did not know what to say. But something in him told him it was important to make some sort of contact with her—if she would allow it.

"Danny and Molly—" he ventured. "They got your telegram. It meant a lot to them."

She gave a faint smile. "Did they have a nice wedding?"

"Fine. They looked real happy."

"Let's hope so. She's a heart of gold has Molly."

"Yeah—well, Danny—they don't come any better."

There was a pause. They faced each other, neither at ease, each one knowing the other was fencing. Clarrie broke the silence first.

"I heard Jean run up. Is anything the matter?"

He hesitated before answering. "If I've made trouble for you,

Mrs. Moreton—I want to apologize. I've never meant to—honest—"

How inadequate the words sounded. He could hear the useless tinny apology clatter to the ground. But to his surprise Clarrie roused herself a little and said, "You couldn't help it. In spite of everything I like you, Matt. Do you believe me?"

"Yes, ma'am."

She had lifted her head a little, but now she dropped it back on the pillow as if the effort had drained her. Her face was the colour of parchment, and when she spoke again he could scarcely hear her voice. "Whatever I have done I did to protect my family. I've Jean at heart—her happiness—"

"I know." There was nothing else for him to say.

They both listened, very still, as the bathroom door opened and Jean's footsteps sounded down the stairs.

"Some things are right," Clarrie went on, "some are wrong. You and Jean—it's just wrong. I can't help believing that." She gave him another smile. "Take care of yourself, wherever they send you."

"And you, ma'am. Rest and take it easy."

He turned to go, but her faint thread of voice recalled him.

"Leave her alone, son—will you?"

At the door he looked back at her, and not for the world could he have kept the bitterness out of his voice.

"Don't worry. The only way I can take her is not my style."

Jean had gone straight downstairs and into the living room to sit with her father. She didn't speak to him, but sat opposite, scrubbed and austere with her hair pulled back as though she was trying to obliterate the loveliness that had helped bring her to this moment. She sat motionless, empty and exhausted.

After studying her without comment for a while her father said, "How are we going to manage, chick? How the hell are we going to manage?"

She didn't ask him what he meant. They both knew Clarrie's death could not be much farther away.

Matt appeared in the doorway. "She wants a drink of water, Mr. Moreton—asks if you'll take it up."

"Aye—right. I will." Looking very old Mr. Moreton got to his feet and pottered into the kitchen. Matt waited for Jean to speak to him, but she turned away as if he was not there. His heart was wrenched with pity for the way she looked.

Mr. Moreton came back, carrying the glass. He hesitated in front of Matt.

"See you again, son?"

"Hard to say, sir—hard to say."

"Well—all the best, son, any road."

Left alone with Jean, Matt still waited in the doorway. When she spoke it was in a faint voice, still not looking at him.

"What did my mother have to say?"

Matt's lips tightened angrily and he refused to answer.

She turned to him. "Well?"

"What *she* had to say. Why don't you ask what *we* had to say?"

She looked back into the fire, and he came and sat in the chair opposite her. The small space of carpet between them might have been a hundred miles.

"She asked me to leave you alone," he said in a tight voice.

"And what did *you* say?"

"Jeannie—I don't *want* to leave you alone. I love you."

"You *love* me." She could almost taste the bitterness in her own mouth. "You wouldn't even risk giving me a baby—our baby. It should have been wonderful but you just couldn't risk it. I knew then. I knew I was just part of your war. When it's over and you go back home you want the lid down good and tight."

He looked at the floor. "I didn't want it to be that way for us. I had different hopes."

"Oh rubbish, Matt," she said fiercely. "You just haven't the guts to take me on—like Danny has Molly—you don't love me enough."

"I'm not ready to have a kid," he said deliberately.

"You're not ready for *me*," she spat.

"You want to believe it, you believe it," he said. A great sense of weariness came over him as he realized that Jean was Clarrie's daughter and like Clarrie implacable. How would it be, this grim certainty, in the years to come?

"I believe it," she said coldly.

He rose to his feet and stood looking down at her. "I want you, Jean—I want to spend my life with you. But you didn't give us a chance to breathe. I'm just not ready for this—" He glanced upwards to where Clarrie lay dying above them. "Her against us—me going off. No, I won't pay that price for you or anyone else."

At the door he turned and said. "And I've never loved anyone else, Jeannie—like I love you."

He went out without waiting to hear if she answered. But she only sat staring into the fire, tightening her arms round her body as if trying to stem the rising tide of anguish that threatened to engulf her.

16

It was hard to subdue the leaping of her heart when she saw John walking towards her. After nearly five weeks without seeing him she had believed she was mistress of her feelings. And now here he was, walking the length of the school hall where she was getting ready for a charity concert, and there was the sudden excitement inside her, jeering that she had been deluding herself. All around her the rest of the orchestra was unpacking for a last-minute rehearsal. Out of the corner of her eye she could see Tim laying out programmes on the seats. She stood up from unpacking her cello as John approached her.

"Hi there!" he said with a smile, and she knew with a swift illogical relief that it was as hard for him to be natural at this meeting as it was for her. "Haven't seen you around camp for a while."

"They assigned me to the new air base."

His look conveyed that he understood what she had not said. Whoever "they" were, "they" had only been carrying out the wishes of Mrs. Helen St. John of Lime Hall.

"Figured something like that." He glanced at Tim. "I see you've got your boy helping out."

"Yes, and he even listens to the music."

Meaningless words, she thought, between us who never needed words. Why had he come?

As if he'd read her mind he said, "I've got some bad news. Well—not really bad, nothing serious, we just can't lend you a truck any more."

"We'll manage," she smiled.

"They need all the trucks now—"

He left the implication hanging in the air. She tried to sound casual. "That means you'll be leaving us."

"Well, you don't expect them to start without me," he said jokingly.

Tim came up quickly, positioning himself in between them. "I won't have enough programmes for all the seats."

"I'll go and get some more in a minute, darling. Just finish those."

The boy laid his remaining programmes on the front seats and returned. He was whistling.

"You sound happy," John said.

"My father's coming home."

"Really. That's great."

"On leave. For a whole month." He bustled away.

John looked at Helen. She nodded.

"Well—I've got to get back to camp. I just wanted to let you know."

He just wanted to let her know something any messenger boy could have told her. There was a warmth about her heart as she smiled and said, "Thank you. For everything."

"Nothing to thank me for."

"Well—" she hesitated.

"Well—" He realized that neither of them was certain what movement would be right for their parting. He was relieved when she solved the problem for him by holding out her hand. He shook hands with her.

"John," the low voice called him back as he turned to go. "Do try not to let anything foolish happen to you."

"I just won't take the war seriously." He gave a smile that was like a salute, and left her.

She became aware that the conductor was ready to start the rehearsal. She listened with half her mind while the rest of the quartet played the opening bars, trying to take in the fact that she would never see him again, never.

She was distantly aware of the conductor's baton bringing her in, and she attacked her opening notes with such passion that one or two of the others, who had privately been of the opinion that Mrs. St. John played like a cold fish, jerked their heads up, astonished. She played blindly, unaware of her companions or her surroundings, pouring out her emotions in the only way left to her.

JEAN WOKE on the morning of her mother's funeral to the sound of trucks rumbling past her window. The sound brought back that other occasion, seven months and a lifetime ago. But she subdued the anguish, making it merge into that other and greater anguish.

Clarrie had slipped away without apparent pain. Jean's father had come out of his room very early four mornings ago and told her tonelessly how he had woken to find his wife dead beside him.

Now, standing in the shop filled with wreaths and flowers, Jean thought of the woman who had covered her natural warmth with a terrible inflexibility that bent and broke everyone around her, and whom in spite of everything, she had loved. Through the windows she could see truck after truck filled with khaki-dressed young men, on their way to war, to death. She stood there in the midst of death and searched the cards and flowers, looking for a name that was not there.

He'd know Clarrie was dead. Molly would have told Danny somehow. But his name was not there.

"Has the Yank sent none?"

It was Auntie Maud, her mother's sister who had recently come to stay and who had become a constant pillar of strength to Jean in all her troubles. She was standing in the doorway. Behind her Jean could see the mourners waiting for the arrival of the cars. "No, Auntie. Doesn't look like it—no."

"Can you blame him?" Maud's tone was gentle.

"I thought he might have—for *me*," said Jean forlornly.

"You're as big a bloody fool as your mother was, God rest her," said Maud frankly. "She's dead, Jean, but you'll never bury her— not now. You know that, don't you?"

Jean retreated into the living room, her heart too heavy to answer. What did it matter now what she knew or didn't know? Matt was going, and he did not love her.

Maud watched her depart with love and frustration written on her face. Something in the commotion outside drew her attention and she went to the window to watch the never-ending stream of troop-filled trucks. "Oh, Yank," she muttered, "where was your flamin' guts?"

The church was full. It seemed that everyone who'd ever known Clarrie or bought from her shop must be there. Jean cast her eyes round slowly: Annie, Mrs. Shenton, Mrs. St. John, with Dr. St. John home for a month's leave, standing beside her. He was in uniform, his cap under his arm. Over and above everything else was the continuous rumble of those trucks. It felt as if every man in the world was being taken south to invade France.

Outside in the graveyard the noise was worse. She could see them now, an endless line, thousands of fresh, young faces above green-brown uniforms, but never the one she was looking for.

How strange it was. Here she was, standing over this hole in the ground and watching as her mother's coffin was lowered into it, but her mind was half on those trucks. It was as if they, not the coffin, were taking her past away.

Something about Helen St. John drew her attention. Without being sure how she knew, she had the feeling that Helen, too, was acutely aware of the passage of the convoy. Tim seemed to think the same thing, for he was gazing up at his mother with what Jean could only call an *old* look on his face. Then Helen looked down and smiled at her son, and his look vanished.

When they got home it was Aunt Maud who was out of the car first, hurrying inside to make a last minute check on the food. Jean climbed out more slowly.

As she went into the shop Aunt Maud reappeared, her face flushed with excitement. She caught Jean's arm. "There's a parcel come—a Yank brought it—said his sergeant couldn't make it."

The moment she said "Yank" Jean felt the colour come and go in her face. She stood staring until Aunt Maud gave an impatient little shove.

"Go on and look at it." It stood on the counter, a square cardboard box, just like that other one, so many lifetimes ago. She knew what she would find inside it.

The iced cake was even more beautiful than the last one had been. Jean stood gaping, wondering how he had managed to produce anything so exquisite in the midst of an army camp in the process of packing up to attack the enemy.

But more than the beauty, and the trouble that had gone into it, was the wording, for with infinite patience and skill Matt had managed to squeeze on—"Thinking of you—Love, Matt".

Unable to speak out of a full heart, Jean turned to face Aunt Maud who was grinning all over her face. Geoff's voice broke in on them. "Jean, me Dad wants to know where—"

"Leave it, Geoffrey." Aunt Maud, her eyes still smiling, turned to her nephew. "Your Auntie Maud will see to it. Jean, love, why don't you—"

She was talking to empty air. Jean had already fled the shop and was chasing the last of the trucks as they vanished into the heart of town. She caught up with them, ran alongside, searching frantically for Matt.

There was no sign of him. Already she was winded. In desperation she threw herself into the path of the last truck which just managed to stop. The young driver gave her a forgiving smile.

"What's up, honey?" he asked.

"The station please—I have to get to the railway station," she gasped.

"You and everybody else. OK. Climb in the back."

She ran to the rear and a dozen young strong arms helped her aboard. Curious eyes took in her mourning clothes and white face, but nobody asked questions.

Cramped as they were they pushed up farther to make a seat for her. She almost collapsed onto it. She had no strength left. It was not merely the effort of running but the sudden shock of emotion. From black despair to dizzying happiness all in a second had left her light-headed.

At that moment the truck did a slight turn on the crest of a hill, and for a moment she had an incredible vista. As far as her eyes could see there were trucks—hundreds of them, snaking down the long winding road to the station. And somewhere down there was Matt, lost among—how many men? Three thousand? Five?

Oh God, she prayed, let me find him in time. Don't let me have discovered him too late. Don't take him away from me without letting me make my peace with him.

She had to leave the truck before it went into the station yard. The station itself was awash with soldiers. Her heart sank in despair. How would she ever find one man in all that? Two

110

trains were already in. One was full, the other one was being boarded.

She began to fight her way through the throng. Then a voice she knew screamed her name at full pitch.

"Jean! *JEAN!*"

She could just make out Molly waving to her from somewhere in the khaki sea. She struggled through to her. "Molly, I've got to find Matt. He's going and I've got to find him."

"It's hopeless, kid. There's thousands of them—it's hopeless."

"I've got to try, Molly." Tears began to run down her face. "Molly, please help me."

Molly looked at her distraught face and made her mind up. "Come on. We'll get where we can see."

She turned, took a deep breath, and barged into the crowd, holding Jean's wrist in an iron grip.

"Excuse me—I'm pregnant," she called cheerfully. "Excuse me—pregnant."

It worked. Miraculously a way was made for them down the ramp that led to the platforms. Their luck held out until halfway down, when a military policeman stopped them. "Sorry ladies, restricted. Sorry."

"But I'm pregnant." Molly tried the charm again.

"Congratulations. But it's still restricted."

Molly wasted no time in further argument. She had spotted a bridge over the lines. It was lined with the privileged wives of officers. Grabbing Jean's wrist she again raised the cry of "pregnant", and by dint of blackmail and pushing she managed to get the two of them up onto the bridge, and to the front of it, where they leaned over at a dangerous angle, desperately scanning the sea of bobbing helmets and kitbags below.

"Have you seen Danny lately?" said Jean.

"Not for a week. They wouldn't let them out. He'll be down there somewhere—they *both* will."

Cupping her hands she screamed, "DANNY—MATT—DANNY—"

None of the heads below looked up, and after a moment Molly turned back to Jean. "Hey," she said, embarrassed, "I'm sorry about your mother, Jean—the funeral—but I wanted to be here—"

111

Jean nodded and touched her shoulder briefly to show she understood, then turned her desperate gaze back onto the brown sea below them. "D'ya think they are together?" she asked.

"I don't know. Jean—a Yank just brought me these—" she held up a tiny pair of boxing gloves "—for the little champ."

Her voice broke on the last word and tears filled her eyes. It was so unlike Molly to give way to sadness that Jean felt ashamed. Molly was seeing off the father of her child—who might never see that child. Impulsively she put her arms round her friend and hugged her.

FOR MATT the journey to the railway station was a misery. He stared fixedly at the Moretons' shop as the truck jolted past it. Perhaps Jean would have got the cake. Perhaps she would be there looking for him, and he could at least go away with her smile to gladden his heart. But the shop was shut up and there was no sign of her. A little farther down the hill they passed the church with funeral cars outside.

As they neared the station Danny began scanning the crowds of faces for a glimpse of Molly. Matt had to guide him onto the platform because Danny's neck was permanently cricked in other directions.

All around them were girls' faces, young faces, pretty faces, but never the right one. They boarded the train. A group of girls broke free of the military police and raced across the railway tracks. Matt and Danny jostled at the window to get a better look at them, then pulled back inside the carriage again, their faces grey with disappointment.

Then the whistle blew. They pushed their heads out again, determined to look till the last moment.

"*Matt! Matt!*" Jean screamed with all her strength, leaning over the bridge. But she knew her voice was lost in the general bedlam. He was going away and she had lost him.

"Jean—" Molly tried to console her, "Danny'll write—you can write back with me. He'll know where Matt is—OK?" Jean nodded through her tears. She was weeping helplessly. "Now come on. Give the lads a wave—wherever they are."

They leaned over and waved as the engine began to creak beneath them, belching out clouds of smoke and steam.

"*Molly! Molly! There they both are!*"

It was almost too late. Their carriage was slipping away under the bridge, but at the last moment Matt looked up and saw her. Danny was waving and shouting, but Matt's voice, shutting out all other noises, seemed to reach her directly, repeating, "I love you," and then, "Don't worry. I'm coming back for you."

When the smoke cleared again he was gone.

114

Christine Sparks

"**Y**ou should be interviewing Colin Welland over lunch, not me. He wrote the script. I just filled in the bits between his dialogue."

Over the telephone, Christine Sparks seemed determined to play herself down. She not only summarily dismissed the achievement of creating what is bound to be one of the year's bestsellers, but she also warned me that she was "very reserved and dour".

She was, I'm glad to say, the antithesis of what she had led me to expect: an obviously warmhearted lady wearing a cuddly big jersey and sporting huge and playful-looking gold-rimmed spectacles. She talked easily and eagerly about her work as a writer and about her home life, married to an ebullient Italian shoe designer in London. ("I met him on a weekend's holiday in Venice, and it was love at first sight.")

Most working days, she attends the editorial offices of *Woman*, where she is employed as a feature writer "specializing in emotional pieces". Special assignments, however, break the routine—once she was nearly stranded for a week in the South African bush. In the evenings, and when her husband can spare her, she does her "other work". She has written the books of four television series, *The Good Life, Accident, Potter,* and *The Enigma Files*, and is currently working on novelizations of two film scripts. Recently she ghosted the autobiography of a distinguished naturalist.

The film *Yanks* stars Richard Gere as Matt, Lisa Eichhorn as Jean, Vanessa Redgrave as Helen and Rachel Roberts as Clarrie. Shooting was done at Twickenham Studios and in Yorkshire.

N.D.B.

The

Capricorn Stone

A CONDENSATION OF THE BOOK BY

MADELEINE BRENT

ILLUSTRATED BY BERNIE FUCHS

PUBLISHED BY SOUVENIR PRESS

Late one night, shortly after receiving news of her father's violent death, Bridie Chance is standing by the window of her bedroom at Latchford Hall. A ground mist swirls across the lawn, enveloping the flowerbeds and shrubbery.

Suddenly, out of the mist, moves a mysterious figure on horseback. Then, almost as quickly, he disappears.

Is the rider reality or illusion?

Many months are to pass before Bridie learns the amazing truth, not only about the rider but also about her father's past. They are months packed with excitement and new experiences as Bridie struggles to save her family from scandal and impoverishment.

Madeleine Brent, author of *Moonraker's Bride* and *Merlin's Keep*, has surpassed herself in this brilliant novel which sweeps the reader from the splendour of a great country house, through the glamour of gaudy nineteenth-century music halls to the terror of a forbidding château in the heart of France.

⚝⚝ Chapter One ⚝⚝

Almost every week, for as long as I could remember, my mother had experienced a premonition and uttered a warning of disaster. Her forebodings were never specific, the calamity was always nameless, so it was strange that she did not speak of any premonition in the week before the two men came from London to Latchford Hall, for they brought with them sudden and terrible disaster which was to crush our family and change my life.

On that hot afternoon in July, when they came to our home just outside the village of Wynford, I was two miles away on the edge of the heath, sitting in the sun outside old Tom Kettle's cottage, lazily pencilling on my sketch pad while he worked with an auger, boring out a log to make an elmwood pump.

Every now and then I would look up at the sky with a scowl of mock anger, annoyed because it was unblemished by a single cloud and too perfect for my liking. If Nannie Foster had been there she would have chided me for the scowl, even though I was now twenty-one. "Exaggerated facial expressions are not ladylike, Miss Bridie." She had been saying those words to me ever since I was old enough to understand, but I had never broken myself of the habit. Surprise or puzzlement, pleasure or anxiety, whatever emotion I felt, my face would always show it much too emphatically.

Nannie Foster had tried hard. So had my teachers.

"For goodness' sake, don't grin so, Miss Bridie."

"I'm sure your eyes will fall out if you raise your eyebrows any higher, young lady."

"Don't grimace as if you were in agony, dear. You're only writing a French translation."

Perhaps I did not try very hard. My friends seemed to find me amusing, and no doubt I played up to this. I was never going to be pretty enough to be admired for my looks, or clever enough to be respected for my brains, so I had to be content with making people laugh, even if the laughter was not always entirely kind. But at least I could always make Bernard laugh with me rather than at me, and this was more important than anything else, for Bernard Page, a rising young architect from Lowestoft, was my fiancé and we were to be married next summer.

Looking up from my sketch pad, I studied the field of ripening corn beyond the cottage, wishing that I could show the heavy scattering of poppies. Scarlet on gold, they were a joy to the eye, but field and cottage were no more than a background to my sketch. The central feature was Tom Kettle himself.

He had been born in the same year as Queen Victoria, so both were now in their late seventies. Tom was a Fenman by birth, but after spending some time as a soldier he had settled here in east Suffolk, two or three miles from the coast; for over half a century he had lived in this cottage alone, making kitchen furniture and elmwood pumps for farms nearby.

It was half an hour since Tom had last taken a rest from his work. Now he released his grip on the massive handle of the auger, wiped his face with his neckcloth and sat by me on the oak bench. Picking up a tankard of ale from the table, he drank deeply, wiped his mouth and looked at my sketch.

"T'ent bad," he said at last.

"No, Mr. Kettle, it's not bad," I agreed, and laughed. "Most things I do aren't bad, but just occasionally I feel it would be nice to do something well for a change."

"Can't all be somethin' pertickler," he chuckled. "You fared lucky, you got learnin', Miss Bridie. You wrought a good tidy time wi' schoolin'."

Tom Kettle had known me all my life. He knew that I had been to a boarding school for young ladies in Colchester, and that now I was a student at Girton College, Cambridge. To a man who had never been to school it would indeed seem that my education had been going on for "a good tidy time".

"Gettin' wed to that feller, then," he announced, and took another swallow of ale. "Going on wi' schoolin' after?"

"Oh, gracious, no. I shall leave Girton at Easter." I had been reading for my Tripos in Mediaeval with Modern Languages, but with no special purpose. I had been happy at Girton, and looked forward to my last months there, but I looked forward very much more to becoming Bernard's wife and beginning a new life.

After a while Tom said, "Lucky feller, your Mr. Page."

I turned to look at him with round-eyed surprise. "Bernard? Oh, I'm sure most folk think I'm the lucky one, Tom."

"Folk," he said with heavy contempt.

I laughed. Tom was a bachelor with a firm dislike of females. It was a rare compliment he had just paid me, and I felt myself flush a little with pleasure. I had long ago resigned myself to the fact that I was a gangling, clumsy, rather plain girl, but there were moments when I could not help wishing that I looked more like my younger sister, Kate, who at eighteen was small and beautiful, with a way of moving like the swaying of a flower. She was also blessed with outstanding musical talent.

If I had not loved her dearly I would have been jealous of Kate, for I lacked all her gifts. As Nannie Foster had often said when we were children, no two sisters could have been less alike. Kate did everything with passion, whether it was playing the piano or writing a letter, laughing or crying, loving or hating. She was a creature of strange moods and contradictions, furiously angry one moment, contrite and full of affection the next. Compared with Kate I was a very prosaic girl, and yet we got on well together. I did not even resent her being my father's favourite child, for this seemed only natural to me.

Beside me, Tom Kettle set down his tankard and got to his feet. "I'll be goin' to hev me tea soon. You'll stay, Miss Bridie?"

I looked at the little gold watch my father had given to me at Christmas. "Thank you, Mr. Kettle, but I must go. This is the day Signor Peroni comes up from London for Kate's weekly piano lesson. I must be there to give him tea before he leaves. Mama is always so nervous about playing hostess to anybody, and she likes me to do it for her during vacation."

Tom stretched, spat on his hands, and resumed his work. I picked up my pencil, but could not concentrate on my sketch. I was still thinking about Kate, and how much my mother would miss her when she went away to London in September to be a student at the Prince Consort College of Music. With my father abroad most of the time, Mama would only have old Nannie Foster for company.

My heart lifted as I thought of my father, who was coming home from Paris next week. Papa was tall, with thick brown hair and wide-set laughing eyes, a man who seemed to carry sunshine with him on the most wintry of days. He was quite unlike the rather stern gentlemen I had met who were the fathers of my college friends. Perhaps it was the Irish in him that made Roger Chance different; certainly he had a gift for talk and a thousand stories to tell.

When my father was with us there was always laughter and excitement in Latchford Hall. Even Mama seemed at peace with the world instead of being in a state of constant anxiety. Nannie Foster pretended to disapprove of Papa's happy-go-lucky manner, but in her heart she was no less delighted than the rest of us to have him at home once more.

Nannie was now nearing seventy. She had been employed in two or three big houses in Norfolk for twenty years before coming to Latchford Hall, and she had been with us for almost as long. "Lord bless us, are you still here, woman?" my father would cry whenever he returned from abroad. "I thought some handsome fellow would have carried you off long since."

Nannie would bridle and purse her lips. "That's no way to speak in front of the young ladies, Mr. Chance. And besides, it's Black Shuck will carry me off, for it's too late for a man."

Black Shuck was a creature of Norfolk folklore, a monstrous black dog with a single flaming eye in the middle of his forehead. Legend had it that he wandered the fields and lanes on wild nights, howling, and to glimpse him was a sure sign that you would die within the year.

A chuckle from old Tom Kettle broke my reverie. "You luke right comical with your 'at loike that, Miss Bridie," he said. I had tipped my straw boater over my nose to keep the sun from my eyes. Now I moved it back with a flourish that made him chuckle again, stood up and walked over to where Daisy stood in the shafts.

"Thank you for letting me sketch you," I said, as he handed me up into the gig. "I'll call again next week."

He nodded. "Savin' trouble."

I had heard him use those words a hundred times before, as perhaps a more devout man might use "God willing". They were a simple countryman's expression that nothing in life was certain, and that no living soul could be sure what tomorrow might bring. Normally I would smile and say, "Yes, saving trouble, Mr. Kettle." But today, as he spoke, a shiver ran through me, and when I looked up it was almost a surprise to see that the sun still shone.

"You all roight, miss?"

"Yes. Yes, thank you. It was just somebody walking over my grave. Good afternoon, Mr. Kettle."

A flick of the reins sent Daisy trotting away at a gentle pace. A curious unease lay upon me now, and I could not shake it off. To drive it away I began to think about my mother, and at once there came the usual twinge of guilt. To my shame, I loved my mother only because she was my mother, and I was lacking in the real warmth of affection I should have felt. For most of my life I had been sorry for her, and I was ashamed of that, too.

Mama had married above her, and found the burden too heavy. I think this had first dawned on me when I was twelve. Kate and I knew nothing of her childhood, but it was clear to us both that she was different from other ladies of similar standing. She spoke correctly but with excessive care, as if afraid of making some error of speech. Her manner was equally anxious, as if she feared committing a breach of etiquette. We had good servants at Latchford Hall, but Mama was never quite at ease with them, and her whole bearing was touched by an air of apology. In recent years she had begun to lose her looks as lines of worry became permanent and an unhealthy pallor stole the colour from her cheeks.

I have no doubt she loved her daughters, but I am equally sure that the centre of her existence and the sun that warmed her life was her husband. When Papa was at home she blossomed, seemed at ease, and was always smiling. She listened to his every word, watching him with something close to adoration.

The feeling between them was not one-sided. During his

visits home I had seen my father look proudly down at her as they walked arm-in-arm in the grounds. "Am I not the luckiest of fellows to have married your beautiful mother?" he would say. The gentry of the district might be rather cool, sensing that Mary Chance was not out of the top drawer, but that made no impression on him whatever.

Once I had asked him where Mama had gone to school and why she had no family. We were standing on the platform at the station, waiting for the train. I had come to see him off, for my mother could never bear the strain of public parting when he returned to Paris. My question was more idle than concerned, for like most children I accepted my family situation with little curiosity. Others might find it strange that Roger Chance should spend so much of his life on the Continent, but to me it was quite natural for it had always been so. I had learned that my father was an art dealer, and that he was based in Paris because that city was the centre of the art world. Other children had fathers who were doctors or lawyers or landowners, but mine was different, and I was rather proud of it.

When I asked about my mother that day, he laughed in the full-hearted way I loved, throwing back his head and twirling his cane. "Why, Bridie dear, do you know I've never asked? I met your Mama, wooed her, married her, and that's all that matters. As for family, I cut adrift from my own before I was twenty and never regretted it. A sober-sided lot they were, and I fancy they were as glad to see me cross the water as I was to leave them behind. And your mother, bless her, she'd long left her family when I met her, so we were two of a kind." He took one of my plaits and tickled my nose with it. "Learn a lesson, Bridie dear. Never look back and never look deep. Just take folk as you find them, and don't ask what they've no wish to tell. Here's the train now, so give me a kiss and be sure to look after Mama while I'm away."

I was much older now than when I had asked that question, and had last seen my father when he came home at Easter. It was then I asked him a question to which I had given more thought. "Papa, why don't we live in Paris, since that is where your work is?"

He had looked at me with a hint of sorrow in his eyes. "Ah

now, Bridie, think what it would be like for your Mama. It's a quiet life in the country she has need of."

"Yes, I suppose so. But she's only truly happy when you're here with us, and it seems such a shame."

"Does she really miss me, Bridie?" he said softly. I was in the library with him, sorting some books, and I looked up in surprise at his words.

"She's a different person, Papa."

He sighed. "She doesn't utter a word of complaint. Perhaps I've never quite realized. . . ." He stood thinking for a moment, then gave one of his quick joyous laughs. "Never mind. Give me another year and I'll be ready to retire, Bridie. Come summer next year and I'll not be going away any more."

My heart lifted. "You really mean it, Papa?"

"When did I ever break a promise to you, Bridie dear? But don't speak of it yet to Mama. You'll make it a long year for her if you do, for she'll be wishing the days away. Promise, Bridie?"

"Yes, of course, Papa."

I had kept that promise, counting the weeks as they passed and rejoicing in my heart that soon my father would come home to be with us always.

As Daisy trotted up the drive I saw that Dr. Carey's gig stood in front of the porch. Beside it was the cab from the railway station. Kate was running towards me, her skirts flying, and some sort of dispute appeared to be going on between George Cooper, who drove the cab, and Henson, our butler.

Kate's face was pale, her eyes very large. "Oh, it's awful, Bridie!" she gasped. "I—I don't know what's happening, but two men came, and then Mama swooned, and Signor Peroni said he would leave early under the circumstances. Nannie sent for Dr. Carey, and the men who came keep saying they must speak with somebody in authority here, and there's only you, Bridie, and we didn't know *where* you were—" She broke off, panting for breath, half crying.

I had brought the gig to a halt, and Henson hurried to help me down. As he did so the cab driver called after him angrily, "A tidy hour I been waitin' fer them Lunnon folk, so you tell 'em they best pay me. Do they don't, I'll set police on 'em."

"They *are* the police, you old fool!" snapped Henson, who had

125

quite lost his usual calm manner. "Begging your pardon, Miss Bridie, but—"

"Police?" I broke in. "Did you say police?"

"Yes, miss." Henson tried to compose himself. "An Inspector Browning and a sergeant. From Scotland Yard, they say."

"If they want fer I to wait," grumbled George Cooper, "then tes on'y roight they hev to pay. A tidy hour I been—"

"How much are you owed?" I said sharply, and was surprised to find my voice so steady.

"Sixpence for the trip an' a shillin' an hour fer waitin', miss."

I opened my purse, took out a shilling and a sixpence with shaky fingers, and gave them to him. Then, trying to hold back the nameless fear that was pressing upon me, I went up the steps and into the big oak-panelled hall. Kate and Henson followed. "I'm sorry, Miss Bridie," Henson said. "It's all been very confusing."

"All right, Henson." I was taking off my hat and coat. "Is Dr. Carey with my mother now?"

"Yes, miss. Nannie Foster got her to bed, and Dr. Carey came a few minutes ago. The two gentlemen are waiting in the drawing room."

I moved to the looking glass and tried to push wisps of hair into place so that I would not look too untidy. Kate was staring at me with a mixture of dread and excitement. "What do you think it's all about, Bridie?" she said breathlessly.

"I can't imagine. You go to the morning room and have a cup of tea. Henson, you escort Miss Kate, please. I'll ring if I need you for anything." Without waiting for an answer I walked across the hall and opened the door of the drawing room. Two men turned from the mullioned windows. One was of middle age, thickset, in a rather rumpled grey suit. His face was square and his gaze placid. The other man was younger, with a short moustache and quick eyes. And he was more smartly dressed in a Norfolk jacket and knickerbockers.

"I have paid your cab driver eighteen pence," I heard myself say. "If you want him to wait longer, it will be a shilling an hour."

The older man studied me for a few moments, then nodded politely and said in a rather deep voice with a London accent, "I'm much obliged to you, miss. We shall be wanting him to take us to The Woodman later where we have arranged lodgings for the night." He glanced at his companion. "Go and speak to him."

"Right, sir. Excuse me, miss." The younger man went briskly out. The other took out a purse, shook some coins into his palm, then placed them on the mantelpiece. "Eighteen pence. Thank you, miss." He put the purse away and held out his warrant card. "Inspector Browning of the Criminal Investigation Department," he said. "I am with my colleague, Sergeant Dean."

I looked at the warrant card without seeing it. I had no idea what words would come from me next, and I hoped my second effort would be less stupid than my first.

"I am Bridget Chance," I said, as the door opened to admit the sergeant. "Would you gentlemen care to sit down?"

"We prefer to stand, thank you, miss," said the inspector. "I understand from your butler that with your mother indisposed, you are the next in authority, as it were?"

"Yes. My father is abroad."

"You have no brothers? No older relatives?"

"No." I was struggling to keep my voice steady. "Whatever you have to say, Inspector, you had better say to me. There is nobody else." A dreadful suspicion was beginning to grow within me. "Does this concern my father?" I asked. "Has he suffered an accident?"

The inspector fidgeted with his watch-chain and then said simply, "It's very bad news concerning your father, Miss Chance. The worst possible news, I'm afraid."

I walked across the room and stared blindly out of the window. No tears came, but I was aching with the most searing pain I had ever known. My father had always been so full of life that I had counted him immortal, but now . . . "My father is dead?" I asked.

"Yes, miss."

The last crumb of hope was gone. I do not know how long the silence lasted, but I was grateful that neither man spoke throughout that time. The pain came at me in waves, gnawing and tearing within my chest. Then, slowly, I gathered my strength and turned. It was a great effort to speak, and the words sounded slurred as I said, "Was there an accident?"

"Well . . . in a manner of speaking, yes," said the inspector. "Your father was a guest at a château in France. He fell from a balcony, and he died instantly."

The inspector stopped abruptly, as if he had been about to continue. Half a dozen questions were all tangled together in my dazed mind, but both men were looking at me strangely now. "Is there something more you have to tell me?" I asked. "Is this a police matter because . . . because somebody harmed him?"

The inspector looked at me steadily for a moment or two, then said, "You're a very intelligent young lady, if you don't mind my saying so, Miss Chance. Yes, it's quite true that this wouldn't be a police matter unless some form of crime was involved, but it wasn't a question of somebody harming your father." He tugged at his collar with an embarrassed air. "I'm sorry, miss. This is bound to be a nasty shock."

My face felt paper-white. My hands were clasped behind me, nails digging into the flesh. The inspector's words seemed strangely meaningless. My father was dead. How could I be shocked further? "Please explain," I said dully.

He took from his inside pocket a piece of stiff folded paper. "I regret to inform you," he said rapidly, "that we have received certain information from the French police. They claim that Roger Chance was engaged in an act of theft on the night he died; that he was caught in that act, and fell to his death while attempting to escape. Affidavits provided by eye-witnesses and evidence supplied by our French colleagues are so conclusive that the assistant commissioner has applied for and received this warrant, which I hereby show you, giving full authority for the police to search the residence of the deceased, namely Latchford Hall."

A full minute must have passed before the meaning of the words finally sank into my brain. For a moment I was swept by an almost overwhelming impulse to scream with laughter, but managed to check it with an effort that made my chest heave. Then came rage, a great black fury such as I had never known before. I marched across the room to stand in front of Inspector Browning.

"How *dare* you!" I said in a trembling whisper. "How dare you say such a terrible thing about my father! He is—he was a gentleman of the highest reputation. He was an art dealer. What you say is wicked! And utterly *impossible!*"

Inspector Browning sighed. Sergeant Dean shook his head slowly and said, "He did a bit of dealing in pictures, miss, but that was just a smokescreen. The Frenchies reckon he'd been a professional jewel thief for twenty years and more, though he didn't come under suspicion until a couple of years ago—"

"That will do," Inspector Browning broke in. "I'm very sorry, miss."

My mind had frozen. After a while I said, "Did you tell all this to my mother?"

"Yes. We had no option."

"The whole thing is a tissue of lies," I said slowly and distinctly. "I shall seek advice from my father's solicitor at once."

"That's very sensible of you, miss," said the inspector. "Now I'm afraid we have to search the house. We'll try to be as unobtrusive as possible."

I looked at him blankly, uncomprehending. "What are you looking for?" I asked.

"We have orders to search for stolen property, miss. My own opinion is that we won't find any here, but—" He broke off as he saw the look on my face. "Well, never mind my opinion."

I felt sick, and there was a bitter taste in my mouth as I said, "I have yet to tell my sister that our father has died. Surely you can leave us alone for a little while, Inspector?"

He bit his lip and looked unhappy. "There's the question that something might be removed, if you take my meaning, Miss Chance." He rubbed his chin. "But, if we make a quick search of this drawing room, miss, and put a seal on the rest of the downstairs rooms, then I'm willing to take a chance with my superiors by not executing this search warrant till tomorrow morning."

Before I could speak there was a tap on the door and old Dr. Carey entered—he had brought me into the world over twenty years ago. He gave the two men a rather puzzled look, then came to me and took my hands. I could tell from his manner that he knew nothing of the dreadful accusation against Papa.

"I'm sorry about your father's death," he said. "Your mother, I'm afraid, is suffering severely from shock. I've given her a sleeping draught, and she'll be asleep soon, but she wants to see you first, Bridie. Do you think you can avoid breaking down?"

I nodded. Somehow I had passed that point.

"There's a good girl," said Dr. Carey, and held my arm as we moved to the door. "I'll come and see you tomorrow morning. Is there anything I can do for you before I go? I'm most uneasy about leaving you to look after your mother and sister when you're suffering such a grievous shock yourself. Perhaps the vicar's eldest girl, Victoria, would be willing to come round and spend the night here with you."

"Oh, no. Please don't arrange anything like that," I said quickly. I was unable to think clearly, but I knew that the last thing in the world I wanted was to have a stranger in the house.

"Very well," said Dr. Carey. "I'll leave you some powders to help you sleep."

I saw him to the front door, and told the inspector he could proceed with his duties. Then I hurried up the stairs.

When L went into my mother's room Nannie Foster was sitting beside the bed, her eyes red-rimmed from weeping. I had expected my mother to look ill, but my nerves jumped in alarm at the sight of her: her face was like wax, the bones standing out to give her an almost skeletal appearance. Nannie got to her feet and took my hand. "Do you know about your poor Papa?"

"Yes, Nannie. Please help me by being brave and not making a fuss. I'd like you to leave me alone with Mama for a minute."

She shuffled out, and I leaned over the bed. My mother looked up at me with haunted eyes. "Your dear Papa is dead, Bridie," she whispered. "I do not know what we shall do. Those policemen are telling terrible lies about him!"

"I know, Mama. But please try to sleep now. I'm going to consult John Whitely—Papa's solicitor. He'll know what to do."

"Yes, dear. You must do whatever you think best. I really can't manage." She put her hands over her face and began to sob. I patted her arm gently and said some stumbling words in a hopeless effort to comfort her. After two or three minutes the crying faded and she lay with eyes closed, her breathing tremulous. I waited until the sleeping draught had taken effect, and quietly left the room.

Ellen, the housemaid, was waiting on the landing at the top of the stairs, looking upset. "Do there be somethin' I can do, Miss Bridie?" she said as I came along the passage.

"Yes, Ellen. Go down to the morning room and tell Miss Kate to come to her room, please. I shall wait for her there."

I had not been long in Kate's bedroom when she came hurrying in, and before I could speak she said, "Is Papa all right? Oh Bridie, has something happened?"

I made her sit down and drink a sleeping draught. Then I told her that there had been an accident, and that Papa had died as a result. She sat with fists pressed to her cheeks, eyes closed, face twisted with grief as tears fell unheeded to her lap. I knelt by her, held her for a little while, and then said that Nannie would get her to bed and stay with her until she slept.

It was a relief to close the door behind me, for I dreaded any questions about how Papa had died. At the moment only my mother and I knew the horrifying accusation made against Papa, and through the haze of grief that engulfed me I had clung desperately to the notion that this must be kept completely secret.

As I came down into the hall, Inspector Browning emerged from the drawing room. He said in a low voice, "I've dealt with this room, Miss Chance, so you can have the use of it. Sergeant Dean is putting a seal on the doors of other rooms."

I said, "Very well, Inspector. We will not enter any of the sealed rooms." After a moment I went on, "There is something I must say to you. The charge against my father is completely false, but my family will be placed in a dreadful situation if this story is given general currency, so I should be very grateful if you would refrain from speaking of it to anybody."

Inspector Browning stared at me with a troubled air. "I'm afraid you don't quite understand, miss," he said apologetically. "There have already been reports in some French newspapers. And it's bound to be quite a big piece of news here as well."

There was a hammering in my head. "Do you mean that the newspapers will print what you have told me? They will name my father and say he was a *thief?*"

"Well, there's nothing to stop them saying what's been alleged, and printing an official statement from the French police." He hesitated, then went on, "And the foreign papers have named your father, all right. Over on the Continent there's been a high-class jewel thief working the big houses for years, but the police could never nail him. The Frenchies even had a fancy name for him. *Le Sorcier*—the magician."

"But it was not my father!" I said in a trembling whisper. "How

131

many times must I tell you that a hideous mistake has been made?"

The inspector pursed his lips, swaying back and forth contemplatively. "I've no wish to cause you more distress, miss," he said slowly, "but it's no kindness to leave you with false hopes. The fact is, there's no mistake. The French police finally came round to suspecting Roger Chance was this *Sorcier* chap. They laid a trap for him and put out a nice bait. Some high-up in the police asked an Italian countess to make a big display of her diamond pendant during this weekend party where your father was one of the guests. He went over the roof and into her bedroom. The police were waiting for him, miss, and they caught him with the jewellery in his hand. He tried to bolt, and he fell. They found two skeleton keys and a miniature jemmy on him, and when they searched his room they found the finest set of burglar's tools they had ever seen. I'm sorry, but there's been no mistake, miss."

I tried to wake up, knowing that I must be in the grip of a nightmare.

After a few moments, when the world of horror in which I found myself remained solid and unchanging, I said, "You expect that all this will appear in the newspapers shortly?"

"I'm quite sure it will be in tomorrow's papers, miss. The Yard asked them to keep quiet until we'd searched Latchford Hall, but there's no need for further secrecy." He paused for a moment as Sergeant Dean appeared from the library. "We'll take our leave of you now, miss, and call again tomorrow morning. I hope half past nine o'clock will be convenient?"

"Yes," I said vaguely, "yes, Inspector. And thank you for your courtesy."

I showed them out myself, then went into the drawing room and sat down in a chair by the window. I had never in my life before wished that I were dead, but I wished it now. Tomorrow the whole county would know the story, and every eye would be upon the Chance family of Latchford Hall. There was nobody in the house I could turn to for help. Thank goodness I had my fiancé to give me the support and comfort I needed. I saw Bernard's face in my mind's eye, strong, assured, and I knew that I was not alone. Sitting at the bureau with a sheet of writing paper before me, I tried to think clearly. Robert, our groom, could catch a train to

Lowestoft and deliver a letter from me by hand this evening. I picked up a pen and wrote hurriedly:

Dearest Bernard,

My father has died, and I am in great trouble which I will explain when I see you. Please come to me by the earliest train tomorrow. I am in desperate need of your help.

With my love,
Bridie

As I sealed the envelope it occurred to me that if Bernard glanced at the morning newspaper tomorrow he would see how truly great was my need. With that thought came another. It was very important for me to speak to Mr. Whitely, the solicitor, without delay. I was desperate to have proper advice before the news came out.

I rang for Henson, and when he came I said, "I'm afraid I have bad news, Henson. My father has died in an accident in France. A wicked story is being told about him, which is why the police were here. I haven't time to explain any more now, because I must drive to Southwold at once to see my father's solicitor. Will you have Robert bring the gig round for me? Then he must take the next train and deliver this letter to Mr. Bernard Page."

"I . . . I'm very sorry, miss." Henson looked deeply shaken. "Your poor father. . . . But you're not fit to go driving out this evening, Miss Bridie. You'll make yourself ill."

"I have to go." My voice started to rise, and I struggled to keep it normal. "I have to, Henson. Now please go and tell Robert I shall be ready in five minutes."

I REACHED THE OFFICES of Whitely and Whitely in Southwold soon after six o'clock. The door was opened to me by the solicitor's clerk. He told me that Mr. John Whitely had gone home, but when I explained that my business was urgent, he suggested that I should call at his private residence. In another ten minutes I was tugging at the bell-pull of a sombre grey house set back from the main road.

A maid answered the door, took my card, and showed me into a large, book-lined study. Five minutes later a tall man with thin grey hair entered the room. He held my card in his hand, and there was no expression either in his face or voice as he said, "Miss Bridget Chance? I am John Whitely."

I had risen as he entered. "I am most grateful to you for receiving me, Mr. Whitely, and I apologize for this intrusion."

He shook my hand, glanced at the back of the card, and said in a dry voice, "You have written, *Daughter of Mr. Roger Chance— on a matter of life and death.* In my experience few matters are quite as urgent as that."

"Forgive me, Mr. Whitely. It is already a matter of death, for we received news only a few hours ago that my father has died. And the accompanying news is so dreadful that unless something is done about it I truly fear for my mother's life."

No flicker of curiosity touched his face. He moved to a speaking tube on the wall, blew it, and then put it to his ear and waited. "Please accept my condolences," he said in the same dry tone as before, "and pray be seated. This has no doubt been a great shock to you." Without a pause in the flow of words, he said into the mouthpiece of the speaking tube, "Be so good as to bring a plate of wholemeal biscuits and a pot of tea to the study, Nelly." Then he put the mouthpiece back in its cradle, moved to a cabinet, and poured a glass of brandy. "You are in need of sustenance, Miss Chance. By the time you have finished sipping this brandy," he handed me the glass, "there will be tea and biscuits to ensure that no untoward effect follows the consumption of alcohol upon an empty stomach."

He sat down in a swivel chair behind the desk. I sipped the brandy obediently, gasping a little at the fiery touch of it in my throat, and drained the last drop just as a maid entered with a tray of tea. She set the tray on the desk and went out. Mr. Whitely poured the tea, placed a heaped plate of biscuits within my reach, picked up a pen, and settled back in his chair. "Now. What is it that you wish to tell me, Miss Chance?"

It was an effort for me to force the story from my lips but I was helped by the realization that in his curious way Mr. Whitely was a considerate and kindly man. He did not interrupt, and not for a moment did he show surprise or shock as my halting tale was told. His pen scratched steadily on the paper, and he paused only twice, to point sternly at the biscuits and encourage me to eat.

After I had said all that was to be said there was silence while Mr. Whitely read through what he had written.

"You are of the opinion that what the French police have said concerning your late father, Roger Chance, is untrue?" he said.

"Yes, of course, Mr. Whitely!" I said hotly. "Surely you agree? After all, my father was your client."

"I have no opinion as yet, and in any event the truth is not a matter of opinion. I must tell you that the firm of Whitely and Whitely has never accepted cases involving criminal law. But, as senior partner, I can also say that if you wish to instruct me I shall do whatever I can to assist you."

I felt a surge of gratitude towards this seemingly dry and unsympathetic man. When the report appeared in the newspapers there would be few if any of our neighbours and acquaintances who would speak to us. But Mr. John Whitely had declared that he would help, and I was more thankful than words could tell.

"This evening I shall speak with the inspector from Scotland Yard, and tomorrow I shall arrange to see the branch manager of your father's bank." He hesitated. "I have no wish to add to your worries at such a time, but financial matters are of some urgency. I have no idea of the extent of your father's substance. May I ask if there are any reserves? Shareholdings? Funds of any nature?"

"I'm not sure, Mr. Whitely, but I don't remember hearing any such matters spoken of by my father."

The solicitor folded his hands in front of him and gazed at me mistily. "It is my recollection," he said, "that your father was an unusual man, Miss Chance. I hope you will not be offended if I describe him as a man of happy-go-lucky disposition, to the extent that he would be generous in the extreme, but with little regard, perhaps, for making financial provisions for the future."

There was a silence as I sat remembering moments with my father, hearing again his careless laughter, and I knew that Roger Chance had indeed been a man who lived for today, though this was something I had never thought about before.

"Yes," I said. "I don't suppose my father was what you would call a prudent man, but as a family we have always had whatever we wished for. I assume that my father would have provided for our needs in his will."

Mr. Whitely sat back in his chair and said mildly, "Your father left no will. I urged him to do so on several occasions, but he merely laughed, and said he would thank me to avoid a topic he considered excessively morbid."

"Oh." I was disconcerted for a moment, but not really surprised. I could almost hear my father teasing this dry, precise solicitor, and brushing his advice aside with a laugh.

Mr. Whitely was looking at me with a hint of concern in his grey eyes. "I think we have discussed as much as is needful for the moment," he said. "We must see about accompanying you home, Miss Chance."

"I cannot tell you how grateful I am to you for the way you have received me," I said as I stood up. "But there's no need to take me home. I don't wish to disturb you."

"Not at all," he said with distant courtesy. "My manservant Frederick will follow us in my gig."

I remember little of the drive through growing dusk from Southwold to Wynford, for I seemed to be in a kind of sleep, my mind dormant. Astonishingly, Mr. Whitely drove like a young blood, feet spread and body leaning forward as he sent the gig rattling along the lanes at a fiery pace. Daisy had never been pushed so hard in her life, and in forty minutes we came to Latchford Hall.

Henson opened the door to me. I thanked Mr. Whitely and waited in the porch until he and Frederick had driven off. Then I said to Henson, "How are my mother and Miss Kate?"

"I understand that they are asleep, Miss Bridie."

"Thank goodness. When do you expect Robert back from Lowestoft?"

"That's hard to say, miss. There's only one train an hour each way. I'll see to Daisy myself."

"Well . . . thank you, Henson." For a butler to do the work of a groom was unheard of, and I realized then how deeply troubled Henson must be. As I took off my boater, he said diffidently, "The staff are wondering what their position is, Miss Bridie. Do you think we shall be staying on at Latchford Hall or might we all have to look for a new situation?"

The question caught me unprepared, and I was ashamed that it did so, for naturally the servants would be concerned about the

possibility that we would move to a smaller house. I lifted my
shoulders in a helpless shrug. "I'm sorry, Henson, but I just don't
know what will happen yet." I felt tears suddenly flood my eyes,
but managed to control my voice as I went on, "Everything is . . .
very difficult and complicated, but I promise to let you and the
rest of the servants know where you stand at the first possible
moment."

"Thank you, Miss Bridie." He went down the steps to the gig,
and I wondered what his thoughts would be when he heard the
dreadful scandal about his master. We might then find it impossible
to employ anyone at all, for the reputation of the master was of
high importance to the domestic staff of any household.

Slowly I mounted the stairs, and as I reached my bedroom
Nannie Foster came along the passage in her dressing gown.
"Heavens, child," she said, "you look worn to a thread. You
take the doctor's medicine and get to bed now. I'll keep an eye
on your Mama and Miss Kate, never fear. I don't sleep much at
the best of times, so it won't hurt me to sit up tonight."

"Thank you, Nannie." I took her hands.

"Those wicked policemen," she said fiercely. "Coming here and
telling lies about their betters. I wish I'd sent them about their
business!"

"They're not the kind to be sent about their business, Nannie.
I know the story is untrue, but it will be in the newspapers
tomorrow, so we have to brace ourselves for an ordeal."

"Dear God, help us all," she whispered.

"Yes, Nannie. And we must help each other. I've never quite
realized before what a solitary family we are, with no relatives to
turn to. It's my mother who will be in greatest need of help, and
you're the one who can do most for her, Nannie."

The grey head nodded. "Yes, dear," Nannie Foster said in a faraway voice, as if thinking aloud. "It's the loneliness, you see, from
being taken out of her station in life. Poor dear soul, she could
always be at ease with me. . . ." Her voice faded to silence, then
she came to herself with a start. "Tell me, Miss Bridie, have you
made arrangements for your poor dear papa to be brought home
to Wynford to be buried?"

I stood gazing at her stupidly, realizing that this question had
not occurred to me. How was such a matter arranged? What

would the vicar say about burying a man declared to be a criminal? The room swayed, and I caught at the bedpost to steady myself. Then Nannie Foster was holding my arm, making me sit down, starting to unbutton my dress, and chattering briskly away as if I were a child again. "There. You've overdone it, Miss Bridie, haven't you? Never mind, Nannie will put you to bed and give you the nice medicine the doctor left, and you'll have a lovely sleep. Here's your nightie. . . ."

The chatter became a blur. I was in bed, somehow swallowing the draught, then lying thankfully back on the pillows. The world swung away. Somewhere within me I tried to cling to consciousness, telling myself that I had left a host of things undone, but my feeble struggle against waves of darkness was shamefully brief, and soon came the peace of oblivion.

I DID NOT KNOW the hour or the day, nor whether the scene before me was dream or reality. I stood by the tall window of my bedroom, pushing aside one of the heavy curtains. I felt hot and stifled. The casement window stood half open, though I could not remember opening it. Even the night air seemed too warm and moist.

The moon and stars were bright, but a ground mist swirled across the lawns, flowerbeds and shrubbery. My eyes rested on the dark line of trees which marked the beginning of the copse on the southern side of the grounds of Latchford Hall.

In my dream, or in reality, I stood breathing deeply, my lungs craving cool fresh air. A pinpoint of fire glowed steadily against the darkness of a tree that rose above a spreading shrub, a strangely misshapen growth which resembled the silhouette of a horse's head. Suddenly the point of fire spun through the air and dropped to the ground with a burst of tiny sparks. I closed my eyes and opened them again. Part of the shrubbery moved, the part that had looked like the head of a horse. From the darkness they moved out amid twisting feathers of mist, the horse and rider who had been so still against the dark background of trees.

If I felt anything at all it was a shadow of surprise that I felt no astonishment or alarm. The horse and rider moved at a steady walk across the grass. The animal was a beautiful creature, deep-chested, with a proud head and high-stepping gait. I was a

fair judge of a horse, and the one I now saw, or dreamed, in the
garden below me had the build of a mount that would carry a
rider far and fast.

I peered at the man in the saddle as for a moment moonlight
shone full upon him. He sat tall, with head a little bowed, and
there was a harmony between him and his mount which told of
the true horseman. His long legs reached down so far that I
wondered if he had stirrups. I saw nothing of his face, for it was in
the shadow of a round hat with a wide brim, the crown low and
flat. I had never seen anyone wearing such a hat before, and yet it
was not completely unfamiliar. In a children's encyclopaedia long
ago I had seen a drawing of a gaucho, one of the horsemen who
herd cattle on the great pampas of Argentina. He had had just
such a hat as the rider below me wore.

Then he moved out of the moonlight and into the trees again.
Soon horse and rider were no more than a black shape becoming
ever more shapeless. Then they were gone. Still I felt no surprise,
no fear, no curiosity. If I dreamed, then my lack of feeling was
part of the dream. If I was awake, then the turmoil and tragedies
of the day had drained me to the point where I was beyond feeling. I have no memory of returning to my bed and to sleep, and if
I dreamed other dreams that night I was never to remember them.

⚜ Chapter Two ⚜

Somebody was shaking me by the shoulder, calling anxiously.
As I started to rouse from sleep all the horrors of the day before
came rushing in upon me, chilling my blood and making me
shrink from the misery of facing a new day.

"Bridie, wake up! *Please*, Bridie!" I opened my eyes and saw
Kate bending over me, her face pale and troubled. My head felt
heavy and there was a sour taste in my mouth, and I wished now
that Dr. Carey's sleeping draught had not been quite so potent.

"Just a minute, Kate," I said thickly. "Give me a moment . . . I
feel rather sick."

"You must hurry, Bridie!" she cried tearfully. "Mama has taken
the governess cart and gone out and I don't know what to do."

I was out of bed, my heart pounding. The clock beside me

showed that it was only twenty minutes past seven. "What do you mean, Mama has gone out?"

"When I went to her room a moment ago, Nannie was alone there, asleep in the armchair. So I went downstairs, and Henson was very upset, telling Robert off. It seems Mama had got up, gone to the stables, and told Robert to harness Daisy to the governess cart. Then she drove off."

I had thrown off my nightie and begun to dress hurriedly.

"Henson was cross with Robert for not stopping her," Kate was saying, "but Robert said it wasn't his place . . . and so I ran to fetch you." She pressed her lovely hands to her cheeks. "Oh, whatever's happening, Bridie?"

I was sitting down, pulling on my stockings. "Did Robert say which way Mama went?"

"She took the Selby road," Kate said in a frightened whisper. This was a small road which forked only half a mile from Latchford Hall. One fork led to the nearby hamlet of Selby, the other was barely used, for it led to nowhere but a bay with only the ruins of a few cottages, long deserted, to show that a small fishing community had once dwelt there.

"Bridie . . . do you think Mama has gone to the sea to. . . ?" Kate left the last words unsaid, but I knew what she was thinking.

"I'm sure she's not gone to drown herself," I said quickly, "but I must catch up with her as soon as possible. Tell Robert to saddle Punch. I'll be down immediately."

Less than five minutes later, with my face unwashed and my hair in a tangled pile, I rode out on the Selby road in the morning sunshine. Robert could have ridden faster, so could Kate, but the groom was an awkward village boy who would have no idea how to deal with a woman half out of her mind with grief. And Kate was too delicate for a task which might well call for physical strength if Mama was hysterical. At least I was quite strong, and for once I was thankful to possess this unladylike quality.

It did not occur to me to take the fork to Selby village, for I knew, somehow, that my mother was heading for the bay road. According to Robert she had left not more than ten minutes before me, but even so, I would be hard put to overtake her before she reached the bay. I dared not urge Punch to a faster pace, for the narrow road had fallen badly into disrepair, and my heart was in my mouth with fear of him putting his foot in a hole and coming down.

With the rising sun full in my eyes I could see almost nothing of the road stretching out to the sea, and it was not until I turned north for the last half mile that I was able to make out the governess cart in the distance, halted near the line of crumbling cottages. I dug my heels into Punch, and three or four minutes later I slid to the ground beside the little trap.

My mother was walking out along the old stone jetty, her hair flying in the breeze and her cloak flapping about her. I tried to call out, but could find no breath. Stumbling on the green algae-covered cobbles I began to run, but I had covered no more than twenty paces when my feet slipped from beneath me and I fell with an impact that jarred my bones and left me dizzy.

I could have screamed aloud with frustration at my clumsiness. I knelt up and called to my mother as loudly as I could, but the wind snatched the sound away. I struggled across more cobbles, then shingle, weed, and crumbled rock. At last I reached the jetty. I looked up and saw that my mother had stopped at the far end, where it was almost awash in deep water. She was gazing down at a small casket in her hands.

Suddenly she swung her arm high over her head, hurling the casket out over the sea. At the zenith of its flight the lid flew open. Tiny glittering things scattered and fell. There was a cluster of small white splashes, then a larger one as the casket struck the water.

My mother stood staring at the sea, then slowly turned, and stood waiting listlessly as I moved towards her. Though I knew how deep her grief must be I was still shocked by the way her eyes had sunk back in that bone-white face, framed by a tangle of wind-blown golden hair.

"Oh . . . there you are, Bridie," she said vaguely. "Whatever are you doing out here at such an hour?"

I took ice-cold hands in mine. "I've come to take you home."

"That was a kind thought, dear. Yes, I really don't feel very well, but at least it's done now, so I can rest."

I slipped my arm through hers, and we began to walk slowly back along the jetty. After a few moments I said, "That was your jewel box you threw into the sea, wasn't it, Mama?"

141

"Yes, dear." Her voice was low and confiding. "All my jewellery, everything your poor dear papa ever gave me. Those policemen can nose about as much as they like now."

I turned to stare at her ravaged face. "But Mama, you mustn't believe what the inspector told you!" I felt tears running down my cheeks. "That was *your* jewellery. It wasn't stolen! You can't believe that Papa would have given you *stolen* jewellery?"

"No, I'm sure he would never do that. It would be foolish, and he always used to say, 'You can't be too careful, Mary darling.'" A furtive look showed for a moment in the sunken eyes.

"Yes, but he didn't mean . . ." I shook my head. "Oh, Mama, you make me so confused."

We came from the jetty onto the beach, then crossed the cobbled road to the cottages. As I helped my mother into the governess cart she said in a faraway voice, "Your father was a very unusual man, Bridie. I always worried about him, but he would laugh and lift me up in the air and tell me stories . . . and in the end I'd find myself laughing with him, and promising I wouldn't worry any more. But I always did, the next time he went away. . . ." She put her hands to her face and began to weep.

There was nothing I could do. From her strange ramblings I feared that her mind had slipped, and I prayed that it would be only temporary. After tethering Punch to the back of the little trap, I climbed in, gathered the reins and circled back onto the Selby road.

It was after half past eight o'clock when we reached Latchford Hall. Kate was on the porch, full of questions, but I hushed her and told her to put Mama to bed.

Scarcely had she gone to do my bidding than Henson's appearance in the hall with a copy of *The Times* reminded me that I had not yet warned Kate of what today's newspapers might say. From the stunned look on Henson's face, I knew that he had read something about my father. He came forward and said in a hushed voice, "Miss Bridie . . . oh, Miss Bridie." I held out my hand to take the paper, and asked him to follow me into the drawing room. When Henson had closed the door I said, "Give me a moment to read this, please."

I unfolded the newspaper. The story was contained in two columns under a title that sent a shiver through me.

A GENTLEMAN JEWEL THIEF

A report which can only be described as remarkable was published by all major French newspapers yesterday. It concerns a Suffolk gentleman, originally from Ireland, who came to a violent end beneath the walls of a French castle whilst engaging in his secret profession of jewel thief.

Our inquiries reveal that Roger Chance, aged 52, of Latchford Hall, Wynford, in the county of Suffolk, was an art expert and picture dealer. He pursued his profession almost exclusively on the Continent, returning to his home in England three or four times a year to spend a few weeks with his family at Latchford Hall. It was here that he had resided since his marriage, with his wife (Mrs. Mary Chance) and his two daughters (Miss Bridget Chance and Miss Kate Chance).

The report of the French police states that unknown to anyone, except perhaps to a fellow criminal who received stolen property, Roger Chance led a second life as a highly accomplished burglar. This report has now been confirmed by our own Criminal Investigation Department at Scotland Yard. The CID have informed us that for many years the police forces of several countries have been baffled by a thief who specialized in stealing jewellery from the houses of the rich. These exploits were not frequent, but always yielded a haul of considerable value, and the methods of the thief were so skilled and mysterious that in time he acquired the nickname of *Le Sorcier*.

I looked up from the newspaper, for the words had begun to dance before my eyes. Henson stood with head bowed, staring down at the floor. I looked down again and made myself continue reading.

Over a year ago the French police made a new study of all the facts relating to these baffling thefts. From this study there emerged certain common factors which gave rise to the theory that the mysterious felon might be none other than Roger Chance, who was a popular guest at many of the best houses on the Continent.

After much discussion, a trap was laid by the police in collaboration with Baron Montpalion and one of his guests, the Contessa Vizzini, at a weekend house party given by the baron. In the weeks preceding the house party, to which Mr. Roger Chance had been invited, reports appeared in a number of French and Italian newspapers concerning a magnificent diamond pendant recently made for the contessa. It was hoped that this would prove a tempting bait for *Le Sorcier*, and these hopes were realized.

In the early hours of Saturday last, his face masked by a close-fitting hood, Roger Chance effected entry to the contessa's boudoir by way of the balcony and began a search for the diamond pendant. He was not to know that French police officials were awaiting him. They allowed him to find a duplication of the pendant in a jewel box on the dressing table, then burst from their hiding places as the miscreant made to depart.

The masked man darted out onto the balcony and leaped from the balustrade to grasp the cornice by which he had presumably traversed the last part of the perilous journey from his own room. In his haste to escape he lost his grip and fell sixty feet to the stone flags below, where he was killed instantly. When the black hood was drawn from his head, the truth of *Le Sorcier*'s identity was revealed at last.

In a statement issued last night, Scotland Yard confirmed that detectives began yesterday to carry out a search of Latchford Hall in the hope of recovering some of the ill-gotten gains of this criminal who had led such an amazing double life. Success in their search would appear highly unlikely, since apparently Chance confined his felonious activities to the Continent, doubtless to protect his family. Further developments in this remarkable case will be closely followed by our correspondent.

I folded the newspaper and rubbed my eyes. Henson said in a shaken voice, "I just don't understand, Miss Bridie. How can they say those things about Mr. Chance?"

"I can't begin to think, Henson," I said heavily. "Our solicitor has spoken to the police, and I hope he will clear things up."

"A solicitor? Ah, that's good, Miss Bridie. And I expect your fiancé will be here soon, with you sending him that note."

"Yes." I had to hold back tears of relief at the thought of Bernard's arrival. "Yes, Mr. Page will know what to do. In the meantime you must tell the servants about this newspaper report, Henson. And you must warn them that things will be very difficult for a while."

145

"Yes, Miss Bridie. The gossip will be awful. I'm afraid people will come to stare at the house, and at anyone coming or going."

"Oh, dear lord," I said, cringing inwardly at the thought. "And we shall have reporters here soon."

"I'll put Robert on the gate, Miss Bridie, and I'll send for his brother. Strong as a bull, Jack is, and looks it. If I give him a shilling he'll make sure nobody troubles you."

"Thank you, Henson. You had better arrange it without delay."

As I crossed the hall I caught sight of myself in the big looking glass. My hair was tangled and my dress smeared with dirt, the skirt torn where I had fallen. I was stiff and sore from the ride, and despite the warmth of the day I was inwardly cold with the dread of breaking the news to my sister.

Kate was in her bedroom with Nannie Foster. I made her sit down, told her that a hideously false report about Papa had appeared in *The Times,* then read it out to her, my voice failing me several times before I finished. Kate had begun to cry quietly halfway through, and now sat with her face in her hands, her shoulders shaking. I patted her shoulder and bent to kiss her head. "I'm sorry, darling," I said wearily. "Stay here with Nannie and try to be brave. I must bathe and change now, before the detectives arrive, and Dr. Carey, too."

Ellen had set my hip-bath in front of the fireplace and had laid out a navy blue dress for me, which would serve for mourning until black dresses were ready. Twenty minutes later, feeling almost calm, I emerged from my room to find Ellen coming up the stairs with Dr. Carey. He gave me a strange, embarrassed look and said, "Good morning, Bridie."

"Good morning, Doctor." I knew that he had seen the newspaper report. Clearly he did not wish to be in Latchford Hall, but felt duty bound to call. I wondered how often in the coming days I would see that look in people's eyes, a look of shocked distaste overlaid with avid curiosity.

I sent Ellen downstairs and led him into my mother's room. Mama was asleep. Her eyes were still sunken and bruised, but the terrible stress had vanished from her face, and she looked almost beautiful again. She stirred when Dr. Carey felt her pulse, but did not wake; he felt her brow, then looked at me. "I take it she slept well?"

"I believe so, Doctor Carey." I had decided to say nothing to him about my mother's wild trip to the coast.

He nodded. "No more sleeping draughts, I think. She's still almost comatose. See that she eats something later, and she should be able to get up tomorrow, if she wishes." He picked up his bag. "I don't think there's any need for me to call again."

We went down to the hall together in silence, and I felt sure that Dr. Carey would not be calling again in any event. Perhaps for the first time I feared that all our acquaintances would now see us as the family of a notorious criminal. We would be stared at, the subject of endless gossip, and avoided as if we carried some plague. Once again I felt a surge of thankfulness that I could count on Bernard for support.

Henson was at the door, and as he opened it I saw the figures of Inspector Browning and Sergeant Dean approaching.

"Well . . . ah, good morning, Bridie," said Dr. Carey.

"Goodbye, Dr. Carey." I could not keep the bitterness from my voice. He went out, clapping his hat on his head, and I stood back as the two detectives entered.

They greeted me politely. "I'm sorry we have to intrude, miss, but I'd like to carry on with the search," the inspector began.

"Of course," I replied. "Did Mr. Whitely speak with you?"

"He did, miss, and I understand he's gone up to London to talk to my superiors at the Yard today. A very sound gentleman Mr. Whitely is, if you ask me."

Inspector Browning turned to the sergeant. "Make sure the seals are intact, then start with the dining room and work your way through on this floor."

"Right, sir." Sergeant Dean marched off, followed by Henson.

The inspector hesitated, then said, "I would like to see your mother's jewellery now, miss, and also any jewellery belonging to you or your sister. Then I regret to say I must search the—um —sleeping accommodation."

It would be useless to withhold the truth from him. I took a deep breath and said, "The shock of my father's death and the terrible accusation you made yesterday caused my mother to act in a completely irrational manner. This morning she gathered her jewellery together, drove out to the bay, and threw it all into the sea. I regret that I was too late to stop her."

147

Inspector Browning whistled faintly on an indrawn breath, then stared at me in silence for a while. At last he said mildly, "Well, thank you for telling me, miss."

I felt a pang of guilt. "I'm sorry, Inspector. I suppose your superiors won't be very pleased with you over this?"

"Oh, don't you worry about that, miss. I'm sure you can give me a description of all the pieces, and that it can be vouched for by your mother's maid."

"Yes. That would not be difficult."

"Mind you, I'm quite sure we won't find that it matches anything on the list of stolen jewellery the French police gave us. I told my superiors that Mr. Chance was much too clever to make a silly mistake like giving bits of the stuff to his family."

I glared at him now. "My father did *not* steal any jewellery!"

"Perhaps not, miss, perhaps not," he said quietly. "But your mother seems a lot less sure about that, doesn't she?"

AT TEN O'CLOCK Bernard still had not come, and the next train would not bring him to Wynford for another hour. I went to Kate's room and sat with her for a while, and Ellen brought me up some breakfast, her face pinched with distress. All the servants knew the worst now, and the house was full of whispering and tiptoeing, as if we were in attendance at a funeral.

From the window in Kate's room, I could see beyond the tall shrubbery to the main gate. A dozen or more village folk stood on the other side of the lane, gawking at the house. Robert was at the gate, and pacing back and forth across the drive was his brother Jack, idly twirling a yard-long blackthorn cudgel. Twice Robert had brought me a message from a reporter on the *East Anglian Daily Times* asking to see a member of the family, and twice I had replied that no interviews whatever would be given.

At eleven o'clock I saw the station carriage trundling up the drive. I flew outside as Bernard climbed from the carriage.

"Oh Bernard, thank Heaven you've come. I've been so dreadfully alone—" I was clinging to his hands, and so overwhelmed with relief that my voice failed me completely. His eyes were steady and his jaw set, as he tucked my arm tightly through his.

"Where can we talk, Bridie?" His manner was crisp and determined, kindling new hope in me.

148

With an effort I gained control of my voice. "Oh, please . . . not in the house. It's so dreadfully miserable, and there are two detectives there, searching."

"Yes. That was in the newspaper. You look ill, Bridie."

I made a little sound that was between a laugh and a sob. "You need not worry about me. I shall be quite all right now, my dearest." The noon sun was warm on my face, and I felt stronger as we walked slowly across the main lawn behind the house. When we halted by a small copse I turned to look up at him, with love in my eyes.

"Are you feeling steadier now, Bridie?" he said quietly.

"Yes, Bernard dear. Thank you with all my heart for coming."

"I had to come, Bridie. I couldn't just write you a letter."

"A letter?" I echoed.

"That's what my father wanted me to do after he read *The Times*. We had rather a row, as a matter of fact, but I felt the only decent thing was to speak to you face to face."

I took my hand from his arm and tried to prevent myself trembling. "What is it you have to say to me face to face, Bernard?" I asked at last in a high, wavering voice.

He ran a hand through his thick fair hair. "Surely you must know that, Bridie? Everything has changed now. Your father was a criminal, and however unjust it may be, you and your family are going to suffer from that for the rest of your lives. The best thing for you to do is to go abroad, change your name, start afresh somehow. Wherever you go in England there'll be a finger pointing at you." He drew a long breath, then went on firmly, "I cannot possibly be your husband in such circum- stances, Bridie. It would put an end to my career, reflect on my own family, and make me a social outcast. That's what I've come to tell you, Bridie, and I'm sure you understand."

I nodded slowly, unable to speak. My hopes of comfort and support had been shattered, and I was alone again. Yet I did understand what Bernard had said, and I could not blame him. It had been foolish of me not to realize just how great a stigma would cling to the family of Roger Chance, a stigma I could not expect any man to share.

I carefully took from my finger the sapphire engagement ring which Bernard had put there only a few months ago. When I held it out to him he hesitated, then put up his hand for me to drop it into the palm. "Thank you, Bridie," he said doggedly. "I'm very sorry. I hope that in the end you will find your way to . . . well, to a satisfactory outcome."

It was still impossible for me to speak without losing all control. I nodded to acknowledge his last words, gave an exaggerated shrug to indicate that there was no more to be said, then gestured with a shaky hand towards the front of the house. I knew that Bernard had not sent the station carriage away, and now I realized why.

He said uncomfortably, "Well, goodbye, Bridie. There's really nothing else I can say."

I closed my eyes in answer, and when I opened them again I found that I was alone in the garden. In those moments of darkness something had happened to me. I was no longer close to tears, and my panic at the thought of bearing my burdens alone had faded. Somehow I would care for my mother and Kate and Nannie, and I would have no time to feel sorry for myself. I was not a very competent person to take charge of the family, but there was nobody else now.

I had been staring down at the grass, and now my eyes focused on a small object at my feet. I bent to look more closely. It was a thin, tightly-rolled, straight cigar of a kind I had never seen before, with black ash at one end where dew had extinguished it. To whom had it belonged? Except for Papa, nobody at Latchford Hall smoked cigars.

I turned away from the dark brown stub, wondering what possessed me to speculate on a matter so trivial when my whole world was crumbling. For a while I stood thinking, planning what I must do in the days ahead. With affection I remembered Mr. Whitely, my one ally. Tomorrow morning I would drive to Southwold again to hear about his inquiries at Scotland Yard. There would then be the funeral to arrange, and many matters to be discussed with my mother once she was well enough.

It seemed to me that we should sell Latchford Hall and move to a more modest house in another part of the country. I felt miserably certain that wherever we went the story would follow us, and I wondered if it might be better for us to settle in London, where we would be more anonymous. In London, Kate could live with us while attending the Prince Consort College of Music. I was convinced that it was very important for her to continue her studies—Signor Peroni had declared firmly that Kate had a truly rare gift—and I also felt that work would help keep her from dwelling on our tragedy.

I walked slowly back to the house, and as I entered I heard Kate playing. She had chosen "Les Préludes" of Liszt, and I had never heard her play better, for it seemed that her heart's sorrow was flowing from her fingers to the keyboard. I went into the drawing room and stood behind her, resting a hand gently on her shoulder. Still playing, she brushed my hand with her cheek, then said, "I'm all right now, Bridie. I won't cry any more."

I squeezed her shoulder, then stood simply listening for a while, letting the music wash through me. At last she said, "Bridie, do you think what the newspapers said about Papa is true?"

"Kate, how could you!" I moved so that I could see her face. "Of course it's not true. Can you really imagine Papa doing anything like that?"

She stopped playing and looked at me. "Yes, I can imagine it, Bridie. He was a reckless man." Her hands pounced down, fingers flashing as she played a dancing, devil-may-care melody from a new work by Dukas, "L'Apprenti Sorcier". "He was like that, Bridie," she said. "Did you never feel that he saw the whole world as a joke to be laughed at?"

It was hard for me to find words, for my heart was pounding with a mixture of shock and indignation. It had never occurred to me for a moment that the dreadful story could be true, yet my sister Kate was in doubt within an hour of hearing it.

As Kate began to play "Les Préludes" again, Henson came to say that the policemen were leaving. I went out into the hall to find the inspector and his sergeant waiting, hats in hand.

"Sorry to disturb you, miss," said the inspector, "but I thought you'd like to know that we've finished here now, and we've found nothing. I'd like to thank you for not making a fuss." He hesitated, then went on: "Might I make so bold as to offer two words of advice, miss?"

I tried to smile as I said, "I welcome advice at this moment."

"Well, don't hide yourself away. Just come and go freely, and those people outside will clear off sooner. As for the reporters,

151

would you like me to tell them that you have nothing to say? I think you'll find they'll take my word for it."

"I should be most grateful, Inspector."

"One more thing, miss. If anything sort of . . . well, sort of strange happens, anything puzzling, I'd be glad if you'd send me a wire at the Yard. I've left my card on the hall table."

I stared at him. "Strange in what way, Inspector?"

"I can't really say, miss. It's just a notion at the back of my head." He gave me a courteous bow. "We'll bid you good day now, miss. Come along, Sergeant." As Henson closed the door after them I reflected vaguely that Inspector Browning had shown more genuine sympathy than my erstwhile fiancé.

I ordered something light and simple for luncheon, and went upstairs to sit with my mother for a little while. She was awake when I entered her room, and she looked strangely young and serene. She gave me a little smile, and beckoned me to sit beside her. "I've been waiting for you, Bridie," she said.

"There were one or two things to see to, Mama." I took her hand and held it. "Are you feeling a little better?"

"Yes, dear." She made a sound that was almost a giggle. "The inspector isn't going to search this room after all."

"He knows about your jewellery, Mama. I told him."

She looked reproachful. "Oh, Bridie, that wasn't very sensible. I'm sure your Papa would have thought you a silly goose."

I did not want to argue with her, so I just nodded and continued to hold her hand. There were many things to be discussed, but I knew this was not the moment. After a few minutes my mother closed her eyes and smiled faintly. "He was so clever, Bridie. I was never frightened while he was here, telling me his stories, and laughing . . . but I would think of the stories when he was away, and then I would be frightened."

For a minute or so she was silent, then spoke again in a whisper. "Such stories, Bridie. In Austria long ago there was a safe in a big house belonging to a titled gentleman, and it had a special kind of lock, you see. But he made two little holes with a drill, and sucked the air out with an air-pump, I think, and he said it drew the gunpowder in through the other hole. Then the door came loose with the explosion. Wasn't it clever of him? Such beautiful emeralds, and the velvet wrapping was barely scorched. That must

152

have been before we were married, because I saw them that day when he took me to the Capricorn Stone. Oh, how he laughed about leaving the special lock of the safe quite untouched. That was the part he liked best, you see . . . the joke of it. . . ."

The voice rambled on. I sat trying to think coherently, to feel any kind of emotion, but I might have been a block of wood. Eventually Mama stopped talking and fell asleep. My numbed brain began to come slowly to life again. Very well, I had been wrong. My father, Roger Chance, had indeed been the notorious thief known as *Le Sorcier*. But the world believed this already, and the fact that I now knew it to be true seemed to make no difference to what lay ahead for my family and for me.

Perhaps I was stupid not to realize that it would make a frightening difference.

I WOKE THAT NIGHT to find myself standing by the window and looking out on the garden. Nothing stirred, and no horseman moved out of the shadows as in my dream of the night before.

As I rubbed my eyes to make sure I was awake, I remembered the half-smoked cigar, which I had seen near the shrubbery that morning. I remembered, too, that the night before I had seen a fiery trail of sparks curve to the ground, just before the rider with the gaucho hat had emerged from the blackness. A cigar, tossed to the ground by a man on a horse, would have appeared to me in just that way. Suppose, then, that it was not a dream? That there had indeed been a horseman prowling in the grounds.

With a shrug I told myself that was nonsense. I had been over-wrought last night, and had dreamed a strange dream. The half-smoked cigar by the trees was no more than a coincidence. I did not know, as I got wearily back into bed, that I had just come to a wrong conclusion for the second time in twenty-four hours.

～❦❧ Chapter Three ❦❧～

The next morning I drove out from Latchford Hall to see a dozen or more men, women and children loitering near the entrance to the drive. They had formed two small groups, gossiping. A woman was knitting a stocking, a small child was licking a toffee-apple, and there was a little air of holiday about the whole scene. As I turned the gig out into the lane, my cheeks flaming, everybody was staring. All through the journey to Southwold my imagination made me feel a thousand curious eyes on me, and I seemed to hear the whispering of a thousand gossiping tongues.

Mr. Whitely, as dry and polite as ever, received me in his office and came straight to the point. "I am bound to tell you, Miss Chance, distressing though it is, that after long discussion with the assistant commissioner I can see no way whatsoever to assert your father's innocence, for we should be attempting to do so in the face of incontrovertible evidence."

I had been prepared for this, ever since my mother had spoken those terrible words yesterday, and now I said, "Very well, Mr. Whitely. I'm sure you won't expect me to believe the evidence, but thank you for all your efforts on my behalf."

"Do you have any further instructions for me?" he asked.

"I should like my father's body to be brought home for burial here. Could I ask you to do whatever is necessary? My mother is not well, and I seem to have nobody to turn to."

He nodded. "Leave the matter with me. I anticipated this request, and my understanding is that there will be no difficulty. As to other matters, I hope that I shall soon be able to make a reasonable assessment of the financial situation. So far the French police have not been able to trace any foreign assets; unfortunately, Miss Chance, it would appear your father kept his substance well hidden." Mr. Whitely sighed. "However, we shall pursue our inquiries and keep you fully informed. I am greatly obliged to you for calling, Miss Chance. . . ."

IN THE DAYS that followed I took the advice of Inspector Browning and went out on household matters openly, armouring myself with dogged resignation against stares and whispers. Latchford Hall had become a sad and sombre place. With an apologetic air Henson asked if I would write references for all the servants. Nannie was indignant, but I could not blame them for wanting to find new positions.

By letter Mr. Whitely told me that arrangements had been made to bring my father home in approximately two weeks' time.

The solicitor also asked if I would call at his office on Friday morning to discuss my father's estate, adding that he hoped my mother had recovered sufficiently to be present, since she was of course the natural inheritrix.

I wrote to confirm the appointment, but said my mother would be unable to attend. She had remained in bed, and seemed to have withdrawn into a long daydream where she found a kind of contentment. In a way I was glad for her, but all the same I worried because she left her food untouched and slept most of the time. By Thursday I was so concerned that I sent for Dr. Carey. It was clear that we no longer held any position in his eyes, for his manner was short and unsympathetic. He examined my mother, then spoke to me. "She is physically sound, but you must get her to eat. If you don't she'll go into a decline."

I said, "We keep trying, Doctor, but she just takes a spoonful or so, then falls asleep. I'm very worried."

"I'll make up a tonic to stimulate her appetite and send it round later today. That will be two shillings, please, plus sixpence for the tonic."

"Oh." I managed to control a silly grimace of surprise. "Oh, I'm sorry. I . . . please wait while I fetch my purse."

When he had gone I shut myself in my bedroom and wept with humiliation. I could have said, "Kindly submit your bill in the usual way, Doctor." But I was Bridie Chance, so I had pulled a face, groped for words, and thought far too late of all the cool, dignified things I could have said.

On the Friday morning I drove out of Latchford Hall to my appointment with Mr. Whitely. Robert's brother, on guard at the gate, saluted me, and I drew up for a word with him.

"On'y two women and a brace o' kids today, miss." He nodded at the little group across the lane. "Don't nobody try coming in like before. Them newspaper fellers was the worst, but they lost 'eart a bit now since I threw one of 'em into the 'edge."

"Thank you for your help," I said, smiling. "Here's an extra shilling for you, and very well earned."

Ten minutes later, as the gig swung round a bend in the lane, I pulled hard on the reins to stop short of a horse and rider standing quite still in the middle of the road. At Daisy's modest pace there was no danger of collision, but the sudden encounter startled me. Before I could speak the man took off his grey top hat and gave me a smile of greeting so warm and direct that I caught my breath.

He was a man of above average height, with dark curly hair above a square face. His hazel eyes glowed with gentle amusement. There was something odd about the cut of his elegant grey suit, and as he spoke I realized that he was not English.

"Forgive me, mam'selle." His voice was rather deep, with a slight French accent.

I noticed that he was riding with long stirrups, like the mysterious night-rider in the flat, wide-brimmed gaucho hat. Confused, I blurted out: "Do you ever wear a different kind of hat?" Then I felt colour flooding my cheeks. Surely nobody but Bridie Chance would have chosen such words in response to a polite apology from a stranger?

The man showed no surprise, but pursed his lips as if giving the matter due consideration. At last he said, "I occasionally wear a cap, mam'selle. Is it a matter of importance?"

"No . . . no, not at all. Please excuse me."

"It is for me to offer excuses, mam'selle," the stranger replied. "I offer my most humble apologies for having intruded upon you, but allow me to introduce myself. My name is Chatillon. Philippe Chatillon, at your service."

It was hard to think clearly with those wide hazel eyes seeming to encompass me, but I forced myself to be wary. "Do you mean that you stopped me on purpose, M'sieur Chatillon? Are you a journalist?"

His smile was disarming. "Ah, please do not insult me, mam'selle. No, I am not a journalist. I am, in a sense, a policeman. To be honest, I did indeed position myself here so that I might speak with you. I was a friend of your father, the delightful Mr. Roger Chance."

"A friend?" My voice was husky with shock.

"In a sense." He gave a shrug of regret. "It is possible to admire an opponent. A few months ago, over a bottle of wine in the Champs Élysées I urged your father to retire from his profession and return to England. He understood me well enough, but chose to pretend that I referred to his dealing in paintings. Ah, well . . . I am glad that I was engaged on other matters, and so was not involved in the final scene. I lost a most entertaining friend the night that you lost a father." His eyes were warm and comforting. "The grief is not to be compared, of course. I offer you my deepest sympathy."

"Thank you." I was so confused that I found myself wondering what to say next. "Well, M'sieur Chatillon," I said finally, "I imagine you have something to ask me."

"No, mam'selle, something to tell you. I knew Roger Chance well, perhaps better than his own family. We called him *Le Sorcier*, and he well deserved such a name, for he was a man of strange fancies. I believe you will find that he has left a riddle to be answered, and when that time comes, I urge you to seek my help, mam'selle."

"A riddle? Your help? I don't understand."

"I have posted my card to you containing my address in Paris. A telegram will bring me to you in less than a day. Please keep the card for the time when you need it."

"You are a most unusual policeman, sir," I said slowly.

He gazed thoughtfully at me. "Yes, I am a most unusual policeman. I do not speak or dress like one; I might almost be mistaken for a gentleman. But there are exceptions everywhere, are there not? Roger Chance, for example, was a most unusual gentleman."

Strangely, I was not distressed by his words. I was glad simply to be with somebody who seemed to have a complete understanding of the man who had been my father. He moved his horse to one side. "I will detain you no longer, mam'selle," he said. "It has been an honour to meet you. I have known your name for a long time now." His eyes danced with sudden humour. "But I had no idea that you were so beautiful."

The feeling of comfort splintered under his mockery, and tears flooded my eyes as I gathered up the reins. With an effort I spoke. "You need not fear being mistaken for a gentleman, sir."

I shook the reins to rouse Daisy from her doze, but the Frenchman leaned down and caught my wrist. "Forgive me, mam'selle, but I cannot let you depart with a wrong impression." His face was very serious now. "It is clear that you believe I spoke in jest, but I did not. Dear young lady, you do not have the prettiness of the china doll, and at this moment your face is drawn with grief. But nothing destroys true beauty, for it is from within, and will be with you if you should live to be eighty." He raised my hand to his lips. "Au revoir, mam'selle."

Smiling, he settled his top hat on his head, touched heels to his horse, and cantered down the lane. After a few moments I gave a brief laugh. "So that was a Frenchman," I thought to myself as I coaxed Daisy to a trot. "I've heard that they pay flowery compliments but I didn't know they could be so convincing."

I drove on in a strange and dreamy state. The encounter had given birth to a feeling of excitement, even of pleasure. By the time I reached Southwold, I was beginning to think that perhaps the worst of our ordeal would soon be behind us.

But when Mr. Whitely greeted me I sensed unease behind his usual dispassionate manner. "I regret adding to your burdens at this time," he said as he took his place behind his desk, "but I am disturbed about your family's financial situation, Miss Chance. No substantial assets have been discovered. The funds in your father's account here in Southwold amount to only a few hundred pounds. We have been in touch with your father's French bank, but the modest balance there will be completely disbursed in settling various debts."

"You were good enough to warn me that this would probably be the case, Mr. Whitely," I replied. "It just means we shall have to sell Latchford Hall, but I'm sure my mother would wish to do so in any event. I have been looking at property advertisements, and it seems to me that Latchford Hall should realize twenty thousand pounds. That would permit us to live very comfortably in a more modest residence."

Mr. Whitely looked at his hands as he said slowly, "Your father did not own the freehold of Latchford Hall, I regret to say. Twenty-one years ago he bought the remainder of a lease which expires at the end of October next. On that date the property reverts to the freeholder, Lord Royston."

There was a very long silence in the big, musty office. I sat looking at a large sepia picture on the wall, and as a wound hurts only after the first numbness has passed, so I did not at that moment feel panic and fear. All that was to come later.

Mr. Whitely broke the silence. "You will wonder why I did not tell you this before, Miss Chance, but the fact is that I did not

158

know. When your father signed the lease, he employed a London solicitor. I only recently became apprised of the situation when I put in hand inquiries concerning the ownership."

I did not take in much of what Mr. Whitely was saying. He was not a man to make mistakes, and I knew that Latchford Hall did not belong to us. The chilling fact was that our family faced a future with no breadwinner and with no more to our name than a few hundred pounds.

I tried to think what to do. We would have to find somewhere to live and money to live on. Somehow I would have to take care of my mother, Kate and Nannie Foster, who had expected to see out her days with us and had no home to go to. I began trying to work out sums in my head, but my mind kept going blank. Stupidly I remembered the eighteen pence which the inspector had placed on the mantelpiece after I had paid the cabbie. I wondered how long it would take me to earn eighteen pence.

Mr. Whitely was speaking, and I dragged my mind from a dreamlike emptiness to listen.

"I fear I have given you most disturbing news, Miss Chance. I shall be pleased to continue to act for you, and you may rest assured that my firm's charges will be—ah—quite nominal."

"You are more than kind, Mr. Whitely. Please believe me to be grateful."

"You have my respect and, if I may say so, my admiration, Miss Chance," he said. "I regret that I am able to do so little. May I speak plainly?"

"Please do."

"Without income, you and your family will shortly be close to penury. Latchford Hall was leased fully furnished, so I doubt that you have many possessions of substantial value to sell. Your mother's jewellery is—ah—no longer available. It will therefore be important for you, Miss Chance, to find some source of income as soon as possible. Fortunately you are a very well-educated young lady, and it should not be difficult for you to secure a good position as governess, despite your family association with—pray forgive me—with the recent scandal."

I was suddenly so weary that I found it hard to speak. At last I said, "Could you give me some idea of the sum a governess might expect to earn, Mr. Whitely?"

He stroked his nose with a finger. "It would vary with circumstances, of course, but she would be fully kept, and would also be paid a sum in the region of sixty pounds a year."

I got slowly to my feet. "I have responsibilities which call for a great deal more than that, Mr. Whitely. Thank you very much for your suggestion, but I feel I must give myself time to digest all the implications of what you have told me before I can think clearly about the future."

He had risen with me. "Please feel free to call upon me, Miss Chance, for any sort of advice."

He had moved to the door when a thought struck me, and I said, "When you had discussions at Scotland Yard, was any mention made of a French police officer named Philippe Chatillon?"

For once Mr. Whitely showed surprise, his eyebrows lifting. "May I ask where you heard that name, Miss Chance?"

"I met the gentleman less than an hour ago, on the road near Wynford. He introduced himself to me." I gave a brief account of our conversation, leaving out the concluding flattery.

When I had finished, Mr. Whitely said thoughtfully, "What a remarkable fellow. Yes, I came to know his name at Scotland Yard. Chatillon is not precisely a police officer. He is a rather well-to-do gentleman with an interest in criminal investigations. A private detective, I suppose. Apparently he is very highly thought of, and has helped to solve some notable cases."

"I wonder if I shall receive his card?"

"I think it most probable." Mr. Whitely opened the door for me. "If so, I would advise you to keep it. The gentleman is said to be very efficient at solving riddles."

I WAS HALFWAY home when panic struck at me. I felt it sweeping through my limbs so that I shook as if with ague, and had to pull Daisy to a halt off the road. For ten minutes I sat shivering in the sunshine, racked by fear, wondering what in heaven's name I could do to save us all from penury.

One thing was certain. As soon as I reached home I would have to give all the servants a month's notice. Every pound, every shilling I could save was suddenly important now. I picked up the reins, but I could not yet summon the courage to go home, and so I took the lane to old Tom Kettle's cottage.

Tom was working on the spout of a pump when I arrived at the cottage. He looked up as Daisy came to a halt, then laid down his mallet and chisel and plodded towards me.

"You'll stay for sharin' a pot o' tea wi' me, Miss Bridie?"

"Yes, please. You know about . . . my father?"

He nodded, grim faced, and said with huge contempt, "Them Frenchies." He took my hand as I stepped down, then led the way towards the cottage. "Do yew mind to come inside, Miss Bridie? Tes cooler, an' there's words to be said."

"All right, Mr. Kettle, but please don't worry about finding the right things to say. I know you liked Papa, and I'm sure we have your sympathy."

"More to it than that, miss." In the cool, dark cottage he pulled forward a beautifully-made wooden armchair for me, and gestured with a calloused hand for me to be seated. "You set quiet now while I make tea."

I had no energy left to wonder what Tom Kettle might have to say to me. For the moment I was glad to be in a place where I could rest and try to recover my courage. Five minutes later he set down the teapot, and for a while we sipped our tea in silence. At last he spoke. "I'd ha' come to the house to see your Mam, but I hear tell she's faring right sick, Miss Bridie. I got something to give her from your Dad, see."

I put down my cup and saucer, astonished. "Whatever can you mean, Mr. Kettle?"

"No more'n I sez, miss." He drank some tea, frowning. "Your Dad, he come to see me every time he was home. It was him who stopped old Briggs turning me out from this cottage. Seventy pounds he give, so's I could see me time out here."

"I'm glad, Mr. Kettle. It's the sort of thing he would do."

"A good 'un, he were. Trusted me, he did, Miss Bridie, better'n them lawyers an' banks, so he give me this letter to take to your Mam if I iver heard he was dead."

My nerves crawled. "A letter? When did he give it to you?"

"Ooh, nine or ten year back now. I got it hid safe away. I told him, I'm nigh seventy, Mr. Chance, so I reckon it's me as'll be dead fust. But he just laughs, an' gives me a sovereign. You're good for twenty years yet, Tom, he sez, and as fer meself, why, I'm the sort that might vanish in a puff of smoke one fine day.

Then he laughs again, as if he'd made a sort o' joke." Tom Kettle shook his head sombrely and set down his teacup.

Not many days ago I would have found it difficult to believe that Papa would entrust an important letter to an uneducated old man, but now, nothing I learned about him could surprise me.

"Do you wish me to take the letter to my mother for you?" I said. "I don't feel she is well enough at the moment to see it, but if you're willing to trust me with it, I'll try to choose the right moment to give it to her."

Mr. Kettle gave a gusty sigh of relief. "Ah. I were hopin' you'd say that, Miss Bridie." He got to his feet and went to the corner of the room where two steps led up to his bedroom. He struck the riser of the lower step and it swivelled back a few inches. Reaching into the cavity, he brought out a dusty oilskin packet tied with string. He blew the dust off carefully, and set the packet in front of me. "There's none too sorry I am to be free of that," he said.

"Thank you very much, Mr. Kettle." I put it in my handbag, wondering what new trouble it would bring. I had loved my father dearly, but there were times now when I felt almost angry resentment at the tribulations he had left me to struggle against by his reckless improvidence.

Ten minutes later I said goodbye to Tom Kettle and drove on to Latchford Hall. Kate met me in the hall with a letter which had come for my mother from Signor Peroni. As I read the letter aloud I felt a tiny spark of comfort. Signor Peroni expressed his deepest sympathy for our sad bereavement and "other afflictions". He went on to say that he did not wish to intrude upon us at a time of trouble, but that he hoped my mother would write when she felt it appropriate for him to resume Miss Kate's lessons, as he considered it a privilege to have such a rewarding pupil.

"Well, that's something to be thankful for," Kate said. "At least he isn't turning his back on us, like everybody else."

I nodded, and summoned up my courage. "Yes, it's heart-warming. But I don't quite know how we shall be placed, Kate dear."

"Placed?" She gave me a puzzled look, and at that moment Nannie Foster came in. We all wore black dresses now, and I felt a stab of panic at the thought of the dressmaker's bill.

"There's some very bad news I have to tell you both," I began. "I've just come from Mr. Whitely, and it seems that all we have in the world is a few hundred pounds."

I went on to explain our situation, while Kate put a hand to her mouth and stared at me in disbelief. When I stumbled to a halt at last she said, "But Papa had plenty of money. His wallet used to bulge with it, Bridie, don't you remember?"

"He always carried a lot of money, dear, but that's not the same thing. Unfortunately it seems Papa wasn't the sort of man to hold investments or buy property."

Nannie's round old face was like a mask. "Is there nothing, Miss Bridie? Nothing?" she asked. "Is it the workhouse for me?"

Suddenly I remembered that her parents had died in a workhouse while she was a girl in service. I put my arms round her and said, "Don't be silly. I'll look after you, Nannie, I promise."

I looked over my shoulder at Kate, who was very pale. "You must neither of you tell Mama about this," I said. "She's not well enough to know yet. I'm going to give the servants notice myself. I'll have Henson get them all together and do it now. There's so much to be done that we shall have no time to fret."

Kate struggled to keep her voice from shaking. "Do you think I shall have to give up my music scholarship, Bridie? I was to live as a paying guest in London, but if we haven't any money. . . ."

"Of course you'll be able to take up your music scholarship," I said quickly. "I'll think of some way to manage."

She gazed at me uncertainly. "You look strange, Bridie. Your eyes are funny, and your face is so white. Are you all right?"

"Yes, quite all right." As I went to the door, I managed a small smile. "It's always been a bit of a funny face, anyway."

In the hall I stopped and pressed my hands to my eyes, wondering what madness possessed me. In the last few minutes I had made two promises without having the haziest idea of how I could possibly keep them.

Later, when I had said what had to be said down in the servants' hall, I spent ten minutes with my mother and then went to my room. I locked the door, lay on my bed, and allowed all the devils of pain, sorrow and fear to have their way with me as I cried into the pillow. When the long spasm was past, I sponged my face with cold water, opened my handbag, and stood weighing in my hand

163

the oilskin package Tom Kettle had given me. I knew that if I went to my mother with a letter from her adored husband, the quietness that now possessed her would be broken, and she would again be racked by all the grief and horror she had known in the first days of our ordeal. Some instinct kept warning me that to open the letter would bring fresh and unimaginable disaster upon us. I realized this was foolish, yet still I could not overcome my dread, and slipped the packet into the bottom of my chest of drawers, empty now that I had turned out my engagement gifts.

The sight of that empty drawer did not bring to my mind the man I was once to have married, Bernard Page. It was as if we had known each other in another world and another time. Strangely, the man I thought of now was one I scarcely knew—the man I had met on the road only a few hours ago.

At six o'clock Philippe Chatillon's embossed card arrived by the evening post. I did not believe I should ever have need of it, but remembering Mr. Whitely's advice I put it in my writing case. As I did so, the Frenchman with laughing hazel eyes and friendly smile leaped into my mind's eye again, so suddenly and powerfully that for a moment I caught my breath.

⤳⤳ Chapter Four ⤳⤳

My mother died two days before my father's coffin reached Southwold station. It was unexpected, for though she had declined steadily, Dr. Carey had not felt that she was in danger when I called him to see her the day before her death. I had the money ready for him that time.

She died quietly during the night, and it was I who discovered it when I went to her room the next morning. To Kate and Nannie Foster it was a most dreadful shock, but I was beyond both, and at first I could only register in a dull sort of way that my mother had gone and that she had surely wished to. Then, to my utter shame, I began to feel a furtive relief that the burdens which were overwhelming me had been reduced in some measure by her passing. I told myself that death had released her from a future of grief and penury, yet I knew in my heart that a part of my feeling was selfish, and I hated myself.

Ironically, my mother's death eased the problem of my father's funeral. I had spoken twice with the vicar about arrangements, and his evasive replies led me to guess that important members of his congregation were protesting at the idea of a criminal being buried in hallowed ground. Now the vicar had a way to follow his conscience without offending his flock, for they could not object to my mother being buried at the church where she had worshipped for twenty years, nor argue against her husband being buried with her, whatever his sins.

I arranged for the double funeral to take place in four days, and paid another visit to Mr. Whitely to discuss the legal situation. He was very kind, and told me that my father's estate would now be deemed to have passed to his two daughters. We would likely receive less than four hundred pounds.

Even earlier, my difficulties had been made more trying by Kate becoming withdrawn and bitter. I was too wrapped up in practical problems to give her the time and sympathy she needed, and to help her I had written to Signor Peroni, saying that I would like him to continue her lessons. With the shock of Mama's death I completely forgot that I had written, and in consequence he arrived at Latchford Hall the day afterwards.

When I told him what had happened he made to withdraw in great distress, but I insisted that he stay for a while. I thought it only fair to tell him that we would soon be leaving Latchford Hall in straitened circumstances, and that we had not as yet been able to make plans for the future.

Signor Peroni was a small dark man in his middle forties, with an English wife and three young children. He had met his wife in Rome when she was a lady's maid to the wife of a British diplomat. The Peronis had married and lived there for a time, but Mrs. Peroni had pined for England, and in the end they came to London. Signor Peroni had inherited enough money to take a modest house in Kensington, and there he had gradually established himself as a teacher of the pianoforte.

He had been giving Kate lessons for four years, ever since Papa had engaged him during a spell at home. Now as I described our situation, his dark eyes widened in alarm. "But the music scholarship, signorina!" he exclaimed. "Surely she must go to the college of music. She has the possibility to be a great

165

artiste. It will be a great sorrow if she misses this chance to study."

"With all my heart I agree with you, signor," I said. "There is nothing I want more, but we shall have no money except what I am able to earn, and I understand Kate's incidental school fees and lodging expenses would amount to almost one hundred pounds a year. At the moment I have no idea how I shall even manage to feed us, so you can see how little hope there is for Kate to go on with her studies."

He lowered his eyes quickly to hide the pity in them. "I am sorry that you have such great troubles, signorina. Please permit me to say that I liked very much your dear father." He groped for words, then gave a small shrug. "I do not regard what has been said or done. I remember him with much liking."

I was deeply touched. "Thank you for those words, signor, and also for coming here today. I'm afraid Kate is too distraught to have a lesson this afternoon, but I hope you will come next week, and until we leave Latchford Hall. I'm sure it will help to take Kate out of herself a little."

"Then I shall come," he said, and stood up. He bowed politely, then hesitated. "I have a small thought, Signorina Bridie. I must speak of it with my wife, but perhaps . . ." He left the sentence unfinished. "I will say goodbye now."

"Goodbye, signor. I look forward to seeing you next week."

Later that afternoon, I went out into the garden. It was at its best just now, with honeysuckle and clematis frothing from the old wall beside the orchard, and the beds full of colour with lupins and border carnations. I had seen the seasons change year after year in these comely grounds, and it made my heart ache to think that soon I would never walk here again.

As I moved round the main rosebed my foot touched something on the grass. When I looked down I saw that it was the stub of a thin dark cigar—not the one I had found earlier, but a fresher, longer stub, a stone's throw from where I had found the first. I stared down at it, thinking of the gaucho horseman, then thinking of the horseman in the grey top hat I had met on the road one morning. Philippe Chatillon at least had not been a creature of my imagination. . . .

Suddenly I thought of the letter from my father, which Tom

Kettle had given me that same morning. It still lay in my bottom drawer, completely forgotten, and now I felt hot with guilt because I had not given it to my mother.

I had no curiosity about its contents—in fact I shrank from reading a private love-letter. Yet it seemed to me that I had no choice but to open it now, for my father would not have been so secretive about it unless it contained something more than words of love and solace. The thought occurred to me now that it might even tell of a hidden source of money.

Five minutes later I sat in my bedroom, taking off the outer wrapping of oilskin. I slit open the envelope within and found sheets of paper covered with my father's handwriting. He had written just as he spoke, so that I could almost hear his voice.

Mary darling,

    I'm sure you'll never read this, for it's just in case I'm unlucky, which I've no intention of being. I'm sorry to spend so much time away from my beautiful girl, but I am what I am as you well know, a fool who can't live without excitement bubbling in his veins like champagne, and that's the truth of it.

    Now here I am sitting at my desk in Paris, and laughing at myself a little to be writing words that I'll be the only one ever to read. So why am I writing them, I wonder? I'm not a pessimistic fellow, or a cautious one either, but I have to think about how you and the girls will be taken care of if the good Lord is absent-minded one day, and sends that creature of Nannie's to carry me off—Black Shuck, is it?

    Now then, you're not to be sad and full of tears, my lovely girl, for if I'm gone for good, then I'll be waiting for my sweetheart in an even better world than this, where the grass is gold and the wind never blows cold.

    Meanwhile, I'm writing this, Mary dear, to remind you of all things said between us when we drove out from the little smithy and up into the high valleys that fine summer day, when I told my secrets and you loved me still. Will you make a pilgrimage there, and remember the poor poetry I spoke? Do that for me, my darling. Walk again where the stream runs golden from the hills, and on to the valley of the Capricorn Stone. Have no fear of the shadow, for the darkness at eventide leads only to the dayspring of rainbow's

167

end. Remember me then, Mary dear, and have no fear of the waiting crow, for it serves only to reveal the emptiness that is filled with brightness.

Remember.
Ever with my love,
Roger

I sat gazing down at the last page of the letter written ten years before by my bewildering and enigmatic father. I read the final paragraph again. The first few lines seemed to refer to a particular place and day when Roger Chance had told his wife the truth about his secret life of crime, and I was not surprised that her love had remained unaltered, for in my mother's eyes my father could do no wrong. Then there was mention of the Capricorn Stone. I had no idea what this might be, and had never heard of it until my mother spoke the words during her ramblings shortly before she died. The rest of the paragraph seemed to be an attempt at what my English teacher used to call poetic prose, but the concept behind the words was too obscure for me even to guess at.

On the third reading I wondered if it might be a secret message which only my mother could understand. According to folklore, a crock of gold was to be found at rainbow's end, but I felt sure Papa was using analogy. What followed must be a cryptic direction indicating . . . what? Suddenly I was swept with irritation, for it was as if my father was reaching out from beyond the grave to tease and harass me. I stared into the looking glass above my dressing table and pulled an angry face, then wrapped the letter in oilskin once again and dropped it back in the drawer. If it did contain a message, then it was one which had meaning only for my mother, and that meaning would never now be unravelled.

THREE OF US attended the funeral, my sister Kate, Nannie Foster, and I. At the church there was no music to ease the silence, for the organist, a man of fiery puritan outlook, had declined to play. The coffins were borne one at a time by Robert and his brother Jack, assisted by two men from the village.

The vicar was kindly in his manner and the service was short, for which I was glad. Nannie Foster was bearing herself very well, but Kate looked waxen and I was afraid she might faint. As we rose

168

to follow the first coffin out, I took her arm and held it tightly. She whispered, "I'm sorry I've been horrid, Bridie."

"It was nothing, silly. Don't worry."

To my surprise I saw now that a few other people were in the church, and were now waiting to follow us out. There was Mr. Whitely, old Tom Kettle in a black suit that looked green with age, and a stranger I had never seen before. He was a man in his middle fifties, short and very broad, with a rubbery face and brown hair plastered to his head with oil. The centre parting of his hair might have been made with a ruler it was so straight. Though his dark suit was well made it sat uneasily on him, and I felt he would have looked more at home in rather loud tweeds.

At last the coffins lay side by side in the grave. When the hand-fuls of earth had been thrown, Kate and I moved among the little group to thank them all for attending. We came finally to the stranger. .Offering my hand I said, "Good morning, I don't think we have met."

He looked at me very hard from pale brown eyes. "Alfred Perkin at your service, miss. I trust I 'aven't displeased you, coming to pay my respects." He had a throaty voice which sounded as if it could be very powerful when he chose to exert it.

"My sister and I are glad to see any friends at such a time, Mr. Perkin," I said. "I take it you knew my father?"

"Slightly, miss." He hesitated. "I knew your mum better, really. We were colleagues, like, before she got married."

I was taken by surprise and did not know what to say. As it was, I felt close to tears. Behind us I could hear the thud of earth being shovelled into the grave, and my skin seemed to contract with sudden cold. "If you will excuse us, Mr. Perkin . . . ?"

I wished him good day and moved away towards our carriage, Kate holding my arm and Nannie Foster following.

I went to the churchyard alone next morning to arrange flowers on the grave. There was one small wreath which had not been there the day before, and also a beautiful little bouquet. The wreath was for my father, and the words on the card were written in a neat, angular hand: *Dormez bien, mon vieil adversaire— Philippe Chatillon."*

Sleep well, my old adversary. . . .

So the Frenchman had arranged for a wreath to be laid on the

169

grave of his old opponent before returning to France. My eyes prickled, and I felt a little touch of gladness at the thought.

The card attached to the bouquet had been written in a very different hand, careful and laborious. It said: *Dear Mary, Yrs. faithfully, A. Perkin.* Suddenly I glimpsed Mr. Perkin himself moving quietly away along the southern wall of the churchyard. He stopped, uncertain what to do, and then, realizing that I had seen him, he came towards me, hat in hand. "Good morning, miss," he said, his voice hushed. "I saw you coming and didn't want to intrude, so I was just slipping away."

I found myself liking this man, for he struck me as having a natural kindness. "Please don't feel that you're intruding, Mr. Perkin," I said. "I'm glad we have met again."

"That's very 'andsome of you, miss. You'll be Miss Bridget, unless I'm much mistaken?"

"Yes, but how did you know, Mr. Perkin?"

"Read the announcement in *The Times* when you were born, miss. Same with your sister, a few years later. My word, but I 'ad a shock when I saw Miss Kate yesterday. Image of your Mum when she was young. Talk about beautiful."

I said rather wonderingly, "Why, yes. And since I think you must have been fond of my mother, you'll be pleased to know that she remained very beautiful all her life."

Mr. Perkin nodded, and then bowed his head. After a moment I said, "Do you mind if I ask where you have come from?"

"London, miss. That's where I spend more than 'alf my time. I travel a lot, too, only I'm resting now for a few weeks."

"Oh, have you been ill?"

He started to smile, then remembered where he was. "No, miss. It's a professional term. In the theatre, if you're not working, you're resting. It usually means you 'aven't got a job, but that's not so with me." He produced a card and handed it to me. "We've got all the bookings we want, but I make sure we take a few weeks off in the summer. It keeps you fresh, so to speak."

The card said:

MR. ALFIE PERKIN & COMPANY
COMEDY SKETCHES
10 GRANT CHAMBERS,
HOLBORN, LONDON.

I stared at him open mouthed. "Good gracious, you're on the stage!"

"On the music halls, miss, yes. Thirty years now. Made my first appearance at the Canterbury back in sixty-seven."

I looked down at the card again to hide the shock I knew would show in my face. It was generally accepted that stage people could not possibly be respectable, and on this question I had heard only one dissenting voice, which was my father's. The previous year there had been a scathing letter in *The Times* concerning the decline of morals brought about by the "salacious" entertainment of the variety turns. He had read the letter, laughing, and said, "Now isn't that fellow a fine ripe prig, Mary? I'll wager he's never sat in the Oxford or the Alhambra and laughed his head off at the comics. How I detest Misery Dicks with not a spark of fun in them."

At the time I had wondered vaguely why he should comment on the subject, but now I realized that it was relevant to my mother's past. I looked up at Alfred Perkin and said, "Thirty years? Were you a music hall comedian when you met my mother?"

"Not exactly, miss. I was still doing the conjuring when your mum came in as my assistant."

I put my fingers to my mouth, and felt my eyes opening wider than ever. "Your *assistant?* On the stage?"

"Why yes, miss. I suppose you didn't know." He twisted his hat in his hands, looking embarrassed. "I do 'ope I've not given offence, saying all this after your Mum married well, but she was a real lady in 'erself, if you know what I mean. In service she was, when we met." He glanced at the headstone, and lowered his voice. "Don't think bad of me, Miss Bridget, but I fell in love with your mum and I asked 'er to marry me."

A few weeks ago I would have been horrified to learn that my mother had once been on the stage and that a music hall comedian had asked for her hand, but now I felt tears pricking at my eyes. "Why should I think badly of you, Mr. Perkin?" I asked. "There's nothing shameful about falling in love."

He nodded slowly, his eyes distant. "She wasn't sure," he said softly. "Then she met your dad, and she was really sure about him. But I never forgot her, miss, and I never wanted to marry anyone else." He drew in a breath and straightened his back. "I read about your dad passing away," he went on, "and I was coming up to see Mary, in case she needed help. But then she passed away, too, so I just came to pay my respects."

I stood deep in thought for a little while. "How long will you be staying, Mr. Perkin?" I said at last.

"I've got a room at The Woodman, for tonight, but I can stay on longer if there's anything I can do to 'elp, Miss Bridget."

"No, I wouldn't ask you to stay on, but I would like to have your advice about the possibility of finding work for myself in London. Would you be so kind as to come and have tea at Latchford Hall this afternoon, say at half-past three o'clock?"

"I'd be delighted, miss." Mr. Perkin looked quite overcome with pleasure as he bowed and said, "I'll take my leave of you now, Miss Bridget, and look forward to this afternoon."

I stood holding his card as he left the churchyard, filled with astonishment at my own temerity. Yet I had to find work, and London would be the best place to begin. There would be more opportunities for employment there than in a country town. Above all, it was important that we should live within easy distance of the Prince Consort College of Music.

Later, when I told Kate of my encounter with Mr. Alfred Perkin, she showed little surprise. "Are you really so astonished that Mama had been on the stage, Bridie? We always knew she wasn't born a lady."

"Oh, don't speak so unkindly, Kate!"

"I don't mean it unkindly. Quite a lot of stage ladies have married into the gentry, so it's not really strange that Mama married Papa, or that Papa married her, for he was a quite extraordinary man. I think it's rather exciting. What do you want to talk to this Mr. Perkin about, Bridie?"

"Kate dear, I've *explained*," I said, trying hard not to be irritable. "Soon there will be no money for us to live on, so I shall have to find a way to earn some."

She gave me one of her beautiful smiles. "Don't worry, Bridie. I'm sure that when we go to London you'll meet a rich man who'll fall desperately in love with you. You'll marry him, and then everything will be perfect. After all, that's what happened with Mama and Papa, wasn't it?"

I did not answer. Kate was sometimes hopelessly romantic,

sometimes severely practical. At the moment she was in one of her romantic moods, and I was content for her to be so if it helped ward off the chill misery of anxiety.

ALFRED PERKIN presented himself promptly at half-past three o'clock. I introduced Kate, and could see after the first few minutes of small talk that she was greatly taken with his natural good manners.

As soon as I had poured tea for us all I said, "Mr. Perkin, can you tell me what sort of work is available in London for an educated young lady?"

He frowned down at his cup of tea. "Well, I've been thinking about that after what you said this morning, Miss Bridget—"

"Please call me Bridie," I broke in.

"Most kind of you—um—Bridie. Well, there's shop work, there's teaching work and there's quite a few young ladies doing office work now. P'raps I can tell you a bit more if I know what you 'ave in mind, see?"

"That's simple, Mr. Perkin. My father's estate amounts to only a few hundred pounds, and apart from that we have nothing. I have to take care of our old nannie, Kate and myself, of course."

Mr. Perkin drew in a whistling breath through pursed lips and looked unhappy. "I 'ate to be a Dismal Jimmy, but I can't see where a young lady can earn that sort of money. With rent, food and clothes, you're going to need . . . let's say a hundred and twenty pounds a year to live anything like decent." He looked about him. "And it wouldn't be like this, neither."

Kate said, "That doesn't seem a great deal, Mr. Perkin."

He looked at her, and his face softened. I knew he was seeing my mother in her, and his voice was very gentle as he said, "I don't suppose you've 'ad to think much about money, Miss Kate. But you take a housemaid. She'll get all found and p'raps twelve pounds a year." He looked at me. "If you taught in a school you'd earn more, but then you wouldn't 'ave bed and board thrown in. Same applies with office work."

"I'm quite a good needlewoman, Mr. Perkin," I said. "Would there be any opportunity in that line?"

He winced as if in pain. "Lord, no. You 'ave a think about what you pay your dressmaker. It's worse in London. You walk around

174

the workshops in the East End—twelve bob a week women get
sewing. Sweated labour, that's all you'll find."

Kate was gazing at Mr. Perkin as if fascinated. "Twelve shillings
a *week?*" she said wonderingly. "However do they manage?"

He gave a shrug of his broad shoulders. "They live like pigs,
my dear," he said simply.

Kate blinked, then put down her cup and stood up. "Excuse
me," she said in a subdued voice, and went from the room.

"It's all right, Mr. Perkin," I said as he looked at me in distress.
"Kate can be realistic, but at times she doesn't wish to be. Now
let us talk about something else. I'd be interested to know how
you met my mother, if you don't mind telling me."

"Why, no," he said slowly, "but there's not much to be told,
really. She was a lady's maid, and a footman brought her to the
Oxford one evening. I was doing an act called Marvo the Mystic
then, and for one trick I usually got a young man from the
audience to 'elp. Well, this pertickler night I spotted your mum
and I got a bit of the devil in me, so I tried to coax her up on
the stage."

"But Mama was such a shy person," I said wonderingly. "I'm
sure you didn't succeed."

"It was only because of all the people around 'er," said Mr.
Perkin. "They were all jollying 'er along, and in the end she
reckoned it was best to come up and get it over with. Anyway, I
was smitten so 'ard I followed 'er back that night to where she
worked. I waited my chance to see her when she came out next
morning, and I introduced myself, and I think she was a bit
impressed, what with me being on the stage."

"And she became your assistant?"

He smiled suddenly. "Three weeks later. Her mistress was going
abroad and Mary was under notice anyway. I offered her a job
at good money, and she never had to say anything on the stage.
She just wore a pretty frock, and passed me bits of apparatus, and
kept smiling. She had a kind of dignity, if you know what I
mean, and she brought a bit of quality to the act." He sipped his
tea. "She knew all about 'ow to behave, from being in service and
taking note of the gentry."

"My sister and I have never known about her early days," I
said. "Did you meet any of her family, Mr. Perkin?"

He shook his head. "There were no real ties, Bridie. She was put out to service when she was twelve. Her mum had died and her dad wanted to be rid of her. Then the son of the 'ouse got married and Mary became lady's maid to his wife."

For a brief while I had forgotten the future, for I was fascinated to hear about this other world in which my mother had lived. "Was she on the stage with you for very long?" I asked.

"Just over a year. We worked three months in London, then went on tour for six months, then back to London again." He looked at me with sudden anxiety. "It was all very respectable, though, with your mum and me. My young sister Ethel lived with us. She wasn't much to look at so she'd never been part of the act, and it was only when I went in for comedy that I brought her in. But what I'm saying is, your mum shared a room with Ethel, and it was all respectable."

"I'm sure it was, Mr. Perkin. I'm surprised she didn't marry you, if you were courting her."

He smiled. "That was a nice kind thing to say, Bridie, but I wasn't surprised myself, not really. Oh, she liked me well enough. But then Mr. Chance càme along, your dad."

"How did that happen?"

"Oh, he saw the act at Gatti's, and he sent her flowers and waited at the stage door for her. Wasn't the first gent to do that, mind you. Your mum 'ad been asked out to dinner several times and she'd always said no. It was easy enough, because she always came out with Ethel and me, and that put the gents off a bit, but your dad was different. He walked up to the three of us, and says he'd be honoured if we'd all come to dinner with 'im at the Café Royal."

"I can imagine him doing it."

"Well, I thought it'd be fun, letting this gent take us out to a posh dinner, so I winked at Ethel and your mum, and said we'd be 'appy to oblige. And it was fun all right, because your dad was a real marvel, telling stories and saying nice things to poor Ethel just as much as to your mum. But your mum was spellbound by Mr. Chance, and I knew I'd lost her."

"That was very sad for you."

"Well, I'd known for quite a while that Mary wasn't meant for me. The thing was, though, I didn't know if Mr. Chance's

176

intentions were honourable, did I? He asked Mary out twice more, and then I buttonholed 'im. And you know what he said? 'It's high time you asked me that, Alfie,' he says, 'for I could be the worst sort of rake. So let me tell you Mary's the one I'll love till the day I die, and I want to marry her as soon as she pleases, and I'm hoping you'll give her away!' "

Mr. Perkin paused, and I saw a hint of moisture in his eyes. "They were married three months later," he said at last, "and went off to live here. I told Mary we mustn't write, because she was going to be a gentleman's wife now, so she'd got to live up to it and couldn't 'ave common friends."

I nodded, remembering. "She did wonderfully well, Mr. Perkin. You would have been proud of her. And my father spoke the truth, for he really did love her."

There was a silence. Mr. Perkin took a watch from his waistcoat pocket and said, "My word, I'm sure I've stayed too long."

"I've enjoyed every moment of your visit, Mr. Perkin," I said. "And it was very kind of you to give me your advice."

He stood up, frowning a little, and then said, "I'm afraid my advice wasn't much 'elp, Bridie, but it's no use me painting a rosy picture when it's not rosy. The thing is, you're Mary's daughter, and I've done not too bad over the years, so I reckon I could 'elp you out a bit—"

"Oh, no!" I came to my feet, my face crimson. "No, Mr. Perkin! That isn't why I told you of our difficulties. Whatever can you think of me?"

"I think very well of you, young lady," he said soothingly. "Now don't take on so."

I rolled my eyes up, exhaled a long breath, and made a shrugging grimace. "Oh, dear. Forgive me for making a fuss, but I just couldn't have you give us money. It would be quite outrageous."

He was studying me with interest as I spoke, and suddenly he laughed. "Sorry, Bridie, but I'm tickled by the way you looked just then, all overcome with sort of comic despair."

"Oh, dear. Whenever I feel something, my face tries to say it. I've always been like that, and I can't seem to help it."

"I wouldn't try, my dear. It gives you character." His smile vanished and he looked down at me soberly. "Now listen, Bridie," he went on. "If you won't let me 'elp in one way,

177

then p'raps I can 'elp in another. It's quite a big flat we've got in Holborn, me and Ethel and young Charlie—that's her son, who's part of the act. Now, when you come down to London with your sister, there's a spare room you can share. Nothing wonderful, but you could use it until you've got your bearings. We're out working every night 'cept Sunday so you'd 'ave the place to yourselves quite a bit."

Quite suddenly I found that tears were running down my cheeks. I did not try to hide them, but impulsively reached out to Mr. Perkin and put my hand on his. "Thank you with all my heart," I said. "I hope we shan't need to trouble you, Mr. Perkin, but it's truly wonderful to know that we have somewhere to go in our new life."

Alfred Perkin looked about the drawing room. "Yes," he said quietly, "it's going to be ever so different, Bridie."

I dabbed my cheeks with a handkerchief, and smiled. "Never mind. I've been so frightened, but you've put new heart into me."

His mobile face creased in a great beam of pleasure. "Well, I'll trot along now, but you just write me a letter when you want to come, and I'll see you're met at the station."

When he had gone I went to find Kate. She was in the library studying the score of a sonata, and she looked up apologetically as I entered. "I'm sorry if I was rude, Bridie," she said. "Somehow that man made me realize how awful it will be to be poor."

"He didn't think you were rude, darling, and I know how you feel. I've been quite frantic, trying to work out ways and means. At any rate, Mr. Perkin may be able to help us."

I sat down beside her and explained his offer.

"That's very kind of him," Kate said thoughtfully. "I don't suppose there will be a piano. But never mind. What about Nannie though? She's so worried."

"Oh, I've decided about Nannie," I replied. "That tiny cottage near the shops in Wynford is for sale with a twenty-year lease for ninety-five pounds, and I'm going to buy it for Nannie. She'll be happier here with her friends. And if I can send her fifteen shillings a week she'll be able to live fairly comfortably."

Kate leaned her head against my shoulder. "Don't forget that rich, handsome man who's going to fall in love with you," she said dreamily. "Someone full of dash and devilment, like Papa."

I said nothing. I too had loved Papa, but the price for his dash and devilment had proved a heavy one for his family, one which I would be paying for far into the future.

Mr. Alfred Perkin's visit had refreshed my spirits, and the following week came another piece of good fortune. When Signor Peroni arrived for Kate's lesson, he said that he and his wife would be happy to have Kate come to live with them in their Kensington home. She could have a room of her own, a piano on which to practise, and would be able to attend the college daily. Signor Peroni and his wife could provide all Kate's needs for fifty pounds a year.

"I must tell you," said Signor Peroni with a gesture of apology, "that my family does not live as Miss Kate is accustomed, neither is our house large with a big number of servants. But she will be cared for, as if to be a relative of our own."

Kate was sitting up straight, her eyes sparkling, and I felt a great wave of relief sweep over me. "Oh, Signor Peroni, I don't know how to find words for such kindness," I said.

"Miss Kate has much talent. I cannot bear that it is lost. Also I have much affection for her, and I hope she will not find it difficult to accept a home more modest."

For answer Kate jumped up, ran to the little sad-faced Italian, and hugged him as she pressed her cheek to his. She choked out a muffled "Thank you!" and hurried from the room in tears.

Signor Peroni said in a low voice, "Poor child. It has been most hard for her. Hard for you both. Forgive me that I have had to request payment, Miss Bridie, but I am not a rich man."

"I understand, signor. I would like to pay you fifty pounds in advance, then I shall have only myself to worry about for a full year. When could Kate come to you?"

He thought for a moment. "Suppose I come on this day next week and escort Miss Kate to London?"

I had no doubt that Kate would be in very good hands with Signor Peroni. We had led sheltered lives, and I had been dreading that the huge change about to take place would prove a crushing affliction to Kate. Now at least she would be in the care of a decent, affectionate family.

"That would be a splendid arrangement," I said. "One thing I must say: while Kate is under your roof, you have the authority to act as you would if she were your own daughter. I shall say this to Kate herself, of course."

Signor Peroni smiled. "We shall not have any troubles," he said. "Miss Kate is not at all a difficult young lady."

ONE WEEK LATER I stood on the platform waving my handkerchief as the train pulled slowly out on its journey to London. Kate waved excitedly from the open window. She had good company, for Signor Peroni had brought his wife with him to Latchford Hall so that I could meet her. I liked Anne Peroni at once, and felt that Kate could not have been more fortunate.

The next few days were very busy. Mr. Whitely put in hand the purchase of the cottage for Nannie Foster, and I saw her comfortably installed there. At the same time I suffered a hard blow. With the ending of the lease at Latchford Hall we faced liability for repairs which proved much greater than expected. This completely swallowed up all that I had been able to produce from the sale of the piano, ponies and carriages. After paying Signor Peroni, the servants, and various bills, I had just over one hundred pounds left.

I spent several evenings working out sums, and the answers I found were very bleak. At the end of a year, if I allowed myself one pound a week, I would have twenty-one pounds left. My liabilities would then continue at the rate of one pound a week for Kate, the same for myself, and fifteen shillings for Nannie. So I would have to earn at least two pounds fifteen shillings a week. Alfred Perkin had opened my eyes to the kind of wages available, and I had lately been studying advertisements which con-firmed what he had said. The brutal fact was that I could not earn enough to meet my obligations.

I told myself that I had a full year in which to solve my prob-lems, and wrote to Alfred Perkin saying that I should be grateful to take up his kind offer. By return of post came a letter in a round, careful hand: Mr. Perkin would be delighted to meet my train, if I would inform him when I expected to arrive. I wrote again, thanking him and giving a date just over a week hence.

The servants completed their month's notice and departed from Latchford Hall. For three days I was alone there, with only family ghosts of my own imagining to keep me company. I slept poorly, and on the second of those three nights, in the early hours, I saw the gaucho horseman again, moving silently across the lawn. Strangely, I felt comforted rather than afraid. When the shadowy figures of horse and man passed from my sight I went back to my bed and slept soundly till morning.

Next day I said goodbye to Nannie Foster, Tom Kettle and Mr. Whitely, who had helped me so much in the long ordeal. Finally the time came to leave Latchford Hall.

At nine o'clock on that warm September morning I sat in the corner of a third-class compartment in the London train. On my wrist was the small watch which had been a present from my father. In my handbag I carried Philippe Chatillon's card and my father's letter. I would have found it hard to give a reason why I had kept them; perhaps I was afraid to throw them away, though I desperately wanted the break with my old life to be complete.

In that moment of departure I felt very lonely, plain, and frightened. Angrily I told myself that it was self-pitying to feel lonely, that I should be used to feeling plain, and that it was cowardly to feel frightened. No doubt all this was true, but where fear was concerned I had yet more to learn.

Chapter Five

At one o'clock on the first Saturday of November I left Lady Grainger's Millinery Establishment in Knightsbridge to ride home on my bicycle to Grant Chambers in Holborn. Usually I worked from eight o'clock till half-past six, but today was the first Saturday of the month, on which I was allowed a half-day off.

Even after six weeks as a shop-girl I still felt leg-weary at the end of the day, and it was a joy for me to be finishing with hats and gloves and difficult ladies following a morning's work. It was Ethel, the sister of Alfred Perkin (or Alfie as I now called him at his earnest request), who had secured this job for me after I had been unable to find a position during my first two weeks in London.

"There's this friend of mine who serves at The White Swan," she said in her high, penetrating voice. "Well, she's got a cousin who's a maid to Lady Grainger what runs a hat shop up the

West End, and this cousin says how her ladyship's looking for another girl to serve there, only she's got to be ever so refined, just like you, Bridie."

I had looked at her long angular face in surprise. "But I didn't know ladies kept shops, Ethel."

Alfie put aside his horse-racing paper and gave me a grin. "Yes, it's funny when you come to think of it. The gentry turn up their noses at anyone in trade, but somehow it's all right for a lady to run a shop selling clothes or flowers. Well, you ought to try for that job, like Ethel says. Leastways you'll be dealing with a nice class of people."

"Will it be best if Bridie doesn't use her own name, Alfie?" Ethel asked. "I mean, people are going to remember about Mr. Chance and all that, and Lady Grainger might not like it."

"She's daft if she don't," said Alfie. "More likely to bring in customers than turn 'em away." He wagged his head with a grimace of regret. "Sorry, Bridie dear, but that's the way it is."

I nodded. I had been gawped at in Wynford, and had learned to endure it. "I won't change my name or use a false one, Alfie," I said. "I made up my mind about that right from the beginning."

Two days later I was interviewed by Lady Grainger and was accepted as a shop assistant at a wage of fourteen shillings a week. The first thing I did was to spend two pounds from my meagre capital to buy a secondhand bicycle, so that I could travel without further expense. I did not enjoy the work. On the few occasions when I saw Lady Grainger she eyed me with dark suspicion, and the two other girls were great friends and made it very obvious that they did not want a third person in the shop. But all this was nothing. I was truly thankful to have a job and grateful to Ethel for her help.

Ethel was a thin woman with a bony face and a great mass of splendid chestnut hair which she wore piled in a tall chignon. Her features were vaguely horsey, and she seemed always to be balancing her chignon as she moved, as if she were afraid it might fall off. Her voice was high-pitched and unvaried, so that she spoke on one long and monotonous note. This was of great effect in the variety act of Mr. Alfie Perkin and Company, but she spoke in just the same way off-stage.

Ethel was known as "Mrs." Perkin, and her son Charlie was the third member of the act. He was twenty-two, and used his mother's surname. I gathered from an idle remark which Alfie let slip one day that Charlie Perkin was a result of the very brief and only romance Ethel had ever known. He was a tall, loose-limbed young man with red hair and a pale face, who was rarely at home and who spent all his time on his private pursuits except when he was on-stage, or rehearsing, or in bed. What those private pursuits were, neither Ethel nor Alfie seemed to know. Charlie spoke little but was quite friendly, and during his few moments at home he communicated mainly by a grin, a wink, or a wag of the head.

Home was at 10 Grant Chambers, Holborn. This was a large flat in a new building of three floors, with a lift and a hall porter. Our flat was on the top floor and we had a pleasant view of St. Paul's. Charlie shared a large bedroom with Alfie while Ethel and I had a small bedroom each. There was also a spacious living room, a kitchen, and a splendid modern bathroom with hot-water taps. Radiators connected to a basement boiler kept all the rooms beautifully warm.

Every morning at nine o'clock, except on Sundays, a brawny woman named Minnie arrived at the flat. She would make breakfast for the Perkins, do three hours of cleaning, and then take away the linen to be laundered. I was quite surprised by the luxury in which we lived, and I sometimes wondered how it was possible for a music hall performer to live in such style. I worried that my contribution to the household expenses was too little, but three shillings a week was as much as Alfie would take.

It was only on Sundays that I was able to spend much more time with my new friends. Every weekday I would arrive home at about seven o'clock, only half an hour before Alfie, Ethel and Charlie left for the first of their nightly appearances. By the time they returned at eleven I was long asleep, and when I left in the morning at eight, they had not woken.

Before I began to work in the shop I had spent several evenings at the theatre with them. Alfie had tried to prepare me for what I would see, and had explained that there were different classes of music hall. "First there's the posh West End 'alls, Bridie, like the Empire and the London Pavilion. Next you've got the second-class London 'ouses and some big music 'alls down into the suburbs, like the Bedford in Camden Town, and last there's the tavern music 'alls for the working class. I've played 'em all, Bridie, but we 'aven't played the bottom end for years now. We've built up a good name, see? Mind you," he went on, "the profession's a bit more respectable than it used to be, really. We get a lot of decent trades people now, shopkeepers and such; they come along regular with their families."

Alfie produced a scrapbook full of photographs, programmes, and yellowing newspaper cuttings. He turned to a page near the front, and there was a sepia photograph of Alfie as a much younger man, in evening dress and a short cloak. He had a conjurer's wand in one hand and a string of flags in the other. Holding the other end of the string, smiling a shy smile, was my mother.

"She should've been born a lady," Alfie said softly. "Right, Ethel?"

Ethel nodded, her eyes misting. "Couldn't be brassy if she tried, Mary couldn't. The men always behaved themselves when she was on-stage."

Alfie closed the book and looked at me. "When she left, it was your dad who put me on the right road. 'Alfie,' he says, 'you're not a bad conjurer but you'd make a much better comic. You've got the face for it, and you might find Ethel a good bet too, with that funny voice. So work out a comic sketch and try it.' "

"We thought it was a barmy idea," said Ethel.

Alfie nodded. "But we couldn't get it out of our minds, and in the end we worked out a sketch with a young chap called Nipper Jennings." He made one of his eye-rolling grimaces. "Got the bird with it when we tried it out first time."

"The bird?" I asked.

"Got booed—fell flat as a pancake, Bridie. Anyway, we changed it round a bit, and suddenly it seemed to take. So we worked out another sketch, and that's what we've been doing for the last twenty years, more or less. Nipper Jennings got pneumonia and died five years ago, but we'd been training Charlie, and he just stepped straight in."

I gaped in astonishment. "Only two sketches, Alfie?"

He grinned. "There's more than forty music 'alls in London and

people don't go to them every night, do they? And anyway the
people out front like best what they know best. I reckon they
laugh more at a joke the second or third time around."

He chuckled as I shook my head wonderingly.

I had my first experience of music hall at the Canterbury in
Westminster Bridge Road, watching from the stalls with the
redoubtable Minnie as my protector. I was quite dazed by the end
of the evening, for it was as if I had suddenly been transported
to another world—raucous, gaudy and vulgar, but somehow honest
and bursting with life.

Minnie and I were seated among the young gentry, some of
them with female companions who laughed uproariously at every
word, from their escorts. We drew a few curious glances from
young men before the performance began, but in general the
atmosphere was friendly and genial. Behind us the hubbub grew
louder with the chaff and chatter of young clerks, local bloods
and some tradesmen with their families, but by far the greatest
noise came from the gallery above, which I could barely see even
when I craned my neck. Here, according to Alfie, was where the
fate of an artiste was really decided, up in "the gods".

Every man in the audience seemed to be smoking, and the air
was thick with it. There was much coming and going with refresh-
ments, and I felt quite shaken by the thought that when the curtain rose someone called Margaret Dane would have the awesome
task of securing the attention of the audience. In the event, this
dark-haired lady finally brought the house to a measure of
silence when she sang a song about a dying soldier, and I was glad
to hear her receive a good round of applause at the end of her
turn.

Mr. Alfie Perkin and Company came on for the last turn before
the interval, and as the show went on I found myself holding my
breath with anticipation. I scarcely knew what I felt about the
programme so far. Of the comedians I had seen, two had gone in
for a great deal of shouting and capering, as if trying to bully the
audience into enjoying itself. Most of what they shouted was
almost meaningless to me. Another comedian was a lugubrious
man who delivered a monologue about The Problems of Being a
Nob, which I thought was very funny, and a baritone sang several
over-sentimental songs which I did not enjoy but which were

warmly appreciated by the audience. Then a vivacious young woman sang a song with entirely innocent words which she managed to invest with far from innocent meaning. The audience was greatly taken with her. Beside me, Minnie guffawed till the tears ran down her cheeks, and I was laughing myself, even though it was scarcely the kind of entertainment that I was used to.

At last the curtain rose on Mr. Alfred Perkin and Company in "The Water Board Man". There was a murmur of gleeful anticipation from the audience as the orchestra ended a short piece of introductory music. The centre of the stage was occupied by a stretch of canvas with a brick wall painted on it. There were one or two pots of flowers representing a garden, and a post with a clothes line attached which ran off into the wings. On the floor a large iron manhole cover had been propped open as if to reveal a hole in the ground. I learned later that the hole was really only a few inches deep, with water pipes and turncocks set in it which were fed from a water churn in the wings.

Alfie Perkin, wearing a uniform slightly too small for him and a cap with a shiny peak, was moving towards the hole, notebook and pencil poised. Behind him followed Charlie, in a uniform too large and carrying a shapeless bag of tools. He walked with a curious chicken-like step, and immediately the audience began to laugh. Alfie stopped by the hole. Charlie went walking on. Alfie watched him, pencil poised over notebook, with silent and dignified irritation. When Charlie finally halted by the hole, Alfie continued to eye him, and as he did so there passed over that rubbery face a whole range of emotions: indignation, outrage, resignation, menace, and finally a kind of hopeless acceptance. After the chuckling of the audience had died down, Alfie spoke, and for the first time I heard that powerful voice used to the full, reaching to the uppermost tiers of the gallery. Pointing down with his pencil he said slowly and deliberately, "Arnold, this is what we call a *hole*."

A roar of mirth went up, and my own laughter was a part of it. Anybody might have gone through the same movements and spoken the same words, but there were a dozen nuances in every move, gesture and expression which gave the act a gloriously comic effect.

186

The idea of the sketch was that Alfie was the man from the Water Board, and Charlie was his assistant. They had come to inspect a water main. Ethel was a householder, the hard-of-hearing Mrs. Fortescue, who was trying to hang out her washing and who misunderstood all the explanations of the Water Board Man. All three were really quite splendid, and I had not dreamed Charlie could be so funny. When a jet of water hit him in the back of the neck, or when he got tangled up in the washing, he would reel about the stage with brilliant displays of eccentric dancing. There was a wild inconsequence about the whole sketch which I found quite hilarious, and certainly the audience enjoyed Mr. Alfie Perkin and Company, applauding rapturously as they stood to take their bows.

I first saw the other sketch in the repertoire from the wings of the Metropolitan, Edgware Road. It was called "The Paperhanger's Mate": Alfie was the paperhanger, Charlie was his mate, and Ethel was the lady of the house, who was greatly concerned for her furniture in general and for a very large picture in particular, a portrait of a man with a huge moustache, whom she referred to as "mai departed 'usband". Dreadful things happened to that picture, and Alfie's harassed attempts to conceal them or put them right were hilarious. When I had seen both sketches several times, I found myself marvelling at the way the Perkins timed their pauses and their interventions to a split second, even taking into account the slightly different response from different audiences.

When I began work at the shop I had no time to visit the music hall, except on Saturdays, when I could sleep a little later on Sunday mornings. After my second week in London I took to cooking Sunday luncheon for the Perkins. I was by no means a wonderful cook, but I had learned the basic art from our cook at Latchford Hall, and I was certainly much better than Ethel. My efforts were much appreciated, and I felt enormously pleased to perform some service for these kindest of friends. Then I would ride my bicycle to Signor Peroni's house and spend the afternoon with Kate and the family. To my relief Kate seemed to have settled in well and was happy in her studies.

On that first Sunday in November, Kate was in one of her practical moods. Signor Peroni always made sure that we were left together for half an hour so that we could discuss any private matters, and as soon as we were alone on this occasion Kate said briskly, "Bridie, are you sure you can manage this sixpence a week you give me for pocket money?"

"Yes, dear, of course. After all, you are entitled to half of what little was left to us."

She smiled. "At least I had enough sense to let you have charge of everything. But I think I could find a few piano pupils, if that would help."

"No, no, Kate, you mustn't do that—it will interfere with your studies."

She nodded reluctantly, and I went on, "We shall be all right for a year, and I'm sure something will turn up before then."

Kate leaned forward and put a hand over mine. "What is it like for you, Bridie, working in the shop and living with those people? It must be . . . well, strange."

"Oh, Kate, please don't call them 'those people'. They've been so good to me, and I'm very happy with them. Strangeness isn't necessarily a bad thing, and I've learned a great deal in these past weeks. Anyway, don't worry about me. Now let's talk about Christmas. Alfie says he'll arrange for us all to go to the pantomime."

We talked for a while, and then the Peroni children came in, full of suppressed excitement, followed by their mother and father. The children had been practising a little Italian song to sing to me, and there was much laughter and chatter in both English and Italian as they urged Kate to the piano. I was thankful that Kate was part of a warm and loving family. I was no less fortunate myself, and when I thought how wretched our situation might have been, I felt an inward shiver.

BEFORE CHRISTMAS my friends were resting, and it was pleasant to spend the evenings with them. During my first few days in London I had felt awkward and embarrassed in their company, because they were not of my kind. I was ashamed when I recalled my feelings, but they had long since passed. I had suffered enough humiliations in the shop to cure me of condescension, and I now regarded Alfie and Ethel as my dearest friends.

One day I arrived home to find only Charlie there. He was about to go out, as usual, but he courteously helped me off with my coat and carried my shopping basket to the kitchen. We then proceeded to have the longest conversation we had ever had together.

"Ma's out with Uncle Alfie," he announced. "Bit o' Christmas shopping, she said. Back by seven, though. Said you was to 'ave your bath an' all that, and then you'd all go out to eat." His words were accompanied by the usual miming. Suddenly it struck me that Charlie and I were two of a kind, though he had had no nannie to admonish him for making "exaggerated facial expressions". Now he squinted thoughtfully up at the ceiling and said, "Chap was asking about you last night."

"A chap?" I said. "Who was it?"

He shrugged. "Dunno, Bridie. Some chap."

"Where, Charlie?"

He looked furtively over one shoulder and said in a conspiratorial whisper, "*Billiard 'all!* Shhh! Don't tell Ma!"

I blinked in surprise. "No. Of course I won't. But is that where you spend *all* your spare time, in a billiard hall?"

He nodded his head. "Daft about it, I am. Cue in me hand, and I'm 'appy for ever." He rolled his eyes. "But Ma don't like billiards, see?" He was still whispering. "*I think it's because of me dad. I think he was a billiards player, see? And he left Ma, you know. . . .*"

"Yes, Charlie, I understand," I said quickly. "I won't speak of it. Tell me more of this man who asked about me. What did he want to know?"

"If you were all right. If you were courting."

"*Courting?* But why?"

"Dunno, Bridie. I just said yes you were all right, no you weren't courting. I was busy playing, see?"

"Did you spare a moment just to look at him?"

"Er . . . 'ad a sort of brown face, 'air a bit longish. Spoke slow. Yankee all right."

"American? Are you sure? I've never even met an American."

"That's about it. Oh, and this chap 'ad a horse. Some other chaps saw 'im go, and they said it was a real beauty."

I stood quite still, remembering the nights at Latchford Hall, and I said, "Was he wearing a low-crowned hat with a wide brim?"

Charlie closed his eyes in a supreme effort of recollection. Then he said, "I never saw any 'at. If I see 'im again, I'll take more notice."

I slept uneasily that night. A man on a horse? I had dreamed of one such man and met another in Wynford. But . . . an American? Charlie could never have mistaken Philippe Chatillon for an American, and if my dream had been reality, then who could the strange night-rider be? Why was he now in London, asking about me? I continued to wonder for many days, and the nagging puzzlement had still not faded completely when it was revived by an encounter which left me dumbfounded.

⚭✌⚭ Chapter Six ⚭✌⚭

Christmas came and went. For me, as for Kate, it was an occasion of very mixed emotions, as we remembered the festivities of previous years. Kate was a little stiff and restrained with Alfie and Company when she was with us on Christmas Day, and I wished especially that she could have been more at ease with Alfie, for it was clear that he adored her as her mother's daughter. By contrast, I felt very much at home with the Peroni family on Boxing Day and our visit to the pantomime was a huge success, with Mrs. Peroni stoutly declaring that the paperhanging scene was the best part of the whole performance.

The new year was a few days old and I was busy in the store room at the back of the shop, when Helen, one of the other assistants, appeared in the doorway, round eyed. "Ai say, there's a *gentleman* customer, asking for you by *neame*, Bridget," she whispered in her over-refined accent. "He insists that he wishes to be served bai *you!*"

A gentleman customer was a rare phenomenon in Lady Grainger's Millinery Establishment, and even more surprising was that the customer had asked to be served by me. I made sure my hair was tidy, and then walked out behind the long shop counter. A man, standing with his back to me, suddenly turned around, and I found myself looking into the smiling face of Philippe Chatillon.

I stopped short, almost knocking a hat-stand over, then stood gazing in astonishment. "Good morning, mam'selle," he said, in the beautifully pitched voice I remembered so well. "I apologize if I have startled you." His eyes held mine without effort, and I could not have looked away if I had tried. "I hoped you would do me the honour of allowing me to take you to luncheon today," he continued.

I felt my cheeks burn with discomfiture. It was quite out of order for a virtual stranger to invite a young lady to take luncheon with him alone.

I managed to steal a glance at Helen and Maude. They were listening breathlessly, eyes shining with excitement, and they both gasped as I said firmly, "It is not my habit to accept such invitations from a gentleman of slight acquaintance."

Philippe Chatillon was unperturbed. "I was hoping to make our acquaintance less slight, mam'selle. May I escort you home at the end of the day?"

"I prefer that you do not, m'sieur." It was an answer given from instinct rather than thought. I did not dislike Philippe Chatillon, in fact I found myself strongly attracted to him, but it rather frightened me that I felt weak when this man looked at me. I had once, in my most desperate hours, shocked myself by wondering how one became a "kept" woman, and the thought came to me now that here was a man who would not find it hard to acquire a mistress whenever he wished. But apart from this touch of fear, I wanted above all to draw a line across the past. Our lives at Latchford Hall had ended in nightmare, and I was determined that nothing should remind us of it.

Philippe Chatillon stood eyeing me with a thoughtful expression, and after a long silence he spoke quietly, in French. "I believe you speak fluent French, mam'selle?"

I replied in the same language. "Reasonably fluent, m'sieur."

"I congratulate you on your accent. May I ask if you have discovered what I suggested you might discover when we last met? That your father had left you a riddle to solve?"

For the first time in weeks I thought of the letter which lay tucked away in my writing case. I said nothing, but kept looking steadily at the French detective with what I hoped was an impassive stare. After a few seconds he said, still in French, "You have not answered my question, mam'selle. I asked if you have found anything which you feel may carry a hidden message."

I felt myself blink. Then I looked down at my hands and told a flat lie. "No, M'sieur Chatillon, I have found nothing such as you describe." I did not feel proud of myself at that moment, but I had no intention of amending what I had said.

As I looked up again he nodded slowly and said, "I see."

I was very much afraid that he did see, and I was wondering apprehensively what he would say next. To my relief, he bowed. "I will take my leave of you, then," he said in English. "But I hope we will meet again."

Our meeting was to be sooner than I expected. At seven o'clock that evening, as I reached Cambridge Circus, I saw Philippe Chatillon step out into the road ahead of me, take off his hat, and hold out his hand. I did not want to stop, but I pulled on the brake and drew my bicycle to a halt beside him.

His face was serious as he said, "Please forgive me for any embarrassment I caused you this morning, mam'selle." He took something from the inside pocket of his jacket as he spoke. "But there are some matters on which I must speak with you. As you know, I am a sort of policeman, and I would be obliged if you would tell me if you have been approached by this man."

I took the photograph from his hand and stared at the half-length portrait of a man in his middle thirties. He had a lean face, very wide-set eyes, and short thick hair above a high fore-head. After a few seconds I shook my head and held out the photograph to Philippe Chatillon. "No, I have never seen him. Why should he approach me?"

"Because he may think that you hold the key to great riches, mam'selle." He took a silver pencil from his pocket, wrote on the back of the photograph, and returned it to me. "Please keep this to remind yourself of what I say now. This man is a fraud, liar, and cheat. He is also clever and very dangerous."

Perhaps because I was so tired, the words made little impression on me. I realized that my father might have hidden a hoard of valuable jewellery, but since nobody was ever likely to discover the truth of the matter there was small chance of the supposed hoard being sought by thieves of the underworld. Then I remembered Charlie's encounter with a stranger. "Is this man an American?" I asked. "What is his name?"

Philippe Chatillon said, "I regret to tell you that the man I am warning you against is a compatriot of mine. I could give you

a dozen names he has used, but he can always find a new one. Please beware of him, and trust no word he may say to you."

I slipped the photograph into the handbag which hung from the handlebar of my bicycle and said as politely as I could, "You are most kind, m'sieur. I shall remember what you have said." Suddenly I felt exhausted. "I really do not know what you want of me," I went on, "but I assure you it has not been easy for me to cope with the problems arising in the last year. And I should be grateful to be left alone, to do the best I may."

For a moment he looked almost harassed as he said in a low voice, "I would be glad to help you in your difficulties, mam'selle, and I will tell you what I want of you. This is not at all the time or place, but you have left me no choice. Since I first met you near your home in Wynford I have been unable to forget you. In simple terms, I wish to call upon Miss Bridget Chance."

I stared at him in astonishment. After a moment I pulled my scattered wits together and said, "I am honoured, M'sieur Chatillon, and taken very much by surprise."

"For that," he said quickly, "I must ask your pardon. I might have written, perhaps, but I prefer to speak with you face to face. I have matters to keep me here in England for some time, but I would have come in any event, to say to you what I have just said. Speech is more honest than the written word."

Again I saw that warm smile, but as he spoke I knew that I had arrived at a decision which had nothing to do with logic, and I broke in quickly, "I must tell you that I wish to sever all links with the past, and that I do not wish you to call upon me. You have been very kind, but, as I said, I simply wish to be left alone. Please accept this as my final word."

He stood gazing down at me with an expression I could not fathom. Then he nodded slowly. "I think you are a very resolute person, mam'selle, and I respect your answer. I ask only that if you have need of my professional help, you will not hesitate to write to me." He slid a card from his wallet. "This will be my address for the next few weeks."

I took the card and managed to smile as I said, "You are very kind, sir, and I will call upon you in case of need. I hope you will excuse me if I leave you now."

He raised my hand to his lips. "Au revoir, Mam'selle Bridget."

I mounted my bicycle and pedalled away, thinking what an undignified way it was to end such a conversation. It was also typical of Bridie Chance.

An hour later, when Alfie and Company had left for the theatre, I lay in the splendid bath, feeling the hot water ease the weariness from my limbs as I thought about the strange happenings of the day. It occurred to me that something at least of what Kate had predicted had actually come to pass. Philippe Chatillon was certainly a very handsome man, and probably rich. He had not exactly asked me to marry him, but he had made the first step. And I had refused. I looked down the length of my too-long legs and sighed. "What a fool you are, Bridie Chance," I murmured. It was true enough. If I had been asked why I had refused I could not have given an answer, for my wish to break with the past was no more than a part of it. There was something else, and it was too deep within me to be discerned.

Chapter Seven

It was at the end of February that the double disaster struck. Alfie Perkin and Company were just finishing their season of pantomime and would then be free of bookings for three weeks while preparing for a tour of the Midlands and the North. I would stay on in the flat while they were away but I knew that I would miss them dreadfully, and I was also troubled by the realization that after five months in London I had managed to save only two or three pounds. In another six months I would need ninety to cover my liabilities to Signor Peroni and Nannie Foster.

The first blow fell when Lady Grainger swept into the shop one morning and told me that she would not require my services beyond the end of the week. I felt ill with shock. Later in the day I learned from Maude that Lady Grainger wished to bring in a girl she had taken under her wing. Helen and Maude were sympathetic, but obviously relieved that I was the victim.

When I arrived home that evening, Ethel took one look at me and opened her arms. I ran to her and sobbed, and haltingly told them both what had happened.

"Miserable old cow," said Ethel indignantly. "Not fair, giving anyone the sack like that." She looked at Alfie. "How about me going along there and giving her a piece of my mind?"

"Oh, no!" I exclaimed hastily. "I have to work there for the rest of the week."

"No, you 'aven't," Alfie said firmly. "You'll only be miserable as sin, and it's not worth it. You 'elp us to get ready for the tour, and I'll pay you the same as what you've been paid at the shop." He lifted a hand as I started to protest. "You'll be earning your corn all right, even if you just do the cooking. And there's letters to be done, and lists to be made, and all sorts of things. My word, you'll be busy all right. Eh, Ethel?"

I ran to kiss him on the cheek. "Oh, Alfie," I said, "I do so hope that one day I can help you in some way, in return for all you've done. I'd be so happy."

He patted me on the shoulder, smiling and embarrassed at the same time. "Well, you never know, do you? Now then, you come along with me to Drury Lane tomorrow morning, with a pencil and a notebook, and I'll get you working on the transport bookings for our scenery."

All next day I spent moving between the Drury Lane Theatre and the warehouse near Blackfriars where Alfie rented storage space for the scenery and props. These had to be dispatched by train when the tour began. It called for considerable organization, and by the end of the second day I was joyfully certain that I was earning my wages. But by the fifth day all our plans were in ruins, for it was then that the second disaster struck.

At nine o'clock in the morning Charlie was walking along Holborn to buy himself some cigarettes. As he passed a brewer's dray which was being unloaded outside a public house, one of the huge casks of ale slipped free. It struck Charlie with great force, hurling him against the wall and breaking his right leg between knee and thigh. He did not lose consciousness, and five minutes later a bystander was at our door, panting out his tale of what had occurred. Within an hour Charlie was in one of the operating theatres in St. Bartholemew's Hospital.

This was a day in which we scarcely knew what to do with ourselves, we were so dazed by the shock. Alfie and Ethel were allowed to see Charlie for a few minutes in the evening, and returned to say that he seemed quite comfortable but rather sleepy from medicine given him to dull the pain. I had made dinner, but none of us had any appetite. As we picked at the food, I asked hesitantly, "Did anyone say how long it would be before Charlie recovers?"

They looked at each other. Ethel, grey-faced, lifted a hand to her chignon. "The sister reckoned three months if all goes well," she said, her penetrating voice strangely subdued.

"It was a clean break," said Alfie, "so the leg shouldn't mend shorter than it was. But even when Charlie's up and about, it'll take the muscles a long time to get back to what they were. Anyway, they'll keep 'im in Bart's for two or three weeks and then he can go to a convalescent place in the country."

"Please don't think I'm being inquisitive, Alfie, but won't that be very expensive?"

His rubbery face twisted into an expression of wry relief. "Well, it would be, 'cept I took out insurance for all of us about five years ago. Got cover for 'ospital expenses and convalescence for a whole year. You should've heard the way some people laughed. They don't think much about tomorrow, not in our business they don't."

Wisdom and forethought were certainly proving their worth. But if Alfie had to rest the act until Charlie returned, then I could not possibly remain as a burden upon his resources. "How difficult will it be for you," I asked, "if you can't work for several months?"

Alfie sucked in air through his teeth and screwed up one eye thoughtfully. "Well, we won't end up broke, because we've put a bit away. But the trouble is, it might finish the act, Bridie. If you drop out of circulation, you get looked on as a sort of has-been." He sat frowning down at the tablecloth, picking idly at a few crumbs beside his plate.

After a silence I said, "Perhaps this is a silly question, but could you get somebody to replace Charlie for a while?"

"It's not silly, dear," said Ethel. "It's just going to be very 'ard to do. Oh, we know a few eccentric dancers who could do the steps, but I can't think of anyone that would fit in with us nice and natural, can you, Alfie?"

He shook his head. "It's deeper than it looks, making people laugh. If you get it just a little bit wrong, they'll sit on their 'ands."

I began to clear the table. This would be a bad moment for me

197

to say I must fend for myself, but I would certainly have to speak soon. Whatever the cost to me, I could impose on my friends no longer.

Next day I bought a small basket of fruit for Charlie, which Alfie and Ethel took with them when they went off to the hospital that evening. At eight o'clock they returned and sat down to the dinner I had prepared. They were both in a mood I found hard to fathom, for they spoke little and seemed distracted, yet I sensed an odd spark of something in them that might almost have been optimism.

When dinner was over, Alfie and Ethel looked at each other, then at me. Alfie rose from his chair and left the room, saying, "Hang on a second, Bridie." When he came back, he was carrying one of the costumes Charlie used for the "Water Board" sketch, which had been brought home for mending. "Will you do something for me, Bridie?" Alfie said. He looked at me very soberly, his eyes anxious yet hopeful. "Will you go an' put it on?"

I could not imagine what he was about. I felt one side of my mouth turning up in a questioning half-smile. "Put it *on?* But . . . ?"

Ethel said, "It was Charlie's idea. It came to 'im in the night, while he was worrying about the act, and he fair burst out with it, soon as we got there. 'Bridie can do it, Ma,' he said. 'She moves right an' she's got the face an' she'll be top-'ole once she's got over 'er nerves.' That's what he said, didn't he, Alfie?"

I stared numbly from one to the other. At last I managed to say, "Me? Acting Charlie's part? *Me?* But—it's impossible! I can't act, and I'd die of fright if I had to go out on the stage. Charlie must have been delirious even to *think* of it!"

When I trailed into silence Alfie said doggedly, "It's the best idea Charlie ever 'ad. We both wondered why we didn't think of it ourselves. You've got the knack of using your face in a way that's naturally comic."

"Oh yes, my face!" I gave a nervous laugh. "But there's the dancing, and that's absolutely vital to the act. If you perform those sketches with someone who can't do the Chicken Walk and the Crab Glide you . . . you'll get the bird!"

"I can teach you enough," said Alfie, "if you're ready to work eight hours a day on it. After all you don't 'ave to speak a word in the act, do you?"

Ethel said diffidently, "It could save the act for us."

I stood mute, pale and inwardly cringing at the enormity of the ordeal I was being asked to face.

"Will you try it for us, Bridie?" said Alfie. "Please?"

I could never do it. Never. I tried not to remember how good Alfie and Ethel had been to me, how loyal, generous, and affectionate. I did not dare think of the debt I owed them, for I was about to refuse them the only help they had ever asked of me.

I drew a breath to speak, and my mouth said, "All right, Alfie. I'll try."

I heard the words with shock and astonishment, but there was no going back. After a long time, and with what felt like a terrible smile, I took the clothes from Alfie and walked to my bedroom on legs which seemed suddenly to have turned to wood.

Ten minutes later I returned wearing the costume: dark blue trousers, a jacket, and with my hair pinned up under a cap.

"Nice long legs," Ethel murmured as they eyed me appraisingly. "We'd 'ave to alter the costumes a bit, but that's nothing. I don't know what's best to do about the hair, though."

"I'll have it cut short if you wish," I said at once, hoping to show my willingness.

Alfie shook his head. "No," he said firmly. "Let's leave it like that. We want to make a big show of 'er being a girl—like a special feature of the act. She'll be a male impersonator."

Alfie was beginning to show increasing enthusiasm as he talked. "We'll spend tomorrow at Mac's rehearsal 'all in Charing Cross Road. I can get Vera to play the piano for us." He patted my arm. "But we can make a start tonight."

It was nine o'clock when Alfie began to count slowly, "One, two, three, four . . ." as he showed me how to perform a sideways, floating step called the Crab Glide. Again and again I tried to imitate the elusively simple movement of Alfie's feet. After half an hour I broke into tears, and by ten I hated both Alfie and Ethel. I had acquired what Alfie called four bars of the Crab Glide, but I did it with leaden slowness, plodding and hopping where Alfie swayed and floated.

By eleven o'clock I could go through the movements of eight bars, enough to take me across the average stage and back, and I no longer hated my friends, for I was too tired to nourish any particular emotion. I had drifted into a strange kind of limbo in which I went on doing the same thing over and over again without thought.

At half-past eleven the breakthrough came. As I stood waiting for Alfie's count, my mind was a blank. He said, "One, two, three, four . . ." and I began to move through the same steps I had now performed several hundred times. But there was something different. I was gliding smoothly . . . almost floating . . . and despite all weariness my body felt lighter, more fluent, more harmonious within itself than ever I had known before. A sense of astonishment and delight touched me as I came to a halt.

"Not bad," Alfie said. "Try it again, Bridie. Your feet and your body know what to do, so let 'em get on with it." The magic remained through the next three attempts. "Right," Alfie said. "You've made a good start, and it's nearly midnight. You 'op off now and have a good 'ot bath. You'll be stiff in the morning, but Ethel can show you exercises to 'elp loosen you up."

In a confused stupor I said goodnight and went to run a bath. Later I lay in it sleepily, feeling the hot water draw the aches from my weary muscles. I had no energy left with which to think, and was aware only of a tiny, pinpoint glow of triumph somewhere deep inside me. I slept very soundly that night.

At breakfast next morning Alfie looked up from his plate and said, "We didn't talk about money last night, Bridie."

I was mentally going through the Crab Glide, and said, "Money? What money, Alfie?"

He grinned. "Stop dancing inside your 'ead for a minute, and listen. If you're going to be in the act, you've got to 'ave a proper wage. I've talked it over with Ethel, and we reckon four pounds a week an' all found."

I let my face run riot with astonishment, and at last I said, "Four pounds? But that's ridiculous!"

Alfie chuckled. "Don't look so flabbergasted, young lady. There's plenty of professional gents like solicitors and doctors who'd be glad to pick up what a good music hall turn can get. Alfie Perkin and Company never take less than thirty-five quid a week, so I reckon we can afford your four quid easy enough, Bridie, and you'll be earning it all right, don't you worry."

I sat staring down the table at him, my head buzzing. Four

pounds a weeks was riches. Certainly it would solve all my money problems, at least for as long as it lasted.

That day was spent with Alfie in a hired rehearsal room over a tavern in Charing Cross Road. On the way we had stopped at a theatrical costumiers to buy me some rehearsal clothes, and as soon as I had changed we began to work. To my infinite relief, I was able to perform the Crab Glide straight away, and with the almost magical effect of floating. I could see myself in the great looking glass at the end of the room, and Alfie spent the first hour teaching me how to use my arms, head, and even fingers to enhance the steps. After an hour, I was able to combine all the elements of the little dance, though in a somewhat rough and ready way. The piano accompaniment helped me far more than I had expected.

"Right," said Alfie at last. "We'll spend 'alf an hour every day polishing that up. Now let's start the Chicken Walk. Watch me now . . . you do a sort of contrary movement with your 'ead and tail, see? The opposite of normal. All right, try it with me."

After half an hour I was in despair again, but Alfie was a patient and encouraging teacher. Slowly but surely I improved. At the end of the day I was tired, but strangely enough not nearly so leg-weary as I had been at the millinery shop. By the end of three days I had learned the Willow Strut, the Stork Step, and the Hesitation Walk, and on the fourth day Ethel came to the rehearsal rooms to view my progress with a fresh eye. I felt nervous, but after I had gone through all my steps to music, Ethel was genuinely delighted. "Oh, my word, you've done wonders, dear, you really have. You've certainly saved our bacon, Bridie."

A wave of panic swept me. I had been concentrating so hard on the work that I had given no thought to the end in view. "Oh dear!" I said. "I'm so worried that if I ever get onto the stage I shall simply freeze, and not be able to move."

"You'll move all right," said Alfie cheerfully. "I'll make sure of that. Now let's work it out, eh? We'll take a few more days to polish up the dancing, but tomorrow's Sunday, and you mustn't miss seeing your sister Kate, so we'll make that a half day. Then Wednesday we'll start doing 'alf a day on dancing and the rest rehearsing 'The Paper'anger's Mate'. You'll have to be 'ere every afternoon for the sketch, Ethel, otherwise we'll never get our timing right. One thing's certain . . ." he hugged me. "We won't 'ave to cancel. Alfie Perkin and Company are going on tour."

That evening I went with Ethel to the hospital to visit Charlie for the first time. He seemed very pleased to see me, and kept assuring me that I was going to be "top-'ole" in the act.

"You make sure you 'ave plenty of practice with the props, Bridie. 'Specially the paper'anger's paste. Mustn't get it on your boots, or it mucks up your dancing. Sticky, see? And make sure your cap has a really stiff peak. I got a very thin bit of wood in mine. Uncle Alfie stands you against the wall an' runs the big paste brush down you from top to toe. If the peak's a bit floppy, you get your eyes pasted, see?"

I said, "Thank you, Charlie. I'll be glad of all the hints you can think of. I'm really very frightened."

He winked. "It's enough to frighten anyone. Tell you what I did first few times I was on. Every time I felt I was going to freeze, I'd think to meself, 'Thank Gawd I 'aven't got to open me mouth!' You remember that, Bridie. It'll 'elp ever so."

"I'm sure it will, and thank you Charlie . . ." Looking at his bright face, I thought how kind and uncomplaining he had been, and I gave him a big smile.

He laughed delightedly. "That's the ticket, Bridie. You'll be all right."

Next day, a Sunday, I went to Signor Peroni's house as usual to spend some time with Kate. She was in a rather strange, absent-minded mood, but when I told her what was happening she collapsed in her chair with a fit of the giggles.

"Oh, Bridie, no! You mean you'll be in that sketch we saw at the pantomime, doing funny dances and getting paste all over you? Won't you die of fright?"

"Quite possibly, but I shall try not to. Now listen," I went on, "I shall be away on tour for several months, and this is the last time I shall see you for a while."

Kate looked a little taken aback. "Oh dear, I shall miss you so much, Bridie."

"I'll write to you every week, and I'll give you a list of dates and theatres so you'll know where to write to me."

"Yes, please do, but you won't be cross if my letters aren't very frequent, will you? I seem to be so busy all the time."

I laughed. Kate had always been a reluctant writer of letters. "No, dear, I won't be cross," I said.

She looked down at her hands, gently massaging the long beautiful fingers, and said slowly, "Bridie, did Mama or Papa leave any message for us? A letter, perhaps?"

I was not sure I wanted to speak of Papa's letter, and to give myself time to think I said, "A message? What makes you ask?"

"Oh . . . I was just wondering about it. I felt certain Papa would have left word for Mama. You know how he adored her."

In those few seconds I made up my mind that Kate was entitled to know the truth, and I said, "Yes, he left a letter for Mama with Tom Kettle, who gave it to me, but Mama was too ill to see it. I read it after she died. It was a kind of love letter. I did wonder briefly if part of it was a cryptic message, but I'm sure it wasn't."

"Have you kept it?"

"I've got it tucked away somewhere. But why?"

"Oh, I was just thinking I'd like to see it. You can't be *completely* sure there's no cryptic message."

I felt suddenly uneasy. "Well, if there is, Mama was the only one who could possibly have understood it. I'll show it to you when I have time. Now tell me how you're getting along at the college."

Her lovely face lit up. "I'm so happy there, Bridie, I really am. As for my music, well, you must listen to me play."

After tea, when I had told the astonished Peronis about my new career, Kate played my favourite Chopin nocturne. There was an exciting new quality in her rendering of it, even to my rather undiscriminating ear. As I watched her play, I knew it would be many months before I saw her again. I could not know that it would be in another country, and in circumstances so cruel for my beloved Kate that my heart would break for her.

✎⊙ Chapter Eight ⊙✎

Holborn was almost deserted and dusk had fallen as I neared home that evening. A little way ahead of me, under a street lamp, a man was hailing a cab. I knew at once that I had seen the man before, but could not think where. I could not place him among

Alfie's friends, I had certainly never seen him at the shop, and I did not remember him from Suffolk or Cambridge.

The puzzle kept nagging me at intervals throughout the evening, despite the fact that we spent two hours going through the sketch, but at three in the morning I came suddenly wide awake with the shock of recollection. Climbing out of bed, I lit a candle, went to my dressing table and took out the photograph Philippe Chatillon had given me. A lean face, wide-set eyes, short thick hair. This was the face of the man I had seen in Holborn, the man Philippe Chatillon had called a fraud, liar and cheat. I turned the photograph over and looked at the words pencilled there in the detective's round, untidy hand. *This man is dangerous.*

For a while I sat wondering what should be done, and then realized that there was nothing I could do. Yet I sat studying the photograph and turning it over to read the words on the back. Something was amiss. It was like hearing a single wrong note in a series of chords, and not quite knowing where it had occurred. At last I shook myself irritably and climbed back into bed, telling myself that I was letting my imagination run away with me.

By the end of the second week of my training I could have performed "The Paperhanger's Mate" in my sleep. I no longer worried about the eccentric dancing, for I now had far greater worries arising from the hundred and one tiny details in my "routine". We were rehearsing with props now, and I had once spent two hours with a plank on my shoulder practising to turn round at exactly the right speed to match the timing with which Ethel, her back to me, kept bending down to speak to Alfie. Each time she bent, the plank had to miss her chignon by inches. During the third week we went through the full sketch dozens of times.

On Saturday morning we went to see Charlie for the last time. That afternoon we left for Nottingham. Harold, the lugubrious man who looked after our scenery, had already gone on ahead to arrange lodgings for us, or "digs" as everybody called them.

As our train pulled out of the station I was suddenly swept with horror. What on earth was I doing? How could I ever have imagined that I might become a variety artiste and replace Charlie Perkin? It was wild lunacy. Bridie Chance was a plain, clumsy girl, and if I had been chuckled at almost all my life it was not because I was witty or clever. Alfie and Ethel knew what

I was suffering, and I was glad that they did not try to allay my fears. Perhaps they knew that such fears simply had to be faced and endured.

When we reached Nottingham we found Harold waiting with two carriages. He reported morosely that all our scenery had arrived safely and that he had secured rooms for us at Mrs. Pratt's.

"That's all right then," said Alfie cheerfully. "Ah, 'allo Maggie, how are you, duckie?" The last words were addressed to a dark-haired young woman who had alighted from the train.

She stopped and said, "I'm all right, Alfie. Sorry about Charlie, though. I hear you're using a girl to replace him?"

Alfie nodded towards me and said, "That's right. Friend of ours, Bridie Chance."

As he spoke I remembered the young woman. I had seen her perform the first time I had gone to a music hall. Now, she looked at me curiously and said. "Chance? Wasn't that the man who—?" She broke off with an apologetic smile and said, "I'm sorry. Good luck with Alfie and Company."

I said, "Thank you," and she moved on.

"That bother you, Bridie?" Alfie murmured.

I shook my head. "No, it doesn't seem very important now."

"Good. You won't find it's important to music 'all people, mostly. They've got better things to worry about."

"She's Margaret Dane, isn't she?" I asked. "Didn't I see her at the Canterbury?"

Ethel said, "That's right, dear. She had the first turn. Not much of an artiste, poor old Maggie, but she's a nice girl."

Alfie looked up and down the platform. "What's 'olding up our luggage, I wonder?"

"Three porters gawping into that van," Harold said irritably. "I'll go and wake them up, Mr. Perkin."

"No, 'ang on, they're getting a horse out. Look."

We were all staring down the platform now, and I saw the most splendid mount step quietly from the open doors of a van. It was a red roan, and it moved with the unruffled arrogance of a creature aware that it was a king among its kind. At first I could not see the man who held the bridle on the far side of the horse, but then he swung up into the saddle, paused to speak to the porters, and began to move at a walk along the platform towards us.

He rode with long legs in long stirrups, wearing narrow trousers and a jacket of fine leather. On his head was a black hat, broad-brimmed, low-crowned, a kind I had seen in the dream which had come to me in the dark of night at Latchford Hall . . . if indeed it had been a dream.

"My word!" said Ethel. "I never saw anyone like that before."

"He's what they call a cowboy, Ethel," replied Alfie.

I scarcely heard them, for I was gazing at the approaching rider and trying to make sure that my telltale face was not showing my astonishment. I could make him out more clearly now. He was tall and loose-limbed, with a very brown and weathered face, and his manner as he rode was completely relaxed. Beneath the brim of the hat I could see a thatch of straw-coloured hair, and he wore a moustache, trimmed short.

"I wonder what a cowboy's doing in Nottingham?" Ethel mused. "Seems funny, doesn't it, Alfie?"

"Well, it would," agreed Alfie, "if it wasn't this Yankee bloke Nathan McFee. Jimmy Samuels, the agent, was telling me about 'im. Says McFee does a novelty act with a horse and a lasso. You know, a rope. He's well down the bill for this tour because he's new, but Jimmy says give him a year and he'll be in the top five."

I could see now that the man's eyes were vivid blue with crow's feet at the corners. He had a nose which looked as if it had been broken at some time, and a square chin, clean-shaven. The man had almost reached us, and now he lifted a lazy hand to the brim of his hat and said, "How do, ladies." The blue eyes rested amiably on Alfie. "Sir."

Alfie said, "Hello, friend. Nathan McFee?"

The man reined to a halt, then swung down from the saddle and took off his hat. "Recognized you, Mr. Perkin. I've seen your act more than once. Didn't figure you'd know me, though." His voice was deep and drawling, with a pleasant twang.

"Jimmy Samuels mentioned your act," Alfie said. "Where are you staying, Mr. McFee?"

"Jimmy fixed up for me to lodge with a Mrs. Pratt."

"Ah, you'll be all right there," said Alfie. "Very nice digs. Always stay there ourselves. We've got a couple of cabs waiting, so we'd be glad to take any luggage for you."

Nathan McFee indicated his saddlebags with a big brown hand.

"That's real neighbourly of you, but I have the habit of travelling light. Be glad to follow your cab, though, if you'll allow. Save me hunting around for Mrs. Pratt's."

The porters approached with our luggage, and as we made our way to the station exit Nathan McFee said, "I was sorry to hear about the accident to the young feller. That was real bad luck."

"It was an' all," Alfie agreed. "Still, we got a first-class replacement for Charlie." He snapped his fingers in annoyance as we halted by the two cabs. "I'm forgetting me manners, not introducing you proper. This is my sister Ethel, Charlie's mum, and this is an old friend of the family, Bridie Chance, who's taking Charlie's place for the time being."

Nathan McFee bowed to Ethel. Then the blue eyes rested on me. "Miss Bridie. Pleasure to make your acquaintance."

I dropped a small curtsy, caught a heel in the hem of my dress, and would have over-balanced if Nathan McFee had not caught me by the elbow. I should of course have tried to remain dignified, but before I realized it I had rolled up my eyes despairingly, and was saying, "Oh, dear. Thank you, Mr. McFee."

He grinned slowly, but his eyes were friendly as he released me. "My pleasure, ma'am." He leaned down to pick up the hat he had let drop to save me from falling. As he slapped it against his thigh to dust it, I said, "Surely that's not a cowboy hat, Mr. McFee. Isn't it a gaucho hat?"

Nathan McFee looked at the hat thoughtfully. "That's correct, Miss Bridie," he said. "I was born in Wyoming, but I'm a wandering sort of man, and I once spent a few years down on the pampas in Argentina." He lifted the hat to put it on, and smiled. "Always liked myself better in this than a stetson."

Harold had finished supervising the loading of the luggage. "All ready, Mr. Perkin. We going to hang around all day?"

Mrs. Pratt's boarding establishment was a tall, four-storey house no more than half a mile from the Theatre Royal where we would open on Monday. The room Ethel and I were to share was large and pleasant, and as we unpacked Ethel chattered away happily in her shrill monotone, needing no comment from me. I remained quiet, and thought about Nathan McFee. It was extraordinary that I should have dreamed of a night-rider in a gaucho hat at Latchford Hall, and now I had met a horseman who must surely be the only man in England to wear such a hat. It was even more extraordinary if what I had seen earlier had not been a dream.

Ethel's voice penetrated my consciousness. ". . . I don't know about you, Bridie, but I could do with an early night, what with all that's to be done tomorrow."

Tomorrrow. Sunday. The last day before my ordeal. At once everything else was swept from my mind, and I could almost feel the blood chill within my veins. Nathan McFee and his hat ceased to exist for me, and I was in the grip of raw fear once again.

I slept fitfully that night, and at ten o'clock on the Sunday morning I was on the stage at the Theatre Royal, looking out over the tiers of empty seats. Again and again we went through the sketch, while a half drunk pianist called Reg pounded on the piano. I mimed, danced, grimaced, and wished that it was I who had broken a leg rather than Charlie.

Towards the end of the morning I passed through the barrier of despair to a grey limbo where I no longer cared about anything, and then things began to go better. For the last two rehearsals we put on costume and went through the sketch with no breaks. I made several mistakes, but Alfie seemed not too displeased. "It's much 'arder when you've got no people out front," he said. "I mean, they're part of it, really. You get a sort of response going between them an' you. It'll be different with an audience, you'll see." I was quite certain it would be different with an audience, and it was this difference which terrified me.

Ethel chatted away quite cheerfully as we left the stage and made our way to the dressing room allotted to us. There was a screen across one corner with a small hip-bath behind it. While I sponged the wallpaper paste off myself, Ethel asked, "What would you like to do for the rest of today, dear?"

"Oh Ethel," I said miserably, "I'm so frightened that I don't know what I want to do. Maybe go into the country for an hour or so. I haven't seen any countryside for so long, and Mrs. Pratt told me there are some nice woods nearby."

"All right, dear, we'll see what Alfie says."

We found him still on-stage with Harold, discussing details of lighting, scenery, and music cues. When Ethel made her request he shook his head with the first sign of impatience I had ever seen him show. "Blimey, 'ave a heart. I got too much to do."

208

I began to say, "No, please don't bother, Alfie—" when a voice spoke from the back of the theatre. "Hope you'll pardon me for butting in, Mr. Perkin, but I'd be happy to escort your two ladies. I had a fancy to look at some country myself today."

We peered across the tiers of seats, as Nathan McFee rose to his feet and strolled down the centre aisle. "Came to get the feel of the house, Mr. Perkin. Didn't want to intrude, so I just sat there and watched your last rehearsal." He reached the orchestra pit and stood looking up at me. "Wasn't easy to keep from laughing out loud. You're going to be fine, Miss Bridie. Just fine."

I felt a small spark of hope come to life within me, and I returned his smile with a glow of pleasure.

Alfie scratched his head. "What about it, Ethel? Do you and Bridie want a run out with Mr. McFee here?"

Ethel had blushed slightly and was almost simpering. "Ooh, well, yes, that would be ever so nice, wouldn't it?"

The blue eyes looked at me. I said, "You're very kind, Mr. McFee. We shall look forward to it."

He gave a little bow. "No more than I shall, ma'am. If you'll excuse me, I'll go and see about hiring a phaeton."

At two o'clock he was waiting for us outside Mrs. Pratt's boarding house, and soon we were moving slowly along a grassy broadwalk in woods where buds of spring were beginning to speckle the dark branches. Ethel had chattered almost without pause for the first twenty minutes, and then lapsed into a sleepy silence. Nathan McFee drove with a sure hand and spoke little except to murmur occasionally to the horses.

Gradually the peace and beauty of the early spring day helped to ease the tension within me. I drew in long breaths of good air such as I had not tasted since leaving Suffolk, and after half an hour the sun broke through some thin white cloud to bring a pleasant warmth to the afternoon.

Nathan McFee half turned and said politely, "Will it trouble you ladies if I smoke?"

Ethel roused and said, "Not at all," and I said, "Please do."

From his jacket he produced a cigar which he clipped between his lips. He then struck a match on his boot, and as he lit the cigar I saw that it was thin and dark, like the stubs I had found in the grounds at Latchford Hall. A kind of wonderment possessed me

209

as I sat looking at those broad shoulders, remembering the occasions when I had seen or dreamed of the night-rider; but I asked no questions now, for I could not think how to begin.

Ten minutes later he drew the horses to a halt where the broad-walk ended in a cluster of small paths. When I started to speak he lifted a finger and nodded towards Ethel, and I saw that she was dozing. He climbed down from the driver's seat and helped me out of the phaeton, then we strolled for perhaps a hundred yards along a grassy path in companionable silence. As we turned I said with a smile, "We're both very quiet today, Mr. McFee."

"I hope you don't think me impolite, Miss Bridie. I figured you were busy with your own thoughts, and I didn't want to intrude."

I made a wry grimace. "I'm busy worrying about going on-stage for the first time, and I should be only too glad if anyone would intrude, but I thought perhaps you were a man of few words."

"Well, sometimes, I guess." We were strolling back towards the phaeton now, and he was looking about with an air of quiet pleasure. "Maybe another reason I haven't said much is because I've been busy taking everything in. First few weeks I was in England I fell in love with your countryside. I know deserts, mountains and plains, and they're good places in their way, but your woods and lanes, your little fields and small hills, bewitched me, Miss Bridie. I just want to go on looking."

His blue eyes were warm as he gazed about him, and I knew he had been speaking from the heart as I said, "Do you not have this kind of countryside in any parts of America?"

"Oh, sure, ma'am. They tell me New England's much the same as here in many ways. It's a part I've never seen, for I've lived and worked mostly in the west. But I'll go take a look when I get back to the States, and if it's all they say, then one fine day I'll buy a nice farm there and settle down."

We stopped short of the phaeton where Ethel was still sleeping, and turned to retrace our steps. I said, "Well, I hope you get your farm in New England, Mr. McFee."

"Thank you, Miss Bridie."

"You don't seem to be worried about your performance to-morrow, but of course you're not a beginner like me. Were you apprehensive the first time?"

"If I wasn't, I guess it was because I don't have the job of

210

making folks laugh, thank the Lord." He chuckled and shook his head. "I just go on and do what I can do easy enough. Spin the rope, do a few tricks with Lucifer, and that's all." He shrugged. "I've never yet got the bird, as you say here, but I guess there's always a first time."

"Yes." I swallowed hard as a wave of fear swept me.

Nathan McFee seemed aware of my thoughts. "You'll be scared pretty bad tomorrow, Miss Bridie, and there's no way round it," he said quietly. "But you have two fine professional artistes to support you, and you have your own courage to see you through."

I gave a nervous laugh. "You overrate my courage, Mr. McFee. I'm only doing it because I owe it to Mr. Perkin."

He drew on the cigar, took it from his lips, and eyed the glowing end. "This job you've taken on for Mr. Perkin would scare the living daylights out of most folk. Especially a young lady with no stage experience at all. You've got courage, all right, and you've shown it in other ways too."

"Other ways? I don't understand."

He hesitated. "Well . . . I hope I won't offend you by speaking of it, Miss Bridie, but I know your story. I was in England at the time. It must have been very tough for you." He looked at the stub of the cigar and tossed it away. Watching it fall through the air, I remembered seeing the small fiery glow in the darkness from my bedroom window, and then the trail of sparks curving down to the ground.

I said, "Mr. McFee, have you ever been in the village of Wynford, in the county of Suffolk?"

As I looked up into his face, I saw a flash of wariness. Then a veil came down behind his eyes and he said consideringly, "Wynford? Yes, I reckon I could have passed through there while I was up in Suffolk last year."

"May I ask where you were staying, Mr. McFee?"

"Little place called Thetcham, as I recall, ma'am. It was just at the time when the trouble hit you, and that's when I read about it in the newspapers."

"Did you have Lucifer with you?"

He smiled placidly. "Sure. We'd been appearing at a music hall in Norwich, and after that we stayed to have a look at Suffolk. Like I said, I fell in love with your countryside."

"Please forgive me for being so curious, but do you make a habit of riding at night?"

"Oh, sure. When I was on a cattle drive I always liked watching over the cows at night. It's a different world. Excuse me, but you're looking mighty fierce, Miss Bridie."

"Oh, I'm sorry. But I really must ask you—did you ever ride through the grounds of my home, Latchford Hall, by night?"

"That's possible, ma'am. I might have let Lucifer just wander where he fancied for a while." He looked at me anxiously, but the veil was still there. "Hope I didn't upset you by trespassing?"

I had asked a whole string of questions, and now I suddenly had nothing more to say. His explanation seemed quite plausible, but I was not convinced. I studied his brown face for a few seconds longer, but his look of polite patience revealed nothing to me. At last I said, "Is there anything more you want to tell me about your visit, Mr. McFee?"

He shook his head. "Why, no, ma'am. But I hope you'll look on me as a friend."

I put my doubts aside, smiled, and said, "Thank you, Mr. McFee. Are you sure it doesn't trouble you to offer your friendship to somebody whose father was the notorious Roger Chance?"

To my astonishment he threw back his head and burst into laughter. "Why, no, ma'am, it doesn't trouble me at all," he said. "You see, my pa was the notorious Hank McFee."

I blinked. "I'm sorry. Should I have heard of him?" I asked.

"I doubt it, ma'am. He was only wanted in two states, and as bank robbers go, he wasn't very successful."

I think my mouth fell open then. "*Bank robber?*"

Nathan McFee nodded, amusement still dancing in his eyes. "That's right. He robbed three banks, in all, according to what my ma told me later. I was just four at the time, and I don't really remember him. We had a patch of ground in Wyoming, but he got tired of hard work and left my mother to do all that while he went off robbing banks. At the third one he got away with a big bag of gold dust, but then his horse went lame and he had to hide in a dry gulch because there was a posse after him."

"Did he give up after the third one?" I asked.

"Yes, ma'am, he gave up sure enough, because that posse found him and they strung him up from the nearest tree."

"They . . . hanged him? How dreadful for your poor mother."

"She was a mite upset at the time, she told me. But she was too busy trying to scratch out a living to have time for fretting."

I shook my head slowly. "It all seems so strange, so different. . . ."

He inclined his head. "We're a new country, and a big one. There hasn't been time yet for us to have settled ways of doing things, like you have here. I can tell you this, Miss Bridie. Nobody gives a cuss that my father was a bank robber. Over there, you start fresh when you're born, so I'm judged as Nathan McFee. Myself, good or bad."

At that moment Ethel's high-pitched voice pierced the quiet woods. "Bridie! Mr. McFee!" As we walked towards her she waved. "Time to go, dear. It's getting a trifle chilly, I think."

As Nathan McFee drove us back to our lodgings, Ethel talked brightly the whole time without saying anything. I usually paid attention to some extent, for I was very fond of Ethel, but today I simply let the noise flow over me, leaving Nathan McFee to say, "Really, ma'am?" or "Well, now!" at appropriate moments. My thoughts and feelings were in great disorder as I digested what I had learned of the man who sat holding the reins.

Nathan McFee had offered me his friendship, but shadowy doubts hung in my mind. I was quite sure that almost all he had told me was true, but I was equally sure that he had been less than honest about the reason for his visit to Latchford Hall. And I did not want a friend I could not fully trust.

I DREAMED WILD DREAMS that night, and spent the next day feeling physically sick with nervousness. At the band call in the morning, we went through our musical cues with the orchestra. Afterwards I could eat no lunch, and felt quite unable to sit still. Every nerve in my body seemed to be twitching and my terror could scarcely have been greater if I had been awaiting a tumbril to take me to the guillotine.

Ethel was reading a book, and I was standing by the window, when there came a tap on the door. Ethel took off her spectacles and called, "Come in." The door opened and Nathan McFee took half a step into our room. "Hope you'll forgive the intrusion, ladies," he said, "but I wondered if Miss Bridie could spare half an hour to play a game of chess?"

I was drawing breath to refuse when Ethel said firmly, "Go along, Bridie. I can't take my nap with you flitting about like a grasshopper every other second." Before I knew what was happening Ethel was ushering me to the door, assuring Nathan McFee that there was nothing I would like better than to play chess with him.

I was still dazed when we settled in a corner of the big sitting room and Nathan McFee unfolded a worn board. He set out wooden chessmen, polished by much handling, and gave me the white pieces to play. Reluctantly, I began, but in spite of myself I enjoyed the game and was only narrowly beaten. When I looked at my watch I saw to my astonishment that an hour and a half had passed in which I had ceased to feel nervous!

"I hope you have time to give me my revenge, Mr. McFee," I said eagerly.

"Surely, ma'am. And if I'm not making too bold, I'd be glad to have you call me Nathan. I think you'll find stage folk aren't quite so formal as others."

I smiled. "Yes. I've noticed. Call me Bridie, if you wish."

"I'll feel honoured, ma'am." He began to set out the pieces for a new game.

"Who taught you to play chess?" I asked.

"My mother. Ma taught me lots of things. She was a woman with a good education. I greatly admired her. She died when I was seventeen. She was pretty much worn out, I guess."

"She must have been a very brave and determined lady," I said. "It seems strange that she—" I stopped short, angry with myself for being so tactless, but he smiled.

"Strange for an educated woman to marry a no-good bank robber? I guess it was, Bridie. My mother came of a good family, farming folk up in New Hampshire. Pa had come from out west and was working on their farm. She met him and fell in love. By all accounts he was a man who could charm a bird off a tree." Nathan centred a pawn on its square, and looked up at me with quiet eyes. "It happens, so they tell me: sometimes a young lady can get swept off her feet by a man who's real bad underneath."

"Did your mother run away with him?"

He nodded. "They ran away, got married, and the family disowned her. She soon found that Pa was a wastrel, and she spent the rest of her life bringing me up and scratching out a living."

I felt suddenly quite near to tears, "How terrible for her. Do you never feel bitter on her behalf, Nathan?"

He shook his head slowly. "The way she taught me was different. You do what you want, but you pay for it. I'll say one thing, though. I'm real proud of the way she stuck out her chin and paid." He leaned forward and moved a pawn forward one square. "Come on now, Bridie, do your worst."

Within three minutes I was absorbed in the new game. We were evenly matched, and finally both became so reduced in strength that we agreed on a draw. I looked at my watch again, found that it was five o'clock, took a deep breath, then looked across at Nathan McFee. "I'm going to start being frightened again now," I said. "But we shall leave for the theatre soon so at least I shall be occupied. I really think that if it hadn't been for you I should have fallen to pieces this afternoon. Please tell me, did you do this to help me?"

"Perhaps that came into it, but it was mostly selfish, ma'am. I was looking for the pleasure of your company."

I stood up, and he rose with me as I said, "Thank you, Nathan. I think you're a very kind man."

To my surprise he looked suddenly uneasy. "You have a generous heart, Bridie," he said quietly, almost as if speaking to himself, "but don't be too ready to trust folk." Before I could say anything he gave me a quick smile. "Thanks for the games, and good luck for tonight."

ᏚᎦᏇᎦ Chapter Nine ᏇᎦᏇᎦ

I stood in the wings, my heart thundering so loudly in my ears that I could barely hear Ethel talking beside me, or even the orchestra playing furiously while two jugglers tossed glittering clubs at each other. The orchestra struck a long loud chord, the jugglers took their bow, the curtain came down, and I saw Harold and two stage hands working quickly to set up the scenery for Alfie Perkin and Company.

Beside me, Alfie patted my shoulder, said something I did not take in, then moved on-stage. Ethel, in a too-large dress with a monstrous floral pattern, touched her cheek to mine and followed him. When the curtain rose, there would be thirty seconds of dialogue before the cue came for me to enter.

I stood alone, though there was all the usual bustle of off-stage activity behind me. My mind was blank, and I could remember nothing. No cues, no moves, no steps, no business. The orchestra played our introduction, the curtain rose, and there was a burst of applause. As it died away, Ethel's splendidly penetrating voice lifted indignantly in the part of Mrs. Prendergast.

"You may say what you laike, Mr. Perkin, but ai will nevah allow mai late 'usband's portrait to be moved. Nevah."

Alfie pushed back his bowler hat and rolled his eyes at the audience in despair. There was laughter, quickly hushed as they waited for the next words. Frozen, unable to move, I heard him call, "Arnold! Fetch the bucket, lad!" Somebody was jabbering furiously in my ear. On the stage, Alfie said, "*Now* what's become of him? *Arnold!*" Then a hand slapped my face and Harold thrust a bucket into my hand. "You're on, Miss Bridie, you're *on!*"

Reality exploded about me. I had missed my cue. The next moment I was on-stage, stepping out in the curious gait of the Hesitation Walk. From the vast black cave beyond the footlights came a blare of sound, part of it from the orchestra picking up the accompaniment of my walk, and part of it laughter from the towering creature with a thousand eyes which crouched beyond, huge as a mountain, unpredictable as an avalanche. The audience.

Sweat was trickling down my neck as I strutted on. Remember Charlie's advice. Think: *Thank God I don't have to open my mouth!* Swivel on one foot and put the bucket down. Do the Willow Walk and fetch the plank. Alfie has just descended the stepladder and got his foot stuck in the bucket. Begin the business of swinging the plank, missing Ethel's chignon by inches each time she bends to help Alfie. Count the tempo, turn two-three, look surprised two-three, turn again two-three. . . . Alfie's foot is free. Dialogue. Laughter. Mrs. Prendergast goes out to make tea. Start to paste and hang paper. Accidentally paper over the portrait. Peel the paper off, and half of the paint comes away from the portrait. Mrs. Prendergast returns, horrified. Miming, dancing, dialogue, and at last the end.

I have been on-stage for a hundred years in eight minutes. The curtain falls, and rises again for our bow. Alfie says sharply from the corner of his mouth, "Cap off, Bridie. Pull the pins out and shake your 'air loose." Steady applause, then a sudden extra surge of applause as I shake my hair loose.

We are in the wings at last. My legs are like jelly and I am sagging with exhaustion as Alfie's big arm clamps about my shoulders. "Oh, Alfie, can you forgive me for missing my cue?"

"Bridie dear, you made a tiny mistake but we covered it. You'll never do the same again." His face split in a great grin of relief and delight. "You didn't bring the 'ouse down, and nobody's going to offer you a solo spot at the top of the bill, but I reckon you were just a bit better than Charlie when he made his first appearance! Right, Ethel?"

Ethel beamed and flung her arms round me. "It's true, dear, honest it is. You've got a funny little style that's all your own." She stepped back to look at me, her eyes moist with tears. "I know we were all a bit nervous, but it'll get better and better now we've broken the ice, you'll see. You were lovely, Bridie, and I'm going to write to Charlie first thing tomorrow, and tell 'im so. He'll be ever so proud."

"I know someone else who'd've been proud of you," Alfie said, "And that's your dad." He reached out to take my sticky hands. "You saved our bacon," he said. "Without you, we didn't 'ave an act. We're never going to forget that, Bridie Chance."

Ten minutes later I was sitting in the hip-bath in our dressing room, barely able to keep my eyes open. Ethel had to help me dry myself and get dressed. Even when Nathan McFee appeared to congratulate me I could not stop yawning, and I left it to Alfie and Ethel to take me home as if I were a sleepwalker.

I SLEPT LATE next day, and ate heartily when I woke. Beneath my sense of relief I was beginning to worry again, and I wondered if music hall artistes ever became so experienced that they felt no apprehension at all. When I put the question to Alfie he grinned. "It'll get easier, Bridie, but I'll tell you one thing. If you don't feel a bit strung up, you 'aven't got the juice to make a real impression on the audience, if you see what I mean."

"Yes, I do, Alfie. No wonder a performance is more tiring than half a dozen rehearsals." I looked across at Ethel. "Shall we go shopping today? I'd like to buy a dress, to celebrate my début."

Alfie tapped a finger on the table. "You've 'ad nothing new since you came down to London, so you're going to buy yourself a whole wardrobe, young Bridie, and at *my* expense. But you won't find time today, because we're rehearsing. Don't forget we'll be doing the Water Board sketch 'alf the time we're playing Sheffield."

As I stood in the wings waiting for my cue on the second night I was still full of trepidation, but in no danger of panic, and by the end of the first week my fears had dwindled to little more than a quickening pulse and a tight feeling under the heart. I could not truly say that I ever enjoyed a performance, but I found great pleasure in the feeling that I was good enough to bring sudden roars of laughter from the audience.

On the third day Ethel and I went shopping in the morning, and that evening, after our performance, we joined Alfie and slipped into the stalls. The second act after the interval was billed as "Nathan McFee—Wild West Artiste", and when the curtain rose I felt almost as nervous as if I were appearing myself.

Nathan was already on-stage in his splendid gaucho costume, a white lasso in his hands. While the orchestra played a cheerful melody, he spun the rope in a wide noose parallel to the floor. He made a seemingly casual jump into the centre of the rope circle, and fed in more rope so that the noose expanded, shooting up above his head and falling almost to the floor. I was entranced.

After several more remarkable tricks with the noose, Nathan sent the lasso flying into the wings. The audience applauded. Lucifer appeared upstage, carrying a coiled rope in his mouth; he moved forward, butted Nathan gently aside, and then went down on one knee as if taking the bow himself. The audience roared and clapped. Lucifer stood up and carried the coiled rope to Nathan, who shook out the noose and started to spin it round himself again. Then, quite suddenly, he sprang into the saddle, still spinning the rope. Quickly the noose expanded to encompass both horse and rider, rising and falling, as Lucifer trotted round the stage. The noose grew larger still, and at last the great circle of rope occupied the whole stage. Then, to a splendid galloping tune, the curtain swept down on the scene.

Nathan took a bow to satisfactory applause. When he did not appear again for a second bow the applause dwindled quickly. Alfie nudged me, and we slipped from our seats.

"It's clever, all right," Alfie said as we rode home to Mrs. Pratt's. "But it could be twice as good. He makes his tricks look too easy and he don't use that horse enough."

Next day, at breakfast, I told Nathan how much I had liked his act, and I was pleased when he asked me to take tea with him that afternoon. After rehearsal I put on my new walking costume, and Nathan drove me to the Fortune Hotel.

When we were settled in the tearoom, I screwed up my courage and said I believed Alfie could help him improve his act. The words were hardly out when I regretted them, and added hastily, "Oh, please don't be offended, Nathan. I only meant—"

"Easy now, easy," he broke in with obvious amusement. "I'm not tetchy about my act, Bridie, and I'm sure Alfie could improve it. I learned to do a few tricks when I was herding cattle, and I figured I could work my way around England by doing a music hall act." He smiled. "But I've never thought about working up a real eye-catching presentation. This isn't a career for me. I'm just passing through."

"Oh." I concentrated on pouring tea, to hide my sudden dismay. "Will you be going back to America soon?"

"I'll be going when I've finished this tour."

I put down the teapot. "I shall miss you, Nathan. Oh dear, that isn't the sort of thing a young lady is supposed to say."

"No? I was glad to hear it, Bridie. And it'll be mutual." He hesitated. "Do you enjoy music? I was wondering if you'd allow me the honour of escorting you to a concert on Saturday."

I could feel my face light up with pleasure. It seemed I had scarcely known a moment of relaxation since I had agreed to take over Charlie's part. It would be a joy to sit in an audience, close my eyes, and simply listen to music.

"Yes, Nathan," I said. "Oh, yes, I would like that very much."

⧆⧆ Chapter Ten ⧆⧆

After three weeks at the Royal, we moved on to Sheffield. I was in some apprehension about my first performance in the Water Board sketch, but my fears were nothing like so great as they had been on that first night at the Royal, and in the event the sketch went down very well. By the time we came to appear at the Empire in Hull I had had six weeks of experience, and I was confident that I could play my parts without letting Alfie and Ethel down.

Every week I wrote to Charlie and Kate. Every week I had a lovely letter from Charlie, the grammar hopeless, the spelling atrocious, but filled with unbounded friendliness and enthusiastic reassurance. I had two rather hasty notes from Kate during those first three bookings. In the second she again spoke of Papa's letter, asking me to send her a copy, so she could see for herself that it contained no cryptic message. I felt unhappy about her suggestion, though I would have found it difficult to say why. After thinking it over, I wrote that I would show the letter to her on my return to London.

In our second week at Newcastle a subtle change happened on-stage during my longest dance, in "The Paperhanger's Mate". In those moments I knew that in some strange way I had moved into another class; it was as if all I had learned and practised suddenly became a part of me. I had never floated so deftly, never glided so smoothly, or strutted so effortlessly. The applause was very big that night, and became even louder when I shook my hair out to show I was a girl. In the wings Alfie gave me a great hug. "Now you know! Blimey, you got there quick, Bridie. Some people never do."

Nathan always watched us from the wings now. He smiled and said, "That was a humdinger of a performance, Bridie."

I was half laughing myself with excitement. "You must tell me what a humdinger is later," I said breathlessly. "Oh, mind the paste, Nathan! You'll get it on your lasso."

The magic stayed with me all through our booking in Newcastle. The Scottish audiences were not quite so enthusiastic, but from the day we opened in Leeds on our way south again, we were a great success. Alfie and Ethel insisted that I had exceeded their highest hopes, and certainly the audiences seemed to find my performance very comical. It was exciting to be on-stage waiting immobile, and then suddenly to take my cue, and for the first time in my life I seemed no longer to be clumsy.

Charlie was now on his feet again and was to join us in Manchester. To my joy, Alfie had said that there was no question of my leaving the act. I was to alternate with Charlie for the rest of the tour, and then Alfie would rewrite the sketches to incorporate an extra character.

"It's about time we put new life into the act," he insisted. "Watching you an' Charlie play off each other will be a real treat."

There was no doubting that his enthusiasm was genuine, and when I reviewed my situation I felt overwhelmed by my good fortune. I had acquired a wonderful new family, I was earning six times as much money as most girls of my age, and I was able to take care of Kate and Nannie Foster. My inward scars from the dreadful shocks of last summer were fading, and in Nathan McFee I had a friend with whom I was completely at ease.

Despite all this I found that I was troubled by a profound melancholy stemming from some nameless cause. I made great efforts never to let it show, but in Leeds and again in Manchester both Nathan and Ethel asked me if there was anything wrong. In Manchester I was able to offer an excuse, for I received a letter from Signor Peroni saying that he was anxious about Kate. She had become, as he put it, "at times contrary, and antagonistic to discipline," and she seemed secretive about her companions at the college. He wondered if I could write to her and try to find out if she was under some disruptive influence there.

I used this as an excuse for my melancholy, but truth to tell I was not greatly disturbed. I knew how capricious Kate could be, and felt sure the mood would pass more quickly if nothing was said or done. I wrote reassuring Signor Peroni, saying that I did not feel it would be wise for me to question Kate by letter, but that on my return to London I would have a serious talk with her.

Two days after writing the letter, I was to realize the reason for my strange melancholy. I came off-stage after a good performance to find Nathan in the wings as usual, chuckling so much that he found it hard to speak.

"What is it, Nathan?" I said.

He shook his head. "Just . . . just you, Bridie. You were so darned funny. Lord knows I've seen the act often enough now, but you really caught me under the ribs tonight."

I smiled and thanked him, but melancholy was like a stone within me. As I sat in my bath, sponging myself free of paste and grime, I suddenly knew the cause. In a small way I had become a successful clown. I was Comical Bridie Chance . . . smothered with paste, falling in a barrel of water,, miming with monstrously exaggerated facial expressions. This was how everybody saw me, even Nathan. But I was a girl. Not pretty or clever, but still a girl, and I longed to feel that one day I would be loved and wanted by a man I loved in return. In my heart I had felt, without realizing it, that this could not happen to a girl who was only a clown.

Then I laughed angrily at myself. No . . . I was lucky to be a clown, enormously lucky. And now that I knew the reason for my strange melancholy I would very quickly bring about a cure.

CHARLIE came up on the Sunday, and we met him at the station that afternoon. When he alighted from the train, we were all watching anxiously to see if he showed any hint of a limp. As we hurried towards him, with Nathan following, Charlie stopped, blinked, mimed surprise and alarm, then went floating back on those long elastic legs as lightly and easily as of old.

I almost wept with delight, and made myself hang back so that Ethel and Alfie could greet him first. Then I put my arms round his neck and kissed him, making him blush to his ears. "Hello, Charlie. You're looking wonderfully well."

"Thanks for the letters, Bridie. Going all right, then?"

"Well, I'm no match for you, Charlie dear, but I'm always trying to improve."

His eyebrows shot up. "No match? You're 'aving me on! I'm dying to see you do the act."

"You will, tomorrow. And I shall be very nervous, knowing that you're watching, but never mind. Now come and meet a friend of ours, Nathan McFee. He's on the programme with us, and he does a marvellous turn with a lasso."

Nathan extended a hand. "Glad to know you, Charlie. Haven't we run into each other before, somewhere?"

"Eh? Did we? Don't remember." Charlie looked almost panic-stricken. "Ah, 'ere's the porter with me luggage. We in digs with Mrs. Curtis as usual, Uncle Alfie? I'm dying for a cup of tea."

I wondered why Charlie was so disconcerted by meeting Nathan, but it was not until after tea that I had the opportunity for a private word with him. When I went up to my room, I found him lurking on the landing.

223

"Bridie," he whispered. "Can I come in for a sec? Something to tell you." He stepped into my room, and muttered hoarsely, "I didn't dare say, but that's *'im*, the bloke I told you about!"

"What bloke, Charlie?"

He drew a hissing breath of exasperation. "Him at the station! The Yankee! Oh, blimey. I thought he was going to say about . . . you know, the billiard 'all. That was the bloke who asked about you!"

"Oh!" The mists of bewilderment cleared suddenly. "You mean that Nathan McFee was the man in the billiard hall in London, who asked if I was courting?"

"M'mm, that's *'im*. I keep telling you, Bridie."

"Well, I expect there's a perfectly natural explanation, but it's surprising he hasn't said anything. I shall ask him about it."

"Oh, crikey, don't do that. I don't want 'im remembering the billiard 'all and spilling it to Ma!" Charlie ran a hand through his spiky red hair. "Please don't say anything, Bridie."

It was impossible to refuse. "All right, Charlie, I won't say a word. And if Nathan ever speaks to me about it I'll make sure he won't mention the billiard hall."

He exhaled a long sigh of relief. "Thanks ever so, Bridie. You're the best girl I ever knew. Well . . . I'd better 'op along now."

When he had gone I sat down and thought about Nathan McFee. Over the months of the tour we had become good friends, and for a few moments I allowed myself to dream that he might have seen me in London, wanted to make my acquaintance, and had first inquired about me. But it was not a very plausible explanation, for as far as I knew our coming together was entirely a matter of chance. I could not ask him about it, for I had given Charlie my promise, but I had to acknowledge that Nathan had concealed the encounter from me, and this raised doubts about one I had felt was a good friend.

Charlie sat in the audience the next night, but he was backstage before I reached the dressing room. His pale face was one huge grin of delight. "Cor, Bridie, you were first class."

I glowed with pleasure, for this was praise from a master of the art. Then I had to thrust back a familiar pang of melancholy at the thought that all he was praising me for was my clowning. Nathan had been in the wings, as usual, and we had exchanged a word or two as I came off, but I noticed that he was rather quiet. Since Charlie's arrival I had felt a little ill-at-ease with Nathan, and I seemed to sense a hint of wariness in him also.

Charlie rehearsed with Alfie all that week to get back in shape. Then he was going to take over from me, while I visited Nannie Foster for a few days. It was during my last performance that calamity nearly befell Mr. Alfie Perkin and Company. We were in the middle of "The Water Board Man" when a valve stuck in the water reservoir off-stage, and the jets failed. In the wings Harold was wrestling with the connections, and Nathan was moving to help him. I froze with horror. Next moment I heard Alfie saying, "'Ello! Look at those ants crawling all round the 'ole. I'll go and fetch some paraffin. You watch out they don't bite you, Arnold."

Then Alfie muttered, *"Dance, Bridie!"* and strode off. A sweat of fear broke out all over my body. I began to dance, as if trying to avoid hordes of ants which might crawl up my trouser legs. My impromptu solo lasted for perhaps a minute, and brought continued bursts of laughter, but my alarm as I dodged the imaginary ants was very little assumed. I could have cried with relief as a thin stream of water suddenly shot up from the manhole. Alfie came stalking back on-stage, dousing the "ants" from an old paint tin, and we were able to pick up the sketch where we had broken off.

The applause was good, and as we came off into the wings Alfie said, "Blimey, you'll never do better than tonight, Bridie. I was too busy to look, but I could 'ear 'em laughing."

Then Nathan McFee was in front of me, on his face a look I had never seen before. There I was in my soaking wet uniform with its too-short trousers looking half girl, half clown, and Nathan McFee put his hands on my shoulders, gazed down at me with a glow in his eyes that set my heart leaping. Alfie and Ethel had halted on either side of me, but he seemed unaware of them. "Bridie Chance," he said, lifting his quiet voice a little above the music, "Bridie Chance, I love you, and will you marry me, please?"

I stood dazed. The world stopped. Tears mingled with the water on my face. Then it was as if something within me opened like a flower, and I knew that I had been falling in love with Nathan McFee for several weeks past, perhaps from the time when I had first been troubled by that nameless melancholy.

Beside me, Ethel exclaimed, "Well I never!" And simultaneously

Alfie said in astonishment, "Cor blimey!" I laughed, put my arms up round Nathan's neck, and said, "Oh, dearest Nathan, yes. But what a time to ask!"

"I couldn't wait any longer," he said simply. Drawing me to him, he bent to kiss me gently on the lips, then held me close, ignoring grinning stagehands and everybody else backstage. "We'll go to supper at the Royston after my turn, to celebrate."

Later, I lay in the hip-bath in a hazy golden dream, letting Ethel's chatter pass me by unheard until I realized she must have asked a question.

"I'm sorry, Ethel," I called. "What was that?"

"I said will you go back with him to America, do you think, or will he stay here?"

"I haven't thought. What about Alfie and Company? He's been planning to change the sketches, and I wouldn't let you down."

"Don't talk daft. It's been lovely 'aving you, but we never thought it was going to last for ever, dear. I mean, it wouldn't do, really. You're a different class."

"Oh, Ethel! You and Alfie are the truest friends I've ever had."

"P'raps so, dear," Ethel said, her voice softer than usual. "But you're a bit special, I think."

For the next three days it was as if I were floating on a cloud. I knew that in another world I had once been engaged to a man called Bernard Page, but I could barely remember what he looked like, and I knew that I had never been in love before. I no longer felt like a clown, fit for nothing but to be laughed at. I felt like a girl who was greatly loved by a wonderful man.

When we took supper in the Royston Hotel that evening Nathan wanted to talk about our future. This proved difficult, for I had taken two glasses of wine, which I was quite unused to, and I kept laughing, partly from the wine and partly because I was so happy. Whatever the cause, it set Nathan chuckling.

"Now be serious a while, Bridie," he said. "How soon do you want us to be married?"

"Oh, dear. I'm dreadfully forward, Nathan, and I'd really like to marry you tomorrow, but I don't suppose that's possible." I sobered a little. "I'd like to finish the tour, of course. Then I'd like to see Kate settled. It depends how far away we would be, I suppose. Would we live in England or America?"

"That's for you to say, honey."

"I don't know. Perhaps America. We'd always be living with the Roger Chance scandal here. You said it wouldn't be like that in America."

"That's right," he grinned. "Maybe we could hang a picture of your Pa and my Pa each side of the fireplace and tell stories about them when we have neighbours in." He reached for my hand. "Lord, but I do love you, my sweet maverick girl."

"Maverick?"

"Not one of the herd. Now, Bridie, we have to talk about money."

I nodded, and made an effort to feel less carefree. I had learned that money was very important. Being rich did not matter, but having enough money to live without fear was something that mattered very much.

It was then that Nathan told me about the farm. Recently, he had heard through a firm of American lawyers that his mother's father, a widower, had died without leaving a will. As the only grandchild, Nathan was sole heir.

"The farm is in New Hampshire," said Nathan. "Eight hundred acres. And the old man looked after the land well, so there's a good living in it and maybe a little more. The lawyers estimate he also left something over eighty thousand dollars. Say twenty thousand pounds in your money."

"My goodness," I said dazedly. "I didn't realize you were rich."

"I don't know about rich. But whatever it is, don't say 'you', say 'we', Bridie."

I tried to take it all in. "Oh, Nathan, I do wish I hadn't arranged to go and see Nannie Foster on Tuesday. I shall be away for three whole days, and I shall miss you so much." I was suddenly overwhelmed by the sadness of parting from Nathan so soon after we had found that we loved each other. "Nathan, I know this sounds silly, but I think I'm about to cry."

The wine had gone to my head, and my memory is vague at this point. I recall being in a cab with Nathan, weeping on his shoulder while he spoke soothing words interrupted by spasms of laughter. I recall entering the boarding house and sailing up three flights of stairs, never once touching them with my feet. The last thing I remember is Ethel trying to undress me while I insisted on demonstrating the secret of the Chicken Walk.

I SLEPT TILL past nine o'clock next morning, and hurried to the breakfast room to find the Perkin family sitting at table with Nathan and the singer, Margaret Dane. They were lingering over coffee, chatting idly.

As I entered Ethel trilled, "Ah, here she is!" and everyone smiled. As Nathan held a chair for me, I made a huge "Arnold" grimace of despair, and said, "I'm so ashamed about getting tipsy last night."

"Ashamed?" It was Alfie who spoke first. "I should 'ope so, young lady. I understand you 'ad two whole glasses of wine!"

Ethel giggled. Charlie got up and reeled about the room, and Margaret started to sing "The Demon Drink Was Her Undoing". Nathan bent to touch his lips to my cheek, smiling and shaking his head reassuringly. "You weren't tipsy, Bridie. You were just happy, and beautiful with it. Now, try to eat a little breakfast."

It rained all that day, and the wind howled round the chimney-pots, but I could not have been happier if the sun had shone from a perfect blue sky. I was with Nathan and could wish for nothing better. In the afternoon we went out for a walk and came home drenched and laughing. The next day I chose my engagement ring. It was not expensive, and Nathan protested on this count, but the small diamonds were beautiful, the design unusual, and I fell in love with the ring as soon as I saw it.

We made tentative plans to be married in the spring, and though we had yet to decide where we would live, I felt that I would like to go to the farm in New Hampshire. It would be hard for me to return to the conventional life in which I had grown up, and I felt that America offered freedoms I could not find in England. Much depended on Kate. I hoped she would come with us, but we could make no decision until we had seen her.

Early on Tuesday morning Nathan saw me off on the train for my visit to Nannie Foster. The journey was a wretched cross-country affair, and I did not reach Wynford until teatime. Nannie Foster wept with delight when she opened the door, and began to fuss over me as if I were a twelve-year-old returning from boarding school. "I've put the kettle on, dear, so we'll have a nice cup of tea and some of Nannie's special *scones!* Gracious me, how pretty you look, Bridie. You've quite changed the way you walk, haven't you? So very nice and elegant, dear. I expect you've been practising with books balanced on your head, the way Nannie tried to teach you."

I did not tell her that my newfound grace came from being a comic dancer in a music hall turn, for it would have upset her deeply. After tea we sat talking, and to my relief she was content to spend most of the time gossiping about life in Wynford. She asked after Kate, and said anxiously that she hoped I was not working too hard, but in general she was satisfied with simple and uninformative answers.

Later, she produced an excellent supper and we washed up together in the tiny kitchen. It was a rather sultry September night, and I felt sleepy from the day's travel when we sat down again. "I've been waiting all this time for you to ask about my ring, Nannie," I said. "Look."

She took my hand as I held it out, and then looked up with shining eyes. "Bridie! You're not . . . ?"

"Yes, I'm engaged to be married, Nannie. It happened only two days ago, and even Kate doesn't know yet. He's American, and his name is Nathan McFee."

"Oh, that's splendid, Bridie," she beamed. "Just think of it, little Bridie getting married to an American gentleman. Oh, that reminds me. I won't be a moment, dear." She went slowly upstairs and came down with a yellowing envelope. "You remember asking me to clean your poor dear Mama's room? Well, there were a few very old magazines in one of the drawers, and I took them to look at later." She paused, sitting down beside me. "I'm afraid I forgot all about them till I was having a tidy-up a week or two ago. Then I found these photographs tucked away in one of the magazines."

"Photographs?"

"Yes. Your Mama showed them to me once, when you were just a baby. They were taken by your Papa when your parents were on their honeymoon. In France, it was."

"Yes. They stayed at a village in the Dordogne valley. I can't remember the name of it. Can you?"

"No, dear. I'm dreadful at foreign names."

There were only two photographs, and I had not seen either of them before. The first showed my mother as a young woman, standing with her back against what appeared to be a rocky cliff.

She was smiling a shy smile, and she was holding her hat in place, as if there might be a stiff wind. The second picture had been taken from much farther away, so that she was quite a small figure. Now it was clear that she was standing against a natural pillar of rock, a rather freakish outcrop that jutted up from barren ground. The background was blurred, but I had the impression of a small dry valley with low cliffs on each side.

"I wonder where this place is?" I said. "It looks high up so it would have been difficult for Papa to carry a camera and tripod. Why would he go to such lengths to take photographs there?"

"Oh, I couldn't say, Bridie. But when your Papa decided to do something, he always found a way, and he was very clever with mechanical things."

"Did Mama not explain when she showed you the pictures?"

Nannie Foster suddenly seemed tired. "It's a long time ago now," she said vaguely. "I think the photographs were just a souvenir, you know. To remind her of the Capricorn Stone."

I sat up straight. "The Capricorn Stone? What did she mean, Nannie?"

"Oh, I don't think she said, dear. I didn't really pay much attention. I know she spoke of the Capricorn Stone, though. Anyway, you must keep the photographs, dear. I meant them for you."

The Capricorn Stone. Those words had been among almost the last my mother had spoken to me, and I had seen them written down in the letter my father had left for her. *Walk again . . . something about a stream in the hills . . . and on to the valley of the Capricorn Stone.* I looked down at the second photograph once more. Here, surely, was the valley, with my mother standing against the Capricorn Stone itself. But what then? . . . *Darkness at eventide . . . rainbow's end . . . waiting crow. . . .*

I could not remember the letter in detail, but of one thing I was now certain. The last part was indeed a message. On reflection it was typical of my father that he should think he had made provision for his wife and family by telling Mama where to look for his spoils —as if she could or would have made use of them. In that moment I might have hated him if I had not known that he loved her so dearly.

Idly I turned the photographs over, and I noticed faint pencil markings on the back of the one which showed Mama against the Capricorn Stone at a distance. The lead had rubbed away over the years, but when I held the photograph under the lamp I saw that my father had written *Tête de Chèvre!*

Head of the goat. I looked at the picture again, but the words seemed to have no connection with it. Suddenly I wished Nannie Foster had never discovered the photographs. I knew that together with the letter they might yield the answer to a mystery, but this was ground I shrank from disturbing. I could tell Inspector Browning what had come to light, or I could write to Philippe Chatillon in Paris. In my heart, however, I didn't want to tell anybody. I hated the thought of the whole dramatic story being reopened in the newspapers.

Nannie Foster smothered a yawn and said, "My, my, I'm a sleepy head tonight."

I slipped the photographs back into the envelope. "Yes, I am too, Nannie. It's been a long day."

We made up a bed for me on the sofa, and though I was tired I lay awake for an hour or more after Nannie had gone upstairs. At last I determined that I would talk everything over with Nathan, so that we could decide together what I should do. I also made up my mind that I ought to tell Kate, for it was as much her right to know as mine.

Next morning after breakfast I wrote Kate a long letter telling her about my engagement to Nathan and about the photographs, adding that she had been right in thinking Papa's letter held a hidden message. We would have a long talk about it, I said, on my return to London.

At ten o'clock I walked to the post office and slipped the letter into the box. Later that morning, I hired a gig and paid a visit to my old friend Mr. Whitely. He was delighted to hear my news, and though his manner was as dry as ever I could tell he was more than a little astonished to learn how I had been earning my living. When I took my leave, he promised he would keep my stage career a secret, and he congratulated me warmly on my engagement.

I returned to Wynford and spent an hour with old Tom Kettle, then drove to the church, where I put a posy on my parents' grave. By teatime I was back at Nannie Foster's house. I was conscious as I drove through the village that more than one pair of eyes were upon me, but I did not much care—I had been stared at by a thousand eyes, six nights a week. I was glad that I would soon be with my friends again, and especially with Nathan.

If I could have known what awaited me before the month's end, I would never have boarded the early train from Wynford so eagerly that fresh September morning.

∽✑ Chapter Eleven ✑∽

It was raining in Manchester, but still a joy to come home. Nathan was at the station, and I knew that wherever in the world I might be, for me "home" was in his arms.

Later I told him what I had discovered, showing him the photographs and the letter from Papa. He studied them quietly, a little uneasily I thought, and said at last, "Yes, Bridie, I guess this letter was some sort of reminder to your mother, telling her where to look for the jewellery."

"Do you think there really was a lot of it?"

"Seems likely. I read the list of big items they reckoned he'd got away with over the years, and that was only part of it."

"Oh, where did you see that?"

"In one of the newspapers. Now don't be upset, Bridie."

"I'm not, Nathan, truly I'm not. It's just that I don't know what to do. If the jewellery my father stole can be recovered, I feel I owe it to the people it was stolen from to do all I can to help. Do you think I should speak to the police? I don't want to, but I keep feeling it's the right thing to do."

He kissed me. "You don't have to make up your mind this minute, Bridie. Take a while to think it over. Whatever your father hid, it's not going to run away by next week or next year."

I felt a sense of relief. "Yes, that's true. A few days can't make any difference, and anyway I ought to wait until I've heard from Kate before I decide."

On Monday I took over from Charlie and played the final week in Manchester. I had felt diffident about this, but Charlie was very reassuring. "'Course I don't mind, Bridie. I found it a bit tiring last week and want to ease meself back gradually."

I was happy to know that Charlie did not feel put out by my

return to the act, for I found to my surprise that I was looking forward to going on-stage again. "You're just a clown, Bridie Chance," I told myself, "that's the trouble with you. But Nathan loves you exactly the way you are, thank goodness."

The sketch went well that Monday evening. Nathan was in his usual place as we came off, and kissed me despite the paste on my face. "You get better all the time, Bridie," he drawled. "Seems a real waste of talent for me to take you away." He smiled. "Not that anything's going to stop me."

"I'll do my comic dancing especially for you, shall I? And I'll do it to make our children laugh, too."

"Really, Bridie!" Ethel said. "You do come out with some shocking things. Whatever's Nathan going to think of you talking about children when you've hardly been engaged for five minutes?"

Nathan said, "I think she's just fine, ma'am."

I laughed with sheer happiness, thinking how wonderful it was that Nathan and I understood each other so well that we could say whatever was in our hearts.

The following Sunday we moved to Birmingham, where we were to end the tour. I still had not decided what to do about the photographs, and in fact had mentally put the matter aside. Nathan had said nothing more, but I felt it was on his mind, for there were times when his thoughts seemed far away.

At the end of the first week, Ethel and I went to a teashop between the Saturday matinée and evening performances. Nathan had said he might join us, but he did not arrive. I was not particularly worried, but when Ethel and I returned to the Empire I asked the stage doorman if he had seen Mr. McFee. "Funny you asking that, miss," he said. "This feller was waiting when Mr. McFee coom out an hour back. Give him this note, he did, and you should ha' seen Mr. McFee's face when he luked at it. Then he steadies himself, like, nods to the feller, and walks off. Then the feller called a cab and asked to go to the station. Red-faced bloke. Shifty, I reckon."

I went in, and told a call-boy to look for Mr. McFee and ask him to come and have a word with me as soon as possible.

Ethel and I had scarcely been two minutes in our dressing room when there was a tap on the door. It was Mr. Chapman, the manager.

"Sorry to trouble you, Miss Chance, but can you spare ten minutes to come to my office?"

I was taken aback. "Why yes, but . . . oh, is it anything to do with Mr. McFee?"

He looked puzzled and shook his head. "No, dear. It's Inspector Browning from Scotland Yard. He's up here on business and saw the show last night. He said he'd like to meet you again, but I was to tell you it wasn't official."

After a moment I said, "Very well, Mr. Chapman." When he had gone I explained briefly to Ethel. "Inspector Browning was really very kind to me at the time, and if he says it's not official, then I can believe him. If Nathan comes, please tell him I won't be long."

When I entered Mr. Chapman's office, Inspector Browning was alone. He rose from an easy chair, looking exactly as I remembered him.

"It's good of you to see me, Miss Chance," he said. "You're looking very well, I'm happy to say."

"Yes, I've been most fortunate. I'm glad to see you looking well yourself. How did you know I was here?"

He looked a shade embarrassed. "Well, the file's never been closed, miss, so the Yard still keeps an eye on you, in a manner of speaking. They took note of that announcement in *The Stage* about Miss Bridie Chance joining Mr. Alfie Perkin and Company."

"Oh, I see."

"Me being here in Birmingham is just a coincidence, but when I saw the playbills I couldn't resist coming along last night to watch you do your turn. You were absolutely splendid, miss."

I was pleased to have impressed the inspector. "I'm very glad you enjoyed the act." I hesitated. "You say a file is still being kept open at Scotland Yard. I was hoping that the whole affair was officially dead and forgotten. Can you say how long it will be kept open?"

"Hard to tell, miss." He gave me a sympathetic look. "It's the stolen property, you see. One day a piece of it might turn up. I'm sure the French police haven't closed the case, and you know yourself that Pinkertons are still on it."

"Pinkertons? I don't understand."

"The American detective agency. They're working for a lady

from Boston who lost a priceless bit of jewellery in Biarritz." He seemed puzzled by my lack of understanding. "Pinkertons have had one of their agents right alongside you for months now."

I shook my head, trying to hold down the fear growing within me. "I have no idea what you mean. Will you explain, please?"

His eyes narrowed in surprise. "I didn't realize you were unaware. I'm afraid I've said too much." He looked troubled, then seemed to make up his mind. "All right, miss," he said in a low voice. "I'm under no obligation to Pinkertons, and I took a liking to you right from the start, so here goes. Pinkertons is a very big detective agency in America, and they'll tackle any kind of robbery for the right price. When the Boston lady engaged them, they put a man into France to try and nail the guilty party. Then, after your father died, the agent came over to Wynford to keep an eye on your family. Everyone thought that sooner or later a clue would turn up as to where the spoils were hidden." The inspector shrugged. "Anyway, you've been under close surveillance ever since. I thought you knew, miss. I'm sorry if this comes as a shock."

I turned away. I was lost somewhere in a dark place in my mind, and I did not want Inspector Browning to see my face. After a moment I said, "Is the Pinkerton man Mr. Nathan McFee?"

"That's right, miss. I fancy you must have had an inkling about him after all."

"No, Inspector," I said, and marvelled that it was possible to feel such racking pain and yet remain so calm, "I had no inkling about him at all. Thank you for explaining to me, and perhaps you will excuse me now."

I saw nothing as I made my way through the maze of passages to our dressing room. Ethel looked up from her book, and for the second time in my life she simply stood up and opened her arms to me. I clung to her, shaking as if with ague.

"What is it, Bridie dear, what is it? You tell Ethel. Was it the inspector? What's he been saying, dear?"

I whispered against her shoulder. "If Nathan comes, I can't see him, I can't. Not yet."

"Whatever you say, Bridie dear. Don't you worry now. Charlie can do the act if you're not feeling up to it—"

"No!" I heard my voice crack. "Of course I shall go on tonight.

I'm a clown, Ethel, only fit to dance about for everyone to laugh at, not fit for a man to love. I've been a fool, Ethel, such a stupid fool."

The tears came suddenly, and I clung to her feverishly. She said nothing, but simply held me until I was quiet. Then she said sadly, "Is it Nathan?"

I nodded. "I've just discovered that he's really a detective who works for an American firm. They think I might know where my father hid a whole mass of jewellery. During all this time Nathan has simply been spying on me. Oh Ethel, I truly thought he loved me. It hurts so much . . . I can't tell you. . . ."

She chafed my hands gently. "I know how it hurts, dear. I know."

I remembered then that she had been abandoned by Charlie's father, a man she must have loved dearly. "I'm sorry, Ethel," I whispered. "It's just such a shock. I'll be all right in a minute."

She sighed and looked troubled. "Are you sure about Nathan, dear? He may be a detective and all that, but p'raps he loves you just the same. He seems such a nice honest young man to me."

I went to the washstand and sponged my face, "Yes, I'm sure, Ethel. I think his conscience troubled him once, and he almost gave himself away by telling me not to be so trusting. But I shall ask him tonight, and he can speak for himself."

"Perhaps it will all come right," Ethel said hopefully.

I kissed her cheek. "No, it won't, I'm afraid." I was still holding the towel, and as I looked down my eye caught the sparkle of the engagement ring on my finger. "This will be the second ring I've returned," I said, with a shaky laugh. "One gets used to most things. I suppose I shall get used to being humiliated."

WE SAID NOTHING to Alfie before our number, and I noted with dull surprise that I performed well that evening. There had been no sign of Nathan in the wings as we went on, and he was still missing when we took our final bow.

"No Nathan?" Alfie said in surprise as we came off. "He's always 'ere to watch you, Bridie. What's up?"

Ethel said, "How should we know? All we know is that he's let our Bridie down, and don't you start asking questions now, Alfie. I'll tell you later." She took my arm and moved briskly off. "Come on, dear, let's get you into the bath."

As Ethel was buttoning my dress, Margaret Dane appeared at the door, looking both troubled and apologetic. "Hello, I just had to come and ask," she said. "Is it true about Nathan McFee? I heard he just broke his contract and walked out. I couldn't believe it, but I thought Bridie would know—being engaged to him."

"We didn't know," I said. "And I think the engagement is ended, Maggie. Do you have any idea where Nathan is now?"

"Oh Bridie, I'm so sorry. I expect he's at the digs, packing up. Oh dear, I'm sorry to bring such wretched news."

I said, "I'm glad to know. Thank you, Maggie. I'd better hurry now. Please excuse me."

Ten minutes later I was at Mrs. Bailey's theatrical digs. The sitting room was in darkness, and I met nobody as I climbed the stairs and tapped on the door of Nathan's room.

Nathan called, "Come in." When I opened the door he was on the far side of the room, his back towards me, fastening the straps of his saddlebags. "Will you take these bags down, please?" he said. "I want to go to the livery stables in Albert Street."

I said, "I'm not the cabbie, Nathan."

He straightened slowly and turned, his face impassive. "Hello, Bridie," he said quietly.

I closed the door behind me and stood looking at him, wishing I could stop myself aching with love for him. "May I ask you some questions, Nathan?"

He nodded, and I could read nothing in his eyes. "This evening a man told me that you work for a detective agency. He said that you were sent here to watch me, in the hope of discovering jewellery hidden by my father. Is it true?"

After a moment he said. "Yes, it's true, Bridie. I'm sorry."

My heart felt like a cold stone. "And did you make friends with me just to win my confidence?"

A muscle in his jaw twitched visibly. "It was business," he said in a flat voice. "My job was to recover a client's stolen property, and we have to handle a case in whatever way seems most likely to get results."

"You could have told me the truth, Nathan." I held up my left hand, showing the ring. "And was this just business too?"

He looked away as I began to ease the ring from my finger. "Well, I've shown you the letter and the photographs, so you

237

know as much as I'll ever know about the jewellery. I suppose you're going to France now, to the Dordogne valley?"

He looked at me again. "No. I've been called to New York urgently. I hope to be in Southampton by tomorrow night."

I put the ring down carefully on the corner of a small table. "I do wish you hadn't given this to me," I said. "It wasn't necessary." I opened the door, then paused to look back at him. The cold stone in my chest had grown so large that I found it difficult to breathe. I said, "I ought to hate you, but I can't. I wish you well, Nathan. I hope you're never hurt as badly as you've hurt me. Goodbye."

He was still gazing at me from brooding eyes as I closed the door quietly behind me. I took a cab back to the theatre. If I had gone to my own room, I would have heard Nathan McFee departing, and that was more than I could bear.

In our dressing room I found Ethel and Alfie sitting on the two bentwood chairs, and Charlie leaning glumly against the wall. Alfie rose as I came in, and took my hands in his own.

"Ethel told us. Did you see 'im, Bridie?"

"Yes." I tried to smile. "He admitted it was true. He's leaving for America this evening, so it's all over and done with now."

Charlie said angrily, "Rotten swine. He's got no right to treat our Bridie like that."

Ethel closed her eyes, and a tear ran down her cheek. "I never dreamed he'd turn out like that," she said.

"No, well, you're not the best of judges, Ethel," said Alfie briskly, "and what's done is done, so stop piping your eye or you'll 'ave us all at it." He looked at me, still holding my hands. "The thing is, what do you want to do now, Bridie?"

I did not need time to think. "Will you have me back, Alfie? I mean, could we rewrite the sketches, and . . ."

"Have you back? Blimey, girl, you never went, did you?" A smile added to the creases on his face. "Right, that's it, then. We'll get down to work on it tomorrow."

Somewhere deep within me I set a heel on all my joyous hopes of the past days. They were dead for ever, and best forgotten quickly. "Thank you, Alfie," I said. "From now on I just want to be part of Alfie Perkin and Company. I'll never think of leaving you again."

Chapter Twelve

For much of Sunday we worked on ideas for the new sketch. I was thankful to be kept busy. On the Monday I played my part in "The Water Board Man", feeling hollow and lifeless, but strangely we had the best Monday night reception I could remember.

As we sat at breakfast on Tuesday morning, Mrs. Bailey's son brought me a telegram. I opened it apprehensively. The only person I could think of who might have sent it was Kate, and I felt that telegrams rarely brought good news. The words danced before my eyes. REGRET MISS KATE HAS RUN AWAY AND WE BELIEVE IT IS ELOPEMENT. PLEASE COME AT ONCE. PERONI.

Alfie's voice said from a distance, "Bridie? You all right? You've gone white as a sheet."

I passed the telegram to him with a shaking hand. Alfie read it aloud, his face haggard, and I remembered that to him Kate had seemed a replica of the girl he had loved more than twenty years ago.

"Oh, dear God, who do you think it is, Bridie?" Ethel asked.

I shook my head. "I've no idea. Kate hasn't spoken of anybody in her letters. But there haven't been many letters."

Ethel said, "If she met someone nice, why didn't she say? Why not bring the man 'ome, and start courting like anyone else?"

"Well, 'im not being nice is just what we're worried about, isn't it?" said Alfie. He looked at me. "You'll 'ave to get down there on the first train, Bridie."

"Yes. I'm sorry."

"Don't worry. It's no trouble for Charlie to step in. I'm just sorry I can't come down with you, but we've got to play out the rest of the booking. Now I'll go and borrow Mrs. Bailey's time-table, so we can see 'ow the trains run. You go and get packed. Just take a suitcase. We'll bring your trunk with us when we go 'ome, Sunday week."

Ten minutes later, as I tried to concentrate on packing, there came a tap on the door. Ethel opened it to admit Alfie, who was carrying what looked like a thin white tube.

"Train leaves at twenty-five past eleven, Bridie," he said. "I'll come and see you off. But before you change into your travelling togs I want you to put this on." He handed me the white tube and I saw that it was a fine suede belt with something inside it. Alfie said, "There's a row of little buttons along the top, Bridie, to keep the money nice and snug inside."

I looked at him blankly. "Money?"

"It's a money-belt, dear. You wear it under your clothes. I've put eighty quid in there in fivers, and twenty in ones—"

"Alfie, no!"

"Be quiet and listen, there's a good girl. You might 'ave to go chasing off anywhere over the next few days, and you'll need ready cash. Tell you the truth, I've got a funny feeling that young Kate's gone abroad. Don't ask me why, because I don't know. But if you need more cash, I've written to my bank in London saying you can draw on my account."

I put my arms round Alfie's neck and wept against his shoulder. No words could have told what I felt.

THE TRAIN BROUGHT ME to London exactly on time, and ten minutes later I was on my way to Kensington. I had sent a telegram to say when I would be arriving, and Signor Peroni had the front door open even before I had paid off the cab.

"Thank Heaven you have come!" he said. "It is so bad. You entrust your sister to me and then this happens."

His wife stood in the hall with hands clutched together. They both looked drawn with worry, and I said, "I'm sure you have nothing to blame yourselves for. You wrote to me that Kate was being difficult, and I replied that it was best to do nothing." I managed a poor smile. "So if anybody is at fault, I'm the one. Can you tell me all that you know about it?"

I was shown into the drawing room, and there Signor Peroni told his tale. Several days ago Kate had announced that she would like to spend the weekend with a college friend, Sarah Patton. Kate had stayed with her once before, remaining away from Friday morning till Monday evening. On that occasion Signor Peroni had first paid a call on the Pattons to confirm the invitation and to assure himself that Kate would be staying in a respectable home.

On this second occasion, Signor Peroni had not felt it necessary to confirm the invitation. Thus it was not until Kate failed to

240

return on Monday evening that he and his wife began to worry. He had taken a cab to the college, where a professor said that Kate had not attended her classes since the previous Thursday.

Shocked and bewildered, Signor Peroni had driven on to the Patton's house, there to learn from Mr. Patton that there was no truth in the story of the invitation. Sarah was summoned by her father. She was clearly startled to hear of Kate's disappearance, but she admitted that she might be able to guess the reason. Kate was in love, and had been for many weeks now. There was a man she often met secretly. Sarah had never seen the man, but had no doubt that Kate was completely enchanted by him. The last thing Kate had confided to her was that this wonderful man had asked her to marry him.

I listened in alarm to Signor Peroni's story. I knew that there was great passion in Kate, and if a man was clever enough to strike the right chord of response in her. . . .

"Did she leave a message for you?" I asked.

Mrs. Peroni shook her head. "We found nothing."

"How unkind to leave you without a word. That's not like Kate."

Signor Peroni waved a hand. "For a young girl in love there are no rules," he said. "My wife and I do not mind for ourselves that Miss Kate left no word, but we have much fear that a man who would take her away in such a manner is not a good man."

"I have the same fear," I said. "Did this girl Sarah Patton learn anything about him?"

"Yes. Of course Miss Kate had told her that the man was hand-some, wonderful, brilliant—" He shrugged. "But apart from this, Sarah could say only one thing of importance. The man is French."

I drew in a quick breath, startled as there came to my mind's eye the image of the man in the photograph Philippe Chatillon had given me. That photograph was in my writing case still, together with those Nannie Foster had found and the letter from my father. I had brought them with me, scarcely knowing why.

"I don't know who the man is," I said slowly, "but I believe I know what he looks like, and I have been warned against him my-self." I found it hard to go on, for my throat seemed to be swelling with fear. "I think he is a scoundrel, a criminal perhaps, who set out to make Kate fall in love with him . . . because he thinks she may be the means of finding some valuables hidden by my father."

Signor Peroni and his wife exchanged a troubled look. My mind had suddenly begun to work very quickly, and I now saw much that I had been unaware of until this moment. Kate's romance with the dangerous Frenchman must have been going on even before I left on tour. I remembered that she had asked about Papa's letter, speculating as to whether it held a hidden message. That question, I was now sure, had come from the Frenchman.

I could not imagine how he had tricked her into trying to worm such a secret out of me, but a clever and unscrupulous man could have done it easily enough with an impressionable girl. Remembering how easily Nathan McFee had deceived me, I could not feel that Kate had been any more gullible than I had been myself. The man had courted Kate, dazzled her, and bided his time. Then, when she received the letter I had written to her from Nannie Foster's cottage, he must have decided to take her away with him . . . to France, of course, to the Dordogne valley.

But no. Kate did not possess the photographs or Papa's letter. So why had the Frenchman not waited till he had access to every detail? And how did he persuade her to go with him? He would have had to offer marriage, for however romantic Kate might be she had too much pride to accept the role of mistress.

I shook myself mentally. Speculation was fruitless, and the important thing now was to find Kate. I could not plan beyond that point, but I knew that the man to help me was Philippe Chatillon. It might well be that the personal interest he had once shown in me had passed, but I knew he would be very much interested in what I had to tell him.

"Miss Bridie?" Signor Peroni's voice penetrated my deliberations. "Will it be possible to find Miss Kate?"

"Well . . . I think there is somebody who can help me, but it means I must go to Paris as soon as possible. I'm sure Kate is in France. Do you have a Bradshaw, Signor Peroni? I would like to look up the times of the boat trains."

There was a night express, which would arrive in Paris early the next morning. A few hours later Signor Peroni escorted me to Victoria Station, greatly troubled at the idea of my travelling alone, but I assured him that I would manage very well. He saw me comfortably settled in a first-class carriage, and when he had gone I sank back and closed my eyes, thankful to be alone. My head throbbed, and although I was desperately weary I felt I would be unable to sleep until I held Kate's hand safely in mine.

For an aching moment I wished I might look round and see Nathan beside me, quiet and strong, a man I could trust to stand with me through whatever might lie ahead. But Nathan McFee was no such man. Better to be alone than to have such a friend; and unless I could win help from Philippe Chatillon I would indeed be alone in my task, as I had been in those days of grief and fear at Latchford Hall.

WHEN THE TRAIN clanked to a halt in the Gare St. Lazare it was not yet seven o'clock. To my surprise and relief I had slept soundly during the journey, and I now went straight to the station hotel to take breakfast and to change some money. I felt thankful that my French was good, for I had never set foot out of England before, and would have felt a little nervous even without the heavy anxiety that pressed down upon me.

At twenty minutes to eight a hotel porter hailed a cab for me. I read out to the driver the address on the card Philippe Chatillon had sent me long ago, and then settled back in my seat as the cab began to rattle along the Rue Lafayette. Twenty minutes later I was speaking to the doleful concierge of a run-down apartment building. It was so poor a place that the cabbie had come in with me. Now I held out the card to the concierge and asked, "Do you have a gentleman here by this name?"

"No, mam'selle." He tapped the side of his nose and leaned forward to whisper. "But sometimes a gentleman will use this address for correspondence, you understand? A gentleman who does not wish his true whereabouts to be known."

"Any such gentleman would have to give you his correct address," I said firmly, "so that correspondence could be sent on. Do you have an address for M'sieur Chatillon?"

The concierge shook his head. "Gentlemen call here for their letters, and I have a poor memory for names and faces."

"Chatillon?" the cabbie said. "Not M'sieur Philippe Chatillon?"

I looked at him hopefully. "But yes. He is a detective, I understand."

"Oh, yes, mam'selle. He is a detective of much fame except to such imbeciles as this." He surveyed the concierge with scorn. "I have driven M'sieur Chatillon in my cab on several occasions. Come, I will take you to him at once."

For the next ten minutes, as we drove, he regaled me with a shouted account of how he had come to know M'sieur Chatillon. Three years ago this gentleman had proved the innocence of a cabdriver accused of murder, who would otherwise have gone to the guillotine. It had been a most dramatic affair, I was assured, and since then M'sieur Chatillon had been a great hero among the cabbies of Paris.

At last we drew up by a small but gracious house on a tree-lined road. I paid the cabbie, tugged the bell-pull and stood nervously before the heavy door. It was opened by a short, grey-haired maid. "Is this the residence of M'sieur Philippe Chatillon, if you please?" I asked.

"Yes," she acknowledged. "Who wishes to see him?"

"Mam'selle Bridget Chance, on an urgent matter."

The maid stepped back and said, "Please enter, mam'selle." She led me across a panelled hall to a beautifully furnished drawing room. "I will inform M'sieur Chatillon."

Less than a minute later the door opened and a man stepped quickly into the room, still buttoning a jacket which he must have been putting on as he hurried through the hall. But the man was not Philippe Chatillon, with those curiously magnetic hazel eyes set in the square face beneath the cap of black curls. This was another man. He was no more than an inch taller than I, well-proportioned and light on his feet. The eyes were wide-set, the hair was light brown, and the face was one I knew. I had seen it under a lamp in Holborn one evening. I had also seen it in a photograph, and on the back of that photograph Philippe Chatillon had written, *This man is dangerous.*

I stared in shock and bewilderment as the man came forward extending his hand, a smile of inquiry on his lips. In excellent English, he said, "I am delighted to see you, Miss Chance. I hope you are in good health, and your charming sister also."

I put out my hand automatically, then drew it back and blurted out, "But you are not Philippe Chatillon!"

There was amusement in his eyes as he said, "I assure you I can bring many witnesses to confirm that my claim is true. May I ask why you think I am not Philippe Chatillon?"

244

With an effort I pulled myself together and said, "But I have met M'sieur Chatillon in Suffolk. He . . . he sent a wreath to my father's funeral. And he said that I should write to him if I discovered any sort of message left by my father. Here is his card." I had been fumbling in my bag, and now held out the printed card sent to me in Wynford.

The man took it, his eyebrows lifting in surprise. "Please continue, mam'selle."

"I did not write to him, but he came to see me again in London. It was then that he . . . he warned me against you, and gave me this." I put the photograph into the man's hand. He looked at it, turned it over, and read the words on the back.

After a moment he said, "I did indeed send a wreath on the occasion of your father's funeral. It was arranged by your local undertaker, to whom I sent a card on which I had written, '*Dormez bien, mon vieil adversaire.*'"

I caught my breath, as I suddenly remembered the neat angular handwriting on the card attached to the wreath. It was quite different from the round, untidy scrawl on the photograph, which I had seen pencilled there myself by the man with hazel eyes.

I looked at the person in front of me, and knew the truth. "I have been greatly deceived," I said slowly as I put out my hand. "How do you do, M'sieur Chatillon."

He took my hand and bowed over it. "I am delighted to make your acquaintance, mam'selle. I think we have much to say to each other. Please sit down." He rang for tea, then stood with hands clasped behind his back, eyes thoughtful. "Well now, it is perhaps a little difficult to know where we should begin."

"Yes, M'sieur Chatillon. Who can he be, this man who claimed to be you? I can describe him to you very easily. He is—"

"Forgive me, but there is no need," interrupted Philippe Chatillon. "He is French, of good height and build, dark curly hair, hazel eyes . . . and a power to charm which ladies are said to find quite irresistible. His name is Victor Antoine Jean-Pierre Sarrazin, and he is a dangerous criminal."

The door opened and the grey-haired maid entered, pushing an elegant trolley bearing tea and cakes. Philippe Chatillon thanked her, then giving me a friendly smile, he drew up a chair, and began to pour tea. "Now, how may I assist you?"

I hesitated to take the cup he was now offering to me, for my hands were suddenly shaking as I said, "I believe this man has taken my sister, Kate. I think she has . . . eloped with him."

Philippe Chatillon stood up, as if he could not bear to remain still. To my surprise, he said in a low voice, "That dog Sarrazin has taken Kate? Oh dear God, no."

I said, bewildered, "You speak as if you know her, m'sieur."

He nodded. "Yes, I know her, though she does not know me. For much of the summer I was in London, watching her . . . because I was watching Sarrazin. Then he seemed to conclude that she could be of no use to him for he returned to France. I realize now that it was a trick. He must have discovered my surveillance, and decided to throw me off the scent. Evidently he went back to England as soon as he had achieved his purpose. What a fool I am!"

I put a hand to my head. "There is much I do not understand, m'sieur, but above all I want to find my sister."

"I do not think it will be difficult to find her," he said quietly. "Sarrazin will have taken her to his home, the Château Valbrison, south of Brive. It is even possible that he has married her. A special licence would not be hard to arrange."

I looked down at my hands. "Why has he done this, m'sieur? When we met in London he said that he wished to court *me*."

"That does not surprise me. Did you find yourself attracted to Victor Sarrazin, mam'selle?"

I lifted my head and looked at him. "Yes, and in a frightening way . . . perhaps that was why I rejected him. He has more than charm, m'sieur, he has power, and if he exerted that power upon Kate, I cannot feel surprise that she yielded to it."

"Poor girl," he said gently, and closed his eyes for a moment. After a pause, he went on in a businesslike manner. "You must have guessed by now that the hoard left by your father is the reason for everything Sarrazin has done. The only two persons who might know your father's secret are your sister and yourself. If you had found a message, and written to Philippe Chatillon at the accommodation address Sarrazin gave you, then *he* would have received it, and his first move would have succeeded. But you did not write, and so he came to you in London. Tell me, did he ask then if you had found any message?"

I cast my mind back. "Yes, he did. In fact I had recently come into possession of a letter my father had left for my mother, but at that time I did not want anybody to know of it, so I lied to him."

Philippe Chatillon shook his head. "From you, that would never deceive Sarrazin. He would have known at once that you were trying to hide something from him, and so he began an attempt to court you. When that failed, he turned his attention to your sister."

"That was months ago, m'sieur. Would he pursue her for so long?"

"Once he knew that the secret existed, yes. For he believes, as I do, that the spoils will be enormous. The Pinkerton agency has had a man working on this case for over a year now, in the hope of recovering just one piece of jewellery for a wealthy client."

I tried to keep the heaviness from my voice as I said, "Yes. Nathan McFee. He has been called back to America. . . ."

Philippe Chatillon gave a frown of surprise. "Strange to withdraw him when he is so familiar with the case. I met him when he first came to France—a very competent man, I would say."

"Yes, I have no doubt." My mouth was dry. I managed to pick up my cup of tea and sip a little without my hands shaking too obviously. "I must accept that the spoils are worth a great deal, m'sieur, but how can it help Victor Sarrazin to make Kate run away with him? She knows something of the letter and the photographs I discovered, but I cannot believe she knows enough for his purposes."

Philippe Chatillon looked at me sombrely. "Mam'selle," he said, "Sarrazin knows that if he has your sister in his hands, then he has you also. I am sure that a marriage has taken place, and the law is very wary of interference between husband and wife. Sarrazin may virtually do as he pleases with her. I am surprised that you have not already received some sort of message from him."

"You mean he would . . . harm her?" It was warm in the room, but I felt shivery with cold. After a moment I said, "Please advise me, m'sieur. I ask your professional help, and whatever your fee I will find a way to pay it."

He shook his head quickly. "No, mam'selle, there will be no fee. I offer you my personal help in this matter." He paused, and then went on quietly. "I am a bachelor of thirty-five, well-to-do, and I have known more than a few young ladies since my youth. Since my return from London, however, I have discovered that my emotions were deeply engaged there by a young lady with whom I never spoke."

I said wonderingly, "You mean . . . Kate?"

"Yes. I spent many days within a stone's throw of her, watching her pass daily between home and college, observing her clandestine meetings with Victor Sarrazin, and feeling tormented by worry as I saw him bring her under his spell."

"Did you not warn her, m'sieur?"

"Can you imagine how a young girl would respond to a stranger who tells her that the man she loves is a criminal?"

"But surely there was something you could do?"

He moved to a bell-pull and tugged it. "You cannot blame me more bitterly than I blame myself," he said quietly. "I involved myself in this case because I wished to bring Victor Sarrazin to book, but that reason has been replaced by one far stronger. I can only say that I now realize your sister has captured a heart I had long thought immune."

He stopped abruptly as the door opened and the elderly maid entered again. "Please tell Raoul to have the carriage ready in ten minutes."

As the door closed, he moved to a bureau and took out a time-table. "I shall go at once to Château Valbrison," he said, flicking through the pages. "Let me see . . . ah yes, there is an express to Toulouse shortly. It stops at Brive, where there is a good connection for Valbrison. I should be there soon after three o'clock."

I stood up. "You must take me with you, m'sieur."

He looked at me, and gave a little nod. "I hoped you would wish to come. Since we are to be colleagues in this matter, may I ask you to do me the honour of calling me Philippe?"

"Thank you. And I am always called Bridie." I hesitated, then went on. "What will you do when we reach Château Valbrison?"

Philippe Chatillon gave a small shrug, "I shall confront Victor Sarrazin and find out if he has married your sister. That being the case, I will offer to give all possible assistance in finding the spoils, with the understanding that Sarrazin may keep them if he will release Kate into your care. Do you agree?"

"Yes, of course. But if he refuses?"

Cold menace flared suddenly in the dark eyes of the quiet man before me. He picked up the photograph of himself he had put down on the table and turned it over. "If Sarrazin refuses," he said in the same polite voice, "then he will learn that the words he wrote here are true." His head came up again. "I will do whatever may be necessary."

WE CAUGHT the Toulouse train with a few minutes to spare, and Philippe Chatillon was able to reserve a compartment. As the train headed south, I began to learn more of Victor Sarrazin, the strangely compelling man I had first encountered in a country lane near Latchford Hall.

Victor Antoine Sarrazin, the youngest son of an aristocratic family, was a gambler, a libertine, and a receiver of stolen property, though this last had never been proved. His family had long since turned their backs on him, but he was still accepted in some sections of European society, for many ladies and gentlemen with too little to do were greatly attracted by his considerable charm. It did not matter that he was arrogant and unscrupulous: such defects even added to his attractions in certain circles. There was one man only he respected, and perhaps to a degree feared, for this man was utterly unimpressed either by Victor Sarrazin's charm or by his sinister reputation. That man was Roger Chance, my father. He used Sarrazin as a receiver of stolen goods and as a spy to keep watch on wealthy ladies, and though Sarrazin would willingly have become a lieutenant of *Le Sorcier*, Roger Chance would have none of him in that respect. My father regarded him with a tolerant amusement: he was of use as a tool, and no more.

Then Philippe Chatillon told me of the extraordinary man who had been my father. "He could not help himself, Bridie. Of that I am sure. When Sarrazin said that I was both friend and adversary of your father, he spoke the truth for once." Philippe smiled. "There are people who must climb mountains even though it will kill them. Roger Chance had just such a compulsion. But he was not a bad man, Bridie."

I said a little tiredly, "No. But I've learned that people don't have to be bad to cause a great deal of hurt. Please tell me, is Sarrazin like my father, or is he truly bad?"

"Oh, he is truly bad." Philippe Chatillon stared out of the window with haunted eyes. After a moment he shook his head as

249

if making an effort to clear it. "I must keep firm hold on my feelings," he said sharply. "May we study your father's letter and the photographs now, please? If we can decipher his message we shall have more to bargain with when we confront Sarrazin."

For two hours we read and re-read the letter and scrutinized the photographs, but we made no progress. After luncheon Philippe said, "It is hard for a Frenchman to perceive English nuances. Let us try again. Your father writes of *the little smithy*. Is there any double meaning there, Bridie?"

I shook my head. "No. I think it must just be a forge, a particular place from which you can go up into *the high valleys*."

"Yes," he said. "The high valleys. We shall be entering such an area towards the end of our journey. Your father asks your mother to make a pilgrimage to this place. Let us take the words in sequence. *Walk again where the stream runs golden from the hills* . . . I would say that a stream would be more likely to run golden toward sunset or shortly after sunrise. *And on to the valley of the Capricorn Stone*. This, surely, is where your mother stands against the stone pillar, but it is not a unique landmark. So *Capricorn* is written to help identify it. . . . But how? Does the word Capricorn have any special significance?"

I thought carefully, then said, "Not that I know of. It's one of the signs of the zodiac. I have heard of people being born under Capricorn. It's the sign of The Goat, isn't it?"

I broke off, and we stared at each other with wide eyes. "Well done, Bridie," Philippe said. "*Tête de Chèvre*. Goat's head. The words your father pencilled on the back of this photograph."

"Yes," I said doubtfully. "I suppose so. But it doesn't really tell us any more, does it?"

"We may find more meaning in it if we can solve other parts of the puzzle." He looked at the letter again. "It continues: *Remember me then, and have no fear of the shadow, Mary dear, for the darkness at eventide leads only to the dayspring of rainbow's end*. No fear of the shadow? The Capricorn Stone would cast a shadow, of course, but why should she fear it?"

"I think," I said slowly, "that some of the phrases are put in simply to link up the important parts, and the important part here must surely be the shadow."

"Which he seems to equate with *the darkness at eventide*. And

250

this leads to—ah, yes! It is a way of saying that the shadow points in a particular direction." He frowned. "But shadows move with the sun."

"He says *at eventide*, so it must mean when the sun is going down. That confirms what you said before, about the stream running golden at either sunrise or sunset."

He gave a quick nod of agreement. "Exactly so. And we can assume that the shadow of the Capricorn Stone at sunset points to the *rainbow's end*, which by tradition is where a crock of gold is to be found. There will be a hiding place, of course, but of what nature we cannot tell until we see the surroundings."

I knew the letter by heart now, and could recall the final words. *Have no fear of the waiting crow, for it serves only to reveal the emptiness that is filled with brightness.* As if echoing my thoughts, Philippe said slowly, "What is *the waiting crow*? There surely cannot be a bird in the hiding place."

My head had begun to ache, and I leaned back, closing my eyes. "I'm sorry, I just can't think. Let's go through it again from the beginning."

We had made no further progress when the train halted at Brive, where we had fifteen minutes to wait for the train to Valbrison. It was warmer here than it had been in Paris, and the sky was without a cloud. A short way from where we sat, three or four French workmen in blue overalls were renewing sleepers in a siding, levering the old ones out with thick steel crowbars. I watched the workmen and looked at the other passengers, but found it more difficult every moment to keep Kate out of my mind and to hold back the panic that threatened to possess me.

At last the local train came in, and two minutes later we were on our way to Valbrison. We were travelling beside the river now, and as I gazed out I knew suddenly that some important thought lay in the depths of my mind. Somewhere, sometime, I had seen something which threw light on the riddle we had just spent hours trying to solve. No . . . not sometime. Recently . . . I wrestled with the will-o'-the-wisp of memory, I closed my eyes and tried to make my mind a blank . . . Overalls. Workmen in blue overalls. I could see the old railway sleepers being prized up out of their flinty beds. Workmen. . . .

The train was beginning to slow to a halt when I jumped as if stung, and clutched the arm of the man beside me. "The *crow*, Philippe!" I gasped. "It isn't a bird, it's a common abbreviation of *crowbar!* Oh, what's the word in French? *Une barre de fer?* A long iron lever for lifting things up. There's a crowbar in the hiding place, Philippe! That makes sense, doesn't it?"

He nodded slowly, excitement lighting his eyes. "Excellent sense, Bridie! Crow . . . crowbar. It is a connection only to be seen by an English person." He leaned forward and took my hand. "Only the precise location is lacking now, but we have everything else to offer Victor Sarrazin. I pray it will be sufficient." After a long silence he said in a low voice, "Dear Bridie. I have dreamed that one day I might call you sister."

I felt close to tears. "That would make me very proud," I said. "Perhaps it will all come right. There must always be hope."

He nodded, and then he said quietly, "I wish Nathan McFee were with us. A good man, that one, with a good head."

I said nothing, but the ache which lay beneath my anxiety for Kate was like a great cold weight within my breast.

CHÂTEAU VALBRISON stood at the head of a high valley, across the foot of which flowed a tributary of the Dordogne. In the heat of the afternoon an ancient cab brought us up the long winding road from the little station to the grim, dilapidated château.

There were no doors at the entrance to the courtyard. The great hinges had rusted through a century ago, our cabbie informed us. He drove between the old pillars, then on through an arch into a smaller courtyard and up to broad steps which rose to a weather-bleached oak door. Philippe paid him off, and as the cab creaked away I felt my heart begin to race with mingled hope and dread.

Philippe pulled the chain bell-pull beside the door. In a moment the door swung open, and a burly man stood looking at us. He was about to speak when Philippe said, "Be so good as to tell Victor Sarrazin that Philippe Chatillon and Mam'selle Bridget Chance are here to see him on a matter of great advantage." As he spoke he stepped forward briskly, his slim cane pointed towards the man's face, causing the man to step back, and in another second I had followed Philippe across the threshold.

The big hall in which we stood was a high-ceilinged, gloomy place which was much in need of thorough dusting and polishing.

A door opened on the far side of the hall, and there came a burst of laughter from the room beyond. A voice I knew said, "Who the devil is it, Felix? If it's that wench from the bakery, bring her in. We can always do with another girl—"

Victor Sarrazin appeared at the door and stopped short at sight of us. His shirt was unbuttoned at the neck, and he wore no jacket. From the clink of glasses, and the laughter coming from the room behind him, I guessed that he had been drinking, but he showed no sign of it. There were two long scratches down his cheek, but the hazel eyes were clear, his face fresh and alert, and his whole manner one of leisurely assurance. Then, abruptly, he threw back his head and laughed. "The devil looks after his own," he said to me in English. "My stubborn wife refuses to invite you here, yet now I .find that you have brought yourself and the great French detective."

Beside me, Philippe said, "Do you have Kate Chance here?"

The hazel eyes gleamed with amusement. "I have Kate Sarrazin here, m'sieur. We were married by special licence three days ago."

"Very well." Philippe's voice held no expression. "We demand that you release her to our care, with a view to annulment of the marriage. In return we offer the information you need in order to lay your hands on the jewellery stolen by *Le Sorcier*."

A dark flame gleamed in Sarrazin's eyes, and his head came up like the head of a listening dog. "So you have the answer, by God!" he said softly. He stepped back, opening the door wide and extending an arm. "Welcome to Château Valbrison!"

Philippe touched my arm and I moved forward into a large, ill-kept room. Three men and three women lounged round a long table on which lay platters of food and bottles of wine. I had no doubt that the men were criminals. The three women were dressed in tawdry finery and had a brazen air—they did not strike me as local girls and I thought they might have come from Brive.

Sarrazin looked towards Felix and said curtly, "I have business to attend to. Take the women down to the station and return immediately."

There were giggling protests from the women as Felix hustled them out of the room. Then Sarrazin flung himself into a chair and refilled his glass. "You will no doubt wish to see your sister," he said mockingly to me. "You shall do so while I talk to the

254

famous M'sieur Chatillon." He glanced at one of the men. "Take her up to Madame Sarrazin's room, Alex."

The man gave a nod and went out of the door, leaving me to hurry after him. We mounted a wide, once-elegant staircase with a worn and grubby carpet, and then walked past several doors until we reached one near the end of a wide passage. He bent to turn the key and told me to enter, and when I passed in front of him he locked the door behind me. The room was lofty, with threadbare carpets and a fourposter bed in one corner. Kate stood by the window, looking out, her back to me. She wore a plain grey dress used for half-mourning. Her hands, hanging by her sides, were tightly clenched, and her whole body seemed rigid.

I managed a husky whisper, "Kate . . . oh, Kate."

She spun round. "Bridie!" A whole range of emotions flickered across her face: gladness and alarm, shame and stubborn pride, relief and despair. There were dark smudges under her beautiful eyes, and a blue-yellow bruise on her right cheekbone. I started towards her, with my arms outstretched, and she ran into my arms.

"There, darling, there. It's all right, I've got you. . . ."

I could feel her sobbing, though she made no sound. After a little while the spasms eased, and I said gently, "Kate dear, I have to ask. He says you're married to him. Is it true?"

She said in a muffled voice, "Yes."

My heart sank. "Has he . . . used you?"

She nodded, "In Paris, before we came here. Before I knew he was . . . a monster. Oh, Bridie, I loved him so. I thought he was so wonderful, I would have died for him. And then, when we came here . . . suddenly it was as if he took off a mask." She lifted a tear-stained face, and anger glinted in her eyes. "He hasn't touched me since, Bridie. He tried, but I tore his face with my nails."

I knew with cold certainty that if I could find a way to kill Victor Sarrazin I would do it. I said, "Was that when he made this bruise on your face?"

She shook her head. "No, he did that when I wouldn't write a letter inviting you here." Her face twisted with alarm. "Oh, dear God, Bridie, you shouldn't have come! That's what he wants."

"It's all right, darling, I didn't come alone." I drew her towards a sofa. "Let's sit down while you tell me what happened."

She spoke haltingly at first, but then the words came tumbling out. The elopement had been planned in the way I already knew, except that she had written to me and to Signor Peroni. Sarrazin had pretended to post the letters in Dover on Friday afternoon, and next day they had been married in Paris under special licence.

They had travelled down to Valbrison on Monday. It was then that Victor Sarrazin let fall the mask he had worn. His cronies were already at the château, the women were soon brought in, and for Kate the unbelievable nightmare had begun. She was Victor Sarrazin's wife, completely in his power, and he meant to use her to lure me into his grasp.

Now Kate looked at me anxiously. "You did say your fiancé was with you, didn't you, Bridie. He's a detective whom Victor fears."

"I told you I wasn't alone, but it isn't Nathan with me. He had to go back to America. I came with another detective called Philippe Chatillon." Then I told her all that Philippe had recounted to me of his surveillance in England, how he had watched over Kate, and found himself falling in love with her. She shook her head in bewilderment.

"I don't suppose Victor will allow me to see this gentleman," she said. "But please thank him for me, and say that I am . . . honoured to learn of his feelings." She pressed my fingers. "Thank God he is with you, Bridie dear. At least it means you will go safely away from this place."

"But we're not going without you, Kate!" I exclaimed. "All Sarrazin wants is the spoils Papa left, and between us Philippe and I have found most of the answers to that riddle. Philippe will offer him all we know in return for you."

She looked at me from eyes that were now far wiser than they had been such a little time ago. "It isn't all Sarrazin wants," she said quietly. "One of the reasons he made me his wife is because he relishes humiliating a daughter of Roger Chance. He envied Papa so much that it became hatred."

I felt a chill of apprehension. At that moment the door opened, and the man Alex stepped into the room. Looking at me, he jerked his head and said in French, "He wants to see you downstairs."

I hesitated, then squeezed Kate's hand and said, "I'll be back soon. Try not to worry, dear. You're not alone any more."

To my surprise Sarrazin was by himself in the dining hall when I followed Alex in. He was lounging in a chair, a glass of wine in one hand. With a tremendous effort I held down the hatred that surged within me. I must do nothing which might jeopardize Kate. Moving forward, I said, "I take it you have discussed with M'sieur Chatillon the matter which brought us here?"

"Yes. He explained what he wanted very concisely, but to my great disappointment he has refused to give me the information I desire until I enter into certain agreements concerning my dear wife." He stood up. "I believe the letter and photographs are in your possession at this moment."

I gripped my handbag tightly. "Yes, but I will show you nothing and tell you nothing until M'sieur Chatillon is satisfied that he has secured Kate's freedom from you. Where is he?"

"You have a hard heart, mam'selle, to speak of taking my new bride from me." He gave a sorrowful shrug. "Before we discuss it further, I would like to show you something which I am sure you will find of interest. Then we will join M'sieur Chatillon—he is with my wife. If you will permit me?"

I said impatiently, "Very well."

We went out of the room, along a passage and into a cluttered kitchen where Sarrazin paused to light a lantern, then turned through an arch into a small dark room. There was a heavy iron bar set horizontally at waist height between two ancient stone blocks. Beyond the barrier, I saw a black hole some nine or ten feet in diameter.

Sarrazin stood by the bar and pointed down. "The Valbrison Well," he said musingly. "A natural shaft which drops sheer for eighty metres into a river which flows underground for some twelve miles before emerging to join the Dordogne."

A sense of dreadful unease gripped me as Sarrazin went on. "Anything which is dropped down that shaft will surface in the river gorge after eight or nine days." He gave a little chuckle. "Even a man. I have put this phenomenon to the test myself. What is most interesting is that the icy cold of the underground river causes the body to be preserved, so that when it is found it appears that death occurred only a few hours before. Thus the impression is given that the unfortunate person died by falling into the gorge far from Château Valbrison."

"Why do you tell me this?"

"Simply as an exercise in imagination, mam'selle. Let us imagine, for example, that my wife married me because she believed I was a rich man, and despite the fact that she had a lover in the person of Philippe Chatillon. Let us imagine that when she discovered I was not rich, she decided to run away with her lover. I would be heartbroken, of course. I would probably go to Paris, and I would be in Paris eight or nine days later, when their two bodies were found in the river, *recently* dead."

In a voice that was an ugly whisper I managed to force out a few halting words. "Where . . . where is my sister?"

"Quite safe, mam'selle." But I could see in his eyes the deep pleasure he drew from my distress. "Let us go and join her now, together with your friend M'sieur Chatillon."

I felt lost and afraid. As I followed Sarrazin out through the kitchen, I knew that he had crossed the border of sanity in pursuit of the plunder he had coveted for so long. I scarcely noticed the route we took, and after two or three minutes I found myself following him into a dark stone cellar. Facing us were several ancient iron-bound doors, and I realized with a shock that this was not a cellar but a dungeon. From a gap beneath one of the doors came a faint light, and on a hook to one side of it hung a great iron key.

Sarrazin walked up to the door and pushed a small panel to one side. He looked into the cell for a moment, and then motioned me to take his place. Through the peep-hole I saw Kate kneeling on the stone floor, cradling Philippe Chatillon's head on her lap. He lay sprawled on his back, unconscious, with blood running from a cut in the side of his head. No doubt she had looked up and seen Sarrazin when he first opened the panel, but she was not looking up now. As I stared numbly, she tore off a piece of her petticoat to press against Philippe's wound.

I whispered, "Kate."

She looked up, glaring defiance, then her face changed. "Bridie, are you all right?"

"Yes," I said shakily. "Is Philippe badly hurt?"

"So this is the man who came with you. I was brought down here only a few minutes ago, and I found him lying on the floor like this. His heart and his breathing seem steady."

Sarrazin laughed. "It will take more than a crack on the head to kill Chatillon," he said. "Who knows, it might even bring him to his senses! The lovesick fool must have been out of his mind to come marching into Château Valbrison."

A look of contempt and loathing touched Kate's bruised face. "Don't trust him, Bridie," she said. "I'm not sure what he's planning now, but don't trust him for a second."

I couldn't help burying my face in my hands and I leaned against the wall, weeping. Behind me, Sarrazin laughed again, and through my stifled sobs I heard the sound of the panel being closed.

"Come," he said briskly, "we have work to do." I drew a deep breath and turned as he smiled insolently at me. "We shall now return to the dining room, dear sister-in-law," he said. "There you will tell me everything you know about *Le Sorcier*'s treasure. If you are tempted to refuse, please remember the Valbrison Well, and what may happen to a deceitful wife and her secret lover."

TEN MINUTES LATER I sat looking at Victor Sarrazin across the long table. I had told him everything, and now he was gazing down at the letter and photographs in brooding silence. Then his head came up, and the hazel eyes were glinting in triumph.

"*Tête de Chèvre*," he said softly. "I knew it at once, but I have been trying to understand how. . . ." His fist thumped down on the table. "By God, that cunning dog had me tricked for years! He would come from Paris with a locked attaché case. I had him followed everywhere in the city before his trips here, but we could never discover when he visited his hoard. And no wonder, because there was no hoard in Paris! Now I remember that he always stayed overnight at the village of Charlet before coming here to do business with me. He claimed he liked to visit Charlet because he spent his honeymoon there but, of course, *it was also because he wanted to visit his hiding place . . . !*"

Sarrazin sprang to his feet, ran to a cupboard, and dragged out a map. "Here!" He jabbed at the map with his finger. "Here is *Tête de Chèvre*. I saw it once when I was a boy. It lies between Charlet and Château Valbrison among high hills of barren rock." He looked up from the map with a wild glare. "Your father would go from the smithy at Charlet during the night to select from his plunder or add to it. And in all the years that I handled the selling for him, I never dreamed that the booty lay no more than an hour's ride from this château." Sarrazin flung back his head and gave a shout of laughter. "But I win at last, my clever colleague! Victor Sarrazin will have the spoils of *Le Sorcier!*" Jumping to his feet he strode to the door and jerked it open. "Alex! Didi! Here, quickly!"

He was folding the map when the two men arrived. "We have it, my friends," he said with a grin of triumph. "Didi, fetch a lantern, some rope, a short jemmy and a pistol. Hurry, man. Alex, go and saddle my horse. One for the girl, also. I'm riding up into the hills with her, to make sure there's no mistake about Roger Chance's treasure being where it should be."

"But we have no sidesaddle for the girl," said Alex.

"You have a *knife*, idiot! She must ride astride. If you slit her skirt and petticoats, then there is no problem."

As Alex reached the door I said, "If you bring scissors and safety pins I will see to my dress without assistance."

Sarrazin spoke from behind me now, his voice grim. "Very well. But let there be one minute's delay and by God I'll show you how quickly a dress can be altered."

Somewhere a clock chimed once. Looking down at my watch I could see that the time was half-past four o'clock. Unbelievably, it was less than an hour since Philippe and I had crossed the threshold of Château Valbrison.

Chapter Thirteen

The horse beneath me was sweating. We had been climbing for more than an hour now, starting our journey along a track which led directly north from Château Valbrison into a small wooded plateau. Beyond the woods there was no trail, only hills which were barren except for the few hardy plants which grew in crevices.

I had cut my skirt and petticoats and pinned the edges to make crude breeches for riding. My wrists were bound, with perhaps fifteen inches of rope between them so that I could manage the reins. Sarrazin rode ahead with my horse on a long leading rein. One pocket of his jacket was weighed down by a heavy pistol, and by his saddlebag hung a cavalry sabre in a sheath. Somehow I held down my terror. Deep within me I clung to a slender thread of hope for Kate and Philippe.

The sun was low in the sky now, and we were moving north along a broad limestone valley with a series of smaller valleys running off at intervals on the eastern side. For the past several minutes Sarrazin had turned his head to look down each valley as we passed its mouth.

Suddenly he gave a great cry of triumph and pointed a quivering finger. "There, girl! There is *Tête de Chèvre!*"

We were looking along a valley to our right, and to me it seemed little different from any of the others. It ran straight between sheer walls and then bent in a dog-leg so that the rest of the valley was hidden from us. But suddenly I saw it, the strange formation of the cliff face at the dog-leg. There, beyond all question, was the giant head of a goat. It was in half profile, and the discoloration in the rock served as much as the freak of natural sculpture to make the features stand out clearly. The horns were black, where two curving furrows ran over a steep rounded slope. The eyes and the nose were blackish-brown hollows. A slight undercut formed the lower jaw of the face, and some wavering cracks beneath gave the effect of a little beard.

Sarrazin glanced back at the red orb of the sun dropping towards the horizon, and gave a jerk on the leading rein. "Come!" he said hoarsely, and we moved into the valley. As the horses picked their way between rocks and we drew nearer to the turn in the valley, the goat's head began to lose its form.

Once round the sharp bend, the valley ran straight again. For as far as I could see, the walls were scarred with cracks and holes, but I was only fleetingly aware of this, for my eyes were held by the Capricorn Stone, and I heard Sarrazin give a gasp of delight.

It was just as I had seen it in the photographs, a weathered crag of hard rock rising from the softer limestone, and no more than a stone's throw from us. Our horses stepped onto smoother ground, and a few seconds later we were before the Capricorn Stone, with the setting sun throwing a great black finger of shadow across the valley bottom. Sarrazin was actually grunting with excitement, making a small ugly noise with each breath. The calm, urbane gentleman was an animal now.

Without a word he nudged his horse along the line of the shadow, and where the shadow ended, he continued in the same direction. In another few seconds we came to the cliff of seamed and pock-marked rock which formed the southern wall of the valley. There we stopped, and Sarrazin snapped, "Get down, girl!"

I swung down from the saddle. There was no stiffness, for my muscles were in perfect condition from months of dancing, and I was fleetingly thankful for this. If by some miracle a chance came to harm Sarrazin in any way, I wanted to be nimble enough to make the most of it.

He was on foot himself now, staring at the wall of rock. Suddenly he whirled round, face distorted, and hit my face with the back of his hand. "Where is it, you—!" He used a French word unknown to me. "Where is it?"

I ducked to one side, taking most of the force from the blow. Even so, it made my face burn and my eyes water with shock. I backed away as he advanced towards me like a cat about to spring. It was then I saw it, the gap in the rock which even at a short distance would look like one of the hundreds of ancient channels blackened by weather.

"There!" I cried frantically, pointing past him with both my bound hands. "It's an opening! There!"

He stopped short, watching me suspiciously, then flicked a glance over his shoulder. Almost at once he looked back, and now his sweating face was agleam with eagerness. "Not quite where the shadow pointed," he said panting. "Different time of year, perhaps. Who cares?" He ran to his horse, took the lantern from the saddlebag, and crouched to light the lantern, cursing as he broke a match in his haste. Then he jerked his head towards the crevice. "You first, little sister, I don't want you behind me."

Sarrazin held the lantern high as I moved through the gap into a tall, narrow passage. After I had taken three cautious paces, the passage turned abruptly and opened out into a cave. Sarrazin thrust me against the wall. "Stand still," he growled, and strode past me, shining the beam from the lantern steadily round. The cave was roughly oval in shape, with the roof sloping steeply at one end. On the floor, there were a few small rocks scattered about amid limestone dust and rubble. The lantern beam fastened on the only rock of any size, a flat-topped piece of stone with a rounded underside which rested snugly in a shallow natural hollow in the ground.

"It's under there," Sarrazin whispered. "Under there, by God!" The beam began to dart wildly about the cave. "Where is the crowbar? The waiting crow? Where the devil has the fool hidden it?" His voice rose in fury and he moved quickly round the cave, crouching, peering, cursing again in his frustration. Then the light came suddenly to rest on a thin tapering crack at shoulder height. Sarrazin moved forward with a gasp of triumph, and drew out a heavy crowbar, almost losing his grip as the end came clear. He stood the lantern down and worked the tip of the crow under the stone. As he strained and grunted in the darkness beyond the pool of lantern light, he seemed even more like some dreadful animal.

At last the stone was clear of the cavity. Sarrazin flung the crowbar aside and lifted out something wrapped in oilskin. As he tore the oilskin away I saw a cylinder of dull metal. He unscrewed the lid and set it aside, tilting the cylinder so that the light shone into it. Carefully, he lifted out an object wrapped in a piece of cloth, and with shaking hands he unfolded the corners. Green, white and red fire glittered from between his suddenly motionless hands. Emeralds, diamonds, rubies lay flashing under the touch of the light. For a long moment Sarrazin did not move, then a high-pitched laugh broke from his lips and he reached feverishly into the cylinder again.

I took a wary step backwards. I was in the shadows, my back to the narrow entrance, and although Sarrazin faced me he was for the moment totally obsessed by the plunder in his hands. I took another step back, and then another, my mind a fever of half-formed thoughts. I could not hope to disable Sarrazin or to reach the valley mouth. My best hope was to hide among the endless jumble of rock. If he failed to hunt me down, I would somehow find my way to Charlet, to the smithy perhaps, and to the police. . . .

I had turned the corner now and was backing out into the light. For a moment I was tempted to mount Sarrazin's horse and take mine on the leading rein, but I was no horsewoman, and knew I could make but painfully slow speed over the rocky ground. As I emerged blinking into the fading sunlight I turned at once and began to run, grateful now for my divided skirt. I made for some

263

huge boulders mingled with rocks of every shape and size. If I reached there safely, I might be able to hide till darkness fell.

I had never been more thankful for my hours of training for the stage, for I was in no measure breathless when I reached my objective. Fine balance and deftness of footwork were instinctive to me now as I leaped to a sloping surface, swung across to the top of a rock beyond, then dropped down into a hollow beneath a boulder. Even as I wriggled through the crevice I heard a great shout from along the valley.

Sarrazin's voice. He was screaming abuse, blasphemy, and threats. I hugged the ground, frozen with fear, then forced myself to wriggle on. Once through the crevice I crawled onto a flat outcrop. Just in front of it, a tapering rock leaned against a crag, with only a hand's-breadth gap between them. Suddenly I realized that I could lie flat on my stomach on the outcrop, and through the gap command a full view of the valley without being seen myself.

I drew myself up warily onto the flat surface, every nerve aquiver. Then I was staring through the slender gap, just in time to see Sarrazin as he vanished from view round the dog-leg bend, urging his horse on at a wildly dangerous pace. He had naturally thought I must have run that way, but would soon discover his mistake.

When Sarrazin did not sight me in the valley mouth, he would return to hunt for me. I would have to leave my vantage point then and find a cranny in which to tuck myself away. Or I could listen for his approach and try to evade him amid the maze of rocks in a game of hide-and-seek . . . with death as the penalty for being found.

I was trying to decide which course was better when Sarrazin reappeared, moving slowly now, allowing his horse to pick its way along the treacherous ground. He dismounted just beyond the Capricorn Stone, and disappeared into the cave entrance. I guessed that he was first going to secure the jewellery before starting the hunt for me. Awkwardly I began to worry loose the knots securing my wrists, lifting my head every two or three seconds to keep watch for Sarrazin.

A hand gripped my ankle gently, and the shock was like a physical blow. Every nerve within me seemed to give a silent scream, and my head snapped round as if on a spring.

Weather-brown face, bright blue eyes with crow's feet at the corners, black gaucho hat pushed to the back of his head, a rope coiled over one shoulder. . . . Nathan McFee. He lay prone on the same outcrop, his head near my left foot, and as I gazed in wonder he wriggled up to me. His hand touched my chin, drawing me towards him a little, and he kissed me gently on the lips. "That's my girl," he said quietly, and smiled. "That's my Bridie."

I wanted to say a dozen things at once, but all I could manage was a bewildered whisper. "Nathan?"

"In person, honey. Tell you everything later, but for the moment just know I really love you and never stopped. Now keep watching for Sarrazin." I turned my eyes back to the crevice, and through my body there surged a great golden tide of joy and relief. The danger remained, but I was no longer alone. Nathan was with me, Nathan, Nathan! My heart sang.

"Tell me what's happening," he said, and reached for my wrists. Something cold touched my flesh, then the rope fell away.

Struggling to control my voice I whispered, "He's in the cave. He brought me up from Château Valbrison this afternoon—"

"I know, Bridie. I trailed you on foot the whole way. Figured he had a gun, so I didn't dare get close. Once he saw me he'd just stick it against your head and give his orders."

Nathan's hand ran lovingly over my shoulder. I kept my eyes fixed on the cave entrance as my feelings seesawed wildly. One second I could feel nothing but joy at having Nathan beside me, the next nothing but fear for Kate and Philippe. "Sarrazin's married Kate," I said, and marvelled that my voice should sound so calm. "She's a prisoner in the château now, along with Philippe Chatillon. I'm so frightened for them, Nathan. Do you have a pistol?"

"Never carry one, honey. Made a promise to Ma, way back, when they strung up Pa. Carry a bowie, though." I glanced down for a second and saw in his hand the big knife he had used to cut the rope from my wrists.

Then I looked again at the entrance of the cave. "He's coming out, Nathan! Carrying the cylinder containing the jewellery."

"Right. Keep watching. And let me have some of your petticoat. I'll need two pieces, each about two feet square." He laid down the knife. "Use this. I'll be back in a minute."

265

He seemed to melt away without a sound. I saw that Sarrazin was moving towards the grey horse. As he began to tie the container securely to the saddle, I picked up the knife, and began to unpin my skirt.

WHEN NATHAN returned, I had managed to cut two pieces from my petticoat. He had brought two rocks about the size of large coconuts and with deft hands he folded each rock into a square of white lawn and knotted it securely. Then he sliced a six-foot length from his lasso and began to tie an end of it to the knotted cloth holding one of the rocks. As he did so, from a hundred yards down the valley, Sarrazin lifted his voice in a penetrating call.

"*Bridie! Bridie Chance!*"

Nathan flicked a glance at me and said, "Here it comes, honey. Brace yourself."

"*Bridie Chance!*" Sarrazin continued. "*I know you are hiding nearby. I know you can hear me. If you do not come from hiding in three minutes, I will return to Château Valbrison. And with the help of my friends I shall begin to make your sister wish that she had never been born! Do you understand, Bridie Chance?*"

I felt the blood drain from my face. Nathan finished tying the other end of the six-foot rope to the second rock, knotting it to the gathered linen. "He means it, Bridie, believe me," he said quietly. "Only one way to save Kate, and that's to finish this business right now. You ready to take a gamble with me?"

I nodded mutely and he kissed me again. "Just keep beside me," Nathan went on. "He'll come at us fast. When I say 'now', you go down on one knee." Again he touched his lips to mine. "The rest is up to me. I love you, Bridie Chance, and I sure hope you're going to love me again."

I put my hand to his cheek and said, "I've never stopped, Nathan." We lay looking at each other, and in Nathan's eyes I found all I needed. Explanations would come, if we lived, but they no longer mattered.

He took my hand and said, "Let's go, Bridie." Next moment he had slithered from the outcrop and was helping me down. The bowie knife was in a sheath on his belt, and in his right hand he gripped the rope connecting the two rocks.

The western sky was red with the dying sun as we stepped from the maze of boulders hand in hand and began to walk slowly forward. Sarrazin had mounted his horse and was silhouetted against the sunset, and suddenly a great shout burst from him, his voice throbbing with triumph.

"McFee! By God, you have presented me with a clean sweep today, Yankee!" His arm swept suddenly high in the air, and for a moment something glinted blood-red in the rays of the vanishing sun. Then there was only the multiple echo of hoof-beats on rock as he set his horse to a gallop, the bared sabre held in the classic position of the cavalry charge.

Beside me Nathan said, "Right, Bridie . . . now."

I released his hand and dropped to one knee close beside him, trembling. The sight of Sarrazin coming hard at us was truly bloodchilling. A single blow of the sabre would cut a man almost in two, and no doubt he expected us to turn and run, so that he could take each of us in turn as his target.

Beside me Nathan lifted his right arm. I looked up to see that he was holding the rope in the middle and swinging the two weights round above his head in a whirling circle. From the depths of childhood memory a word came back to me, a word associated with Argentina and the pampas . . . *bolas!* The *bolas* consisted of two or three iron balls with a length of rope between, skilfully thrown to wrap round the legs of wild cattle or large game. . . .

Sarrazin was thirty yards away when Nathan released the make-shift *bolas*. The two cloth-covered rocks flew through the air, gradually separating until the rope between them was fully extended and horizontal. But Nathan had not thrown for the horse's legs, he had thrown for the man. I think Sarrazin saw nothing of the rope in the fading light, only the bulk of the two weights at each end as they flew towards him. He had opened his mouth in a whooping cry of exultation when the rope caught him across the chest. The flying rocks snapped viciously round each side of him, and the rope tightened in a flash, pinning his left arm to his chest so that he lost control of the reins. The twin weights whipped round again across his chest and his back, one weight finally thud-ding against his chest and the other catching the back of his head.

As Sarrazin fell from the saddle, his head struck a rock and the sabre clattered away. His left foot was still caught in the stirrup,

267

and as the galloping horse came on at a furious pace, his body bumped across the unforgiving rock. Beside me Nathan crouched a little and jumped. For a moment he clung to the horse with one hand on the pommel and one on the mane, then he bounded into the saddle and wrenched the animal to a halt. After soothing the frightened creature, he slid to the ground, where he freed Sarrazin's foot from the stirrup and dropped on one knee beside him. Then he looked up and shook his head. "He's dead, Bridie. I guess he died when he first hit the ground."

As I stood up, I felt nothing but relief. Nathan rose to his feet. "Will you go and bring the other mount please, honey? I'll tie Sarrazin on that and we'll ride double on this one."

"Yes, Nathan." I began to walk back to the cave, then I caught my breath in alarm and broke into a run. Kate and Philippe. I had forgotten them in the last few minutes. As I came hurrying back with the grey I called, "We must go to Kate quickly, Nathan!"

"Sure, Bridie." He had brought his lasso from among the rocks, and now he lifted Sarrazin's body onto the grey. "Don't fret too much, honey," he said. "Sarrazin's men won't touch your sister without his orders. But we'll be down there in well under an hour, anyway."

I said, "But there are four of those brutes waiting for us, Nathan."

He slid an arm round my body. "They've no leader, Bridie. And I have you back now, so I'm riding tall tonight."

DUSK BECAME DARKNESS as we were on our way down from the high valleys, but then came a clear moon to ease our going. In that time we scarcely spoke except to murmur a loving word. I rode with Nathan's arms about me, my back against his chest. For a while I wanted nothing more than to be close to him with all anxiety shut away, simply feeling in his presence a happiness and contentment beyond description.

At last I gave a long sigh and pressed my hand over his. "Tell me, Nathan dear."

He held me yet more tightly, and when he spoke his soft drawl was a little ragged. "That day, Bridie, the day I left you, a man brought a message to me at the stage door. It was from Sarrazin. It said by the time I read it, he would be in France and married to Kate. If I valued her welfare, and yours, I was to get out of

England by the first possible boat. The message said I'd be under observation, and he'd be told by telegraph if I didn't act right away. So I took passage from Southampton to New York. Then I quit ship at Le Havre and headed down here. He had me figured as the biggest threat to his laying hands on the jewellery. That's why I couldn't tell you, honey. I didn't dare. If I did, and somehow you came face to face with him, he'd soon find out I was still around, and then he'd go loco. I was scared of what he might do then."

I said, "Yes. He was insane." Then, after a pause: "When you were in London, why did you ask Charlie if I was courting?"

"Wanted to know if Sarrazin was trying to get at you. I'd heard he could charm any girl, if he set his mind to it."

"Yes. He did try with me, but . . . I didn't want to be charmed." I pressed his hand. "Nathan, was it very hard for you that day—I mean, pretending you didn't love me?"

"I never had to do a harder thing in my life, Bridie," he said slowly. "I cabled my resignation to Pinkertons from Manchester when I first knew I loved you. I guess they were mad as wet hens. It was too late to put a new man in, so they cabled back and said they'd be glad if I'd just stay on guard to keep any criminal parties away from you. That was fine with me."

"Why ever didn't you tell me then?"

"Tell you I'd struck up acquaintance under false pretences? That I'd started out by working for a detective agency, trying to prize information out of you? Bridie, I was afraid you'd hate the sight of me. Afraid you'd think I was just trying a new line to find out what I wanted to know."

I shook my head. "No. I would have believed you, Nathan. I love you."

"Those are the best words I ever heard." He was silent for a moment. Then, "Bridie, you know what nearly broke me? It was when I pretended I'd never loved you and was only doing a job. You could easily have cut me to pieces for being a lowdown skunk, but you didn't. You just said goodbye and wished me well . . . and nearly tore my heart out." He bent his head to kiss my neck.

As we rode on, I learned that he had come down from Le Havre by train for there had been no time to arrange transport for Lucifer. From Brive he had travelled on foot over the hills to

270

Valbrison, where he had made a small camp in the woods from which he could watch the château. Nathan had missed seeing my arrival with Philippe, but he had seen me leave with Sarrazin, and had then trailed us up into the valleys to the Capricorn Stone.

There were lights burning in the windows of the château as we rode through the outer courtyard and dismounted under the archway. Nathan untied Sarrazin's body and heaved it over one shoulder without ceremony. "Stay close behind me, honey," he said, his voice calm and gentle.

He walked with long strides towards the porch, and continued up the steps. I felt no fear now, for I had put my whole trust in him, and I did as he had said, keeping close behind him all the way. Reaching out, he heaved on the bell-pull, and we heard the loud jangling within. A full minute passed. At last there came the rattle of a bolt being drawn and the voice of a man calling in French. "Victor! Thank God you are back! They've broken out—"

The door was open no more than six inches when Nathan smashed his foot against it in a tremendous kick. I heard a cry of anguish as the door was hurled back, and I followed Nathan into the poorly-lit hall. The thickset man called Didi lay sprawled on his back half a dozen paces away, one hand clasped over a bloody face, the other groping for a pistol which lay where it had evidently fallen beside him as he was flung to the floor. Without apparent haste Nathan kicked the pistol and sent it slithering across the floor. Then he dropped Sarrazin's body beside Didi. "There is your master. He is dead. Do you wish to follow him to hell?"

To my surprise, Nathan had spoken in French. The accent was quite the most astonishing I had ever heard, the kind that makes a Frenchman wince or laugh. But no man alive could have looked into Nathan's face at that moment and laughed. Didi gave a strange whimper and crawled frantically away from the body.

Two lamps were burning in the hall, but there were no lights on the gallery above and the staircase rose into a pool of darkness. Nathan moved to the foot of the stairs and stood listening, and I saw that the big knife was in his hand now. Lifting his voice he called, "Monsewer Chatillon?"

From above there came a sudden scuffling noise, and then a limp figure tumbled down the stairs. Nathan stepped aside as it sprawled to a halt. Sarrazin's henchman Felix lay face up, un-

271

conscious, a short black club attached to his wrist by a leather loop.

A voice from the darkness said, "There is only one man in the world with such an accent, and I am more than glad to hear it, Mr. McFee." Philippe Chatillon emerged from the gloom at the top of the stairs as he spoke. He had a stained bandage round his head and a heavy black poker in his right hand.

Nathan sketched a mock bow and said, "Glad to see you, mon-sewer. Bridie tells me there were four men here."

"No longer. When that rogue Sarrazin left, one of his henchmen was foolish enough to visit our dungeon and I managed to disable him and later overpower one of his colleagues. Then your arrival made a diversion which enabled me to do the same with that one." He nodded down at Felix. "But I am most grateful to you for dealing with Didi. He was the one with a pistol—"

Philippe broke off and half turned, reaching out a hand. "Yes, come, *ma petite*," he said gently. "It is finished now." Kate appeared from the darkness of the gallery, and took his out-stretched hand.

"Where is Sarrazin?" she said in a low voice.

"He is dead, ma'am," Nathan said quietly.

Kate nodded slowly, and the fierce tension seemed to drain out of her. She looked past Nathan to where I stood, and her voice broke as she said, "You were so kind before, Bridie. Don't be cross with me now it's over."

I opened my arms to her for the second time that day. She gave a little sob, came flying down the stairs, and threw herself into my arms.

"Bridie, thank God you're safe. I was sure he meant to kill you. Oh Bridie, I've been so wickedly stupid . . . caused so much trouble and pain. I'm so ashamed I wish I could die. And Philippe has been so good to me. Nobody could have been more gentle, comforting, and brave. But I'm too ashamed to face him now. Hold me tight, Bridie. . . ."

I did not try to stem her outpouring of sorrow and humiliation. There would be time enough later to try to heal the cruel wounds she bore within her. For the moment it was enough that she could say all that was in her heart. I led her to a sofa and made her sit down, and just kept gently patting her shoulder until at last her muffled voice trailed into the silence of exhaustion.

After a while I closed my eyes. When I roused I saw Philippe standing watching us, his face weary, but his eyes alert. Kate did not stir.

In a low voice I said, "Please can we go soon, Philippe? This is a place of horror for my sister. For us all, I think."

"In a very few minutes we will leave, Bridie." He turned his head to look towards the dining hall. "Sarrazin lies in there, and we have locked the others in the cell below. My good friend Nathan has ridden to fetch his belongings from his camp in the woods. He will bring the carriage from the coach house, and we shall drive down to the station at Valbrison. I will tell the local gendarme to take charge here until men can be sent from the Sûreté. We ourselves can take the next train to Paris."

My head ached, and it was an effort to think. "The police won't ask questions of Kate tonight, will they?" I asked. "She's endured so much, Philippe."

He shook his head quickly. "Have no fear of that, Bridie, I will arrange everything. You won't even be involved in court proceedings. The examining magistrate will certainly find that Victor Sarrazin brought about his own death. Beyond that, there is nothing to answer. The newspapers will mention the recovery of the jewellery, of course, but very soon . . ." he spread his hands and smiled, "very soon it will all be finished. Tomorrow we shall be in Paris, and I hope that you all will be guests in my home."

"Thank you, Philippe. You're very kind, and it would be a great relief to be under your wing until this affair is over."

"It will be my pleasure." He made a little gesture towards Kate. "Is Miss Kate asleep?"

She stirred in my arm, and pressed her face more closely into my shoulder. In a barely audible voice she said, "No . . . but I'm ashamed to look at you, Philippe. I have brought you all close to death by what I have done."

"No, that was Sarrazin's work. Do not blame yourself for being deceived by him."

There was a little silence, and I sensed that this was a moment of very great importance.

Philippe said reflectively, "Your dress is smeared with my blood, Miss Kate. When I was hurt, you cared for me, and when I moved against our captors, you put your trust in me. Between those who have passed through the shadow of death together, as we have, there is a bond which might otherwise take a thousand days to forge. Until three hours ago we had never spoken, but surely we are close friends now, you and I?"

For a moment Kate's head was bowed, then she lifted it and looked towards Philippe, her eyes weary and older than her years now.

"I am a secondhand woman, Philippe," she said.

He smiled. "Rubbish, *ma petite*. You are a young, talented and beautiful girl with more than enough intelligence to realize that you have been the victim of a monster, and that you have the whole of life before you. Let the past lie dead, and the future begin tomorrow." He extended a hand. "Please."

She closed her eyes for a moment. When she opened them again I saw tears run down her cheeks, and then she stood up and took Philippe's outstretched hand. A wave of thankfulness swept through me. "All will be well, Kate," Philippe said quietly.

I rose and moved to the open door. A carriage and pair stood in the starlit courtyard at the foot of the steps. From the outer courtyard came the sound of hooves, and next moment Nathan cantered through the archway. He reined in, slid to the ground, and threw a knapsack into the carriage. Then he slipped an arm round my waist. "Where's Kate?"

"In the hall, Nathan dear." I pressed his hand. "Philippe is looking after her."

"Ah. That's good." He grinned, lifted his voice and called in his excruciating French, "*La voiture vous attend, monsewer!*"

I heard Philippe laugh, and a few seconds later he led Kate out. Nathan was holding the carriage door open, but she paused, turning to him.

"I have not thanked you yet, Mr. McFee." She put her hands on his shoulders and kissed his cheek, then turned and climbed into the coach. Nathan blinked, pushed his hat back on his head, and looked at Philippe.

"There's something about these Chance girls," he said.

Philippe laughed, then gestured towards the carriage door. "Please to ascend, Bridie, and then let us be away."

I shook my head. "You go with Kate, please." I took Nathan's arm and hugged it to me. "I'm going to ride with the driver."

274

✺ Chapter Fourteen ✺

Early on a morning of golden weather in my second summer in New England, I rose from the splendid bath in our newly-installed bathroom, and reached for one of the big white towels. As I dried myself I smiled at the memory of the times I had sat in a battered hip-bath in dressing rooms from Edinburgh to Birmingham, sponging paperhanger's paste from my body.

Excitement bubbled within me, for yesterday had brought two letters and there was much to look forward to, even beyond the everyday happiness that life had given me. When I had towelled myself dry I put on a clean shift, then padded on bare feet to the nursery where six-month-old Philip Nathan McFee lay sound asleep in his cot. His wrath if woken up to be fed was terrible to behold, so I crept silently back into our bedroom, where Philip Nathan McFee's father lay sprawled face down beneath a rumpled sheet.

Quietly I moved to the dressing table and picked up Kate's letter to read it again. She wrote now with unfailing regularity, but this letter held special news.

Nathan said suddenly, "Morning Mrs. McFee, ma'am."

I gave a start of surprise, then floated back across the room in a reverse Willow Strut, eyes wide and mouth round as I conjured up "Arnold" of Alfie Perkin and Company. Nathan propped himself up on his elbow with a laugh of delight. "Hey, it's better when you're just in a shift, Bridie. Your legs show more. Do the Crab Glide for me."

I hitched up my shift and went undulating across the room towards him, my face wearing an expression of wanton menace. Nowadays I never worried about the way my face behaved, for Nathan loved what Nannie Foster had always called my "exaggerated expressions".

As I reached the bed he gave a shout of laughter, and I flung myself upon him, kissing him hard and long. When I lifted my head he said a little breathlessly, "How's the young master?"

"Still asleep. Oh Nathan, isn't it wonderful news from Kate? Could we go to Paris after Christmas, so we could be there when she has her baby?"

"Sure, Bridie. Young Philip Nathan will be a year old by then. High time he started to see some of the world."

Kate had married Philippe Chatillon three months ago. We had been unable to go to the wedding, for our baby was then only twelve weeks old.

"It will be so lovely to see her," I said. "And Philippe, too. I suppose it's a pity she isn't going on seriously with her music, but after all if she'd wanted to be a concert pianist, she'd have had to make it her life."

He gave me a little squeeze. "Well, I figure she's got something better. She can play for herself, her family, her friends. Let someone else be famous."

"Yes, Nathan. And isn't the other letter exciting?"

This other letter was from Charlie, and also carried special news. Alfie Perkin and Company had been booked to tour the major East Coast cities and they had arranged for a break of two weeks before playing Boston, only forty miles from our home.

"I'm so fond of them, Nathan," I said. "I'll never forget all they did for me."

"Nor shall I, honey," he said soberly. "Now listen, you write today and say they're to be our guests for those two weeks."

Just then, a faint wail found its way through from the nursery, growing steadily more demanding. Nathan sighed, kissed me, and let me go. I rose from him reluctantly and moved to open the blinds so that bright sunshine lit the room.

"Fetch him in to feed him, Bridie, huh?" Nathan urged softly.

"So you can just lie there watching, while we do all the work?"

"That's what I had in mind." He reached out his arms.

I went to him, ruffled his hair, and bent to be kissed again. Then, with my heart singing, I went through to the nursery to fetch our son.

Madeleine Brent is a pen-name, one of the best-kept publishing secrets of the decade. Here, this highly successful author, who is known to be well established in at least one other field of literary endeavour, recalls two "fragments of memory" that led her to write her latest novel of romance and high adventure.

Some years ago I read a newspaper report about a man who was caught after twenty-five years as a professional thief. He lived with his wife and two teenage children in a detached house in Surrey, went off to work by car each morning and returned in the early evening. During that time he would normally rob one house, sometimes two. They were always well beyond the Surrey borders. He took only cash, jewellery, and small objects of value.

Throughout all these years of crime his wife believed him to be a self-employed insurance consultant.

The second memory. In the nineteen-thirties, when I was in my early teens, I was constantly doing battle with my older brother, Tim. He was a male chauvinist long before the phrase came into common use. All boys were in those days. Tim belonged to a troop of Scouts who were to put on a show at a local hall. He and a friend undertook to contribute a five-minute turn. It was to be a tap-dancing horse, an idea stolen from a pantomime we had seen.

The hiring of a horse costume was arranged, and during the next two weeks Tim and his friend learned a simple tap-dancing routine from a lady who ran a school of dancing and had a child in the Brownies. The boys practised hard on a big sheet of plywood in our garden. Then the friend broke his leg by falling off a moving bus.

I could not believe my ears when Tim announced that I would have to be the hind legs of his horse because the other Scouts were all taken up with their own contributions to the show. I was not a Scout, or even a boy, and I indignantly refused even to contemplate the idea. To this day I cannot recall how I eventually came to be hopping about on a sheet of plywood under Tim's instructions for two hours every evening and endlessly throughout three weekends. I suppose I loved him.

Astonishingly, I was quite good at the routine by the time of the show, and our turn was a real success. My brother and I, true to form, managed to have a wordy battle inside the horse, for he felt that the applause called for an encore. I disagreed, for I had been hinged forward at the hips for a very long time and my back felt close to breaking. We did the encore, of course. The hind legs of a horse are not a position of power.

Well, there are my two fragments of memory, one from long ago and one more recent. These were the seeds of the story I have called *The Capricorn Stone.*

The
MASSACRE
at
FALL
CREEK

A CONDENSATION OF THE BOOK BY

Jessamyn
West

ILLUSTRATED BY TOM HALL

PUBLISHED BY MACMILLAN

In Indiana in 1824, red men were
still considered fair game for white men's
rifles. Then one day two Indian families
who camped every spring by Fall Creek
were shot down in cold blood. Incredibly,
four white men found themselves on
trial for murder.
With her rare insight into the human heart,
Jessamyn West has woven from the settlers'
terrible dilemma a novel as vibrant as the
American frontier which forms its dramatic
background. And in Hannah Cape, the
fiery young daughter of Fall Creek's
preacher, she has created one of
literature's most unforgettable
heroines.

BOOK ONE
The Crime   I

Jud Clasby, hidden in the yet-unleafed sassafras clump, watched the work going on in the camp. The three squaws and four children were as pretty as does with their fawns, he thought. He did not actually think—he spoke silently to his listening self. He was a long hunter, alone for months at a time harvesting pelts, and though he never said a word aloud, he continuously commented to himself. Because of this habit, he never knew the loneliness other long hunters spoke of.

The three women were busy, as squaws always were about camp. If Indian men had been half as industrious as their women the whole country would have been cleared, planted, and built up long ago. And where would he be then? Jud had no more farmer or storekeeping blood in him than an Indian. He too was a hunter and trapper. If the government tried to tie him to a hoe or latch him to a plow the way it had Indians, he would move on west ahead of the government. Just what the Indians were doing, too, he supposed.

This was a Seneca camp—though one of the squaws was half white, and old Tall Tree was at least half Miami. The Senecas had been pushed westwards from New York, until now here they were halfway across Indiana. And they still weren't planting and reaping. They were hunting; as he was.

The hunters of this party had not had much luck so far; but the spring was late. Now, in mid-February of 1824, the raccoons were just beginning to leave their holes in the trees; and the Indian bucks, Tall Tree and Red Cloud, had complained to him that whites were springing the traps their squaws set. Jud didn't doubt this was true. There were only ten or twelve white families living around Fall Creek, and if they had all trapped and hunted twelve hours a day seven days a week they wouldn't have skimmed the cream off the game. But the amount of game taken wasn't what bothered the settlers; it was the Indians themselves, moving down from the north to the sugar camp as if they had a right, as in the old days, to go where they pleased.

These particular men and their families had been meek as Moses, not even going into Pendleton, where other Indians were trading pelts and baskets for calico and beads and whiskey. But who knew what went on in an Indian's mind?

Red Cloud's squaw (in her thirties or forties—age was hard to judge in a squaw) was rubbing deer brains into a green hide to cure it. Tall Tree's squaw, no longer young or comely, was chewing a tanned hide to supple it. The pretty young breed was tending a pot of boiling maple sap. Yank that calico dress over her head, Jud thought, and he'd find skin as white as his own.

Which didn't make her white. There were two ways of being an Indian: to be born one, or to be raised one. This girl was fifty percent the first and a hundred percent the other. That made her a hundred and fifty percent Indian.

The wind that had been blowing into Jud's face was shifting. He had been able to smell the Indians and he supposed they would be able to smell him soon. Smell was as important for a hunter as sound. Only once in his life had he missed Indian smell, and that failure had almost cost him his life.

He had been hunting and trapping when half a dozen Sioux began to close in on him, planning to get his hair and his packload of pelts at one swoop. He out-maneuvered them, and hid in a canebrake, quiet as a coiled snake who had lost his rattle. There was no sound from the Indians, either. But if they were near, he would have smelled them. Then, between one long breath and another, they were upon him. They hadn't killed him at once because their plan for him was something more entertaining: torture the next day with the whole tribe as audience.

He hadn't been prepared for Indians he couldn't smell. Torture he had been prepared for since he had left home in York state at the age of fifteen. He believed he could make as good a showing when the fire and the slicing started as any brave. So he, knowing what was going to happen, and the Sioux, anticipating it, had traveled south together in comradely fashion.

"Why didn't I smell you?" Jud asked.

They told him. It was an advantage they had counted on. They had been fasting and had ended their religious rite with a session in the steam hut. They were as cleaned out as a wasp nest in winter. "A man smells of what he eats."

"I should have eaten Indian before I started this hunt," he told them, and they laughed, as he had known they would.

"Tomorrow," they said, "we eat you and smell white."

That was no joke. If he was brave, he would be eaten. A man became what he took into his body: the deer made him fleet; the bear, fierce; the courageous enemy, brave.

Clasby didn't hold against them the prospect of being eaten. Every hunter ate what he hunted. He had eaten Indian. Perhaps that accounted for his escape that night. He didn't smell white and he wasn't as noisy as a white. His hands were tied, but he was able on an ember of the still-smoldering fire to burn the thong that bound him. Burned his wrists, but that had been a small price to pay for freedom, then slipped into the river, soundless as an otter.

THE SQUAWS smelled him now. He could tell by the looks they exchanged. He had no wish to make them suspicious. His intention from the first had been to walk in, talk casually, and have a careful look around. But he was a hunter. He approached a camp as carefully as he approached a herd.

Before he was out of his sassafras clump, the two hunters, Tall Tree and Red Cloud, with Black Antler, the Seneca Faithkeeper, returned to the camp. Tall Tree was heavyset in the middle-aged Seneca way. Red Cloud was an Indian in his prime. Black Antler was all beak and Adam's apple.

Black Antler was a follower of Handsome Lake, the Seneca prophet. He preached the old faith of the Senecas. They had no writing for their scriptures. The prophet's teaching had to be memorized. Folded Leaf, Red Cloud's son, who was eleven or twelve and a magpie for picking up words, was being trained to be a faithkeeper.

The men had returned for their one cooked meal of the day, usually eaten in midmorning, and usually a soupy stew of meat and vegetables. Tall Tree's squaw handed the bowls around, and when Clasby stepped into the camp, he, too, was given a bowl.

"Where is Folded Leaf?" Red Cloud asked the women.

"I saw him down by the creek," Clasby told him in their own language. "Playing duck-on-rock with his brother and sisters."

Red Cloud put two fingers in his mouth and gave a blast that Clasby felt inside his nose like a gust of red pepper.

The soup was good. He had tasted and made many a pot like it. "How's the hunting?" he asked.

"Bad. Whites still spring our traps. They want to drive us out."

"You've moved in pretty close to them."

"Close to *them*. We were here before they were born."

Clasby didn't want to waste breath on this old argument. White men who had never owned an acre or been allowed to run a deer or even hunt a rabbit might not push an English squire around, but they'd found that they could push the Indian. And if he wouldn't push, why, shoot him.

Black Antler, when the children returned, took Folded Leaf to one side and had him recite what he had memorized the day before. The rigmarole the prophet Handsome Lake had preached took four full mornings to repeat. Clasby had heard enough of it to know it was nine-tenths Indian, one-tenth Christian. Handsome Lake had been influenced by the Quakers.

Listening now to Folded Leaf made Clasby uncomfortable. He had no stomach for the sight of a young savage mouthing "scriptures." He said thank you for the food he had eaten, and left.

Once Clasby was out of earshot, Talking Crow, Tall Tree's old wife, said, "Watch that one."

Red Cloud answered, "I have known him a long time. It is the other way around. He watches us."

"Like the game he hunts."

Tall Tree asked his wife, "How would you stop him?"

"In the old days, you would not ask that question." Talking Crow's eyes were arrow-shaped. Tall Tree felt the wound of her looking. "We were the Seneca nation, the keepers of the western gate. We keep no gates now. We run."

Red Cloud spoke up. There were truths there was no use raking over. He gestured toward his son, his eyes glowing with pride. The boy was a born faithkeeper.

"Some of the old ways we keep. Wherever Folded Leaf goes the words will go with him," he said.

"And you let the whites laugh at the sacred words he speaks."

"Clasby did not laugh."

"Not for you to see. But I saw. Folded Leaf was like a chipmunk to Clasby. Inside, he laughed to hear a chipmunk speak."

"Do you want me to tomahawk Clasby? Have all the men here from the falls with long guns one sun later?"

"No. We have many to their few. Rouse our tribesmen. The river was ours. The falls were ours. Make them ours again."

"You do not understand, Talking Crow. This is a time of peace. We have signed treaties."

Deep out of Talking Crow's throat came a rumble of disgust. "You will die signing treaties." She turned away from him.

Red Cloud watched her enter the lean-to. There was truth in what she said. Twenty-two years ago Handsome Lake, the prophet, spoke to Jefferson, the "Great White Chief of our white brothers," asking him for a "writing on paper" so that "we can hold fast our land against the seizure of our white brothers."

The Great Chief had sent the writing on paper. "I said to you last winter that the land you then held should never go from you except when you should be disposed to sell. . . . We wish you prosperity as brethren should do."

Wishes were not enough. The Seneca had accepted that paper, and their property had vanished. But Talking Crow need not think it was lack of manhood that kept Red Cloud from bringing home the dripping scalps of those who were their enemies. It was manhood that caused him to keep his word. He had agreed to the paper of the Great Chief. He would rather die than not keep his word.

He listened to the quick, sure voice of his son repeating after Black Antler, "The Great Spirit has given us a mother: the earth. Our mother we must love. The Great Spirit has given us brothers. To them we must be brotherly. The white man has Jesus. We have Handsome Lake. If the white man follows Jesus and the red man Handsome Lake, the brothers will dwell in peace."

He was pledged to the way of Handsome Lake, not of Talking Crow.

WHEN JUD CLASBY showed up at the Cape house an hour after he left the Indian camp, Hannah Cape lit out to call on the Woods. Actually she was going to court John Wood, Jr. She hoped the others did not know what she was doing. Her mother knew, but her mother approved. Since boys didn't come to court Hannah, the next best thing was to have Hannah court a boy. This was no place for a woman without a man. John Jr. wasn't the man Hannah's mother would have picked. He was seventeen, just Hannah's age, and she had seen mullein stocks with more pith to them than John Jr. had. But Hannah, more than likely, wasn't Mrs. Wood's idea of a perfect daughter-in-law, either. Mrs. Wood probably thought Hannah would wear the pants in the family.

It wouldn't be true. Hannah's husband would wear the pants, if Hannah had to sew them onto him. Hannah wouldn't marry a man she didn't worship. She'd fetch and carry for the man of her choice, the way she did for her father and her fourteen-year-old brother, Ben. Her height and her great swag of red hair might count against her, but she had plenty to count for her. Her face was almost as creamy as her bosom; and her bosom was prominent enough to offset anybody's idea that, because she could use a bucksaw and axe as well as a man, she wasn't womanly.

Her mother wondered why Hannah wasn't courted. Hannah didn't. She knew. The minute a man sashayed up to her, he undermined her faith in his judgment. She wanted a man who dreamed of something better than Hannah Cape, a backwoods girl. A man who wanted her didn't have his sights set high enough to suit her.

Jud Clasby didn't hide where *his* sights were. His staring made her uncomfortable; and his talk of killing animals and Indians made her queasy.

"I'm going over to the Woods'," she told her mother.

"You set your cap for that milksop boy?" Clasby asked.

"Milksop" made Hannah mad. "No," she said. "It's the old man I've taken a shine to."

Her mother was sorry to hear her speak so pertly. It was what people expected of a redhead. But Clasby laughed.

"You going to lose either way. The boy don't want a wife and the old man's got one wife too many already." Old Mr. Wood was a widower remarried not so long ago to Reba Reese, a widow young enough to be his daughter.

286

Hannah knew that bandying words with Jud Clasby would be like trying to outgrunt a pig. In the first place, he knew more than she did; and in the second, he didn't care what he said.

"Good-by, Mama," she said. "I'll be back before suppertime."

"I'll bring you home," Jud said. "I got an errand at the Woods'."

Hannah gave Clasby her bullet stare, but he was too tough for anything but true lead.

HANNAH was bold, but not a bold wooer. She couldn't go to the Woods' without some excuse. When Reba Wood opened the door, Hannah held out a willow basket, its contents neatly covered with a napkin. "Molasses cookies," she said. "Mama sent them."

"Johnny's favorites," Reba said. "How did you ever guess?"

"Everybody likes molasses cookies," Hannah answered coolly.

Mr. Wood was stretched out for a rest on the bed that filled one corner of the room. The Woods had more furniture than most of the people at Fall Creek, because their cabin contained the belongings of two families. The Woods and the Reeses had headed west together after both had been suckered by land agents in York state. On the way, Hosmer Reese had drowned, and John Wood's wife, Abbie, had died of a bloody flux. It was the most natural thing in the world for the widow and widower to combine forces.

Hannah didn't think that lovemaking could have been in Reba Reese's mind when she married John Wood. He looked to be all bone and gristle, his skin as gray as his long beard and hair, his mouth as thin as the cutting edge of an axe. He and Reba didn't get along and made no bones about it, even before company.

Reba would be hard for anybody to get along with, Hannah thought. She was afraid for herself when she looked at Reba. Would she look that way when she was forty? Reba's hair was the red of maple leaves after heavy frost had smirched their color. Her cheeks were cobwebbed with veins. She was sharp and mean to a man old enough to be her father; sharp and mean to the boy she had inherited from Abbie Wood. Was that what happened to pert and saucy girls when they got to be middle-aged?

"I reckon you want to see Johnny?"

"I thought we might read some more together."

The best gift Johnny got from his stepmother was the tin box of books that had belonged to Hosmer Reese. There were spellers and arithmetics in the box—Hosmer had been a schoolteacher—but there were storybooks, too, and these Johnny read aloud to Hannah. Hannah could read all right, but he liked to read, and she loved to listen. It was a good thing. Johnny wasn't much of a talker.

"Do you want to go up and get him?" Reba asked.

The loft was Johnny's bedroom, and Hannah was too well brought up to go alone to a boy's sleeping room. "No. Maybe he's resting up."

"Resting?" Reba exploded. "What's he got to rest up from? He's a spoiled do-nothing. Been carried around on a chip since he was born." Reba went to the ladder that led to the loft. "Johnny," she shouted, "you've got company."

Everything about Johnny Wood made Hannah's heart ache. Half an orphan, a stepmother who hated him, a father soured on life. Hannah wanted to be both a mother and a father to him—and something else besides, because he was so beautiful.

Johnny came down the ladder from the loft like a man walking onto a stage—though Hannah was his only audience. Reba was noisily stirring up corn pone for supper; the old man still had his eyes closed. Johnny was a statue that breathed; all cream ivory, with black carved curls and a narrow, long-limbed body. Was he bashful? Was his mind so occupied with deep thoughts he had no time to talk with her? He liked to read to her, anyway, and she didn't ask for more.

It was too early for candlelighting, so Hannah pulled the bench close to the Dutch door and opened the top half enough of a crack to let in some light. They were reading *Ivanhoe*. Had people really lived like that? Worn such rich clothes, fought and died for such noble causes? Was the world going downhill? No shining armor now; nothing but linsey-woolsey and an unfelled forest stretching for untold miles.

One thing hadn't changed: love. Johnny wasn't anything like Ivanhoe; perhaps he was like the man who wrote the book and was silent because his head was full of words he wanted to put on paper. Whether or no, Hannah loved him. He never touched her, but if he did, she would more than likely faint dead away.

Clasby came at twilight. "I've come to fetch Hannah home."

"There was no need," Hannah said.

"I promised your mama, and I want to talk to John and Reba."

Mr. Wood shook himself awake and sat on the bench across the table from Jud Clasby. While the men talked, Johnny read on, but Hannah couldn't listen, for Clasby was talking about her family.

"Cale Cape thinks there's no point getting stirred up about the redskins moving in here now."

"Cale Cape is so kindhearted he'd share his wife with a grizzly," said Reba.

Hannah had to bite her tongue at that. Her father was a peaceable, God-fearing man, but he knew right from wrong.

"The reds are treacherous." Old Mr. Wood was an Indian-hater. That was his religion. "Run 'em out," he bellowed.

"Hush up about Indians," Reba ordered her husband. "You'd be the first one under the bed if a redskin showed up at the door." She turned to Clasby. "If you want somebody who means business, go talk to my brother, George Benson. Don't waste your time here. The old man's lost his sap and the boy never had any."

Johnny stopped his reading, went to his stepmother and, with his open book pressed under her chin, pinned her to the wall.

"Have I got any sap?" he asked, giving the book a forward shove that brought Reba's pop eyes farther out of their sockets. "Answer me!"

Reba's tongue waggled, but the sounds she made were not speech. Clasby wrenched Johnny away.

"Junior," he said, "if you want a woman to talk to you, don't half choke her to death first." He helped Reba to a bench and got her a dipperful of water. Johnny ran up the ladder to the loft.

Restored, Reba said, "Goes up like a monkey, don't he?"

"Best not tease monkeys," Clasby advised, "or a courting boy."

"Courting? The girl's the one doing the courting."

Hannah felt her cheeks flame up like red-hot stove lids. "I visit Johnny," she said. "Is that courting?"

Clasby said, "We'd better be on our way, Hannah. I've got some other visits to make tonight."

"Stop and see George Benson," Reba insisted. "What's on your mind is on his."

Hannah was pulled in more directions at once than were comfortable. How could Johnny, book reader, kind to animals, have turned on his stepmother that way? She wanted to tell him, I don't understand what you did, but whatever you do, I'll love you. She wanted to say to Clasby and the Woods, The Indians haven't done a thing against us.

It was more than she could bear. She ran outside to hide her tears. Jud Clasby followed with her shawl.

WHEN FEBRUARY came, you thought winter's back was broken. But winter could still drop down out of a clear sky.

"You aiming to shake yourself to death?" Jud Clasby asked.

"No," Hannah said. "I wasn't even aiming to shake. I didn't know I was. It smells like spring, don't it?"

"You put this on," Clasby said. "No sense not being warm while you smell spring." As he adjusted the shawl over her shoulders his hand brushed lightly across her breast. Hannah started to say something, but shut her mouth. There was no sign Clasby even knew he had touched her. Where was her mind, anyway? First in love with a boy who didn't love her; now thinking that every man who adjusted a shawl for her had other ideas than her comfort in mind. Were other ideas what she wanted him to have?

"Thank you," she said.

"I thought for a minute you were going to bolt."

"Oh, I've worn shawls before." It crossed Hannah's mind that they both might be thinking of the same thing, after all.

"I'd thought to stop at George Benson's and the Bemises' on the way to your place. If you don't want to, I'll take you home first."

"Ora Bemis's my best friend," Hannah said, leaving Benson out of it. She'd as lief visit a bull buffalo as George Benson.

Luther and Ora Bemis lived half a mile up the creek. Ora was a couple of years older than Hannah and she was expecting a baby. Some people were surprised when a wandering dandy like Luther Bemis had taken to a girl as swarthy as Ora, with a scar on her face, too. Some weren't. They said that a man who'd spent ten years hunting far from all whites must've had an Indian wife or two, and that Ora's color and decorations made him feel right at home.

However Ora made Lute feel, he'd been a changed man since he married her. Lute had grown up in the same town as Hannah's folks. At eighteen he had broken loose in all directions at once: gave up farming and took up drinking, fighting, and hunting. After he half scalped his stepbrother in a drunken fight, he lit out west.

In the ten years before he reached Fall Creek, he had calmed

290

down considerably. He still looked like a rakehell instead of a Baptist elder, which he'd become since marrying Ora, but he'd given up drink, farmed hard, and hunted only for meat for the table. Whatever he might have felt about Indian girls before, he now had eyes only for Ora.

He'd have been crazy, Hannah thought, otherwise. Ora was as sleek and pretty as a dove, so plump and lustrous she hardly seemed human. And her acts were those of a Christian woman. Hannah's father, who was the nearest to a preacher the settlement had, said that Ora lived in the Light.

The two girls sat together beside the fire. The two men faced each other across the table. Lute brought out a jug of cider. Jud Clasby swallowed his first mouthful and looked as if he'd had a helping of quinine. "Sweet cider? Ain't you got anything better'n this, Lute?"

"Springwater."

"When I think of the jugs you and me's emptied!"

"I've changed."

"Well, there's nothing so strong as a pretty woman's apron strings to tie a man down." Clasby smiled at Ora, but it was a gibe nevertheless. As if Lute had been more of a man before.

Lute didn't turn a hair. "It's a fact. Tied the strings myself and don't plan to ever unloosen them of my own free will."

Hannah couldn't keep her mind on Ora's talk. She listened to Jud.

"What I came about," he was saying, "is I need your help in tracking a lost horse of mine. I reckon you can still track."

Lute ignored the soft soap. "Strayed, you mean?"

"Stolen's likely the name for it."

"Got any idea who?"

"The Indians down at the sugar camp. I seen tracks there."

"I'm through fighting Indians."

"Who's talking about fighting? You through helping friends?"

"I ain't reformed that far yet. When do you want to look?"

"The sooner the better. I'm on my way out of here and I need that horse. If you're willing, I'll pick you up tomorrow morning."

HANNAH wouldn't have gone to the Bensons' with Clasby except that the Bensons lived on her way home. And whatever she thought of George Benson, Sarah and her six children were good neighbors.

At the Bensons', supper was late, and they were asked to join the family meal. The fare was good: stewed squirrel, johnnycake, and hot, sweet sassafras tea.

George Benson was a big-shouldered, heavy-handed man. When he clapped a hand down on the table, the crockery jumped.

"Jud," he said, "how about the sugar camp?"

"I been sounding out folks. About got it lined up, I think."

"Wasn't you going to ask me?"

"What do you think I'm here for?"

"Sparking Hannah, maybe. She needs a full-grown man, not that weedy Wood young un."

"George," Sarah Benson warned. "Hannah's company."

Benson gave Hannah's broad shoulder a hearty slap. "Hannah knows I'm teasing her. Why, if I hadn't met you first, Sarah, I'd be courting her myself."

"She's man-shy," Clasby said. "I've found that out."

"What man's she known? Father's nine-tenths a preacher, and John Jr.'s nine-tenths a girl."

Hannah wanted to sail into George Benson, talking that way about her father and Johnny. But she wanted even more to get the talk turned away from herself.

"What are you planning to do at the sugar camp?"

"Break up the camp."

"Break it up? Why? What harm have they done?"

"Harm? If a man asked me that question, I'd flatten him. What harm? They killed my grandfather. They're animals. We kill wolves, who do us less harm. Nothing's safe as long as they lurk around. They ought to be given their walking papers. And the only walking papers they understand is lead."

"What harm have *these* Indians done?" Hannah persisted.

"They're Indians. That's the harm they've done. If you're so Indian crazy, go be a squaw. You don't belong here."

"Then I'm going home." Hannah slid off the bench. "Don't come with me, Mr. Clasby. It's no more than a step. Good night, Sarah."

"I'll see you across the crick," Clasby said. "Then you can go on home alone. George and me's got more talking to do."

In the middle of the footbridge, Clasby said, "If you make a wish over running water, you'll get it."

"I wish I was home," Hannah said, half crying because of what George Benson had said. Her shawl on one side hung almost to her knees. Clasby pulled the shawl even, crossed the ends neatly, then circled each breast with a hand. Hannah's first inclination was to throw herself crying into his arms. But was she going to ask this man, who had said nothing of love, to handle her again in his free and easy way? But she had to do *something*. She hit him, a half shove, half hit. He was on a slope, on the other side of the bridge, no more expecting to receive a blow than she was to give one. It was either slide into the creek or sit down. He sat.

"You damn little wildcat."

"I'm not little."

"You damn *big* cat. The next time you want to rassle, give me some warning, and we'll have a real tussle."

Then Hannah turned and ran.

The fire was banked and her father and mother were in bed when she got home. She felt her way up the ladder to the loft, where she and Ben slept. There was a window at her end, a nicety given to her because she was a girl and glass was too precious for everybody to have his own. Now she opened that window and leaned out, trying to put the evening's happenings out of her mind. She wanted to think how small she was under the distant stars. What was the fire Jud Clasby had stirred up in her, compared with them? What was the hurt of Reba's calling her a courting girl and George Benson's calling her a squaw?

There was a rustling from Ben's cornhusk bed. "Shut that window, Hannah. You want to freeze us to death?"

As she pulled the window shut, an owl hooted.

"It could be an Indian. Ben, could you shoot an Indian?"

"If he was going to shoot me," Ben grunted sleepily.

"But not in cold blood."

"No."

"They're our enemies. Everybody says so, except Papa."

"You can shoot 'em. I'm going to leave them alone."

Hannah wanted to tell him everything that had happened that night. But Jud Clasby's touch had changed her baby brother; it had made Ben a man. She couldn't, now, throw her arms about his neck and tell him her troubles. They weren't troubles she proud of.

She put on her nightgown and knelt by her bed. Most times, praying was as natural to Hannah as breathing. But tonight all she could say, over and over, was, "Help me, God. Help me."

THE NEXT DAY was Saturday. Hannah's mother, Lizzie, spent the day cooking. Since there was no church in the settlement, church-goers met at the Cape cabin. It was the one chance of the week to see a face that didn't belong to your own family, and to hear, in addition to whatever news was making the rounds, one of Caleb Cape's sermons. What Caleb had that made people willing to ride ten miles, fording streams and picking their way around fallen trees, was a God-blessed gift of gab. Listening to him, people thanked God they were alive and living in such a paradise.

Each Sunday Caleb promised his wife that *next* Sunday he would not ask everybody to stay and have a bite. But the next Sunday he did ask them. So Lizzie spent her Saturdays cooking. The neighbors, in any case, had taken to bringing in some food of their own.

Lizzie was thirty-four, Caleb thirty-six. They thought of themselves as middle-aged. If Hannah hadn't been so stand-offish, they'd have been grandparents by now. Lizzie had no trouble seeing herself as a grandmother. Caleb as a grandfather gave her imagination quite a stretch. Caleb was a jackanapes, a cutup, a clown. There was nothing he liked better than making people laugh. Lizzie endured and Hannah winced when Caleb started playing the fool. He didn't think that man, made in God's image, glorified his Maker by looking like he'd just bit into a green persimmon.

The Sunday feeling began to boil up in Caleb as soon as Saturday dinner was over. By midafternoon, where they were now, the love of God was fizzing up in him, too high for corking. Since the only congregation he had at hand was Lizzie and Hannah, they got the full force of his pre-Sabbath jubilation. Hannah was taking a pudding from the oven—dried pumpkin, sweetened with maple sugar, thinned down with milk, and thickened up with four precious eggs.

"Never seen a prettier dish," Caleb said.

He picked up Lizzie and kissed her on the mouth. She squirmed in his arms like a hooked eel. "Hannah," she reminded him.

Caleb kissed her again. "High time that girl learned that there are worse things in this world than kissing."

294

Hannah, her cheeks flaming, bent over her pudding.

Caleb was no namby-pamby preacher too delicate for the world the Lord had put him in. He knew Lizzie liked to be kissed, and he hadn't married his wife to suit his daughter. But he was not coarse-grained. He put Lizzie down, didn't say anything further to embarrass Hannah, and went outside. Ben, puffed up from some business of his own back in the woods, said, "Pa, can I go hunting with Johnny Wood?"

"Ben, I don't like the sound of guns popping off on Sabbath eve."

"Can I go if I don't do any shooting?"

"If you want to go for a run through the woods, I got no objection."

"I'll be back before dark."

He kept his word. They had just settled down to their supper of milk gravy and corn bread when Ben came in. One look at him stopped all forks in midair. "What happened to you?" his father asked. "You meet a bear?"

"Maybe he met an Injun," Hannah teased.

Ben, who had been about to pull out his stool, jumped like he was bee-stung and ran out the door. All forks at the table were put down at the sound of his dry retching.

"Hannah, take him a dipperful of water," Caleb said.

Hannah carried the water to Ben. He was on his knees, his head resting against a rick of wood, his sides going in and out like a horse with the heaves. "Is it something you ate?" Hannah asked gently.

Ben shook his head. "Let me alone," he whispered.

Hannah ran inside. "He's sick, Mama, and he won't get up."

Lizzie half rose. Caleb said, "Best leave him alone."

But when bedtime came, Caleb said, "He'll have to come in, if I have to lug him. Whatever ails him, lung fever won't help."

Lizzie and Hannah half expected some struggle from Ben, but there was none. After a few minutes he walked into the house a step or two ahead of his father.

"What's the trouble, son?" Caleb felt his son's forehead.

"I'm sick."

"You don't feel hot. Touch of the ague, like as not. Now you get up to bed. A night's sleep's the best medicine."

Ben climbed the ladder to the loft without a word.

II

This Sunday morning the Sabbath feeling was gone from Caleb's heart. Ben lay in his bed refusing to move, speak, or eat. But it wasn't just Ben's sickness. The day was too warm for February, more like May. He liked nature to hold steady, not make you sweat in February. Such weather brought deaths in March.

His uneasiness caused Caleb to start the morning service off in a quieter manner than customary. Usually, when about half of those expected to attend were in their places, he led them in singing. Today he hadn't the heart for singing. The senior Woods were there, the Bensons, the Pryces. Luther Bemis, faithful churchgoer, hadn't yet arrived. Jud Clasby, no churchman, but who had come to the meeting (for the home cooking, likely) the last two Sundays, was absent. And four or five families who lived down near the north fork of Fall Creek were not yet here.

Caleb said, "We'll put off our singing until we're all together. Meanwhile, I will read to you the Twenty-third Psalm." He was hoping the comforting words would raise his spirits. *"The Lord is my shepherd; I shall not want. He maketh me to lie down in green pastures . . ."* Caleb's heavyheartedness was easing up. He was speaking directly to God. A shout brought him back.

"Get her out of here!"

In the door of the cabin, carried on a quilt held by four men and two women, lay a blood-soaked squaw.

"Get that squaw out of here. Don't you know this is a church meeting?" Benson shouted again.

The North Fork people hesitated; then Caleb, with a voice more carrying than Benson's, said, "Bring her in. She's hurt."

Caleb went to help the men place the woman he knew to be Talking Crow on his and Lizzie's bed. He was sorry for the bloodstains, but he didn't value a coverlet more than a human being. The squaw had a bullet hole near the base of her throat.

Caleb need not have worried about Lizzie's coverlet. Talking Crow, gray with loss of blood, rose slowly to her feet, and no one wanted to use force on a woman whose throat bubbled bloody air as she breathed.

"You kill me," she said in English. "I not die on your bed."

She faced George Benson. She spat at him, a bloody froth.

"Woman killer. Child killer," she said hoarsely.

Benson rose, reaching for a wooden ladle on the table. Caleb wrestled him down. "George, this is a church meeting."

"Not when the savages come in."

The disturbance brought Ben halfway down the ladder from the loft. He looked fully as sick as Talking Crow.

"What's going on?" he asked blankly.

"Nothing you had backbone for," Benson said.

Talking Crow looked at Ben. "You no help Folded Leaf."

Ben did not appear to hear her. He came on down the ladder as if sleepwalking. At the bottom he fell with a sodden thump of flesh onto the floor and lay there, face down.

Talking Crow watched him fall. "You kill me," she told the others. "I not die in your house." She passed her hand over the flowing wound on her throat and pointed a finger dripping blood at Benson. "When you die, you remember."

Slowly, but without wavering, the old squaw went out the door and down the two log steps. On the bottom step she gave a last cry, the cry of a brave at death. Then she fell forward.

Caleb bent over her. "Her troubles are over," he said.

Hannah, while the others were watching Talking Crow, went to Ben. He was clammy, limp as a dead snake. But alive. She sat on the floor beside him, waiting.

Everyone in the room was talking at once. The North Fork folks were trying to tell where and how they had found Talking Crow.

Caleb put an end to the hubbub. "This is not the Tower of Babel," he said. "We need to know what you saw, and one at a time is all we can hear. Ebon Hall, you tell us."

"All of us was on our way to church. You know the trace we follow—a hundred yards or so from the sugar camp. There was no one around, but I didn't think anything of it. Along about the old Jessup place Maggie Bushnell said, 'I hear something.' It was a human voice. Sick or hurt. We followed the sound to the filled-up well. The voice was coming from there. From down under a lot of dead bodies. We pulled them out."

"How many?" a neighbor named Brewster asked.

"Two girls. Two boys. Three women. The woman we brought here was at the bottom of the heap."

George Benson got to his feet. "Why did you bring her here?"

297

Ebon Hall's wife, Phoebe, spoke up. "She's an old woman. When I'm an old woman, I wouldn't want to be left to die like that."

Benson had an answer to that. "She's the mother and grandmother of men that killed my folks. She's likely hacked white prisoners to death with her own hands. I shot the old squaw, and you'll thank me for it. Next year the redskins'll keep their distance and you'll all breathe easier."

George Benson's sister, Reba Wood, jumped up. "One thing George left out. He didn't do it all single-handed."

"I wasn't meaning to hog the credit, Reba. But in this sort of thing, every man's got the right to speak for himself."

"Well, my husband's one to hang back when it comes to claiming credit. But I want you to know he was right there and he done every bit as good as brother George. Young John did his part, too. My two men gave a good account of themselves."

Hannah, who had been huddled over Ben, half hearing, did hear Reba. "What did you say about Johnny?" she called out.

"I said Johnny killed Indians with the best of them."

Hannah, not believing, asked, "Johnny did that?"

"You been doing your best to make a man of him, ain't you, Hannah? Well, he's a man now. He's been blooded."

"I wasn't trying to get him to kill anybody."

Ben, hearing the argument, if that was what it was, pulled himself, unnoticed, back up the ladder to the loft.

Ebon Hall said, "What I worry about is what Colonel Johnston, the Indian agent, is going to do when he hears about it."

"Who's in charge of this country?" Benson shouted. "Indians and their softhearted agents, or us? Move in with the redskins if you're so sweet on them, Eb Hall. You'll never be missed."

"We'll all be missed if the tribes to the north take it into their heads they got a little revenge coming."

George Benson erupted like a wounded bear. "I never thought I'd see the day when men of my own country and color would take the side of the Indians against me!"

"Let's clear out of here, George," Reba said. "These folks want to have a powwow, not a church meeting."

"You're right, Reba. The place has got an Indian stink."

George and Sarah Benson, their six children, and the two Woods left the meeting. A hot gush of feeling ran along Hannah's veins.

Her father, his church, and God Himself were being discredited. She called out, "This has stopped being a church. But it's still Sunday, and if we pray, maybe God will forgive us."

CALEB and Lizzie urged upon their neighbors the food they had brought. But they left it behind, as if it, too, had been sullied by what had been said and done.

The Capes weren't hungry, either. Lizzie had gone up to reason with Ben. They had some idea now of what ailed the boy.

Caleb and Hannah carried Talking Crow to the bed of the wagon. They put the bloody quilt over her.

"We can't leave her here," Hannah said.

"For a while we can," Caleb answered. "I'm going to walk over to Rocky Point. I want to see for myself what happened."

"Can I go with you?" She was too upset to stay home.

"What you'll see won't be very pretty."

"I know that."

It was a three-mile walk, with nothing but the woods: oak, walnut, and the sugar maples that brought the Indians back each year. The trees weren't leafed out yet, so they walked through bars of sunshine. It was a day to rejoice in. "It shouldn't have happened on Sunday," Caleb said. Then he took it back. "The day don't matter. The deed makes the day, not the other way round."

Hannah said, "Reba drove Johnny to help Benson. I heard her tell him he was a weakling. She shamed him into it."

"There are other ways of proving your strength."

"That's the way that come up first."

There was no arguing with Hannah about Johnny Wood's reasons for doing what he did. If he did anything. They had nothing but Reba's word for it that he did.

Then Caleb sighted what he'd come to see: bodies sprawled at the edge of the filled-up well where they'd been laid in the haste to get at the woman who still lived. For a minute he couldn't go on. "Well, George didn't lie about what had been done," he said.

Hannah faced away from the bodies, staring at a beech tree as if her life depended on memorizing the number of its limbs.

"There's no call for you to come, Hannah," Caleb said.

She listened to her father's retreating footsteps, then ran after him. "I don't want to be left alone."

Hannah had never seen death before. At first sight these dead were as lifeless as boulders. As she came closer they became human beings asleep in awkward positions. All except Folded Leaf, a boy she'd seen playing in the creek. He wasn't a boy anymore. Where his face had been there was a clot of offal like she'd seen at butchering time when the job had been botched. A pain sharp and sickening went through her. "Ben saw this?"

"Saw it done, maybe."

"Where were the Indian men? Why didn't they help?

"How do I know?" Caleb could figure only one answer. "The men must have been ambushed," he told her. "I'm going to take a look around. You don't need to come."

She needed to. She couldn't stay there alone with the dead bodies. But the bodies went with her, filling her mind.

Her father spoke. "There." She followed his pointing finger. Up the trace ahead of them, kneeling, forehead to ground, was a man. He was dead, his shirt black with dried blood. "It's Tall Tree, shot in the back. Tolled away from camp on some trumped-up excuse so they'd be free to finish off the women and children."

"There were two men," Hannah reminded him.

"The other is probably nearby. Hannah, I can't leave these people lying here like scraps thrown out for dogs. I'm going to put them back in the well. Tomorrow I'll bury them all. You'll have to help me carry Tall Tree. I can't heft a man his size."

Caleb took the bulk of the load; even so, Tall Tree's legs angled downward in Hannah's grasp. She staggered under the weight. The effort kept her mind off the burden she carried.

Red Cloud was where her father had thought he might be—in the opposite direction and about the same distance from the camp. He lay on his back, a bullet hole in his stomach, a knife wound in his throat. He was lighter than Tall Tree, easier to carry.

It was full dark when Caleb and Hannah got home, bloodstained and bone-tired. Lizzie didn't pester them with questions until they'd washed and changed. They sat down to the good food that hadn't been eaten at midday, and that they couldn't eat now.

"What did you find?" Lizzie asked when she saw there was going to be no eating.

"Just what George said we would. Dead Indians, shot down in cold blood. I'm going to bury them in the morning."

"That'll be quite an undertaking, Caleb."

"Ben can help."

"Ben's still sick."

"Try Lute Bemis, Papa," Hannah said. "I was at the Bemises' when he told Jud Clasby he was through fighting Indians. He'd be just the one to help you."

III

Caleb took Hannah's advice. After the supper he couldn't eat, he set out in the cold clear night for the Bemis cabin.

The Bemises had no candles lighted, no fire burning. Caleb thought twice about rousing them if they'd gone to bed. While he was thinking it over, Ora called out sharply, "Who's there?"

"Cale Cape. If you're in bed, I'll come in the morning."

Ora unbolted the door. "Come in. Lute's feeling poorly, but I'm up." She put a couple of sticks on the fire and sat in the rocker, hunched up like a bird in cold weather. Lute lay face to the wall.

"Nothing serious, I hope," Caleb said.

"He can't hold anything on his stomach. He's got no fever, but he was in no shape to put in an appearance at church. And he didn't want me to make the walk by myself."

"We didn't have any church. The folks from North Fork brought in a half-dead squaw from the sugar camp. She said a few words and died. Benson and old Wood, or at least Reba Wood, boasted they'd done it. Whoever done it, they're all dead. Men, women, and children."

"Did Hannah tell about Clasby being here night before last?"

"That's why I'm here. I'm going to give those folks a resting place underground, not leave them for wolf bait. I come, knowing from Hannah how Lute felt, to get his help."

"He's so poorly—" Ora began, but Lute interrupted her.

"I'll be at your place tomorrow at sun-up, Cale."

"If you don't feel like it . . ."

"I'll feel up to it. Did anybody at church mention Clasby?"

"Nobody. Reba was so anxious to claim all the glory for her men, nobody else could get an oar in once she'd started."

Lute, with an unexpected movement, threw all the bedclothes aside and stood tall and white in his long underwear.

301

"Pray for me, Cale. I missed church today. I ain't so steady in the Light as I'd like to be. I need help."

Caleb said, "There was no church to miss today."

"Where two or three are gathered together in His name," Ora reminded them, "that's church."

So the three had a little church of their own then and there, and Caleb walked home easier in his heart than he'd been all day.

CALEB and Lizzie were at the breakfast table next morning when Ora arrived in a cold drizzle of rain. "I come to tell you Lute's had a setback. He's feverish and got the shakes. I set my foot down against his coming. I'm in no shape to be a widow." She was the only one who laughed at her joke.

She wouldn't eat or linger. She wouldn't hear of anyone walking home with her. "The baby's snug," she assured them, "and Lute needs me. All that talk of killing was too much for him."

"Sounds like Lute and Ben both been hit by the same complaint," Caleb said, as he watched her leave. He went to the loft ladder. "Ben, Hannah, get down here. We're leaving in fifteen minutes."

They came down at once, Hannah first. Ben looked like a man ready to walk to his own grave. When the corn dodgers and syrup were put in front of him, he shook his head. "My stomach's still unsettled."

"You can't work on an empty stomach, son."

"It'd be empty, anyway, the next minute after I swallowed."

"Ben, you got some reason for not wanting to help me?"

"I want to help you. I'm going to. I never said not."

CALEB sat on the floor of the wagon beside Talking Crow's body and told Ben to drive. "Up by the old well," he directed.

Before they were there, he saw that branches that he and Hannah had placed over the well lay scattered about. Hannah, there first, exclaimed, "The bodies are gone!"

Animals had not been there. Indians had. There were tracks of moccasins and unshod horses. The hair on the back of Caleb's neck rose as his skin tightened. Decent burial for a dead Indian was one thing. The presence of live Indians was a different matter. He peered into the trees. Was there any movement there?

"How did they know where they were?" Hannah asked.

"Indians keep pretty good track of each other."

"You got a gun with you, Papa?" Ben asked.

"You know I have. I never leave the house without one. But this is a burying party, not a shooting party. We'll put Talking Crow in the well and cover her up. The Indians'll be back for her."

Hannah, while Ben and her father put Talking Crow back where she'd been found, walked up toward the sugar camp. She wasn't frightened by the thought that Indians might be near. Since Friday evening she had felt that the course of her life had gone out of her hands. Two days and a few hours; yet in that time either she was a changed girl or was only becoming acquainted with the girl she really was. On Friday her heart had been engraved on every cookie she gave to Johnny Wood. Two hours later the touch of Jud Clasby's hands had turned her to jelly. On Sunday she had seen a dying squaw spitting blood, then today dragged dead men to their graves.

She stumbled, without noticing where she was walking, onto what she took at first to be a boulder. It was a big deerskin bag, the top held close by a rawhide drawstring. Burned in the skin were the initials J.C. Hannah drew her hand across the soft suede bulge of the bag. It was his. She lifted it up; it was heavy. Slowly she carried it back to her father.

Caleb, who never swore, said when he saw her, "In God's name, Hannah, don't go wandering off that way without letting us know. What've you picked up?"

Hannah pointed to the initials. "Jud Clasby's, I reckon."

"Ben, was Clasby there?"

Ben looked at the ground.

Caleb stared at his son. "I can't thrash you into talking. You know that. But the sooner you tell me what you know, the better."

He untied the drawstring. What spilled out were the best peltries of the Indians' trapping, knives, beaded decorations, bowls. Clasby had skinned the camp of its valuables.

"Thievery," Caleb said.

Killing Indians was one thing. Benson could boast of that. But "I stole" was a confession nobody was likely to make.

Caleb left the bag and its contents where it had fallen.

"Won't the Indians find it?" Ben said.

"Let them," said Caleb. "It belongs to them. They were likely chasing Clasby when he dropped this."

IT WAS hailing as they drove home. The horses walked with lowered heads and at a good pace, barn-eager. No one spoke.

Hannah tried to draw herself into a knot of unfeeling flesh—not against the hail, but against memory. On a single day she had been ready to clasp two different men: one a killer, the other a thief and killer. She was riding with her eyes shut. She would not have known that they had turned into their own lane except for her father's wild shout and the sudden jerk of the wagon. She opened her eyes to see him already halfway to their door, in which an arrow was planted, standing straight out.

Hannah leaped out of the wagon after her father, screaming, "Mama, Mama!"

Lizzie herself opened the door, alarmed by all the commotion. "Caleb, what's happened? What's the trouble? Is somebody hurt?"

Caleb grabbed his wife in his arms. Hannah circled around, patting both. She had something she could cry for now without having to explain, so she sobbed, "Mama, Mama."

"Oh, thank God, praise God," Caleb said. "You're all right?"

"I may have a cracked rib soon if you don't let up your hugging. But I was pretty sound till you got home."

Caleb loosened his arms. "You didn't see or hear anything?"

"I heard the hail. What else was there to see or hear?"

Caleb pulled his wife outside and closed the door. When she saw the arrow, the color went out of her face. "What's the meaning of it, Caleb?"

"I thought I'd find you scalped," Caleb said.

Lizzie looked at the arrow again. "Is there any need for us to be standing out here in the hail?"

"No," said Caleb, "there ain't." It took a hard tug to get the arrow out of the double oak door. It had been sent with force.

When they were all inside, Lizzie, who now was as upset as she had been calm, bolted the door. Caleb stood turning the arrow in his hands. It was feathered with red-hawk tail and tipped with chipped quartz. He could not help admiring its beauty. It was the nearest to a bird a man had ever made; but it flew to kill.

"Burn it," Lizzie begged. "Throw it in the fire."

"No, I'm going to keep it, Lizzie. In the first place, the killing part wouldn't burn. In the second place, it was sent to us by a friend."

"It was sent to us by an Indian, wasn't it?"

305

"I judge so. But he sent it to warn us. Considering what's been done, that's more than we've got any right to expect."

"But we didn't do anything," Hannah said.

"We're part and parcel, as far as Indians are concerned, of the murders at the sugar camp."

"Murders," Hannah repeated, shocked. "Is killing an Indian murder?"

"If all he's doing is boiling a pot of maple sap, I don't know what other word fits."

AFTER an hour's rest and a bowl of hot bean-and-venison soup, Caleb and Ben set out to tell the neighbors that the bodies had been taken from the sugar camp, and that someone had put an arrow in Cale Cape's door. They were home before candlelighting time, and after an early supper Caleb shooed the young ones up to bed. He didn't himself go to bed that night. Oh, he took off his outer clothes and stretched out now and then beside Lizzie. But mostly he stood in front of the fire and rehearsed what he thought he should do. After he knew what he thought, he was accustomed to weigh his conclusions against Lizzie's convictions. She was no "as my husband says" woman.

"The Brewsters," he told her, "are already packing to move into Pendleton until this blows over."

"There's no blockhouse there."

"No, but there're two hundred people instead of twenty. Of course, the Bensons and the Woods say that arrow wasn't any warning. Just somebody trying to throw a scare into us."

"Don't it enter their heads that what they did may stir up the tribes to the north?"

"Nobody except the Brewsters thinks it could come to that. They're all so used to these peaceful sugar-camp, calico-buying Indians, they think some trinkets and a jugful of rum would settle things."

The sleet had let up and now the room was filled with the soft owl-feather swish of falling snow. Lizzie dozed off. When she woke Caleb was dressed, had a kettle boiling, and sliced mush frying.

"No need to be up so early on a day like this, Caleb," she said. "What can you do?"

"I'm going to Piqua. To see the Indian agent. If Brewster's

306

right, Colonel Johnston's likely the only man who can head the Indians off if they're thinking of making a sweep down here."

"Wait till the weather moderates," Lizzie urged. "Piqua's two hundred miles. 'Bout as well stay home and be scalped as go out and die in a snowbank."

Caleb laughed and didn't know why. "No, I'd choose the snowbank any day—and take you with me, if I thought that was the choice. But I'm not intended for snowbanks, nor you for scalping. We're going to have to tough it out along more everyday lines."

The mush was overfried and the sassafras tea had steeped too long. Lizzie couldn't swallow a bite and Caleb didn't want to. He filled himself full, anyway. He wasn't going to fizzle out for lack of fuel. When he had finished, he said, "I'm going up and have a few words with Hannah."

Hannah, at the sound of her name, was awake. Caleb sat down on her bed and kept his voice low. No use rousing Ben.

"Hannah, I'm going to ride to Piqua to tell the Indian agent there what happened. I don't think there'll be trouble here. . . ."

"Trouble?" Hannah whispered.

"Indians. If there is, if you get warning, get your mother and Ben into Pendleton. If there's no warning, give up. You and Ben are young; if you don't fight, they'll likely adopt you."

"Make a squaw out of me?"

"There's been more than one child adopted by the Indians who wouldn't go back to their families when they had a chance."

"If we don't fight, what's to become of Mama?" When Caleb didn't answer, Hannah said, "They'll kill her, won't they?"

"They'll kill all of you if you fight. Burn you alive in this house. None of this is likely, Hannah. I wouldn't leave if I thought it was. I told you because I trust your good sense."

Hannah followed her father down the ladder. There, with Lizzie, they knelt before the fire, and Caleb prayed. Then he folded Lizzie in his arms, kissed Hannah and gave her a hearty handshake. "Ben's too young and your mother's too ladylike for the job, so I appoint you man of the house while I'm gone."

A few hours after Caleb left, there was a heavy rapping on the door and George Benson's shout. "You home, Mrs. Cape?"

"We're home," Hannah answered, and opened the door.

Jess Abernathy, a tall man, part Indian himself, people said, who lived a mile or so beyond the Bensons', was with George. The men, wet from the icy drizzle, stood steaming in front of the fire.

"Mrs. Cape," George Benson said, "where's Cale?"

"On his way to Piqua. He's gone to ask the agent to quiet the Indians," Lizzie said.

Benson gave the table a slap Lizzie knew he would rather have given her husband. "The agent! All that man Johnston does is baby the Indians. What Cale'll do is to get us forbidden to drop a hook in Fall Creek or trap a muskrat on its banks."

"Caleb's risking his own life in this weather to try to save your life," Lizzie said sternly.

Benson snorted. "Preachers would be better off to stay home and pray. Cale's not satisfied to leave matters in the Lord's hands. Oh, no. Cale wants a finger in everybody's pie."

Hannah grabbed the heavy twig broom and swung it in a semi-circle that caught Benson across the side of the head.

"What's going on here?" he shouted. "You lost your senses?"

"You get out of here, or I'll knock *you* senseless."

Benson made a move toward Hannah, but Abernathy held his arm. Hannah, using the broom as a battering ram, shoved Benson toward the door. "You get out of my father's house before you say another word against him."

"I'll get out, but I'll ride after your father and bring him back before he ever lays eyes on Piqua."

Hannah closed the door with a bang, then returned the broom to its place by the hearth. "He's just talking big," she reassured her mother.

HANNAH was right. Abernathy talked Benson out of trying to follow Caleb. "He'll never make it in this weather, anyway."

Caleb made it; but not in the three or four days he had planned. It was a matter of weeks before he entered Johnston's office in Piqua. Johnston wasn't in. There was only a dark-haired young clerk.

The young man leaped to push a chair toward Caleb. "Have a seat, sir. You look pretty peaked."

"I been sick," Caleb said. "Lung fever. I been in and out of my head for four weeks. I'd of died, except for a family outside Winchester who took me in. I set out in a storm to tell Johnston that nine Indians had been killed at a sugar camp in Fall Creek."

"We got that news right after it happened," the clerk said. "There's been more than Indians killed now."

"Where?" Caleb whispered. "Where? Not at Fall Creek?"

"No, no. Fifty, sixty miles north of there. The tribes up north, when they heard of the sugar-camp killings, burned a couple of homesteads and killed everybody in them."

"How do you know that?"

"Indian friend of Johnston's, Black Antler, sent a runner. Wanted Johnston to smooth down the Indians up north."

"Can he do it?"

"He couldn't, till the government promised that the men who murdered the Indians would be tried and punished the same as if they'd murdered white men."

"Murdered." Caleb remembered Hannah's shock at his use of that word. "Who is promising this trial? The governor?"

"You folk up in the woods don't know our governor very good, do you? Woodsies vote. The Indians don't. The governor is not about to call voters murderers."

"Then who did promise it?"

"The United States Government, that's who. Calhoun, the Secretary of War."

"The Indians have heard a lot of promises."

"They'll believe Johnston. He's never broke his word to them yet, and he says these men are going to be tried. Better a few men in jail than the whole settlement wiped out. Captain Berry didn't have the least trouble getting the accused to jail, either. The burnings up north wasn't wasted on your folks."

"Jail! We ain't got a jail."

"You got one now. Or Pendleton has. They built one on purpose. Trial starts as soon as the circuit court meets there."

"Those men don't have money to hire lawyers."

"Calhoun knows that. Seven thousand dollars have been set aside for this. Four of the best lawyers from Ohio state are on their way to Pendleton to defend them right now. The regular state prosecutors will handle the case against the murderers."

The contents of Caleb's stomach started roiling about. He had come here to save bloodshed, not cause it. "Has any white man ever been convicted of murder for killing an Indian?" he asked.

"Not to my knowledge."

"But that's what Johnston's up there telling the Indians? White men will be tried for murder?"

"Yes."

"And if guilty?"

"You're sick, Mr. Cape. You know what happens when a court finds a man guilty of murder."

Caleb stood, but felt as if he was standing on air and sat down quickly. The clerk's hands bored into his shoulders. Caleb looked up at the man supporting him. "Do I know your name?"

"Hardesty, Jacob Hardesty."

"Thank you, Mr. Hardesty. I was weaker than I thought. I don't know what to think about what I just heard. I didn't want to get my neighbors thrown in jail for murder."

"You didn't do that. Black Antler and Mr. Calhoun did."

The man who killed a man ought to be hanged, Caleb thought. He had never doubted that. But wispy old John Wood? The Wood boy, who had no notion of right or wrong outside a book? Benson, a big ox who needed somebody saying gee-haw and whoa if he was to be kept on any straight path? Hang them? Praying church-goers? And he the one, no matter who got there first, who went to Piqua to carry the news. What was he? Some kind of a Judas?

BOOK TWO
The Trial   IV

Hardesty was not exaggerating when he told Caleb that the federal government was supplying the accused men with superior counsel. Up from Ohio to Pendleton came Patrick Conroy, Noah Beazley, Isaac Vickers, and Charles Fort. All were able, eloquent lawyers with every intention of winning a decision for their clients. They were also men of a city that had earned its stability, they believed, by conquering the Indian population. If they could help it, no white man was going to be hanged for trying to protect Pendleton in the same way their forebears had protected Cincinnati.

The government had one paramount purpose: *not* to give Indians the impression that this was a powwow called to belittle the red man. The defense lawyers were well known. They had to be. But

310

the prosecution lawyers were famous: Senator James Noble, former soldier and Indian-fighter; his son-in-law, Abel Trask; Jonathan Armitage, the state's prosecuting attorney, and his assistant, Oscar Achilles Dilk, a black-haired, bullet-headed young man with a mind like a bear trap. Dilk was obviously headed for the Senate.

The Indian agent, Colonel Johnston, had been instructed to have Indian chiefs present to observe the trial and send the news back to the tribes: "White men are being tried for murder for killing Indians. It is a fair trial. If found guilty, they'll be hanged."

CHARLIE FORT, the youngest of the defense lawyers, twenty-four, had the best lodging in town. He had been offered, by the widow Culligan, the loft room in her Pendleton home because, she told him, "you look like my late son."

Charlie was accustomed to having lonesome widows tell him that he reminded them of their late husbands. "Late son" was more to his liking. His fellow lawyers, the senator among them, were piled two in a bed in less commodious lodgings.

When his family had been killed by Indians, Charlie, the sole survivor, age two, had been found, carried into Cincinnati, and adopted there by the man he thought of as father, Enoch Leverett. Leverett had sent him east to Harvard, where the bright Yankee boys went, planning for him to take over the Leverett newspaper, the *Western Spy*, when he graduated. In spite of himself, Charlie became a lawyer. A newspaper writer has to tone things down. A lawyer could tell the jury facts that would lose an editor every subscriber. So Leverett made use of what Charlie *could* do: send facts that he could cut, dress up, water down, until they were fit for print.

When Charlie moved into the widow's room, he sat down to write Enoch a report in what he considered newspaper style of this outlandish place and this outrageous trial.

Extracts from a letter by Charles Fort to Enoch Leverett:
Pendleton is a town of two hundred souls. I made the mistake when I first arrived of calling it a settlement. The Pendletonians wasted no time setting me right. A settlement is a place like Fall Creek, twenty miles upriver—no stores, streets, or taverns there. Pendleton is a town. My idea of a town naturally is Cincinnati. Two theaters, three thousand books in our library, boardwalks,

streetlights. I doubt if half a dozen books could be scared up in this entire settlement. Excuse me, I mean town.

Three judges sit here: a presiding judge, appointed by the state legislature, and two elected side judges, who are local. The presiding judge is Amos McGowan. Giddings, a man much respected here, is one of the side judges, as is Omer Oursley, the town blacksmith. Oursley ironed the prisoners after they all climbed over the walls of the prison stockade on the first night of their incarceration. Nobody here, including the prisoners, takes this trial seriously. They look at it as a kind of play-party to impress the Indians. But that Indian agent, Johnston, intends another kind of party.

Samuel Brady, the sheriff, in buckskins, moccasins, and with a side knife the size of a pigsticker, is a sight to scare wrongdoers. Bigger than most men, he is actually no different from the others here in dress, or his lack of shoes. Every man, woman, and child is in moccasins. They look at me as I go clip-clopping along in my brogans as if I was half horse.

On my first day here, Judge Giddings invited me to midday dinner. Also present were Jonathan Armitage, the circuit prosecutor, and a friend of his, Dan McGowan, brother of the presiding judge. A very large, nicely browned goose was on the table.

Dan McGowan, after his first bite, said, "Judge, this is a damned fine goose."

Giddings, to my astonishment, replied, "Yes, it is a fine goose, and you are fined a dollar for swearing."

It seems that Pendleton has a statute imposing a fine of one dollar on any person who should "profanely curse, swear, or damn." Not another word was spoken during the entire meal. When we finally pushed back our chairs, the judge said, "Squire McGowan, pay me a dollar."

I was beginning to get some idea of the kind of man I was going to have to plead my case before. Invite a man to dinner and fine him a dollar for complimenting your goose!

After the dinner I went over to talk with my clients. The jail, thrown up in short order since what they have been calling "the massacre" took place, is square, built of heavy beech logs, with one door and no window. A stockade manned by guards surrounds it. I was let into the stockade and through it into the jail room itself. No furniture, straw on the floor; a bucket in the corner. The

312

prisoners, though heavily ironed, were in good spirits. Wood Sr. was reading his Bible. Wood Jr. was reading a novel. The guards let them crack the door enough to get a sliver of light for reading.

They were not much fazed by being accused of murder. Mad that their neighbors had gone chickenhearted about the possibility of Indian revenge, but not fazed. What really galled them was that the Indian Bureau they all hated took the charges seriously enough to provide them with defenders like myself.

Benson, clanking like a gristmill, strode about, bellowing at me. "What's this country come to? My father was praised for doing what I done. Now you lock me up for it. Iron me like a mad bull."

I tried to quiet him down. "Mr. Benson, I'm here to get you out of irons. Undoubtedly there was some reason, some reason a jury will understand, for your shooting those Indians. Now if they shot at you first—or threatened you . . ."

"Threaten? Hell, no. Except breeding the way they do."

"So there was no reason for the shooting?"

Benson jumped a foot in the air. "They were Indians. Fishing in our streams. Killing off the deer. Pushing in right next to our homes. These are facts. Every man you can set on a jury knows it."

George Benson was about like a man who's shot wolves all of his life in the belief that he's protecting himself and his neighbors and who's suddenly told *wolves* must be protected—unless by chance the wolf has got his fangs at your throat. Nothing Calhoun or Colonel Johnston could say was going to change his upbringing.

Wood Sr. was the opposite of Benson: calm, understanding. "After the burnings up north, I guess our neighbors didn't have much choice," he said. "Better for us to have a little spell of setting here than for them heathen to sweep down on our women and children."

"There's going to be a trial," I said. "That's why I'm here."

"I never been in a trial, but I've seen more'n one and I'll know how to handle myself. I've got all my wits about me still."

The boy reading the novel said something like, "Hrrumph."

"That's my son. *He* thinks I lost my wits marrying again."

I wasn't interested in the home affairs of the Wood family.

"I heard down at the tavern that others besides you three were at the shooting," I told Wood.

"Clasby, you mean? He's clear to Texas by now," said Wood.

313

"Was he the leader in this? Did he put you up to it?"

"What do you mean, put us up to it?" Benson, who had clanked over, asked. "We been fighting Indians all our lives. We're grown men. We don't need anybody to put us up to anything."

"I heard there was another man there besides Clasby. Is that right?"

"Ain't three of us enough to satisfy the redskins?" he stormed.

"There was a boy there," old Mr. Wood put in. "But he didn't have a gun or take any part in it."

"Who was this boy?"

Benson replied, "Ben Cape. The preacher's son. Nothing but a soft pile of guts . . ."

Wood Jr. said, "Shh," and Benson, who wouldn't bat an eye at old split-foot himself, said, "Well, speak of the devil!" Not the most courteous way to address your pastor, but Caleb Cape had lived too long among these rough Indian-killers to take offense.

"Well, George," said he, "your body may be in chains but your spirit, I see, is still free and soaring."

Caleb Cape's a tall, lean man. I can see God-searching in his eyes, but there's a sardonic turn to his mouth that looks more like punning than praying to me. He is a preacher only by virtue of the fact that he preaches. But the settlement couldn't hold him in higher regard.

He introduced himself. "Mr. Fort, I understand. I've come over to pray with these men. You're welcome to stay if you like."

I thanked him and said he'd likely prefer to be alone with his parishioners. *I'd* prefer to be absent when Benson prayed.

"My daughter's outside. The guards didn't think the jail a place for a young girl. You might keep her company for a while."

He was right. The jail *wasn't* any place for her. Cape's daughter is a redheaded girl I had caught sight of earlier. The place for her was out in the open, with plenty of cooling air for all. I said who I was and she said who she was. "Hannah Cape."

I just stared, and she stared back.

Pa, I know the subscribers to the *Western Spy* don't give a tinker's damn as to whether Charlie Fort has or has not fallen in love. And, as a matter of fact, Charlie Fort doesn't know himself. But it seems I can't resist putting my feelings in this story. Well, you'll edit me, anyway.

I don't know how long the staring match went on. The lawyer

wasn't the first to speak. Hannah said, "Which side are you on?"

The correct answer would have been, "The side of justice." But that would sound pompous. "I'm a defense lawyer," I said.

"You're going to get these men off?"

"I'm going to try. Do you want them to be hanged?" I asked.

"The boy in there shouldn't be."

"He your sweetheart?"

"He never kissed me or anything. He was just trying to be a man at the sugar camp. His stepmother hounded him into it."

"I had a stepmother." If she pitied boys with stepmothers, she had as well spread some of her tenderness around.

"It didn't hurt *you* any, did it?"

"No."

"I wish you'd talk to my brother."

"He was there, too, wasn't he?"

"He didn't do anything. But he saw it all. He's sick from not telling someone."

"He'll have to tell someone. They'll subpoena him."

"What's subpoena?"

"Come to court and tell what you know or go to jail."

"There's something he's ashamed of."

"Everybody has something. Haven't you?"

I shouldn't have asked that. She dropped her head.

"I have, anyway. Most of us have." I took her hand. I didn't want her to be ashamed of anything. She didn't jerk her hand away but let me fold it up in mine like a young kitten. Kisses would have been next in order if her father hadn't come back.

"We're going to have a singing service now, Hannah. The guards say you can come in for that. Mr. Fort, won't you join us?" My singing, as you know, sounds about like a strangled bullfrog's. So I said I had other business—which was to get over here, write this, and think about Hannah.

End of extracts from a letter by Charles Fort to Enoch Leverett.

V

Lizzie Cape, having cleaned up after the Sabbath worship and eating, sat in front of the fire with her tired feet on a footstool. If God had listened to that morning's praying, she thought, His head must be spinning. He had been asked to release the imprisoned; to punish the redskins for their killing up north; to bless Colonel Johnston in his efforts to appease the heathen; to have Colonel Johnston scalped; and to have Caleb Cape himself either blessed or shut up.

She was glad to be alone in the house after the morning's turmoil. She hadn't Caleb's faith. Or his high spirits, which made him feel, she believed, that even if God didn't help him he would be able to make out on his own. Caleb had made her a rocker which had as much bump as rock, but the movement was soothing, and she dozed off. She dreamed she heard a voice calling, "Lizzie, Lizzie." This did not awaken her, but her own voice answering, "Who is it?" did.

"It's Lute, Lizzie. I hope I didn't scare you."

"No, I was only dozing. Come in and warm yourself." Bemis was rubbing his hands like a man bone-cold. "You're not still sick?"

"The only sickness I had, Lizzie, was heartsickness." Lute pulled his bench right up to the edge of the fire.

Lizzie and Lute were at home with each other. They were about of an age, but she couldn't tell herself she felt sisterly toward him. She felt like a woman in the presence of a pleasing man. Perhaps most women felt that way with Lute. She was easy in her feeling because the bond with Caleb was so strong.

Caleb had converted Luther Bemis, seen him settled, expecting now a young one born of a Christian marriage. Lizzie was Caleb's right hand in his work—he himself said so—and in this way they were both Luther Bemis's spiritual parents.

"I came looking for Cale. He around someplace?"

"He and Hannah rode over to visit the men in jail."

"They're still holding them? I thought the government might've come to their senses."

"It makes sense to the government to try the men who did the killing, if that'll stave off an Indian uprising."

"They're our own folks, Lizzie."

"The ones the Indians'd scalp would be our own folks. Us."

"Lizzie, sometime last week the world went round a bend."

"Went round a bend? What happened last week?"

"We suddenly caught sight of a world where an Indian is a human being who can't be killed like a wolf. What's to come's too far ahead to see."

IT WAS full dark when Lizzie heard the horses come into the yard. Both Caleb and Hannah were wet with a drizzle that had started up after Bemis left. Lizzie could feel the tiredness in Caleb as she helped him out of his coat. Hannah was as lit up as if she'd made the whole trip on wings under angel-kindled starlight.

Lizzie pulled her rocker to the fire for Caleb and brought him a cup of hot sassafras tea and a slice of sweet cake. "How are they?" she asked. She didn't need to say who.

"Dry," Caleb said. "That's more than I can say for myself. Could I have a little hot milk with some rum in it?"

"I'll fix it for you, Papa," Hannah said.

"The ride don't seem to have tired Hannah," Lizzie remarked.

"She don't know she rode. There was a young defense lawyer there too busy making eyes at her to pay much heed to his clients."

After Caleb drank his hot milk and rum, Lizzie told him about Bemis's visit. "I told him you'd be played out."

"I am. But I'll have to go over there."

"You know what's the trouble?"

"I've got an inkling."

Extracts from a letter by Charles Fort to Enoch Leverett:
The town of Pendleton, after building itself a jail, has now also built itself a courthouse. It is, I *suppose*, a courthouse—a log building with two rooms, one for the court, one for the jury. The courtroom is about twenty by thirty feet long with a platform at one end enclosed by a heavy railing. Inside this railing is a bench and table for the judges, a deal table and chair for the clerk. In front of the platform is a long bench for counsel. Here I will sit. Near this bench is a little pen for the defendants.

Feeling is running very high here. Half the populace is so fearful of retaliation by the Seneca that they would, I verily believe, roast every prisoner alive to calm the Indians down. The other half are friends and relatives of the prisoners and those who believe that trying whites for killing Indians will be taken by the red men as a sign of weakness that will bring upon us the worst massacres ever at their hands. Persons of these convictions would like to free the prisoners, and are prepared to fight off any reprisals, shot for shot.

But the government is very firm in its determination to hold this trial. And the employment of Senator Noble to prosecute the accused will convince the Indians that the Great White Father is on their side. We defense lawyers have our work cut out for us.

There are some few who regard this trial like any other. Men have killed men. Let the law prevail. Caleb Cape is no doubt one of these. Black Antler, the Seneca Faithkeeper, doesn't want *any* executions. But I don't expect him to have a hearing.

At the time I met Cape and Hannah, I heard from my clients that Hannah's brother, age fourteen, had been at the sugar-camp fracas, so on Wednesday I rode over to Cape's place. If the boy could report some threatening word or gesture by the Indians, my case would be greatly strengthened. Seeing Hannah again didn't go against my grain, either. So I saddled Bay Boy at sun-up, and my little pacer stepped off the near to twenty miles in something less than three hours.

Pause in extracts from a letter by Charles Fort to Enoch Leverett.

At this point Charlie knew that he wasn't going to be able to stop talking about Hannah. So he took a fresh sheet of paper and prepared to write on, not for the *Spy* at all but just for the pleasure it gave him to talk to his father. His father would laugh and say, This is a story I've heard before, Charlie, but the heroine is new.

Continuation of extracts from a letter by Charles Fort to Enoch Leverett:

I had ridden twenty miles, more or less, to see this girl. Now the minute I saw her a couple of hundred yards away—she was outside in the sunshine making soap—my heart gave such a jump I was half of a mind to turn and head back for Pendleton. She had some boyish straightforwardness that made me jump down and greet her like a team mate, handshake and all. And then I talked. It's our great human cover-up. Nice mess of soap if I ever saw one, said I, staring into a huge pot of lye and grease. Was her brother home?

"He's at home. Do you think he can tell you something that will make things easier for Benson and the Woods?"

"I hoped he might."

"He can't. He told me all he knows."

"Then you tell me. Just what he wouldn't mind my hearing."

"I won't. I don't even like him to see us talking."

"Let's walk down to the branch. Can you leave your soap?"

"You don't know anything about soapmaking, do you?"

But she did start to walk toward the branch that circles the knoll the Cape house is built on. We walked in step, not touching. With some girls, you can't keep step. You're as mismatched as a pacer hitched to a trotter. Hannah and I advanced right foot with right foot, left with left.

When we got to the branch, we naturally stopped. Wading wasn't on the program. Soap was a finished subject. She refused to get started on brother Ben. There was nothing to say.

I didn't ask. She didn't offer. When we kissed we were up off the ground for a while, like creatures of air.

End of extracts from a letter by Charles Fort to Enoch Leverett.

ORA BEMIS arrived at the Cape house soon after Charlie left. She was on foot, downcast, bigger each day with child. Lizzie came to the door. "Ora, you think you should be traipsing around the countryside, as far along as you are?"

"I came over slow and careful as I could. It's Cale I want to see."

"He's out milking, Ora. He ought to be in any minute."

"What I've got to say is private, Lizzie. I'll go on out to the cowshed now. That'd be all right, won't it?"

"Caleb'd be glad for company."

Caleb was down to stripping the cow when Ora came into the shed. "Sit down," he said, motioning to a mound of hay. "If I don't take all Daisy's got, she'll get the idea she can let up."

"Cale," Ora asked, "have you told anyone? What Lute told you when you came over?"

"Not a living soul."

"You think Lute has to go through with it?"

"I think Lute's got to do what he thinks right. You know that. He's God's man. We can't tell him what to do."

"I can pray, can't I?"

"You can pray. But don't ask God to upset His own laws."

"What law has God got about this?"

"About half the Ten Commandments. There're some prayers God can't answer, Ora. Why don't you pray that Lute does what he thinks is right? And ask God to give you the strength to stand by him?"

"Yes. Pray for me, Cale."

Caleb got down on his knees. He didn't know a thing he could ask the Lord but to strengthen Lute, and to comfort Ora in what likely lay ahead. He ended his prayer, "Bless this babe-to-be here in the straw as Thou blessed another Babe born in the straw."

Before he could say amen, Ora was up on her feet. "Don't make a prayer like that for my baby. That Babe was killed. Why do men put killing and dying and blessing so close together?"

"What would you have, Ora?"

"No killing, no killing. Then blessings wouldn't matter."

"We need God's blessing."

"No, we don't. All we need is to love each other. Cale Cape, Lute was a happy man until you started him worrying about his soul. I will pray that Lute forgets he ever laid eyes on you."

She ran out of the shed, and Caleb didn't try to stop her. He picked up the milk pail and went into the house slowly, head lowered. He was heartsick and couldn't use his regular remedy for that disease: tell Lizzie all about it.

NEXT Sunday morning, a couple of hours before sun-up, Caleb and Lizzie were still in bed, Lizzie's head on Caleb's shoulder, the last comfort she would have that day—the way things were going.

The fit of man and woman always surprised her. It was a detail you might have thought God wouldn't have had the time to arrange. The heavy bone of a man's big shoulder left a hollow before it reached the bulge of the muscle in his upper arm that just fitted a woman's head. *My* head, Lizzie thought comfortably.

"When was the last time we had a real Sunday, Lizzie? Got to sleep a little late and could look forward to the peace and fellowship of a church service to follow?" Caleb asked.

"Before the killings," Lizzie said, then wished she hadn't. Now they'd have to face the day that was ahead of them. "At least the meeting's not set till eleven," she added.

"The time set ain't going to carry a pennyworth of weight with folks who want to see this day's meeting. There'll be people here who've been traveling all night."

"Why is Johnston having the people here at all? Why don't he take them straight to Pendleton?"

"Here's where it happened, Lizzie. If anybody's liable to fly off the handle about the trial, it's the people here. And if I don't miss my guess, the Indians Johnston will bring here will make everybody think twice before they decide to tangle with them."

"What kind of a man is the colonel?"

"He's nothing special to look at. Not at first glance. Second glance tells you here's a man that don't back up. He's hewn out of old rock. The Indians know this. They don't fool with him. They ain't got no cause to. He's worked for them."

"Couldn't a fight break out? So many men hating the Indians."

"It'll be a fistfight if it does. Nobody's bringing a knife or a gun into our place. Johnston's got militia down at the foot of the lane to see to that. But you listen to me, Lizzie. Don't start asking people in. The house won't hold them, in the first place. In the second place, the Indians don't want to come inside. They'd think what we had in mind was to get them in and set the place on fire—the way we did at—"

Lizzie stopped him before he could finish. "Well, I don't want Indians in my house, anyway. A lot of them are light-fingered."

"You only know those poor town reds down around Pendleton—drunks and beggars. They weren't that way till we came along. Today you'll see Indians we ain't touched yet. Chiefs and braves in furs and skins and warbonnets till we'll all stand chopfallen before them in our calicoes and linsey-woolsies."

"We're all equal in the sight of God," Lizzie said.

Caleb laughed till the bed shook. "God save me from arguing with women."

BEN, WHO HAD tried to hide himself from himself, felt at home with the crowd of strangers who were filling the yard. To them he wasn't the Cape boy, who had been at the sugar camp at the time of the killing; to them he could be an onlooker. No one paid him the least heed, not even Hannah, who usually kept an eye on him. Today she was so busy talking to one of the trial lawyers, she wouldn't have noticed if he'd dropped dead in his tracks.

He had chosen the best place to watch: the angle where barnyard fence met the barn. He had a wall to lean against and a squared-off rail to sit on. In case of any trouble he could be up and into the barn at the first click of a trigger—or war whoop.

Ben was so interested in the crowd he scarcely noticed that he had been joined on the rail, until he began to feel pushed through the barn wall. The man who had crowded in beside him looked, except for his clothes, like a blacksmith—big, dark, and somehow sooty-looking because of the stub ends of beard under his skin.

"You feeling pinched?" the man asked kindly.

He was, but some soft fiber in him made him hesitate to tell people that they were in the wrong. He was ashamed when he was in the wrong, and he had had too little experience to understand that the world wasn't made up of duplicates of Ben Cape.

"I'm O. A. Dilk," the man said. "I shoved in here on purpose. I'm a lawyer for the state. You're Ben Cape, aren't you?"

There was no way of avoiding a yes to that.

"Who's the beauty over there talking to Charlie Fort?"

"That's my sister, Hannah," Ben had to admit.

Dilk scanned him, searching for a family resemblance that wasn't there. "You know these people? Are the prisoners' families here?"

"Mrs. Benson's over there." Ben pointed her out.

"With all those young uns? I'd think they'd stay home."

"They want to see the Indians."

"Their pa didn't have any love of Indians."

"Who told you?"

"Why do you think he's in jail?"

Ben looked at O. A. Dilk. If I was in trouble, I'd like him on my side, not against me, he thought.

"Clasby ought to be in jail," Dilk said. "Your sister, Hannah, found Clasby's saddlebag with stuff he had stolen from the sugar camp. Thieving as well as killing."

"How do you know about that?"

"That's what I'm here for, to find out facts like that. Then to prosecute the guilty. See that they are punished."

Then all the people in the yard turned as if by a single lever. "Here they come."

It was the Indian chiefs who were coming. They moved into the lane where the other visitors had been forbidden to come.

"People aren't supposed to ride in," said Ben.

"*They* can," Dilk told him. "Johnston arranged it. If you were a dozen Indians, would you walk into a crowd of whites after some of them had killed your women and children?"

Ben kept his mouth shut. He wasn't sure what sound would come out if he opened it. Maybe he'd yell a warning like any boy seeing

Indians. Maybe he'd cry for Folded Leaf, who'd never grow up now to ride a horse like this.

"You never seen the like, did you?" Dilk said.

He never had. Fourteen men, not on half-starved Indian nags, but on big, arch-necked stud horses, all colors, all high-stepping, came up the lane. At the head of the line were two white men.

"They squaw men?" Ben asked.

Dilk snorted. "Back here in the woods you think anybody who says howdy to an Indian is a squaw man. The first horseman in that line is James Noble, United States senator. You want to call him a squaw man?"

Ben didn't. Senator Noble was thin and straight as a musket.

"Who's that coming next?"

"Colonel Johnston. The agent."

Johnston was as big and heavy as Dilk himself, but colored yellow and white like a miller instead of dark like a smith, his face sharp and his eyes going everywhere.

Behind the white men came the Indians, who, because of their headdresses, looked as much like birds or beasts as men. There was no war paint. This wasn't a war party. There were eagle feathers made into a cap and the cap finished off with a beak and glaring eyes. Hawk feathers held in place with a silver band. Owl feathers shaped like a pinwheel. Earrings, shoulder-long, swinging. White doeskin. Spotted lynx. Ermine paws.

"Are they all one tribe?" he almost whispered.

"Mostly Senecas. There's a Miami there. A breed or two. One of the women killed was mostly white."

Ben made a sound, soft and broken.

"You choke on something?" Dilk asked.

He had choked on his tears.

The horsemen were all in the yard now, and Ben was able to see the faces under the feathered headdresses: beaks stronger than eagles' beaks and eyes harder than owls'.

"They make us look like a bunch of sick muskrats," he said.

"Nonsense," said Dilk. "They're savages. These men you see have eaten dogs. And worse than that. They'll keep a man alive for twenty-four hours just so they can roast him longer. They—"

Ben wouldn't let him finish. "If I was an Indian, I wouldn't have you for my lawyer."

"I'm not *their* lawyer. I'm the state's lawyer, prosecuting men for breaking the law. It's against the law to murder human beings. The law don't say that if the human being ate dogs, or men's livers, he can be murdered."

"Folded Leaf wasn't a savage. He never ate dogs." Ben was crying now. "He didn't even have a gun or a tomahawk. His teacher, Black Antler, taught him not to kill. I studied with Folded Leaf."

"Studied how to scalp?"

"No. I learned verses like Bible verses, only Indian."

"Well, Folded Leaf made a mistake when he fought the whites."

"He didn't fight the whites. You said you came here to find out what happened. Why don't you ask people who really know?"

"I am," Dilk said. "I'm asking you."

Ben took one look at Dilk, then jumped down from the top rail and pushed his way through the crowd into the barn.

O. A. Dilk wasn't a man who liked to hurt others, but better the boy suffer some now, and because of it decide to tell what should be told, than keep the truth from being known.

THE INDIAN CHIEFS and the two white men didn't dismount. Down on the ground some shoving might start; and shoving led to blows, and finally what happened at the sugar camp might seem a frolic compared with this. There were no Indians so vengeful as the Seneca. They believed that the spirits of their slain tribesmen would never rest until those responsible for their killing were themselves slain. It was a duty the Seneca accepted with enthusiasm.

Dilk had no idea how Johnston had persuaded these masters of retaliation into letting the white man take care of the punishing. It was possible that to the Indians the nasty business of white men letting other whites dangle at the end of a rope was a revenge sweeter than any they could devise. And if Johnston had lied, this time, there would be nothing to prevent the Indians carrying out their first plan: burn, scalp, slaughter. Johnston was counting on the settlers to remember this. Dilk was, too.

The agent was the best mounted there: a fifteen-hand blood bay with a long black switch tail. He sat in front of the band and spoke first, slowly. Every person with two ears and a brain between them could understand what he was saying.

"What has taken place here you all know about. It's not my

task to determine who were the killers, or why they killed. A court of law will decide that. The Indians know who the dead are. They know that kin of theirs were killed by men of this neighborhood. Nine people died. Seven of the dead were women and children. They know that.

"They know—you do, too—what happened over in Hancock County a few years back. A Wyandot chief with his wife was on a hunting expedition. Three white men came to his camp and asked to spend the night. The Wyandots were Christians. They shared their camp with those they supposed to be their Christian brothers. They fed them. They said their prayers with them. Then they went to bed. As soon as they were asleep, these white men rose up, killed them, robbed their camp, and stole their horses.

"These murderers were caught and put in prison. But soon after, while the officials were looking the other way, they escaped. And that was all the punishment they had: a few days in jail.

"I have told the chiefs with me that this will not happen here. That if the accused are found guilty, they will hang in public. Only because they believe me have these chiefs been able to keep their young men from descending upon you.

"One of the chiefs will speak to you now. His English name is Sun Fish. Two hundred braves look to him for command. He will speak in his own language; what he says will be interpreted for you. You should listen well."

Sun Fish was a young chief, his face full of pride and his eyes aglitter with hatred. He didn't need to say a word to convince anyone there that, except for Johnston's promises, he and his two hundred braves would avenge the deaths of his kinsmen.

His speech was short, clanged out in a rush of brassy sounds. The translator, his mind trained to retain words, spoke as if the speech were his own. Even his voice had the clang of Sun Fish's.

"There is a treaty between your people and mine. We are not at war. This was not a fight between warriors. There was a time when we called each other brothers. I do not call you brothers today. Brothers do not kill each other's women and children. We have been promised that the murderers will be punished. We have promised that we will wait and see. We are waiting."

Colonel Johnston let the words sink in before he spoke again. "Now we ride to Pendleton to say what we have said here. The chiefs will then depart for their homes and the trial will begin."

The horsemen rode off through a quiet crowd. Dilk thought he could hear a sound like that of a hive of disturbed bees: a sound of breaths sucked in, of heart thumps. What could they say, or do? The agent had asked nothing unreasonable. "You made these laws. Keep them." Now the Indians—had they the right?—could say, "When you kill us, you murder. Hanging is your way with murderers. Keep to your ways."

The trial would be a mortal tussle, and Dilk felt the power rise in him to win it. He saw the Cape boy, his redheaded sister, and defense lawyer Fort standing together over by the wellhead. He had to see the Cape boy again. And Hannah: he had never expected to find as reward here a girl like Hannah Cape. She would grace any marble staircase, Indiana or Washington.

He introduced himself. "Miss Cape, may I make myself known? I'm O. A. Dilk, lawyer for the prosecution."

Hannah said, "I'm pleased to meet you, Mr. Dilk."

"Oscar, isn't it?" Fort said, not waiting for formalities.

It was. But Dilk preferred to hide it behind initials.

"Those Indian dandies didn't help my cause any," Fort went on.

"What do you consider your cause, Fort?"

"Save white men from being hanged for defending themselves against the savages who have been molesting them for a hundred and fifty years. What's yours?"

"The law. But I'm sure that Miss Hannah doesn't want to have the trial argued here."

"I don't want to have it argued ever," Hannah said.

Dilk smiled. He wouldn't have himself seem a sobersides before her. The trial would be time enough to lock horns with Fort. Let it be seen then who was the better man.

"Miss Hannah," he said, "Ben and I had our talk cut short by the speechmaking. If you'll excuse us, we'll go on with it."

VI

Charlie Fort could charm a bird out of a tree. Mrs. Culligan, his landlady, was fully aware of the charm. She was also too honest to fool herself into thinking that her feeling for him was maternal. She *was* able to fool Charlie.

Charlie was eating at eight o'clock on a mild April evening a dish of fresh, tender-grained clabber, which Mrs. Culligan had brought to him with no more than, "I thought this might help you through your evening's work."

He had a long evening's work ahead of him, so he eased into it with his father's letter. It made him laugh.

> If you want to write a story called "Hannah, the Hoosier Maiden," I'll try to get it published for you. But readers of the *Spy* generally are not interested in the girls you spark. Now I know you didn't intend parts of your letter for printing; but I tell you, son, it doesn't even make proper reading for me. I'm not trying to stopper you up. Just telling you a fact: the words haven't been invented that'll tell one man what another man feels about a woman.
>
> What I suggest is this. If you have to write about Hannah, put her on a sheet marked personal. Otherwise, if I'm down with the ague, I wouldn't put it past old Ames, who doesn't love either of us, to print the lot just for the fun of seeing your face red.

Charlie finished the letter, then picked up his pen. Pa was right. No more about Hannah.

Extracts from a letter by Charles Fort to Enoch Leverett:

On the day the trial began, Judge McGowan ordered that the trial jury be chosen.

The trial jurors are all hardy, heavy-bearded fellows. Not one is without a side knife in his belt. The first sight of them gave me considerable confidence. These are men, I thought, who know what it means to stand off the savages; men who have managed to bring Christianity and civilization westward with them.

The courtroom was crowded. Friends and families of the men I will be defending, their faces drawn with anxiety, were there. People I have come to know, clustered together like sheep in a storm, on the front benches with their minister, his wife, and children. Next to the minister sat Luther Bemis and his wife, Ora.

There's more to tell, Pa, much more. But I'm too sleepy tonight. Enough to say now that the defense received a great shock—and setback—in the testimony heard by the court today.

End of extracts from a letter by Charles Fort to Enoch Leverett.

THE COURTHOUSE was already crowded when Caleb Cape, with his family and the Luther Bemises, arrived. The turnout for the trial turned Caleb's stomach. It always did. Let a churn be stolen or a coon dog shot and, if the matter came to trial, settlers for miles around traveled to hear the lawyers' spiel. It was not to be expected that this trial, the first of its kind ever, would not bring out ten times as many onlookers. Caleb knew that the speechifying of the city lawyers would be in itself a seven-day wonder. And then there were those Indians, upright as trees, at the back of the room, their slit-stone-agate eyes seeing every move that was made. To settlers from lonely crannies of the woods, it was what playacting was to townfolk. Caleb understood all this. Still, he didn't like the flushed, staring faces. Was anyone there praying? For the men in jail? For the Indian dead? For the jury that would have to search its heart about right and wrong? Gawking and gaping, that was about the size of it. Caleb reached over, put a hand on Luther Bemis's.

Lute knew what that meant. Armitage was about to call him to the stand, and Caleb was giving him comfort. Or would give him a shove if he saw any signs of faltering.

But Lute wouldn't back down. He kept his eyes on Ora. He wasn't sure what she might do now. She had never denied that what he planned to do was right. But she had never been two-faced enough to pretend (though she knew pleasing God came first with him) that *she* felt at one with God if that meant prison for Lute.

"Will Luther Bemis please take the stand," said Armitage.

Lute moved through this scene like a man through a dream remembered. Ora did not cling to him. Caleb did not have to shove him forward. He floated past faces of neighbors as featureless now as bleached winter cabbages. Only the Indians were truly visible. What he had to say would be said to them.

Fenton, the clerk, asked him to tell the truth, the whole truth, and nothing but the truth. In God's name, did they think he had got up here to tell them some tall tale? Lute intended to tell the truth. If that convicted him, and it would, so be it.

"Mr. Bemis, where were you on the evening before the day of the alleged killings?"

"I was at home."

"Did you have any visitors that evening?"

"I did. Jud Clasby, accompanied by Hannah Cape. He was

329

seeing her home from a visit she had made to the Woods'. Our house is between the Woods' and the Capes'."

"So the call was just a social one?"

"For Hannah, it was. Jud was sounding me out about the Indians."

"What do you mean by sounding you out?"

"He asked me if I didn't think the Indians at the sugar camp ought to be cleared out. He thought they'd stolen his horse."

"What did he mean by cleared out?"

"Killed."

"Did he say so in so many words?"

"I don't remember his exact words. That was his meaning."

"What was your answer?"

"My answer was that I was finished with killing Indians."

"You had killed Indians before?"

"Yes."

"Why?"

"To save my life sometimes. Sometimes because they were Indians. We were pardners, Clasby and me, hunting out west. It don't make sense to wait for a dangerous animal to attack you."

"That's how you considered an Indian? A dangerous animal?"

"Out west when I was younger—yes. Since I came here, I've become a Christian. Mr. Armitage," Bemis said, "it would maybe save time if I'd tell the court what I did and you ask questions only when you think I'm leaving out something."

"Proceed along those lines, Mr. Bemis."

At this point the chief defense counsel got to his feet. "Judge McGowan, may I address a question to the witness?"

"Address your question, Counselor."

"Luther Bemis, did Mr. Armitage promise you that if you gave testimony helpful to the prosecution, he would see that you had a light sentence?"

Luther Bemis's hand instinctively went to his belt, where ordinarily he carried a knife. "That's a damn lie, and you know it."

Judge McGowan gaveled, and the courtroom, which was in an uproar at this exchange, went silent. "Mr. Bemis," the judge said, "you will be held in contempt if there is any more profanity. Defense counsel is trying to help you recognize the facts."

"Judge McGowan," Bemis said, "I am trying to tell the truth."

Caleb Cape rose. "Judge McGowan," he called out.

Caleb was well enough known to be permitted this interruption. "Mr. Cape," the judge said, "you have relevant testimony?"

"I have."

"Step down, Mr. Bemis. Mr. Fenton, call up the witness."

Duly sworn, Caleb said, "Before Luther Bemis ever saw Mr. Armitage, he came to me with the account which he now wishes to give the court. My advice to him was to tell Mr. Armitage what he had told me. It was Mr. Bemis who sought out Mr. Armitage. Not the other way around. No deal was made."

"Mr. Cape," asked McGowan, "why didn't you advise Mr. Bemis to make his report to the defense lawyers?"

"I didn't think the defense lawyers wanted to hear what Luther Bemis had to say. I thought Jonathan Armitage did."

. After this interruption, Judge McGowan ordered the questioning of Bemis by Armitage to continue.

"Mr. Bemis," Armitage asked, "what happened after you told Jud Clasby you were finished with killing Indians?"

"Jud asked would I just come with him to look for his horse. Well, there was no question about my doing that. So the next morning Jud came to the house and he and I set out."

"Did you take a gun with you, Mr. Bemis?"

"I did," answered Bemis.

"Why?" asked Armitage.

Fort was on his feet at once. "I object. By asking why, Mr. Armitage would like the jury to believe that Mr. Bemis went out armed for the purpose of killing Indians. Mr. Armitage knows as well as I do that no man up here and in his right senses goes five hundred feet from his house without a gun."

"Objection overruled," said McGowan.

Armitage repeated his question. "Why the gun, Mr. Bemis?"

"Habit, mostly," said Bemis. "And good sense."

"Where did you go after leaving the house?"

"We went toward the shack where Clasby has been living since he came back here. On the way he showed me two small piles of corn. Clasby said he figured they had been put there by the Indians to toll the horse away from his place."

"Did you see any tracks around the corn?"

"Yes. Horse and moccasin tracks. At the time I thought the moccasin tracks were Indians'. I think now I was tricked."

"Why? How?"

"I was tricked by somebody's putting that corn there and seeing that some horse come to it. The idea was to make my blood boil at Indian thievery—and it did boil. Then Clasby said, 'Let's go to the sugar camp and see if my horse is there.'

"Before we started out, Clasby asked me into his shack. He got out a bottle and took a pull on it. Then he handed it to me. When I was converted, I gave up drink. I'm not myself when drinking. I do things and afterward I don't know why I done them. But I thought, maybe going without it for so long, whiskey wouldn't work on me the way it used to. I was wrong. If anything, it worked on me harder. I was drunk. While we were still at the shack, Benson, the two Woods, and the Cape boy came along."

"Did these men have guns?"

"All but the Cape boy. He was just traipsing along because young Wood is his friend."

"What happened next?"

"We went to the sugar camp. It was agreed that the others would stay in camp with the women and children, while me and Clasby, with the help of the two Indian bucks, hunted the horse."

"What made you think the Indians would lead you to the horse?"

"We didn't think that. The plan was to kill them."

"Whose plan was this?"

"Clasby's. But I went along with it. I was took in by the corn and the tracks. And by the whiskey. I was thinking the way I did when I was out west and every redskin was my enemy."

"What happened when you got to the sugar camp?"

"First of all, the Indian squaws gave us food. That sobered me up some, but not enough. Clasby told the Indians his horse had strayed. Would the men help us look for it? Tall Tree and Red Cloud said they'd be glad to help. So Red Cloud went with me, Tall Tree with Clasby. Clasby had told me what to do. When I heard his gun, it would be a signal that he had killed Tall Tree and that I was to kill Red Cloud."

"Didn't you have any second thoughts about this plan?"

"I did, yes. But by now I was bound. I'd told Clasby what I'd do, and I've never been a man to back down on my word."

"You thought it was better to murder than to break your word?"

"I was drunk. And nobody up to then had ever called killing

Indians murder. Keeping my word seemed the right thing to do."

"Mr. Armitage," Judge McGowan intervened, "let's move to what the witness did after he left the camp."

"Well," Bemis resumed, "I let Red Cloud range on up ahead. He was about thirty steps in front of me when I heard my signal—Clasby's shot. At the sound of it Red Cloud turned toward me, and I bungled my shot. I hit him in the belly. I wish I could forget his look. He couldn't believe I'd done it." Bemis, who up to this point had spoken without emotion, buried his face in his hands.

Judge McGowan said, "Mr. Bemis, you'll have to take your hands down so that we can hear what you are saying."

Bemis straightened up at once. "What came next ain't easy to tell. I walked toward Red Cloud. He had sunk to the ground. Just sat there, dying like an Indian. They don't beg for mercy. I took my knife from my belt, and Red Cloud nodded. He was asking me to do what I done."

"What was it you did?" Armitage asked.

"I cut his throat. And he thanked me with his eyes till they closed. That's one reason I'm here. To say Red Cloud done no wrong. I killed him while drunk, and he died like a brave man."

"Why have you made this confession?" McGowan asked.

"I made it to get some peace with God and my soul."

There hadn't been a sound in the courtroom during Bemis's confession. The listeners held their breaths as if they'd been out there in the woods watching the whole affair—the tracking, the gunshot, the knife at the throat, the closing eyes.

Armitage asked the judge if, in view of Bemis's confession, the formality of a grand jury indictment might be waived.

Before McGowan could agree or disagree, Charlie Fort was on his feet. Caleb Cape had also risen, and both began to speak together. Judge McGowan, an old hand at outbreaks in rural courtrooms, pounded his gavel. "The court is adjourned for two hours," he said. "Sheriff Brady, take Mr. Bemis into custody."

VII

The day after Bemis's confession was Thursday. Judge McGowan had come down with a bout of sickness. At his request, both side judges moved to postpone the trial until the next morning. A stunned silence lay over Pendleton. People were uncertain what the confession meant and how they felt about it. But by Thursday afternoon some of the shock had worn off and the town began to chatter like a family facing a new, unexpected problem.

Charlie Fort had prevailed upon his landlady to provide a little supper for him and Hannah Cape that evening.

"Norry," he said (Mrs. Culligan's name was Norah), "I know you're not running a boardinghouse and that you only took me in out of the kindness of your heart. But I wonder if you could give me and Hannah Cape a little supper tonight?"

"As you said, Charlie, I'm not running a boardinghouse."

"It's this way, Norry. Along with her family and that raft of cousins they're staying with here in town, she now has O. A. Dilk pawing around her like an ox. So my only chance to talk to Hannah alone is here. Or take her out for a little walk in the woods."

Norry's preference would have been to cook a supper that she and Charlie could eat alone together. That being out of the question, why send him traipsing off to the woods with that big redhead? Who would be the gainer by that?

"You courting this girl, Charlie?"

"I haven't asked her to marry me, if that's what you mean."

"That's what I mean."

"Not yet. I don't want to scare her to death."

"I guarantee you won't. What would you like for supper?"

WHAT THEY HAD for supper Charlie didn't know. The table was set pretty, not in the kitchen where Norry ate, but in the sitting room in front of a nice slow-burning fire. Norry had covered the table with a cloth and decorated it with a little jug filled with the first Johnny-jump-ups of spring.

Hannah made Charlie proud. She wasn't a preacher's daughter for nothing. She was accustomed to putting strangers at their ease. She admired the table, smelled the flowers, helped Norry bring the food from the kitchen.

When the supper was on the table, Norry said, "Now you help yourselves. I've promised to go sit with old Sam Randall for a spell. He's down with a fever and his poor wife hasn't had any rest for a week. If I ain't back before you leave, Hannah, I'm pleased to have met you."

Norry shut the door firmly behind her and went down the path toward the Randalls'. She had done unto others as she would be done by. Die a Christian if not a sweetheart.

When the door closed, Charlie and Hannah, moving slowly, as if carried by a wave, went into each other's arms. They did not kiss. That was too special, too concentrated.

After a time they remembered the table. "What're we going to do with all this food?" Charlie asked.

"It would hurt Mrs. Culligan's feelings to leave it untouched," Hannah said.

They could not unclasp hands. So they ate, or tried to eat, one-handed. Finally Hannah gave up trying and watched Charlie.

She wanted to say, My darling love, you are so beautiful. I will never be separated from you. But he hadn't said I love you yet. A woman who said that first could drive a man off with her forwardness. The game was hide-and-seek, and it was the woman's place to hide and the man's to seek. Otherwise, no game.

Instead she said, "What do you think that row of Indians is standing in the back of the courtroom for?"

"To see that we are keeping our word about having a trial. And don't think Colonel Johnston doesn't want everyone to have a good look at the customers the folks here might have to deal with if the murderers aren't hanged."

"Hanged? They wouldn't hang poor Johnny Wood, would they?"

"If he's found guilty . . ." Charlie put down his fork, took both Hannah's hands in his, and groaned. "Oh, Lord, I've lost my mind. Hanging! I didn't ask you here for any talk like that."

"What kind of talk, then?" Hannah asked, so bold her eardrums pounded with blood.

Charlie closed his eyes and laughed. Then he opened them wide. "You want me to say it?"

"I think so."

"My darling Hannah Cape, I love you."

"I love you, Charlie Fort."

They leaned across the table, ready to kiss now. Charlie's cuff dragged in the gravy bowl.

"We've got to get rid of this damned table," he said.

Hannah's startled look reminded Charlie that he was talking to a preacher's daughter. "I didn't mean the cuss word," he said. "I

335

told you I was out of my mind. Let's carry the table into the kitchen. We'll give the leftovers to the dog."

When they came back from the kitchen, they stood in the sitting room like actors waiting for a cue. They had said "love" and Hannah expected "marry me" next, to which she would instantly say yes; go home, and start plucking geese for feather beds.

He said, "You're the most beautiful girl I've ever seen."

This wasn't a proposal, but it was perhaps the kind of talk that should come before a proposal, like grace before a meal. It made Hannah tongue-tied. She hid her face against Charlie's shoulder— he was tall enough so she could do that. The minute she did so, she didn't care about proposals. Or anyone speaking. Her body spoke, and Charlie's heard and answered.

NORRY came home at ten. There in front of the fire lay Hannah Cape and Charlie Fort, sound asleep and fondly entwined. Norry stared for a time, then closed the door.

What did you expect? she wondered. She sat down at the table where the two had eaten. Tom, Tom, she said to herself, thinking of the husband of her youth, not the Tom dead and in his grave. It was you and me I saw there. She put her head on the white linen tablecloth and cried a big wet splotch of tears. Then she got up. Those two must be roused. Charlie must get Hannah home.

She took the poor cat out of its crib in the woodbox and set her on the step. "Run for your life, Goldie," she said. Scooter could never catch the big cat, but he'd sit under the tree Goldie climbed and bark for an hour. If that didn't wake the young people up, she'd clatter around the kitchen until she did it herself.

Goldie ran, Scooter after her, baying. Norry went behind the springhouse, out of sight from the house. She heard the front door close, then watched as the young people, arms around each other, moved off quickly under the light of a moon growing full.

Inside the house, she went to bed, leaving a night-light burning on the table by the door—as she always did when Charlie came in after her bedtime. She went to sleep at once. The light was gone when sometime later she awakened and turned over.

Upstairs in his loft, Charlie got ready for bed. Tomorrow, he thought, he must write to his father and tell him to prepare to meet a Hoosier daughter-in-law.

ON FRIDAY, Judge McGowan was still sick. He therefore moved that the trial be postponed until Monday.

Caleb Cape and his family, together with Ora Bemis, left Pendleton Friday morning when the second postponement was announced. Ora wouldn't ride in the same buckboard with Caleb. Except for Caleb's meddling, Lute wouldn't be in jail now, and she alone. Ben and Hannah drove her home in the rig the Bemises had driven over to Pendleton. Ora didn't hold Caleb Cape's making a Christian out of her husband against his children. They would spend the night with her, Ben doing the barn work, Hannah doing housework and keeping Ora company. Ora was within a month of her time, and what she had gone through in the past few days might speed things up.

That night, after Ben had gone to bed, Hannah pulled a stool to Ora's bedside.

"Is there anything more I can do?" she asked.

"Bring Lute home," Ora said.

"I don't think he will be away long."

"What makes you think so?"

"I was talking to Mr. Fort, the defense lawyer."

"If there were ladies on the jury, I'd banter Mr. Fort could get this case dismissed out of hand if he wanted to."

"You think he's a masher?"

"Maybe not. But when a man's as good-looking as Charlie Fort, women can't keep their hands off him. And men can't help liking that."

"Did Lute ever love anybody besides you?"

"Hannah, I never laid eyes on him until he was twenty-six. He was out west, a lot of the time with Clasby. He and Lute both had Indian wives. More than one."

"Did they have babies?"

"Of course."

"How soon do babies start to come . . . after you're married?"

"If you don't want one, it comes quick as a wink. If you do, you can wait for years. It's all hapchance. I think God Himself keeps pretty clear of such matters." Ora sighed. "I never thought I'd be able to sleep on a night like this—Lute in prison laying on straw. But I'm dead beat."

Ora slept. Hannah couldn't. She walked in her bare feet up and

338

down the room. Finally she knelt and prayed. "God forgive me" was what she intended to pray. "God, I thank Thee" was the way the prayer came out.

At ten the next morning O. A. Dilk arrived at the Bemis cabin. Hannah answered his knock. For a young girl she looked stately, better turned out at ten on a Saturday morning than many a cabin woman at four on Sunday afternoon. She knew, and Dilk was glad to see it, that appearances counted in this world.

She immediately protected Ora. "Mrs. Bemis is feeling poorly."

"I didn't come to see Mrs. Bemis. I came to see Ben. And you, too, if you'll join us."

"Ben's down at the barn, cleaning out the stable."

"It's such a nice spring day. Isn't there someplace out-of-doors where we could talk?"

"Has something more come up about Lute?" she asked.

"Nothing more about Lute. You can tell his wife that he said this morning that he'd had two of the best nights' rest since the shooting. He feels he's clear with God now."

"I don't know's that's a message she'd like to hear."

"You use your own judgment about what you tell her. I'm going down to get Ben now. I'd like you to be with us when I talk to him. He puts a lot of store in what you say."

Dilk fetched Ben from the barn, and they used upended chunks of logs, sawed but not yet split, for seats. The sun brought out the sweet smell of the freshly cut oak. Frogs down in the branch were tuning up for tadpole time. It was the weather and the place for a picnic, Hannah thought, not a talk about killing.

There were no fireworks about Mr. Dilk. He was steady and thoughtful. Pleasant as a basket of chips, her mother would say. Nor did he have that mortal sweetness that makes folk keep their distance for fear of a heartscald they'd never get over. My heart is already scalded, Hannah thought. She loved and was loved. What she and Charlie had done was wrong, and they would never do it again. And yet it was very strange that an action so wicked could make her feel so full of grace; as if she had been somehow sanctified. She was just a moon reflecting Charlie's warmth onto this other lawyer. Anvil-hard, this one seemed to her, however agreeable.

Ben seemed as much changed as a boy as she was as a girl, and with nothing more to help him than some sensible talk with O. A.

Dilk. To Ben, the hardness of this man must feel reliable. He was going to do whatever O. A. Dilk wanted. She could tell. Testify in court, if Dilk thought that right.

"I'm not saying it'll be easy," the lawyer told him. "I am saying it'll be simple. Just tell what you saw. It's your duty, and you'll feel better afterward. If they cross-examine you—"

"What's cross-examine?" Ben asked.

"It's what the defense lawyers may do. After you've told your story, they may try to mix you up by asking a lot of questions."

"Well, they can't mix me up," Ben said. "I'll tell it the same way every time. They'll get sick and tired of hearing me."

"They'll be sick all right," the young prosecutor said.

VIII

Court resumed on Monday morning. George Benson, who would be tried that day, was in the prisoners' pen. He was noticeably thinner and paler. Sitting over there in the jail, cussing and fuming, had worn him down.

O. A. Dilk, as assistant to Armitage, wasted no time in asking Ben Cape, the preacher's son, to come to the witness stand. This caused a gasp in the courtroom. Caleb Cape had had a hand in getting Bemis to confess. Was the preacher now going to hear a confession squeezed out of his own son?

Dilk handled young Cape as tenderly as a china dish. He all but carried the big lunk of a boy to the witness stand. Moved his own lips in the swearing in, as if to show Ben anybody could do it. Once under way, the boy didn't need any more help than a sledder going downhill on glazed ice.

"How did you happen to go to the sugar camp on the afternoon in question, Benjamin?" Dilk asked, using the full dignity of the Biblical name.

"Johnny Wood came by our house with a gun. I thought he was going squirrel hunting and I asked if I could go with him. Pa said I could, but not to do any shooting."

"Why not?"

"Saturday afternoon is getting close to Sunday, and Pa thinks that on Saturday afternoon you shouldn't go frolicking."

"But he let you go with Johnny Wood."

340

"Just to watch and pick up squirrels for him."

"Did you pick up any squirrels?"

"No. Johnny didn't shoot any. He was in a hurry to meet his father and uncle at the sugar camp."

"George Benson and Wood Sr.?"

"Yes, sir."

"Were these men glad to have you with them?"

"No. Old Mr. Wood wanted to send me home. But Johnny's uncle George said, 'Let him stay. It will do him good.' "

"Did he say what it was that would do you good?"

"No, sir."

"Who else was at the sugar camp?"

"The Indians. One was my friend, Folded Leaf. I was learning Indian gospel with him from Black Antler, the preacher."

"How did your father feel about your memorizing Indian gospel?"

"He said that what Black Antler preached was about what he preached. Except the names was different."

"Benjamin," Dilk said, "why did you think Benson and the Woods went to the Indian camp?"

"To visit them."

"What did you think happened to the squirrel hunt?"

"I thought we would hunt after we ate."

"The Indians fed you?"

"Indians always do."

"What happened next?"

"We just talked around for a while . . . till we heard the shots."

"What shots? Where?"

"I can't remember." Ben dropped his head into his arms.

Dilk tried another approach. "Benjamin," he said, "was the first shot from the river side or away from it?"

Ben looked up. "The first shot was from the river side. Then a single shot from the other direction."

"After that, Benjamin?"

"It was then they started killing the women and children."

"Who did the killing?"

"They all did it."

"Did you see anybody in particular?"

"I saw two. First of all, I saw what Johnny Wood did."

Charlie Fort was on his feet at once. "Judge McGowan, we are now considering the case of George Benson. If the boy has any testimony relevant to actions of George Benson on the afternoon in question, let him continue. If not, let him step down."

Dilk turned his anvil face toward Judge McGowan. "Your Honor," he said harshly, "I ask the court to remember that the witness is a young lad, and the events he witnessed did not happen in any order which Mr. Fort may feel most suited to the defense's case. We will, I assure you, get to Mr. Benson. But I beg of you, Judge McGowan, out of consideration for the boy, that you permit the witness to tell the court of the happenings in the order that they happened."

"Permission granted, Mr. Dilk. Continue with your witness."

"Benjamin," Dilk said, "which deaths did you witness and who was the killer?"

"When the shooting started, two squaws and the children fell down right away. Everybody thought they were dead. But one of the squaws wasn't dead. She died at our house the next day."

"There were three Indian women at the camp, Benjamin. Do you know the name of the third, the one who didn't fall down right away?"

"Yes, sir. Wide Eyes. George Benson told Johnny he was leaving her for him because she was younger than the other women."

"Hadn't Johnny done any shooting?"

"No. He hadn't lifted his gun. When Mr. Benson said, 'What are you waiting for, Johnny?' Wide Eyes said, 'I am a Christian. The Lord Jesus Christ is my Saviour. Don't shoot me.' Then Mr. Benson said, 'She's a redskin, Johnny. Let her have it.' Then Wide Eyes tore open the front of her dress so that all of her skin down to her waist showed. She said, 'Brothers, my skin is white as yours.' And it was. Johnny raised his gun and fired. It hit one side of her chest—right in the center. But she just stood there and not even any blood came out. So Mr. Benson said, 'One more will do it, Johnny.' So Johnny shot her again—on the other side. She went down to her knees like she was going to say her prayers. Then she fell on her face and died. When she died, Johnny raised up his gun and ran at Mr. Benson."

"To shoot him?"

"No, the gun wasn't loaded then. To hit him. But Mr. Benson took hold of the gun and threw Johnny to the ground."

Ben leaned over, his face in his hands. Dilk said quietly, "So all the Indians were then dead?"

Ben shook his head. His face was glazed with tears. "Everyone looked dead," he said. "But Folded Leaf was alive." On his feet now, he was repeating in a strangled voice, "Alive. He was alive." Then he bolted from the stand and headed for the door. As he passed the bench where the Cape family sat, Caleb shot out an arm and pulled his son down next to him. The crowd murmured, but not enough to require the judge's gavel.

Ben leaned forward in the seat, head to his knees, and rocked soundlessly backward and forward. He could feel his father's arm across his shoulders, supporting him, so his rocking was easier.

"Ben," Caleb whispered, "this is a big test for you. The hardest you've had yet. Now you do what you ought to do here—tell the whole truth. It don't matter what people think. This is between you and Folded Leaf and God. And me. I set some store in you—and what you got the backbone to do. Telling the truth, no matter how much you wish it could be different, will clean the slate. It'll make everybody who loves you proud."

Caleb murmured so low Ben hardly knew whether it was his father or his own mind speaking. Maybe it was Folded Leaf, forgiving him and whispering to him to tell what had happened. The pain in his chest let loose of him and he sat up straight.

Dilk said, "Is the witness ready to resume his testimony?"

Ben's voice had a cracked sound, but it carried. "I am ready."

When Ben had reseated himself in the witness chair, Dilk said, "Benjamin, you have told us that though everyone *looked* dead, one was not. My question for the record is, 'Who was alive?'"

"Folded Leaf. He'd been shot in the leg and was stunned. But when Wide Eyes was shot, he sat up and tried to crawl to her. He couldn't because of his leg. The bone was sticking out. Then Mr. Benson yelled, 'The damned little bastard is alive!'"

"There are ladies present, Benjamin. Bad language has no—"

"I'm keeping back most of the bad language. There was lots."

"Thank you, Benjamin. What did Mr. Benson then do?"

"He started toward Folded Leaf, and Folded Leaf called to me, 'Help me, Ben!' I ran toward him. But Mr. Benson slung me down and said, 'Preacher's boy, if you don't want the same medicine, stay out of here.' Then Folded Leaf called again. But I didn't go. . . ."

"Why?" Dilk asked.

"I was scared. Mr. Benson's eyes were popping and spit ran out of his mouth. He lifted his foot like he was going to kick me."

George Benson, eyes once more bulging, got to his feet. The chains rattled as he stamped his feet. "That's a lie," he bellowed. "I was trying to save the boy. The redskin was crawling toward him. Ben, you know that's a lie. It was your safety I was thinking of."

"Mr. Benson," Judge McGowan said, "you will be given all the time necessary to tell your story. But now you must sit down and be quiet or I will instruct the sheriff to remove you."

Benson sat down.

"Resume, Mr. Dilk," the judge said.

"Benjamin"—Dilk put his hand on Ben's shoulder—"Mr. Benson was right, wasn't he? Folded Leaf tried to kill you."

Ben jerked away. "He didn't, he didn't. I told you, he couldn't move. His leg was shot in two. When Mr. Benson saw he had me buffaloed, he walked over and picked Folded Leaf up by the heels and swung him around in a circle so that he fetched his head up against the trunk of a big beech. Then he swung him the other direction and did the same thing."

"Did this kill the boy?"

"He didn't have any head left. Mr. Benson smashed his head like an egg."

"What did Mr. Benson do then?"

"He threw what was left of Folded Leaf away. Then he said, 'I reckon that finishes the job.' "

"What did you do?"

"When he said that, I got up and run home."

"Did you hear any more shots back at the sugar camp?"

"I couldn't hear anything but Folded Leaf asking me to help him. And how quiet he was when Mr. Benson picked him up. He didn't make a sound. But his head made a sound . . . like—"

Judge McGowan said, "You don't need to repeat that. Mr. Dilk, unless you have more questions, ask your witness to step down."

Dilk put his arm around Ben and led him back to his family.

THE COURTROOM was silent. No one moved. Judge McGowan stared out at the crowd. They had come to see the monkey show. Well, they had seen it. McGowan gaveled sharply.

"The court will adjourn for two hours."

The prisoner, his wife and six children trooping behind him, was taken out. Judge McGowan watched him go. Benson would pass through that door someday hearing dreadful words he, Amos McGowan, had spoken. God in heaven, why did he ever become a judge? He watched the jury leave. Those twelve men had listened to something they could not forget. Finding guilt or innocence was their responsibility. Life or death was his.

The lawyers, talking, but quiet for lawyers, left together. Then the onlookers filed out, their faces heated and their eyes bright. Judge McGowan had seen this time and time again. Considering the vein of cruelty that pulsed in all men, the love of violence, the fascination with death, it was a wonder so few heads were broken, so few breasts mangled with bullets.

He did not believe the Indians were different in nature from the white men. They, too, were brutal, but their training was different. Their faces were not open books. The Indian boy had not cried out; nor had his kinsmen, hearing the manner of his death. They left the courtroom, their faces as sealed as old tree butts around the living sap that fed them. Amos McGowan envied them.

When he was alone, he did put his arms on the table and his head in his arms. He was not an old man—thirty-eight. But he was not ambitious, like Fort and Dilk. He was judicious by nature. Judicious in practice, he had learned, was another kettle of fish.

A hand on his shoulder roused him.

"Amos, I hope I didn't wake you up." It was Johnston, the Indian agent. "Will you come eat dinner with me?"

"Thank you, Colonel. I don't feel like eating just now. My stomach turns at the very thought."

"That wasn't a very pretty story."

"That's not what makes me bilious. I've got a troubled mind. No one man can hand out justice the way a judge is asked to."

"No one man is asked to, Amos. Besides the juries, you've got a framework of law and of court practice to support you."

"Court practice won't help me in this case. You know as well as I do no court has ever handed down a judgment against a white for killing an Indian."

"Don't you think it's about time the law recognized the Indians as human beings?"

"Oh, it's time, all right, Colonel. God knows it's time. But for two hundred years it was time to kill Indians. How were Benson and the Woods to know the time had come to stop?"

"Something told Bemis. This court can teach the others."

"What lesson will the Indians learn?"

"They'll learn there's justice for them, too. They'll learn they don't have to raid and scalp and burn to get it."

"Colonel, it won't be justice that hangs these men. If they hang. It'll be chance. The chance that put an Indian agent like you in the territory at the time of the killings."

"Leaving chance and justice out of it, Amos, you know what this trial can mean in the matter of saving lives?"

"Oh, I know that. But this court, while I preside, won't be providing victims to appease attackers. I'd rather we'd all be wiped out than sentence any man to save our own necks."

McGowan looked up at the chunky colonel. The *colonel's* decision had been made from the minute he heard of the killings. Get the killers hanged and stave off an Indian uprising. Backing up the colonel were the Secretary of War, Calhoun, and Monroe, the President. And what did *he*, McGowan, have? The terrible knowledge that all courts up to this time had ignored the law. And that Benson, the Woods, and Bemis had killed out of their knowledge of this fact.

CHARLIE FORT didn't feel like eating, either. He didn't know what anyone could have done about the Cape boy's story. In the long run it didn't make much difference how a man died. There was no law providing clemency for tidy killers. But a jury was inclined to find a savage killer guilty faster than one who hadn't bloodied up the landscape. This afternoon, though, when he put Benson on the stand, Charlie had a thing or two to bring out that might undo some of the harm of the morning's testimony.

It was June in April. No June flowers or leaves yet, of course, but June's breath, warm and sweet. Charlie had two hours before he had to be in court. He headed out of the town to the Baldwin house, where the Cape family was staying—all sitting outside, eating a cold picnic dinner. Dilk was with them, acting cozy as a member of the family. Hannah was handing out the victuals. When she saw him, he felt in his veins the impulse he knew was in hers to do away with all distance between them. Jump stumps, send fried chicken flying. Clout the sanctimonious Dilk in the process.

Yet Charlie was able to greet them all like a lawyer, not a lover. Congratulate Dilk. Tell Ben that he had done the right thing (he had, though Charlie wished he had kept his mouth shut).

"Have you eaten yet?" Caleb Cape asked. "Join us."

"I thought I'd walk out in the woods. There's a number of things I'd better think over before court this afternoon."

Lizzie Cape said, "Hannah, fix the poor man some lunch. You can think while you eat, can't you, Mr. Fort?"

"Think better, maybe," Charlie said.

Hannah brought bread, chicken, and sweet cake wrapped in a fringed napkin. "If you don't mind, Mrs. Cape," Charlie said, "I'll take Hannah with me to listen to me practice my plea."

Dilk said, "Pleading's not going to change facts, Charlie."

"The facts are maybe less one-sided than you think, Oscar."

Charlie headed himself and Hannah toward the woods. When the trees shielded them from sight, he threw the food away and took Hannah in his arms.

"My love, my Hannah, where have you been?"

"I've only been away three days."

"Does it seem that short to you?"

"No," said Hannah. "It seems forever."

They moved two steps forward, deeper into the woods, then kissed; two more steps, then kissed again.

"Let's sit down and rest," said Charlie.

Sitting down was the last thing Hannah intended. She had already decided how to see and talk to Charlie without encountering the danger of what had already happened once: always stand up.

She was no ignorant backwoods girl who thought that babies were delivered by storks. Ora had taught her more. She had no intention of being pitied because of a watermelon under her apron. There was no way she could stop loving Charlie, but from now on she would stay on her feet when with him. Always. Lying down was when the trouble began.

Charlie didn't ask her to lie down. He simply put his knee into the back crook of hers and she folded up like a jackknife. She went down and Charlie with her, into a nest of leaves. She remembered, Always stand up. But they were nothing but words now.

LATER THAT DAY, after court was adjourned, Charlie was back in Norry Culligan's loft, writing his article for the *Western Spy*. He sketched in Ben Cape's testimony of that morning. Then, because he was tired, because he had the notes from which he had spoken, he decided to finish the piece with his own defense of Benson. He wrote of himself in the third person, as lawyer observed, not reporting. It made the writing more objective.

Extracts from a letter by Charles Fort to Enoch Leverett:

In the afternoon, when court resumed, George Benson was tried for the first of the two crimes for which he had been indicted, the murder of the Indian woman, Talking Crow. Before putting Benson on the stand, Charles Fort, for the defense, reminded the jury of facts they must not forget: i.e., that the trial of a white man for killing an Indian could not and must not be separated from the two-hundred-year relationship of these two races.

"What happened at the sugar camp cannot be judged except as history," he began. "I would like to recount for the jury a happening within the lifetime of many of you, in the state of Ohio, from which Mr. Benson and I hail.

"A family by the name of Ferguson lived on a farm some forty miles from Cincinnati. Adam Ferguson and his fourteen-year-old son were slaughtered by Indians while harvesting the corn crop. Mrs. Ferguson, her babe, and three older children were captured, tied to horses, and made to travel furiously to escape pursuers. The babe began to sob. The Indians, fearing that its cries would alert followers, snatched it from its mother and brained it.

"When the lodges of the Indians were reached, the mother and her two daughters, ages fourteen and sixteen, were bestowed as spoils of war on leading chiefs. They were passed from chief to chief. I will not dwell on their experiences. The younger girl died in captivity. The seven-year-old boy was taken farther west and never heard from again. Mother and daughter, after three years, escaped. When I was a boy, it was still common for mothers to warn their children against straying too far from the house by saying, 'Remember the Fergusons.' "

After this speech, Fort immediately called George Benson to the stand. Duly sworn, Mr. Benson was asked by Mr. Fort if he, too, had been warned in his childhood to "remember the Fergusons."

"No," said Mr. Benson. "What the young uns in the Benson family were told was, 'Remember Grandpa.'"

"Did you, when so admonished, 'remember Grandpa'?"

"Nobody had to remind me. I saw it happen to Grandpa."

"What was it you saw?"

"When I was seven years old—that was in 1784—the Benson family was living in Virginia near the banks of a creek called Little Muddy. In October of that year, my grandfather, a man near seventy, was down at that creek, getting a load of dauby mud to use in caulking our log cabin. Pa was nearby, bringing in a load of pumpkins, gun with him, of course. I was playing in the cattails. They was well over my head, so I heard what was happening before I saw it. I heard Pa's gun fire, then I heard him yell to Grandpa, 'Injuns. Run for the house.'"

"Didn't he call to you?"

"He didn't know I was there. And Grandpa was deef and didn't hear anything. Pa made it to the house, but Grandpa didn't have a chance. They put more arrows in him than a porcupine has quills. They scalped him while he was still alive. Then he died."

"How did you get back to the house?"

"When all the Indians had left, Pa came down and found me."

"Did you remember this when you were at the sugar camp?"

"I remember it all the time."

Mr. Fort then turned his witness over to the prosecution for cross-examination. Senator Noble had but few questions.

"Mr. Benson, had your grandfather ever killed any Indians?"

"Of course he had. He had lived on the frontier all of his life. A man don't live there without killing Indians."

"Whose land was he living on?"

"His own."

"Who owned it before he did?"

"Nobody."

"Didn't Indians own it?"

"Indians don't own land. They roam it. Hunting and killing."

"And getting killed."

Mr. Fort here objected. "The means by which the citizens of the United States got a foothold on this continent have no bearing on this case. Mr. Benson is to some degree responsible for the westward march of civilization in this country. But if we turn our attention to that subject, we'll be here till the Fourth of July."

After Fort had spoken, Judge McGowan gave the jury an able charge. They were out no more than twenty minutes when they returned with a verdict of manslaughter. This verdict, after a recess for deliberation, was followed by a sentence from Judge McGowan: "Two years in prison at hard labor."

Patrick Conroy, the leading lawyer for the defense, immediately upon the sentencing sprang to his feet and said, "If the court please, we are ready for the case of Benson for killing the Indian boy in camp."

Judge McGowan, though the state also was ready for a continuation of the trial of Benson, adjourned the court for the day. It was growing late, the hearings had been exhausting, and McGowan had every reason to call for a halt. He instructed the court to reconvene Tuesday afternoon at two.

End of extracts from a letter by Charles Fort to Enoch Leverett.

IX

On Tuesday, though it was noontime, nobody seemed of a mind to eat. The open space around the courthouse had for an hour been filled with many of those who had listened to Monday's proceedings, too restless now to light and stop talking. Was what had happened right? they asked each other. And right or wrong, what would be the outcome for them? The Indians were impassive as they spoke together. What were they saying?

Thomas Gunn, jury foreman, hair sheep-curly and sheep-colored, came up to Charlie. "Mr. Fort," he said, "you want to know why we decided the way we did? Way back there when that boy saw his grandfather hacked up by the redskins, something took hold of him and was his master. So what he did was manslaughter. It was his nature speaking: nothing he planned. That's the way I seen it, and it was the way I persuaded the other jurors to vote."

Before Charlie could thank Gunn, Sarah Benson, with children at her heels, threw her arms around the foreman. If a man's character is to be decided by the appearance of his wife, Benson was not a bad man; Sarah would never see forty again, but to judge by her unlined face she had enjoyed the last twenty of those years.

She was crying now, cheeks like plum blossoms in the rain.

"Mr. Gunn," she said, "I can't reward you, but God will, for saving my husband's life. Me and my children will forever be in your debt. Oh, Tom Gunn, God bless you."

Charlie, knowing that Benson's troubles were not yet over, turned to Norry Culligan, who was standing close by, as though waiting to speak to him. She said, "I fixed a pickup dinner for you and Hannah, if you want to invite her to the house." Norry didn't expect a miracle, but if Charlie said, I'd like to talk over the trial with a woman of more experience than Hannah, she wouldn't argue. It wasn't the reply she got.

"I haven't seen Hannah," Charlie said.

Norry pointed. Hannah was surrounded by men—her father, Colonel Johnston, a couple of the jurors. Charlie was of two minds about joining the crowd, when Hannah came to him.

"Norry has fixed us a bite to eat at her place," he said.

Norry was heading quickly away. Hannah watched her resolute departure. "Why is that woman so good to us?" she asked.

"She's an old lady without any children left at home," Charlie said. "We take their place."

Hannah looked at Charlie. It was easy for her to see in Charlie what Norry saw. "She's in love with you," Hannah said.

"My God, Hannah," said Charlie, "she's a *grandmother*."

"She don't think of you as a grandson. Likely she had a young husband, just your spit and image. She looks at you and remembers him—and forgets all the time in between."

"I look at her and remember you. And the difference. Come on, let's eat."

Norry had left the food on the table. Custard pie; deviled eggs; pickled beets. Food pretty to look at, but look was all they could do. They sat down, then rose immediately, clasped each other, and kissed away most of the hour they had.

"Charlie," said Hannah, "we mustn't make love anymore."

"Because it is wrong?"

"It *is* wrong. But wrong wouldn't stop me. Besides, afterward, I don't feel like I've done wrong. As I would if I lied . . ."

"Afterward—how do you feel, Hannah?"

"Blessed," she said, startling herself with the holy word.

"We're going to be married, you know, Hannah."

"I don't want to *have* to be married."

"You and I have to be married. There'd be no sense in not. As soon as this trial is over."

"Then we mustn't anymore—until the trial is over."

"No, we mustn't, Hannah. You're right." Charlie held her in his arms. No kissing now. "But you must help me, Hannah."

"I will, Charlie. I'll always help you. You know that."

JUDGE MCGOWAN WAS in his tall fanback chair a quarter of an hour before the afternoon session. He leaned his head back and closed his eyes. If people thought he was sleeping, they might let him alone. How a jury had decided that shooting a woman point-blank was manslaughter was beyond him. But a judge didn't over-ride his jury, so he had no choice in his sentencing. Men are not hanged for manslaughter.

A feeling of warmth near him made him open his eyes. Three inches away was the bulk of Black Antler, hot with feeling, trembling with conviction. "Judge, you did right not to condemn Benson to die."

"With the verdict what it was, I didn't have much choice."

"No one should be killed for killing. It is not the Indian way. Or the way of Handsome Lake and the old longhouse faith."

"What do you do with your killers?"

"The man is cast out, not spoken to or fed."

"Doesn't he die?"

"If the Great Spirit wills. We do not kill him."

McGowan nodded toward the Indian line that had once again formed at the back of the room. "Killing is their way."

"With your people, not our own. They have been at war with your people. They want them killed because that is war."

"What if they knew you were here asking me to spare them?"

"They think I am crazy."

"My people would say that you're crazy like a fox. That you'd persuade us not to hang the killers so the tribes up north could claim, 'They did not have a fair trial.' Then they would kill every settler in the Fall Creek valley."

"I know, but I say what is right. Right is what you want to do."

"My God, Black Antler, you don't help me much. I can't sentence according to what strikes me or you as right or wrong. I sentence according to law. I have sworn before God to do so. And before

352

God I will do so." McGowan rose and struck the table in front of him with his closed fist.

Black Antler took a seat by himself in the courtroom. The people he knew best had been killed. Neither whites nor reds trusted him. But he sat at ease. He had done what he could.

JUDGE MCGOWAN gaveled the courtroom into silence. Then George Benson was put back on the stand. Fort had no intention of spoiling the effect Benson's account of the death of his grandfather had had on the jury the previous afternoon. He wanted *that* to stay in the jurors' minds, not Benson's admission that he had killed a stripling. He kept his questions brief.

"Mr. Benson, you have been accused of killing the Indian boy named Folded Leaf. Did you do so?"

"I did."

"Wasn't the death of the squaw sufficient revenge?"

"I didn't kill Folded Leaf for revenge."

"What was your motive, then?"

"Self defense. He was crawling toward me."

Charlie, doubting that Benson would do himself any more good, said, "The defense rests." O. A. Dilk then took over.

Judge McGowan, who had seen many a lawyer perform, felt sorry for Benson. Dilk was no natural orator like Fort. But he would take that jury over the logical jumps of the killing so smoothly it would end up with "murder" in its mouth without knowing how the word got there.

Dilk made no reference to the verdict—except to praise the jurors for their devotion to duty. They fairly blossomed.

There was not a jot of difference in law between the two killings. McGowan knew it and knew that Dilk knew it. What those jurors knew was hard to say.

"Did you kill Folded Leaf?" Dilk was asking.

"I did," said Benson.

Then Dilk produced something from a carpetbag he was carrying. "Do you recognize this garment, Mr. Benson?"

The garment Oscar Dilk held up was a calico blouse. This one had been red, but it was now so stiffened and discolored that little of the original red was visible.

"No," said Benson. But his face did not say no.

"Could you identify the shirt if you could see the color?"

"Well, I can't see the color."

"Do you know why you can't?"

"The shirt's dirty."

"Do you know what that dirt is?"

Benson sat in silence.

"I'll tell you, Mr. Benson, and the jury, what that dirt is. The rusty brown stains are blood. Great gouts and spurts of blood fell, probably from the head, onto this garment. Notice here, Mr. Benson and gentlemen of the jury, where the color is gray. That discoloration is a boy's brains, spilled onto his pretty red blouse. Now, Mr. Benson, do you remember Folded Leaf's red shirt as it looked before you smashed his skull against a tree?"

Benson got to his feet. He was a sick-looking man again. "You know why I killed that boy. I explained it all. My grandfather . . . This boy would grow up and do the same thing."

Dilk, without replying, took from his bag a pair of buckskin pantaloons. One leg was intact; the other had been sheared off at the thigh. What was left hung in tatters of bloodstained buckskin.

"A boy with a leg like this would be a threat?"

"He was crawling toward Ben Cape right then. . . . You heard me say so."

"I heard Ben Cape say he was trying to get some help."

"I killed him out of pity. Yes, I did. He was suffering. I did it to put him out of his misery. I took the quickest way—"

Judge McGowan stopped his ravings. "Sit down, Mr. Benson."

Benson sat and Dilk then addressed himself to the jury.

"Gentlemen of the jury, I see I need not tell you that the case you had to consider yesterday and the one you have to consider today are very different. In the first, you found the prisoner guilty of manslaughter for using his rifle on a grown squaw. In the second, a boy, who went where his parents went, with no choice of his own, had his brains knocked out against a tree."

Dilk held up the bloodstained garments again. "Poor helpless child. Taken by his heels like a rabbit and brained. Was this not the act of a brutal murderer?"

The jury retired for its verdict. The courtroom was silent.

After an absence of not many minutes, the jury returned, silent as before. "Have you reached a verdict?" asked Judge McGowan.

356

Gunn, the big Scot with sheep-textured hair, rose. "We have."

"What is the verdict, Mr. Foreman?"

"Guilty of murder in the first degree."

The prisoner was remanded, and the court adjourned.

AFTER THAT VERDICT, the strength appeared to have gone out of the onlookers' legs. Many still sat as if felled by a blow. What kind of a sentence could McGowan give after a verdict like that? The boy had died a terrible death: no two ways about it.

The Cape family was strong enough to stand on its feet and start toward the Baldwin home. Hannah knew she should go with them: she was expected to help at her cousins'. Instead she lingered in the courthouse yard, striking up conversations with one person and another, looking for Charlie. She knew she should be feeling sorrow for George Benson, and she did, but at the moment she was grieving more for Charlie. He had done nothing worse than lose a case—his life wasn't at stake—but she loved Charlie, and you hurt where your heart was. And now she couldn't even find him. As soon as her family was out of sight, she searched in earnest.

He was still in the courtroom, backed into a corner with McGowan and Noble. At last he saw her over the heads of his companions and left to join her. "I know a place where we can be alone," Hannah said.. "Where we can talk. It's a leaf cave."

Charlie had had his fill of talk. The verdict clanged in his head like a fire bell. Murder. Murder. "What's a leaf cave?"

"Come on and see."

She and her Baldwin cousins had discovered the leaf cave. Fox grapes, climbing a sycamore tree at the edge of a branch, had reached the top limbs, then spilled downward, making a green umbrella clear to the water's edge. "It's a little leaf house," she said. "Look, we marked off the rooms with pebbles."

"Which room is mine?"

"Every one is yours. Lie down. Rest. I'll sit beside you."

He felt like lying down. The land sloped gently toward the branch in the right way for resting. Hannah, with some idea of being a nurse to a man who had suffered a setback, kissed his closed eyes, made him a mustache out of her braid, and finally picked up his head and rocked it against her breasts like a baby.

He forgot there ever had been a trial. Rocked like a baby, he

357

responded like a baby, and Hannah yelled, "You *promised.*" He had her bodice half unbuttoned.

"*You* promised to help me," Charlie said. "Then you lie down with me and hold me and kiss me. What help is that?"

"It is helping you to forget the trial—and Dilk and Benson."

"Dilk and Benson?" he asked. "Who are they?" He unbuttoned and she buttoned. This was becoming less lovemaking and more wrestling. "I love you, Hannah," Charlie said, trying to recall to her the purpose of these embraces.

He, not Hannah, relaxed when he said that. She sat on top of him and looked him in the eye.

"I hate you, Charlie Fort. You are not a man of your word. You are not strong in body or soul. I never want to see you again."

Having said this, Hannah leaped to her feet and ran, hair streaming, out of the house of leaves. Charlie's first impulse was to follow her. Then he thought better of it. If he did catch up with her someplace on the outskirts of Pendleton, what would people think? They'd think that what had not happened had.

He started walking home, home being Norry Culligan's house.

ENOS BALDWIN, Lizzie's brother, had a big family, set a good table, and there was always plenty of slop for the hogs. The washup that evening was big. Caleb helped Hannah carry the scraps to the pen out behind the privy where Spot and Pinky lived.

A pig with his snout in the gruel of dishwater and cabbage leaves may not be the prettiest sight in the world, but it ought not move anyone to tears. Nevertheless, Hannah was crying.

Caleb said, "There ain't been no sentence set yet."

But Hannah wasn't crying about George Benson. She was crying about Charlie. Told he was weak in body and soul. His defense of Benson gone to pieces. She saw him now, stretched out on his attic bed, recalling every painful word that had been spoken that afternoon.

She said, "I'm never going to give any pig I'm going to eat a name. I think if it's going to be meat, you should treat it like meat from the beginning. Not give it a human name, then go out one day, knock it on the head, and fry it. I'll never do that." And she threw her apron over her face and sobbed.

Caleb doubted his daughter was crying her heart out over a pig.

"There was no way in the world," he said, "Charlie Fort could have got a decision for Benson in the face of the evidence Dilk showed the jury. Charlie's a good lawyer. But a jury's got to judge by law, not smooth talk."

Hannah uncovered her face. "That's what I told him he was, this evening. Just a smooth talker."

"That was piling the punishment on pretty high."

"I know it. I'm sorry for it now. But he made me mad."

"That temper is going to get you in trouble someday, Hannah."

"I'm in trouble now. Charlie hates me, I think."

"Well, you go tell him you're sorry for what you said, and he'll stop hating you, I expect."

"Tell him right now?"

"It's no more than first dark—and less than a five-minute run to Mrs. Culligan's. You'll feel better, and he will, too, like as not, if you sashay over there and say, 'Charlie, my tongue ran away with me.' Then you can run back home with a clear conscience."

Hannah took off her apron, threw it to her father, and left.

THE RUN went out of Hannah when she saw the glimmer of light at Mrs. Culligan's. It was one thing to know that she'd like to tell Charlie she was sorry. *Charlie, you are not weak. I love you with all my heart.* It was another thing to walk bald-faced up to Mrs. Culligan's door and ask to see Mr. Fort, please. She climbed the porch steps noiselessly, so that, if at the last minute her courage failed, she could turn and run home and no one need be the wiser.

There was no answer to her whisper of a knock, or to the second knock, which was a murmur. Silently she went along the porch to the window of what, besides the kitchen, was the one downstairs room. The glimmer of light she had seen came from a candle set on the night table in that room. At first, in the gloom of its flicker, she saw only dim outlines of furniture. Then, she saw the two white bodies on Norry Culligan's bed, across from the window. They were male and female. If Norry in the light of day was an old lady, in candlelight she didn't show it. Short, plump, and white as a squab. She was on one elbow, her back to the window, watching Charlie Fort as he slept.

Hannah crept home. There was no run left in her. She hadn't known anyone could feel so sick without being on his deathbed.

X

The courthouse was filled an hour before the trial was to begin next morning. The prisoner to be tried that day, Johnny Wood, had not yet been brought over from the jail. Judge McGowan was not yet in his place. The word was around that the judge alternated these days between praying and drinking glasses of water spiked with baking soda. No one envied him his job. The jury, with eleven other jurors to back up each individual juror in his decision, was not in a place so stony lonesome as the judge. It is easier to say "We all did it" than "I did it."

But the defense attorneys were there, having a conference. Charlie Fort had arrived first, hoping to see and talk to Hannah. He saw her all right, talking to, or being talked to by, O. A. Dilk. When he caught her eye, she looked at him with a vacant stare. He was glad to give his attention to the problem that faced the defense. Looking at Hannah, he might cry.

Noah Beazley said, "Is there any point getting that Cape boy up here and having him repeat his story?"

"Not for us," Charlie said, "but the prosecution may insist."

"You know Dilk, Charlie. Why don't you ask him if he'll agree to a stipulation that the boy's testimony be made a part of the record and that we spare the boy a repetition of that bloody story? Dilk ought to be willing—looks like he's trying to stand in well with the boy's sister."

Charlie wanted to get away from that subject. "Say they agree to the stipulation," he said, "what's our next move?"

"Put young Wood on the stand. He's got a right to defend himself, however you look at it. That he'd have shot an Indian woman, first in one breast, then the other, don't make good sense."

"He is the unlikeliest-looking murderer I ever saw," Charlie agreed. "The jury's going to have a hard time finding that sweet-faced boy guilty of murder in any degree. Let alone first."

"Then are we of the same mind about putting him on the stand?"

"We are," said Isaac Vickers. "Charlie, you talk to Dilk."

Charlie hoped to talk to Hannah as well, but as he approached, she walked away. Dilk, as Beazley had suggested, was eager to spare the Cape boy any further torment.

"I think I can promise you, Charlie, that the prosecution will agree to the stipulation. You put the Wood boy on the stand now and then we'll cross-examine. But I'd never let a witness like that testify if I was representing him."

"What worse can be said than what we've already heard?"

"Something worse can always be said," Dilk replied.

BEN CAPE'S testimony as to what he had seen Johnny Wood do at the sugar camp was read into the record. Then Noah Beazley, solid and fatherly, took over for the defense.

Beazley called Johnny to the stand. The boy put down a book he had been reading and was sworn in. Could a young man guilty of murder be that nonchalant? He went into the questioning as if all he had to do was to make his whole story known to be understood and excused.

BEAZLEY: Did you accompany your father and your uncle to the Indian sugar camp?

JOHNNY: Yes, sir.

BEAZLEY: Did you have a gun?

JOHNNY: Yes, sir. I was going squirrel hunting.

BEAZLEY: You didn't take the gun so you could kill Indians?

JOHNNY: No, sir. I was going hunting. You can ask Ben.

BEAZLEY: We have asked Ben. He says you gave up your squirrel hunt and joined your father and uncle in an Indian hunt.

JOHNNY: No, sir. I never did that.

BEAZLEY: Well, what do you call it, then? You shot and killed an Indian woman.

JOHNNY: No, sir. I never shot and killed any Indian woman.

When Noah Beazley finished his questions, Johnny looked into space, waiting for Mr. Armitage to begin his.

Jonathan Armitage, as if he understood that any rough handling of this soft-spoken stripling would prejudice his case with the jury, talked to Johnny like a kindly uncle.

ARMITAGE: I'm Jonathan Armitage, Johnny. I'd like to talk to you some more about what happened at the sugar camp. How many Indians were killed in all?

JOHNNY: Eight, all together.

ARMITAGE: Eight? There were nine dead bodies at the camp.

JOHNNY: You said Indians. There was one white woman.

ARMITAGE: Who shot the white woman?

JOHNNY: I did.

ARMITAGE: Why?

JOHNNY: I shot her because she was doing what was wrong, and she was trying to get me to do what was wrong. When a woman does that, I have to protect myself, or I'll join her in wrongdoing.

ARMITAGE: Wide Eyes? The Indian woman?

JOHNNY: I don't know her name. But she was white. She showed me she was white. She was no Indian.

ARMITAGE: How did she show you she was white?

JOHNNY: She tore open her dress and did what a woman shouldn't do. Showed me those two things a woman has. I shot one and that didn't stop her. So I shot the other. I seen a woman pointing those things at me once before and I know what she has in mind when she does that. I won't let it happen again.

ARMITAGE: What happened the first time, Johnny?

There was a muffled outcry from the courtroom, and Reba Wood, standing, addressed the prosecutor. "Armitage, you stop hounding my boy. Stop your prying. Johnny ain't no more responsible here for his past life than you are. And I don't reckon you're about to spill all that, are you?"

The courtroom exploded. Even the Indians broke their rigid line to face each other and talk.

Judge McGowan gaveled them into silence. Then he said, "Sheriff Brady, I think you'd better remove the prisoner from the room." Johnny Wood went with Brady as if happy to get out of the limelight and back to his book.

Reba Wood followed. McGowan was inclined to tell her what she had told Armitage: Don't hound that boy anymore. But there was no precedent for a judge to instruct a stepmother about her conduct with her stepson. When the two were out of the room, he gave his charge to the jury.

"You have heard a clear-cut confession of murder. The young man believed he was killing a white woman, though in fact he was shooting a woman who was at least half Miami. She was in no way threatening his life. He believed she was doing something wrong. The law does not empower us to shoot those whose ways are different from ours, or whose conduct we condemn. The law does not give us the right to excuse killing by the conclusion that the killer, if brought up in a different manner, might not have killed.

362

"The law is very clear on one point. If this was a premeditated killing—not self-defense, not accidental—the defendant is guilty of murder in the first degree. That is all you have to decide."

The jury, given their charge, was not out long. Brady brought the prisoner back into court to hear the verdict. Tom Gunn delivered it: "Guilty of murder in the first degree."

If this meant anything to Johnny Wood, his face didn't show it. The words might have come from the page of a book he was reading. Those in the courtroom had no fault to find with the verdict. A man who thought he had license to shoot loose women— white women—was better punished early than late.

No one knew what the Indians, except Black Antler, thought of the decision. Black Antler was against "murder for murder," and he let everyone know what he felt. Because he was a faithkeeper, the Indians let him talk. The whites believed him crazy.

One other Indian, a Miami chief, the most resplendently dressed Indian at the trials, did make his convictions known. He was named Lone Fawn, and like his tribe's woman, Wide Eyes, he had more than a dash of white blood. Lone Fawn approved wholeheartedly of the death sentence for those who had murdered the Indians at the sugar camp. But what he particularly liked was the method of the punishment. Indians had never used hanging, which, from what he had heard of it, was a manner of killing, slow and dignified. All took place at a height where the hanging could be well viewed— and the punishment, he understood, went on often for as long as ten minutes, with a considerable amount of convulsive twitching and jerking to entertain the onlookers. It was not exactly a religious occasion, but the whites' priests were present and there were prayers for and by the man to be strangled, if he felt like praying.

Lone Fawn, like the other Indians, had been invited to attend the hangings if they took place. It was an event he did not intend to miss. Justice would be done; but, beyond this, Lone Fawn had a natural bent toward the solemn, ceremonious, and fatal.

THAT NIGHT CHARLIE FORT sat at his attic table trying to put together something appropriate for the *Western Spy*. He was determined to keep out of his report everything about his breakup with Hannah. He couldn't, or wouldn't, write his father, Girl thrown me over; case gone to hell.

Hannah, heart of my heart. He tried to prevent himself from rehearsing that last meeting in an effort to create a new scene in which he and Hannah would walk away from that leaf house hand in hand, an engaged couple, as he had planned. Actually, what had he done that was so terrible? Unbutton a few buttons and kiss what the buttoning had covered. What had that fondling girl expected? Whatever it was, he wished he had done it.

The pain had never ceased except for that night, when Norry, nurse and mother and mistress, had made him forget and sleep. Norry kept clear of him now. Food on the table, bed made, but she herself always gone. It would have helped to talk to her.

He finally managed to get onto paper a bare account of Johnny Wood's trial. What was left to report was sad and short.

Extracts from a letter by Charles Fort to Enoch Leverett:
John Wood, Sr., after he learned of his son's testimony and the jury's verdict, refused the services of his lawyers and pleaded guilty.

The old man was impressive. Tall, thin, gray, his Bible in his hand, his face, as we judge faces, righteous. His speech, addressed to Judge McGowan, was very moving. He said that he was as guilty as his son of killing a squaw; and that if his son had been found guilty of first-degree murder for this act, he should also be found guilty. In fact, he said he was four times as guilty as his son. Johnny had killed one Indian squaw. He had killed one squaw and three Indian children.

He said that he was an old man, that his son was the only tie that he had to life; that his present wife hated him; that he had been able to survive thus far in life in part because he had always fought Indians; and that he would consider his death now, if the judge so decreed, as the often-expected termination of many of those fights. What he had never expected was that his death in such a fight would come from the hands of white men. If his countrymen had come to such a pass, he would rather be dead.

Judge McGowan rose, picked up his gavel, but did not use it. He stood turning it over and over in his hand. Finally he spoke: "On Monday at ten in the morning Luther Bemis, George Benson, John Wood and John Wood, Jr. will appear before me for sentencing. Until that time the court stands adjourned." Judge McGowan

364

then brought his gavel down with so much force his real desire appeared to be to smash courthouse, lawyers, onlookers, the whole sorry lot.
End of extracts from a letter by Charles Fort to Enoch Leverett.

XI

It was Sunday and Caleb was determined that there should be a regular hour-long meeting for worship. Tomorrow Judge McGowan would pass sentence on four residents of Fall Creek. These four men needed prayers; and Judge McGowan needed prayer perhaps more than any of them. So it was going to be church for one full hour, and God have mercy on them all.

Oscar Dilk had made the ride over to the Capes' for two reasons. First, he wanted to see Hannah. Once this trial was over, he would move on and, he had no doubt, up. His feeling was that Hannah would be the woman to go with him.

She would need a little "gentling," as these Westerners called breaking fractious horses. Slow down her movements, put a little more dignity in her speech. But she was the most strikingly beautiful woman he had ever seen. No matter where he went, eyes would not stray from them if that woman was by his side. So the wooing of Hannah Cape was his first reason for coming.

The second was also important: to smell out the settlement's feelings. If there was to be any attempt at a jailbreak, here where the four men lived is where it would start.

Hannah was already dressed when he arrived an hour before church time. "Your shoes too fancy for a walk, Hannah?" he asked.

Hannah had one pair of shoes, and they were designed for walking. What else? "No, Mr. Dilk. Walking won't hurt them."

"Don't call me Mr. Dilk. My name's Oscar. I don't like it, but it's better than Mr. Dilk."

"Did anyone ever call you Ossie?"

Dilk was delighted. "No one ever did. Would you like to?"

Hannah hadn't the heart to disappoint him. "Yes, Ossie."

Dilk led Hannah to the bridge that crossed the branch below the Capes' house. "If you make a wish over running water, you get your wish, Hannah; did you know that?"

Hannah, remembering when she had stood here with Jud Clasby, thought, What I should wish is that some man like Dilk would fall in love with me and marry me and save me from falling in love with men like Jud Clasby and Charlie Fort. "Yes, I know."

"Have you got a wish?"

"I just wished it."

"Can you tell me?"

"No, of course not. If you tell, it won't come true."

Dilk took one of Hannah's hands and put it solemnly on the left side of the good broadcloth of his jacket.

"Can you feel that, Hannah?"

"Yes," said Hannah. "It is your heart."

"Do you know what it says? It says, 'Ossie loves Hannah.' "

For a second Hannah feared she would laugh. That is your trouble, Hannah, she told herself. You laugh at good men and let mashers have their way with you.

"Does Hannah say she loves Ossie?"

The wish took hold sooner than she had expected.

"I will when I know you better."

That was exactly the kind of answer Dilk wanted. He didn't care for girls who leaped before they looked. Hannah wouldn't say "love" like "good morning" or "pass the salt." When she knew him better, she would say it. But now the Capes' dinner bell, which served on Sundays as church bell, was ringing.

Summer in April was gone that morning. April, too, for that matter. It was now May, which had arrived with a cloudy sky and a raw wind. "A blackberry winter shaping up," they said, that season when freezing weather, or snow itself, matches the creamy blossoms of the berry vines.

Inside, the cabin was crowded, every bench filled, and children either sat on their parents' laps or squatted between their feet. Here sat the families of men who would at ten a.m. on the morrow hear a judgment of life or death.

There were present not only those fearing that the sentencing would be harsh, but those who feared that without death sentences, all of them would die at the hands of the northern tribes.

And Black Antler was there. He had Caleb's permission to preach, after church services were over, his own kind of sermon to as many as would listen. He stood alone against the wall, no head-dress, plain moccasins, breechclout and apron, and a doeskin jacket.

Caleb stood before them. Last night he had searched his Bible for the right text. Finally God had led him to it. Nothing except the Twenty-third Psalm would speak to the condition of all who were present this morning. The verses had come to him like a gift. Now he poured them forth like a gift. *"Yea, though I walk through the valley of the shadow of death, I will fear no evil: for thou art with me; thy rod and thy staff they comfort me."* The words filled his mouth like a draft of cool water. The words a man speaks are always more comforting than the words he hears. Caleb knew that. He labored to put the taste of these words on the tongue of every man present. *"Surely goodness and mercy shall follow me all the days of my life."*

Caleb was never sure whether the words that were in his heart then got spoken or whether they simply thundered in his veins.

"We are met as Christians. We say, *Thy will be done.* We have made laws which we believe will bring the kingdom of heaven nearer to earth. We must abide by them. We must pray for Judge McGowan as well as for the men who await his decision. We must remember that all things work for good for those who love the Lord."

These, he believed, were the words his lips said. Inside, others pounded to the beat of his heart: God, let this hour pass. It is more than we can endure.

Kill for killing. Or refrain and be killed for not killing. His final prayer was tears, with a few broken words floating on that tide.

Hannah, seeing the state into which her father had fallen, rose and said, "Let us sing." Many could not. The sides of their throats clung together like slices of meat hung in the sun to dry. Hannah sang. Oscar Dilk, with his lawyer's throat, sang. Lizzie sang. Caleb sat with his head in his hands. He was no true Christian. Why was the prospect of men going home to Jesus so horrifying? It was how they were being sent there.

The singing stopped, and Black Antler took the preacher's place.

They were against him before he could say a word. His heavy-boned face hung above them like the mask of all the bogeymen they had been taught to fear from childhood days: the Indians! Dark, like the devil; slant-eyed. Hair plucked to form a scalp lock—an act of bravado—for easier scalping. And such a one here in a Christian church while white men, because of his kin, were threatened with hanging. And not content to be here listening, but rising to speak of forbearance, long-suffering, forgiveness. Such words in a heathen mouth, in God's name! It was more than they could stomach. Shouts of "Out, out!" grew to a chant.

Black Antler stood his ground, holding out his arms.

"I offer you myself. I will not run. Strike. You will feel better. I will not be harmed."

"We'll see about that," yelled a huge woodsman, who was carrying an axe handle. But Caleb put himself in front of Black Antler. "Who are the savages here?" he thundered. "Black Antler came because I asked him. He will eat with us. Those who want to join us are asked to. Let us all break bread together and pray for strength for tomorrow."

Oscar Dilk and two families from down near Pendleton stayed. The others left the place at once. Eleven whites and one Indian sat down to a repast prepared by the Capes for half a hundred.

JUDGE MCGOWAN arrived at the courthouse nine o'clock the next morning and closed the door behind him. On the sheets of paper he carried were the sentences he would pronounce. McGowan put the sheets on the table and got onto his knees, with his face on his chair. "God, God," he prayed, "help me."

Outside, the lawyers, defense in one group, prosecutors in another, knotted together, both groups long in the face. What would McGowan do? They did not know. They did know he was honor bound to judge the taking of life, white or red, in the same way. If he did, four men would hear within the hour a sentence of death.

Charlie Fort, whose heart had received its own death sentence, decided to appeal. Hannah, wrapped in a big doeskin cape, was with her family, separated, happily, from Oscar Dilk.

Charlie went to her, greeted her parents and Ben, then said, "Hannah, may I speak to you alone for a few minutes?"

Hannah, the redhead, had her father's gray eyes, and when she looked at him, Charlie drowned in them. He could not speak.

"I'm waiting," Hannah said when they had left her parents.

"Hannah, we love each other. We were going to be married."

"We did love each other. We were going to be married."

"What did I do?"

"You know."

"I told you we wouldn't make love again till we were married. We didn't."

"No," said Hannah. "We didn't."

"You don't love Dilk, do you?"

"Not the way I did you. But I can trust him."

"You can trust me."

Hannah's eyes filled with the whole of herself. She was without protection of any kind. "Charlie," she cried.

As she spoke, Oscar Dilk came to her side.

"Charlie trying to appeal his case, Hannah?"

"I'm not the winner today, Oscar. In court or out."

"Maybe your luck will change back in Cincinnati." Dilk turned to Hannah. "Court's opening. Let's not straggle."

Charlie watched the crowd pour into the courtroom. He felt he had already heard the sentence.

THE COURTROOM WAS so packed there was not enough space to breathe in except when your neighbor breathed out. Judge McGowan rapped his gavel.

"Sheriff Brady," he said, "bring in the prisoners."

When the four men were in front of him, the judge rose. He gazed at them for a long time before he began to speak.

"I have no wish to unnecessarily harrow your feelings," he began. "We are a civilized and Christian people. That is what we call ourselves—Christian, civilized. As such we have sent missionaries to the Indians so that they, too, might become Christian and civilized. There is no record of any hostile act by any Indian against a white before they were mistreated by us.

"How did we mistreat them? You know as well as I do. We took away their land, first of all. Oh, we paid for it sometimes. Not enough. But meanwhile we gave them a taste for whiskey, so we got most of the money back that way. We cut down their forests so that the game their lives depended upon vanished. And even when two families came to boil maple sap in what was their old home, we did not have the heart of decent men, let alone Christians, to say, We have more than enough. It was once yours. Share.

"No. Instead, we fell upon them. We killed women and children. In horrible ways I ask you not to forget.

"These murders would not have been committed, except that the murderers expected the approval of the people of this community. Four men alone will suffer under the law of the land. Everyone here must suffer under the law of heaven for making it possible for those men to believe that it was no sin to kill an Indian."

McGowan sat down in his fanback chair. "Luther Bemis."

Bemis, rigid, white, walked to the judge's bench.

"Luther Bemis, I hereby sentence you, for the murder of the Indian Red Cloud, to be hanged by the neck until dead."

Bemis, head high but staggering a little, returned to his place.

"George Benson." Benson moved not an inch. The sheriff stepped in his direction, but Judge McGowan shook his head. "Let him alone, Sam. George Benson, for the murder of the boy Folded Leaf, I sentence you to be hanged by the neck until dead."

John Wood, Sr., stepped forward without being summoned.

McGowan's voice trembled for the first time. "John Wood, for the death of three Indian children and the woman Bright Water, I sentence you to be hanged by the neck until dead."

Wood Sr. returned to his fellow prisoners almost jauntily.

"John Wood, Jr., step forward, please."

Johnny looked at his father as if asking, Which direction is that? Wood Sr. gave his son a gentle push forward.

Judge McGowan leaned back momentarily and closed his eyes. Then he leaned forward. "I must speak to you, John. You killed the Indian woman Wide Eyes—"

Johnny interrupted the judge. "She wasn't an Indian."

McGowan said, "You are not to speak, John, but to listen. For the killing of Wide Eyes, the Indian, you are sentenced by this court to be hanged by the neck until dead."

Before this sentence was finished, a woman's scream drowned out the final word. Reba Wood was trying to make her way to McGowan. "Stop it," she shouted. "You can't kill a boy for that."

"Take the woman outside, Sheriff," Judge McGowan said.

Johnny Wood went back to his father's side. "Take her out," he echoed. "She's a bad woman, too."

CALEB CAPE received permission to spend the nights before the impending execution, set only ten days in the future, in jail with the prisoners. Caleb could have found no rest away from these men of his church, particularly since one of them, Luther Bemis, would never, except for Caleb's word, have been in jail at all.

He did not know that his presence gave much comfort to anyone except John Wood, Sr., who, brought up in Bible reading and prayer, valued the nearness of his pastor in his final hour.

George Benson paid no heed to Caleb. He had ears for only one thing: the sound of a posse come to set them all free. Restore the country to its rightful ways of thinking. He had depended upon his sister, Reba, to stir up action for the rescue, but something had happened to Reba. He didn't understand what, but he waited for others to take up his cause.

Luther Bemis had not faltered in his belief that he had been right to confess. That hadn't lifted his spirits, however. He thought constantly of Ora and the child, due now at any time.

Caleb gave him what consolation he could. "Lizzie and Hannah are with her," he told Lute, "every minute. And Ben's going over every day to look after the stock. Ora's in good hands."

"They ain't my hands, though," Lute said. "Oh, God, Cale, my son will be born and I will never touch him."

"I had a son," Caleb said. "My firstborn. Died when he was four."

"What was his name?"

"Named for me."

"We plan to . . . we planned to call our first for me."

"You might have a girl."

"Ora don't think so from the way the baby kicks."

"Shut up, you two," George Benson said. "The court's robbing us of our lives. You rob us of sleep."

It was a cold night, and there was no means of heating the jail. Caleb wrapped his blanket about him and went as far into his own conscience, his own self-knowledge, as he could.

Greater love hath no man . . . Would he take Lute's place on the gallows if permitted? He thought he could. He'd had more years of life than Lute. Lizzie, with Hannah and Ben, would make out better than Ora alone with a new baby. He thought he could do it. Then he wondered, Could you take his sin on your shoulders? No, I could not. Only one man was able to do that.

"I ain't afraid for one minute of the noose," Lute said. "Nobody who's been out in Indian country and fought Indians could be. A twitch at the end of a rope is a play-party game compared with the things they do. But then there was no Ora. There was no son. It's *now* that's tearing my heart out. Now. Now. Why now?"

Caleb turned face down in the straw. He kept silent, he believed, but his shoulders went up and down with his crying.

Bemis reached out a hand to the man who had brought him to God. "I'll tough it out, Cale. I'll tough it out."

BOOK THREE
The Verdict   XII

O. A. Dilk believed in morning constitutionals. Lawyers' work required sharp brains and an iron butt. Those Oscar possessed. But he had no intention of letting legs and lungs rust from non-use. Also, he'd be stout if he neglected his constitutionals. He wouldn't neglect a thing that might advance him.

All the lawyers, except Noble, who had had to return to Washington, were staying on for the execution. Their presence would dignify the occasion. The defense would stay to show the men they had defended unsuccessfully where their hearts were, the prosecution to see that what they had argued for was carried out. Everyone who had come to town for the trials had stayed, and others had arrived. The trials, whatever the results for the prisoners, were a goldmine for everyone with a loft to rent or a meal to sell.

Oscar, out early for his exercise, had walked a mile into the woods, two thousand paces—he always counted them—when he saw a rider, a long-legged boy on a big roan, approaching at a thundering pace. He thought, They're storming the jail. Find Brady. Oscar began to run. At the edge of the woods he intercepted the rider, who pulled up to avoid running him down. "Hannah," he shouted, "what're you doing here? And in that getup?"

Hannah had on a pair of Ben's buckskin trousers, a little tight in the bottom and short in the leg.

"What getup? Oh. Well, I had to dress in a hurry."

"Surely you had time to put on a skirt? I don't like my sweetheart riding astraddle, legs uncovered for anybody to see."

"Not unless they can see through buckskin. Ossie, something wonderful has happened. Help me to get into the jail."

"You can't get into the jail—with all those men. It wouldn't be decent. And not in that outfit."

"I've got to see my father. Luther Bemis has a new son. I was up all night with Ora. I promised her I'd get the news to Lute."

"You could stop at Mrs. Culligan's and borrow a skirt."

"I don't want her skirt. If you won't help me, I'll ask the sheriff."

Hannah left Oscar gazing after her as she galloped off. He liked spirit in a girl, but britches were a mite too spirited.

SHERIFF BRADY was perfectly willing to fetch Caleb Cape for his daughter. If he saw anything unbecoming in a woman in trousers astride a horse, he didn't say so.

"Papa," she said when Caleb reached her, "Lute's baby was born last night. It's a boy, black-haired and big like Lute."

"How's Ora?"

"Fine. She wanted Lute to have the news as soon as possible."

"Lute ought to hear this firsthand."

"Ossie said they wouldn't let me in the jail."

"Ossie?"

"Mr. Dilk."

"So it's Ossie, now? Well, he's probably right. But they ought to let Lute out of the jail into the runway. He can't climb the stockade without help. You could talk to him there."

Sheriff Brady agreed to Caleb's suggestion. Hannah followed Brady inside the stockade and waited there for him to bring Bemis out. Neither she nor Lute spoke until the stockade door slammed on them.

"Ora?"

"Fine. You've got a baby boy."

Luther Bemis clasped Hannah in his arms and rubbed his bearded face against hers. Hannah was startled but knew what he was doing. She was Ora and Luther Bemis, Jr., all rolled into one. She was life, and he was about to lose life. But she was glad that Ossie, who might not understand such things, couldn't see.

"Oh, thank God, Hannah. Thank you for coming. Tell me everything. Did she have a hard time? What's the boy look like?"

"In the beginning. But she said she'd have this baby in time for me to get the news to you this morning. And she did."

"That Ory! What's the baby look like?"

"He's got your hair, Lute. A big mop of black hair. He's ten pounds and not fat. Ora said to tell you he had your appetite."

"Ory, Ory."

"She's all right. Mama's with her and won't leave her."

"That's about long enough, Hannah," the sheriff called.

Bemis took Hannah's hands in his. "Tell Ory that she's carried my life and that she is my life. And that because of her I'm glad I was born—even to come to this end. God bless you, Hannah, for bringing me the word."

Oscar Dilk was waiting with her father when Hannah came outside the stockade. "You go on over to your aunt Rebecca's," Caleb told her. "I'm going to talk with Lute for a while."

Oscar said, "I'll walk you over to the Baldwins'. Your aunt can fix you up with some proper clothes, I expect."

"Who can care about clothes at a time like this? Men going to die. One never to see his son. I wouldn't care if I was naked."

"Now, Hannah, you're overwrought. One reason I've been so proud of you is that you're always so neat about your person."

"Neat about my person?" Hannah repeated. No girl had ever been loved, had she, for being neat about her person?

"Neat about your person," Oscar repeated firmly. "Fastidious, I might say. And where we're going, that'll be important."

Hannah wanted to say, Where *are* we going? But she was too proud to ask. And she was too obstinate to forgo her belief that Ossie was the one man who could save her from running headlong back to a two-timer.

LUTE KNEW WHAT he had to do, and knew that he couldn't do it without help. On the second day after Hannah's visit he asked Caleb to his corner of the room to talk. The room had been divided by choice into individual living areas. The Woods in one corner, Benson in one, Lute and Caleb in the third. The fourth corner held wash bench, pitcher, and water bucket. And a bucket chamber pot, emptied four times a day—not quite often enough.

In Lute's corner, Caleb leaned against the wall and Lute paced in front of him. "Cale, I've got to see that baby."

"I've been thinking. I don't know if what I've got in mind will work, but this is it. They never put any leg irons on you. You can get over the stockade, but not without help."

Lute took a deep breath. "You mean you'd help me?"

"I'll help you. Not to escape. You keep that in mind. One look at your son—then you hotfoot back here. A day for the trip, a day for the visit, a day to return. It'll be hard to come back, Lute."

"It wouldn't be any harder coming back than it was coming in. I knew the baby was coming. And what the sentence might be. I ain't changed my mind about what I did. I'll be back."

"We got to get you out first."

JOHNNY WOOD seemed to do all of his living at night. In the daytime he was far away, not in the jail, scarcely in life itself. At night he dreamed, talked to himself, screamed.

The night after Caleb's talk with Bemis, Johnny had one of his screaming dreams. The minute it started, Caleb, disregarding contents, emptied water bucket and chamber pot, ran with them to the jail door, and clanged them together, crying, "Guard, Guard!"

Matt Holmby, the guard on duty, was inside the jailhouse in seconds. "What's going on here?"

Caleb, at his side, said, "The boy is having a fit, Matt. Grab his tongue. He'll choke to death."

Holmby had rushed in without a lantern, and in the dark it was hard to find the boy, let alone his tongue. Holmby's handling awakened Johnny. The screaming stopped; tongue swallowing was no longer a danger.

Caleb was at Holmby's side when Johnny quieted down.

"You all right now, boy?" Holmby asked.

"It was just a bad dream. I'm all right when I wake up."

Holmby said, "Everyone else ready to settle down now?"

Only Benson answered. "Nobody's keeping us awake but you."

Caleb went to the jailhouse door with Holmby, like a courteous host. "Never knew the boy to have such a fit before."

Matt said, "What's he scream about?"

"Something he did in the past, likely."

"The shooting?"

"I couldn't say as to that."

"Well, good night, Reverend. Get inside. It's freezing."

"Good night, Matt. You maybe saved a life tonight."

Two hours later Benson got up to use the chamber pot. He went bellowing to Caleb's corner. "What did you do with the pot?"

Caleb, sitting up, said, "I'm afraid I left it outside when I went out to rouse up Matt."

"What d'you expect me to do now?" Benson leaned over Caleb menacingly, then straightened up. "Where's Lute?"

Caleb said nothing. "Where is he, Cale? He sleeps beside you."

Johnny woke up. "What's wrong? I ain't screaming again, am I?"

"No, you ain't, Johnny, but I am. I'm about to scream my head off." Benson went to the jail door and bellowed, "Matt, Matt. Man loose. Come running, Matt. Man loose."

Matt came running, this time with a lighted lantern in his hand. "What's wrong now?"

"Luther Bemis's gone."

"That can't be. He was here just a while back."

"Well, he ain't here now. Look for yourself."

Holmby looked. He kicked up the loose straw, he shook Bemis's blankets. "He's gone," he finally agreed, and ran to get Brady.

The sheriff was there in ten minutes, nightshirt tucked into his pants and a big bearskin coat on top of his nightshirt. The night was bitter cold and there were occasional splatters of sleet.

"Matt, did you lock the jail door when you came here?"

"I locked the stockade door. Even if he run outside, that's as far as he'd get."

"It's as far as he'd get without help."

"Who'd help him? Everyone was right under my nose."

Caleb stepped into the circle of lantern light.

"Sheriff, I boosted Bemis up so's he could make the climb."

Holmby said, "Reverend, you're crazy. You was right beside me."

"Matt, while you were hunting around for that boy's tongue, I was outside with Bemis."

"Cale," Brady said, "you know what you've done? Helped a condemned prisoner escape. That's obstructing justice. That's punishable under law. What in God's name got into you?"

"That man come to the jail of his own free will. He'll come back the same way. I helped him so's he could have one look at his newborn son. I couldn't do less for a dying man."

"I reckon God knew what He was doing when He put preachers in the world, Cale. But even He didn't figure on their lacking common sense. Bemis won't be back. Not once he gets a look at his wife and child. I'm going to set men to tracking him right now."

FOR THE FIRST TWO or three miles Luther Bemis thought he had wings. He didn't notice the weather. All he knew was that he was outside, running home. To Ora and their baby. Ory, my Ory. A man with a good woman oughtn't to get mixed up with God. God and a good woman got in each other's way for a man who wanted to please both.

He'd have to slack up. He'd run four miles without being winded. Twenty miles at that pace he couldn't do. He knew the way, but by eye, and in dark like this you could run in circles.

When he slowed down, the cold hit him. He was sweaty from running, and soaked through by sleety rain. He had on his moccasins and linsey-woolsey pants, and a deerskin jacket over a calico shirt. The sleet was freezing around his face and butt. He'd have to take a commonsensical pace, slower than he'd been going, but fast enough so he didn't end up an icicle.

He had covered perhaps another mile when he heard horsemen behind him. There was only one explanation of horsemen here on a night like this: they were hunting him. He got off the trace and back into the woods as quietly as he could. Soaked through and dog-tired, he stumbled to his knees against a fallen tree—a hollow tree, it proved—and he was almost startled into an outcry when a nest of young raccoons ran from the log. He explored the opening with his hand. Big enough for him to crawl into.

He didn't know how cold he had been until he got into the dryness of that great fallen beech. He was aware then of an uncontrollable shivering, which meant, he knew, that his body was in danger of freezing. Inside the log, where the chips and leavings of the animals' nesting made him a mattress, the shaking finally stopped. The log wasn't long enough to cover his feet, but some of the warmth that was returning to his body would surely be carried down to them.

He thought he heard more horsemen go by up on the trace. No use exposing himself to another band of searchers. He had as well snuggle down amid the leaves for a little rest.

THE MEN Brady had dispatched in the search party were back at Pendleton by noon—without Bemis. It was still storming, well below freezing, and the men were gray with cold and weariness.

A dour Brady met them outside the jail. "No luck?"

"Sam," Jim Mullins said, "in this blinding storm we couldn't've seen a buffalo if it didn't bump into us."

"Did you go to his house?"

"We did. His wife had a new baby, but we looked under and in her bed. He wasn't there and hadn't been there."

Brady went directly to Caleb, who was stretched out on his pallet in the jail. "No trace of Bemis," Brady said. "He's given us the slip. I'm taking your word that you believed he'd go home."

"I still believe it."

"It won't make any difference, as far as you're concerned, which way he headed. You helped him escape. There's a prison sentence for that. And that ain't the half of it. We let one condemned man escape and every buck in the Six Nations will claim a right to lift the hair of every white man between here and the Lakes."

"I'm ready to hang in Bemis's place. That ought to satisfy the Indians. Four men sentenced and four men hung."

"If you can get yourself sentenced to hang, I'll hang you. If not, you're going to have to tough it out as a preacher who got the wool pulled over his eyes by one of his backsliding church members." Brady shook his head. "Cale, up to now you were in here through my good-heartedness. You're a prisoner now. The grand jury will meet to indict you for helping a condemned man to escape."

"That's no more than fair."

"It's legal, and that's my lookout."

XIII

Luther Bemis knew exactly where he was when he woke up—and knew that he had slept longer than he had intended. From inside the log he could tell it was no longer night, but there was no sunshine in the day. He was cold and stiff. He had better get out before he was permanently log-shaped and immobile.

He squirmed out of the log, and after he was clear of it he lay still for a few minutes, listening for searchers. The sleet had been replaced by a ground fog, rolled up from the warmer creek. He could hear the drip of water from trees, ice melting, nothing else.

He sat up carefully. He had to move slowly, but he felt no pain. Encouraged, he put his hand to the ground, preparing for the same slow rise to his feet. He was half up, had one foot under him, when he collapsed. His feet were frozen clods, clumps of unfeeling flesh as incapable of supporting him as a cowpat.

He sat there, filled with a sardonic humor. Life hangs upon hinges of chance. He met Caleb Cape and got converted. Converted, he had to confess his sin. Confession put him in jail. Caleb got him out. And here he sat in worse case than bedded down on straw and with death ahead at the end of a quick clean jerk.

He had no way of judging how far he'd traveled toward home— not a landmark to be seen in the smother of ground fog. He was not in pain now, but would be as soon as blood in his calves, blocked off from its regular flow, began to pound in his veins. He could crawl. He didn't have the pants for it. But he *would* crawl. There was still a chance of getting home and seeing that baby.

Animals on all fours can make good time. But not man. Long before nightfall Lute's kneecaps were raw and bleeding. He took his jacket off and tried using it to cushion his way.

The ground fog had thinned out, but a small icy wind had sprung up and went through shirt and skin clear to his heart. He could now make out where the sun was: halfway down the afternoon sky. If tonight was as cold as last night, he'd have lost more than his feet by morning. But he wasn't a man to die sitting down. By God, he wouldn't. He'd die crawling. He threw the jacket ahead of him and crawled onto it.

CHARLIE FORT and Norry Culligan sat in Norry's kitchen drinking tea. They, or at least Charlie, had passed beyond self-consciousness, shame. Someone had been kind to him when he was desperately unhappy. Some bond attached him to this woman; he would be hard put to give it a name. Loving-kindness, perhaps.

Norry had a name for what she felt for Charlie: just plain yearning love. But she was a hardheaded Irishwoman, and she had no intention of throwing away what she had in pursuit of what she knew she could never get. Charlie held her hand sometimes, patted it gently in the way he would a kitten. She was at least as smart as a well-trained kitten: she didn't try to climb up his arm.

Charlie said, "What in God's name got into Cale Cape, do you think, to help Bemis break jail?"

"It's always been there. Milk of human kindness."

"Milk of human kindness is going to get him a jail sentence,

379

unless I do a better job of defending him than I did those others."

"You think you'll get to see Hannah more, defending him?"

"It entered my head."

"It's an ill wind," Norry said. "What's she see in that Dilk, anyway? Hannah ain't going to be more than a crutch to him, helping him climb the steps to the statehouse."

"Maybe Hannah'd like to climb some statehouse steps."

Norry looked at the young man with blue eyes still life-filled. "Don't run the girl down just because she gave you the mitten. And if you want to climb statehouse stairs, you can. No need of a crutch, either. I'd like to tell that girl a thing or two."

"There's a thing or two you'd better be quiet about, Norry," Charlie said. He'd gotten that easy with Norry.

BETWEEN losing the case and losing Hannah, Charlie'd about dried up as a source of news for his father. If he wasn't careful, he'd soon add another ache to his miseries: How did I fail my father?

After he left Norry, he set about remedying that one.

Extracts from a letter by Charles Fort to Enoch Leverett:

Perhaps those most outraged by Luther Bemis's escape are the Indians. Lone Fawn, a Miami chief, and Bent Arrow, a Seneca brave, representing the Indians who have gathered here to see that the executions take place per government promises, went to Sheriff Brady and accused him of doing what has been done before in such cases involving the murder of Indians: locking the criminals up for a while, then seeing to it that they get loose. Brady was as mad at this accusation as the Indians were at the escape. What he told them, in unprintable language, was to head for the woods if they thought they could do a better job of finding Bemis than his men had. The two Indians left at once.

Brady is having erected the most impressive gallows ever heard of hereabouts—let alone seen. Platform of oak timbers, twelve feet above the ground. The hanging beam, a walnut timber a foot through, rising about eight feet above the platform. Brady has been scoffed at for the size of it, and for the rope and hangman, both imported from Cincinnati. It is a little odd for the most solid structure in town to be the gallows tree. But the prisoners can be thankful that nobody's going to have to be hanged twice, as has happened before, when beams or ropes break.

The gallows site is a rolling meadow on the north bank of Fall Creek, just above the falls. It is spacious enough to accommodate the more than a thousand spectators who are expected. Rising above the meadow is a low but extensive ridge. Colonel Johnston, the Indian agent, is offering this to his Indian observers, so they can clearly see that the government's word has been kept. He no doubt also wants to keep the Indians and the whites from being elbow to elbow at a time of so much emotion.

Thus matters now stand, with the execution date only four days distant: Clasby vanished; Bemis escaped; the preacher in jail with the three remaining condemned men; the gallows waiting.

End of extracts from a letter by Charles Fort to Enoch Leverett.

Charlie put down his pen. The *Western Spy* was now as up-to-date as he was. And he didn't care. He had to face it. All he cared about was Hannah. What *could* he do? She wouldn't listen to a word he had to say. He leaned his face against the window. It might have been ice. He could hear the rising wind in the spruce trees, and floor joints creaking as the cold deepened. If I cried, he thought, my face would freeze to the glass.

NIGHTFALL was at hand. Luther Bemis had given up crawling. His knees were worn down to raw bone. The throb in his feet had passed beyond pain and become a sickness that filled his whole body. He knew what was happening. His feet were dying, and the poison of their death was being passed into his entire body. This was going to be a harder way to die than with a broken neck at the end of a rope. But Ora would know why he had chosen it.

The pain of his knees, or the poison, or lack of food, had caused him to faint—not to the point of unconsciousness, but to the point of leaving his body behind. He could see it stretched out on his jacket, his knees bloody, his eyes sunken. This man is dying, he thought. Now he saw figures he knew were imaginary: two Indians.

One of them spoke in English to the body stretched out on the ground, "This would have been your last night, if we hadn't found you." To his companion, a younger man, the Indian spoke in Seneca, and the young man trotted away. The Indian who

381

remained said, "He will bring ice from the stream. I will bind it to your feet with sycamore leaves. You will have less pain."

"Who are you?" Lute asked.

"Lone Fawn. Wide Eyes was my niece."

Lute was moving in and out of his sick body. "It should not have happened. Why are you helping me?"

"I want to see you hang." Lone Fawn took off his fur-lined cape and put it around Lute's shoulders. "It is shameful to hang. Killed by your own people. I want my people to see that."

"I am willing."

The younger Indian returned with foam ice held in a cup of leaves. Lone Fawn removed Lute's moccasins and filled each one with the ice and leaves, then shoved Lute's feet back into them. If the Indians hadn't been there he would have screamed. A shoe of red-hot steel couldn't have hurt more. But he was determined from childhood to equal Indians' endurance. Lone Fawn watched him closely. "Your feet will feel better soon."

"You are very kind, Lone Fawn. What's your plan for getting me back to the jail?"

"A travois. We will make one."

They made it before his eyes. Two poles. Lone Fawn's jacket and Bent Arrow's extended between the poles by their sleeves. The two Indians were left in shirt sleeves. Lute was lifted onto the travois and tucked under Lone Fawn's cape as if he were a babe.

The Indians handled him as if he were a featherweight. They carried him smoothly, moving fast even in the darkness.

When they reached the trace and began to pull the travois, the passage was less smooth. The ice around his feet had melted, and he could feel the throb of his shattered knee bones deep in his groin. But he kept his mouth clamped shut.

Lone Fawn stopped and put some jerky in his mouth. "You might have escaped if you had headed in the other direction."

"I know that Clasby went that way, and escaped."

"Clasby is still running. Yes."

"I wanted only to see my son. Then I would come back."

"Why come back?"

"I had done wrong. I was willing to die."

"How old is your son?"

"One week."

"You kill at the wrong time."

"I was drunk."

"You are as bad as the red man."

"Worse."

"We will bring your woman and boy to you."

LONE FAWN and Bent Arrow returned Luther Bemis to the prison on the morning of the third day before the execution. Bemis's knees were healing, but his feet were dead flesh. Norry, who knew through Charlie of his pain, sent a bottle of opium painkiller.

The spoonful Caleb gave Lute at noon that day kept him asleep until nightfall. When he awoke, he couldn't remember where he was. "Ory," he said, "I'm better. What time is it?"

"It's Cale, Lute. You're in Pendleton jailhouse. Ora ain't here."

"I was on my way home. I dreamed two Indians carried me."

"It wasn't a dream. They did. And they're going to bring Ora and the baby here to see you."

It all came back to Lute. "Why are they going to do that?"

"Don't ask me to explain Indians to you. They liked the way you talked on the way back, for one thing."

"How they going to get Ory in? She can't climb that wall."

"Brady will let her in. The Indians did him a good turn. Brought you back so he could have a proper hanging. And he don't cotton to the idea that any savage has a kinder heart than Sam Brady."

"But, Cale, what if Ory won't come with the Indians? It's nothing she'd ever do in ordinary times. Nothing I'd let her do. She'll lock the door and shoot one of them through it."

"If I could send Hannah with them, she'd warn Ora. But I can't. I'm as much a prisoner here now as you are."

"What'd you do, Cale?"

"Helped a condemned man escape."

"Me? They put you in prison for that? I wouldn't have done it if . . . Well, I reckon I would. How long'll they keep you in?"

"I don't know. But don't shed any tears. For a spell I figured you weren't coming back at all. Thought I'd end my days here."

"My God, Cale, I'd never run out on you. You know that."

Cale took Lute's hand. "I know that. And I've figured out how to get word to Hannah. Fort's my lawyer now. I got a right to see him, and he'll take the word to Hannah."

"Hannah may be afraid of the Indians herself."

"The shoe'll more likely be on the other foot."

Lute laughed. He'd supposed he'd never laugh again. But he had. He had a wife and a son and a friend. And he'd done the right thing finally, and he didn't doubt the Lord would honor him for it. There were a lot of men laughing with less.

THERE'S no use planning in this world, Charlie thought on his way to the Baldwins'. While he was sitting in his attic room trying to figure out whether his chances would be harmed or helped by seeing Hannah again, fate gave him no choice. He had to see her now. At the Baldwins', the old folks and the young uns, including Oscar Dilk and Hannah, were sitting in a semicircle facing the fire.

After paying his respects to the Baldwins, Charlie said, "I have an urgent message for Hannah from her father."

"Well, what is it, Charlie?" Oscar asked, as if he were empowered to speak for Hannah.

"Hannah's father asked me to talk to her alone. If she'll step outside with me, I'll tell her what he wants her to know."

"Charlie, Hannah and I have an agreement—what concerns one of us concerns the other. I'll just step outside with you two."

"Is this true, Hannah?"

"Yes, it is true. We agreed on that."

"Hannah, since you and Oscar have this agreement, I reckon your father'd be willing for him to hear it, too."

Hannah put on a shawl. Oscar, showing his hardihood, went outside in his shirt sleeves.

"Cale Cape is crazy," Dilk said when he heard the message.

"Don't you say that about my father, Ossie."

"I apologize, Hannah. But your father's too trusting. How's he know what two red men's intentions are toward you?"

"He trusts them, Ossie, just as you said."

"Well, trust apart, how's it look? One girl riding off with two men. It don't *look* good, whatever their intentions may be."

"What do looks matter, Ossie? What matters is that Lute gets a chance to see his wife. I don't care about looks."

"Well, I care. What you do, no matter how good your intentions are, will be judged by how it looks. No, Hannah. I forbid you."

"I am going. You tell Father, Charlie. My mind's made up."

385

XIV

The two Indians, with Ora, Ora's baby, and Hannah, rode into Pendleton in the late afternoon the day before the hanging was to be. Sam Brady was outside the jail stockade awaiting them, with the additional guards he had ordered for the night. Brady didn't fear a rescue posse as much as George Benson hoped for one, but he didn't plan to be taken by surprise, either.

Lone Fawn addressed the sheriff in his elegant English.

"Mr. Brady, I have here with me the wife and newborn child of one of your prisoners. We have come in the hope that you would permit the father to step inside the stockade for a few minutes so that he can see his wife and infant son."

"Not a single prisoner is coming outside that jailhouse," said Brady. "Last time that happened, your husband, Mrs. Bemis, made his getaway. I don't figure on letting that happen twice."

"Bemis no longer has feet to walk on," said Lone Fawn.

"I hadn't finished, Lone Fawn, if you'll be kind enough to let me get a word in edgewise. There's no law says I can't let prisoners' wives in. Mrs. Benson is already in there, and has my permission to spend the night with her husband. Mrs. Wood could have been, but her husband didn't want her. You, Mrs. Bemis, can be with your husband tonight—if you want to."

Ora, at that, jumped from her saddle and threw her arms about the sheriff's neck. "God will reward you, Mr. Brady."

Brady said, "After what I've gone through in the last few weeks, I deserve some reward."

The Indians, responsible for this reunion, were left unregarded on the outskirts of the rejoicing. Hannah, the baby in her arms, reined her horse close to them.

"Lone Fawn," she said, "I thank you and Bent Arrow. I will never forget. If I can ever help you, remember that."

"Thank you, Miss Cape. Tell your people that Indians are gentlefolk when they meet whites who are gentlefolk."

The single street was crowded with people, like sightseers come to a fair. One man, his face unsmiling, tipped his hat. "Ossie," Hannah called. He shook his head and stepped back into the crowd.

"You must say good-by to the red men before your white man will be friends again," said Lone Fawn.

BRADY HAD bent over backward letting the two women spend the night with their husbands. He hadn't bent far enough to permit candles or lamps. He was determined to have four men to hang in the morning. A candle turned over in that straw and he wouldn't have men, wives, or jail. Or me, Caleb Cape thought. The thing Caleb wished was that the roof was off the jail so that the men could, on this last night, see stars. On *his* last night, he'd want a look at sky and earth.

But what did Luther Bemis care about stars? When Ora had knelt to put that baby in his arms, Lute had made a sound the like of which Caleb had never heard before. Maybe God had made a sound like that when he first saw Adam. Lute nuzzled his face against his son's. Then Ora bent down so their three faces touched.

Caleb had doled out enough medicine to cut down Lute's sharpest pangs, but yet leave him sufficiently awake to know who he was and who was with him. No harm if he forgot *where* he was.

It was full dark outside as well as in when the guard gave the squalling baby back to Hannah, who came for him in an hour.

"He's hungry," Ora apologized for her son.

"Don't you suckle him, Ory?" Lute asked.

"No. I had a reason not to."

"You never told me."

"No. I will, though. You'll see I was right."

Caleb gave Bemis another small dose. "You don't figure there's enough in there to quiet down Benson, do you?" Lute asked.

"It would take the whole bottle to do the job."

Benson was screaming at the top of his lungs. What he was bellowing against was not the prospect of his death. He could face death. But in jail, condemned to die because his neighbors and friends wouldn't raise a hand to help him, that cut him to the quick. "I'm crying for my country. What's it coming to? God!" He banged his head against the log wall of the jail. Sarah tried to stop him, put her arms around him. But Benson only banged his head more.

Ora came to Caleb, who was leaning against the door where he could catch a whiff of the fresh cold air that blew into the room.

"Cale, I did a wrong thing, but it might help George. I didn't know there'd be medicine for Lute's feet and I knew he'd be in pain, so I brought this." She held up a pint of whiskey.

387

"How'd you get it in?"

"Hanging on a cord under my skirt. I know it was wrong."

"Ora, there's such a mix-up of wrong and right in this jailhouse tonight, I don't know as God Himself could sort things out. George thinks he's forsaken by all. A remembrance from you would touch his heart. You take it to him. It may quiet him."

It did that. George greeted Ora like the only friend who had kept him in mind, downed the whole bottle, and took Sarah's suggestion to rest his head in her lap and snooze.

Ora talked with Sarah for a minute, then returned to Caleb.

"Cale, I'm not mad at you anymore. Lute's at peace with himself. He never would've been if he'd done what I wanted—run. He'd of hated himself, and me, too, likely, before long. Your words didn't save me, Cale, nor your prayers. Only Lute's example's done that."

"Ora," said Caleb, "don't make me cry. Preachers just preach. But it takes men like Lute, who live out the words, to bring the Light home to others." He gave her the spoon and medicine bottle. "You dole this out to him, Ora, as you think he needs it."

"What're you going to do?"

"Me and John Wood are going to say Bible verses."

Before going to the Woods' corner, Caleb stood again at the crack of the door, where the whiff of the outside world came to him. He, not fated to die in the morning, savored the earth to the bottom of his lungs. He wished he belonged to some church that had thought out long ago words and acts suitable for men's last hours on earth. Words the dying believed in; words that would make a bridge between jail tonight and paradise tomorrow. He felt the need of more than he, with only his memory of the Scriptures and his heartache, could provide.

Over in the Bemises' corner, Ora was saying, "Did you like our baby, Lute?"

"I never seen his equal. Ory, one thing you got to promise. Don't you stay a widow. You was meant to be a mother."

"I am a mother. And I'll never marry again. I don't want to and it wouldn't be fair to any other man."

"But why don't you nurse the baby? I always figured I'd like to see you nursing our baby."

"I wanted you to give me another baby. A nursing mother

can't get in a family way. You know that—except now and then."

"How'd you figure, nursing or not nursing, there'd be any way for me to give you a baby—me locked up in a jailhouse?"

"I knew I'd see you. I trusted in the Lord. I'm a Christian now, Lute. And I'll bring our children up to be Christian."

"Children?"

"Our little boy and our little girl."

"You even know the denominations?"

"I called the turn last time, didn't I? Lute, we haven't said one word about love."

"When we live it, we don't have to say it."

"We could say it, anyway."

"I can tell you the truth. You're the woman I waited ten years to find. I love you, Ory. The mother of my children."

"You said children."

"That's what I said. Give me a quarter spoonful."

She measured the medicine with great care.

"Ory," Lute said, "I'm man enough for both of us from the knees on up. So if you and the medicine work together, I think I could just about make us an eight-pound girl. You understand, Ory?"

"I understand. What'll the preacher think?"

"In the first place, he can't see you. In the second place, he don't expect you to sleep with all your clothes on."

"Lute . . . Oh, my Lute."

BEFORE he got to Bible verses, old John Wood wanted to do some remembering, and Caleb listened. Wood said, "I reckon I've got a chance to go down in history as the first man to have his neck in a noose for killing an Indian. It'll seem a sudden thing to the rest of the country. Not to me. I been heading for that noose for some time. Ever since I bought that land in York state the developers had cheated the Indians out of. Land that was useless except for trapping and hunting, and we was farmers. Why did we buy it? Because we could get it for next to nothing. We didn't give a passing thought to the Indians we drove out.

"Next I headed west. More easy money. Free land, nothing to do but clear it and kill Indians. I lost my wife on that trip. That's the price I paid for free land. And I married Reba. That was more of the price. I ain't blaming Reba, I'm blaming myself. I went out with brother George to kill Indians to show her I was still as much a man in some lines as anyone else. And she done what she done with John Jr. to show me she was still a woman in some lines.

"For myself, what's to come tomorrow will be a relief. I believe in the Lord Jesus and I believe that He forgives those that believe on Him. Though whether He can forgive me for what I done to John Jr.'s going to test Him some. Cale, you know what Scripture's being going through my head?"

"No, John."

"His birth! All that rejoicing. That's what I'll do tomorrow. Be born again. Rejoice."

Johnny, who had been lying on his pallet, listening but not joining in the conversation, sat up.

"I am going to die tomorrow."

Caleb did not know any honest way of denying this. "Those who believe on Him have everlasting life, Johnny."

"I don't want everlasting life. I've had enough of it. Tomorrow I'm going to go to sleep. I been looking forward to it. What I'd like is one good game of jackstraws before then."

"The verses I've been thinking of," John Sr. repeated, trying, Caleb knew, to turn the talk to something less painful to him than his son's wanderings, "are those of the birth." And old Wood began. "*My soul doth magnify the Lord, And my spirit hath rejoiced in God my Saviour. . . .*" And then Johnny joined him.

When they finished, Caleb said, "Johnny, I had no idea you remembered all that."

"I remember everything I read."

"Now," said Wood Sr., "I'm going to get a little sleep."

Caleb told the two Woods good night and returned to the door crack. There Johnny later came to him.

"There's a prayer my mother taught me, my real mother, not the woman living at our house. Say it with me. You'll feel better."

"Maybe I don't know it."

"Everybody knows it.

"Now I lay me down to sleep.
I pray the Lord my soul to keep.
If I should die before I wake,
I pray the Lord my soul to take.

"I'm going to sleep now," Johnny said. "You do the same. You've said your prayers. There's nothing more you can do."

Johnny was right. There was nothing more Caleb could do—but he didn't leave the door crack until a knife blade of gray morning came into it. With the light came Matt Holmby.

"The women are to be out in half an hour," he said. "Rouse them up. There'll be a good breakfast for the men. We leave here at eight. The hanging's set for ten."

"Will they let me go with the men?"

"You can go. Say a prayer with each man. But after that you have to come back here till the grand jury meets."

ORA BEMIS didn't need any waking up. She was wide-awake and fully dressed. Lute looked drowsy.

"I gave him enough to see him through the ride out there. He don't want any at the last minute."

When Caleb went to wake the Bensons, Ora said, "Lute, I won't do it if you set your foot down. But I'd like the last thing for you to see to be the look of love in my eyes. And that's the last thing I want to see from you. And I'm going to bring the baby. He won't know what's going on. But afterward I want to tell him he seen how brave his father died. The other'll be there, too."

"You pretty sure about that, Ory?"

"Sure as sure. She's there. I've got her named."

"I'd like to know, if it ain't a secret."

"Laura. That's as near to Luther as I can get for a girl."

"You come then, all of you, if your heart's set on it."

"You just look in my eyes when the time comes, Lute. I'll fix myself where you can. All you'll see is love, then a little wait and we'll all be with you. That's the sum of it."

XV

Judge Amos McGowan was at the jailhouse at fifteen of eight. "Cale," he said, "you know I'll have to convene a grand jury for your part in Bemis's escape."

"I know that," Caleb said. "I'm prepared."

"Well, no use being overprepared. A judge hearing the case could suspend sentence."

It took a minute for Caleb to take in all that McGowan was saying. Then he took the hand the judge held out to him.

"You going out to the hanging?" Caleb asked.

"I am. When I sentence a man to hang, I sentence myself to be present at the hanging. It tears me apart. But when I can't observe what I've ordered, I'll resign from my judgeship. What's too much for the law to see is too much for the law to require." He turned abruptly from Caleb. He'd said more than he intended.

McGowan made himself a part of the crowd waiting to see the men come out of the prison. Either Colonel Johnston or the sheriff or both had brought in state militia—around twenty—to see that the proceedings were orderly. There was no telling what spark might light when this rabble caught sight of the gallows.

Judge McGowan was speculating on the possibilities when he was roused by a voice. "I didn't expect to see you here, Judge."

"Fort! I supposed you would have gone back to the civilized comforts of Cincinnati long before this."

"One thing and another has held me. For one thing, if I had had Dilk's power over the jury, these men wouldn't be riding out to the gallows this morning. I feel I belong with them."

"It's the same with me," McGowan said.

A flatbed wagon, pulled by a matched pair of black carriage horses, came through the crowd, which parted silently to let it pass. Matt Holmby and Sam Brady climbed down from the wagon seat. The militia lined up, separating the two men from the crowd, which was pressing in closer. Holmby went inside the stockade. Brady stood, gun in hand, by the wagon.

A few minutes later Holmby and Caleb Cape brought Luther Bemis, seated on a chair, out of the jail.

"My God," said McGowan, "what have they done to the man?"

"He escaped and his feet froze. They should be amputated. But why cut a man's feet off one day and hang him the next?"

Sam Brady beckoned to Fort. "We'll need your help to get his chair up onto the wagon, Charlie."

Just before the four of them, Caleb, Holmby, Brady, and Fort, put their backs into the hoist, Brady said to Bemis, "Lute, you can lead off. You're in pain, and I won't keep you waiting."

"Thank you, Sheriff," Lute said.

They placed Lute near the tail of the wagon; then Brady and

Holmby brought the two Woods through the stockade doors.

John Wood, straight as an arrow, Bible in hand, was everyone's idea of a God-fearing patriarch. When a man like John Wood was headed for the gallows, something had gone amiss with the country. The crowd's murmur became angry, like bees swarming.

Johnny Wood didn't make the crowd any happier. He had a book, too. Not a Bible, but some storybook, and he read as he walked, like a man so caught up in what's happening in the story, he stumbles upstairs to bed not knowing where he's going.

At the wagon, he looked up and saw someone in the crowd he knew. He waved, called, "Good-by, good-by."

Charlie turned to see who was receiving Johnny's farewell. There was Hannah, hat off in spite of the cold, threatening weather, waving, crying, and calling, "Good-by, Johnny. Good-by."

Benson, hands tied behind his back, leg irons on, came out of the stockade next, bucking like a colt who has for the first time felt the touch of leather. For a minute the crowd forgot what was to come, caught up in the excitement of what was happening. How a man so bound and ironed could still manage to plunge and lunge was beyond imagining. They loaded him, with two of Brady's men on each side of him, and then Caleb got in.

HOLMBY kept the two mares down to a walk. The militia was ahead, behind, and on both sides. Behind the wagon rode or trudged a hundred or more persons. A few friends and relatives. Many more, those making a day of it.

The road they followed was an old logging track, and when they came through the woods to where the huge gallows was visible, the crowd pulled up at the sight. There was a sound, not angry buzzing, but a hundred people sucking in their breath at one time.

The men on the wagon bed were faced away from what they were approaching, and, though the crowd must have told them what had come in sight, no man turned his head to have a look.

Charlie and Judge McGowan stood to one side to let the sight-seers pass on. The meadow surrounding the gallows was already filled with people. Five or six hundred of them.

"It looks more like a crowd come to a picnic than a death-watch," Charlie said. Small fires had been lighted to offset the numbing wind and to heat water for tea.

"Up there on the ridge is no picnic," McGowan said.

The ridge above the meadow was a long one. At its top, like rimrocks, stood a double line of Indians, straight, quiet, not talking. They had come to see what none of them had ever seen before: white men punishing white men for the killing of red men.

The wagon had come to a stop at the foot of the gallows. On the gallows platform the Cincinnati hangman was already stationed, black-peaked hood, with its cat-slit eyeholes, covering his face.

All the men were walked up the steps to the gallows platform—with the exception of Bemis, who was carried up on his chair.

Near the platform, almost at its edge, Charlie saw Ora Bemis and her baby, Lizzie Cape at her side, Hannah at her mother's elbow, and Oscar A. Dilk at Hannah's elbow. "If you don't mind, Judge," Charlie said, "I think I'll move back a little."

Judge McGowan said, "That suits me to a T. I'll go with you."

THE CONDEMNED MEN knew the order of what was to come. Bemis, old Wood, Benson, young Wood. A prayer for each by Caleb, parting words from each, if anyone had anything to say.

The hangman told Bemis, "We'll set your chair on the trap, pull the latch—you'll go through as smooth as a man standing."

"No," said Bemis. "I don't go to my death on any chair. How long does it take you to pull that latch?"

"One second."

"I can stand for one second." Bemis was white with pain. "Cale, you say the Lord's Prayer. That's what I want to hear. Ory and the baby are right down front. Put the chair on the trap. I'll set while you're praying. Then the minute you finish, pull the chair back. I'll stand, and go to my death on my feet, the way a man ought to."

The hangman didn't argue. Who had more right than a dying man for a last request? The chair was moved forward. Lute's hands were tied and the noose's knot was placed just back of his ear.

Caleb's voice was strong and steady. "Our Father, who art in heaven, Hallowed be thy Name. . . ."

Lute looked down, as Ora had said, and it was the way she had said it would be: lost in love everlasting. As Lute looked, Ora held up their baby. They had told themselves they would both say the last words, "For thine is the kingdom, and the power, and the glory, for ever and ever. Amen." Their voices mingled with Caleb's.

At "Amen" the chair left him, and Lute did more than stand. He went—up toward God, or out toward Ora—in a kind of swoop before he fell that made the crowd gasp.

"How could he do that? Nothing to stand with?"

Ora answered. "He was a good man going home to God."

Lute, after the fall, hung perfectly still, a young man dead before thirty. Below the platform, in sight of all, the doctor listened for a heartbeat. When he heard none, the militiamen loosened Luther Bemis, born in Ohio, died in Indiana, from the rope and placed him in one of the four coffins that were lined up next to the gallows. Only then did Ora, crying, run to press her face against his. Lizzie, carrying the Bemis baby, went with her.

BIBLE IN HAND, John Wood walked to the center of the platform. "You don't need to tie my arms behind my back," he told the hangman. "Let me go holding my Bible."

The hangman said, "Nobody can prepare in his head for a noose. Your hands will decide in spite of you to fight for life."

Caleb had an idea. "John, put the Bible over your heart. That's where it belongs, anyway. The belt to your britches will hold it in place. You think God cares where you carry it?"

"No, Cale. God don't care." Caleb took the Bible and placed it inside John Wood's shirt. The hangman tied the old man's hands.

"You want something from the Bible, John? Or a prayer?"

"I'm going to die saying the same words I said last night."

Hands tied, noose adjusted, John Wood, Sr., stepped onto the trapdoor. When the latch was pulled, there was just enough weight to the old man to tauten the rope, but that was enough to kill him.

THE MINUTE John Wood was stretched out in his coffin, George Benson went to the hangman. "Put the rope on me." His hands were already tied behind his back. "Let's get it over with."

"There's time for prayer, George."

"You pray for yourself, Cale, you blasted hypocrite."

Benson raised his voice till it carried to everyone in the meadow. "Friends and neighbors. I called you that once. No man ever asked George Benson for help and got a no. I helped raise your barns, shuck your corn, cut your trees. I was fighting for *you*.

"Did the government ever help us? Whose side is the government on today? The redskins'. Look there." Benson nodded to the coffins. "Two good white men dead as doornails to please men taking their ease in Washington: Calhoun and Monroe—"

The hangman stepped forward. "You've had your say, Benson."

"I'm just started."

"I've got to be in Cincinnati tomorrow."

Benson shouted to the crowd. "The hangman's got a date in Cincinnati tomorrow. He wants to hurry this up."

The crowd responded to that. "Let him wait. A condemned man's got a right to make a speech. Go on, George."

Benson went on. "Here's our chance. A thousand of us here. A hundred of them up there on the ridge. It'd all be over in ten minutes. Let's show those men sitting behind their desks in Washington how we handle things out here in the West."

There was not a whisper from the crowd. Not a movement. Benson listened to the silence. For a half minute, a whole minute.

Then he shouted, "You dirty yellow bastards. You Indian-lovers. If ever I called you friends and neighbors, I take it back. You're lower than the red men. They fight for their own. *Love thy neighbor as thyself.* That's what you been preaching, Cale Cape. Let it sink in how much anybody's listened to you. Failed, failed. You've all failed. May God have mercy on your souls. Now, hangman, I've had my say. Spring your trap."

Before the trap dropped for him, George Benson whose hands had appeared to be tied behind him, brought them up in front of him untied, and yanked at the rope around his neck. Before the hangman got to him, his feet were already off the platform.

The crowd screamed. Benson was the underdog, and in the contest between life and death, he was life. Even the Indians on the ridge broke their silence as he grappled with the hangman. The Indians wanted Benson killed. If the whites couldn't manage the affair, they would kill him themselves with pleasure.

Hannah put her hands over her face. "God help him."

"Hannah, what are you saying?" Oscar rebuked her.

"I don't want to see people die."

"Why did you come here?"

"For Johnny's sake. I didn't know it was so terrible."

"Take your hands down. It doesn't look right for the promised wife of one of the prosecuting lawyers to be sobbing because a man he won a verdict against is going to be hanged."

"I'm not sobbing. I'm praying."

"I'm talking about the looks of it—a prosecutor's wife taking on so over a legal execution. Now take your hands down."

She took them down. "I'm not your wife."

George Benson's moment of freedom was a moment only. In an instant Brady and the hangman had his hands retied, and Benson was sent through the trapdoor, his life three minutes longer than Brady had planned.

One of the four condemned to be hanged still remained alive: young Johnny Wood. Below him in their coffins lay Luther Bemis, and Johnny's father and uncle.

"Why do they keep him waiting, Ossie?"

"There's a rumor the governor may be bringing a pardon."

"If he is, it's cruel to keep Johnny waiting. He can't stand it."

"The governor has other things to do than to save murderers."

A half hour went by. No governor. An hour. No governor. The hangman picked up the black hood, which the other men had refused, and approached Johnny.

"Looks like the pardon's not coming," said Oscar.

At that word, Hannah, moving quickly, left Oscar, scooped the remains of a little bonfire into an empty iron kettle, overlaid the coals with a handful of twigs that had been gathered for tea making, and, with this pot of fire blazing in one hand, ran up the steps of the platform. She was gone before Oscar could forbid her.

On the platform, the twig bonfire leaping above the pot's brim, she faced the Indians on the ridge. "Spare the boy," she screamed, "spare the boy!" She held her hand unflinchingly in the flame, trusting in the Indians' respect for bravery.

"Spare the boy," she pleaded and held the pot higher, so that all on the ridge could see what she was doing. Some on the ridge understood English, she knew. But even if they did not, Hannah hoped all would understand her request.

Fort understood. He gave the judge a shove, tripped up a militiaman, and would have knocked down Dilk, except that Dilk, appalled by Hannah's outlandish act, had melted into the crowd.

Charlie snatched the kettle and threw it away. "Lard, lard," he shouted as he took Hannah in his arms. "Bring me some lard."

Neither he nor Hannah saw the Indians on the ledge make their sign, "We are satisfied."

Nor did the governor, who, without much regard for the safety of the crowd, came riding in at a hard gallop, his horse much lathered. The impression he gave—he had done this before—was that of a man sparing neither himself nor his mount to come at breakneck speed to save a life. The crowd loved their governor. Judge McGowan said under his breath a word he would not permit in court.

Dismounting, the governor ran up the gallows steps to Johnny. "Young man, do you know who now stands before you?"

"No." Johnny could not take his eyes off the coffins below.

"Well, sir, there are but two persons in the universe who can save you from the noose. One is the great God of heaven; the other is the governor of the sovereign state of Indiana, who now stands before you. Here is your pardon. I have ridden long and hard to bring it to you. Now go, and sin no more."

The governor handed Johnny his pardon. Johnny let the rolled parchment slip from his hand. "What is my sin, sir?"

The governor turned to Brady. "What's wrong with the boy?"

The sheriff said, "Sir, we've all been through a lot. This boy's father and uncle are lying below you. Johnny had a long wait, not knowing what was to come next. He's not in his right mind just now."

Johnny said, "I know the difference between right and wrong."

The governor descended the steps, mounted his horse, and rode slowly through the crowd, taking the salutes of the electorate.

BY EARLY afternoon the meadow was almost deserted. Charred remains of fires dotted the meadow. Families had started for their homes. With what they had seen there so recently still in their minds, the meadow had lost its appeal as a place for picnicking.

Lizzie gathered Ora, her baby, and Johnny Wood for the ride back to Pendleton. Oscar Dilk had disappeared.

"I think Black Antler's still on the ridge," Caleb told Lizzie. "I'm going up to talk to him. I promised Brady to go straight back to the jailhouse afterward."

"We'll be all right, Caleb. Charlie's going with us."

Hannah and Charlie, before they climbed in the wagon, drew Caleb a little apart. "Hannah," Caleb asked, "how's your hand?"

Hannah held it up. It was inside a pillow sham filled with pure leaf lard. "It still throbs."

"That was a brave act, Hannah. Charlie, you could use a little lard yourself."

"I haven't had time to think about *my* hand yet. Mr. Cape, Hannah and I've got a favor to ask you. When Hannah's hand is healed enough to wear a wedding ring, will you marry us?"

"Marry you? Hannah, I thought you and Oscar Dilk were keeping company?"

"We were keeping company, but we don't love each other."

"Not much point getting married, then. And you two do?"

"We do," answered Charlie, as if already in the midst of a marriage service. "We had a misunderstanding, but we understand each other now. Isn't that true, Hannah?"

"It is. Papa, I love Charlie and will never marry anyone else."

"That being the case, I guess it's lucky Charlie wants you."

"Papa! You talk that way and he'll change his mind."

Caleb reached out to take Charlie's hand but remembered the burns. "You're a lucky man, Fort. She's the apple of my eye."

On their way to the wagon, walking with their stride that fitted, Charlie said, "Hannah, there's something I've got to tell you."

"You're sure it's something you want to talk about?"

"I don't want to talk about it. But you've got to know."

"I already know. I saw it."

"My God, my God. Oh, Hannah, I did that to you?"

"What you did was to prove to me I was going to marry you, Charlie, no matter what."

"Hannah," Lizzie called, "you and Charlie can spoon right here in the wagon and not keep the rest of us waiting."

CALEB did want to have a word with Black Antler. But more than that he wanted to climb out of this valley of death.

As he neared the top of the ridge, he recognized three of the dozen Indians who had lingered on: Lone Fawn, the powerful Miami; Bent Arrow, the Seneca, and, standing a little apart from his tribesmen, Black Antler.

Caleb greeted them, then spoke, in Delaware so that none would miss his meaning. "What you saw this morning was ugly. It was right. This will be remembered as a great day both for the red man and the white man. On this day three white men gave their lives so that the killing between whites and reds would be finished. It *is* finished. Now we will live peacefully together. Handsome Lake's prophecy will come true."

Caleb shook hands with all, except Black Antler. To him, Caleb raised his arm in the Indian salute of farewell. Black Antler responded in kind. Then Caleb started down the slope slowly, loath to pass the spot where the price of peace had been paid.

Black Antler spoke to the Indians who remained. "Leave me."

"This is the appointed place," they replied. "He will be here soon. We will leave then, after we hear his message."

Two messengers, not one, arrived. Plains Indians—Osages, well mounted on horses which bore the marks of hard riding.

"We have caught him at the junction of the Illinois and the Mississippi, but they will not begin the feasting until you get there. Clasby killed your kin. It is your right to partake of the feast."

Caleb, halfway down the slope, heard the laughter. They have much to rejoice about today, he thought.

BLACK ANTLER waited silently until Caleb and the Indians were out of sight. He could still see the slow swing of the killing rope. He could still hear the jubilation of the red men in anticipation of the pleasures to come. He was able to shut both from this mind. For the first time since Folded Leaf's death, tears covered his face.

Black Antler was bereft, but not alone. The spirits of Folded Leaf and the old prophet, Handsome Lake, lived and spoke to him. The bodies of men vanished, but their words and wisdom lived on. Their spirits did not die. The sun and the earth remained. The animals were his brothers. The willow, the birch, the elder comforted and protected him. He was sad, but not alone.

He knelt and scooped up a handful of sun-warmed earth. He kneaded with it the leaves at hand, aspen and maple and dogwood. He held his two fists clenched on earth, then turned earth's bounty sunward in the old Indian gesture of worship. Black Antler's hands, reaching upward, blotted out the rope. The smell of the crushed leaves was sweet. The sun was warm. He said the two names. "Handsome Lake. Folded Leaf."

The earth his hands held, the names his spirit honored: what else did a man have?

Jessamyn West

The extraordinary literary career of Jessamyn West, or Mrs. H.M. McPherson as she is known in private life, began almost by accident. A bout of tuberculosis confined her to bed for several years and she took to writing to pass the time. She was thirty-eight when her first book, *The Friendly Persuasion*, was published. It now ranks as a classic.

Miss West has lived in California since 1913, but she was born in Indiana, and returns again and again in her stories to her native territory. This latest book is based on one of the most controversial trials of frontier history, held in Pendleton, Indiana, in 1824.

"It was twenty years ago that I came across a reference to 'The Massacre at Fall Creek'," Miss West recalls. "I remained haunted by it and the dread dilemmas it must have thrust upon whites and Indians alike; the more so perhaps because I had an Indian grandmother."

Most of the characters are, Miss West says, her own invention, with a few notable exceptions: Colonel Johnston, the Indian agent; Senator Noble, the prosecutor; and the governor of the state, who did make just such a last-minute appearance. The prophet, Handsome Lake, is also real. He died in 1815 and still has a devoted following.

"So much for the evidence of history," Miss West sums up. "The massacre had no significant impact upon the increasingly violent relationship between whites and Indians. My intention was not to reveal historical facts in a fictional setting, but to open questions of more abiding truths. And that is quite a different matter."

WHIP
HAND

A CONDENSATION OF THE BOOK BY
Dick Francis

ILLUSTRATED BY NEIL MCDONALD
PUBLISHED BY MICHAEL JOSEPH

Sid Halley, ex-jockey turned special investigator, finds himself driven to the limits of human endurance. While struggling to come to terms with his broken marriage, he tackles two cases that lead him into an underworld of fraud and violence, forcing him to confront his ex-wife's bitterness—and his own naked fear.

Whip Hand is Dick Francis's latest and most exciting book. And Sid Halley, destined to become one of television's outstandingly popular heroes, is his finest and most memorable creation.

Prologue

I dreamed I was riding in a race.

Nothing odd in that. I'd ridden in thousands.

There were fences to jump. There were horses, and jockeys in a rainbow of colours, and miles of green grass. There were massed banks of people, with oval faces, indistinguishable pink blobs from where I crouched in the stirrups, galloping past at speed. Although I could hear no sound I knew they were shouting.

Shouting my name, to make me win.

Winning was all. Winning was my function. What I was there for. What I wanted. What I was born for.

In the dream, I won the race. The shouting turned to cheering, and the cheering lifted me up on its wings, like a wave.

I woke in the dark, as I often did, at four in the morning.

I could still feel the way I'd moved with the horse, the ripple of muscle through both of the striving bodies, uniting in one. I could still feel the irons round my feet, the mane blowing in my mouth, my hands on the reins.

There came, at that point, the second awakening. The real one. The moment in which I remembered that I wouldn't ride any more races, ever. The wrench of loss came again as a fresh grief. The dream was a dream for whole men.

I dreamed it quite often.

Damned senseless thing to do.

Reality was so different. When what one had as a left hand was a matter of metal and plastic, not muscle and bone, one discarded dreams, and made what one could of things.

1

I took the battery out of my arm, fed it into the recharger and fitted the spare. Then I pulled my tie off and flung it haphazardly onto my jacket, which lay over the leather arm of the sofa; stretched and sighed with the ease of homecoming; listened to the familiar silences of the flat; and as usual felt the welcoming peace unlock the gritty tensions of the outside world.

Contentedly padding around in shirtsleeves and socks, I switched on the tablelights, encouraged the television with a practised slap and poured a soothing Scotch. I tended nowadays to do most things one-handed, because it was quicker. My ingenious false hand, which worked via solenoids from the tiny natural electrical impulses in the nerve-endings of what was left of my forearm, would open and close in a fairly vice-like grip, but at its own pace. It did *look* like a real hand, though, with shapes like fingernails, and ridges for tendons, and blue lines for veins.

I shaped up to that evening as to many another. On the sofa, feet up, knees bent, in contact with a chunky tumbler and happy to watch the small screen; and I was mildly irritated when halfway through a decent comedy the doorbell rang.

With more reluctance than curiosity I went into the hall and took a look through the spyhole in the door. There was no trouble on the mat, unless trouble had taken the shape of a middle-aged lady in a blue headscarf and loose fawn raincoat. I opened the door and said politely, "Good evening. Can I help you?"

"Sid," she said. "Can I come in?"

I looked at her, thinking that I didn't know her. But then a good many people whom I didn't know called me Sid, and I'd always taken it as a compliment.

Coarse dark curls showed under the headscarf, a pair of tinted glasses hid her eyes, and heavy crimson lipstick focused attention on her mouth. There was embarrassment in her manner. She still appeared to expect me to recognize her, but it was not until she looked nervously over her shoulder, and I saw her profile against the light, that I actually did.

Even then I said incredulously, tentatively, "Rosemary?"

"Look," she said, brushing past me, "I simply must talk to you."

While I closed the door behind us she stopped in front of the looking glass in the hall and started to untie the headscarf.

"My God, whatever do I look like?"

I saw that her fingers were shaking too much to undo the knot, and finally she stretched over her head, grasped the points of the scarf, and pulled the whole thing forward. Off with the scarf came all the black curls, and out shook the more familiar chestnut mane of Rosemary Caspar, who had called me Sid for fifteen years.

"My God," she said again, putting the tinted glasses away in her handbag and fetching out a tissue to wipe off the worst of the lipstick. "I had to come. I had to."

"Come on in and have a drink," I said, knowing it was what she both needed and expected, and sighing internally over the loss of my quiet evening. "Whisky or gin?"

"Gin . . . tonic . . . anything."

Still wearing the raincoat she followed me into the sitting room and sat abruptly on the sofa as if her knees had given way beneath her. I switched off the television and poured her a tranquillizing dose of mothers' ruin.

She was forty-fivish, I supposed, thinking about it as I gave her the tumbler. In the days when I was a jockey, before I turned into a sort of all-purpose investigator, I had ridden a few times for her husband. I had known her casually for years. The general impression of thin elegance had always been strong, but now the eyebrows and eyelids fell in drooping lines and there was fine down noticeable at the sides of the jaw.

"So what's the problem?" I said.

"Problem!" She was transitorily indignant. "It's more than that. Why do you think I came creeping around at night searching for your damn flat in this ropey wig?"

"Well . . . why?"

"Because the last person I can be seen talking to is Sid Halley."

"Why don't you take your coat off?" I said. "Sit back on the sofa, and tell me what you want done."

As if dazed she stood up, undid the buttons, shed the coat, and sat down again. The newly revealed clothes were a cream silk shirt under a rust-coloured cashmere sweater, a heavy gold chain, and a well-cut black skirt: the everyday expression of no financial anxieties.

"George is at a dinner," she said. "We're staying here in London overnight . . . . He thinks I've gone to a film."

George, her husband, ranked in the top three of British race-horse trainers and probably in the top ten internationally. On race-courses from Hong Kong to Kentucky he was revered as one of the greats. At Newmarket, where he lived, he was king. If his horses won the Derby, the Arc de Triomphe, the Washington International, no one was surprised.

"He mustn't know," she said nervously. "You'll have to promise not to tell him I came here."

"I'll promise provisionally," I said.

"That's not enough," she said. "You'll see why . . ." She took a drink. "I tell you George is worried to death." The shrillness of her voice seemed to surprise her. She took some deep breaths, and started again. "What did you think of Gleaner?"

"Er . . ." I said. "Disappointing."

"A damned disaster," she said. "One of the best two-year-olds George ever had. Won three brilliant two-year-old races. Favourite for the Guineas all that winter. Going to be the tops, everyone said. Going to be marvellous."

"Yes," I said. "I remember."

"And then what? Last Spring he ran in the Guineas. Fizzled out. Total flop."

"It happens," I said. "Just one of those things."

She looked at me impatiently. "And Zingaloo?" she said. "Was that, too, just one of those things? The two best colts in the country, both in our yard. And neither of them won a penny last year. Just stood in their boxes, looking well, eating their heads off, and totally damn bloody useless."

"It was a puzzler," I agreed, but without much conviction. Horses which didn't come up to expectations were as normal as rain on Sundays.

"And what about Bethesda, the year before?" She glared at me vehemently. "Top two-year-old filly. Favourite for months for the One Thousand. Terrific. She went down to the start looking a million dollars, and she finished tenth. *Tenth*, I ask you!"

"Surely George must have had them all thoroughly checked," I said mildly.

"Of course he did. Vets crawling round the place for weeks.

410

Dope tests. Everything. All negative. Three brilliant horses all gone useless. Heart murmurs, the vet suggested. On all three? It doesn't make sense."

I sighed slightly. It sounded to me more like the story of most trainers' lives, not a matter of melodramatic visits in wigs.

"And now," she said, "there's Tri-Nitro."

I drew in an involuntarily audible breath. Every racing page hailed Tri-Nitro as the best colt for a decade. His two-year-old career the previous autumn had eclipsed all competitors, and his supremacy in the approaching summer was taken for granted.

"The Guineas isn't far away," Rosemary said. "Two weeks on Saturday, in fact. What if he fails, like the others . . . ?"

She was trembling again, but when I opened my mouth to speak she rushed on at a higher pitch. "Tonight was my only chance to come here . . . and George would be livid. I suggested he call you in to guard the horse and he nearly went berserk. He says no one can get at him, the security's too good. But he's scared, I know he is."

"Rosemary," I began, shaking my head.

"Listen," she interrupted. "I want you to make sure nothing happens to Tri-Nitro before the Guineas. That's all. Please do it. Say how much you want, and I'll pay it."

"It's not money," I said. "Look . . . . There's no way I can guard Tri-Nitro without George knowing and approving. It's impossible."

"You can do it. I'm sure you can. You've done things before that people said couldn't be done. I had to come. George can't face it . . . not three years in a row. Tri-Nitro has got to win."

She was suddenly shaking worse than ever. More to calm her than from any thought of being able in fact to do what she wanted, I said, "Rosemary . . . all right. I'm no superman. But I'll try to do something."

"He's got to win," she repeated.

I said soothingly, "I don't see why he shouldn't."

She picked up unerringly the undertone I hadn't known would creep into my voice: the tendency to discount her urgency as the fantasies of an excitable woman.

"My God, I've wasted my time coming here," she said bitterly. She stood up, slid into her raincoat and moved towards the door. "I'll have to go and see that film. George will ask . . ."

I followed her into the hall, almost feeling her tension in the air. She put the black wig back on her head, tucking her own brown hair underneath with fierce jabs. She painted on a fresh layer of the lipstick with unnecessary force, replaced the scarf with a savage jerk, and fumbled in her handbag for the tinted glasses.

"I changed in the lavatories at the tube station," she said. "It's all revolting. But I'm not having anyone see me leaving here. I shouldn't have come. I see that now. But I thought . . ."

She stood by my front door, waiting for me to open it: a thin, elegant woman looking determinedly ugly. It came to me that no woman did that to herself without a desperate need. And I'd done nothing to relieve her distress.

"Rosemary," I said flatly. "I've said I'll try, and I will."

But her mind was already on the film, on her return to George. She turned abruptly and walked away without a backward glance. With a continuing feeling of having been inadequate I shut the door and went back into the sitting room.

I switched on the television again; but Rosemary had come between me and the comedy. With a sigh I switched off, and cooked a steak, and after I'd eaten it I picked up the telephone to talk to Bobby Unwin, who worked for the *Daily Planet*.

"Information will cost you," he said immediately, when he found out who was on his line.

"All right," I said. "You wrote a long piece about George Caspar in your Saturday colour supplement a couple of months ago. Bring a copy of that magazine to Kempton tomorrow, and I'll buy you a bottle of your choice."

"Oh boy, oh boy. You're on."

His receiver went down without more ado, and I spent the rest of the evening reading the flat-racing form books of recent years, tracing the careers of Bethesda, Gleaner, Zingaloo and Tri-Nitro, and coming up with nothing at all.

I HAD FALLEN into a recent habit of lunching on Thursdays with my father-in-law. To be accurate, with my *ex*-father-in-law: Admiral (retired) Charles Roland, parent of my worst failure. To his daughter Jenny I had given whatever devotion I was capable of, and had withheld the only thing she eventually said she wanted, which was that I should stop riding in races. We had been married for five years: two in happiness, two in discord, and one in bitterness; and now only the itching, half-mended wounds remained—those, and the friendship of her father, which I had come by with difficulty and now prized as the only treasure saved from the wreck.

We met most weeks at noon in the upstairs bar of the Cavendish Hotel, where a pink gin for him and a whisky and water for me now stood on prim little mats beside a bowl of peanuts.

"Jenny will be at Aynsford this weekend," he said. Aynsford was his house in Oxfordshire. "I'd be glad if you would come down."

I looked at the fine, distinguished face and listened to the drawling, noncommittal voice. A man of subtlety and charm whose integrity I would trust to the gates of hell.

I said carefully, without rancour, "I am not coming to be sniped at."

"She agreed that I should invite you."

He looked with suspicious concentration at his glass. "I'm afraid she's in some sort of trouble," he said finally.

I stared at him, but he wouldn't raise his eyes.

"Charles," I said despairingly, "you *can't* . . . you can't ask me . . . you know how she speaks to me these days."

"But you'll come?"

"No . . . some things, honestly, are too much."

He sighed and sat back in his chair, looking at me over the gin. I didn't care for the blank look in his eyes, though, because it meant he was still plotting.

"Dover sole?" he suggested smoothly. "Shall I call the waiter? We might eat soon, don't you think?"

He ordered sole for both of us, and off the bone, out of habit. I could eat perfectly well in public now, but it had been difficult to learn to take into account the two-second delay between mental instruction and electrical reaction in my left hand. During which long and embarrassing period I had used the marvels of science as little as possible.

The waiter told us our table would be ready in ten minutes and went quietly away. Charles glanced expansively round the big, light room, where other couples, like us, sat in beige armchairs and sorted out the world.

Then he cleared his throat and addressed himself to nowhere in particular. "Jenny has lent some money . . . and her name, I'm afraid . . . to a business enterprise which would appear to be fraudulent."

"She's done *what?*" I said.

His gaze switched back to me. "She was attracted to a man," he said dispassionately. "I didn't especially like him, but then I didn't like you, either, to begin with . . ."

I ate a peanut. He had disliked me because I was a jockey, which he saw as no sort of husband for his well-bred daughter; and I had disliked him as a snob. It was odd to reflect that he was now probably the individual I valued most in the world.

He went on, "This man persuaded her to go in for some sort of mail-order business . . . all frightfully up-market and respectable, at least on the surface. A worthy way of raising money for charity . . . you know the sort of thing. Like Christmas cards, only in this case it was a sort of wax polish for antique furniture. One was invited to buy expensive wax, knowing that most of the profits would go to a good cause."

He looked at me sombrely. "The orders rolled in," he went on. "And the money with them, of course. Jenny and a girl friend were kept busy sending off the wax."

"Which Jenny had bought in advance?" I guessed.

Charles sighed. "You don't need to be told, do you?"

"And Jenny paid for the postage and packing and advertisements and general literature?"

He nodded. "She banked all the receipts into a specially opened account in the name of the charity. Those receipts have all been drawn out, the man has disappeared, and the charity, as such, has been found not to exist."

I regarded him in dismay. "And Jenny's position?" I said.

"Very bad, I'm afraid. There may be a prosecution. Her name is on everything, and the man's nowhere."

My reaction was beyond blasphemy. "Couldn't you have stopped her? Warned her?"

He shook his head regretfully. "I didn't know about it until she came to Aynsford yesterday in a panic. She had done it all from that flat she's taken in Oxford."

We went in to lunch. "The man's name is Nicholas Ashe,"

414

Charles said, over the sole. "At least that's what he said." He paused. "My solicitor thinks it would be a good idea if you could find him."

AS I DROVE to Kempton my thoughts were uncomfortably on Jenny. Divorce itself had changed nothing. The legal line had been drawn—no children, no maintenance disputes, no flicker of reconciliation, petition granted. But it had not proved a great liberating open door. The recovery from emotional cataclysm seemed a long, slow process, and the decree was barely an aspirin.

I had spent eight years in loving, losing and mourning Jenny, and although I could wish my feelings were dead, they weren't. Neither were hers. Indifference was a weary way off.

If I helped her in the mess she was in, she would give me a rotten time. If I didn't help her, I would give it to myself. *Why*, I thought violently, in impotent irritation, had she been so *stupid!*

THERE WAS a fair attendance at Kempton for a weekday in April. Outside the weighing room there were the same old bunch of familiar faces and conversations. Who was going to ride what, and who was going to win. There were the failures making brave excuses, and the successful hiding the anxieties behind their eyes. All as it had been, and would be, as long as racing lasted.

I had no real right any longer to wander in the space outside the weighing room, although no one ever turned me out. I belonged in the grey area of ex-jockeys: barred from the weighing room itself but tolerantly given the run of much else. The cosy inner sanctum had gone down the drain the day half a ton of horse landed feet first on my metacarpals.

George Caspar was there, talking to his jockey, with three runners scheduled that afternoon; and also Rosemary, who saw me at ten paces and promptly turned her back. I could imagine the waves of alarm quivering through her, although that day she looked her usual well-groomed elegant self: mink coat for the chilly wind, glossy boots, velvet hat. If she feared I would move over to talk to them, she was wrong.

Farther away, Bobby Unwin, notebook and pencil in evidence, was giving a middle-rank trainer a hard time. His voice floated over, sharp with northern aggression. "Can you say, then, that you are

415

perfectly satisfied with the way your horses are running?" The
trainer looked around for escape and shifted from foot to foot.

Presently Bobby released the miserable man and steered his
beaky nose in my direction. Tall, forty, and forever making copy
out of having been born in a back-to-back terrace in Bradford. We
ought to have had much in common, since I too was the product
of a dingy back street, but temperament had nothing to do with
environment. He tended to meet fate with fury and I with silence.

"The colour mag's in my briefcase in the Press Room," he said.
"What do you want it for?"

"Just general interest."

"Oh, come off it," he said. "What are you working on?"

"And would you," I replied, "give me advance notice of your
next scoop?"

"All right," he said. "Point taken. I'll have a bottle of the best
bubbly in the members' bar. After the first race. OK?"

"For smoked salmon sandwiches extra, would I acquire some
background info that never saw the light of print?"

He grinned nastily and said he didn't see why not; and in due
course, after the first race, he kept his bargain.

"You can afford it, Sid, lad," he said, munching a pink-filled
sandwich and laying a protective hand on the gold-foiled bottle on
the bar counter. "So what do you want to know?"

"You went to Newmarket, to George Caspar's yard, to do this
article." I indicated the magazine, which lay beside the bottle.
"What did you think of George as a person?"

He spoke round bits of brown bread. "I said most of it in that."
He looked at the magazine. "He knows more about when a horse
is ready to race and what race to run him in than any other trainer
on the turf. And he has as much feeling for people as a block of
stone. He's got forty lads working for him and he calls them all
Tommy, because he doesn't know tother from which."

"And Rosemary . . . what does she think about things?"

I poured a refill into his glass, and sipped at my own. Bobby
finished his sandwich with a gulp and licked the crumbs off his
fingers.

"Rosemary? She's halfway off her rocker."

"She's here today," I said. "And she looks all right."

"Yeah, well, she can hold on to the grande dame act in public still, I grant you, but I was in and out of the house for three days, and the goings-on there had to be heard to be believed."

"Such as?"

"Such as Rosemary screaming that they hadn't enough security and then George telling her to belt up. Rosemary has some screwy idea that some of their horses have been got at." He drank deep and tipped the bottle generously to replenish his supply. "One day in their hall she literally seized me by the coat and said I should be writing some stuff about Gleaner and Zingaloo—you remember, those two spanking two-year-olds who never developed —and George came out of his office and said she was neurotic, and right then and there in front of me they had a proper slanging match." He took a breath and a mouthful. "Funny thing is, in a way I'd say they were fond of each other. As much as he could be fond of anybody."

I ran my tongue round my teeth and looked only marginally interested, as if my mind was on something else. "What did George say about her ideas on Gleaner and Zingaloo?" I said. She'd left out Bethesda and so did I.

"He took it for granted I wouldn't take her seriously, but anyway, he said it was just that she had the heebie-jeebies that someone would nobble Tri-Nitro. He said the security round Tri-Nitro was already double what he considered necessary, because of her nagging. He told me that Rosemary was quite wrong, anyway, about Gleaner and Zingaloo being got at. It seems that both the horses developed health problems as they matured, which accounted for their rotten performances. So that was that. No story." He emptied his glass and refilled it. "Well, Sid, mate, what is it you *really* want to know about George Caspar?"

"Um," I said. "Do you think he is afraid of anything?"

"George?" he said disbelievingly. "When I was there, I'd say he was about as frightened as a ton of bricks."

"You don't think then," I said slowly, sounding disappointed, "that he'd be wanting any extra protection for Tri-Nitro?"

"Is that what you're after?" He gave a leering grin. "No dice, Sid, mate. Try someone smaller. George has his whole ruddy yard sewn up tight. For a start, it's enclosed by a high wall, like a fortress. Then there's ten-foot-high double gates across the entrance, with spikes on top."

I nodded. "Yes . . . I've seen them."

"Well, then." He shrugged, as if that settled things.

We watched the second race on a closed-circuit television in the bar. The horse which won by six lengths was one trained by George Caspar, and while Bobby was eyeing the two inches of fizz still left in the bottle, George himself came into the bar. Behind him, in a camel-coloured overcoat, came a substantial man bearing all the stigmata of a satisfied winning owner. Cat-with-the-cream smile, big gestures, have one on me.

"Finish the bottle, Bobby," I said.

He made no objections. Poured, drank, and comfortably belched. "Better go," he said. "Got to write up these colts in the third. Don't you go telling my editor I watched the second in the bar. I'd get the sack." He didn't mean it. He saw many a race in the bar. "See you, Sid. Thanks for the drink."

He turned with a nod and made a sure passage to the door, showing not a sign of having dispatched seven-eighths of a bottle of champagne. His capacity was phenomenal.

I tucked the magazine inside my jacket and made my own way slowly in his wake, thinking about what he'd said. Passing George Caspar I said, "Well done," in the customary politeness of such occasions, and continued towards the door.

"Sid . . ." he called after me, his voice rising. "Want you to meet a friend." I went back and shook the hand offered: snow-white cuffs, gold links; smooth pale skin, faintly moist; well-tended nails, onyx and gold signet ring on little finger.

"Your winner, Mr. Deansgate?" I said. "Congratulations."

"You know who I am?"

It was the first time I'd seen him at close quarters. There was often, in powerful men, a give-away droop of the eyelids which proclaimed an inner sense of superiority, and he had it. Also dark-grey eyes, black controlled hair, and the tight mouth which goes with well-exercised, decision-making muscles.

"Trevor Deansgate," I said. "Bookmaker in the big league."

"There you are, Trevor," said George, pleased. "I told you he knew everything."

I didn't enlarge. Deansgate's name at birth had been Trevor Shummuck. He'd been born in a Manchester slum, and changed his name, accent and chosen company on the way up.

We civilly discussed his winner until it was time to adjourn outside to watch the colts.

"How's Tri-Nitro?" I said to George, as we moved towards the door. "No problems?"

"None at all," he said. "In great heart."

We parted outside, and I spent the rest of the afternoon in the usual desultory way, watching the races and talking to people. I didn't see Rosemary again, and calculated she was avoiding me. After the fifth race I decided to go. If I was really going to help her it was time I called up the troops.

2

From the car-telephone I rang the North London Comprehensive School and asked to speak to Chico Barnes.

"He's teaching judo," a voice said repressively.

"His class usually ends about now."

"Wait a minute."

I waited, driving towards town with my right hand on the wheel and my left round the receiver. The car had been adapted for one-handed driving by the addition of a knob on the steering wheel's rim.

"Hullo?" Chico's voice, cheerful, full, even in one single word, of his general irreverent view of the world.

"Want a job?" I said.

"Yeah." His grin travelled distinctly down the line. "It's been too dead quiet this past week."

"Can you go to the flat? I'll meet you there."

"No. I've been lumbered with an extra class. Fill me in now, Sid. Where do I go? And what do I do?"

"Newmarket. Spot of pub-crawling."

"Can't be bad."

"You'll be looking for Paddy Young. He's George Caspar's head lad. Find out where he drinks, and drift into conversation. We want to know the present whereabouts of three horses. Are they still in his yard? He shouldn't have any reason for not telling you."

Chico clicked his tongue. "Why don't you ask George Caspar right out? Be simpler, wouldn't it?"

"At the moment we don't want George Caspar to know we're asking questions about his horses," I said. "Anyway, the three horses are Bethesda, Gleaner, and Zingaloo."

"OK. I'll go up there on Saturday. Shouldn't be too difficult. You want me to ring you?"

"Soon as you can."

I put the phone down with the feeling of satisfaction that Chico nearly always engendered. As a working companion I found him great: funny, inventive, persistent, and deceptively strong. Many a rogue had discovered too late that young, slender Chico could throw a twenty-stone man over his shoulder with the greatest ease. When I first met him we were both working in the Radnor detective agency, where I had learned my new trade. Then I had gone freelance, and he had left for a part-time job teaching judo. The first time I'd asked for his help he joined up with enthusiasm, and he had sort of stayed with me ever since.

On Saturday I went to Aynsford, as Charles had known I would, driving down in the afternoon and feeling the gloom deepen with every mile. For distraction, I concentrated on Chico's news from Newmarket, telephoned through to my flat at lunchtime.

"I found your Paddy Young," he had said. "The pub's nearly next door to the yard: very handy. Anyway, if you can understand what he says, and he's so Irish it's like talking to a foreigner, what it boils down to is that all three horses have gone to stud."

"Did he know where?"

"Sure. Bethesda went to Garvey's in Gloucestershire, and the other two are at a place just outside Newmarket, which Paddy Young called Traces, or at least I think that's what he said."

"Thrace," I said. "Henry Thrace."

"Yeah? Well, maybe you can make sense of some other things he said, which were that Gleaner had a tritus and Zingaloo had the virus and Bruttersmit gave them both the tums down."

I tried turning "Gleaner had a tritus" into an Irish accent in my head and came up with Gleaner had arthritis, which sounded a lot more likely. I said to Chico, ". . . and Brothersmith gave them the thumbs down . . ."

"Yeah," he said. "You got it. This Brothersmith is George Caspar's vet." He gave me the address. "If that's all, then, Sid,

420

there's a train leaving in half an hour, and I've a nice little dolly waiting for me round Wembley way who'll have her Saturday night ruined if I don't get back."

I paused. "Chico, did Paddy Young give you any impression that there was anything odd in these three horses going wrong?"

"Can't say he did. He didn't seem to care much, one way or the other. I just asked him casual like where they'd gone, and he told me, and threw in the rest for good measure. Philosophical, you could say he was."

"Right, then," I said. "Thanks."

The more I thought about Chico's report and Bobby Unwin's comments the less I believed in Rosemary's suspicions; but I'd promised her I would try, and try I still would, for as long as it took me to check a little further, and talk to Brothersmith the vet.

AYNSFORD still looked its mellow stone self, but the daffodil-studded tranquillity applied to the exterior only. I stopped the car gently in front of the house and sat there wishing I didn't have to go in.

Charles, as if sensing that even then I might back off and drive away, came purposefully out of his front door and strode across the gravel.

"Sid," he said, opening my door. "Welcome."

I climbed out and looked up at the front of the house, seeing only blank windows reflecting the greyish sky. "Is she here?" I said.

He nodded. I turned away, went round to the back of the car, and lugged out my suitcase.

"Come on, then," I said. "Let's get it over." We made the short journey in silence, and went through the door.

Jenny was standing there, in the hall.

I had never got used to the pang of seeing her. I saw her as I had when I first loved her, a girl not of great classical beauty, but very pretty, with brown curling hair and a neat figure, and a way of holding her head high, like a bird on the alert. The old smile and the warmth in her eyes were gone, but I tended to expect them, with hopeless nostalgia.

"So you've actually arrived," she said. "I said you wouldn't."

As always, we gave each other a brief kiss on the cheek. We had maintained the habit as the outward mark of a civilized divorce. Charles shook his head impatiently at the lack of real affection, and went ahead of us into the drawing room, where he introduced me to a stocky young-old man whose austere eyes were disconcertingly surrounded by a rosy country face.

"This is my solicitor, Oliver Quayle," Charles said in his most ultra-civilized voice. "Gave up his golf to be here. Very good of him."

"So you're Sid Halley," the young-old man said, shaking hands. There was nothing in his voice, but his gaze slid down, seeking the half-hidden hand that he wouldn't have looked at if he hadn't known. It often happened that way.

Charles made courteous sit-down motions with his hands, and the four of us sank into comfort and pale gold brocade.

"I've told Oliver," Charles said, "that if anyone can find this Nicholas Ashe person, you will."

"Frightfully useful," Jenny murmured, "having a plumber in the family when the pipes burst."

It was a fraction short of offensiveness. I gave her the benefit of a doubt I didn't have, and asked nobody in particular whether the police wouldn't do the job more quickly.

"The trouble is," Quayle said, "that technically it is Jenny alone who is guilty of obtaining money by false pretences. The police have listened to her, of course, and the man in charge seems to be remarkably sympathetic, but . . ." he slowly shrugged the heavy shoulders in a way that skilfully combined sympathy and resignation. ". . . one feels they might choose to settle for the case they have. And ignorance, even if genuine, is a poor defence."

I said, "If there's no evidence against Ashe, what would you do, even if I did find him?"

Quayle looked my way attentively. "I'm hoping that if you find him, you'll find evidence as well."

"I'll do my best," I said. "What did he look like?"

After a pause Charles said, "Young, personable, dark haired, clean-shaven. Something too ingratiating in his manner for me. I would not have welcomed him as a junior officer aboard my ship."

Jenny compressed her lips and looked away. But it couldn't be shirked. I said directly to her, neutrally, "Jenny?"

422

"He was *fun*," she said vehemently, unexpectedly. "My God, he was fun. And after you . . ." She stopped. Her head swung round my way with bitter eyes. "He was full of life and jokes. He made me laugh. He was terrific. He lit things up. It was like . . ." She suddenly faltered, and I knew she was thinking, like us when we first met.

I swallowed. "How tall was he?" I said.

"Taller than you."

"Age?"

"Twenty-nine."

The same age as Jenny. Two years younger than I. If he had told the truth, that was. A confidence trickster might lie about absolutely everything as a matter of prudence.

"Where did he stay, while he was . . . er . . . operating?"

Jenny looked unhelpful, and it was Charles who answered. "He told Jenny he was staying with an aunt, but after he had gone, Oliver and I checked up. The aunt, unfortunately, proved to be a landlady who lets rooms to students in North Oxford. And in any case . . ." he cleared his throat, ". . . it seems that fairly soon he left the lodgings and moved into the flat Jenny is sharing in Oxford with another girl. A Louise McInnes."

"He lived in your flat?" I said to Jenny.

"So what of it?" She was defiant.

"Do you want him found?" I asked her the question directly, but she didn't answer.

"He's done you great harm," I said.

With stubbornness stiffening her neck, she said, "Oliver says I won't go to prison."

"Jenny!" I was exasperated. "A conviction for fraud will affect your whole life in all sorts of horrible ways. I see that you liked him. Maybe you even loved him. But he's not just a naughty boy who pinched the jampot for a lark. He has callously arranged for you to be punished in his stead. *That's* the crime I'll try to catch him for, even if you don't want me to."

Charles protested vigorously. "Sid, that's ridiculous. Of course she wants you to find him."

I sighed and shrugged. "It's by no means unknown for women to go on loving scoundrels who've ruined them."

Jenny rose to her feet, stared at me blindly, and walked out of the room. Charles took a step after her but I said with some force, "Mr. Quayle, please will you go after her and tell her the consequences if she's convicted? Tell her brutally, make her understand, make it shock."

He was on his way before I'd finished.

Charles watched his departing back and said, with a tired note of despair, "I don't understand her." He looked at me gloomily. "Do you think you can find him? How on earth do you start?"

 3

I started in the morning, having not seen Jenny again, as she'd driven off the previous evening at high speed to Oxford, leaving Charles and me to dine alone, a relief to us both. She had returned after we went to bed and had not appeared for breakfast by the time I left.

I went to Jenny's flat in Oxford, following directions from Charles. The address was a large Victorian house in a prosperous side street, with a semi-circular driveway and parking room at the back. I rang the doorbell. The lock, I thought, would give me no trouble if there was no one in, but in fact, after my second ring, the door opened a few inches, on a chain.

"Louise McInnes?" I said, seeing an eye, some tangled fair hair, a slice of jeans and a baggy blue sweater.

"That's right."

"Would you mind if I talked to you? I'm Jenny's ex-husband. Her father asked me to see if I could help her."

"You're Sid?" she said, sounding surprised. "Sid Halley?"

The door closed and opened again, this time wide, and the whole girl was revealed. She had English-rose skin, and a face that had left shyness behind.

"Come in," she said.

The first-floor flat, as I might have guessed, was spacious. It had been bought, Charles told me, with some of Jenny's divorce settlement. It was nice to see that my money had been well spent.

The girl led the way into a bay-windowed sitting room which still had the day before's clutter slipping haphazardly off tables and chairs: newspapers, letters, coffee cups, some dying daffodils, a typewriter with its cover off, some scrunched-up pages that had missed the wastepaper basket.

The mess was the girl's. Jenny was always tidy, clearing up before bed. But the room itself was Jenny's. One or two pieces from Aynsford, and an overall similarity to the sitting room of the house we'd shared. Love might change, but taste endured.

"Want some coffee?" Louise said. "I'll have some anyway."

"Can I help you?"

"If you like."

She led the way through the hall and into a bare kitchen. As she fussed with the kettle, her manner was cool. Not surprising, really. Jenny would have said what she thought of me, and there wouldn't have been much that was good.

"Your coffee," Louise said. She picked up her own mug by its handle and out of the corner of her eye saw my left hand closing round the side of mine. "Look out," she said urgently, "that's hot."

I gripped the mug carefully with the fingers that couldn't feel. "One of the advantages," I said.

She looked at my face, but said nothing; merely turned away and went back to the sitting room.

"I'd forgotten," she said, as I put down the mug on the space she had cleared on the low table in front of the sofa.

"False teeth are more common," I said politely.

She came very near to a laugh, and although it ended up as a doubtful frown, the passing warmth was a glimpse of the true person living behind the slightly brusque façade. "What can you do to help Jenny?" she said.

"Try to find Nicholas Ashe."

"Oh . . ." There was another spontaneous flicker of smile, again quickly stifled by subsequent thought.

"You liked him?" I said.

She nodded ruefully. "I'm afraid so. He was such tremendous fun. I find it terribly hard to believe he's just gone off and left Jenny in this mess."

"Look," I said, "would you mind telling me all about it?"

"But hasn't Jenny . . . ?"

"No."

"I suppose," she said slowly, "that she wouldn't like admitting to you that he made such a fool of us."

"How much," I said, "did she love him?"

"Love? What's love? I can't tell you. She was *in* love with him." She sipped her coffee. "Up in the clouds."

"Have you been there? Up in the clouds?"

She looked at me. "Do you mean, do I know what it's like? Yes, I do. If you mean, was I in love with Nicky, then no, I wasn't. In any case, it was she who attracted him. Or at least . . ." she finished doubtfully, ". . . it seemed like it."

I said, "How long have you known Jenny?"

"We were at school together. Quite by chance we met again in Oxford when I was looking for somewhere to stay while I wrote a thesis. She said she'd like some company in this flat. So I came like a shot. We've got on fine, on the whole. I don't know why I'm telling you all this."

"It's very helpful." I paused. "How did Jenny meet Ashe?"

"I don't really know," she said, "except that it was somewhere in Oxford. I came back one day, and he was here, if you see what I mean. They were already interested in each other."

She got to her feet. "It might be as well for you to see all the charity stuff. I've put it in Nicky's room to get it out of sight."

As I followed her through the hall, she pointed at doors. "That room," she said, "is Jenny's. That's the bathroom. That's my room. And this one at the end was Nicky's."

"When exactly did he go?" I said, walking behind her.

"Sometime on Wednesday. Two weeks ago." She opened the door of the end room. "He was here at breakfast, same as usual. I went off to the library, and Jenny caught the train to London to go shopping, and when we both got back, he was gone. With all his belongings. Jenny was terribly shocked. Wept all over the place. But, of course, we didn't know then that he'd cleared out with all the money."

"How did you find out?"

"Jenny went to the bank on the Friday to pay in the cheques, and they told her the account was closed."

I looked round the room. It had thick carpet, Georgian dressing chest, big, comfort-promising bed, upholstered armchair, pretty, Jenny-like curtains, fresh white paint. Five large brown boxes of thick cardboard stood in a double stack in the biggest available space. The room looked as if it had never been lived in.

She went to the pile of boxes and opened the topmost. "The stuff in here will tell you the whole story. I'll leave you to read it . . . I can't stand the sight of it. And anyway, I'd better clean the place up a bit, in case Jenny comes back."

"You don't expect her today, do you?"

She tilted her head slightly, hearing the faint alarm in my voice. "Are you frightened of her?"

"Should I be?"

"She says you're a worm." A hint of amusement softened the words.

"Yes, she would," I said. "And no, I'm not frightened of her. She just distracts me."

With sudden vehemence she said, "Jenny's a super girl." Genuine friendship, I thought. A statement of loyalties. But Jenny, the super girl, was the one I'd married.

I said, "Yes," without inflection, and after a second or two Louise turned and went out of the room. With a sigh I started on the boxes, shifting them clumsily and being glad neither Jenny nor Louise was watching. They were large, and their proportions were all wrong for gripping electrically.

The top one contained two-foot-deep stacks of office-size paper, good quality, and printed with what looked like a typewritten letter. At the top of each sheet there was an embossed and gilded coat of arms. I lifted out one of the letters, and began to understand how Jenny had fallen for the trick.

"Research into Coronary Disability" it said, in engraved lettering above the coat of arms, with, beneath it, the words *"Registered Charity"*. To the left of the gold embossing there was a list of trustees, mostly with titles, and to the right a list of the charity's employees, one of whom was Jennifer Halley, Executive Assistant. Below her name, in small capital letters, was the address of the Oxford flat.

The letter began a third of the way down the paper. It said:

So many families nowadays have had sorrowful first-hand knowledge of the seriousness of coronary artery disease which, even where it does not kill, can leave a man unable to continue with a full, strenuous working life.

Much investigation has already been done into the causes and

427

possible prevention of this scourge of modern man, but much more remains still to be done. Research funded by Government money being of necessity limited in today's financial climate, it is of the utmost importance that the public should support directly the programmes now in hand in privately-run facilities.

We do know, however, that many people resent receiving straightforward fund-raising letters, however worthy the cause. Accordingly, the Trustees, after much discussion, have decided to offer for sale a supply of exceptionally fine wax polish, which has been especially formulated for the care of antique furniture.

The wax is packed in quarter-kilo tins, and is of the quality used by expert restorers and museum curators. We are offering the wax at five pounds a tin; and you may be sure that at least three-quarters of all revenue goes to research.

If you should wish to, please send a donation to the address printed above. (Cheques should be made out to Research into Coronary Disability.) You will receive a supply of wax immediately, and the gratitude of future heart patients everywhere.

Yours sincerely,
Executive Assistant

I folded the letter and tucked it into my jacket. Sob stuff: the offer of something tangible in return, and the veiled hint that it could one day happen to you. And, according to Charles, the mixture had worked.

The second big box contained several thousand white envelopes, unaddressed. The third was half full of mostly handwritten letters, orders of wax, all saying "cheque enclosed".

The fourth brown box, half empty, and the fifth one, which was unopened and full, contained numbers of white boxes about six inches square by two inches deep. I lifted out a white box and looked inside. Contents, one flat, round, unprinted tin. The lid put up a fight, but I got it off in the end, and found underneath it a soft mid-brown mixture that certainly smelled of polish. I took it with me and went quietly back down the hall, opening the closed doors one by one, and looking at what they concealed.

Jenny's room was decisively feminine: pink and white, frothy with net and frills. Her scent lay lightly in the air, the violet scent of *Mille*. No use remembering the first bottle I'd given her in

428

Paris. Too much time had passed. I shut the door on the fragrance and the memory and went into the bathroom.

A white bathroom. Huge fluffy towels. Green carpet, green plants. Looking glass on two walls, light and bright. Everything very tidy. Very Jenny. Roger & Gallet soap.

The snooping habit had ousted too many scruples. With hardly a hesitation I opened Louise's door and put my eyes round, trusting to luck she wouldn't come out into the hall and find me.

Organized mess, I thought. Heaps of papers and books. Clothes on chairs. A washbasin in a corner, no cap on the toothpaste, pair of tights hung to dry. A haphazard scatter on the dressing chest. A tall vase with horsechestnut buds bursting. No long-term dirt, just surface clutter.

I pulled my head out and closed the door, undetected. Louise, in the sitting room, had been easily sidetracked in her tidying, and was sitting on the floor, intently reading a book.

"Oh, hello," she said, looking up vaguely as if she had forgotten I was there. "Have you finished?"

"There must be other papers," I said. "Letters, bills, invoices, cash books, that sort of thing."

"The police took it all. Someone had complained to them that the charity wasn't registered."

I sat on the sofa, facing her. "Who?"

"I don't know. Someone who received one of the letters, and checked up. Half those trustees on the letterhead don't exist, and the others didn't know their names were being used."

I thought, and said, "What made Ashe bolt just when he did?"

"We don't know. Maybe someone telephoned here to complain, as well. So he went while he could. He'd been gone for a week when the police turned up."

I put the round tin on the coffee table. "Where did the wax come from?" I said.

"Some firm or other. Jenny wrote to order it, and it was delivered here. Nicky knew where to get it. We had stacks of it. It came in those big brown boxes . . . sixty tins in each. They practically filled the flat."

"These begging letters . . . . Who got them printed?"

She sighed. "Jenny, of course. Nicky had some others, just like them, except that they had his name in the space where they put

430

Jenny's. He explained that it was no use sending any more letters with his name on, as he'd moved and had no permanent address. However, he was keen, you see, to keep on working for the cause . . ."

"You bet he was," I said.

She was half-irritated. "It's all very well to jeer, but you didn't meet him. You'd have believed him, same as we did."

I left it. "These letters," I said. "Who were they sent to?"

"Nicky had lists of names and addresses. From the charity's headquarters, he said. Thousands of them."

"Have you got them? The lists?"

She looked resigned. "He took them with him."

"And who addressed the letters and sent them out?"

"Nicky typed the envelopes. Yes, don't ask, on my typewriter. He could do hundreds in a day. Jenny signed her name on the letters, and I put them in the envelopes. She used to get writers' cramp doing it and Nicky would often help her."

"Signing her name?"

"That's right. He copied her signature. He did it hundreds of times. You couldn't really tell the difference."

I looked at her in silence.

"I know," she said. "Asking for trouble. But he made all that hard work with the letters seem such fun. And when the cheques started rolling in, it was so obviously worth the effort."

"How long did all this go on?" I said.

"A couple of months, once the letters were printed and the wax had arrived."

"How much money," I said, "did Jenny bank?"

She looked at me sombrely. "In the region of ten thousand pounds. The money just came pouring in. It still does, every day. But it goes direct to the police from the post office."

"What about that box of letters, saying 'cheque enclosed', in Ashe's room? Do you mind if I take them?"

"Help yourself . . ."

After I'd fetched the box and dumped it by the front door, I went back into the sitting room to ask her another question. Deep in the book again, she looked up without enthusiasm.

"How did Ashe get the money out of the bank?"

"He took a cheque and letter of authorization, both signed by

Jenny, which enabled him to withdraw every penny from the account in cash. I've seen the letter and the cheque. You can't tell it isn't Jenny's writing. Even Jenny can't tell the difference."

She got gracefully to her feet, leaving the book on the floor. "Are you going?" she said hopefully. "I've got so much clearing up to do."

She came and opened the door while I awkwardly picked up the brown cardboard box, balancing the tin of polish on top. She went with me to the Scimitar, and opened the boot. I dumped the box inside, and she shut it in.

"Thank you," I said. "For everything."

The faintest of smiles came back into her eyes.

"If you think of anything that could help Jenny," I said, "will you let me know?" I forked a card out of an inner pocket and gave it to her. "My address is on there."

"All right." She stood still for a moment. "I'll tell you one thing," she went on. "From what Jenny's said . . . you're not a bit what I expected."

 4

From Oxford I drove west to Gloucestershire and arrived at Garvey's stud farm in the late morning.

Tom Garvey, standing in his stable yard talking to his stud groom, came striding across as I braked to a halt.

"Sid Halley!" he said. "What a surprise. What do you want?"

I grimaced through the open car window. "Does everyone think I want something when they see me?"

"Of course, lad. Best snooper in the business now, so they say."

Smiling, I climbed out of the car and we shook hands. A big strong bull of a man, with unshakable confidence, a loud domineering voice, and the wily mind of a gypsy.

"What are you after, then, Sid?" he said.

"I came to see a mare you've got here, Tom. Bethesda."

There was an abrupt change in his expression. He narrowed his eyes and said brusquely, "What about her?"

"Well . . . has she foaled, for instance?"

"She's dead." He paused. "You'd better come into the house."

He turned and scrunched away, and I followed. His house was old and dark and full of stale air. All the life of the place was outside, in fields and foaling boxes and the breeding shed.

"In here." It was a cross between a dining room and an office: heavy old table and chairs at one end, filing cabinets and sagging armchairs at the other. Tom perched against his desk and I on the arm of one of the chairs.

"Now then," he said. "Why are you asking about Bethesda?"

"A client wants to know what has become of her."

"Don't fence with me, lad. What client?"

"If I was working for you," I said, "and you'd told me to keep quiet about it, would you expect me to tell?"

He considered me with sour concentration. "No, lad. Guess I wouldn't. And I don't suppose there's much secret about Bethesda. She died foaling a month ago. The foal died with her."

"I'm sorry," I said.

He shrugged. "It happens sometimes. Not often, mind. The foal was lying wrong, see, and the mare, she'd been straining longer than was good for her. Her heart just packed up, sudden like."

"Did you have a vet to her?"

"Aye. I called him when she started, because there was a chance it would be dicey. First foal, the heart murmur, and all."

"Did she have a heart murmur when she came to you?"

"Of course she did, lad. That's why she stopped racing. She came from George Caspar's yard. He wanted to breed from her on account of her two-year-old form, but there you are."

"Well, thanks, Tom." I stood up. "Thanks for your time."

He shoved himself off his desk, and walked with me across to the car. I got in, sketched a thank-you salute, and drove away.

AT AYNSFORD they were in the drawing room, drinking sherry before lunch: Charles and Jenny.

Charles gave me a glass of fino. Jenny told me she had been talking to Louise on the telephone.

"I thought you had run away. You left the flat hours ago."

I chose to ignore the provocation and sipped the sherry. "Where did you buy all that polish from?" I said at last.

"I don't remember." She spoke distinctly, spacing out the syllables, wilfully obstructive.

"Jenny!" Charles protested.

I sighed. "Charles, the police have the invoices, which will have the name and address of the polish firm on them. Can you ask your friend Oliver Quayle to get the information from the police."

"Certainly," he said.

There was an awkward silence; Jenny broke it. "Louise said you were prying for ages."

"I liked her," I said mildly.

Jenny's nose, as always, gave away her displeasure. "She's out of your class, Sid," she said.

"In what way?"

"Brains, darling. She took a first in mathematics at Cambridge."

Lunch came and went in the same sort of atmosphere, and afterwards I went upstairs to put my few things into my suitcase. Jenny came into the room and stood watching me.

"You don't use that hand much," she said.

I didn't answer.

"I don't know why you bother with it."

"Stop it, Jenny."

"If you'd done as I asked, and given up racing, you wouldn't have lost it."

"Probably not." I threw my spongebag with too much force into the suitcase.

"You don't seem to care."

I said nothing. I cared, all right.

She walked to the door and I wondered numbly what else there was left that she could say.

Her voice reached me quite clearly across the room. "Nicky has a knife. He carries it in a little sheath, strapped to his leg, under his sock."

I turned my head fast. She looked both defiant and expectant. "Adolescent," I said.

She was annoyed. "And what's so mature about hurtling around on horses and knowing . . . *knowing* . . . that pain and broken bones are going to happen?"

"I don't do it any more."

"But you would if you could."

There was no answer to that, because we both knew it was true.

"And look at you," Jenny said. "When you have to stop racing, do you look around for a nice quiet job? No, you damned well don't. You go straight into something which lands you up in fights and beatings. You can't live without danger, Sid. You're addicted."

"I was a jockey when we met. You knew what it entailed."

"Not from the inside. Not all those terrible bruises, and no food and no drink, and no sex half the time."

The knife was a safer subject. "Did he show you the knife, or did you just see it?"

"What does it matter?"

"But you told me," I said. "So was it a warning?"

She seemed suddenly unsure and disconcerted, and after a moment simply frowned and walked away down the passage.

If it marked the first crack in her indulgence towards her precious Nicky, so much the better.

MOST OF Monday I spent looking through the box of letters— nearly eighteen hundred of them. I picked Chico up on Tuesday morning and drove north to Newmarket. We were going to see Henry Thrace. A windy day, bright, showery, rather cold. I mentioned I'd been over to Aynsford.

Chico whistled. "How did you get on with the wife, then?"

He had met her once and had described her as unforgettable, the overtones in his voice giving the word several meanings.

"She's in trouble," I said. I told him about Ashe and the fraud.

"Gone and landed herself in a whoopsy," Chico said.

"Face down."

"And for dusting her off, do we get a fee?"

I looked at him sideways.

"Yeah," he said. "I thought so. Working for nothing again, aren't we? Good job you're well-oiled, Sid, mate, when it comes to my wages."

Amicably, we drew nearer to Newmarket, consulted the map, asked a couple of locals, and finally arrived at the incredibly well-kept stud farm of Henry Thrace.

"Sound out the lads," I said, and Chico said, "Sure," and we stepped out of the car onto weedless gravel. I went in search of Henry Thrace, who was reported by a cleaning lady at the front door of the house to be "down there on the right, in his office." Down there he was, in an armchair, fast asleep.

My arrival woke him, and he came alive with the instant aware-
ness of people used to broken nights. A youngish man, very
smooth, a world away from rough, tough, wily Tom Garvey.

"Sorry. Been up half the night . . . foaling. Er, who are you,
exactly? Do we have an appointment?"

"No." I shook my head. "I just hoped to see you. My name's
Sid Halley."

"Is it? Any relation to . . . Good Lord. You're him. What can I
do for you?"

"It's very vague, really," I said. "I just came to inquire into the
general health and so on of two of the stallions you've got here.
Gleaner and Zingaloo."

We went through the business of why did I want to know, and
why should he tell me, but finally, like Tom Garvey, he shrugged
and said I might as well know.

"I suppose I shouldn't say it, but you wouldn't want to advise a
client to buy shares in either of them," he said, taking for granted
this was really the purpose of my visit. "They've both got bad
hearts."

"Both?" With Bethesda, that made three. Curious.

"That's right. That's what stopped them racing as three-year-
olds. And I reckon they've got worse since then."

"Somebody mentioned Gleaner was lame," I said.

Henry Thrace looked resigned. "He's developed arthritis
recently. You can't keep a damn thing to yourself in this town."
He yawned, took a battery razor out of his desk drawer, and
attacked his beard. "Is that everything then, Sid?"

"Yes," I said. "Thanks."

CHICO pulled the car door shut, and we drove away towards the
town. "Bad hearts," he said. "Proper epidemic, isn't it?"

"Let's ask Brothersmith, the vet."

Chico read out the address, in Middleton Road.

We drove across the wide heath and past the racecourse towards
the town. There weren't many horses about: a late-morning string,
in the distance, going home. I swung the car round familiar
corners and pulled up outside the vet's.

Mr. Brothersmith was out seeing to a horse. He would be home
for his lunch, probably, in half an hour. We sat in the car, and

436

waited. Eventually a muddy Range Rover came along Middleton Road and turned into Brothersmith's entrance. Chico and I removed ourselves from the Scimitar and went towards the tweed-jacketed man jumping down from his buggy.

"Mr. Brothersmith?"

"Yes? What's the trouble?" He was young and harassed, and kept looking over his shoulder, as if something was chasing him. Time, perhaps, I thought. Or lack of it.

"Could you spare us a few minutes?" I said. "This is Chico Barnes, and I'm Sid Halley. It's just a few questions . . . ."

His brain took in the name and his gaze switched immediately towards my hands, fastening finally on the left.

"Aren't you the man with the myoelectric prosthesis?"

"Er . . . yes." I said.

"Come in, then. Can I look at it?"

He turned away and strode purposefully towards the side door of the house. I stood still and wished we were anywhere else.

"Come on, Sid," Chico said. "Give the man what he wants and maybe he'll do the same for us."

Payment in kind, I thought: and I didn't like the price. Unwillingly I followed Chico into what turned out to be the surgery. Brothersmith asked a lot of questions in a fairly clinical manner, and I answered him in impersonal tones learned from the Roehampton limb centre.

"Can you rotate the wrist?" he said at length.

"Yes, a little." I showed him. "There's a sort of cup inside there which fits over the end of my arm, with another electrode to pick up the impulses for turning."

I knew he wanted me to take the arm off and show him properly, but I wouldn't have done it, and perhaps he saw there was no point in asking.

"Thinking of fitting one to a horse?" Chico said.

Brothersmith raised his still-harassed face and answered him seriously. "Technically it looks perfectly possible, but it's doubtful if one could train a horse to activate the electrodes, and it would be difficult to justify the expense."

"It was only a joke," Chico said faintly.

"Oh? Oh, I see. But it isn't unknown, you know, for a horse to have a false foot fitted. I was reading the other day about a prosthesis fitted to the fore-limb of a valuable broodmare. She was subsequently covered, and produced a live foal."

"Ah," Chico said. "Now that's what we've come about. Damaged horses. Only there doesn't seem to be anything that can be done about ours."

"It's a couple of stallions I'm interested in," I said, rolling down my sleeve and buttoning the cuff. "Can you remember treating Gleaner and Zingaloo by any chance?"

Brothersmith detached his attention reluctantly from false limbs and transferred it to horses with bad hearts. "Yes, of course. Those two. Wretched shame for George Caspar. So disappointing. Your purpose in asking?"

"A client," I said, lying with regrettable ease, "wants to know if he should send George Caspar a sparkling yearling. He asked me to check on Gleaner and Zingaloo."

"Oh, I see. Well, nothing much to tell, really. Nothing out of the ordinary, except that they were both so good as two-year-olds. Probably that was the cause of their troubles, if the truth were told."

"How do you mean?" I said.

His nervous tensions escaped in small jerks of his head as he brought forth some unflattering opinions. "Well, one hesitates to say so, of course, but it is all too easy to strain a two-year-old's heart, and if they are good two-year-olds they run in top races, and the pressure to win may be terrific, because of stud values and everything. A jockey, riding strictly to orders, mind you, may press a game youngster so hard that although it wins it is also more or less ruined for the future."

"Gleaner won the Doncaster Futurity in the mud," I said thoughtfully. "I saw it. It was a very hard race."

"That's right," Brothersmith said. "I checked him thoroughly afterwards, though. The trouble didn't start at once. In fact, it didn't show at all, until he ran in the Guineas. He came in from that in a state of complete exhaustion with a very slight fever. So at first we thought it was a virus, but then after a few days we got this very irregular heartbeat, and then it was obvious what was the matter."

"What percentage of horses develop bad hearts?" I said.

Some of the anxiety diminished as he moved confidently onto

neutral ground. "Perhaps ten per cent have irregular heartbeats. It doesn't always mean anything."

"So how often do horses stop racing because of bad hearts?"

He shrugged. "Perhaps two or three in a hundred."

George Caspar, I reflected, trained upwards of a hundred and thirty horses, year after year.

I said, "Thanks, then," and stood up. We shook hands. "I suppose there's no heart trouble with Tri-Nitro?"

"None at all. Sound, through and through. His heart bangs away like a gong, loud and clear."

 5

"That's that, then," Chico said over a pint and pie in the White Hart hotel. "End of case. Mrs. Caspar's off her tiny rocker, and no one's been getting at George Caspar's youngsters except George Caspar himself."

"She won't be pleased to hear it," I said.

"Will you tell her?"

"Straightaway. If she's convinced, she might calm down."

So I telephoned to George Caspar's house, and asked for Rosemary, saying I was a Mr. Barnes. She came on the line and said hello in the questioning voice one uses to unknown callers.

"Mr. . . . Barnes?"

"It's Sid Halley," I said. "Can you meet me in Newmarket. I've things to tell you. And I don't honestly think there's any need for disguises."

The alarm came instantly. "I can't be seen with you in the town."

She agreed, however, to drive out in her car, pick Chico up, and go where he directed: and Chico and I worked out a place on the map which looked a tranquillizing spot for paranoiacs. The churchyard at Barton Mills, eight miles towards Norwich.

We parked the cars side by side at the gate, and Rosemary walked with me among the graves. She was wearing the fawn raincoat and a scarf again, but not the false curls.

I told her I had been to see Tom Garvey and Henry Thrace at their stud farms; I told her I had talked to Brothersmith; and I

439

told her what they'd all said. She listened, and then shook her head.

"The horses were nobbled," she said obstinately.

"How?"

"I don't know how." Her voice rose sharply. "But they'll get at Tri-Nitro. You've got to keep him safe till the Guineas."

As we walked along the path beside the grey, weatherbeaten headstones, I was wondering if it would be sensible even to suggest the one way-out theory at the back of my mind. At last, I said reluctantly, "In the normal course of events, George will be giving Tri-Nitro some strong work before the Guineas."

"I suppose so. What do you mean?"

"Well . . ." I hesitated. "You could . . . er . . . make sure he takes precautions when he gives Tri-Nitro that last gallop." I paused. "Inspect the saddle . . . that sort of thing."

Rosemary said fiercely, "What are you saying? Spell it out, for God's sake. Don't pussyfoot round it."

"Lots of races have been lost because of too-hard training gallops too soon beforehand."

"Of course," she said impatiently. "Everyone knows that. But George would never do it."

"What if the saddle was packed with lead? What if a three-year-old was given a strong gallop carrying fifty pounds dead weight? And then ran under severe pressure a few days later in the Guineas? And strained his heart?"

"My God," she said. "My God."

"I'm not saying that it did happen to Zingaloo and Gleaner. Only that it's a distant possibility. And if it's something like that, it must involve someone inside the stable."

She had begun trembling again. "Please go on trying," she said. "I brought some money for you." She plunged a hand into her raincoat pocket and brought out a brown envelope. "It's cash. I can't give you a cheque."

"I haven't earned it," I said.

"Yes, yes. Take it." She was insistent, and finally I put it in my pocket, unopened.

"Let me consult George," I said.

"No. He'd be furious. I'll warn him about the gallops. He thinks I'm crazy, but if I go on about it long enough he'll take notice." She looked at her watch. "I have to go back now."

We retraced our steps with some speed towards the gate. When we reached the cars, she said goodbye, and drove off in a great hurry. Chico, waiting in the Scimitar, said, "Quiet here, isn't it? Even the ghosts must find it boring."

I got into the car and tossed Rosemary's envelope onto his lap. "Count that," I said, starting the engine. "See how we're doing."

He tore it open, pulled out a wad of banknotes, and licked his fingers. "Phew," he said, coming to the end. "She's bonkers."

"She wants us to go on."

"Then you know what this is, Sid," he said, flicking the stack. "Guilt money. To spur you on when you want to stop."

"Well, it works."

WE SPENT some of Rosemary's incentive in staying overnight in Newmarket and going round the bars—Chico where the lads hung out and me with the trainers. It was very quiet everywhere. I heard nothing of any interest and drank more than enough whisky, and Chico came back with hiccups and not much else.

"Ever heard of Inky Poole?" he said.

"Is that a song?"

"Inky Poole," he said, "is George Caspar's work jockey. Not much good in races but can gallop the best at home. Did you ask me to find out who rides Tri-Nitro's gallops?"

"Yes, I did," I said. "And you're drunk."

"Inky Poole, Inky Poole," he said.

ARMED WITH raceglasses on a strap round my neck I walked along to Warren Hill at seven thirty in the morning to watch the strings out at morning exercise. The smell and sight of them on the heath was like a sea breeze to a sailor. I filled my lungs and eyes, and felt content.

Each string was accompanied and shepherded by its watchful trainer. Several smiling faces seemed genuinely pleased to see me, and some that weren't in a hurry stopped to talk.

"Sid!" exclaimed Martin England. I'd ridden for him on the Flat in the years before my weight caught up with my height. "Sid, we don't see you up here much these days."

"My loss," I said, smiling.

"Why don't you ride out for me sometime?"

"Do you mean it?"

"Of course I mean it. Tell you what, come the Friday after the Guineas, stay the night with us, and ride work on Saturday morning."

There wasn't much, I reflected, that anyone could give me that I'd rather accept. "Martin, I'd love to."

"Great." He seemed pleased. Then he wheeled away, to shout to a lad who was slopping in the saddle like a jellyfish.

A moment later, George Caspar rode up. "Morning, Sid."

His eyes were on a distant string walking down the side of the heath from his stable in Bury Road.

"Morning, George." I paused. "Is Tri-Nitro in that lot?"

"Yes, he is. Sixth from the front." He looked round at the interested spectators. "Have you seen Trevor Deansgate anywhere? He said he was coming up here early from London."

"Haven't seen him." I shook my head.

"He's got two in the string. He was coming to see them work." He shrugged. "He'll miss them if he isn't here soon."

I lifted my raceglasses and watched while the string, forty strong, approached and began circling, waiting for their turn on the uphill gallop. The stable before George's had nearly finished, and George would be next.

The lad on Tri-Nitro wore a red scarf in the neck of his olive-green Husky jacket. As he circled, I looked at his mount with the same curiosity as everyone else. Tri-Nitro: a good-looking bay colt, with strong shoulders and a lot of heart room.

"Do you mind photographs, George?" I said.

"Help yourself, Sid."

I seldom went anywhere these days without a camera in my pocket. Sixteen-millimetre, automatic light meter, all the expense in its lens. George shook up his patient hack and went across to his string. I walked over and took three or four photographs of the wonder horse and a couple of his rider.

George began detailing his lads into the small bunches that would go up the gallops together. As I walked back to the fringes of things, a car arrived very fast and pulled up with a jerk. It alarmed some horses alongside and sent them skittering, with the lads' voices rising high in protest.

Trevor Deansgate climbed out of his Jaguar and for good

measure slammed the door. He was dressed in a city suit, in contrast to everyone else there. Black hair rigorously brushed, chin smoothly shaven, shoes polished like glass.

"Hello," he said, seeing me. "I met you at Kempton . . . . Do you know where George's horses are?"

"Right there," I said, pointing. "You're just in time."

He strode across the grass towards George, raceglasses swinging from his hand, and George said hello briefly and apparently told him to watch the gallops with me, because he came straight back, heavy and confident.

"George says my two both go in the first bunch. He said you'd tell me how they're doing, insolent bastard. Got eyes, haven't I? He's going on up the hill."

I nodded. Trainers often went up halfway and watched from there, the better to see their horses' action as they galloped past.

Four horses were wheeling into position at the starting point. Trevor Deansgate applied his binoculars, twisting them into focus. The well-kept hands, gold cuff links, onyx ring, as before.

"Which are yours?" I said.

"The two chestnuts. That one with the white socks is Pinafore. The other's nothing much."

They set off together up the gallop at George's signal. Pinafore romped it all the way to the top, and the nothing much lived up to his owner's assessment. Trevor Deansgate lowered his binoculars with a sigh.

"That's that, then. Are you coming to George's for breakfast?"

"No. Not today."

He raised the glasses again and focused them on the string circling nearby. The search came to an end on Tri-Nitro and Inky Poole; he lowered the glasses and followed them with the naked eye. "That horse looks a picture," he said.

I supposed that he, like all bookmakers, would be happy to see the hot favourite lose the Guineas, but there was nothing in his voice except admiration for a great horse. Tri-Nitro lined up in his turn and at a signal from George set off up Warren Hill with two companions at a deceptively fast pace. Inky Poole rode with a skill worth ten times what he would be paid. Good work jockeys were undervalued. Bad ones could ruin a horse's mouth and temperament and whole career. It figured that for the stableful he'd got,

443

George Caspar would employ only the best. Tri-Nitro cantered up the incline without a hint of effort, and breasted the top as if he could go up there six times more without noticing.

Impressive, I thought. Trevor Deansgate looked thoughtful, as well he might, and George Caspar, coming down the hill and reining in near us, looked almost smugly satisfied. The Guineas, one felt, were in the bag.

The horses walked down the hill to join the still circling string where the work riders changed onto fresh mounts and set off again up to the top. Eventually the whole lot of them headed for home.

"Right, then," George said. "All set, Trevor? Breakfast?"

They nodded farewells to me and set off, one in the car, one on the horse. I had eyes mostly, however, for Inky Poole, who was walking off a shade morosely to a parked car.

"Inky," I said, coming up behind him. "The gallop on Tri-Nitro, that was great."

He looked at me sourly. "I've got nothing to say."

"I'm not from the Press."

"I know who you are. Saw you racing. Who hasn't?" Unfriendly: almost a sneer. "What do you want?"

He fished the car keys out of his pocket, and fitted one into the lock. I wondered if his unhelpful manner was the result of his not getting on as a jockey, and I felt sympathy for him.

"How does Tri-Nitro compare with Gleaner, this time last year?"

"I'm not talking to you."

"How about Zingaloo?" I said. "Or Bethesda?"

He opened his car door and slid down into the driving seat, taking out time to give me a hostile glare.

"Push off," he said. Slammed the door. Stabbed the ignition key into the dashboard and forcefully drove away.

CHICO HAD arisen for breakfast but was sitting in the pub's dining room holding his head.

"Don't look so healthy," he said when I joined him.

"Bacon and eggs," I said. "That's what I'll have. Or kippers, perhaps. And strawberry jam."

He groaned.

"I'm going back to London," I went on. "But would you mind staying here?" I brought the camera out of my pocket. "Take the film out and get it developed. There're some pictures of Tri-Nitro and Inky Poole. We might find them helpful. You never know."

"OK, then," he said. "But you'll have to ring up the comprehensive and tell them that my black belt's at the cleaners."

I laughed. "There were some girls riding in George Caspar's string this morning," I said. "See what you can do."

His eyes seemed suddenly brighter. "What am I asking?"

"Things like who saddles Tri-Nitro for exercise gallops, and what's the routine from now until Saturday week and whether anything nasty is stirring in the jungle."

"Do you really think anything dodgy's going on?" Chico said.

"A toss-up. I just don't know. I'd better ring Rosemary."

I went through the Mr. Barnes routine again and Rosemary came on the line sounding as agitated as ever.

"I can't talk. We've people here for breakfast."

"Just listen, then," I said. "Try to persuade George to vary his routine for Tri-Nitro's last gallop. Put up a different jockey, for instance. Not Inky Poole."

"You don't think . . ." Her voice was high, and broke off.

"I don't know at all," I said. "But if George changed everything about, there'd be less chance of skulduggery. Routine is the robber's best friend."

"All right. I'll try."

CHARLES and I met as usual at the Cavendish the following day, and sat in the upstairs bar.

"You look happier," he said, "than I've seen you since . . ." He gestured to my arm, with his glass. "Released in spirit. Not your usual stoical self."

"I've been in Newmarket," I said. "Watching the gallops."

In due course we ate scallops in a wine and cheese sauce, and he gave me the news of Jenny.

"Oliver Quayle sent the address of the polish firm." He took a paper from his breast pocket and handed it over. "Oliver is worried. He says the police are actively pursuing their inquiries, and Jenny is almost certain to be charged. They'll give her bail, of course."

"Bail!"

"Oliver says she is, unfortunately, very likely to be convicted,

445

but that if it is stressed that she acted as she did under the influence of Nicholas Ashe, she'll probably get some sympathy from the judge and a conditional discharge."

"Even if he isn't found?"

"Yes. But of course if he *is* located, and charged, and found guilty, Jenny would, with luck, escape a conviction altogether."

I took a deep breath. "Have to find him then, won't we?"

"How?"

"Well . . . I spent a lot of Monday looking through a box of letters. They came from the people who sent money and ordered wax."

"How do they help?"

"I've started sorting them into alphabetical order, and making a list." He frowned sceptically, but I went on, "The interesting thing is that all the surnames start with the letters L, M, N, and O."

"I don't see . . ."

"They might be part of a mailing list," I said. "There must be thousands of mailing lists, but this one certainly did produce the required results, so it wasn't a mailing list for dog licence reminders, for example."

"That seems reasonable," he said dryly.

"I thought I'd get all the names into order and then see if anyone, like Christies or Sotheby's, say—because of the polish angle—has a mailing list which matches. A long shot, I know, but there's just a chance."

"I could help you," he said.

"All right. I'd like that." I finished the scallops and sat back in my chair, and drank the good cold white wine.

Charles said he would come to my flat in the morning, and I gave him a spare key to get in with, in case I should be out for a newspaper or cigarettes when he arrived.

I WENT home in a taxi and paid it off outside the entrance to the flats, yet not exactly outside, because a car was parked there on the double yellow lines.

I scarcely looked at the car, which was my mistake, because as I reached it and turned towards the entrance its nearside doors opened and spilled out the worst sort of trouble.

Two men in smart clothes grabbed me. One hit me dizzyingly on

446

the head with something hard and the other flung a lasso over my arms and chest and pulled it tight. They bundled me into the back of the car where one of them tied a cloth over my eyes.

"Keys," a voice said. "Quick. No one saw us."

I felt them fumbling in my pockets. There was a clink as they found what they were looking for. The cloth over my eyes was reinforced by a sickly-smelling wad over my nose and mouth, and anaesthetic fumes made a nonsense of consciousness.

I WAS AWARE, first of all, that I was lying on straw.

Straw, as in stable, rustling when I tried to move. I was lying on my back on some straw, blindfolded, with a rope tied tight round my chest, above the elbows, fastening my upper arms against my body. I was lying on the knot. I didn't know why I was there . . . and had no great faith in the future.

Damn, damn, *damn*.

My feet were tethered to some immovable object. It was dark, even round the edges of the blindfold. I sat up and tried to disentangle myself: a lot of effort and no results.

Ages later there was a tramp of footsteps outside on a gritty surface, the creak of a wooden door, and sudden light on the sides of my nose.

"Stop trying, Mr. Halley," a voice said. "You won't undo those knots with one hand."

I stopped trying. There was no point in going on.

"A spot of overkill," he said, enjoying himself. "Ropes *and* anaesthetic *and* blackjack *and* blindfold. Well, I did tell them to be careful, and not to get within hitting distance of that tin arm."

I knew the voice. Undertones of Manchester, overtones of all the way up the social ladder. The confidence of power. Trevor Deansgate. Last seen on the gallops at Newmarket.

"Take the blindfold off," he said. "I want him to see me."

Fingers took their time untying the cloth. When it fell away, the light was temporarily dazzling; but the first thing I saw was the double barrel of a shotgun pointing my way.

"Guns, too," I said sourly.

It was a storage barn, not a stable. There was a stack of straw bales to my left, and on the right, a few yards away, a tractor. My feet were fastened to the trailer bar of a roller.

"You're too bloody clever for your own good," Deansgate said. "Well, I knew how close you were to getting me nicked. Asking questions everywhere. Just laying your snares, weren't you? Just waiting for me to fall into your hands, like you've caught so many others." He stood for a while without speaking: simply watching. I didn't say anything either. What could one say? Especially sitting trussed up at the wrong end of a shotgun.

He was dressed, as before, in a city suit. Navy, chalk pin-stripe, Gucci tie. The well-manicured hands held the shotgun with the expertise of many a weekend on country estates.

"No bloody nerves, have you?" he said at last. "None at all."

I didn't answer.

Two other men were behind me to the right, out of my sight. I could hear their feet as they occasionally shuffled on the straw. Deansgate switched his attention to them. "Untie that rope round his chest. And do it carefully. Then get two other pieces of rope. Tie one to his left arm, and one to the right. Watch out for any tricks."

He lifted the gun a fraction as the chums tied bits of rope to both of my wrists.

"Not the left wrist, you stupid bastard," he said. "That one comes right off. Tie the rope high, above his elbow."

The chum in question did as he said and pulled the knots tight.

"I don't want to kill you," Deansgate said. "I could dump your body somewhere, but there would be too many questions. I can't risk it. I've got to shut you up. Permanently."

Short of killing me I didn't see how he could do it; but I was being stupid.

The chums completed their task. It didn't make much difference to my chances of escape. They were wildly exaggerating my ability in a fight.

"Lie down," he said to me; and when I didn't at once comply, he said, "Push him down," to the chums. One way or another, I ended on my back. "Pull his arms away from his body," he said.

The chums hauled on the ropes so that my arms finished straight out sideways, at right angles to my body.

Trevor Deansgate stepped towards me and lowered the gun until the barrel was pointing straight at my right wrist. Then he carefully lowered the barrel another inch, making direct contact

on my skin. I rolled my head that way and tried not to beg. I could feel the metal rims hard across the bones and nerves and sinews. Across the bridge to a healthy hand.

I heard the click as he cocked the firing mechanism. One blast from a twelve bore would take off most of the arm.

A dizzy wave of faintness drenched all my limbs with sweat.

I might have given the impression earlier of having no nerves, but I intimately know about fear all right. Not fear of racing or falling, or of ordinary physical pain. But of humiliation, rejection, helplessness and failure . . . all of those.

All the fear I'd ever felt in all my life was as nothing compared with the liquefying, mind-shattering disintegration of that appalling minute. It broke me in pieces. Swamped me. Brought me down to a morass of terror, to a whimper in the soul. And instinctively, hopelessly, I tried not to let it show.

He watched motionlessly through uncountable silent seconds. Making me wait. At length he said, "As you see, I could shoot off your hand. Nothing easier. But I'm probably not going to. Not today." He paused. "Are you listening?"

I nodded the merest fraction.

His voice came quietly, seriously, giving weight to every sentence. "You will give me your assurance that you'll back off. You'll do nothing more against me, in any way, ever. You'll go to France tomorrow morning, and you'll stay there for the next ten days, until after the Two Thousand Guineas. After that, you can go where you like. But if you break your assurance, I'll find you, and I'll blow your right hand off. Do you understand?"

I nodded, as before. I could feel the gun as if it were hot. Don't let him, I thought. Dear God, don't let him.

"Give me your assurance. Say it."

I dredged up a voice. Low and hoarse. "I give it."

Another silence lengthened for what seemed a hundred years. Then he took the gun away, broke it open, removed the cartridges. I felt physically, almost uncontrollably, sick.

He knelt on his pin-striped knees beside me and looked closely at my face. I could feel the treacherous sweat trickling down my cheek. He nodded, with grim satisfaction.

"I knew you couldn't face that. Not the other one as well. No one could. There's no need to kill you."

450

He stood up again and stretched his body, as if relaxing a wound-up inner tension. Then he put his hands into various pockets, and produced things. Evidently the chums had been in my flat.

"Here are your keys. Your passport, your cheque book, credit cards." He put them on a straw bale. To the chums, he said, "Untie him, and drive him to the airport. To Heathrow."

 6

I flew to Paris and stayed right there where I landed, in an airport hotel, with no impetus or heart to go farther. I stayed for the ten days, not leaving my room, spending most of the time by the window, watching the aeroplanes come and go.

I felt stunned. Disorientated. Overthrown and severed from my own roots. Crushed into an abject state of mental misery, knowing that I had run away.

It was easy to convince myself that logically I had had no choice but to give Deansgate his assurance. I could tell myself, as I continually did, that sticking to his instructions had been merely commonsense; but the fact remained that when the chums decanted me at Heathrow they had driven off at once, and it had been of my own free will that I'd bought my ticket, sent Chico a telegram getting him off the hook, waited in the departure lounge, and walked to the aircraft.

There had been no one there with guns to make me do it. Only the fact that, as Deansgate had truly said, I couldn't face losing the other one. I couldn't face even the risk of it. The thought of it, like a conditioned response, brought out the sweat.

As the days passed, the feeling I had had of disintegration seemed not to fade but to deepen. I wished I could sleep properly, and get some peace.

When Saturday came I thought of Newmarket and of all the brave hopes for the Guineas. Thought of George Caspar, taking Tri-Nitro to the test, producing him proudly in peak condition and swearing to himself that nothing could go wrong. Thought of Rosemary, jangling with nerves, willing the horse to win.

Saturday was the day I learned about despair and desolation

451

and guilt. I heard in the evening they had run the Two Thousand Guineas, as scheduled. Tri-Nitro had started hot favourite at even money; and he had finished last. Somehow, in some mysterious, incomprehensible way, Trevor Deansgate had fixed him.

THE NEXT MORNING, I paid my bill and went to the airport. The urge to escape was very strong and there were aeroplanes to everywhere, to escape in. But wherever one went, one took oneself along. From oneself there was no escape. Wherever I went, in the end I would have to go back. I thought that what I had lost might be worse than a hand. For a hand there were substitutes which could grip and look passable. But if the core of oneself had crumbled, how could one manage at all?

It took me a long lonely time to buy a ticket to Heathrow.

I landed at midday and took a taxi home. Before I'd even shut the door of the flat behind me, I heard a rustle in the sitting room, and then Chico's voice. "Is that you, Admiral Roland?"

Chico usually checked on the flat when I was away, and this time Charles had obviously been in and out, too. I simply didn't answer. In a brief moment Chico appeared. "Ah, you," he said. "About time." He looked, on the whole, relieved to see me.

"I sent you a telegram."

"Oh sure. *Leave Newmarket and go home shall be away for a few days will telephone.* What sort of telegram's that? Sent from Heathrow. You been on holiday?"

"Yeah." I walked past him, into the sitting room. There were files and papers everywhere, with coffee-marked cups and saucers holding them down.

"You went away without the charger," Chico said. "You never do that, even overnight. The spare batteries are all here. You haven't been able to move that hand for nine days."

"Let's have some coffee." I paused. "What's all this mess?"

"The polish letters. You know. Your wife's spot of trouble."

I stared at them blankly.

"Look," Chico said. "Cheese on toast? I'm starving."

He went into the kitchen and started banging about. I took the dead battery out of my arm and put in a charged one. The fingers opened and closed, like old times. I had missed them more than I would have imagined.

Chico brought coffee and the cheese on toast. He ate his, and I looked at mine. I'd better eat it, I thought, and didn't have the energy. There was the sound of the door of the flat being opened with a key, and after that my father-in-law came into the room. He took a long slow look at me. Very controlled, very civilized. "We have, you know, been worried." It was a reproach.

"I'm sorry."

"Where have you been?" he said.

I found I couldn't tell him. If I told him where, I would have to tell him why: and I shrank from why. I just didn't say anything at all.

Chico gave him a cheerful grin. "Sid's got a bad attack of the brick walls." He looked at his watch. "Seeing that you're here, Admiral, I might as well get along. I promised the little bleeders at the comprehensive an extra lesson. And Sid, before I go, there's about fifty messages on the phone pad. There's two new insurance investigations waiting to be done, and a guard job. And Rosemary Caspar has been screeching fit to blast the eardrums. It's all written down. See you, then. I'll come back here later."

I almost asked him not to, but he'd gone.

"You've lost weight," Charles said.

It wasn't surprising. I looked again at the toasted cheese and decided that coming back also had to include things like eating.

"Want some?" I said.

He eyed the congealing square. "No, thank you."

Nor did I. I pushed it away. Sat and stared into space.

"What's happened to you?" he said.

"Nothing." I stood up restlessly, to escape his probing gaze. "Leave me alone, Charles."

He paused, considering, then said, "You went dead like this before, when you lost your career and my daughter. So what have you lost this time? What could be as bad . . . or worse?"

I knew the answer. I'd learned it in Paris, in torment and shame. My whole mind formed the word "*courage*" with such violent intensity that I was afraid it would leap of its own accord from my brain to his. He showed no sign of receiving it. He was still waiting for a reply.

I swallowed. "Ten days," I said neutrally. "I've lost ten days. Let's get on with tracing Nicholas Ashe."

He shook his head in disapproval and frustration, but began to explain what he'd been doing.

"This thick pile is from people with names beginning with M. I've put them into strictly alphabetical order, and typed out a list . . . are you paying attention?"

"Yes."

"I took the list to Christies and Sotheby's, as you suggested, and persuaded them to help. But the 'M' section of their catalogue mailing list is not the same as this one."

"You know," I said, "I've just realized we don't have to go trailing from place to place to find out whose list that is." I nodded towards the "M" stack. "All we do is ask the people themselves what mailing lists they are on. The common denominator would be certain to turn up."

"It's an awfully big project," Charles said doubtfully. "And even if we do find a magazine with an 'M' list that matches ours, what then? The magazine wouldn't be able to tell us which of the many people who had access to their list was Nicholas Ashe, particularly as he is almost certain not to have used that name."

"Mm," I said. "But there's a chance he's started operating again somewhere else, and is still using the same list. He took it with him, when he went. If we can find out whose list it is, we might go and call on some people who are on it, whose names start with A to K, and P to Z, and find out if they've received any begging letters recently. Because if they have, the letters will have the address on, to which the money is to be sent. And there, at that address, we might find Mr. Ashe."

Charles put his mouth into the shape of a whistle, but what came out was more like a sigh.

"You've come back with your brains intact, anyway," he said.

Oh God, I thought, I'm making myself think to shut out the abyss. I'm in splinters . . . I'm never going to be right again.

"And there's the polish," I said. "There can't be many private individuals ordering so much wax in unprinted tins. We could ask the polish firm to let us know if another lot is ordered. It's just faintly possible that Ashe will use the same firm again. He ought to see the danger . . . but he might be a fool."

I turned away wearily. Thought about whisky. Went over and poured myself a large one.

"Drinking heavily, are you?" Charles said from behind me.

I shut my teeth hard, and said, "No." Apart from coffee and water, it was my first drink in ten days.

"Your first alcoholic blackout, was it, these last few days?"

I left the glass untouched on the drinks tray and turned round. "Don't be so bloody stupid," I said.

He lifted his chin a fraction. "A spark," he said sarcastically. "Still got your pride, I see."

I compressed my lips and turned my back on him, and drank a lot of Scotch.

After a bit I deliberately loosened a few tensed-up muscles, and said, "You won't find out that way. I know you too well. You use insults as a lever, to sting people into opening up. You've done it to me in the past. But not this time."

"If I find the right sting," he said, "I'll use it."

"Do you want a drink?" I said.

"Since you ask, yes."

We sat and drank in unchanged companionship.

WHEN CHARLES had gone home I wandered aimlessly round the flat, tie off and in shirtsleeves, trying to be sensible. I told myself that nothing much had happened, only that Trevor Deansgate had used a lot of horrible threats to get me to stop doing something that I hadn't yet started. But I couldn't dodge the guilt. Once he'd revealed himself I could have stopped him, and I hadn't.

Because I was afraid to.

Chico came back from his judo class and set to again to find out where I'd been; and I didn't tell him, even though I knew he couldn't despise me as much as I despised myself.

"All right," he said finally. "You just keep it all bottled up and see where it gets you. Anyway, you missed all the fun. Did you know that? Tri-Nitro got stuffed after all in the Guineas yesterday, and they're turning George Caspar's yard inside out. Our Rosemary, she wasn't bonkers after all, was she? How do you think it was done?"

"I don't know."

."I stayed in Newmarket on Friday night," he said. "Yeah, I know you sent the telegram about leaving, but I'd got a real little dolly lined up. One more night wasn't going to make any difference, and besides, she's George Caspar's typist. Into everything, she is, and talkative with it."

The new scared Sid Halley didn't even want to listen.

"There was a right old rumpus all day Wednesday in George Caspar's house," Chico said. "It started at breakfast when that Inky Poole turned up and said Sid Halley had been asking questions that he, Inky Poole, didn't like."

He paused for effect. I simply stared.

"Then Brothersmith the vet turned up and heard Inky Poole letting off, and he said funny, Sid Halley had been around him asking questions too. About bad hearts, he said. Same horses as Inky Poole was talking about. Bethesda, Gleaner and Zingaloo. And how was Tri-Nitro's heart, for good measure."

Trevor Deansgate, I thought coldly, had been at George Caspar's for breakfast, and had heard every word. That was when he had been put on to me.

"Of course," Chico said, "they checked the studs, Garvey's and Thrace's, and found you'd been there too. My dolly says your name is mud. George Caspar's real touchy about those horses."

I sat on the arm of the sofa and stared at the carpet.

"On Thursday," Chico said, "I had the morning off and went up to watch Tri-Nitro's last gallop." Chico had evidently paid little attention to my telegram. "Your photos came in very handy. Hundreds of ruddy horses . . . but there was Inky Poole, scowling like in the pictures, so I just zeroed in on him and hung about. There was a lot of fuss when it came to Tri-Nitro. They took the saddle off and put a little one on, and Inky Poole rode on that."

"It was Inky Poole, then, who rode Tri-Nitro, same as usual?"

"They looked just like your pictures," Chico said. "Can't swear to it more than that."

The doorbell rang with the long peal of a determined thumb. "We're out," I said; but Chico went and answered it.

Rosemary Caspar swept past him, through the hall and into the sitting room, advancing in the old fawn raincoat and a fulminating rage. "So there you are," she said. "Skulking out of sight. Your friend kept telling me when I telephoned that you weren't here, but I knew he was lying."

"I wasn't here," I said. As well try damming the St. Lawrence with a twig.

"You weren't where I paid you to be, which was up in New-market. And your ideas about changing the routine were useless. And I told you from the beginning that George wasn't to find out you were asking questions, and he did, and we've been having one God-awful bloody row ever since, and now Tri-Nitro has disgraced us unbearably and it's all your bloody fault."

Chico raised his eyebrows comically. "Sid didn't ride it . . . or train it."

She glared at him with transferred hatred. "And he didn't keep him safe, either." Then she swung round to me again. "I want my money back."

"Will a cheque do?" I said.

"You're not arguing, then? You admit that you failed?"

After a small pause, I said, "Yes."

"Oh." She sounded as if I had deprived her of a good deal of what she had come to say. While I wrote out a cheque, she started to tremble. The pain in her face was acute. So many hopes, so much work had gone into Tri-Nitro, such anxiety and such care. I understood what the lost race meant to George, and to Rosemary equally, because she cared so much.

"Rosemary . . ." I said, in useless sympathy.

"It's pointless Brothersmith saying Tri-Nitro must have had a viral infection," she said. "He's always saying things like that. And it was his job anyway to check Tri-Nitro and he did, over and over, and there was nothing wrong with him. He went down to the post looking beautiful, and then in the race . . ." There was a glitter of tears for a moment, but she visibly willed them from overwhelming her.

"They've done dope tests, I suppose?" Chico said.

It angered her again. "Dope tests! Of course they have. What do you expect? Blood tests, urine tests, saliva tests, dozens of bloody tests. But it will be like before . . . absolutely nothing."

I gave her the cheque, and she glanced at it blindly. "I wish I'd never come here in the first place," she said. "I don't want to talk to you again. Don't talk to me at the races, do you understand?"

I nodded. I did understand. She turned abruptly to go away. "And for God's sake don't speak to George, either." She went alone out of the room, and out of the flat, and slammed the door.

Chico clicked his tongue, and shrugged. "You can't win them

457

all," he said. "What could you do that her husband couldn't, not to mention his private police force and half a dozen guard dogs?" He was excusing me, and we both knew it.

"I don't know that I'm going on with it," I said. "This sort of job."

"You can't give it up," he protested. "You're too good at it. Look at all the awful messes you've put right. Just because of one that's gone wrong . . . ."

I got up and went into the bedroom. Shut the door. Went purposelessly to the window and looked out at the roofs and chimney-pots, glistening in the beginnings of rain. The pots were still there, though the chimneys underneath were blocked off and the fires long dead. I felt at one with the chimney pots. When fires went out, one froze.

The door opened. "Sid," Chico said. "You've got another visitor."

"Tell him to go away."

"It's a girl. Louise somebody."

I rubbed my hand over my face and head and down to the back of my neck. Eased the muscles. Turned from the window.

"Louise McInnes," I said. "She shares the flat with Jenny."

"Oh, that one. Well then, Sid, if that's all for today I'll be off. And . . . er . . . be here tomorrow, won't you?"

"Yeah."

He nodded. We left everything else unsaid. The amusement, mockery, friendship and stifled anxiety were all there in his face. Maybe he read the same in mine. At any rate he gave me a widening grin as he departed, and I went into the sitting room thinking that some debts couldn't be paid.

Louise was standing in the middle of things, looking around her in the way that I had, in Jenny's flat. Through her eyes I saw my own room afresh: its irregular shape, high-ceilinged, not modern; and the tan leather sofa, the shelves with books, the prints framed and hung, and on the floor, leaning against the wall, the big painting of racing horses which I'd somehow never bothered to hang up. There were coffee cups and glasses scattered about, and piles of letters everywhere.

Louise herself wore a brown velvet jacket, a blazing white sweater, a soft mottled brown skirt with a wide leather belt.

Shining fair hair, and rose-petal make-up on the English-rose skin.

"Mr. Halley."

"You could try Sid," I said. "You know me quite well, by proxy."

Her smile reached halfway. "Sid."

"Louise."

"Jenny says Sid is a plumber's mate's sort of name."

I smiled. "Very good people, plumbers' mates."

She came into the kitchen and watched me make tea and made no funny remarks about bionic hands, which was a nice change from most new acquaintances. When the tea was ready I carried the tray into the sitting room and put it on top of the letters on the coffee table. "Sit down," I said, and we sat.

"All these," I said, nodding to them, "are the letters which came with the cheques for the wax."

She looked doubtful. "Are they of any use?"

"I hope so," I said, and explained about the mailing list.

"Good Heavens." She hesitated. "Well, perhaps you won't need what I brought." She picked up her brown leather handbag, opened it, and pulled out a paperback book. She could have posted it, I thought; but I was quite glad that she hadn't.

"I was trying to put a bit of order into the chaos in my bedroom," she said. "I've a lot of books. They tend to pile up. Well, this was among them. It was Nicky's."

She gave me the paperback. I glanced at the cover and put it down, in order to pour out the tea. *Navigation for Beginners*. I handed her the cup. "Was he interested in navigation?"

"I've no idea. But I was. I borrowed it out of his room. I don't think he even knew I'd taken it. He wouldn't have minded, he was terribly easy going. Anyway, I put it down in my room, and put something else on top, and just forgot it."

I picked up the book again and opened it. On the flyleaf someone had written "John Viking", a firm legible signature in black felt-tip. I flicked through the pages. It was, as it promised to be, a book about navigation, sea and air, with line drawings and diagrams. Nothing of note except one line of letters and figures, written with the same black ink, on the inside of the back cover.

$$\text{Lift} = 22.024 \text{ x V x P x} \left(\frac{1}{T1} - \frac{1}{T2} \right)$$

I handed it to Louise. "Does this mean anything to you? Jenny said you've a degree in mathematics."

She frowned at it. "Nicky needed a calculator for two plus two."

He had done all right at two plus ten thousand, I thought.

"Um," she said. "Lift equals 22.024 times volume times pressure, times . . . . . It has to do with temperature change. Not my subject, really. This is physics." She concentrated. A fast brain, I thought, under the pretty hair. Finally, she said, "It just possibly refers to how much you can lift with a gas-bag." She relaxed into the armchair, handing back the book. "I don't suppose it will help," she said. "But you seemed to want anything of Nicky's."

"It might help a lot. It's John Viking's book. John Viking might know Nicky Ashe."

"But . . . you don't know John Viking."

"No," I said. "But he knows gas-bags. And I know someone who knows gas-bags. And I bet gas-bags are a small world, like racing."

She looked at the heaps of letters, and then at the book. She said slowly, "I guess you'll find him, one way or another. Jenny says you never give up."

I smiled faintly. "Her exact words?"

"No." I felt her amusement. "Obstinate, selfish, and determined to get his own way."

"Not far off." I tapped the book. "Can I keep this?"

"Of course."

We looked at each other as people do, especially if they're youngish, and male and female, and sitting in a quiet flat at the end of a spring day.

She read my expression and answered the unspoken thought. "Some other time," she said dryly. "I'm on my way to visit my aunt."

She stood up, then, and I also, after her.

"I hope," I said, "that you're fond of your aunt?"

"Devoted." She gave me a cool smile. "Goodbye, Sid."

"Goodbye, Louise."

WHEN SHE'D gone I poured a whisky and switched on a tablelight against the slow dusk. No one else would come, I thought. They had all in their way held off the shadows, particularly Louise. No one else real would come, but he would be with me, as he'd been in Paris . . . . Trevor Deansgate. Inescapable. Reminding me inexorably of what I would rather forget.

Humiliation and rejection and helplessness and failure . . . .

 **7**

Next morning, after stacking cups in the dishwasher, I telephoned my man in gas-bags, read out the equation, and asked if it meant anything to him. He laughed and said it sounded like a formula for taking a hot-air balloon to the moon.

"Thanks very much," I said sarcastically.

"No, seriously, Sid. It's a calculation for maximum height. Balloonists are always after records . . . the highest, the farthest, that sort of thing."

I asked if he had ever heard of anyone called John Viking, and he said of course, everyone in ballooning knew John Viking. He was a madman of the first order.

Madman?

John Viking, he explained, took risks which no sensible balloonist would dream of. If I wanted to talk to him, the voice said, I would undoubtedly find him at the balloon race next Sunday at Highalane Park in Wiltshire.

I thanked him for his help and rang off. Suddenly I remembered that today was the May Day holiday. National holidays had always been work days for me, as for everyone in racing; providing the entertainment for the public's leisure. I tended not to notice them come and go.

Around lunchtime Chico arrived with fish and chips for two in the sort of hygienic greaseproof wrappings which kept the steam in and made the chips go soggy.

"Did you know it's the May Day holiday today?" I said.

"I'm here, aren't I? Let out from the little bleeders?"

He tipped the lunch onto two plates, and we ate it, mostly with fingers. "You've come to life again, I see," he said.

"It's temporary."

"We'd better do some work then, while you're still with us."

"Nicholas Ashe," I said.

461

Chico shook salt on his chips. "We're not getting paid for this, didn't you say?"

"Not directly."

He shrugged. "You're the boss. But that makes two in a row, counting Rosemary getting her cash back, that we've worked on for nothing."

"We'll make up for it later."

"You're going on in this line of country, then?"

I didn't answer at once. Apart from not knowing whether I wanted to, I didn't know if I could.

"Sid!" Chico said sharply. "Come back."

I swallowed. "Well . . . er . . . we'll do my wife's little business. Then we'll see."

CHICO AND I spent the rest of the day separately traipsing around all the London addresses on the "M" list of wax names, and met at six o'clock, footsore and thirsty, at a pub we knew in Fulham.

"We never ought to have done it on a bank holiday," Chico said. "More than half of them were out."

We carried his beer and my whisky over to a small table, drank deeply, and compared notes. Chico had finally pinned down four people, and I only two, but the results were there, all the same.

All six, whatever other mailing lists they had confessed to, had been in regular happy receipt of *Antiques for All.*

"That's it, then," Chico said. "Conclusive." He looked at his watch and swallowed the rest of the beer. "So long, Sid, boy."

"Can't you stay?"

"Have a heart. The girl in Wembley." He grinned and departed.

I more slowly finished my drink and went home, where I pottered about restlessly, sorely missing the peace that usually filled me there. I tried to watch the television. Couldn't concentrate. Switched it off. Ate some cornflakes. Changed the batteries.

At around eight I gave up trying to settle down, got into the car, and drove to Aynsford. If Jenny was there, I thought, I would just turn right round and go back to London, and at least the driving would have occupied the time. But there was no sign of her as I eased up the drive and walked quietly into the house.

Charles was in the small sitting room he called the wardroom, sitting alone, sorting through his much-loved collection of fishing flies. He looked up. No surprise. No effusive welcome. No fuss. Yet I'd never gone there before without invitation.

"I wanted some company," I said.

He squinted at a dry fly. "Did you bring an overnight bag?"

I nodded.

He pointed to the drinks tray. "Help yourself. And pour me some brandy, will you?"

I fetched him his drink, and my own, and sat in an armchair.

"Come to tell me?" he said.

"No."

He smiled. "Chess, then?"

We played two games. He won the first, easily, and told me to pay attention. The second was a draw. "That's better," he said.

The peace I hadn't been able to find on my own came slowly back with Charles, even though I knew it had more to do with the ease I felt with him personally, and the timelessness of his vast old house, than with a real resolution of the destruction within. In any case, for the first time in days, I slept soundly for hours, and didn't wake till nearly nine.

At breakfast I told him about John Viking and *Antiques for All*, and he smiled with his own familiar mixture of satisfaction and amusement, as if I were some creation of his that was coming up to expectations. It was he who had originally driven me to becoming an investigator. Whenever I got anything right, he took the credit for it himself.

He glanced at me sideways. "Jenny's here," he said. "Turned up an hour ago."

Just then Jenny marched belligerently into the dining room and sat down. "I don't like you coming here so much," she said.

A knife to the heart of things from my pretty wife.

Charles said smoothly, "Sid is welcome here always."

"Discarded husbands should have more pride than to fawn on their fathers-in-law."

"You're jealous," I said, surprised.

She stood up fast, as angry as I'd ever seen her.

"How dare you!" she said. "He always takes your side. He thinks you're bloody marvellous. He doesn't know you like I do, all your stubbornness and your meanness."

"I'm going back to London," I said.

"And you're a coward as well," she said furiously. "Running away from a few straight truths. I . . . I hate you, Sid."

I went upstairs to fetch my overnight case, to the bedroom I thought of as mine: the one I always slept in nowadays at Aynsford.

You don't have to hate me, Jenny, I thought miserably: I hate myself. And made up my mind, suddenly, once and for all, to do something about it. After all these years I would *not*, I thought, I would damn well *not* be defeated by fear.

CHARLES WENT out with me to the Scimitar. I asked him if he'd follow up on the wax polish firm, and he said he'd be glad to.

"Sid," he said, as I got into the car. "Don't pay any attention to Jenny. Come to Aynsford whenever you want. I mean it."

I nodded.

"Damn Jenny," he said explosively.

"Oh, no. She's unhappy. She . . ." I paused. "I guess she needs comforting. A shoulder to cry on, and all that."

He said austerely, "I don't care for tears."

"No." I sighed, and waved goodbye, and drove down the drive. The help that Jenny needed, she wouldn't take from me; and her father didn't know how to give it. Just another of life's bloody muddles. But at least my own mess was something I could deal with.

I thought about it on the way back to town. I knew now which hurt the worst, not amputation from without, but amputation from within. Somewhere on the North Circular I stopped the Scimitar, got out my briefcase and wrote a letter. I addressed the envelope, stamped it, and pushed it into the next box I came to.

Then knowing I had planted a landmine and would presently step on it, I drove on into the city and round in a few small circles and ended up in the publishing offices of *Antiques for All*, which proved to be only one of a number of specialist magazines put out by a newspaper company. To the *Antiques* editor, a fair-haired, earnest young man in heavy-framed specs, I explained both the position and the needs.

"Our mailing list?" he said doubtfully. "Mailing lists are strictly private, you know."

464

I explained all over again, and threw in a lot of pathos. My wife behind bars if I didn't find the con man, that sort of thing. I finally persuaded him to give me part of the list: P to T.

I waited patiently for a computer print-out, and received in the end a stack of paper setting out several thousand names and addresses, give or take a few dead ones.

"We must have it back," he said severely. "Unmarked and complete."

"How did Nicholas Ashe get hold of it?" I asked.

He didn't know, and neither the name nor the description of Ashe brought any glimmer of recognition.

Back in the car, I telephoned Chico and got him to come to the flat. His May Day holiday had been extended, it seemed. He was there when I pulled up at a vacant parking meter and we went upstairs together. The flat was empty and quiet.

"A lot of leg work, my son," I said, taking out the mailing list and putting it on the table. "We'll go halves. Meet me back here on Thursday morning, ten o'clock. OK?"

He eyed his half unenthusiastically. "Suppose our Nicky hasn't got himself organized yet, and sends out his begging letters next week, after we've drawn a blank?"

"Mm . . . . Better take some sticky labels with this address on, and ask them to send the letters here, if they get them."

"May as well get started, then." He picked up his part of the mailing list, and looked ready to leave.

"Don't lose that," I said. "Or the editor of *Antiques* will be cross."

I TRUDGED around all that day and the next, visiting the people on the mailing list, but no one had received a begging letter from Ashe within the last month. Thursday morning, as arranged, Chico came by. He'd drawn a blank, too.

"Tell you what, though," he said. "I left sticky labels everywhere with your address on, and some of them said they'd let us know, if it came. But whether they'll bother . . ."

"It would only take one," I said. I'd done the same.

"That's true." He shrugged. "Anyway, that's me for today," he said. "I got the judo this afternoon, don't forget."

"The little bleeders," I said, "are welcome."

CHARLES CAME at twelve, sniffing the air of the unfamiliar restaurant like an unsettled dog. "I got your message," he said. "But why here? Why not the Cavendish, as usual?"

"There's someone I don't want to meet," I said. "He won't look for me here." By rights my letter couldn't have borne fruit yet. But where Trevor Deansgate was concerned, I wasn't taking any chances. "Pink gin?"

"A double."

I ordered the drinks. He said, "Is that what it was, for those ten days? Evasive action?"

I didn't reply.

He lit a cigar, sucking in smoke and eyeing me through the flame of the match. "I see it still hurts you, whatever it was."

"Leave it, Charles." I sighed. "How did you get on with the wax?"

He waited until after the drinks had come to tell me. "The wax is made," he said finally, "in a sort of cottage industry flourishing next to a plant which processes honey."

"Beeswax!" I said incredulously.

He nodded. "Beeswax, paraffin wax, and turpentine, that's what's in that polish." He smoked luxuriously, taking his time. "A charming woman there was most obliging. We spent a long while going back over the order books. People seldom ordered as much as Jenny had done, and very few stipulated that the tins should be left unlabelled." His eyes gleamed over the cigar. "Three people, all in the last year, to be exact."

"Do you think it was Nicholas Ashe, three times?"

"Always about the same amount," he said, enjoying himself. "Different names and addresses, of course." He pulled a folded paper out of an inner pocket. "There they are."

I looked at it. "No orders within the last few weeks, I see."

"Give him time," Charles said. "There was a policeman there on the same errand. He came just after I'd written out those names. It seems they really are looking for Ashe, themselves."

"Good. Er . . . did you tell them about the mailing list?"

"No, I didn't." He looked at his glass. "I would like it to be you who finds him first."

"Hm." I thought about that. "If you think Jenny will be grateful you'll be disappointed."

"But you'll have got her off the hook."

"She would prefer it to be the police."

She might even be nicer to me, I thought, if she was sure I had failed: and it wasn't the sort of niceness I would want.

 8

On Friday afternoon, depressed on many counts, I set out for my stay with Martin England at Newmarket. Still no response to my letter. Which might be a good sign. But then again, it mightn't. The day was hot, the weather reportedly stoking up to the sort of intense heatwave one could get in May. I drove in shirtsleeves with the window open.

Martin England was out in his stable yard when I got there, also in shirtsleeves and wiping his forehead with a handkerchief. He hadn't forgotten his invitation.

"Sid!" he said, seeming truly pleased. "Great. I'm just starting evening stables. You couldn't have timed it better."

We walked round the boxes together in the usual ritual, the trainer visiting every horse and checking its health, the guest admiring and complimenting and keeping his tongue off the flaws. Martin's horses were middling to good, like himself, like the majority of trainers: the sort that provided the bulk of all racing, and of all jockeys' incomes.

"A long time since you rode for me," he said, catching my thought. "What do you weigh now, Sid?"

"About ten stone, stripped." Thinner, in fact, than when I'd stopped racing.

We went from the fillies' side of the yard to the colts. He had a good lot of two-year-olds, it seemed to me, and he was pleased when I said so.

"This is Flotilla," he said, going to the next box. "He's three. He runs in the Dante at York next Wednesday, and if that's OK he'll go for the Derby."

"He looks well," I said. "Should do you proud."

He nodded with the normal hint of anxiety showing under the pride, and we continued down the line, patting and discussing, and feeling content. Perhaps this was what I needed, I thought,

467

forty horses and a hard routine: a businessman on horseback.

It would be no public disgrace if I gave up investigating and decided to train. A much more normal life for an ex-jockey, everyone would think. A sensible, orderly decision, looking forward to middle and old age. I alone . . . and Trevor Deansgate . . . would know why I'd done it. I could live for a long time, knowing it. I didn't want to. And the letter, if it worked, wouldn't let me.

IN THE MORNING at seven thirty I went down to the yard in jodhpurs, boots, a pull-on jersey shirt and a borrowed helmet. Early as it was, the air was warm. Martin, standing with a list in his hand, shouted good morning, and I went over to see what he'd given me to ride. There was a five-year-old, up to my weight, that he'd think just the job.

Flotilla's lad was leading him out of his box, and I watched him admiringly as I turned towards Martin.

"Go on, then," he said. There was amusement in his face, enjoyment in his eyes. "Ride Flotilla."

"What?" I said, totally surprised. His best horse, his Derby hope, and I out of practice and with one hand.

"Don't you want to?" he said. "My jockey's gone to Ireland to race at The Curragh. It's either you or one of my lads, and to be honest, I'd rather have you."

I didn't argue. One doesn't turn down a chunk of heaven. He gave me a leg-up, and I pulled the stirrup leathers to my own length, and felt like an exile coming home.

"What about a whip?" he asked.

In the old days I'd always carried one automatically, because a jockey's whip was a great aid to keeping a horse balanced and running straight: a tap down the shoulder did the trick, and one pulled the stick through from hand to hand, as required. I looked at the two hands in front of me. If I took a whip I might drop it: and I needed above all to be efficient.

I shook my head. "Not today."

With me in its midst the string pulled out of the yard and went through Newmarket along the back roads, out to the wide, sweeping Limekilns gallops to the north. Martin, riding the quiet five-year-old, pulled up there beside me.

"Give him a warm-up canter for three furlongs, and then take

468

him a mile up the trial ground, upsides with Gulliver. It's
Flotilla's last work-out before the Dante, so make it a good one."

"OK," I said.

He rode away towards a vantage point more than half a mile
distant. I wound the left-hand rein round my plastic fingers and
longed to be able to feel the pull from the horse's mouth. It would
upset the lie of the bit and the balance of the horse if I got the
tension wrong. In my right hand, the reins felt alive, carrying
messages, telling Flotilla, and Flotilla telling me, where we were
going, and how, and how fast. A private language, shared,
understood.

Let me not make a mess of it, I thought. Just let the old skill be
there, one hand or no. I could lose him the Dante and the Derby
and any other race you cared to mention, if I got it really wrong.

The boy on Gulliver circled with me, waiting for the moment to
start, answering my casual remarks in monosyllables and grunts. I
wondered if he was the one who would have ridden Flotilla if I
hadn't been there, and asked him, and he said, grumpily, yes. Too
bad, I thought. Your turn will come.

Up the gallop, Martin waved. The boy on Gulliver kicked his
mount into a fast pace at once, not waiting to start evenly
together. To hell with your tantrums, I thought. You do what you
like, but I'm going to take Flotilla along at the right speeds.

It was absolutely great, going up there. It suddenly came right,
as natural as if there had been no interval, and no missing limb.
I threaded the left rein through bad and good hands alike and felt
the vibrations from both sides of the bit, and if it wasn't the most
perfect style ever seen on the heath, it at least got the job done.

Flotilla swept over the turf in a balanced working gallop and
came upsides with Gulliver effortlessly. I stayed beside the other
horse then for most of the way, but as Flotilla was easily the
better, I took him on from six furlongs and finished the mile at a
good pace that was still short of strain. He was fit, I thought, pulling him back to a canter. He'd do well in the Dante.

I said so to Martin, when I rejoined him, walking back. He was
pleased, and laughed. "You can still ride, can't you? You looked
just the same."

I sighed internally. I had been let back for a brief moment into
the life I'd lost, but I wasn't just the same. I might have managed

one working gallop without making an ass of myself, but it wasn't the Gold Cup at Cheltenham.

We walked back through the town to his stable, and after breakfast, we sat in his office and drank coffee and talked for a bit.

The telephone rang. Martin answered it, and held out the receiver to me. "It's for you, Sid."

I thought it would be Chico, but it wasn't. It was Henry Thrace, calling from his stud farm just outside the town.

"Rumour had it that you were riding work on the heath this weekend for Martin England," he said. "So I rang on the off-chance."

"What can I do for you?" I said, my mouth as dry as vinegar.

"It's your letter," he said. "Asking me to let you know at once if Gleaner or Zingaloo died, and not to get rid of the carcass."

I closed my eyes.

"Gleaner has, in fact, just died," he said.

"When?" I asked. My heart rate had gone up to at least double. And fear stabbed through me like toothache.

"This morning. An hour ago, maybe," he said. "A mare he was due to cover came into use, so we put him to her. He was sweating a lot. It's hot in the breeding shed, with the sun on it. Anyway, he served her, and got down all right, and then he just staggered and fell, and died almost at once. I left him in the breeding shed. We're not using it again this morning."

I took a shaky breath. "A post mortem, wouldn't you agree?"

"Essential, I'd say. Insurance, and all that."

"I'll try and get Ken Armadale," I said. "From the Equine Research Establishment. I know him . . . . Would he do you?"

"Couldn't be better," he said, and disconnected.

I stood with Martin's telephone in my hand and looked into far, dark spaces. It's too soon, I thought. Much too soon. Then I rang Ken Armadale who agreed to do the autopsy. My hand, I saw remotely, was actually shaking.

I thanked Martin for his tremendous hospitality. Put my suitcase and myself in the car, and picked up Ken Armadale from his large modern house on the southern edge of Newmarket.

"What am I looking for?" he said.

"Heart, I think."

He nodded. He was a strong, dark-haired research vet in his

middle thirties, a man I'd dealt with on similar jaunts before, to the extent that I felt easy with him and trusted him, and as far I could tell he felt the same about me.

"Anything special?" he said.

"Let's see what you find."

Gleaner, I thought. If there were three horses I should definitely be doing nothing about, they were Gleaner and Zingaloo and Tri-Nitro. Not if I had any sense, that is.

But sense had nothing to do with it.

I drove into Henry Thrace's stud farm and pulled up with a jerk. He came out of his house to meet us, and we walked across to the breeding shed. The day, which was hot outside, was very much hotter inside. The dead horse lay where he had fallen on the tan-covered floor, a sad brown lump with milky grey eyes.

"I rang the knackers," Ken said. "They'll be here pretty soon."

Henry Thrace nodded. It was impossible to do the post mortem where the horse lay, as the smell of blood would linger for days and upset any other horse that came in there. We waited until the lorry arrived with its winch, and when the horse was loaded, we followed the lorry to the knackers' yard. It was a small hygienic place: very clean.

Ken Armadale opened the bag he had brought and handed me a washable nylon boiler suit, like his own, to cover trousers and shirt.

The horse lay in a square room with whitewashed walls and a concrete floor. In the floor, runnels and a drain. Ken turned on a tap so that water ran out of the hose beside the horse, and pulled on a pair of long rubber gloves.

"All set?" he said.

I nodded, and he made the first long incision. When the chest cavity had been opened he removed the whole heart-lung mass and carried it over to a table under the single window.

"This is odd," he said, after a pause. "Take a look."

I went over beside him and looked where he was pointing, but I hadn't his knowledge behind my eyes, and all I saw was a lump of tissue with tough-looking ridges of gristle in it.

"His heart?" I said.

"That's right. Look at these valves . . ." He turned his head to me, frowning. "He died of something horses don't get."

"There's another horse at Henry Thrace's that may have the same thing," I said.

He straightened up and stared at me. "Sid," he said. "You'd better tell me what's up. And outside, don't you think, in some fresh air."

We went out, and he stood listening, while I tried to speak with flat lack of emotion.

"There are . . . or were . . . four of them," I said. "They were all top star horses, favourites for the Guineas and the Derby. They all came from the same stable. They all went out to race in Guineas week looking marvellous. They all started hot favourites, and they all totally flopped. At least three of them suffered from a mild virus infection at about that time, but it didn't develop. They all were subsequently found to have heart murmurs."

Ken frowned heavily. "Go on."

"There was Bethesda, who ran in the One Thousand Guineas two years ago. She went to stud, and she died of heart failure this spring, while she was foaling."

Ken took a deep breath.

"There's this one," I said, pointing. "Gleaner. He was favourite for the Guineas last year. He then got a really bad heart, and also arthritis. The other horse at Henry Thrace's, Zingaloo, went out fit to a race and afterwards could hardly stand."

Ken nodded. "And which is the fourth one?"

I looked up at the sky. Blue and clear. I'm killing myself, I thought. I looked back at him and said, "Tri-Nitro."

"Sid!" He was shocked. "Only a week ago."

"So what is it?" I said. "What's the matter with them?"

"I'd have to do some tests, to be certain," he said. "But the symptoms you've described are typical, and those heart valves are unmistakable. That horse died from swine erysipelas, which is a disease you get only in pigs."

"I see," I said. Dear God, I thought, as we went back indoors.

Ken said, "We need to keep that heart for evidence. Get one of those bags, will you?" He put the heart inside, and we peeled off our overalls. "Heat and exertion," he said. "That's what did for this fellow. A deadly combination, with a heart in that state. He might have lived for years, otherwise."

He packed everything away, and we went back to Henry

Thrace. We told him we needed to do some tests, accepted reviving Scotches with gratitude, and afterwards took our trophy to the Equine Research Establishment along the Bury Road.

Ken's office was a small extension to a large laboratory, where he took the bag containing Gleaner's heart over to the sink and told me he was washing out the remaining blood.

"Now come and look," he said.

This time I could see exactly what he meant. Along all the edges of the valves there were small knobbly growths, like baby cauliflowers, creamy white.

"That's vegetation," he said. "It prevents the valves from closing. Makes the heart as efficient as a leaking pump."

Later I sat on a hard chair in his utilitarian office while he searched through his veterinary journals for a paper he had on erysipelas. I looked at my fingers. Curled and uncurled them. This can't be happening, I thought. That barn, Trevor Deansgate. *If you break your assurance, I'll blow your right hand off.*

"Here it is," Ken exclaimed, flattening a journal open. "I'll read you the relevant bits. Swine erysipelas—During 1944 a mutant strain of erysipelas rhusiopathiae appeared suddenly in a laboratory specializing in antisera production and produced acute endocarditis in the serum horses."

"Translate," I said.

He smiled. "They used to use horses for producing vaccines. You inject the horse with pig disease, then wait until it develops antibodies, draw off blood, and extract the serum. The serum, injected into healthy pigs, prevents them getting the disease. Same process as for human vaccinations, smallpox and so on. Standard procedure. But in this case instead of growing antibodies as usual, the horses themselves got the disease."

"How could that happen?"

"It doesn't say, here. You'd have to ask the pharmaceutical firm concerned—the Tierson vaccine lab in Cambridge. I know someone there, if you want an introduction. A Mr. Livingston. He looks a dried-up old cuss, but he's got a mind as sharp as a razor."

"It's a long time ago," I said.

"My dear fellow, germs don't die. They can live like timebombs waiting for some fool to take liberties. Some of these labs keep virulent strains around for decades. You'd be surprised."

He looked down again at the paper, and said, "You'd better read these next paragraphs yourself. They look pretty straightforward." He pushed the journal across to me, and I read the page where he pointed.

(1) 24–48 hours after intra-muscular injection of the pure culture, inflammation of one or more of the heart valves commences. At this time, apart from a slight rise in temperature, there are no other symptoms unless the horse is subject to exertion, which would occasion severe distress.

(2) Between the second and the sixth day pyrexia (temperature rise) increases and white cell count of the blood increases and the horse is listless and off food. This could easily be loosely diagnosed as "the virus". However, examination by stethoscope reveals a progressively increasing heart murmur. After about ten days the temperature returns to normal and, unless subjected to more than walk or trot, the horse may appear to have recovered.

(3) Over the next few months vegetations grow on the heart valves, and arthritis may or may not appear. The condition is permanent and progressive and death may occur suddenly following exertion or during very hot weather, sometimes years after the original infection.

I looked up. "That's it, exactly." Then I said slowly, "Intramuscular injection of the culture could not occur accidentally."

"Absolutely not," he agreed.

I said, "George Caspar had his yard sewn up so tight this year that no one could have got within screaming distance of Tri-Nitro with a syringeful of live germs."

He smiled. "You wouldn't need a syringeful. Here, I'll show you." He went into the lab and fetched a box, which proved to contain a large number of smallish plastic envelopes. He tore open one of the envelopes and tipped the contents onto his hand: a hypodermic needle attached to a plastic capsule, only the size of a pea. The whole thing looked like a tiny dart with a small, round balloon at one end, about as long, altogether, as one's little finger.

He picked up the capsule and squeezed it. "Dip that into liquid and you draw up half a teaspoonful. You don't need that much pure culture to produce a disease."

"You could hold that in your hand, out of sight," I said.

He nodded. "I use these for horses that shy away from a syringe." He showed me how, holding the capsule between thumb and index finger, so that the sharp end pointed down from his palm. "Shove the needle in and squeeze," he said. "Done in a flash."

"Could you spare one?" I asked, and he gave me an envelope. I put it in my pocket. Dear God in heaven.

Ken said slowly, "You know, we might just be able to find an anti-biotic which would cure Tri-Nitro."

"Isn't it too late?" I said.

"Too late for Zingaloo. But I don't think those vegetations would start growing at once. If Tri-Nitro was infected . . . say . . ."

"Say ten days ago, after his final working gallop."

He looked at me with amusement. "Then his heart will be in trouble, but the vegetation won't have started. If he gets the right antibiotic soon, he might make a full recovery."

"What are you waiting for?" I said.

 9

The next day was Sunday. The day of the balloon race.

Highalane Park was a stately home coming to terms with the plastic age. The house itself opened to the public only half a dozen times a year, but the parkland was always out for rent for game fairs, circuses and horse shows. The numbers pouring onto the showground were impressive. I paid at the gate in my turn and bumped over some grass to park the car in the roped-off area.

There were a few people on horses cantering busily about in haphazard directions, but there was no sight of any balloons. I got out of the car and locked the door, and thought that two o'clock was probably too early for much in the way of action.

One can be so wrong.

A voice behind me said, "There he is."

I turned and found two men advancing into the small space between my car and the one next to it: large unsmiling men from a muscular brotherhood. Brass knuckles and toecaps.

If you sneezed on the Limekilns, they said in Newmarket, it was heard two miles away on the racecourse. The news of my attend-ance at Gleaner's post mortem must have spread like wildfire.

Even so, it had taken Trevor Deansgate a surprisingly short time to wheel out the heavies. They must have been waiting outside the flat and followed me here.

I ran.

They weren't going to catch me on the open showground, that was for sure, and when I went back to my car it would be with a load of protectors. Maybe, I thought desperately, they would see it was useless, and just go away.

I reached the outskirts of the show-jumping arena, and looked back from over the head of a small girl sucking an ice-cream cornet. The heavies were still doggedly in pursuit. So I went on, deeper into the show, circling the ring. The arena itself was on my left, with show-jumping in progress inside, and ringside cars encircling it outside. On my right, the stalls one always gets at horse shows. Tented shops selling saddlery, riding clothes, pictures, toys, hot dogs. Among the tents, the vans: ice-cream vans, a crafts display, a fortune-teller, a charity jumble shop, and a mobile cinema. Crowds in front of all of them and no depth of shelter inside.

"Do you know where the balloon race is?" I asked someone.

"In the next field, I think, but it isn't time yet."

"Thanks," I said. The posters had announced a three-o'clock start, but I'd have to talk to John Viking well before that, while he was willing to listen.

My pursuers wouldn't give up. They weren't running, nor was I. They just followed me steadily, as if locked onto a target by a radio beam. I'd have to get lost, I thought, and stay lost until I found John Viking.

I was on the far side of the arena by that time, crossing the collecting-ring area with children on ponies, looking strained as they went in to jump, and tearful or triumphant as they came out.

Past them, past the commentator's box, past the little private grandstand for the bigwigs, past a refreshment tent, and so back to the stalls. I dodged in and out of those, ducking under guy ropes and round dumps of cardboard boxes. From inside a stall hung thickly with riding jackets I watched the two of them go past, hurrying, looking about them, distinctly anxious.

They weren't like the two Trevor Deansgate had been with last time, I thought. Those had been clumsier, smaller, and less professional. These two looked as if this sort of work was their daily bread;

and for all the comparative safety of the showground, where as a last resort I could get into the arena itself and scream for help, there was something daunting about them. Rent-a-thugs usually came at so much per hour. These two looked salaried, if not on the board.

I looked at my watch. After two thirty. Too much time was passing. I had to find my way to the balloons. I slithered out of the stall and into the crowd, asking for directions.

"Up at the end, mate," a decisive man told me, pointing. "Past the hot dogs, turn right, there's a gate in the fence."

I nodded my thanks and turned to go that way, and saw one of my pursuers coming towards me, searching the stalls.

In a second he would see me . . . . I looked around in a hurry and found I was outside the caravan of the fortune-teller. There was a curtain of plastic streamers, black and white, over the open doorway. I took four quick strides, brushed through the plastic strips, and stepped up into the van.

It was quieter inside, and darker, with daylight filtering dimly through lace-hung windows. A Victorian sort of décor: mock oil lamps and chenille tablecloths. Outside, the tracker went past, giving the fortune-teller no more than a flickering glance.

"Do you want your whole life, dear?" said the fortune-teller. "Or just the future?"

"Er . . ." I said. "I don't really know. How long does it take?"

"A quarter of an hour, dear, for the whole thing."

"Let's just have the future."

I looked out of the window. Two strange men in my future were searching among the ringside cars, asking questions and getting a lot of shaken heads.

"Sit on the sofa beside me, dear, and give me your left hand."

"It'll have to be the right," I said absently.

"No, dear," her voice was quite sharp. "Always the left."

Amused, I sat down and gave her the left. She felt it, and looked at it, and raised her eyes to mine. She was short and plump, dark-haired, middle-aged, and in no way remarkable.

"Well, dear," she said after a pause. "It will have to be the right, though we may not get such good results."

"I'll risk it," I said; so we changed places on the sofa, and she held my right hand firmly in her two warm ones, and I watched one of the heavies moving along the row of cars.

"You have suffered," she said.

As she knew about my left hand, I didn't think much of that for a guess, and she seemed to sense it. She coughed apologetically, and looked down again at my hand.

"You are a kind person," she said. "Gentle. People like you. People smile at you wherever you go."

Outside, the two men, twenty yards away, had met to consult. Not a smile there, of any sort.

"You are respected by everyone."

Regulation stuff, I thought, designed to please the customers. Chico should hear it. Gentle, kind, respected . . . he'd laugh his head off.

She said doubtfully, "I see a great many people, cheering you, clapping and shouting. Does that mean anything to you, dear?"

Her dark eyes watched me calmly. I didn't believe it. I didn't believe in fortune-tellers. I wondered if she had seen me before, on a racecourse or talking on television. She must have.

"That's the past," I said.

She bent her head again over my hand. "You have good health, and physical stamina . . . . There is much to endure."

Her voice broke off, and she frowned. I had a strong impression that what she had said had surprised her.

After a pause, she said, "I can't tell you any more."

"Why not?"

"I'm not used to the right hand."

"Tell me what you see," I said.

She shook her head slightly. "You will live a long time."

I glanced out through the plastic curtain. The heavies had moved off out of sight.

"How much do I owe you?" I said. She told me, and I paid her, and went quickly over to the doorway.

"Take care, dear," she said. "Be careful."

I looked back. Her face was still calm, but her voice had been urgent. I didn't want to believe in the conviction that looked out of her eyes. She might have felt the disturbance of my immediate problem, but no more than that.

I pushed the curtain gently aside and stepped from the dim world of hovering horrors into the bright May sunlight, where they might in truth lie in wait.

478

THERE WAS no longer any need to ask where the balloons were. No one could miss them. They were beginning to grow like gaudy monstrous mushrooms on an enormous area of grassland beyond the actual showground. I had thought vaguely that there would be five or six balloons, but there must have been twenty.

Among a whole stream of people going the same way, I went down to the gate and through into the far field, and realized that I had absolutely underestimated the task of finding John Viking.

There was a rope, for a start, and marshals telling the crowd to stand behind it. I ducked those obstacles at least, but found myself in a forest of half-inflated balloons, which billowed immensely all around and cut off any length of sight.

The first clump of people I came to were busy with a pink and purple monster into whose mouth they were blowing air by means of a large, engine-driven fan. The balloon was attached by fine nylon ropes to the basket, which lay on its side, with a young man in a red crash helmet peering anxiously into its depths.

"Excuse me," I said. "Do you know where I can find John Viking?"

The red crash helmet raised itself to reveal a pair of very blue eyes. "That bloody idiot," he said. "He's here somewhere. Flies a Stormcloud balloon. Yellow and green. Now would you mind getting the hell out, we're busy."

I walked along the edge of things, trying to keep out of the way. Balloon races, it seemed, were a serious business and no occasion for questions. There were balloons advertising whisky, marmalade, towns, and major oil companies. Balloons in brilliant primary colours and pink and white pastels. I circled a soft, billowing black and white monster and went deeper into the maze of balloons, searching fruitlessly for a yellow and green one.

As if at a signal, there arose a chorus of deep-throated roars, caused by flames suddenly spurting from the large burners which were supported on frames above the baskets. The flames roared into the open mouths of the half-inflated balloons, heating and expanding the air already there and driving in more. The gleaming envelopes swelled and surged, the tops reaching slowly and magnificently towards the hazy blue sky.

As the balloons filled they began to heave off the ground and sway in great floating masses, bumping into each other. Under each balloon a bunch of helpers clung to the basket to prevent it escaping too soon.

With the balloons off the ground, I saw a yellow and green one quite easily. There was one man already in the basket, with three people holding it down. As I ran in his direction, there was the sound of a starter's pistol. All around me, the baskets were released, and began bumping over the ground; and a great cheer went up from the watching crowd.

I reached the cluster of people I was aiming for and put my hand on the basket. "John Viking?"

No one listened. They were deep in a quarrel. A girl in a crash helmet stood on the ground, with the helpers beside her looking glum and embarrassed.

"I'm not coming. You're a bloody madman."

"You must." He was very tall, very thin, very agitated. He made a grab at the girl and held her waist in a sinewy grip. It looked almost as if he were going to haul her into the basket, and she certainly believed it. She screamed at him, "Let go, John. I'm not coming."

"Are you John Viking?" I said loudly.

He swung his head and kept hold of the girl. "Yes. What do you want? I'm starting this race as soon as my passenger gets in."

"I'm not *going*," she screamed.

I looked around. Most of the baskets were airborne, rising in a smooth, glorious crowd. Every basket carried two people.

"If you want a passenger," I said, "I'll come."

He let go of the girl and looked me up and down.

"How much do you weigh?" And then, impatiently, as he saw the other balloons getting a head start, "Oh, all right, get in."

I gripped a stay, and jumped, and wriggled, and ended standing inside a rather small hamper under a very large balloon.

"Leave go," commanded the captain of the ship, and the helpers obeyed. The basket momentarily stayed exactly where it was. Then John Viking reached above his head and flipped a lever which operated the burners, and there at close quarters, right above our heads, was the flame and the ear-filling roar.

The girl's face was still on a level with mine. "He's mad," she yelled. "And you're crazy."

The basket moved away, bumped, and rose quite suddenly. The

girl ran after it and delivered a parting encouragement. "And you haven't got a crash helmet."

What I did have, though, was a marvellous escape route from two purposeful thugs.

John Viking was operating the burner almost non-stop. He was almost the last away. Suddenly he started cursing. I saw a belt of trees dead ahead. Our balloon seemed set on a collision course.

John Viking yelled at me over the roar of the burner, "Hold on bloody tight. If we hit the trees you don't want to spill out."

Our balloon rushed forward with the burner roaring over our heads like a demented dragon. The basket hit the tree tops, and tipped on its side. I grabbed right-handed at whatever I could to stop myself falling out, as the majestically-swelling envelope above us carried on with its journey regardless. It tugged at the basket, which crashed and bumped through the tops of the trees, flinging me about like a rag doll. My host, made of sterner stuff, had one arm clamped round one of the metal struts which supported the burner, and the other twined into a black rubber strap. His legs were braced against the side of the basket, which was now the floor, and he changed his footholds as necessary, at one point planting one foot firmly on my stomach.

With a last sickening jolt the basket tore itself free, and we swung to and fro under the balloon like a pendulum. I was by this manoeuvre wedged in a heap in the bottom of the basket, but John Viking still stood rather splendidly on his feet.

There really wasn't much room, I thought, disentangling myself and straightening upwards. The basket was only four feet square, and reached no higher than one's waist. Along two opposite sides stood eight gas cylinders, four each side, fastened to the wickerwork with rubber straps. The oblong space left was just big enough for two men to stand in.

John Viking gave the burner a rest at last, and into the sudden silence said forcefully, "Why didn't you hold on like I told you to? You damned nearly fell out, and got me into trouble."

"Sorry," I said, amused. "Is it usual to go on burning when you're stuck on a tree?"

"It got us clear, didn't it?" he demanded. He was about my age: perhaps a year or two younger. His face was craggy, with a bone structure that might one day give him distinction, and his

blue eyes shone with the brilliance of the true fanatic. John Viking the madman, I thought, and warmed to him.

"Do you have to finish first, to win a balloon race?" I said.

He looked surprised. "Not this one. This is a two-and-a-half-hour race. The one who gets farthest in that time is the winner." He frowned. "Haven't you ever been in a balloon before?"

"No."

"My God," he said. "What chance have I got?"

"None at all, if I hadn't come," I said mildly.

"That's true. But if I didn't have to have a passenger, I

wouldn't. Passengers always argue and complain." He looked at me, frowning. "What's your name?"

"Sid," I said. "Why wouldn't your girl come with you?"

"Who? Oh, you mean Popsy. She's not my girl. I don't really know her. She was going to come because my usual passenger broke his leg when we made a bit of a rough landing last week. I guess she just got scared at the last minute."

"Where do you expect to come down today?" I said.

"It depends on the wind." He looked up at the sky. "I'm going higher. There's a front forecast from the west, and there will be some useful activity higher up. We might make it to Brighton."

"*Brighton.*" I had thought in terms of perhaps twenty miles, not a hundred. And he must be wrong, I thought: one couldn't go a hundred miles in a balloon in two and a half hours.

Once free of the trees we had risen very fast, and now floated across country at a height from which the cars on the roads looked like toys. Noises came up clearly. One could hear the cars' engines, and dogs barking, and an occasional human shout. People looked up and waved to us as we passed. I was in a child's world, I thought, idyllically drifting with the wind, free and rising and filled with intense delight.

John Viking flipped the lever and the flame roared, shooting up into the green and yellow cavern. The burn lasted for twenty seconds and we rose perceptibly in the sudden ensuing silence.

"What gas do you use?" I said.

"Propane."

He was looking down at the countryside, as if judging his position. "Get the map out, will you. It's in a pouch over your side. And for God's sake, don't let it blow away."

I looked over the side, and found it. A satchel-like object strapped on through the wickerwork. I undid it, gripped the large folded map, and delivered it safely to the captain.

He was looking fixedly at my left hand, which I'd used as a sort of counterweight on the edge of the basket while I leaned over. I let it fall by my side, and his gaze swept up to my face.

"You're missing a hand," he said incredulously. "How the *hell* am I going to win this race?"

I laughed. "I like winning races. You won't lose because of me."

He frowned disgustedly. "I suppose you can't be much more useless than Popsy," he said. "But at least they say she can read a map." He unfolded the sheet I'd given him. "Look," he said. "We started from here." He pointed. "We're travelling roughly northeast. You take the map, and find out where we are."

He handed it over and started another burn. I worked out where we should be, and looked over the side. The spread-out vistas around us looked all the same, defying me to recognize anything special, proving conclusively I was less use than Popsy.

Dammit, I thought. Start again.

We had set off at three o'clock, give or take a minute or two.

We had been airborne for twelve minutes. On the ground the wind had been gentle, but we were now travelling faster. Say . . . fifteen knots. Twelve minutes at fifteen knots . . . about three nautical miles. There should be, I thought, a river; and in spite of gazing earnestly down I nearly missed it, because it was a firm blue line on the map and in reality a silvery thread that wound unobtrusively between a meadow and a wood. To the right of it, half hidden by a hill, lay a village, with beyond it a railway line.

"We're there," I said, pointing to the map.

He squinted at the print and searched the ground beneath us.

"Fair enough," he said. "So we are. Right. You keep the map. We might as well know where we are, all the way."

He flipped the lever and gave it a long burn. The balloons ahead of us were lower. We were looking down on their tops.

"How high are we?" I said.

"Five thousand feet and rising," he said. "I don't mess about. When I race, I race to win. That's why Popsy wouldn't come. Someone told her I would go high. She didn't want to."

He pulled a packet of cigarettes out of his pocket and lit one with a flick of a lighter. We were surrounded by cylinders of liquid gas. I thought about all the embargoes against naked flames near any sort of stored fuel, and kept my mouth shut.

The flock of balloons below us seemed to be veering away to the left; but then I realized that it was we who were going to the right. John Viking watched the changing direction with great satisfaction and started another long burn. We rose faster, and the sun, instead of shining full on our backs, appeared on our starboard side.

In spite of the sunshine it was getting pretty cold. A look over the side showed the earth very far beneath, and one could now see a very long way in all directions. I checked with the map, and kept an eye on where we were.

"How high are we now?" I said.

He glanced at his instruments. "Eleven thousand feet."

"And still rising?"

He nodded. The other balloons, far below and to the left, were a cluster of distant bright blobs against the green earth.

"All that lot," he said, "will stay down at five thousand feet, because of staying under the airways." He gave me a sideways look. "You'll see on the map. The airways that the airlines use are marked, and so are the heights at which one is not allowed to fly through them."

"And one is not allowed to fly through an airway at eleven thousand feet in a balloon?"

"Sid," he said, grinning. "You're not bad."

He flicked the lever, and the burner roared, cutting off chat. I checked the ground against the map and nearly lost our position entirely, because we seemed suddenly to have travelled much faster, and quite definitely to the southeast. The other balloons, when I looked, were out of sight.

In the next silence John Viking told me that the helpers of the other balloons would follow them on the ground, in cars, ready to retrieve them when they came down.

"What about you?" I asked. "Do we have someone following us, too?"

Did we indeed have Trevor Deansgate's thugs following, ready to pounce again at the other end?

John Viking gave a wolfish smile, and said, "No car on earth could keep up with us today." He looked at the altimeter. "Fifteen thousand feet," he said. "We'll stay at that. I got a forecast from the air boys for this trip. Fifty-knot wind at fifteen thousand feet, that's what they said. You hang on, Sid, pal, and we'll get to Brighton."

I thought about the two of us standing in a waist-high, four-foot-square wicker basket, fifteen thousand feet above the solid ground, travelling on the wind, with no feeling of speed, at fifty miles an hour. Quite mad, I thought.

From the ground, we would be a black speck. On the ground, no car could keep up. I grinned back at John Viking with a satisfaction as great as his own, and he laughed aloud.

"Would you believe it?" he said. "At last I've got someone up here who's not puking with fright."

He lit another cigarette, and then he changed the supply line to the burner from one cylinder to the next. This involved switching off the empty tank, unscrewing the connecting nut, screwing it into the next cylinder, and switching on the new supply. He held the cigarette in his mouth throughout, and squinted through the smoke.

486

I had seen from the map that we were flying straight towards the airway which led in and out of Gatwick, where large aeroplanes thundered up and down not expecting to meet squashy balloons illegally in their path.

His appetite for taking risks was way out of my class. He made sitting on a horse over fences on the ground seem rather tame. Except that I no longer did it. I fooled around instead with men who threatened to shoot hands off . . . and I was safer up here with John Viking the madman, propane and cigarettes, mid-air collisions and all.

"Right," he said. "We just stay as we are for an hour and a half and let the wind take us. If you feel odd, it's lack of oxygen." He took a pair of wool gloves from his pocket and put them on. "Are you cold?"

"Yes, a bit."

He grinned. "I've got long johns under my jeans, and two sweaters under my anorak. You'll just have to freeze."

"Thanks," I said, and I put my real hand deep into the pocket of my anorak and he said at least the false hand couldn't get frostbite.

He operated the burner and looked at his watch and the ground and the altimeter, and seemed pleased with the way things were. Then he looked at me in slight puzzlement and I knew he was wondering, now that there was time, how I had happened to be where I was.

"I came to Highalane Park to see you," I said, pulling the paperback on navigation out of my pocket. "I came to ask you about this. It's got your name on the flyleaf."

He frowned at it, and opened the front cover.

"Good Lord! I wondered where this had got to. How did you come to have it?"

"Um . . ." I said. "If I describe someone to you, will you say if you know him?"

"Fire away."

"A man of about twenty-eight," I said. "Dark hair, good looks, full of fun and jokes, easy going, likes girls, great company, has a habit of carrying a knife strapped to his leg under his sock, and is very likely a crook."

"Oh yes," he said, nodding. "He's my cousin."

 10

His cousin, Norris Abbott. What had he done this time, he demanded, and I asked, what had he done before?

"A trail of bouncing cheques that his mother paid for."

Where did he live, I asked. John Viking didn't know. He saw him only when Norris turned up occasionally on his doorstep, usually broke and looking for free meals.

"A laugh a minute for a day or two. Then he's gone."

"Where does his mother live?"

"She's dead. He's alone now. No parents or brothers or sisters. No relatives except me." He frowned. "Why do you ask?"

"A girl I know wants to find him." I shrugged. "It's nothing much."

He lost interest at once and flicked the lever for another burn. By my reckoning the airway was not far off.

"Won't you get into trouble?" I said.

The wolf grin came and went. "They've got to see us, first. We're too small to show up on radar. With a bit of luck, we'll sneak across and no one will be the wiser."

There were no signposts in the sky to tell us when we crossed the boundary of the airway. We saw an aeroplane or two some way off, but no one came buzzing around to direct us downward. We simply sailed straight on, blowing across the sky as fast as a train. At ten past five he said it was time to go down, because if we didn't touch ground by five thirty he would be disqualified.

"How would anyone know exactly when we touched down?" I said.

He directed his toe at the small box strapped to the floor beside one of the corner cylinders.

"In there is a barograph. The judges seal it, before the start. It shows variations in air pressure. Highly sensitive. On the ground, the trace is flat and steady. It tells the judges just when you took off and when you landed. OK. Down we go."

He reached up and pulled a red cord. "It opens a panel at the top of the balloon," he said. "Lets the hot air out."

His idea of descent was all of a piece. The altimeter unwound like a broken clock. He seemed quite unaffected, but it made me

488

queasy and hurt my eardrums. Swallowing made things a bit better, but not much. I concentrated, as an antidote, on checking to see where we were going. The Channel lay like a broad grey carpet to our right, and it was incredible, but whichever way I looked at it, we seemed to be on a collision course with Beachy Head.

"Yeah," John Viking casually confirmed. "We'll try to avoid those cliffs and land on the beach farther on." He checked his watch. "Ten minutes to go. We're at six thousand feet. That's all right. Might come down in the sea . . ."

"Not the sea," I said positively.

"Why not? We might have to."

"Well," I said, "this . . ." I lifted my left arm. "Inside this hand-shaped plastic there's actually a lot of fine engineering. Dunking it in the sea would be like dunking a radio. A total ruin. And it would cost me two thousand quid to get a new one."

He was astonished. "Better keep you dry then. And anyway, now we're down here, I don't think we'll get as far as Beachy Head." He looked at my left hand doubtfully. "It'll be a rough landing. The fuel's cold from being so high . . . the burner doesn't function well on cold fuel. It would take time to heat enough air to give us a softer touchdown."

"Win the race," I said.

His face lit into sheer happiness. "Right," he said decisively. "What's that town just ahead?"

I studied the map. "Eastbourne."

He looked at the altimeter and at Eastbourne, then at his watch. "Three minutes," he said.

The sea lay ahead again, fringing the far side of the town, and for a moment it looked as if we would have to come down there after all. John Viking, however, knew better.

"Hang on," he said. "This is it."

He hauled on the red cord which led upwards into the balloon. Somewhere above, the vent for the hot air widened dramatically, the lifting power of the balloon fell away, and the solid edge of Eastbourne came up with a rush.

We scraped the eaves of grey slate roofs, made a sharp diagonal descent over a road and a patch of grass, and smashed down on a broad concrete walk twenty yards from the waves.

"Don't get out," he yelled. The basket tipped on its side and began to slither along the concrete, dragged by the half-inflated silken mass. "Without our weight, it could still fly away."

As I was again wedged among the cylinders, it was superfluous advice. The basket rocked and tumbled a few more times and I with it, and John Viking cursed and hauled at his red cord and finally let out enough air for us to be still.

He looked at his watch, and his blue eyes blazed with triumph.

"We've made it. Five twenty-nine. That was a bloody good race. The best ever. What are you doing next Saturday?"

I LEFT John Viking organizing the collection of his green and yellow balloon, found a phone, then rang Charles.

"You went on the balloon race," he repeated disbelievingly. "Did you enjoy it?"

"Very much," I said. "Nicholas Ashe now has a name, by the way. He's someone called Norris Abbott."

"Will you tell the police?"

"Let's see if we can find him first."

I TOOK a train to London, risked a quick stop at the flat to pack a suitcase, then checked into a hotel for the night. It would be wise, I thought, not to sleep at home, where Trevor Deansgate and his thugs could find me all too easily.

In the morning I went back to Highalane Park by train and taxi to pick up my car. It still stood where I'd left it, though surrounded now by acres of empty grass. There was no Deansgate in sight, and no thugs waiting in ambush.

I could still go away, I thought. It wasn't too late. Travel. Wander by other seas, under other skies. I could still . . . run away.

I left the car park and drove numbly to Cambridge. I went to Tierson Pharmaceuticals Vaccine Laboratories. I asked for, and got, a Mr. Livingston who was maybe sixty and greyishly thin. Ken Armadale's dried-up old cuss, with a mind as sharp as a razor.

"Mr. Halley, is it?" Livingston said, shaking hands at the entrance. "Mr. Armadale phoned me, explaining roughly your area of interest. I hope I can help you. Come along, this way."

Livingston led me through a labyrinth of passages into a large laboratory which looked through glass walls into the passage on one side, a garden on another, and another lab on the third.

"This is the experimental section," he said, his gesture embracing both rooms. "Most of our laboratories just manufacture the vaccines commercially, but in here we potter about inventing new ones. Now, ask me what you want to know."

"How did the serum horses you were using in the nineteen forties get swine erysipelas?"

"Ah," he said. "That was before my time. But I've heard about it. Yes. Well, it happened. But it shouldn't have. Sheer carelessness, do you see? I hate carelessness. Hate it."

Just as well, I thought. In his line of business, carelessness might be fatal.

"Do you know anything about the production of erysipelas antiserum?" he said.

"You could write it on a thumbnail."

"Then I'll explain as if to a child," he said. "Will that do?"

"Nicely," I said.

He gave me an amused glance. "You inject live erysipelas germs into a horse. I am talking about the past, now, when they did use horses. We haven't used horses since the early nineteen fifties. The horse's blood produces antibodies to fight the germ, but the horse does not develop the disease, because it is a disease pigs get and horses don't. Are you with me?"

"A child," I assured him, "would understand."

"Very well. Now the live virulent germs were grown in blood agar plates, dishes containing blood, where they multiplied, thus producing a useful quantity for injecting into the serum horses."

"That's fine," I said.

"All right," he nodded. "Now the blood on the dishes was bull's blood. But owing to someone's stupid carelessness, the plates were prepared one day with horse's blood. This produced a mutant strain of the disease." He paused. "Mutants are changes which occur suddenly and for no apparent reason throughout nature."

"Yes," I said.

"No one realized what had happened," he said, "until the mutant strain was injected into the serum horses and they all got erysipelas. The mutant strain proved remarkably constant. The incubation period was always twenty-four to forty-eight hours after inoculation, and inflammation of the heart valves was always the result."

A youngish man in a white coat, unbuttoned down the front, came into the room next door, and I watched him vaguely as he began pottering about. He was opening cupboards, looking for something.

"What became of this mutant strain?" I said.

Livingston nibbled his lips, but finally said, "We could have kept some, I dare say, as a curiosity. Of course, it would be weakened by now, and one would have to restore it to full virulence."

I said, "Would there be any of this mutant strain elsewhere in the world. I mean, did this laboratory send some of it out?"

The lips pursed themselves and the eyebrows went up. "I've no idea," he said. He looked through the glass and gestured towards the man in the next room. "You could ask Barry Shummuck. He would know. Mutant strains are his speciality."

He pronounced "Shummuck" to rhyme with "hummock". I know the name, I thought. I . . . *oh my God*. The shock of it left me breathless. I knew someone too well whose real name was Shummuck.

I shivered. "Tell me more about your Mr. Shummuck," I said.

Livingston was a natural chatterer and saw no harm in it. He shrugged. "He came up the hard way. Still talks like it. He used to have a terrible chip on his shoulder. The world owed him a living, that sort of thing. Shades of student demos. He's settled down recently. He's good at his job."

"You don't care for him?" I said.

Livingston was startled. "I didn't say that."

He had, plainly, in his face and in his voice. I said slowly, hesitantly, "Do you know if he has . . . a brother?"

Livingston's face showed surprise. "Yes, he has. Funny thing, he's a bookmaker." He pondered. "Some name like Terry. Not Terry . . . Trevor, that's it. They come here together sometimes, the two of them . . . . Thick as thieves."

Barry Shummuck gave up his search and moved towards the door.

"Would you like to meet him?" Mr. Livingston said.

I shook my head. The last thing I wanted, in a building full of

492

virulent germs which he knew how to handle and I didn't, was to be introduced to the brother of Trevor Deansgate.

Shummuck went through the door, walked purposefully along the glass-walled corridor, and pushed open the door of the lab we were in. Head and shoulders leaned forward.

"Morning, Mr. Livingston," he said. "Have you seen my box of transparencies anywhere?"

The basic voice was the same: self-confident and slightly abrasive. Manchester accent, much stronger. I held my left arm out of sight, half behind my back, and willed him to go away.

"No," said Mr. Livingston, with just a shade of pleasure. "But Barry, can you spare . . ."

Livingston and I were standing in front of a work bench which held various empty glass jars and a row of clamps. I turned left-wards, with my arm still hidden, and clumsily, with my right hand, knocked over a clamp and two glass jars.

More clatter than breakage. Livingston gave a quick nibble of surprised annoyance, and righted the rolling jars. I gripped the clamp, which was metal and heavy.

I turned back towards the door.

The door was shutting. Barry Shummuck was striding away along the corridor, the front edges of his white coat flapping.

I let a shuddering breath out through my nose and carefully put the clamp back at the end of the row.

"He's gone," Mr. Livingston said. "What a pity."

I DROVE BACK to Newmarket, to the Equine Research Establishment and Ken Armadale.

I wondered how long it would take chatty Mr. Livingston to tell Barry Shummuck of the visit of a man called Halley who wanted to know about a pig disease in horses. I felt faintly sick.

"IT MUST have been made resistant to all ordinary antibiotics," Ken said. "A real neat little job."

"How do you mean?"

"If any old antibiotic would kill it, you couldn't be sure the horse wouldn't be given a shot as soon as he had a temperature, and never develop the disease."

I sighed. "So how do they make the disease resistant?"

"Feed the germs tiny doses of antibiotic until they become immune."

"All this is technically difficult, isn't it?"

"Yes, fairly."

"Have you ever heard of Barry Shummuck?"

He frowned. "No, I don't think so."

The craven inner voice told me urgently to shut up, to escape. "Do you have a cassette recorder here?" I said.

"Yes. I use it for making notes while I'm operating." He fetched it, loaded it with a new tape, and set it up on his desk. "Just talk," he said. "It has a built-in microphone."

"Stay and listen," I said. "I want a witness."

I switched on the recorder, and for introduction spoke my name, the place, and the date. Then I switched off again and sat looking at the fingers I needed for pressing the play and record buttons.

"What is it, Sid?" Ken said.

I glanced at him and down again. "Nothing."

Finally I reached for the buttons.

I had to do it, I thought. I absolutely had to. I was never in any way going to be whole again if I didn't.

 II

I telephoned Chico at lunchtime and told him what I'd found out about Rosemary's horses.

"What it amounts to," I said, "is that those four horses had bad hearts because they'd been given a pig disease. There's a lot of complicated info about how it was done, but that's now a headache for the Jockey Club."

"Pig disease?" Chico said disbelievingly.

"Yeah. That big bookmaker Trevor Deansgate has a brother who works in a place that produces vaccines for inoculating people against smallpox and diphtheria and so on, and they cooked up a plan to squirt pig germs into those red-hot favourites in Caspar's yard."

"Which duly lost," Chico said, "while the bookmaker raked in the lolly."

"Right," I replied.

"Well, Sid, mate," Chico said. "This is results day all round. We got a fix on Nicky Ashe."

Nicky Ashe. A pushover, compared with . . . compared with . . .

"Hey," Chico's voice said aggrievedly through the receiver. "Aren't you pleased?"

"Yes, of course. By the way, his real name's Norris Abbott. I traced his cousin. What's the fix?"

"He's been sending out some of those damn fool letters. I went to your place this morning, and there were two envelopes with our sticky labels on. I opened them. They'd both been sent by people whose names start with P. All that leg work paid off."

"So we've got the begging letter?"

"We sure have. It's exactly the same as the ones your wife had, except her name and the address to send the money to have, of course, been changed."

He read out the address, which was in Clifton, Bristol. I looked at it thoughtfully. I could either give it straight to the police or I could check it first myself. Checking it, in one certain way, had persuasive attractions.

"Chico," I said. "Ring Jenny's flat and ask for Louise McInnes. Ask her to ring me here at the Rutland Hotel in Newmarket."

"Scared of your missus, are you?"

"Will you do it?"

"Oh sure." He laughed and rang off. When I was called to the telephone a minute later, however, it was not Louise on the other end, but Chico again.

"Louise has left the flat," he said. "Your wife gave me her new number. It's still Oxford." He read it out. "Anything else?"

"Bring your cassette player to the Jockey Club, Portman Square, tomorrow afternoon. We have an appointment at four o'clock."

LOUISE, to my relief, answered her telephone. When I told her what I wanted, she was incredulous.

"You've actually *found* him?"

"Well," I said. "Probably. If so, then his real name's Norris Abbott. Will you come and identify him?"

"Yes." No hesitation. "Where and when?"

"Some place in Bristol." I paused, and said diffidently, "I could pick you up this afternoon, and we could go straight on. We might spot him this evening . . . or tomorrow morning."

There was a silence at the other end. Then her voice, quiet and committed. "All right."

SHE WAS waiting for me in Oxford, and she had brought an overnight bag. "Hello," I said, getting out of the car and kissing her cheek. She smiled with what I had to believe was enjoyment, and slung her case in the boot beside mine.

I drove to Bristol feeling contented and carefree. No one except Chico knew where I was going. The shadowy future, I thought, was not going to spoil the satisfactory present. I decided not even to think of it, and for most of the time I didn't.

We went first to a country-house hotel which someone had once told me of, high on the cliffs overlooking the Avon gorge, and geared to rich-American-tourist comfort.

"We'll never get in here," Louise said, eyeing the opulence.

"I telephoned."

We parked the suitcases in our respective bedrooms and went back to the car. Then we drove to the new address of Nicholas Ashe/Norris Abbott. It was a prosperous-looking house in a prosperous-looking street. A solid five-or-six-bedroomed affair, white-painted and mellowed in the early evening sun.

I stopped the car on the same side of the road, where we could see both the front door and the gate into the driveway. Nicky, Louise had said on the way down, often used to go out for a walk at about seven o'clock. Maybe he would again, if he was there.

We had the car's windows open because of the warm air. I lit a cigarette, and the smoke floated in a quiet curl through lack of wind. Very peaceful, I thought, waiting there.

"Where do you come from?" Louise said.

I blew a smoke ring. "I'm the illegitimate son of a twenty-year-old window cleaner who fell off his ladder just before his wedding. And you?"

"The legitimate daughter of the manager of a glass factory and a magistrate, both alive and living in Essex."

We consulted about brothers and sisters, of which I had none and she had two, one of each. About education, of which I'd had

496

some and she a lot. About life in general, of which she'd seen a little, and I a bit more.

An hour passed in the quiet street. A few birds sang. Men came home from work and turned into the driveways. Distant doors slammed. Seven o'clock came and went: and Nicky didn't.

"How long will we stay?" Louise asked.

"Until dark."

"I'm hungry."

Half an hour drifted by. I learned that she liked curry, hated rhubarb and that the thesis she was writing was giving her hell.

"I'm so far behind schedule," she said. "And . . . oh my goodness, *there he is!*" Her eyes had opened very wide. I looked where she looked, and saw Nicholas Ashe.

Coming not from the front door, but from the side of the house. My age, or a bit younger. Taller, but of my own thin build. I took my baby camera out of my trouser pocket and pulled it open with my teeth as usual, and took his picture.

When he reached the gate he paused and looked back, and a woman ran after him calling, "Ned, Ned, wait for me."

"Ned!" Louise said, sliding down in her seat. "If he comes this way, won't he see me?"

"Not if I kiss you," I said.

The woman with Ashe looked older: about forty, slim, pleasant, excited. She tucked her arm into his and looked up at his eyes, her own clearly, even from twenty feet away, full of adoration. He laughed delightfully, then he swung her round in a little circle on the pavement, and put his arm round her waist, and walked towards us with vivid gaiety and a bounce in his step.

I leaned across and risked another photograph from the shadows of the car, then kissed Louise with enthusiasm.

Their footsteps went past. Abreast of us they must have seen us, or at least my back, for they both suddenly giggled, lightheartedly, lovers sharing their secret with lovers. They almost paused, then went on, their steps growing softer until they had gone. I sat up reluctantly.

Louise said "Whew!" but whether it was the result of the kiss, or the proximity of Ashe, I wasn't quite sure.

"Well," I said. "That's that. Let's find some dinner."

I drove back to the hotel. Louise wanted to change before we

ate. We went upstairs together and I told her to knock on my bedroom door when she was ready.

I had a large, wood-panelled room with antique polished furniture, and a huge fourposter bed decked with white muslin frills. Louise's knock came just when I was in the middle of changing the battery in my arm. I let her in and she watched as I completed the operation.

I said, "Are you . . . revolted?"

"No, of course not."

I pulled my sleeve down and buttoned the cuff. We went down

498

to dinner and ate sole and strawberries, and if they'd tasted of seaweed I wouldn't have cared. We sat side by side on a sofa in the hotel lounge, drinking small cups of coffee.

"Of course," she said, "now that we have seen Nicky, we don't really need to stay until tomorrow."

"Are you thinking of leaving?" I said.

"About as much as you are," she said smiling.

She looked calmly at my left hand, which rested on the sofa between us. I couldn't tell what she was thinking, but I said on impulse, "Touch it."

She tentatively moved her right hand until her fingers were touching the tough, lifeless, plastic skin. There was no drawing back, no flicker of revulsion in her face.

"It's metal, inside there," I said. "Gears and levers and electric circuits. Press harder, and you'll feel them."

She did as I said, and I saw her surprise as she discovered the shape of the inner realities. She also felt some sort of tension relax in me, and looked up, accusingly. "You were testing me," she said.

I smiled. "I suppose so." I felt an unaccustomed uprush of mischief. "As a matter of fact," I said, holding my left hand in my right, "if I turn it this way several times the whole hand will come right off at the wrist."

"Don't do it," she said, horrified.

I laughed with absolute enjoyment. I wouldn't have thought I would ever feel that way about that hand.

LATER, we lay drowsily in the huge fourposter. She had been warmly receptive and generous, and had made the act of love an intense pleasure for me. "Louise," I said.

No reply. I shifted a little, and drifted, like her, to sleep.

A while later, awake early as usual, I watched the daylight strengthen on her sleeping face. The fair hair lay tangled round her head, and her skin looked soft and fresh. When she woke, even before she opened her eyes, she was smiling.

"Good morning," I said.

She moved towards me in the big bed, the white muslin frills on the canopy overhead surrounding us like a frame.

"Clouds," she said contentedly. "What do you think of when you're making love?"

"I feel. It isn't thought."

"Sometimes I see scarlet roses on trellises. Sometimes spiky stars. This time it will be white frilly muslin clouds."

I asked her, afterwards.

"No. All bright sunlight. Quite blinding."

The sunlight, in truth, had flooded into the room, making the whole white canopy translucent and shimmering.

WE WENT BACK to Oxford, and had lunch at *Les Quat' Saisons*, which kept the shadows at bay a while longer. With the coffee, though, came the unavoidable minute.

"I have to be in London at four o'clock," I said. "But I can be down here again in two days' time. Will I see you then?"

"Unless you're blind."

CHICO was propping up the Portman Square building with a look of resignation, as if he'd been there for hours. He shifted his shoulder off the stonework at my on-foot approach and said, "Took your time, didn't you?"

"I had to take a film to a twenty-four-hour development place."

From one hand he dangled the black cassette recorder, and he was wearing jeans and a sports shirt with no jacket. The hot weather had settled and I was also in shirtsleeves, though with a tie on, and a jacket over my arm.

On the third floor all the windows were open. Sir Thomas Ullaston, sitting behind his big desk, had dealt with the day in pale blue shirting with white stripes. He was the Jockey Club senior steward.

"Come in, Sid," he said, seeing me appear in his open doorway. "I've been waiting for you."

"I'm sorry I'm late," I said, shaking hands. "This is Chico Barnes, who works with me."

He shook Chico's hand. "Right," he said. "Now we'll get the others." He pressed an intercom button and spoke to his secretary.

The office slowly filled up with more people than I'd expected, but all of whom I knew at least to talk to. The top administrative brass in full force, about six of them, all urbane, worldly men, the people who really ran racing. Chico looked at them slightly nervously as if at an alien breed, and seemed relieved when a table was provided for him to put the recorder on. He sat with the table between himself and the room, like a barrier. I fished into my jacket for the cassette, and gave it to him.

"Well, Sid," Sir Thomas said. "On the telephone yesterday you told me you had discovered how Tri-Nitro had been nobbled, and as you see, we are very interested." He smiled. "So fire away."

I made my own manner match theirs: calm and dispassionate, as if Trevor Deansgate's threat wasn't anywhere in my mind.

"I've put it all onto tape," I said. "You'll hear two voices. The other is Ken Armadale, from the Equine Research. I asked him to clarify the veterinary details."

The well-brushed heads nodded. I glanced at Chico, who pressed the start button, and my own voice, disembodied, spoke loudly into a wholly attentive silence.

"This is Sid Halley, at the Equine Research Establishment, on Monday, May eighth . . ."

I listened to the flat sentences, spelling it out. The identical symptoms in four horses, the lost races, the bad hearts. My request to Henry Thrace that I be informed if either of his two still alive should die. The post mortem on Gleaner, with Ken Armadale explaining how horses had come to be infected by a disease of pigs, and how he had found active live germs in the lesions on Gleaner's heart valves. And my voice continuing, "A mutant strain of the disease was produced at the Tierson Vaccine Laboratory at Cambridge in the following manner . . ."

It wasn't the easiest of procedures to understand, but I watched the faces and saw that they did, particularly by the time Ken Armadale had gone through it all again, confirming what I'd said.

"As to motive and opportunity," my voice said, "we come to a man called Trevor Deansgate . . ."

Sir Thomas's head snapped back from its forward, listening posture, and he stared at me bleakly from across the room. Among the other listeners the name had created an almost equal stir. All of them either knew him or knew of him: the big up-and-coming influence among bookmakers, the powerful man shouldering his way into top-rank social acceptance. They knew Trevor Deansgate, and their faces were shocked.

"The real name of Trevor Deansgate is Trevor Shummuck," my voice said. "There is a research worker at the vaccine laboratory called Barry Shummuck, who is his brother. The two brothers have been seen together on several occasions at the laboratory where the mutant strain originally arose . . . unlikely after all this time for there to be any of it anywhere else . . . .

"Trevor Deansgate is on good terms with George Caspar . . . owns two horses in his yard, watches the morning gallops and goes to breakfast with him. Trevor Deansgate stood to make a fortune if he knew in advance that the favourites for the Guineas and the Derby couldn't win. Trevor Deansgate had the means— the disease; the motive—money; and the opportunity—entry into Caspar's well-guarded stable. It would seem, therefore, that there are grounds for investigating his activities further."

My voice stopped. Chico switched off the recorder, ejected the cassette and laid it carefully on the table.

"It's incredible," Sir Thomas said, but not as if he didn't believe it. "What do you think, Lucas?"

Lucas Wainwright was Director of Security to the Jockey Club. A pepper and salt man, I thought. Brown and grey speckled hair, brown and grey eyes, brown and grey shirt. He cleared his throat. "I think we should congratulate Sid on an exceptional job."

They did so, to my embarrassment, and I thought it generous of him to have said it at all, considering their own security had done negative dope tests and left it at that. But then their security, I reflected, hadn't had Rosemary Caspar visiting them in false curls and hysteria; and they didn't have the benefit of Trevor Deansgate revealing himself to them as a villain before they even positively suspected him.

Sir Thomas and the administrators consulted among themselves. Then Lucas Wainwright asked a question.

"Do you really think, Sid, that Deansgate infected those horses himself?" He seemed to think it unlikely. "Surely he couldn't produce a syringe anywhere near them?"

I dipped again into my jacket and produced the packet containing the needle attached to the pea-sized bladder. I gave the packet to Sir Thomas, who opened it, tipping the contents onto his desk. They all looked. Understood. Were convinced.

"He'd be more likely to do it himself if he could," I said. "He wouldn't want to risk anyone else knowing, and perhaps having a hold over him."

"It amazes me," Sir Thomas said with apparent genuineness, "how you work these things out, Sid."

"But I . . ."

"Yes," he said, smiling. "We all know what you're going to say. At heart you're still a jockey."

There was a long pause. Then I said, "Sir, you're wrong. This . . ." I pointed to the cassette . . . "is what I am now. And from now on."

His face sobered into a long frowning look in which it seemed that he was reassessing his whole view of me, as so many others had recently done.

Lucas Wainwright said briskly, "Do you have any plans, Sid, as to what to do next?"

"Talk to the Caspars," I said. "I'll drive up there tomorrow."

"Good idea," Lucas said. "I'll come with you. It's a matter for our Security Service now, of course."

"And for the police, in due time," said Sir Thomas, with a touch of gloom. He saw all public prosecutions for racing-based crimes as sources of disgrace to the whole industry.

Lucas Wainwright bustled off to his office to telephone the Caspars, and came back shortly to say he had made an appointment with them for eleven tomorrow.

"Pick me up here, then, at nine?" he asked me.

I nodded. "OK."

All the administrators shook my hand and also Chico's; then we walked back to the Scimitar. As Chico folded himself into the passenger's seat, he said, "I brought that begging letter for you . . ." He dug into a trouser pocket and produced a much-folded and slightly grubby sheet of paper. I read it through. Exactly the same as the ones Jenny had sent, except that it bore the name and signature of a new Executive Assistant, "Elizabeth More", and was headed with the Clifton address.

I put it in the glove box, started the car, and drove Chico back to his place in Finchley Road.

"Come to Newmarket with me tomorrow?" I asked.

"Sure, if you want. What for?"

I shrugged, making light of it. "Bodyguard."

"Afraid Trevor Deansgate'll duff you up?"

I shifted in my seat a bit, and sighed. "I guess so," I said.

 12

I found a hotel for the night. Then I rang Ken Armadale. He sounded smugly self-satisfied, and not without reason.

"That erysipelas strain has presumably been made immune to every antibiotic in the book," he said. "Very thorough, Barry Shummuck. But there's an obscure bunch he won't have bothered with, because no one would think of pumping them into horses. Rare, they are, and expensive. Anyway, I've tracked some down."

"Great," I said. "Where?"

"In London, at one of the teaching hospitals. The pharmacist there promised to pack some in a box and leave it at the reception desk for you to collect."

"Ken, you're terrific."

"I've had to mortgage my soul to get it."

I PICKED UP the parcel in the morning and arrived at Portman Square to find Chico again waiting on the doorstep. Lucas Wainwright came down from his office. We set off for Newmarket, reaching there in good time, and came to a smooth halt in George Caspar's well-tended driveway.

George was not at all pleased to see me, and Rosemary looked as if she wanted to throw me out bodily. But they led us into their elegant drawing room, where Chico and I sat lazily in armchairs, while Lucas Wainwright talked about pig disease and bad hearts.

The Caspars listened in growing bewilderment and dismay, and when Lucas mentioned Trevor Deansgate, George stood up and began striding about in agitation.

"It isn't possible," he said. "Not Trevor. He's a friend."

"Did you let him near Tri-Nitro, after that last training gallop?" I said.

George's face gave the answer.

"Thursday," Rosemary said, in a hard cold voice. "He and George walked round the yard." She paused. "Trevor likes slapping horses. Some people pat necks. Trevor slaps rumps."

Lucas said, "In due course, George, you'll have to give evidence in court."

"I'm going to look a damned fool, aren't I?" he said sourly.

"Filling my yard with guards and then taking Deansgate in myself."

Rosemary looked at me stonily, unforgiving. "I told you they were being nobbled. I told you. You didn't believe me."

Lucas looked surprised. "But I thought you understood, Mrs. Caspar. Sid did believe you. It was Sid who did all this investigating, not the Jockey Club."

Her mouth opened, and stayed open, speechlessly.

"Look," I said awkwardly. "I've brought you a present. Ken Armadale at the Equine Research thinks Tri-Nitro can be cured, by a course of some rather rare antibiotics. I've brought them with me from London." I took the box to Rosemary and kissed her cheek. "I'm sorry that it wasn't in time for the Guineas. Maybe the Derby . . . but anyway the Irish Derby and the Diamond Stakes. Tri-Nitro will be fine for those."

Rosemary Caspar, that tough lady, burst into tears.

WE DIDN'T get back to London until nearly eight, owing to Lucas insisting on going in the afternoon to see Henry Thrace and Ken Armadale himself, face to face. The Director of Security to the Jockey Club was busy making everything official.

He was visibly relieved when Ken absolved the people who'd done blood tests on the horses after their disaster races.

"It's an obscure disease," Ken said. "You wouldn't find evidence of it in a blood test unless you knew exactly what you were looking for."

Lucas thanked Ken happily, and disappeared into the Jockey Club rooms in the High Street while Chico and I drank in the White Hart.

"How much do you reckon we'll get?" Chico said.

"More or less what we ask."

George Caspar had promised, if Tri-Nitro recovered, that the horse's owner would give us the earth.

Chico said, "What will you ask, then?"

"I don't know. Perhaps five per cent of his prize money."

"He couldn't complain."

We set off southwards, finally, in the car. Once in London, I dropped Chico and Lucas Wainwright, then picked up the photographs from the twenty-four-hour development service, and went on alone to Aynsford.

CHARLES opened the door.

"It's nearly ten," he said.

I smiled. "You said I could come any time."

I followed him into the house, sat sideways on the gold sofa, shoes off, feet up, as I often did.

"Coffee?" he offered. "Or a drink?"

"Tea," I said.

He went and made it, and brought two big steaming mugs, naval fashion. He put mine on the table which stood along the back of the sofa, and sat with his in an armchair. The empty-looking eyes were switched steadily my way.

"Well?" he said.

I rubbed my forehead. "When you look at me," I said, hesitatingly, "do you see a lot of fears and self doubts, and shame?"

"Of course not." He seemed to find the question amusing, and then sipped the scalding tea, and said more seriously. "You never show feelings like that."

"No one does," I said. "Everyone has an outside and an inside, and the two can be quite different."

"Is that just a general observation?"

"No." I picked up the mug of tea, and blew across the steaming surface. "To myself, I'm a jumble of uncertainty and fear and stupidity." I took a tentative taste: as always when Charles made it, the tea was strong enough to rasp the fur off your tongue. I quite liked it. Then I asked, "Is Jenny here?"

He nodded. "She went up early. But she's sure to have heard us."

I sighed, got out the photographs, and handed them to him. "Nicholas Ashe," I said. "And his new ladyfriend. There's a begging letter too, with his new address."

He shook his head at the foolishness of Nicholas Ashe.

Then, right on cue, Jenny walked in, saw me, and was immediately annoyed. "Oh no, not you again." She sat at the other end of the sofa, beyond my feet. "What are you doing here?"

"Drinking tea."

She looked at me moodily. "I'm going to sell that flat in Oxford," she said. "I don't like it anymore. It reminds me too much of Nicky."

After a pause I said, "I saw him. Two days ago in Bristol. He's living with another woman."

She stood up. "Are you telling me that to be beastly?" she demanded.

"I'm telling you so you'll get him out of your system before he goes on trial and to gaol. You're going to be damned unhappy if you don't."

"I hate you," she said.

"That's not hate, that's injured pride."

"How dare you!"

"Jenny," I said. "I'll tell you plainly, I'd do a lot for you. I loved you once, and I still care what happens to you. It's no good finding Ashe and getting him convicted of fraud instead of you, if you don't wake up and see him for what he is. I want to make you angry with him. For your own sake."

"You won't manage it," she said fiercely.

Charles cleared his throat. Handed her the photographs.

"Her name is Elizabeth More," I said slowly. "His real name is Norris Abbott. She calls him Ned."

The top picture showed them laughing and entwined, looking into each other's eyes, the happiness in their faces sharply in focus. Silently, I gave Jenny the letter. She looked at the signature at the bottom, and went very pale. I felt sorry for her, but she wouldn't have wanted me to say so.

"All right," she said after a pause. "Give it to the police."

She sat down again in a sort of emotional exhaustion. Her eyes turned my way.

"I suppose one day I will thank you," she said.

"There's no need."

With a flash of anger she said, "You're doing it again."

"Doing what?"

"Making me feel guilty. I know I'm pretty beastly to you sometimes. Because you make me feel guilty for leaving you. For our marriage going wrong. I want to get back at you for that."

"But it wasn't your fault," I protested.

"No, it was yours. Your selfishness, your pigheadedness. Your bloody determination to win. I couldn't live in the sort of purgatory you make of life. I wanted an ordinary man."

She got up from the sofa and bent over and kissed my forehead.

507

Then she turned to her father. "Tell Mr. Quayle I'm cured of Nicky, and I won't be obstructive from now on. I think I'll go back to the flat in the morning. I feel a lot better."

She went with Charles towards the door, then paused and looked back, and said, "Goodbye, Sid."

I DIDN'T see her next day. But then I left for London pretty early. What was done, was done. It was time we both moved on. And I had an appointment in Oxford in the evening with Louise.

When I got to London it was raining. At the flat I went round to the lock-up garages in the back, to leave the car there out of sight. I wouldn't have come here at all, except that I'd been on the move for several days, ever since the balloon race, in fact, and I'd run out of clean shirts and such.

I unlocked the roll-up door, and pushed it high. Drove the car in. Got out. Locked the car door. Put the keys in my pocket.

"Sid Halley," a voice said.

A voice. *His* voice.

Trevor Deansgate.

I stood facing the door I'd just locked, as still as stone. I suppose I had known it would happen.

Oh God, I thought. Let him not see the terror I feel. Let him not know. Dear God . . . give me courage.

I turned slowly towards him.

He took a step inside the garage, the thin drizzle like a dark grey-silver sheet behind him.

He held the shotgun, with the barrels pointing my way.

I had a brick wall on my left and another behind me, and the car on my right; and there were never many people around the garages. If anyone came, they'd hardly dawdle.

With eyes and gun facing unwaveringly my way, he stretched up his left hand and found the bottom edge of the roll-up door. He gave it a sharp downward tug, and it rolled down nearly to the ground behind him, closing us in. Both hands, clean, manicured, surrounded by white cuffs, were back on the gun.

"You got away last time," he said, "so I decided to see to this myself. I've been waiting for you, on and off, for days."

I didn't say anything.

"Then yesterday two policemen came to see me in the office.

508

George Caspar telephoned. The Jockey Club warned me they were going to take proceedings. My solicitor told me I'd lose my bookmaking licence. I would be warned off from racing, and might well go to gaol."

His voice, as before, was a threat in itself, heavy with the raw realities of the urban jungle.

"The police have been in the lab. My brother is losing his job. His career. He worked hard for it."

"You both gambled. You've lost. Too bloody bad," I said.

The gun barrels moved an inch or two.

Gambled . . . lost . . . so had I.

"I knew you'd come back, some time or other," he said. "All I had to do was wait. I knew you'd come, in the end."

I said nothing.

"I came here to do what I promised. To blow your hand off." He paused. "Why don't you beg me not to? Why don't you go down on your bloody knees and beg me not to?"

I didn't answer. Didn't move.

He gave a short laugh that had no mirth in it at all. "It didn't stop you, did it, that threat? Not for long. I thought it would. I thought no one would risk losing both their hands. Not just to get me busted. Not for something small, like that. You're a bloody fool, you are."

I agreed with him, on the whole. I was also trembling inside, and concerned that he shouldn't see it.

"You don't turn a hair, do you?" he said.

He's playing with me, I thought. He must know I'm frightened. No one could possibly, in the circumstances, not be frightened to death. He's making me sweat . . . wanting me to beg him . . . and I'm not . . . *not* . . . going to.

"This morning," he said, "I started thinking about myself. I shoot off Sid Halley's right hand, and what happens to me?" He stared at me with increased intensity. "I get revenge . . . And what else? Ten years, perhaps. You can get life for GBH, if it's bad enough. Your only hand . . . that would probably be bad enough. I might as well kill you. That's what I thought."

I thought numbly that I wasn't so sure either that I wouldn't rather be dead.

"Then," he said, "I thought of rotting away in gaol wishing I'd had the bloody sense to leave you alone. I reckoned it wasn't worth years in gaol, just to know I'd fixed you. So I decided not to do that, but just to get you down on the ground squealing for me not to. I'd have my revenge that way. I'd remind you of it, all your life."

Jesus, I thought.

"I'd forgotten," he said, "what you were like. You've no bloody nerves. But I'm not going to shoot you. Like I said, it's not worth it." He turned abruptly, and stooped, putting one hand under the garage door; heaved; rolled it upwards and open.

The warm drizzle outside fell like shoals of silver minnows. The gentle air came softly into the garage.

He stood there for a moment, brooding, holding his gun; and then he gave me back what in the straw barn he'd taken away.

"Isn't there *anything*," he said bitterly, "that you're afraid of?"

Dick Francis

Unlike his hero in this book, when Dick Francis retired from his brilliant career as a jockey after a particularly bad fall, he didn't turn to the investigation of crime. He turned to the writing of crime fiction instead. Now, seventeen books later, all of them highly acclaimed and all with a horse-racing background, he has obviously found a second career as successful as the first, and surely as satisfying.

He and his wife Mary live in a charming bungalow in Oxfordshire, close to the heart of England's horse-racing country. Mary is closely involved with him in the writing of his books—and in the research for them as well. Even on his recent hot-air balloon ride, when he gained useful first-hand experience for the balloon sequence in this book, Mary went too. And both of them have maintained strong connections with the world of horses: they often enjoy a day at the races together, their son is a trainer, and Dick himself is a much sought-after judge at horse shows up and down the country.

Whip Hand's hero, Sid Halley, first appeared some years back, in a book called *Odds Against*. When recently Yorkshire television proposed making a six-part television series about the private detective, starring Mike Gwilym, Dick's imagination was rekindled—he'd always had a soft spot for Sid, he says—and *Whip Hand* was the welcome result.

During his racing career—he was Champion Steeplechase Jockey in 1954—Dick was the rider of innumerable winners for the Queen Mother. Now, perhaps unsurprisingly, it is said that he is her favourite author. Possibly the title of his fascinating autobiography acknowledges that fact. He called it *The Sport of Queens*.